THE GATEKEEPER

DONALD PETERS

WORKBOOK PRESS LLC
187 E Warm Springs Rd,
Suite B285, Las Vegas, NV 89119, USA

Website: https://workbookpress.com/
Hotline: 1-888-818-4856
Email: admin@workbookpress.com

Ordering Information:
Quantity sales. Special discounts are available on quantity purchases by corporations, associations, and others. For details, contact the publisher at the address above.

Library of Congress Control Number:

ISBN-13:   978-1-958176-94-8 (Paperback Version)
                978-1-952754-02-9 (Digital Version)

REV DATE: 08/31/2022

THE GATEKEEPER

Second Book of 'The Mark Taylor' Series

Donald Peters

By the same author:

Covert Decisions

The Iran Affair

Donald Peters
www.donaldpetersbooks.nz

There are countries in this world that are still mysterious and remote despite the rapid and invasive developments in the art and technology of communications.

Some people point to such countries and proudly say, 'I have been there.'

Others point to such countries and proclaim, 'A friend of mine died there.'

Then others say nothing, maybe out of fear, maybe out of dread.

Fear and dread of memories and experiences that they strive to forget.

But they never will forget.

Such memories will always be in the minds of those who have witnessed firsthand all the brutal and savage realities of countries and peoples at war.

(D. P. Smith)

PROLOGUE

Pakistan is an extraordinarily complex country, as are its neighbors—Afghanistan and Iran in the west, India to the east, and China in the northeast. It became an independent home—two independent homes actually—for Muslims when the British ended their rule of the Indian subcontinent in 1947. Until the region of Bangladesh, the remote eastern half of what was Pakistan, itself gained independence.

In its history, what is now known as Pakistan had been invaded or settled by Indo-Aryans, Persians, Greeks, Arabs, Turks, Afghans, and Mongols, making the British's arrival seem like a peaceful interlude in an otherwise violent history. When the British left in 1947, making Pakistan a Dominion in the Commonwealth of Nations, it should have heralded the arrival of more permanent peace.

But it did not.

The division of the provinces of Punjab in the west and Bengal in the east could be best described as an ill-timed and ill-conceived plan—conceived as it was out of arrogance and ignorance of the British lawmakers thousands of miles away in Westminster. It resulted in massive riots in both India and Pakistan. One result was that millions of Muslims moved from India into Pakistan, and millions of Hindus and Sikhs moved from Pakistan into India. Another result was the first Kashmir war between the fledgling nations of Pakistan and India. And that war has been going on, in one form or another, ever since.

In 1956, there was another twist. Pakistan became the Islamic Republic of Pakistan, and then things started to turn pear-shaped. Since then, the nation's history has been characterized by periods of military rule, political instability, civilian riots, sectarian violence, various coup d'état, various assassinations, and various military scraps with India.

Pakistan is also a nuclear-armed state, which makes for political instability, the involvement of the military in politics, and major talking points in the United Nations and elsewhere.

Strangely, Pakistan has, for most of its short life, been an ally of the United States of America—except, that is, during a brief period in the 1990s when relations between the two nations soured over Pakistan's refusal to abandon its nuclear activities. But politics being what they are, the two nuclear powers agreed to differ and to get on with what in later years became the primary job of fighting the Taliban in neighboring Afghanistan and to rid the world of al-Qaeda and the various groups that went on to pursue the same or similar objectives.

At least, that was the intention of the United States.

There was, however, an imminent problem—in fact, several problems. Many thousands of people from Afghanistan had fled their homeland to escape the Taliban and the never-ending wars and were housed in refugee camps throughout Pakistan. But most of the later problems stemmed from the fact that the initial onslaught in the United States-led Operation Freedom caused the Taliban and al-Qaeda to move from Afghanistan into the north-western provinces of Pakistan.

Once there, they were virtually untouchable by the combined military might of Pakistan and a coalition of various US-led allies. In the case of Pakistan, this was because of corruption and divided loyalty among the Pakistani forces. In the case of the coalition countries, this was simply because of geography. These problems were known to both the US and Pakistani governments. But they had vastly different ways of handling them.

However, what was not known was far more insidious.

As the war in Afghanistan and the north-western border provinces of Pakistan continued, some people took advantage of the situation, as in all wars.

Drug dealers.

In the northeast part of Pakistan, which was somewhat remote from the struggles that were currently going on elsewhere, there was good business, especially among the younger people. And the use of drugs, mainly originating in the south of Afghanistan, had spread across Kashmir and into India. These regions had become a fertile ground for recruitment by terrorist groups and potential suicide bombers. The people had nothing else to do. And were too stoned to care.

This contributed to a situation in which Pakistan was beginning to fall apart and come under the influence of forces that had interests other than the more normal religious differences.

The Islamic Republic of Afghanistan is similarly complex. It is a landlocked country surrounded by Pakistan in the south and east, Iran in the west, China in the northeast, and the old soviet republics of Turkmenistan, Uzbekistan, and Tajikistan in the north. Since the late 1970s, Afghanistan has been in a continuous state of civil war.

This was just as well because had the protagonists gone to war, it would have turned into a nuclear conflict, and that would have been the end of life as we know it on planet Earth.

In the middle years of this Cold War, the Government of Afghanistan was pro-Soviet Union. The Government of the United States saw this as an opportunity to weaken the Soviet Union and began to covertly fund the various forces that were fighting against the Afghanistan government. The troops that they chose to support, using the perverse logic that 'the enemy of my enemy is my friend,' were the Mujahideen. This group consisted of Islamic fundamentalists. Although the word *Mujahideen* more correctly translates into 'Muslim fighters' or 'strugglers' rather than 'fundamentalists, ' The United States was warned of the risks of adopting this position. The significant threat was that the Soviet Union might ultimately be forced to intervene.

The United States chose to ignore the warning.

The national security advisor in the Jimmy Carter administration at that time of this impasse was a gentleman called Zbigniew Brzezinski, and you would be forgiven for thinking that sounded improbable. He asked a relatively simple question of the detractors of the then policy of the United States about international affairs and the struggle going on in Afghanistan:

What is most important to the history of the world? The Taliban or the collapse of the Soviet empire? Some stirred-up Muslims or the liberation of Central Europe and the end of the Cold War?

The Central Intelligence Agency of the United States of America (the CIA) and the Komitet Gosudarstvennoy Bezopasnosti (or Committee for State Security of the Soviet Union, otherwise known as the KGB) decided to continue playing games, and their chosen playing field was Afghanistan.

In February 1979, the United States Ambassador—a gentle named Adolph Dubs, lieutenant commander (retired)—was killed after being kidnapped in Kabul by Islamist extremists. There are many theories as to *how* or *why* he died. Afghan security forces, supported by their Russian advisors, swarmed into the Kabul hotel where the Ambassador was being held, ostensibly to secure the freedom of Dubs. But the negotiations with the kidnappers stalled. In the ensuing firefight, Adolph Dubs was killed.

Years later, in documents released from Soviet archives, it was said that the Afghan government authorized the assault despite demands by the United States that they continue peaceful negotiations. The United States believed that the KGB advisor, who went by the name Sergei Batrukihn, may have recommended the assault and the summary execution of at least one of the kidnappers before the CIA could interrogate him. While relatively trivial in the overall international scene, that obscure event did not exactly improve the relationship between the two superpowers.

The relationship turned entirely on its head.

The Afghan President at that time was a gentleman by the name of Nur Muhammad Taraki, who had come to power in a bloody coup. The immediate prior President, Abdul Qadir Dagarwal, and his family had been murdered. In addition to President Tarakis unconventional method of coming to power, his presidency was also somewhat controversial. He was a founding member of the People's Democratic Party of Afghanistan (the PDPA), an avowed Marxist-Leninist organization and pro-Moscow. The alternative—pro-China—did not bear thinking about the United States and the Soviets. The PDPA became split into two factions: the Khalq faction, which was more militant and somewhat independent of the Soviet Union, and the Parcham faction, to which Taraki belonged and aligned with the Soviets.

Taraki introduced some radical communist reforms, which, among other things, had two particularly disastrous effects. Firstly, there were massive uprisings throughout the barren, landlocked country. Secondly, the Afghan Army at the time suffered mass desertions. Even among the Army personnel who remained, there was a significant swap of allegiances depending on imponderables that western cultures had difficulty understanding. And so, the Afghan Army was of doubtful value.

The dichotomy was not surprising. Afghanistan was a country with a profound Islamic religious culture, and, apart from having a long history of resistance to any form of centralized government control, the communist policies challenged the traditional Afghan values in such things as land ownership, forced marriages, sharia laws, traditional power structures, to mention a few.

Eventually, on the way back from a visit to Communist Cuba, President Taraki stopped by Moscow and asked for Soviet ground troops to intervene in an increasingly unstable Afghanistan. At the time, the prime minister of the USSR, Alexei Nikolayevich Kosygin, made one of his more remarkable and confusing statements:

'We believe it would be a fatal mistake to commit ground troops. If our troops went in, the situation in your country would not improve. On the contrary, it would get worse. Our troops would have to struggle not only with an external aggressor but with a significant part of your people.'

But Taraki did get some concessions from Kosygin. He got some armed support—helicopter gunships with Soviet pilots and maintenance crews, 700 Soviet paratroopers—disguised as technicians to defend the Kabul airport. He got 500 military advisors or KGB officers disguised as *military* advisors. Taraki also managed to get significant food aid out of the Soviets, which merely provided him with another means of moving his favoured friends into positions of more considerable influence.

In March 1979, while President Taraki was busy conducting his negotiations in the Union of Soviet Socialist Republics, Hafizullah Amin became Afghanistan's prime minister and vice-president of the Supreme Defence Council. He was also a member of the People's Democratic Party of Afghanistan and a prominent member of the Marxist Khalq faction.

Consequently, the relationship between Taraki and Amin was not exactly cordial, primarily because Taraki saw Amin as becoming a serious threat to his authority.

The chairman of Soviet Russia, Leonid Ilyich Brezhnev, advised Taraki to remove this prime minister and warned him of a possible assassination attempt. At the same time, he advised Taraki to case up on his more drastic social reforms to get 'broader support' from his people. Any support would have been good.

Brezhnev again warned Taraki about the consequences of any full Soviet intervention: 'It will only play into the hands of our enemies—both yours and ours.'

It is hard to determine whether any part of this advice was acted on by Taraki or was believed by the Soviets. It was reported in the *Kabul Times* on 10 October 1979 that the former leader, who had been hailed in Afghanistan as the Great Teacher, Great Genius, Great Leader, had died quietly of a severe illness that he had been suffering from for quite some time. Well, he would have passed peacefully. A pillow over the head, held down by the commander of the palace guard acting on instruction from Amin, would be a quiet way to depart this life.

And so, Hafizullah Amin became the fourth President of Afghanistan or the second President of the Democratic Republic of Afghanistan.

Amin's rule was notable for two things—its brutality and its brevity.

His first step was to carry out a purge of the PDPA, which probably made him more enemies than friends, at least among those still alive to witness the purge. And he launched a brutal military operation against a resistance group at Sayid Karam in the eastern province of Paktia and virtually obliterated sympathetic villages and villagers. One result was that many Afghans fled across the border into Pakistan and set up a base in Peshawar. Another result was that those who had fled formed a resistance group against the Communist regime.

At the same time, Amin tried to implement a part of Brezhnev's advice to Taraki—promising greater religious freedom, repairing mosques, and declaring that the Saur Revolution, which occurred on 27 April 1978 when the Communist PDPA took power in Afghanistan, was based on the principles of Islam.

Many Afghans would be forgiven for failing to see the logic of that.

But the Soviets failed to see the logic in it as well.

Finally, Soviet patience wore thin.

The Soviets invaded Afghanistan.

The first thing that the Soviets had to do was get rid of Amin. And that act proved not particularly hard to do. The Soviets claimed that Amin was a CIA agent, improbable though that may have seemed to, among other players in the international security scene, the CIA.

The Soviet KGB succeeded in infiltrating a chef who went by the name of Mitalin Talybov into the kitchen at Amin's Presidential Palace. Then it was simply a matter of poisoning the food. Unfortunately, they got the wrong man, and Amin's son-in-law got seriously ill. Amin got suspicious, and he moved the presidential offices to the Tajbeg Palace. So, the Soviets decided to try a more subtle approach. Elements of the KGB Alpha Group and Spetsnaz from the Glavnoje Razvedyvatel'noje Upravlenije—the GRU military intelligence—stormed the palace and killed Hafizullah Amin.

The Soviets explained the execution of Amin as the action of the Afghan Revolutionary Central Committee—the same committee that elected Babrak Karmal as the new head of the government—while Western intelligence sources were more likely to point the finger at the Soviet colonel Alexander Poteyev. Babrak was exiled in Moscow at the time, so it could be assumed that he was not responsible for the death of Amin.

And it could also be assumed that he would be more compliant with Soviet wishes.

Babrak lasted as the head of the Afghani government for quite some time, at least by Afghan standards, until the Soviets got tired of propping him up in Kabul. Despite the presence of the Soviet military, Babrak had little control over much of the country apart from those places where there was a military—that means Soviet company. So, he was replaced by Mohammad Najibullah—a nasty piece of work who made his claims to fame running the Afghan State Information Agency (known by the acronym KHAD, for Khadamat-e Etela'at-e Dawlati). And Mohammed outlasted the Soviet occupation of his country, even though the KHAD had been under the firm control of the Soviet KGB.

Throughout the Soviet occupation of Afghanistan, the United States CIA had a considerable interest in the country, as did China, Saudi Arabia, and Egypt.

But then the Soviets withdrew from the country in 1989.

Whether it was political pressure that caused them to withdraw from Afghanistan or simply because they were fed up with going nowhere, we will probably never know. The United States, of course, claimed an ideological victory, having effectively countered Soviet influence in the region—as perceived by the West to include most of the Middle East, which just so happened to include the oil-rich Persian Gulf.

The problem just did not end there.

After the Soviet withdrawal, the United States and its allies turned their attention to other matters and lost interest in the war-ravaged and remote country. Without the Soviets to counter, the strategic importance of Afghanistan was no more. And nothing was done by either of the two superpowers to rebuild Afghanistan despite the carnage and chaos they left behind. Although the Soviets continued to support Afghan President Najibullah in numerous ways, they eventually gave up on him, and the country descended into anarchy.

The various Mujahideen factions that the CIA had initially supported in the conflict with the Soviets turned on each other as the so-called warlords fought for influence or power, or just for the hell of it.

While this was going on, there was a far blander development—the rise of the Taliban. The very same people who had been fighting with the Mujahideen simply morphed into the Taliban with hardly a second thought.

Pakistan's Inter-Services Intelligence Agency, or ISI, was entirely instrumental in guiding the Taliban to power in Afghanistan and did so without any direct involvement from the CIA. By 1996, the Taliban had captured Kabul; and by the end of 2000, their forces were in control of 95 percent of the country.

At least Afghanistan had a stable government after years of conflict. There were a few other issues, of course—women were banned from jobs, girls were forbidden from attending schools or universities, communists were hunted down and eradicated, thieves were punished by the amputation of a hand or foot, and opium production was virtually, although not entirely, wiped out.

The other minor issue was that the Taliban provided an operating base for their friends.

The principal among those was one by the name of Osama bin Laden.

During the war with the Soviets, the CIA had quite happily funded the Mujahideen and anyone else, including Osama, who was opposed to the perceived archenemies of the free world. While there was concern about the changing nature of Afghanistan, and the development of a haven for terrorists, the United States had other more pressing issues to worry about and did nothing to counter the growth of the Taliban.

Then, on the other side of the world came the event that put Afghanistan very firmly and brutally back on the map.

The terrorist attack on the United States on that fateful day.

September 11, 2001.

There was little doubt that the al-Qaeda group headed by Osama bin Laden was responsible for the attacks in the United States. Indeed, the al Qaeda group claimed and boasted full responsibility for that event. The al-Qaeda group had the full support of the Taliban-led Afghanistan. And the Taliban claimed their share of responsibility for the event as well.

So, the United States displayed all its pent-up anger by invading Afghanistan, under the banner of Enduring Freedom, with the avowed intention of getting rid of Osama bin Laden, getting rid of the Taliban, and ensuring that the haven that Afghanistan had provided for terrorists was finally removed.

But the problem just did not end there.

The problem just spread like cancer.

Would Afghanistan ever be at peace?

The United States sought to win the hearts and minds of these battle-weary people of Afghanistan. They built roads to open up Afghanistan and the western provinces of Pakistan. They invested millions of dollars in infrastructure—instead of what they did back in America when they used railroads to open the Wild West. But knocking down houses that stand in the way of such progress could be counterproductive and could give the Taliban another nail to hammer into the coffin.

The sad thing is that the Taliban as a group did not start as your normal jihad. However, through association with their friend Osama bin Laden, and pushed out of power in Afghanistan after the 9/11 debacle. Under threat from the United States and their coalition partners, they took a different view.

Sure, some of their recruits were now a little surprised

when they became aware of the new political agenda. They became involved in almost-daily terrorist activity, but they also got involved in such action against some of their own people. The Taliban took advantage of anything that they could, such as distributing videos of the beheadings of police officers or their families to discourage people from joining a group that could bring some stability to fragile communities, training and indoctrinating their recruits to become suicide bombers, blowing up their people to make some political point—basically to do what terrorists do: strike fear into everyone. And do it all while hiding among the general population, including women and children.

While the initial strike of Enduring Freedom by the US forces did have a positive effect—the influence of the Taliban was significantly reduced, and Osama bin Laden was driven into hiding—things gradually turned against the United States and their coalition partners. Like many others before them in the long and brutal history of the region, the United States-led coalition was beginning to accept a strategic situation that was becoming a stalemate.

It was a war that no one could win.

This was the hellhole that Mark Taylor and his small team were to enter, and to do what?

Follow a man who was a high-ranking official in the CIA and who was suspected of being involved in drug trafficking.

It seemed illogical and, at the same time, terrifying.

But someone had to do it.

Chapter 1

Afghanistan

The young boys were playing football. There was no defined pitch. There were no lines to mark the limits on where they were or could go. There were no defined goalposts. And there was no referee to oversee their game.

Not that having a referee mattered. Boys tend to get on with their games, and interruptions by some officials would tend to hinder them rather than assist them, no matter where they were or what the circumstances were. They rarely hit the ball in the direction of the wall that stretched for close to a mile down one side of their playing area. If they did, and the ball bounced over it, they were unlikely ever see it again.

Under a clear blue sky, the dust rose beneath their bare feet as they battled with each other in the dry heat. It created a temporary haze across the open ground. That haze settled against the rough stone wall, ending its brief life. It was as though it had never existed, like life and death. One minute we are here; the next minute, we are gone.

Like everywhere else in the Helmand province of Afghanistan, life was fragile. The scenery in this part of

Afghanistan was a little more pleasant than in much of this war-torn land. Helmand was to the north of an area where at least things could grow and to the immediate south of a vast area of this country where there was little to distinguish it from the surface of the moon.

Yet even in this oasis, there was evidence that war was never far away.

The battles raging in this land for many years were brutal and savage. They seemed to have no end. They affected everyone. Their effects were indiscriminate and occurred without any warning.

At this time of the year, the temperatures around the middle of the day are relatively warm and pleasant. It would turn bitterly cold at night, which could be very unpleasant. At any time of the year, life was hard, either due to the weather or because of man's efforts to pursue their personal goals or to better themselves at the expense of others.

On the other side of the stone wall was the enclosure, or compound, which was the local headquarters of the North Atlantic Treaty Organization and the United States Allied forces that had come to protect the local population from the Taliban. At least, that was the stated mission of the foreigners who were the latest non-believers to occupy this land.

The guards on the gates stared out on the lookout for trouble but not expecting any. There rarely was. The men were amongst the most highly trained. And here they were, miles from home, in a foreign land, and nothing to do! They could have watched a basketball game back in the States, but these heathens had not yet been educated in that superior sport.

The boys who were playing football were too young to

appreciate the extent to which they needed any protection, and they were a little suspicious of the people who came out of the fortress and usually, but not always, came back.

The area surrounding the compound was flat and clear of any obstructions. In military terms, this was an area known as the killing fields where the armed defenders had free sight of anyone approaching from any direction and where their guns would be trained. The term dates back to the Killing Fields in Cambodia in the 1970s, where vast numbers of innocent people were killed and buried by the infamous Khmer Rouge immediately after the end of the Vietnam War. That was another war that the United States of America had become involved in with the best of intentions. Another battle that had turned to chaos. And now they were involved in yet another war in which the United States would eventually and inevitably be declared the *loser*.

The fact that the boys were using the area outside the compound as a football field left unanswered the question of what would happen if it returned to its true purpose—a killing field—which was a situation that could arise swiftly and with little or no warning.

The boys were too young to understand the state of war or their elders' embarrassment at having to have the foreigners come to defend them against some of their people. Their people were chameleons—fighting a war yet hiding in plain sight. This war had no rules and no one to judge what was right or wrong, what was allowed or not, and who would live or die.

The steady noise from the blade slap of an approaching American helicopter brought a brief halt to the game of football. The boys stared up at the massive machine as it lumbered over the wall, causing more dust to scatter around, and they briefly dreamed the dreams that only boys of their age could.

Where had the killing machine been? Who was onboard? What adventures had it been involved in? How many men had been wounded? How many innocent bystanders had suffered? How many men, women, and children had died? And for what purpose?

Sitting on a rock observing all the activity around the compound entrance was another boy whose age could not have exceeded fourteen years. Yet his features indicated a young life that had seen more than its fair share of sadness and hurt. Apart from that, he looked like any other boy in this godforsaken place—thin from the rigors of the constant struggle to stay alive and from an inadequate diet; dark lined skin from the rigors of the weather; sad, almost-lifeless eyes from what they had witnessed during their short but brutal time on this earth. He was wearing baggy, featureless clothes and headgear, all hand-me-downs from another long-past generation.

He did not play football with the other boys. His crude crutches tended to get in the way. He was, or more correctly had been, right footed. And he was pretty philosophical about the loss of his right leg. He had lost it courtesy of a roadside bomb, hidden by some of his fellow citizens. But despite the incapacity, he had a job to do. He felt fortunate even to have the job. And he was particularly good at that job.

Being oppressively a disabled persona cripple did not mean that the boy was not intelligent or did not have an excellent memory. He had no idea what the people who paid him at the rate of one Afghani per day to pass on the seemingly pointless information he hoped to gain from his work. All he did know was that he would save his money and build a better life for himself, his sisters, and his mother. He was the sole provider, so what choice did he have? His father had departed this earth courtesy of yet another insane and seemingly pointless act in the never-ending battle between ill-defined sides fighting for equally ill-defined principles.

It would take Naeem Sediqyar a fair while to reach his goal, given that the exchange rate between the Afghani and the United States dollar was about fifty to one, but of such things, dreams are made.

They were in the town of Marjah, situated in the Helmand province in the south of Afghanistan. Well, Marjah was not so much a town as a district in Nad Ali, just to the southwest of the city of Lashkar Gah. Estimates of the population ranged from 85,000 to 125,000 people who lived in the area, but no one could ever be sure. The coalition troops claimed to have rid the area of the Taliban, an action that should have reduced the population somewhat. But the population remained about the same. Consequently, it was anyone's guess what the actual resident population was or what the coalition forces had achieved.

The people in this town were chameleons. One day they were fighting a ruthless and bloody war, dressed in ill-defined uniforms and with weapons that were at best unreliable. The next day, they were simple village folk struggling through life, fighting against the harshness of this country that some called home, with primitive tools, with little or no hope of ever improving their lot.

How many of the grand coalition claims were made for the consumption of their people in their own countries, sitting in their cosy living rooms, flicking through TV channels looking for entertainment, far removed from the drudgery of this war?

There were several wars—well, wars within wars— raging in this part of the world, and the district of Marjah seemed to be right in the middle of all of them.

The coalition of NATO, the United States, and other allied troops claimed that they were trying to get rid of the Taliban. The Taliban, on the other hand, was anxious to remain. Some Afghanis did not want the coalition troops or the Taliban to remain. Some Afghanis had to protect their livelihoods, albeit in this part of the country, mainly in the drug trade. The so-called local warlords were forever bickering with each other, the residents, the central government, and the foreigners. A constant battle was being waged between the various factions seeking control. On the one hand, they just wanted peace. Then others just wanted power at any price. And then others just wanted money.

The mixture of these diverse objectives was probably an almost-insurmountable problem.

A conflict of religious, political, and commercial objectives did not mix now, as it had not done for countless years, in numerous places. That applied at the national and international levels. It is also applied at the individual level.

One problem for Naeem was that he did not know which of the various groups embroiled in these conflicts he was passing his information on to. That was probably because no one else seemed to know which side they were on—at least with any degree of consistency. It was a fair assumption that drugs were the major contributor to this dilemma. While Naeem was a bright boy, he could not be expected to understand what went on in the elders' minds in his community. But he could appreciate inconsistency.

His instructions were provided by a man named Nurul Hadi. This man looked as though he was not long for this world and gave his instructions in the tired voice of someone who had no interest in the message he was conveying or whether the instructions would be carried out. But Naeem knew better than to do anything other than carry out Nurul's instructions. Naeem had seen a few and heard of many more who had perished by failing to follow instructions. Like Naeem, Nurul was simply in it for the money. So as instructed, Naeem watched and reported, received snippets of information, and passed that information on to people who knew what to do with it. Or so he assumed.

Naeem was convinced that Nurul was on the payroll of the Taliban. The fact that he was wrong did not matter. There was more to fear in this land than just the Taliban.

Nurul Hadi was working under instructions that came from someone in Kandahar, the spiritual home of the Taliban but also the home of some of the more ruthless crooks in a land of many.

Even had Naeem known this, it would not have explained the other riddle. Why did the instructions require him to pass the information on to Jacob Dutton? And who in the name of Allah was Jacob? That is, apart from the few facts known to the boy. He knew that Jacob was a white American and that Jacob resided in the fortress on the other side of the compound wall. This suggested to Naeem that there was some conflict going on, the implications of which made him fearful. This was a land in conflict with the world, in conflict with itself.

There was a long history of conflict in this part of the world. In more recent years, the Soviets had fought a war in Afghanistan to maintain their influence in the areas bordering the Persian Gulf. The Soviet conflict, which lasted over nine years and ended in an embarrassing withdrawal by the Soviets in 1989, was only partly because the Afghanis were religious. At least 99 percent of them are Muslims.

And that was only the start of the current trouble.

The Soviets engaged in military operations against the Afghani Mujahideen, and for no other reason than that the Mujahideen were anti-Communist, and therefore anti-Soviet; they had support from the CIA, as well as other allied countries like the United Kingdom, some not so allied like China and Egypt, and probably many others, including Israel. Many Afghans have their origins in Iran—of both Sunni and Shi'a sects—and are split into various ethnic groups of mostly Pashtun or Tajik origin, but many others. Consequently, you have the seeds of many conflicts in Afghanistan even without the involvement or interference from the world powers.

Amid all this, there was also Osama bin Laden. He was a Saudi, and he had not been a significant player in the war against the Soviets; he provided training, arms, and funding to the Mujahideen. Consequently, he also had the support of the United States CIA and their fellow travellers, which naturally included the government of his native Saudi Arabia. The Israeli intelligence agency Mossad and the Government of Israel supported the Mujahideen. Still, it would not support Osama bin Laden was simply another irony that besotted the complex politics of the time.

But then came the event that reshaped the world and redefined political agendas, forever. As far as the Afghans were concerned, it happened on the other side of the world and was hardly any concern of theirs. But in modern-day politics, that hardly mattered.

September 11, 2001—9/11.

The people of Afghanistan must have wondered what they had done wrong, moving from one conflict to another without a pause for breath. Their country had already become one of the most populated—that is, saturated—with land mines on the planet while the Soviet occupation ran its course. Now, with the Soviets gone, there were still more mines. But the problem was more a result of *who* was doing the mining than anything else. The *who* kept changing sides, usually for monetary considerations under the guise of ethnic, religious, tribal, or several other transient reasons. Add to this the fact that Afghanistan is one of the most corrupt nations globally, second only to Somalia. The chances of anyone getting control of the country, at least with any degree of consistency and anytime soon, were remote.

As far as anyone could tell, NATO and the United States forces were unlikely to add to the scattered land mines. If you did not count the aerial bombardments carried out mainly by the United States, which often left a variety of unexploded ordnance just lying around, waiting for a trigger. There were so many haphazard groupings of people and objectives in Afghanistan that there was no reliable map of what went on and who was doing what and where. Therefore, it was crucial that the many and various organizations in the country fighting on one side, or another moved around covertly, and some not so covert operations had good intelligence.

But the collection of that intelligence was often crude and doubtful reliability. And who was getting what intelligence? And at the end of another miserable day, did it matter?

Suddenly, the football game on the killing field was violently interrupted. The first thing that Naeem saw was one of the players. He crumpled to the ground to the accompaniment of the rattle of gunfire. The boy was probably dead before his body had completed its fall.

The M1117 Armoured Security Vehicle, which, along with various other US vehicles, had been taking a leisurely approach to the compound's gates, was suddenly under fire. A couple of jeeps came out of the left side of the field—one seeking to engage the Americans in a firefight, the other heading straight for the gates, which had begun opening to let the small convoy in. The M1117 swung around to engage the first jeep but was soon under fire from a group of Taliban insurgents who had appeared as if from nowhere. Everyone else scattered. It was a brutal and hopeless contest.

The M1117 used only its secondary armament—an M240H machine gun—to mow down four of the insurgents as the rest dived to the ground and then crawled crablike away from the withering fire. Then it fired a grenade from its Mark 19 launcher that brought the Jeep to a sudden and fatal end. Meanwhile, the second Jeep had almost made it to the gates, but it did not get much farther. About a dozen heavily armed marines rushed out of the compound, and one of them was carrying a shoulder-mounted grenade launcher. The training of the marines was too much for the attacking band.

The second Jeep rolled over and over as a grenade hit it and eventually ended life in a crumpled heap of vehicles and body parts at the base of the compound wall. The marines methodically and rapidly made their way out across the killing field, spraying anything that was moving with withering fire. They captured two of the insurgents, who they just dragged back into the compound to the accompaniment of their screams from their injuries. The rest of those few who remained alive fled and vanished into the chaos of shacks that surrounded the base. And then the M1117, the accompanying vehicles, and the marines rapidly all withdrew back into the compound.

The gates were shut, leaving the five dead bodies lying on the ground and the four who had occupied the two Jeeps. The remains of the two Jeeps and the bodies were the only evidence that there had been a fight. The Jeep that had crashed into the wall burned on, fuelled by little more than the recently occupied seats. The bodies of the two occupants lay in crumbled heaps where they had been flung from the vehicle, barely recognizable. The other Jeep sat at the far side of the field, the driver still sitting in his seat, the gunman still hanging on the pedestal. Their clothes were shredded and barely covered what remained of their owners. Both men were undoubtedly dead and stayed as a silent testimony to the futility of this brief and one-sided fight.

Yet slowly, the grounds returned to their previous state.

But what of the other one? He was only a boy! An innocent bystander.

A lady emerged from the shacks and hesitantly made her way to where the boy lay, ignoring the other bodies apart from frightened glances, suspicious that they may inexplicably be resurrected. She tried vainly to get the boy to respond until she realized she was dealing with a corpse. Then the tears started to flow, and the wailing began. The distraught lady finally crumpled to the ground in her despair, rocking back and forth, muttering prayers, the total grief etched on an already care-worn face. Another life was lost. One that would appear on no scoreboard.

When the firing started, Naeem had dropped flat to the ground, unable to run away. The boys who had been playing football scattered. Now Naeem staggered back to the rock he had been sitting on and looked around at the carnage. The boys emerged from their hiding places. They stood around, unsure whether they were now safe.

Gradually things began to return to normal.

It was as though nothing had happened.
Nothing had changed.

A man came out of the compound, and for a while, he just leaned against the wall, watching the boys at play. At the same time, the man was very much aware of everything around him. He looked quite at home. He was dressed in casual clothes, but he would have been at home anywhere with a hat on his head to protect him from the sun. Except that he was a Westerner, and this was Afghanistan.

Seemingly satisfied that all was now relatively peaceful, that there were no Taliban in the vicinity, that this was not one of those days when some mindless person would seek to blow himself and many innocent bystanders into the next world strolled across to where Naeem was sitting.

He looked at the boy, and there was a look of pity and concern on his face just for a moment.

It was a harsh world. People did what they had to do to survive. Some were able to get into a position of influence to take advantage of whatever they were privy to, to the disadvantage of others. Some people would never be in such a position—some like Naeem. But life had to go on, and you had to accept the roles that everyone played in the grand scheme of things.

Wars had to be fought—some won, some lost, some we would never know about.

Drugs had to be shipped; some got to their ultimate destination, some did not, and some just vanished.

The man sat down on a rock close by Naeem, still watching the game, still watching for the slightest hint that he had been observed, still watching to see who else was watching. Nothing escaped his attention.

'Is everything set?' he eventually asked the boy.

'Yes' was the simple reply from Naeem.

The man nodded his head, then rose to his feet, patted Naeem on the shoulder, and wandered back toward the compound gates.

Once back inside, Dutton would send an innocuous e-mail to his masters in the secure, air-conditioned peace of the CIA headquarters at Langley, Virginia.

The CIA had always appeared paranoid about its communications systems. And justly so, for you could never know if, or when, the Russians, or whoever, wanted to break the latest encryption. The fact that the algorithms used in the encryption were worked out by some of the best mathematicians that money could buy did not mean that others could not do the same thing but in reverse. The modern encryption systems used 256-bit or even 512-bit logic, meaning anyone wanting to break the code would need serious computing power. Gone were the days when you merely looked for patterns or where people stumbled upon the key. Although it was improbable, it was still possible—hence the paranoia.

Consequently, any messages sent between CIA offices were phrased assuming that some unauthorized person may read the message. Whether to confirm that they were about to launch World War III on an unsuspecting enemy or merely wanted to order a new toilet roll, every note was encrypted. And so, Jacob's message, duly encrypted, would drive anyone who read it stark raving mad—first trying to read it and then trying to understand what it could mean.

Everything is set.

Naeem had no idea how important this simple message was.

Jacob Dutton had just played one more small part in this never-ending game, the repercussions of which would affect many.

Nothing else mattered.

Nothing ever changed.

Chapter 2

CIA Headquarters – Marjah

The CIA office in Marjah was stifling. The building was a converted house consisting of four barren rooms, only two of which had any windows. The rooms were connected via a simple passageway that led to the only door to the outside world. The fans, which some procurement systems had insisted on supplying, were broken. But that did not matter. There was no electrical power to drive them anyway. The supply of utilities, things that you took for granted in the more civilized western world, rarely happened in Afghanistan with any degree of consistency, whether or not there was a war going on.

The three people who shared this *office* did not speak to each other. It was not as though there was nothing to talk about. There were plenty of things happening in their area of jurisdiction, and most of what was happening were chaotic and scary. It was just that the three people had long since exhausted personal issues, and there was nothing left to talk about other than their work. And much of the latter could hardly be described as optimistic.

There would be much more happening positively if

only the politicians and government officials in Kabul and back in Washington DC could make some decisions. But they did not. If the primary group of bureaucrats in Washington DC could convey some decisions to the secondary group of bureaucrats in Kabul—and hopefully do so without too much distortion—that would be good. The difference between the two groups was that one was safely nestled in Washington's relative peace and tranquillity, and the other was in this hellhole called Afghanistan. So, there was little hope for the three people in this third and much lower group in an even worse place called Marjah. But at least this, the operational side of the organization, would have been charged with something to do and to report back through 'channels,' albeit that 'something' was probably ill-conceived and probably doomed to failure.

Initiative and bureaucracy do not mix too well. And with the primary bureaucracy being in entirely different time zones did not help. Neither did having instructions filtered through other people in their 'in-country' headquarters in the relatively stable city of Kabul. And then there is the mission to consider. A mission statement looks good only on paper and to the people who write it. When filtered down the ranks, the information loses most of its clarity. The underlings charged with its implementation have far more critical things to worry about.

However, the problems of getting a clear mission statement out of their masters in Washington were not the only reason why the three people in Marjah were not talking to each other.

Communications among the three people who shared the sparsely furnished and ill-equipped office appeared to have broken down long before the lack of decisions from the bureaucrats back in Washington led to the inevitable delusions that filtered down through such structures the world over.

The organization that they worked for, the CIA, was large by any standards but was nonetheless lost in the tangle of the United States intelligence services. Security of information was only one of the issues faced by the CIA and others in the security business. The number of people, and the many and varied organizations they worked for, made a farce out of trying to keep anything secret, at least for long. It is a simple fact that a secret is no longer a secret if more than one person knows it. Passing information or sharing data between organizations makes it even more difficult to maintain some semblance of secrecy. But then someone else, other than the favoured one or two, who is not privy to the workings of this bureaucratic jungle may need to know *the* secret to stay alive.

The related problem is that the so-called administrative staff numerically exceeded the so-called operational staff of the CIA by some ridiculous figure. And wrestling information out of such an organizational structure can be a nightmare. All three of the people in the Marjah office were, at least technically speaking, operational field intelligence officers. The extent to which this translated into *experienced* field intelligence officers was a moot point. Being in a job for any time was an experience of a kind. But what kind?

In any case, they continued to feed what information they gathered into the monolithic structure. And got nothing back.

Against this background, the problem was that the three people charged with intelligence and security in this part of the world were no longer sure who they could trust.

It had long been known that someone in, or associated in some way with, Afghanistan was passing CIA intelligence information on to the Taliban. That had to be the case; otherwise, how did the Taliban appear to know almost everything that went on? The United States, which boasted of having the most incredible fighting machine that the world had ever seen, was rendered impotent by someone passing information on to the enemy!

Of course, there was always the possibility that the Taliban were simply getting their information from the same sources—that just went with the territory. But it was plain that the Taliban were getting much more. Information, or intelligence, was one thing. Analysis of that information was something quite different. The Taliban were generally not credited with having much in the way of analytical skills. Therefore, it had to be assumed that there was a leak somewhere in the monolithic organization, such that thoroughly analysed information was being shared. But where was the leak?

From the point of view of the intelligence services, whether it was one of the three agents in Marjah, someone in Kabul, or someone in Washington, no one could be sure. From the point of view of the whole US operation, the recipients of the intelligence information could have leaked it.

It could have been all three of the people in the Marjah office.

It could, of course, have been all four of the organizations mentioned above.

In which case, the entire mission was stuffed from the start.

The small CIA field office, located in the military compound on the outskirts of the so-called city of Marjah, had its origins in the arrogance of the United States security and intelligence service.

Millions of dollars were spent on training and outfitting probably the most efficient, at least technically, and meanest fighting machine that the world had ever seen. Yet this elite force still required to be accompanied by CIA field operatives. The CIA operatives' job was to gather intelligence from the front line (which may *or* may not be in the field and which may *or* may not have been from the front line), analyse *that* intelligence, and then pass the relevant parts of that intelligence on to the people they were there to support. That is, provided the people they passed it on to were cleared to receive it in the CIA's view.

The CIA had initially been set up an office in Kabul, the capital of Afghanistan, but had since expanded to have various cells in many other parts of the country. And that expansion had all the problems usually associated with the spread of a bureaucracy—the timely analysis, coordination, and dissemination of information, and then the timely communication of that information to the people who needed it.

The senior CIA agent in the Marjah cell was Glen Weiner, a veteran of the Somali and Iraq conflicts. He had been there, mostly sitting in an office in Mogadishu in Somalia and Bagdad in Iraq. He was too scared to go outside the protective shield that the troops provided. But this minor irritation had been overlooked by the Human Resources Department at CIA headquarters in Langley. Now he was in yet another hellhole in a remote province in the south of Afghanistan.

Weiner was not known as the best communicator in the service. He was divorced, in his late forties, measuring just under six feet, weighing in at about forty pounds overweight, and heading for a heart attack. Every day he came to the office dressed in an immaculate suit, clean white shirt, and a tie. Every day he left jacket-less, tie-less, a shirt soaked in dust and sweat. He was utterly disgruntled with his lot; his only aim was to get the hell out of Afghanistan. But he still had another five months to go on his present rotation. There was the possibility of another tour of duty if no resolution was reached in the conflict. Or if some bureaucrat in Washington decreed that his skills, aptitude, and experience were still essential in Afghanistan to pursue some vague goal that neither the assigner nor the assignee was aware of. Glen's greatest fear was that there was little chance of the conflict reaching any resolution in the near future. He could not imagine anyone standing in a queue anxiously waiting to take his place.

Weiner had a few serious problems that he had to deal with. In his discussions with the military commanders, he was constantly reminded of the effect leaked information had on their role in the field. And, because the information had all the appearances of having been sourced from good intelligence, the assumption was that the person doing the leaking was on the CIA payroll.

It was not within Weiner's purview to point out that the information could just as easily have come from either military intelligence sources or military personnel to whom the data had been provided. However, the problem was worse than that.

He had a strong suspicion that there was a mole somewhere in the upper echelons of the US security and intelligence network, which made the leaks relatively insignificant.

He could not know whether that was part of the same problem, but it made his task more difficult. How could he report on the subject to his masters, who may or may not be the source of the problem? To add to that was the rumour that someone was facilitating the export of drugs from Afghanistan to the United States. Since the Drug Enforcement Administration (DEA) had little representation in southern Afghanistan, it was left to the CIA to follow up on this. While the area around Marjah had its fair share of poppies, Glen had neither the resources nor the inclination to put much effort into the subject.

He did know that the two staff members working with him were most unlikely to be involved in any of these issues. One of his staff he could not personally stand, but that was the price you paid for working in so remote a region. The other was too naïve, inexperienced, and did not have the aptitude to participate in such silly games. And, like him, they would be just pleased to go home.

Of the other two agents who shared this excuse for an office, the younger of them was a lady who was fresh from spy school and appeared to treat every single snippet of information as hot and the gospel truth. It was very unusual for the CIA to even contemplate posting a female officer to the Afghanistan provinces, given the locals' sensibilities and the attitudes of the US military. The *locals*, and the Taliban, had a total lack of respect for people of the female variety. And in the military, the gender bias, which had dogged the US forces for generations, was very much alive and well. However, somehow or another, she had got the posting. And now her senior officer, Glen, had to deal with that and all his other problems.

Cindy Johnston was a stunning lady—five feet six, brown hair, perfect milky-white skin, a figure that Ellie McPherson would have been jealous about, and a smile that would melt the hearts of most grown men. And she was deeply religious. This latter attribute, to the members of the other sex— lonely and so far from the usual comforts of home—cancelled out all her other features. She had no field experience, which she tried to make up for with her enthusiasm. And by asking so many stupid questions of the other officers, they stopped answering her.

The third field officer was far from enamoured with his other two colleagues, which had nothing to do with the Taliban or the CIA. He was experienced, and he had learned how to survive in this festering place. He had little respect for Glen because he regarded him as a wimp. And he had little time for Cindy because she was a threat. She was not interested in anything other than work, and her constant questions unsettled him. On a personal level, he was young and horny. He was about six feet tall and overweight, mainly brought about by his affinity for the bottle and his liking of recreational drugs. He was attractive and single, but unlike many of the young men who had been dragged away from the comforts of home, he had another and more urgent agenda. He was hell-bent on doing his work to the best of his ability for the CIA and his country on a business level. On a more personal level, his primary purpose in this hellhole was to gain access to the local produce.

Opium.

His name was Jacob Dutton.

The intelligence that the three agents had been able to gather so far did not reveal, on first evaluation, any more than the CIA already knew. The Afghanis were displeased with their foreign visitors, making it difficult for the CIA to use their standard methods of obtaining information. There was little point in the CIA trying to deploy deep undercover agents from within the local population. The odds were not good that those local agents would remain loyal to the CIA long enough to be of much use. Worst case, they could be of more use to the very people that the CIA was trying to gather information about. Such was the nature of the Afghani psyche.

Because of the shortage of agents, the difficulties of the service, and the need to make an organization out of the chaos, the tasks of the three agents were roughly divided to reflect their purpose of the CIA having a presence in Marjah.

As Weiner was the senior agent, he was responsible for coordinating intelligence, dissemination, distribution, and subsequent forwarding reports to his masters in Kabul. Once in Kabul, the information was again appropriately analysed by people who had little idea of the realities of life in Marjah and then fed through channels to the sponge that was Washington. And once there, it would perhaps be filed as necessary, or more likely filed as irrelevant. At least it was filed. And as is the way with bureaucracies, the lowest-level staff did the filing. Therefore, it would rarely become exposed again once filed.

Weiner rarely, if ever, got any feedback on what use, or otherwise, his information had been and what his contribution was to the cause. But he kept sending it, as is the way with bureaucrats the world over.

The task of attempting, at least, to gain intelligence from the local population in the surrounding areas was assigned to Jacob. That gave Jacob one excellent reason to be out of the office most of the time. That suited him simply fine.

There were no DEA personnel in Marjah, and so the task of finding out what went on in the drug trade was left to Cindy Johnson. How this was justified did not bear scrutiny. As far as could be ascertained, Johnson knew nothing about drugs—either the use, making, or distribution of drugs—so she was a highly trained filing clerk.

However, because the military operations that the Marjah cell was there to support were ongoing and could not, or would not, wait for the CIA to get its shit together, they had to ensure that their little office was virtually staffed twenty-four hours a day, seven days a week. That made the formal division of responsibilities almost irrelevant.

The most challenging job of the three was that of Weiner's, as indeed it should be. The CIA had a slightly different position from Iraq and the earlier days in Afghanistan. It had taken on a more military role, which included, but was not limited to, flying RQ-1 Predator drones. The *R* was the United States Department of Defense designation for Reconnaissance, and the *Q*, not so logically, was the title for an unmanned aerial vehicle (UAV). These drones could and did fire Hellfire missiles. The drones were usually controlled by an Air Force sergeant sitting at a play station somewhere in Colorado, USA, with a ten-plus-hour difference in time, did nothing to improve inter-service relationships on the ground. There was little or no drone activity in Marjah, but that did not stop the flow of information to the CIA cell, which Weiner chose not to pass on because it was simply *not* irrelevant.

This had, among other things, resulted in tension between the military chiefs in the Pentagon and the spooks at Langley. At the lower level, this tension should not have reached Marjah since it was so far removed from the real action mainly taking place across Pakistan's border. But it did. Military people tend to move around and feel entitled to receive the same information wherever they are. Because of this plain fact in the military, there was tension between Glen and the local area commander. Glen's attitude and inability to communicate certainly did not help.

Add to this the fact that the CIA was trying to distribute cash to people who it was felt could assist the United States war effort did not help. The media referred to these people as 'warlords,' which the military happily accepted since it strengthened their claim for more resources. However, these warlords were village elders who would do the bidding of their CIA paymasters if the money kept coming. Many of the identities of such people were primarily unknown to the military since that kind of information had to be kept secret. The result was one of almost total confusion. It was impossible to work out which warlords they were supposed to be dealing with. And were the military on the same page as the intelligence gatherers? And how did the CIA intelligence, or the military with its own intelligence staff, really know whether the warlords were doing anyone but their bidding?

There was another result of this situation. The Marjah CIA operation was regarded as a bit of a joke by the military and believed to be going nowhere. The military people tended to rely on their intelligence sources, which were not so inept. This situation led to inevitable frustration such that Glen's role simply became that of a conveyor of messages.

This position happened to suit Jacob Dutton fine. Jacob's job was much simpler than it appeared, or at least it should have been. He just had to talk to the locals, establish a rapport, and listen. To make his task much more manageable, the CIA had given him a crash course in the languages and culture of Afghanistan, if four years at the Farm back in Camp Peary York County in Virginia could be called a crash anything. Jacob was particularly good at languages, so he was ideal for the position he now found himself in. But there were two minor problems. Firstly, who could Jacob trust? Secondly, could Jacob be trusted? And, of course, there was another problem that someone would have needed to go on an FBI course to have any hope of resolving. That course would have been about making the best use of informers. But the Federal Bureau of Investigation's concept of what an informer is had little to do with the realities of life in Afghanistan.

Most of the informers in this part of the world would not be described in anyone's language as the most reliable. It was the same as dealing with your regular out-and-out criminals in a more civilized part of the world. The FBI and others in the law enforcement business believed that informers could usually be trusted to deliver what the police or the authorities wanted to hear, complete with lies, deceit, exaggerations, and any combination of all three that happened to suit their objectives at the time.

To overcome this type of problem, the CIA and their friends at the FBI had a theoretical answer. That answer was profiling. The interpretation of whether that profiling was accurate or not depended on the culture in which it was to be applied. And on the ability to read body language was difficult for someone in the country because of cultural differences and almost impossible if you were in a different country.

If you had people able to speak the local language, and you taught them all there was to know about the local culture, they should be able to profile people and read the body language of their informants. But it was asking a bit too much. All Jacob could realistically do was pay people for information. The more—money and people, which is—the better. And then, by analysing what they produced, you could, hopefully, see a pattern emerging. Some informers tell you the truth some of the time. The ones who told the truth none of the time were helpful, provided you could correctly interpret what they were trying to steer you away from or inform you what not to look at.

That was the trouble with paying people for information. It would be far better to have people provide information for free—out of anger, out of passion, out of a sense of righteousness, or out of principle. Such people gave information because they wanted to, or needed to, achieve something. And they usually gave the whole story, plus a little bit more. On the other hand, two things were likely to occur when you paid for information.

From the point of view of the recipient of the information, in this case, the CIA, the objective was to get something for the money; otherwise, what was the point of spending it?

From the point of view of the provider of the information, in this case, a chaotic collection of people from a wide variety of ethnic and religious backgrounds, the objective was to get money; so, anything would do, provided someone could put a value on it.

The odds were always with the provider. The process was as old as time: withhold the information until you saw the money. Then provide the information to the extent necessary—no more, no less. It did not matter whether it was new or old. It did not matter whether it was true or false. What mattered was that you got paid and left behind a hint of more to come.

And that was mind-numbingly frustrating to the small group in the CIA Marjah office.

The job assigned to Cindy Johnston was even more of a joke. Since the Americans had attempted to take over the country, it appeared that the whole economy of Afghanistan had become dependent on drugs. And the wars that had gone on in this landlocked country during the last fifty or more years had used and abused this simple fact. What a girl raised in Tennessee and who had trained in spy school back in the comfort of Langley could hope to achieve against this background was anyone's guess.

The Taliban and the CIA were on the same page regarding their official position on drugs, albeit for entirely different reasons. The Taliban were vehemently opposed to drug use and, had circumstances been different, would have stamped out the drug trade long ago. But the Taliban had to get money from somewhere to be able to fund their war, and what better means to do so than by selling drugs to their archenemy. The Taliban controlled vast areas of the country, and most of those areas were made up of poppy farms. On the other hand, the CIA was officially committed to stamping out the drug trade, and the US Government had poured billions of dollars into another kind of war to do just that. That war, within a war, had achieved precious little. And drugs continued to pour into the United States, often courtesy of schemes funded by the CIA.

Apart from these issues, the task of keeping track of the size and harvesting of the poppy crop was simply one of observation. The yield was enormous. It was merely a matter of reading a calendar when it was to be harvested. Where it went to, however, did present the odd minor problem. Most of the crop simply vanished. And then Johnson had to contend with the issue of the strategic position taken by the various people who were aware of the crop—the local government, such as it was; the local warlords who did not recognize any government; the local Afghanistan Army and police who would be responsible, or not, for the enforcement of the law; and, lastly, her masters, the CIA. Apart from the complexity of the task, there was a problem of perception that people, public and official, failed to comprehend.

From the peace and tranquillity of a living room in New England, it was simple to perceive a demarcation a line between the authority of the military, the authority of the police, the assistance being provided by the CIA and other the United States and allied forces, and their assigned roles in the war on drugs.

In Afghanistan, there was not the respect usually accorded to the likes of the FBI in the United States, the NYPD in New York, or the Bobbies of Scotland Yard in London.

The Afghan police were a joke. Most of the Afghan police recruits could not shoot straight. Most police personnel were happy to sell their weapons to the Taliban or anyone else who came up with the right money. Most of them were young, with little or no education and no prospect of becoming educated. Such people applied to join the Afghan National Police because they would get paid. Or, at the very least, sometimes they would get paid. Their applications to join the police were invariably accepted because the ANP had to maintain numbers, which it did by simply replacing those that had left. It was just a numbers game. Many of the recruits were on drugs—mainly Hashish, a cannabis drug—which they smoked when they had something to worry about most of the time.

The people who were responsible for the training, discipline, and welfare of the Afghan police were aware of the shortcomings of their forces. They simply exploited their weaknesses—to make money for themselves at the expense of their country.

This situation was hopeless, and the police were no hindrance to the people who ran the drug trade. Anyone observing the goings-on could only despair at the lack of official action. In the case of Cindy Johnson, for all her enthusiasm, she could only report on the chaos and wait for a response.

From whatever source and whoever was ultimately responsible, all the information that came to the group in the CIA field office had to be shared, and that meant that they had to keep up to date on everything that was going on. Depending on who provided the information, some were true; some were false. But which? So, they had to double and sometimes triple check the information; they also had to check the source and correlate each story with what they had heard previously from other sources.

This was not only frustrating.

It was tiring.

The CIA personnel were tired of going around in ever-decreasing circles. Tired of the war. Tired of the demands of the military. Tired of the Afghanis. Tired of each other.

Fortunately, they had one solution to this problem.

Drugs.

Both Weiner and Dutton were drug users: Glen preferred smoking Hashish, and Jacob preferred something more sophisticated like heroin. Johnston was not a habitual drug user, but, despite her role in the Marjah cell, she was too inexperienced to see the vital signs of drug use in her partners and too naïve not to be tempted. Unfortunately, drugs in their work environment had a disastrous effect on the operation.

The lack of harmony in the Marjah CIA office suited Dutton. He relied on information, mainly information that his co-inhabitants might wish to pass up the line, so his analysis he kept to himself. If either Weiner or Johnston got even a whiff of what Dutton was up to concerning drugs in Marjah, he would have a problem.

At present, Johnston seemed hell-bent on observing

and reporting what the authorities would already know—those vast quantities of drugs were being produced, and most of those drugs ended up in the US. She had made little progress in finding out how they got distributed. She relied on information, most of which was provided by Jacob and his network of informants. This was ideal for Jacob's purposes. However, should she stumble upon the area Jacob wished to protect, she would need to be dealt with swiftly and permanently.

Fortunately, such things were easily arranged in Afghanistan.

On a more practical note, it would be nonsensical for a young and inexperienced employee of the CIA like Cindy Johnston to interfere in any aspect of the drug trade endorsed by some members of the very organization that she was working for. This was way above her pay scale, so she took the practical course and ignored it.

One way or another, this whole mess was likely to be sorted shortly. There were rumours that some bigwig from Langley was due to visit them to review *their progress* or lack of it. Glen was doing his best to keep the story to himself because he knew of another problem that was the most likely reason for the review.

Someone was passing information to the Taliban. Theoretically, it was doubtful whether any of the three operatives in the Marjah cell was the one responsible for the simple reason that the information the Taliban seemed to be getting was good intelligence rather than raw data. Nevertheless, it was not inconceivable that someone was independently analysing the data rather than waiting for it to pass through the grinder that was the bureaucratic jungle of the CIA and other organizations that made up the US security and intelligence network. This would explain why the Taliban seemed to have information before the US troops. It did not matter if the Taliban's information was right or wrong. The Taliban were not the ones spending billions of dollars and trying to be proactive.

Weiner withheld information about the impending visit from the other team members did not matter to Dutton. He had a direct line of contact which bypassed the usual command structure and reporting procedure, and he, therefore, knew who would be coming.

And he knew the real purpose of the visit.

It did not matter to Johnston either.

But for vastly different reasons.

As with many others that found themselves in this hellhole, Cindy Johnston had her own little secrets.

It was not that it mattered very much, but she was not the religious zealot she had portrayed. Nor was she a virgin. Faced with the prospect of at least six months in Marjah with no chance of a remotely everyday social life, she did the next best and obvious thing.

She slept with the boss.

Chapter 3

The Tajiks

It was a small house that could best be described as little more than a hovel in the barren, thorny, bomb-strewn farmland that was the southern district of Marjah. The outside of the house was made of rocks held together with what looked like dried mud. Inside the house, it had no freshwater, electricity, sanitation, or other amenities that could distinguish it as belonging to the current, or even the last, century.

The house had been chosen at random from one of the many totally or partially abandoned buildings that littered the settlement. The number of men who had been killed in the conflict was more committed to fighting rather than family or had simply fled meant that there were families without husbands or fathers. The families had also left to return to their own families or simply to turn their backs on a place and a period of their lives that they would rather forget.

There were no paved roads in this part of the district. Such were the tracks that meandered through the area that it was unlikely that there would be any motorized traffic. Most people travelled on foot. The more sensible people didn't go outside or travel, especially at night.

Outside of the designated building, three men were continuously patrolling. They checked that no one ventured near the house that they were guarding. Any strangers would be discouraged by the AK-47 rifles that all the three men carried. But still, they had to be sure by making their presence and intentions clear.

Another three men, similarly armed, had clambered up onto the roof. There they lay prone, guns at the ready, just in case someone should foolishly approach the house with the apparent intent of disrupting what was going on. It was pitch-black. Unusually for Afghanistan, there were clouds in the sky at this time of the year, so there was no moon and no starlight on this night.

And that was good.

The men had been instructed that nothing that happened in the house's proximity should escape their notice. However, despite their weapons, they had been ordered not to get into a fight. If anyone approached the building with the explicit intention of disrupting the meeting, the guards would hope to have ample warning. They would simply disappear into the night, along with the people they were guarding. The guards did not have the night-vision magic that the allied forces had. Usually, they made up for that in stealth and the brutal way they dealt with anyone that dared to stray into their path. But not on this night.

There could be no listening devices or other gadgets chosen for this meeting in the house. The choice of this house had been random, so its use could not have been predicted by anyone intent on listening in on the conversations that were to occur. It had no known connection to any form of Taliban or any other insurgent group. And that was also good. The building would not be a target of the dreaded drones.

No one in Marjah was supposed to know that a meeting was even taking place or who was attending, and the secret was known by only the few who had travelled from out of town.

Security was absolute.

Of course, the whole thing was ridiculous because nobody cared.

But it would play a prominent role in the lives of others who had no apparent connection to it.

The guards outside the building and those on the roof were all members of the Afghan Army. They were also from the Tajik people—Sunni Muslims who were more related by ethnicity, custom, and tradition to Iran rather than to Afghanistan. Of the six men who attended the meeting inside the house, five were also Tajiks, and the other was a foreign infidel but a significant one.

His name was Jacob Dutton, and he worked for the CIA in Marjah.

Of the five bearded Tajik elders, two of the men had made the perilous journey across the border from Quetta in Pakistan. The older two were Abdul Hadi Arghandiwal, and the younger one was his brother, Zalmay. They were the originators of a plot to kill a member of the central government. They needed help from the locals to travel from Marjah to Kabul, on the correct assumption that the member of the government in Kabul was unlikely to come to them.

The target of their plot, along with every other member of the Afghanistan government, rarely, if ever, left the relatively secure confines of Kabul and was extremely unlikely to travel this far south. The Taliban, al-Qaeda, and various other insurgent groups inspired that reluctance. But even the Taliban would not suspect that the Tajiks presented a severe threat to any government officials. This could be based on the Tajiks' lack of numbers. It was more likely to be found in the Tajiks' lack of organization. It could be found in the Tajiks' lack of information. It was most probably based on entirely the wrong reason—discrimination.

The Tajiks recognized their lack of information and sought assistance to make up for it from those who would have intelligence. The Tajiks needed help from someone closer to the central government in Kabul to make sure that they could know their target's movement and *when* and *where* it would be best to strike that target. Early in their planning, they had identified the CIA as a possible ally, given that they could not trust anyone else in this godforsaken country. Not that they could entirely trust the CIA. But there was one advantage. If you crossed the CIA, you could probably live to fight another day. If you crossed the Taliban or any of the numerous insurgent groups that littered the scene, you would most likely die.

The incentive for the plot was based on simplicity. Abdul, the leader of this small group, had decided to make a statement to his friends—the desperately poor Afghani exiles in the refugee camps that had sprung up all over Pakistan, the country that lay to the east. Abdul studied the strategies and tactics of the many assassination plots implemented in this part of the world, including in Pakistan, especially in Afghanistan. Some had been successful. Some had not. But from his observation and study of history, the principal objective should be clear.

Go for the man at the top.

Anything else would be a complete waste of time. And it had to be done so that the man knew, and the world would know, what this was all about. No suicide bomber would create mayhem and have only a fifty-fifty chance of getting to the man who was the primary target and a 100 percent probability of killing innocent people. Abdul would announce who his group was and what they represented in a public place and then shoot their target dead. So be it that Abdul himself would probably not survive. He would be a martyr for a just cause and die knowing that he had rid the earth of another corrupt politician who had failed his people.

The unfortunate man at the top, who was to be their target, was not exactly new to a situation where he was the subject of an assassination attempt.

He was the President of Afghanistan—Hamid Karzai.

Some years before the events unfolded, Hamid Karzai lived in exile in Pakistan. There he had married a doctor working with the millions of Afghan refugees who had fled to that country to escape the carnage. Hamid was a highly educated man. His many speeches while in exile about freedom, plus his tireless work with the anti-Taliban movement, impressed the refugees and many others, both outside Afghanistan and inside that war-ravaged country.

Over many years, the Tajik people and the Taliban had not been on friendly terms. The Panjshir province to the northeast of the capital, Kabul, predominantly Tajik, had been the centre of anti-Taliban resistance during Taliban domination of Afghanistan. Abdul Hadi and his Tajik friends had fully supported Hamid Karzai when he first became a leader and then President of their homeland after the fall of the Taliban.

However, despite all the grandstanding and the flowery speeches, Karzai had not achieved much, apart from his appearances on the world stage. Rarely, if ever, did he travel outside of Kabul. And the feelings grew among the Tajiks that he had become hopelessly out of touch with his people.

The rumours were that he was trying to cut a deal with a rejuvenated Taliban. In the opinion of the Tajiks, which could only mean one thing—the Taliban would fight, scheme, and crawl their way back into power in Afghanistan.

There were, of course, other reasons that tended to complicate things.

Abdul Hadi had developed a thriving business, which he was using to make some money to help the refugees, help his own Tajik faction, and help himself. The fact that the business was not strictly legal did not matter, given the objective. And, at least initially, and certainly inadvertently, President Hamid Karzai had significantly helped in that business.

The President had rejected various attempts by the US authorities to take more decisive action to stop the Afghanistan drug trade, most of which was destined to feed the constant and inexhaustible demand for drugs in the United States. One reason that could plausibly have been given for Karzai's rejection of these attempts was the feeling that the US authorities would have been better advised to deal with the demand for drugs in their own country rather than worry about the supply of drugs from Afghanistan. The United States was the largest consumer of illicit or illegal drugs on the planet. It was old but an elementary lesson of economic theory that controlled what went on in the world—demand and supply.

The fact that rumours were rife that Hamid Karzai had only rejected the moves by the United States to protect the considerable drug-based interests of his younger brother, Ahmed Wali Karzai, was really beside the point and of only limited concern to the Tajiks. That was just politics.

Sure, the brother (more correctly, the paternal half-brother) of Hamid was a significant player in the local politics of the southern city of Kandahar. In this position, he could, and did, acquire considerable wealth. On many occasions, Ahmed Karzai had been known to help both the British and the Americans in their ceaseless attempts to infiltrate the darker depths of the drug world.

And he did that for free.

But still, he accumulated wealth.

It was hard to tell whether that wealth came from drugs or other means. There was extraordinarily little convincing proof that Ahmed was either a drug dealer or a drug trafficker.

There could, of course, be other reasons for his accumulation of wealth. Money was flooding into Afghanistan by the truckloads—most of it from the United States—and when vast amounts of money are involved, you get truckloads of something else.

Corruption.

That aside, the facts were that the drug trade was still very much alive and well. And, right now, no one seemed to be willing or able to do anything about it, from either the demand side or the supply side.

However, in all this, there was one overriding consideration.

If the Taliban came to power again in Afghanistan, then that would be the end of the drug trade as we know it.

In the complex world that Afghanistan was a part of, the simple solution to the Tajik problem was to get rid of Hamid and get someone else in charge. That would achieve two things.

Firstly, that *someone else* would leave the drug trade alone.

Secondly, *someone else* would not be so amicable

towards the Taliban.

In the eyes of Abdul, the apparent person to achieve these things was Mohammed Fahim—a member of the leadership council of the United National Front of Afghanistan.

There was, of course, no guarantee that Fahim would emerge from all of this as the replacement leader, but in the view of Abdul, Fahim had a couple of things going in his favour.

Firstly, and foremost, Fahim was a Tajik.

Secondly, and of equal importance, Fahim had a solid military background and was unlikely to become as docile as Hamid had been.

This man, also known as Marshall Fahim, had spent most of his adult life fighting against the Soviets and the Taliban. Along the way, Fahim had also successfully, and obviously, avoided many attempts to assassinate him. Abdul knew Fahim as one who could be very unpleasant if someone happened to annoy him. But he was Tajik. And, uncharacteristically for a politician in this country, he was not known to have divided loyalties. A part of Abdul's plan was to acquaint Fahim with what he intended to do. But before he could do that, Abdul just needed to make sure that Marshall Fahim would not use his knowledge of the assassination attempt on Hamid Karzai simply to promote himself in the government by revealing the existence and the perpetrators of the plot.

Faith in the man was one thing.

Trust in the man was something else entirely.

This was Afghanistan.

It never occurred to Abdul to question the motives, or the reliability, of the CIA in consenting to this obscure logic. Of course, the CIA had other reasons that Abdul could not be privy to. The United States would not be opposed to a change in leadership since Hamid was becoming a bit of a problem. And if some group offered to do the deed by ridding them of another problem, they could take advantage of that opportunity. Circumstances may change, but for the present, they could choose to provide what assistance they could and see where that leads. The CIA was known to have sharpshooters ready on the site of other assassinations to either ensure that the assassination was successful or of ensuring that the assassins did not get away.

Such was the complexity of life or death.

This meeting would not take long. After the initial exchange of greetings, most of which were conducted in Farsi, Hadi turned his attention to Dutton. Much to everyone's surprise, including Jacob, he addressed him in English.

'Will you take some tea?' he asked, while, as is customary in this part of the world, the host proceeded to serve all who were assembled six small cups. He kept his eyes on Dutton the whole time with a curious smile. When he had finished serving the tea, he squatted down and addressed the CIA representative in English again.

'You must be a particularly important man to be representing your country in these discussions?'

Dutton nodded and smiled at Abdul in acknowledgment of the tea. He nodded his head in recognition of the implied compliment. He smiled to hide the panic that was welling up inside him.

Jacob knew how this game was to be played. He would need to be careful, or there could only be one loser.

This was the first time that Jacob and Abdul had met. And Abdul would first need to establish a relationship before starting their discussion. However, Abdul's comment about Jacob's importance was not meant to be flattering. It was a simple statement that required Jacob to state his position. If he did not get it right, or if Abdul even had a suspicion that something was amiss, then it was unlikely that Jacob would live for much longer. Despite their lack of organization and intelligence, the Tajiks still had weapons and were extremely willing to use them.

When Jacob had first been made privy to what the Tajik plan was, he was a little sceptical. The CIA had met with Abdul in Pakistan, and it was there that it had been agreed that it should proceed. As things developed, the 'in-country' CIA regretted having made those arrangements, and it was left to Jacob to try to make some sense out of the mess. Of course, he was pretty willing to do so because there was a good chance that it would suit his other needs. However, that was not so easy.

In their infinite wisdom, the people in Washington had decided that the CIA was committed to this task. To pull out now would leave the CIA, and therefore the Government of the United States, losing face and consequently vulnerable. The Tajiks would be annoyed and could reveal the 'understanding' they had come to with the CIA to the entire world. The Tajiks were unlikely to do so since that would mean almost-certain death for Abdul and his co-conspirators. But who knows what factors were considered in Washington DC? The authorities may have felt that they were dealing with a group of inexperienced amateurs who would not consider the implications of anything they did or said. If that were the case, they had one thing right: they were dealing with a bunch of fruitcakes.

Dutton held his nerve and adopted a calm and business-like attitude that he certainly did not feel. Reading body language in unfamiliar cultures was always tricky. But dealing with eleven men armed with AK-47s and countless knives would not be his idea of a fair fight. He had to play the game very carefully. They had all the advantages, and the game would be played by their rules.

At least for now.

'I represent the United States Government, and everything that I say will have the full backing of our forces here in Afghanistan. You will appreciate that, for security reasons, I will not disclose any of the personnel we will employ. But it is sufficient for me to say that I will be your main contact and attend to whatever your needs are.'

Abdul also chose his words very carefully in reply.

'By using the term security reasons, you say you do not trust us?'

The eyes usually told the story, but reading the Tajik was hard. Abdul could either be seeking assurance or simply challenging what had been said.

Jacob reached across the table, lightly touching Abdul on his sleeve. He hoped that the Tajik could not see the fear in his eyes.

'No ... no, this mission is being handled by a special group set up specifically for this purpose. Many of our people outside that group will not know about it. Because some of our people must work alongside the Afghani intelligence, and indeed, Pakistani intelligence, it is essential that we retain the strictest security.'

The two men stared at each other for a moment, and then Abdul smiled and turned to the other Tajiks. He spoke to them in Farsi. They all laughed. Jacob remained deadpan. He had often heard similar comments passed about *deniability*. Jacob had often experienced situations where the people he was dealing with forgot, or were unaware of, his proficiency in the local languages. Maybe they were aware and just did not care. Either way, the Tajiks were confident in the discussions, even if they regarded him as an infidel and simply as a messenger.

Jacob had passed the first test. They were treating him as a messenger did not mainly concern Jacob at all. The point was that he was as high up the totem pole as they would get.

'What can you tell us about the arrangements in Kabul?' was Hadi's next question.

Dutton was happy to be speaking in English. He had lost track of the number of times he had conveyed a message to the Afghans in Farsi, only to hear that his words had a different interpretation. Knowing the Afghanis as he did, most of the time, which would have been a matter of convenience rather than just a matter of his translation or their interpretation of it.

Jacob had long since gotten over the hang-ups that most of his fellow citizens had in dealing with people in this part of the world. The beards, the headgear, and the dress-like clothes that most men wore were just that. Beneath it all, they were just human beings going about their lawful or unlawful business. They were just trying to survive in a harsh and unforgiving environment.

Except there was one slight difference.

The Afghanis did not seem to distinguish too much between life and death. The sanctity of human life, so dear in most Western cultures, was irrelevant.

While in Western society, life was precious and had to be protected, the Afghanis would slit your throat for very little cause. They would willingly give their own life provided their death would be furthering the reason—whatever the local imams decided was a worthy cause, and that cause was in the name of Allah or the name of the Prophet.

To someone from the Western culture, which meant

that they were just too unpredictable. Consequently, Jacob had two purposes that he now had to achieve.

Firstly, he had to convey his masters' messages and then handle any side issues by providing answers that the Tajiks would wish to hear.

Secondly, he had to do so without upsetting these highly volatile people.

He had to try to stay alive.

'Well,' Dutton began, 'President Hamid is reviewing a group of soldiers at their passing-out parade a couple of weeks from now. He will use the opportunity to make a speech, which Hamid has advertised as significant to all Afghanis. So, both international and local media will be in full attendance, which is good for our purposes. We can get you to within about 100 yards of where Hamid Karzai will be standing. You will be in front of him and to his right. There should be no problem with the security people. They will not be expecting any danger from within the crowd. They will be looking to the sides and at the buildings that overlook the crowd, but not out in front.'

Dutton was merely passing on the message that he had received from his CIA contacts in Kabul. The scheme sounded OK. He did not care whether or not it was. The Tajiks had a distorted view of their ability to use weapons. The fact that the Tajiks would be some distance away from Hamid and would need to push their way forward to have any real chance of achieving their objective meant that they would be long dead before they caused any damage— at least in Jacob's view. An expert sharpshooter with a sophisticated sniper rifle and a stable platform would have at least a fair chance of hitting the target from up to a thousand feet away. These Tajiks would be lucky if they could hit a barn door from a few feet.

'And what can you tell us about Marshall Fahim? Is he with us?' Abdul asked, apparently content that their positioning for the assassination was all arranged.

'Yes, we have got Fahim,' Dutton began. 'He will do exactly what we tell him to do. He does not, of course, know any of the details of who you are or what your exact plans are. It should stay that way until after the event. There is a risk in telling him too much. The Presidential minders can be quite brutal and persuasive in dealing with any assassination attempt. And we would be foolish to place Fahim in any danger. We have not taken him completely into our confidence on this one.'

On this subject, Dutton was also vulnerable. Fahim had not been consulted at all. And there was another overriding issue. Jacob's advice from his masters in the CIA Kabul office was that there was just no way that the Government of the United States could, or would, support someone as devious as Marshall Mohammed Fahim in a bid to be the President of Afghanistan. At least that was the current official United States Government and CIA position. The United States and their coalition partners had enough issues with the current President, as indeed they did with many of the world's regimes that they provided support to. You could not have everything all the time!

A stable government often carried a cost—especially in countries where democracy was not the norm. In a place as volatile as Afghanistan, when Hamid came to power, the Government of the United States had a simple decision to make: Do they support him, or do they not support him? It did not mean that they had to like him or trust him. But they trusted Fahim even less and would have preferred someone else of their choosing. And that someone would *not* be a Tajik.

If Abdul Hadi believed that Fahim would inherit the leadership, let him think that. After all, the CIA intended that whatever else may happen, Abdul and his brother would not be around to know whether or not Fahim did rise to be the next President. The other issue of whether Fahim could be trusted with details of the plot and with more information about any CIA involvement was much more straightforward.

He could not.

And he was not.

The CIA would know that Abdul and his co-conspirators would be, or should be, scared about the possibility of a double-cross by Fahim. And with excellent reason. So, saying that the CIA would not wish to place Fahim in danger was a good ploy. And it was reasonable for Fahim, or anyone else, to deny any knowledge of the plot, even if he talked to Abdul himself. If Abdul knew how this game was played, he would note the duopoly. There was no harm done if he did not know, was there?

'Excellent!' Hadi exalted, oblivious to the well-known characteristics of Fahim that made him an unlikely choice for the next President, at least in diplomatic circles and down to and including the lowest-paid cleaner in the present administration.

'And will Fahim be attending the same event as the President?' asked the excited Abdul. 'Will he witness our revenge?'

The answer to that question was like Crazy Horse making a luncheon appointment with General Custer for the day after the battle of Little Bighorn.

'We don't think so!' Dutton replied. 'We think it is better if Fahim stays away and that he makes his observations on the sudden death of his President from some other place. More particularly, there is a risk that Fahim could be caught up in the crossfire—and we would not want that to happen.'

'No, we would not!' Abdul blurted out. For a moment, there was fear in his voice. From the CIA's viewpoint, which would solve two problems if Fahim did get killed.

But then again, you cannot have everything, can you? At least not at the same time.

Hadi had never been involved in anything as complicated as an assassination plot, and Dutton suspected that he would have conflicting emotions. Abdul was both excited and scared. Not quite the cold, calculating type of person Jacob had assumed he would be. Still, it was too late to change the plan or the principals. All that was necessary now was to ensure that the CIA involvement was minimal in the planning stages and non-existent at the time of execution.

It was only a simple assassination, after all.

The FBI had indoctrinated all the crime-busting organizations in the world to the concept that there were only two kinds of assassinations—*ideological* assassinations and *functional* assassinations.

In the latter case, a functional assassination was simply a matter of it just being inconvenient for the target of the assassination to still be around. Alternatively, it was just timely and more convenient for someone else to take the subject's place, which amounted to the same thing.

In the case of an ideological assassination, emotion plays a much more significant role—and the more feeling, the more passionate the attempt is. But more importantly, the less the people directly involved would be concerned with the actual science of removing life from the body. The assassinator was likely to parade the corpse for all to see on the erroneous assumption that everyone agreed with what had transpired.

To the CIA, this planned assassination of President Hamid Karzai was purely functional, almost clinical. Bang!

Job done. Thanks. What's next?

To these Tajiks, they were more interested in making some political statement and were, at the same time, trying to achieve a whole cascade of unrealistic goals. They had a whole myriad of plans that suited their ideology. They expected to reach them because of a single shot from a rifle. Well, get real! We live in the real world, where things do not just drop into place like some well-oiled machine.

But that was not Dutton's problem.

Jacob Dutton was only the messenger.

'How are we to get from Marjah to Kabul?' was the following question from Hadi.

Much more of this, and Jacob could happily shoot Abdul and forget the whole deal! It was their country! So why did they ask the CIA to take care of such trivial matters?

Dutton retrained himself.

'We have convoys regularly moving up and down the highway between Kandahar and Kabul. We will have no difficulty slotting your little group into one of those,' Jacob said. Then he had an afterthought. Heaven forbids that they wanted to leave now! More than enough people in Kabul that the CIA had to keep an eye on without complicating matters by adding these nutcases to the mix!

'The timing is important because you do not want to spend too much time in Kabul before or after the event,' Dutton cautioned.

Now that was a laugh as well. The timing, and a few other minor things, would be significant. Traveling along the road between Kandahar and Kabul would be no picnic. With or without the protection provided in convoys supported by Afghan troops with a smattering of allied forces to ensure that the Afghanis did not head for the hills when any fighting broke out, the country was still involved in a war. No one could guarantee that the convoy would arrive, and even if they did, no one could ensure how long the journey would take.

Still, they were not planning a functional assassination, so it did not matter.

'Who knows of our plans?' was Hadi's next question.

This was the question that Dutton had been waiting for because this was the real issue that could make or break this plot.

Deniability.

Jacob Dutton knew that he had to be careful here.

Yes, someone from way up in the hierarchy of the CIA at Langley had advised the CIA in Kabul, who had advised the CIA Marjah branch, who had advised Jacob, that the United States had agreed to support the attempt on the life of the President of Afghanistan, Hamid Karzai. Or, more correctly, the advice was to *advise* the Tajiks that they had the support of the United States.

No, this was *officially* not the official position of the Government of the United States.

Yes, the Tajiks would need the assistance of the CIA to carry out the plot successfully.

No, the Tajiks could not be trusted to keep the involvement of the CIA quiet for long.

The problem was that Dutton did not know how high up in his organization and the various other agencies within the United States Government this information had been spread. For all he knew, the President of the United States himself may have authorized the kill. And, if the President had, he would, of course, deny it. Presidents of a country—well, most democratic countries—did not usually agree to the violent disposal of the presidents of other countries. It was just not done! And if the United States President denied it, then somewhere down the chain of command, someone would risk being fingered as the guy responsible for the deal. At this moment, that someone would probably be Jacob Dutton. Whether or not the attempt succeeded, he could end up being reassigned. To somewhere much more peaceful like Somalia!

Dutton tried to stay focused.

Did it matter if the President of the United States did, or did not, know? He should act as though the President did know, but he was on his own. That is what *deniability* meant. If the United States were conducting the assassination, it would be either a covert operation or an undercover operation. The difference between the two types of operation would mean jack-shit to the plotters. Even less to their target, Hamid Karzai.

'We have kept these plans very carefully compartmentalized,' Dutton began, talking with the total weight of the Marjah cell behind him. 'At the moment, only I know who you are. Our people in Kabul will only be told what to expect when you are safely on your way north, and then they will only be given enough information to ensure your success. Although our organization has the highest security globally, we cannot risk even the slightest hint of your plans reaching Hamid Karzai. And we will keep it that way!'

'Excellent!' Hadi proclaimed.

Maybe that was the only adjective that Abdul knew. What did this guy expect? The whole of the Marjah CIA cell was supposed to know everything that had been said because that was the only way it would work. Still, it was difficult to envision anywhere lower in the CIA hierarchy than the Marjah cell. And what did Abdul know about security?

The only way you could keep anything secret would be to tell no one. Then nothing would ever get done. It was no longer a secret when you told someone—be it work-related or more intimately related, as in between the sheets.

There were just too many people, and people had mouths. People love the fact that they know something that others do not. And they all cannot wait to give something away as a titbit to prove it.

Meanwhile, Jacob was not paid enough money to make decisions that would affect the lives of presidents. While the organization he worked for may want to pin the blame somewhere down the line, there was nothing surer than that it would not end up on his desk if he could help it. Somalia did not sound like a reasonable proposition. When he got back to the office, he would file a report making it clear that he was just a messenger.

The security classification of that report would be the highest that he could give it so that only those who were cleared to receive information at that level would see it. But from a purely practical point of view, that group would need to include Glen, and for other reasons, it had to include Cindy. Glen would read the report and then send it by secure means to Kabul, where the same logic would be applied. Weiner would, of course, in due process, tell Cindy. He would say to her that he was sending a report to Kabul. And there was no point in telling her that much if he did not at least hint at the report's contents. And thereby imply his importance in the grand scheme of things and less important things.

It is not often realized that security classification, and the need-to-know things, are not the same as seniority, the right to know something. The problem is that these two factors—the *need* to know and the *right* to know—are assumed to work along parallel lines. They are the boss. Therefore, they must be entitled to know more than me. As far as Jacob could understand, the ultimate responsibility for security was a corporate thing. If someone let some secret slip to someone from another organization, then that secret would make its way through that organization as well.

The only way to keep something genuinely secret was to make it sound so trivial that it was not worth talking about. But then, that would defy all that was inherent in human nature.

One thing Dutton could not do was to question the Tajiks' security or Abdul Hadi and his brother. Maybe it was a cultural thing, maybe not. If Abdul had spoken to any of his friends or family of his plans, or his reason for this visit to Marjah, then any problems that might stem from the security arrangement at the CIA paled into insignificance.

The meeting ended, and the men all shook hands and said goodbye. And with all the stealth that was typical of such events, the Tajiks disappeared as if they had never been there.

Dutton was satisfied that the meeting had gone as well as expected. He was not quite so satisfied with the Tajiks. They were so out of their depth. But the funny thing was, Jacob felt that they could pull this thing off for the straightforward reason that no one would ever suspect that they would have the gall to attempt what they intended to do.

Not that the meeting had been in the format and with an outcome, the CIA and its operatives would typically be involved in. For no logical reason, the CIA usually would not commit to anything at such a meeting, even if they only had to decide who served the tea. It was more or less a tradition that they would only commit to reviewing the matter(s) discussed with some unnamed superior and advise the other party the following day at the earliest. Jacob did not know about any meeting in the history of the CIA where there had been apparent agreement on a course of action at the first meeting between the parties.

There were, however, some factors that made this meeting so different from anything that had gone on before. Firstly, to have a meeting with so unlikely a bunch of misfits as the Tajiks. Secondly, and as a direct result of the first factor, if anyone found out about the meeting, questions would be raised in several quarters that the CIA would be very reluctant to answer. Therefore, thirdly, there was no way that they would want a repeat of the meeting.

And that was quite understandable. The authorities were nervous about the Russians getting a hint that there was such a plot somewhere in the making. Jacob put this down to fear of the relatively usual Russian paranoia, being a race that always assumed the worst in every situation.

Hadi was also not so satisfied with the infidel Jacob Dutton, although he had no idea that the meeting had achieved an unheard-of conclusion.

Abdul had some difficulty understanding the Americans. They were like mercenaries, always considering the money and not much else by way of principles. But they were *non-believers*, so anything was possible. Yet they were so open! It is evident to Abdul that the CIA, and therefore the President of the USA, wanted Hamid Karzai removed and that they would support this plot for that reason, and for that reason alone. But this plot was equally obviously one that the CIA and others of their ilk termed a black operation. They would pretend that the operation never existed. And all that talk by the infidel about Marshall Fahim, and his not being informed of the plot's details, showed the Americans' arrogance.

Fahim was a Tajik. Did they think that Abdul would have advanced his planning so far without consulting the most powerful and influential Tajik in the country?

Fahim was a Tajik. Did they think that Abdul would

have advanced his planning so far without consulting the most powerful and influential Tajik in the country?

Fahim was an essential part of the plot to get rid of Hamid and probably already knew as much, if not more, than the CIA. All that Abdul needed the CIA for was to get him to Kabul without the interference of his archenemy—the Taliban. And then Abdul and Fahim were required to be sure that the Tajiks had someone else to point the finger of blame at.

The world, and especially the American media, would willingly believe that the death of President Hamid Karzai was CIA sponsored rather than a do-it-yourself job by a couple of lowly Tajiks. Conspiracy theories would abound. And the brilliant thing about the American media was that the conspiracy theories would never go away.

Had not the Americans learned anything from recent and not-so-recent history?

The other elders looked equally grim-faced, having attended the meeting, and making critical decisions. Behind the grim faces, there was a lack of trust, but that did not matter much. Because the discussions had been conducted mainly in English, none of them, other than Abdul, had any clear idea of what had been discussed and what had been agreed upon. They would need to rely on Abdul to tell them later. And the later he left it to tell them, the more embellished his story would be to secure his position—at the cost of clarity and to the benefit of his colossal ego.

Yet, on balance, both sides in the meeting had achieved what they had wanted to achieve.

Just as secretively as they had arrived, they all disappeared.

Chapter 4

Another Party

Dutton walked back to his vehicle, which he had left quite some distance away from the meeting house. He had left it in a place where people on his payroll could watch it. He followed the same pattern on his return journey that he had on his arrival. There was no direct route in the haphazard assembly of buildings that made up the community. And that made countersurveillance much easier. Anyone following Jacob would have found it extremely difficult to remain concealed or above suspicion. Still, Jacob practiced what he had been taught back at the Farm. He had to ensure deniability. But in this neighbourhood, he could not know who would be following whom.

The CIA, the British M16, the Pakistani ISI, the Russian SVR, the virgin Afghan intelligence, the Taliban, plus various other organizations all had a stake in knowing what the other players were up to. Jacob was a tiny cog in a huge wheel, but he still had to stay below the radar. All intelligence organizations had the same problems—some large, some small. Some followed others: some led the others. But who knew who was following or who was being followed? And from all of this, which of them had managed to find a solution?

And to what?

Jacob would not have dared leave a vehicle unattended in so rundown an area in a more civilized part of the world. In Marjah, he had done so for four reasons. Firstly, it was just a pool vehicle from the military compound and recognized by the locals. Secondly, no one would have anywhere to hide a 3-ton Humvee other than perhaps the Taliban. Thirdly, the roads in this part of the world made walking the easier of the two alternatives. Fourthly, it was much easier to lose anyone on foot, especially those who would expect him to park closer to his intended rendezvous.

Maybe no one would be the least bit interested in an obscure plot being hatched in the outskirts of Marjah. The problem was you never could know.

On balance, Jacob felt that it was an even contest between the British and the Russians who could stand up to the plate with the CIA. All the rest were woefully left in their wake. But experience showed that assumption was the giant killer. And at least most people in the intelligence business would agree on two things.

They did not believe in coincidences.

They could not rely on assumptions.

A couple of Tajiks come from across the border from Pakistan into Afghanistan and on to Marjah. They are surrounded by a group of Afghan troops, which suggests either that they are important or that they would need some form of protection. A CIA agent from Marjah goes out at night to meet with them at a location that suggests their meeting is secret.

Coincidence?

If no one knows why these things are happening, you must find out.

Or you must make assumptions.

As he moved back towards his vehicle, he exchanged glances with one of the locals walking in the opposite direction.

Dutton did not break his stride. But the hairs on the back of his neck were raised.

Was the man a local?

There was something about the man's demeanour that suggested otherwise. And what was it about the eyes?

It was always in the eyes!

Dutton shrugged. If you tried to second-guess everyone else before you moved, you would never get anything done. He was fairly sure that nobody would have followed him. And what if they had? His job was to talk to informants, which he had just done. Of course, he had not checked whether any of the Tajiks were wired! Probably not. And did it matter anyway?

Jacob followed his strict routine and checked around the Humvee for any sign that anyone had interfered with it. There were no signs, but still, he was nervous as he climbed in. At the same time, his people were told to watch the vehicle. Who knew what others would pay the same people to blow it up? The nervous expectation as he pressed the starter, the panic he felt as the engine coughed and then spluttered into life. The sharp expulsion of breath as he realized the vehicle would not blow up—this time.

Dutton drove off in the direction of the Marjah compound, confident, on balance, that his trip had gone unnoticed.

Olezhka Demidov, otherwise known as Oleg, was one of many Russians who remained in Afghanistan after the Soviet Union had withdrawn in disgrace and defeat. He was initially an agent of the KGB. That body had been disbanded after a failed coup attempt in 1991. Now the Russian foreign intelligence service was in the hands of the Sluzhba Vneshney Razvedki, or simply the SVR. Same people, different names.

Although the Russians employed Olezhka, he was expected to keep himself busy in *other* areas. He did that by offering security and other services to the inhabitants of this chaotic country—not necessarily to the highest bidder.

The Americans had flooded Afghanistan with private security personnel, but there was plenty of work in other areas. Especially those areas in which the Americans could not be trusted or where there would be an apparent conflict of interest.

At present, Demidov was on the payroll of a Kandahar gentleman who went by the name of Ahmed Karzai.

In real life, Demidov was as plain as anyone could be. He was only five feet seven and a little under 150 fifty pounds. If it wasn't because he had no facial hair, he could have been a local. His face was so weathered he could have been any age. He was, in fact, sixty-four years of age.

The Russian was puzzled.

Olezhka had been following Jacob Dutton for several weeks. This time he had followed Jacob, first by vehicle and then on foot, to what appeared to be a kind of safe house on the outskirts of Marjah. He had watched as the various visitors had arrived, together with their protective detail. He was not worried about being spotted by the enthusiastic but hopeless guards. Nor was he worried about being spotted by that arrogant Dutton. Oleg was dressed in Afghan clothes to hide in plain sight. And many years in this festering hellhole meant that he had become particularly good at surveillance and countersurveillance.

He now knew that Dutton had been to a meeting, but it was who he had met with that was the puzzle.

Why had Jacob Dutton met with a bunch of Tajiks?

With his two sidekicks—Mohammed and Omar—his masters had instructed Oleg in Kandahar to determine when the next shipment of drugs would occur. Not just any shipment. Kandahar wanted to know about a specific load. Oleg knew from Naeem that everything had been *arranged*, but neither knew the finer details. Oleg also knew that Jacob would be involved, and he was also tasked with finding out the extent of that involvement.

As for the meeting between a representative of the CIA and a bunch of little-known Tajiks, that was a puzzle because they had not previously been involved in the drug business. Given the relatively low level of the Marjah CIA cell, the meeting was possibly about finding an alternate route out of Afghanistan. Oleg would have found it quite improbable that Jacob was trying to get the Tajiks to sign up as informants. But there were other issues to consider. The Russians had recently secured a deal with someone of high rank in the US security and intelligence network, presumably a member of the CIA, to get information on the various goings-on in Afghanistan. Not sufficiently critical to cause a stir, but knowledge, nonetheless. And that had been arranged in exchange for the Russians keeping quiet about what they knew about another deal that the CIA had got itself involved with. Oleg did not know the details of either *agreement* or, as was the way with Russian intelligence, he was probably better off not knowing. But he was still curious.

Oleg would need to talk with his friend Yuri Alexseyev in Kabul and update himself on the latest arrangements.

But now, that was not high on his list of priorities. File a report and see what happens next.

Dutton made his way back to the 'office' to complete his report. He also had other more important business to attend to, and that business was secret. And this would not be a secret that he would share with Weiner and Johnston, even though it impinged on their areas of responsibility.

He had to make sure that the next shipment of opiates was ready for its trip north, up the road from Kandahar to Kabul, onwards into Pakistan, and ultimately to the United States.

His immediate responsibility was to get the drugs to Pakistan. He had recommended that the trucks carrying the drugs go in a convoy for safety. He could even envisage the Tajiks traveling up to Kabul in the same US- and Afghan- controlled convoy.

Now wouldn't that be a laugh!

But the boss had said no on both counts.

The Tajiks would not be in convoy.

Neither would the drugs.

Chapter 5

Road to Kabul

The three Humvees of the Afghan Army left the confines of the enclosure at about four o'clock in the afternoon. The drivers and their passengers were all uniformed members of the Afghan National Army. All six of them—two in each vehicle—had been trained by the coalition military and should have been capable of carrying out this assigned task.

The Humvees, which had the cumbersome official description of high-mobility multipurpose wheeled vehicles, had been provided by the United States military, which, after all, would not be taking any of its heavy equipment and military hardware back to the United States when their involvement in Afghanistan was finished.

That is, if it ever was finished.

On this trip, the Afghan soldiers were not accompanied by any United States or NATO military personnel, nor were they accompanied by some private security company that worked in this country courtesy of the Pentagon. That was unusual, except that the coalition resources were so stretched that there was just no one who could be assigned to babysitting the Afghans on this day on what was supposed to be a routine and straightforward training patrol.

At least, that is what the paperwork said.

In the chaos of the security arrangements in Afghanistan, many of the contracts for the various security services were held by private companies. These mainly were United States-based companies. And they were mostly paid for by the long-suffering taxpayers of the United States. The money did not matter. It was only money. What mattered was that a large chunk of the money found its way into the hands of the Taliban through a variety of mechanisms.

And that was something that someone would eventually get around to doing something about.

Still, the coalition forces were not overly worried about the Taliban on this trip. And the Afghanis did not have that much fuel in the tanks of their vehicles, and at a rate of consumption of fuel of five miles to the gallon, the Humvees could not go very far. The fact that they did not have that far to go, but that it was neither a simple nor a routine trip, was known only to a few.

At least one member of the CIA contingent knew of the trip, which may or may not have meant that the entire CIA office in Marjah knew. It depended on whether they had all read all the reports and what bias they had placed on yet another seemingly innocuous piece of information.

Jacob Dutton certainly knew and would carefully monitor the situation. He was the one who had ensured that the Afghan troops would do this job *unsupervised*. Glen probably knew about it but could not have cared less about so trivial a matter. Cindy would assume that it was the start of World War III.

Naeem Sediqyar made a mental note that the small convoy of three Hummers had left the enclosure. No doubt he would later take note of the fact that they would return.

At least he could expect that some of them would return. He had no idea where they were going or why. And when the convoy returned, he would be none the wiser. He would make a note of it and pass that on. Naeem was only a messenger.

The first objective of the convoy was to assemble at an old, dilapidated warehouse just on the northern outskirts of what was euphemistically called the city of Marjah. There they were to meet a relatively young man who went by the name of Wakil Hekmatyar. Behind the beard and the clothes was an obnoxious and impatient wiry little man whose eyes never ceased to flicker, taking everything in and leaving nothing to chance. He may have been young, but he was well known and well respected in the local community. Well, *feared* rather than respected would have been a better description. Wakil had control of the opium trade in this part of the world, and the word *control* was usually translated into other adjectives, none of which had much to do with being nice to people.

At the warehouse, twelve packages were meticulously weighed, numbered, and then loaded into the vehicles, four boxes to each Humvee. There was no labelling other than the sequential number of each box and the batch number S346. There was no point of origin, no delivery address, and no statement of the contents. The packages appeared to be just bundles of textiles, as was indeed the intention. This shipment contained opiate raw materials, but apart from that fact and the fact that there was absolutely no documentation, it was no different from any other shipment. It certainly had much farther to go than most shipments coming out of Marjah. It would be guarded by armed guards to its destination across the border with Pakistan. And the recipients would be very particular about the number of packages that arrived while not the least bit concerned about any documentation that could trace the origin of the shipment.

And that was to be expected. Very few people were supposed to know about it, even though there was a considerable sum of money to be paid out because of this activity.

By the time the job of checking and loading the packages into the trucks was completed, it was almost dark. The warehouse was locked behind the Afghan Army personnel as they left—not that the locks amounted to much, and not that it mattered. The opium trade was the primary source of revenue in the region, so the local Afghan police were unlikely to interfere with what went on at this warehouse. The police have been well paid to look the other way, to be sure. To be certain, the police were informed, even though it was common knowledge that the Hekmatyar family owned this warehouse. Wakil did not take too kindly to any form of interference by officials or others. This warehouse was probably the safest place in Afghanistan to be dealing with opiates.

The little convoy made its way east through the remaining tracks of the district until they were clear of any signs of human habitation onto what was little more than the marks left by others that distinguished a worn path leading towards the mountains to the north and east.

Despite their all-terrain characteristics, the Humvees struggled as the track twisted and turned, as loose rocks scattered across their path. The discomfort of the trip was not, however, a problem for the drivers who were used to the condition of the roads around Marjah, although their traveling companions were better off. They stood hanging on to the machine guns to better ride the bumps.

There was no other reason to operate the M240G/B machine guns mounted in each of the Hummers on this trip.

Or so they thought.

The most likely assault would come from a roadside bomb, commonly known as an IED (improvised explosive device), and the gun was of no use in that scenario. Not that they expected any such event. What they had on board and where they were going was likely known to the people most likely to attack them. They were also known for who they were temporarily working for, so that should have been an end to that.

Even the Taliban would be ill-advised to tangle with a convoy sponsored by Wakil Hekmatyar. But they were in Afghanistan, it was night-time, and the three vehicles were now farther from their base and the protection it provided than was wise. While in the region of Marjah, Wakil Hekmatyar was the kingpin. In the wilderness, where the population was composed of various factions, Hekmatyar's influence did not count. So, the sooner this minor task was completed, the sooner the soldiers could return to their compound's safety and comfort.

The lead driver knew where they were headed because just before they reached the city of Lashkar Gah, he drove off the track, instructed the men to kill their engines, and waited there. He must have been confident. Afghanistan probably had more landmines than anywhere else on the planet, and the area south of Kandahar had more than its fair share of them.

After an exchange of radio messages, during which the nervous tension that had gripped the group during their journey from the district of Marjah increased, they eventually contacted the people they were to meet. These people did not particularly like the thought of approaching Afghan National Army vehicles, and despite the meticulous

Another group of two vehicles appeared out of the darkness—an ex-Soviet military truck that had seen better days and a jeep of about the same vintage but looking in better condition—and came to a halt about a hundred yards from where the Humvees had parked. The Afghan troops just shrugged and shifted the packages across the intervening space, two soldiers going each packet, the four remaining soldiers operating their guns in the Humvees. No attempt was made by the men who had arrived in the truck, or its accompanying vehicle, to offer any assistance.

Eventually, each package was unloaded from the Hummers, carefully checked, and ticked off, and then bundled into the back of the truck to take them on the next leg of their journey.

There were no handshakes or other formal acknowledgments of the deal between the two groups. They just each turned away—the Hummers headed back to Marjah relieved of their cargo and the old ex-Soviet truck with its load of packages and the escorting four-wheel-drive vehicle headed north-east and into the city of Lashkar Gah.

The ultimate destination for the shipment was the city of Peshawar in the north-western provinces of Pakistan, and it was thought that the smaller the convoy, the less attention it would attract. These decisions were supposed to be too complex for the eight Afghani civilians who now shared the driving of the truck and the guarding of its precious cargo. The decisions had been made on the other side of the world by the people who would authorize the payment, so that was that.

To get into Pakistan, it should have been a relatively straightforward journey to have gone south-east from Kandahar, where there was only a desert to worry about. The border between the two countries was relatively clearly defined in the southeast, at least on a map. This did not mean that there would not be problems crossing the border and getting to the Pakistan city of Quetta, with or without drugs. But at least you would be able to see where you were going. In the northeast, the border consisted of rugged mountain passes. Beyond that was a landscape where few ventured, except the many tribes that led a rugged lifestyle and had a wide variety of allegiances.

The more normal method for smuggling drugs out of Afghanistan would have been to head northwest into the Herat province and then across the border into Iran using well-known and paradoxically secret smuggling routes that had been in use for centuries.

But neither of these options would exactly please the Americans who were, after all, paying for this shipment. The city of Quetta was teeming with Taliban who had made it their new, if temporary, home after being pushed out of southern Afghanistan. To the west, the United States had more than enough trouble with the people and the Government of Iran, especially a gentleman named Mahmoud Ahmadinejad, to risk going that way. So, the journey would be from Kandahar, on to Kabul, from there to Jalalabad, into the infamous area known as Tora Bora, then across the border into Pakistan, and finally into the city of Peshawar.

Whether this amount of trouble was worth, it was debatable. The opiates would be processed, first into opium, and then the opium had to be processed into heroin. Laboratories were springing up all over the Helmand province of Afghanistan to do just that, and it was far simpler, by volume at least, to move the finished product than to move the opiates. Admittedly, some of these laboratories were being closed by the authorities. But just as quickly, others opened, as is the way in the world of drugs.

For reasons best known only to themselves, the Americans wanted their drugs processed in a laboratory in Pakistan and specifically in Peshawar. The reasons for this had probably got something to do with how the product was to be subsequently shipped or was to be distributed. That could have been arranged too in Afghanistan if someone could be found who could be trusted.

For the right kind of money.

Still, money is king, and the Americans were paying good money. So, the shipment just had to go made. That meant it had to go through some very rugged and hostile country. It had to travel through a land littered with countless landmines. And the process of the shipment would be watched by people who would show no respect for someone else's property.

The journey would take several days, and there could be no guarantee that it would be satisfactorily concluded. The last shipment had entirely simply disappeared off the face of the earth. That shipment did get as far as Jalalabad to the east of Kabul, but then it went into the notorious Tora Bora and had not been seen again. And neither had the people who had been assigned to take the opiates over the border into Pakistan. Whether the opiates and the people went to the same place was not, and probably never would be, known.

While the Americans were extremely annoyed about the loss of the shipment, they had a simple answer and a brutal solution to this dilemma. Since they received no goods, they paid no money. They had, of course, spent a percentage upfront, but that was used in disbursements— or so the story goes. Undoubtedly, not all were used to meet the actual costs of the shipment because Hekmatyar would want his cut.

Everything is relative. The real money changed hands at the trail's end when the goods made it to Peshawar.

The message had gone out along the trail.
This shipment must go through.

Naeem noted the return of the three Hummers to their enclosure in Marjah. The drivers and their guards seemed more relieved than usual for a returning patrol, which was recorded as well. Where they had been at this time of the evening would be known by someone else, and the various pieces of information would be tied together. But that was not any concern of Naeem. He had done what he had been asked to do, and he would be paid, irrespective of the outcome, at the rate of one Afghani per day.

The difficulty with traveling near Kandahar was that the city, of just under half a million people, was still infested by the Taliban. Not that their presence was as evident as it once was. And not that the Taliban alone should take all the blame for making other people's lives both difficult and miserable. In any other town on the planet, other groups would have been described as criminals who were extremely keen to relieve anyone of what they possessed. It was important that the current custodians of the opiates first made sure that they contacted their friends to make certain that they could transit through the city unmolested. And to have their vehicles refuelled before proceeding north.

The next stage of the trip would take them to Kabul, and it was just a matter of joining the Kandahar–Kabul highway—at least their orders, which ultimately came from Washington DC, said that was what they had to do. The people who issued the orders assumed that the highway was the equivalent of getting on Interstate 195 and driving from Washington DC to New York City. The Kabul highway had only recently been upgraded to something more resembling a roadway than the original goat track by a massive cash infusion from the Americans. While probably well over half of the money so infused was filtered off by various corrupt officials into far fewer worthy causes, the building of the road was quite an achievement—at least by local standards.

There were two vehicles in the S346 group. One was a ZIL-131 three-and-a-half-ton truck with a V8 gasoline engine that was not particularly reliable and difficult to service. The other was a UAZ-469 four-wheel-drive all-terrain vehicle with a four-cylinder petrol engine, which was reliable and easy to maintain. The truck could withstand most forms of small to medium arms fire, and so could the ex-Soviet military 4WD, provided someone did not aim at the driver. Both vehicles had been equipped with CBS (citizens band radios) to communicate and not much else.

The highway was about 300 miles long, but it was not built for speed, although speed would have been helpful. The farther north you travelled, the hillier it became did cause some problems. The eight men—two in the 4WD and six in the truck—were armed as was the way with travellers in this part of the world, whether on legitimate business or otherwise. As was typical for people not directly involved with the United States military forces, the arms were Avtomat Kalashnikov Model 1947, otherwise known worldwide as AK-47s. They were ex-Soviet rifles that used 7.62x39mm cartridges. The AK-47 was usually reliable, but they were not the most reliable because of the age of these weapons. However, if they needed to use them, they were no different from the arms they would be up against. That, of course, depended on whether the group of criminals they encountered had traditional or recently stolen weapons.

The road from Kandahar to Kabul was one of the most dangerous stretches of highway on the planet, frequently interrupted by man-made damage by roadside bombs and the destruction of bridges, and more frequently by what was politely referred to as insurgents.

This shipment—known by the batch number S346—was sponsored by someone from the United States and did not mean that the drivers and their escorts were provided with US military M16 rifles. There were plenty of debates in military circles, both in Afghanistan and the United States, about which of the two was the better rifle and much scientific study into the projectiles they fired—the 7.62mm of the AK-47 versus the 5.56mm of the M16. But who cared? The purpose of a rifle is to kill or maim, and if you can see who you are aiming at, the odds were that you would either hit them or give them one hell of a fright.

The person on the receiving end of a rifle shot would not be overly concerned about the size of the cartridge, what it came from, where it came from, or who fired it.

The small convoy rested up just to the south of Kandahar until the sun rose over the arid and hostile mountain peaks in the east. Then they commenced their journey north.

They were prepared for but did not expect any trouble.

The word should have gone out that a particular member of the Hekmatyar family would be particularly annoyed if anyone chose to interrupt another of his shipments.

Whether that word had reached all the potential troublemakers that lay along the tortuous and challenging route was debatable.

On balance, probably not.

Chapter 6

CIA Headquarters – Langley, Virginia

The assistant inspector in the Office of Inspector General (OIG) of the CIA was puzzled. Harold Taylor had not been in the job for long and was still coming to grips with the confining routine and the idiosyncrasies of what was a whole new experience in the bureaucratic quagmire.

Taylor had worked for the CIA for more years than he cared to remember. He went through his initial training in what is known as the Farm with dogged determination, neither standing out nor failing in what was a rugged, unforgiving, and, in many respects, frightening environment for a young man. Then, as a rookie field agent, he had proved to be quietly competent, hardworking, and honest. His ruthless efficiency and meticulous attention to detail made him stand out from the crowd.

He slowly made his way up through the ranks, serving his country in various locations around the globe until he finally ended up as head of station in Wellington, New Zealand.

But then came the event known as the second 9/11, when someone tried to replicate the original crime by setting off bombs in the identical sequence of explosions, on the same calendar day, at the same time, and in the same city—New York City. This time, though, it was not al Qaeda. This time bona fide residents of the good old USA were responsible. And people who were on the Government's payroll did nothing to prevent it. The reasons for this were unclear and were even fuzzier now that Harold Taylor had been promoted to a position that was way above his previous paygrade.

He felt that he had been appointed to this new position more by accident and haste than by the result of any rational thought. And in it, he felt as though he had deserted all the friends, he had worked with for all those years. Now he seemed to be working against them.

Taylor was tall and thin; he always wore pinstriped suits with a matching waistcoat and tie and reading glasses whenever he was behind a desk, giving him the look of a typical, more English bureaucrat. He looked much older than his sixty-two years. He could put it down to the stress resulting from his many years in the CIA; it did not overly worry him. He was as devoted to his country, and his masters as anyone could be. He loved his job, and he loved his country. Everything that he had ever done was by the book. Well, almost. He respected his superiors and was loyal to those who worked under him. The position baffled him that he was now in.

The nature of this new job was that all the friends he had made during a long and distinguished career could no longer be treated as his friends. Likewise, those who had been his friends began to treat him differently. They still spoke to him, called him Harold or Mr. Taylor, depending on the formality necessary; asked after his wife and son; discussed basketball, baseball, or football; and talked about the weather. But these days, they were not the same conversations. It was as though he were now conversing with people from another planet.

Harold Taylor was now a pariah.

This situation came as a surprise to a man who had proudly accepted the job in the Office of the Inspector General—known by the three-letter acronym the OIG—in the belief that in taking the role, he could do some greater good in the service of his country. Now it was as though he was playing a game of cards without a full deck.

On the face of it, the OIG had enormous power within the CIA and could investigate anyone and anything. However, he was still subject to controls within the colossal bureaucratic jigsaw.

Taylor looked around his plush office. It was much larger and better appointed than his previous one had been. His desk was now bigger than his last office. The room was an odd shape being at a corner of the building so that it narrowed as it funnelled into the doorway. On entering, you looked out through the windows over the Potomac and towards Bethesda from the reverse angle. The walls were finished in a matte burgundy that gave the impression of a richness that was somehow false. The desk was over on the right, tucked against the wall, and the rest of the furniture was scattered around to give the impression of a much more social environment than this office was meant to have. And the desk was now devoid of all the paper that he had previously accumulated in his past life as an agent in the field.

He had a very efficient secretary whose job it was to tell him where he was to be, what he had to do, and when he had to do it. He could hardly take a leak, or a dump, without her permission. Washington seemed to have an endless supply of such middle-aged or much older women who were similar. People who knew everything, on occasions even more than their masters, had security clearances that even God himself would have envied. Because of this, they were constantly monitored and *reviewed* by the security service to make sure that they warranted the clearances that they held. The same ladies were, of course, always watched by the spooks from the intelligence and security services of other countries just in case they developed a craving or a lust that would distract them from their formal duties and which others could then take advantage of. It was always much easier to turn a frustrated lady into a spy than turning a dedicated career professional.

If Taylor cared to think about it, he would probably miss the glamour of being involved in the actual business of being a spook. On the other hand, in his new role, the only people he had to worry about were supposed to be on the same side. In recent times, the spook business had become more diplomatic; and it was rare for there to be any actual conflict. A couple of years previously, the Russians had dumped on Western intelligence assets in Russia, which caused the Moscow CIA head of station to return to Washington unscathed quietly but with an extensive list of agents who had not been so lucky. Many of these agents were unknown to the CIA, so they were assumed to be working for other intelligence agencies. Since the Russians only made mention of a British infiltration, it was assumed that MI6 had been the real target. But you could never know. It was possible that the Russians had not targeted the CIA directly out of fear of a like-for-like retaliation, which could have disrupted some of the assets that they thought were well hidden in the United States.

The CIA was now in the process of having a relatively new head of station in Moscow establish a new network, and the problems from this were twofold. Firstly, to avoid employing assets, the Russians had deliberately dangled to act as double agents. Secondly, making sure that the identities were carefully protected to prevent any chance of their becoming too widely known within the CIA itself. Of course, Harold had heard snippets about a possible mole somewhere in Washington. There were always grumblings from the Pentagon about intelligence leaks that affected what was happening out in the real world. Taylor was glad that these things were not within his purview.

In an independent and detached way, his job was to look into the reliability of the CIA's personnel and procedures. That, at least theoretically, meant everyone and everything past, present, and future who sought to enter or continue in the service of the Government of the United States of America through the doors of the CIA. Consequently, his responsibilities included looking at people from the bottom of the bureaucratic ladder up to the people who held the most senior positions. He was the ultimate Government auditor in the CIA. Looking at things with cold, clinical, and detached eyes. Looking for differences or omissions that should not be there and looking for the odd person who may stray, for monetary or other reasons, from the straight and narrow path required of those who served their country. The CIA was a bureaucracy, and it had files on every person, the living, and the dead, that its tentacles reached out to and touched. And the CIA often knew more than was known by the spouse, fathers and mothers, sons, and daughters of every employee on its payroll and beyond.

But since 9/11, a rather strange thing had happened in the intelligence and security business. There had been a massive increase in the amount of data being gathered, and the sheer volume of that data had the opposite effect of what had been intended. There was now so much data being collected that no one had the time to absorb it, let alone analyse it.

Taylor had access to all this information and could demand more at the simple click of his fingers.

However, despite all the power, knowledge, efficiency, and clinical nature of his job, his latest file was going nowhere. A part of that was that it had not yet reached the stage where he could officially claim that the file existed.

And it was difficult for Harold Taylor to stay independent and detached in the case that was now before him.

Stephen Rodriguez.
Assistant deputy director of intelligence, CIA.
Five eleven.
One hundred and eighty pounds.
Born in the Philippines to a father from New York who had worked for the United States Foreign Service and a mother from the back blocks of southern Arkansas.
Now aged fifty-three. Did not carry his age particularly well—looked ten years older than that.
Married with two children. (Two girls – one a student at a Washington law school, the other somewhere in Africa working with the poor, trying to save the world.)
Educated at the University of Pittsburgh.
He was graduated with a degree in Psychology.
No known political or religious affiliations
Like most security and intelligence services members, Rodriguez had no declared allegiance to any political party, Democrat or Republican. Rising in the bureaucracy allegiances could be bad for your career every four years or so.
Rodriguez was probably a Republican.

Religion was a little different: if this were the FBI, then, had he been a Roman Catholic, which would presumably have helped. But you were never asked to vote for any God!

Rodriguez was probably a Catholic.

A social drinker but not known to over-imbibe.

He had a long history with the CIA, first as a field agent, and was recognized early on in his career as having the potential for higher honours.

Risk assessment: zero.

Not a single blemish on what had been a stellar career.

Except that there was one minor blemish that had appeared unexpectedly.

And that had only recently been brought to Harold Taylor's attention.

Someone had suggested that Stephen Rodriguez maybe into drugs. Not necessarily, or only, as a user. But as a supplier, distributor, or trafficker.

For someone in a powerful position as an assistant deputy, such a suggestion was a grave matter. It would certainly need to be thoroughly investigated. It would also need to be treated with caution. There was the risk that the suggestion may be false—in which case a career and a person could be destroyed for entirely the wrong reasons. There was also the risk that, should the suggestion be valid, he could react somewhat unpredictably if Stephen Rodriguez gets word of an investigation into his activities.

For instance, to kill or threaten to kill those involved in the investigation.

As an assistant inspector at the OIG, Harold Taylor

received information of much of a personal nature. He had the daily reports that his minions produced and reviews of how every 'case' was proceeding. They indicated the next steps to be taken, which files would be closed for lack of any conclusive evidence, and a minutely small number that would involve taking some further investigative or corrective action.

The conclusion that Taylor had reached so far was that the officers of the CIA did a surprisingly decent job of informing, instructing, and inspiring in the country that they served—apart, that is, from the occasional 'bad apple' that could be found in every barrel. In an organization that was as vast as the CIA bureaucracy, it was inevitable that there would be some people who did not fit in. Most of these people would idle away their time collecting their pay and not causing any harm. But some were people who would cause damage. The problem was that they would be buried deep in the organization. And they would generate such an array of misinformation that it was unlikely they would ever be found.

Taylor also had reports from the Federal Bureau of Investigation outlining progress on matters they had been asked to investigate by the inspectorate. He also had a tiny percentage of reports where the FBI had unearthed bits of information concerning the CIA or its officers, which they felt might interest an assistant inspector.

Useful in weeding out those who had the potential for corruption.

Helpful in making sure that their sister organization was aware of the FBI's relative power in the bureaucratic jungle that both the FBI and the CIA lived and worked in, occasionally on the same side.

The OIG also received reports from the Drug Enforcement Administration, which was an equal mixture of matters raised either by the FBI, the inspectorate, or the

DEA themselves concerning employees of the CIA.

This was all routine stuff.

The kind of information that most interested Harold Taylor was that concerning significant investigations, and he suspected that he had one simmering in the background right now. And that would not be an easy task for the various parties involved because it concerned them all—the CIA, FBI, DEA, and probably others who worked in the protected environment of the federal government and in the vast organization that encompassed the security and intelligence services of the United States Government.

Before Harold Taylor had been appointed to the job of the assistant inspector in the OIG, both the FBI and the CIA had been involved in what could best be described as a god-almighty cock-up. The United States security and intelligence services had somehow let an apparent terrorist plot—to explode three suicide bombs in New York City on the anniversary of 9/11—achieve its primary objective. One of the three bombs that had failed to cause any damage was of little comfort to the people affected by the other two who had lost loved ones or had to carry on now living with less than their normal faculties intact.

The plot had been executed with perfect timing. The timing of the explosions had precisely matched the timings of the original events. This meant that the entire scheme had been well planned and well implemented. Yet, one of the chief planners had committed suicide shortly afterward. And certain members of the FBI and the CIA had tried to kill people trying to reveal the truth of what had occurred.

But for the intervention of one man, they would have got away with that as well.

And that one man, albeit aided by a considerable element of good luck and the use of some influential friends, was Mark Taylor, the only son of Harold and Elizabeth Taylor.

The initial investigation into the cock-up was relatively straightforward. Certain people in the FBI and the CIA simply wanted money to buy drugs. In exchange for money with which they bought drugs, they agreed to keep certain information from reaching the right kind of people, namely, those employed by the Director of National Intelligence. The DNI reports directly to the President of the United States for intelligence matters relating to national security. Even so, hiding information, or preventing it from reaching the appropriate level, turned out to be ridiculously easy to achieve.

All organizations in the security and intelligence business receive millions of bits of information every day from sources which would include how many times Osama bin Laden has a dump and all sorts of other meaningful intelligence information from loony crackpots at the local funny farm up to events that could lead to the start of World War III.

Because of the sheer volume of data being received, its disparate sources, and its many languages, most of the data is processed by computers. Vast machines with immeasurable storage and processing capability—but still computers. Being dumb and being programmed by mere mortals, computers search for keywords—like 'terrorist' or 'bomb' or 'kill the President'—but on a more deadly scale than your more mundane search engines. Then the bits of information that have these keywords are referred to human beings who will presumably do something with it. And then anything can happen, ranging in scale again from absolutely nothing to the declaration of the aforesaid World War III.

But even though these vermin that Mark Taylor had been instrumental in uncovering within the CIA and the FBI were able to divert or distract the relevant bits of disparate information, they did eventually get caught.

Pending the authorities making some final decisions, these people were locked up. An ex–FBI deputy director named Nicholas Gagarin was now held in the United States Penitentiary in Leavenworth, Kansas. An ex-secretary to the CIA assistant deputy director of intelligence (ADDI) called Hilary Trembath was held in Georgia's Arrendale women's prison. In addition to these two, who were believed to be the ringleaders, several of their ill-advised associates were also locked away.

The two ringleaders had initially been incarcerated on the USS *Bataan*, a Wasp-class amphibious assault ship that had a history of being used by the CIA as a black site for the imprisonment and interrogation of terrorists and all that it that entailed. Presumably, keeping them on the *Bataan* was done to keep Gagarin and Trembath away from other criminals and, more probably, away from the media. However, for a variety of reasons, none of which made much sense, they had been transferred relatively quickly to their present so-called temporary homes, albeit kept in isolation in case some criminal might take advantage of being locked up with an FBI agent (in the case of Nicholas), or a woman (in the case of Hilary). Despite the peculiarities of the American justice system, which meant that their conviction would take so long that the authorities probably wouldn't bother seeing it through, these two were unlikely to return to everyday life anytime soon. They would never again sit in the positions of power and influence they had once enjoyed.

That file on this unsavoury episode in the life of the US intelligence services should have been closed. The perpetrators had been arrested. As the matter was unlikely ever to make it into a public court and would certainly be kept out of the media unless somebody leaked the news, that should have been the end of the sad affair.

But the file was not closed because someone thought that there was more to the affair than had been revealed by the original investigation.

After all the dust had barely settled on this sordid affair, the ADDI, one Stephen Rodriguez, had himself been implicated. That is if a brief conversation between father and son could be taken as an implication. Mark Taylor had received information that involved Rodriguez in something unbefitting of a man in his position.

And that was where Harold Taylor saw another example of the limitations that even the most powerful bureaucrats face: *What do I do with this piece of information?*

And more importantly,

Who do I share it with?

There were two fundamental problems with this scenario.

The first problem was that Stephen Rodriguez, the assistant deputy director of intelligence at CIA's Langley headquarters, had, until recently, been Harold Taylor's boss.

Which led to the second problem.

The ADDI had been paramount in the moves to unscramble the mess that had ensued in New York City, and he had been seen to be the one who had ruthlessly rooted out the criminal factions in the higher echelons of the CIA and the FBI.

Coincidentally, Stephen Rodriguez had also been the immediate boss of Hilary Trembath. And Trembath had said nothing to implicate Stephen, so it would appear, on face value, that he was not involved. It would certainly seem strange in this age where deals could be struck, lies were cheap, and the cost to the incarcerated so high that Trembath had implicated no one.

Coincidentally, Stephen Rodriguez had also been at least on first name speaking terms with Nicolas Gagarin of the FBI. And Gagarin had also said nothing to implicate the CIA assistant deputy.

At the time of this activity, Stephen Rodriguez had the chance to bring it all to a very rapid and presumably spectacular conclusion. But he did nothing other than to ensure that the two chief perpetrators were locked away and that their stories would never be told.

Was this deniability in its ultimate form?

Was Stephen involved in some other way?

From Harold Taylor's point of view, he was left with at least one dilemma: Was Stephen Rodriguez, a part of the original plot that everyone thought, had been resolved? Or was he a part of some other more dangerous subterfuge? It was assumed that no one else was involved for the aforementioned reasons. And that could well be so. But what if Stephen was involved in an unrelated scheme? Or what if his involvement was so well hidden that the earlier investigation had failed to detect it? Or what if his involvement concerned drugs at a level that Gagarin and Trembath quite simply knew nothing about? Or what if someone even more powerful than a lowly ADDI had threatened another and even more unpleasant outcome?

He trusted his son implicitly, and it was unlikely that the tip that Mark had given him was anything but rock solid. But before Harold could make inroads into this very confusing situation, he had to have a little more in the way of plausible evidence.

There was one avenue of inquiry that Harold could try—through the Drug Enforcement Administration.

He had several reasons for considering this approach.

The DEA had not been involved in the open-and-shut case that the CIA and the FBI had most recently concluded. Drugs were involved, but the criminals were users and not suppliers or traffickers. If the DEA were to follow every user they came across in the course of their investigations, then they would require a massive increase in their resources. And they would get hopelessly buried in their own paperwork. Trying to follow the chameleons who operated on the supply side of the drug business appeared to be quite simple from a quantitative point of view. It was infinitely more difficult in practice.

Also, the question had not previously been asked: If the FBI and the CIA officers using drugs had been linked in a scheme that would have required cautious cooperation and coordination. That would be almost unprecedented in relations between the FBI and the CIA. After their long history of interdepartmental squabbles, was it possible they had the same cooperation and coordination with their source and the supply of their drugs?

Then there was the matter of involvement with drugs. The CIA had a somewhat bad history when it came to drug dealing. There was an apparent link between drugs and the funding of terrorist groups, irrespective of any principles that may tend to get in the way. Therefore, the CIA had a genuine interest in drugs and drug dealers. But how far did that go? Way back in the far-off days of the civil war in China, the CIA was known to have helped the Kuomintang forces loyal to General Chiang Kai-shek smuggle opium from both China and Burma into Bangkok to gain covert funds for the Chinese KMT. In Vietnam, the CIA was purported to have been involved not only in drug trafficking but also in drug production. Again, the claimed objective was to fund covert military activities, which it would have been difficult, if not impossible, to support by more conventional means. And the list of CIA involvement in drug affairs goes on—the Iran Contra affairs, the particular unit set up in Haiti to disrupt that country's links to Colombia, the Panama affair, to name a few—all examples where the CIA got its hands dirty. And where the rumours of corruption and conspiracy abound.

The problem is that where drugs and, therefore, obscene quantities of money are involved, principles and objectives can get very rapidly and quickly blurred.

And now there was another problem - in the form of Afghanistan.

The CIA's role at the time of the Soviet occupation of that country involved various forms of collaboration, or tolerance, of the drug trade to enable the Mujahideen to gain covert funding for their battle with their vastly superior enemy—the Soviet Union. After the Soviets withdrew, Afghanistan has not exactly been at peace. Since the United States positioned forces there to keep the Taliban under control, the drug trade had shown no sign of diminishing. The essential characteristic in all the CIA involvement in the drug business is covert. Significantly few people within the CIA, or for that matter, the whole US security services, were complicit in its execution. So, who knew what went on?

Another reason for considering inquiries through the DEA was more personal and paramount importance in the scheme of things. Harold Taylor's son Mark was known to the DEA due to his involvement in operations in Colombia and elsewhere in the never-ending war against drugs and drug traffickers. And usually, that counted for something in the bureaucratic jungle.

Harold could not be sure of the details, but he did

know that Mark had been to Colombia on a couple of occasions as part of a special operations group. And the Pentagon did not usually send covert forces into such places on anything other than drug-related issues. They always went with the knowledge and assistance of the CIA and usually with the understanding of the DEA. Mark would never talk about such covert activities other than to allude to the incompetence of the CIA. He had never mentioned any names. But since his retirement from the military, he had been involved with Stephen Rodriguez on a more personal level. And with all the experience and training that Mark had, he could reach and had reached some logical conclusions.

So now Harold Taylor had a new file, simply headed 'Drugs – CIA.'

But it may have been headed 'The Taylors versus Rodriguez.'

One of the problems faced by bureaucrats the world over was getting information in a virgin state, which is mainly a problem in the security and intelligence business. When any information reaches a senior level, where decisions can be made, the source is lost or hidden, so it is hard to get what is euphemistically referred to in the trade as the correct 'feel' for the information.

Harold bided his time and waited until he was taken to lunch by the director of the Intelligence Division of the DEA for a typical inter-government departmental get-to-know-you session.

Their first meeting was enjoyable. It was made more so by the DEA director of intelligence was, a lovely lady named Karen Marshall. She was unusual for a lady who had had to fight her way to the top in what was very much a man's world. She certainly did not dress like a man. She tipped the scales at a little under 130 pounds and stood five feet six in height. She dressed in a neat charcoal-grey jacket and skirt, white blouse, and shoes that gave a hint of lift that accentuated ankles and legs that would not be out of place on a catwalk. Her hair was dark, tied back for work, hinting that it could be let down to reveal the fun-loving girl held in check only by practical considerations. Her makeup was soft and applied to accentuate the clear, light-blue eyes, which were very much alive. The smile was genuine if a little mischievous.

They discussed various aspects of a personal nature: where born, which schools, how many kids, where have you travelled to in pursuit of a better America, and how did you get to be where you are now in this bureaucratic quagmire? As is the way when government-employed strangers meet, previously known only by their positions and by the names of people they had trampled over on the way up the ladder.

Did Karen Marshall get a hint that all was not well in the Taylor household? Harold mentioned his wife, Elizabeth, as one might mention a piece of furniture. Karen had been at a similar stage with her ex-husband before she had managed to get rid of him. That was what saved her career. It did not keep her ex from premature and spectacular death.

But eventually, they got around to talking business; surprisingly, it was Marshall who ventured into the darker world of spooks.

'It must have been quite traumatic to take up your new position so soon after that horrible event in New York. I also heard about the trouble with the CIA and the FBI having yet another turf war,' Marshall began. And then she laughed.

'And what was all that about?'

'Oh, just the usual bickering between two powerful groups!' Taylor replied, as was usual in interdepartmental discussions avoiding answering that question. He also laughed. But he had seen an opening where he could steer the conversation in the direction that would suit his purpose. He continued in a more serious tone.

'I have not been long enough in my present position yet, so I am still sorting out the trees from the forest. But I have been around long enough to see where the CIA could make life tough for you people. I have been away overseas for most of my career with the CIA and have not taken much notice. But when you eventually come back to Washington, you can sense the immense power in this town. Then you step back and see the rivalry that must exist! Then you think about the problems of jealously guarding territory, and the mind shudders to consider what they could achieve if they just cooperated!'

Taylor shrugged and leaned forward across the table, playing with a napkin. Their hands almost touched. He hesitated as though preferring to do something else and then continued.

'Speaking hypothetically, if you have the CIA getting involved in the world of drugs under the guise of funding some covert missions, how do we handle that? Who has an ultimate say on what is right or what is wrong? Do we ignore certain things that some organizations like the CIA may get up to yet bring the wrath of our justice system crashing down on others who do not have that power? I do not know. How do you handle it?'

Marshall looked across the table with a look on her face that was a mixture of questions, her eyes focused on him, searching for answers.

Was this guy for real?

What Harold Taylor had just said was tantamount to

criticizing the organization he represented. And he was not exactly a tiny player, having risen to his position in the OIG, which had a considerable amount of power and influence. The subject that he had briefly touched upon was very much in the minds of the DEA—absolutely, permanently, and as a major cause of ongoing concern. And it had never been raised to her knowledge at previous meetings between the two organizations, casually or otherwise. OK, Harold Taylor was a part of the inspectorate and new at the job. Therefore, he would view things from a distinct perspective. That was until the system ground him down, and he would eventually meekly and politely toe the corporate line.

But for now, this was something out of the left field.

As is the way with bureaucrats, Karen Marshall would produce a report to the DEA on this meeting. And Harold Taylor would do the same for the inspectorate and probably the CIA. The two reports would be filed and probably not read by anybody other than the filing clerk - only to ensure that they got buried in the correct place.

In the case of Marshall's report, as is the way with bureaucrats everywhere, she could also leave trivial matters like the CIA's involvement in drugs out of her report.

However, this subject was just too explosive to be buried.

She mused that it might need to be the subject of a separate report. This report would need to go up the chain of command to the administrator rather than down the chain of command to the filing clerk. However, it had best be left on balance until she had a better understanding of this shy but attractive assistant inspector.

'Do I read you correctly?' Marshall asked, unable to pass up the chance to make a pleasant but routine lunch more exciting.

'Are you saying that you suspect the CIA of continuing to run operations involving drugs? I thought we have moved on from that!'

Of course, she knew the truthful answer to this question. The CIA was always involved in drugs. That is where there were truckloads of money to be had, so terrorists went to get their funding, irrespective of the fact that drugs may be against their principles. That was where the CIA could get funds to assist whatever events they wanted to support. And without the public exposure that came from seeking formal approval, and therefore funding, from Congress. So, Marshall knew that the truthful answer would be in the affirmative.

She also knew that she probably would not get a straight answer.

And it wasn't.

And she didn't.

It was nothing personal.

'I do not know!' protested Taylor, throwing his hands up by way of defence but lacking the venom and mock sincerity that would usually be associated with such a conversation.

It was times like these when he envied his son Mark's ability to read body language and control his own body language. On the other hand, Taylor had to accept that Marshall had not risen through the ranks of the DEA by being a fool. She had probably read him anyway, and he felt the colour come to his cheeks as he wondered if she had read another side to his take on their meeting.

Harold Taylor was more than a little enamoured with this lady.

Fortunately for Harold, the feeling was mutual.

Still, it was a working lunch, so there was still work that had to be done. He had to find a way of turning the conversation around to matters of drugs that were at a more personal level.

There was a connection between the intelligence community and the drug business, which did not make the task faced by the former any easier. Terrorists and criminals had to have funds. Although the financial needs of terrorists were not significant, they could hardly seek sponsorship on the open market, so they looked for secretive and easier ways of raising money. So irrespective of principles, the terrorists had got involved in the drug trade. Hence, the CIA had little choice but to be involved, along with the FBI and everyone else connected to the war on drugs.

It was also not unknown for people in the CIA and the FBI to be drug users. There was a rising rate of substance abuse, which was one of the more polite terms in current jargon, and an increasing rate of alcohol probably caused by stress.

There was also any number of examples of rackets run by government employees, particularly in the military service and in quasi-military organizations such as the CIA, the FBI, and the DEA, to name a few of the many that made up the country's security apparatus. When bureaucrats deal in billions of dollars' worth of funds, goods, and even bribes, there must be the temptation to cream something off the top. It only needs one tiny lapse, and they can be either stupid or clever, and the dominoes start to fall, only to be replaced by the next generation of dominoes.

The lack of substantive evidence that any such abuse of power and privilege was going on in the CIA—and in their sister organizations, FBI, DEA, and the like—was a severe concern to Harold. But he could not solve all the problems at once.

At least not yet.

Taylor brushed aside the issues clouding his thoughts and continued his course.

'Just imagine: if I suspected that there were people in the Company involved in the drug trade for their own benefit, how do you bring them to justice? In our organization, people are so used to keeping and protecting secrets. They are also trained to deceive and lie, to the extent that they would make the Mafia and their ilk sound like fibs at a kids' tea party. Who knows what web of deceit and lies we would be up against?'

Karen laughed again but then got serious and leaned forward, playing with the napkin that Harold had temporarily discarded.

'You are in a unique position to do something about that. But I get the drift of what you are alluding to. Apart from the damage they cause both directly and indirectly to the people who use them, the major problem with drugs is the money that changes hands. The drug barons have so much money that they can buy almost anything and anyone that they care to target. And they can apply and maintain enormous pressure that the unfortunate people cannot resist. If they do resist, then they just dispose of them.'

She smiled to herself as she realized that she now had his undivided attention.

'The easy fix to the problem is to get people to stop taking drugs, and then the market would disappear overnight. But that is neither practical nor possible. The option in the case of the CIA, and for that matter, the DEA, is to pay your people enough money that they would not be tempted. But that also is not possible, is it? The political answer is to have people working for you dedicated to the task. But that is also unrealistic. So, you put in place systems that seek to identify the people who will give in to the temptation or make it difficult for the crooks to identify those who they should seek to corrupt. But is that realistic?'

Harold just nodded his head, too intrigued to interrupt. He let her continue, unsure whether he was more intrigued by the lady than her story.

'I do not know either,' Karen continued. 'As for bringing those who fail our systems to justice, we must follow every lead, hint, comment—anything and everything—down every blind alley, and who knows what we will find? In most cases, we will find nothing, yet in the process, we take the grave risk that we may destroy people's careers or their lives! More significantly, we run the risk of our people losing faith in the very organizations that they work for!' she concluded with a shrug.

At least Harold could smile at that. The CIA had had more than its fair share of blind alleys. Only when some items became known to the media could a link be made—most of them erroneous, all of them used to unfairly criticize those charged with extracting the needles out of the haystacks. And usually with the benefit of hindsight.

But the drug business was a whole different world, continuously changing, evolving, and adapting.

The drug business measured profits in numbers that made even telephone numbers look small. The people who controlled the supply of drugs at their source were compelling, filthy rich, and were virtually untouchable. Like any other chief executive officers in charge of large businesses, the leaders were subject to the economic realities of the division of labour. They employed lawyers, accountants, operations, production, shipping, security managers, and Minders. They had people who were solely responsible for defining and monitoring their supply routes through the many shipping and air corridors, including the payment of bribes at the border controls, including the mules who risked long jail sentences, and their lives, to get the drugs to where they were needed.

Mules could be used to overwhelm the border checks, and so what if there was an occasional hiccup? If 10, or even 20, percent got caught, that meant that between 80 and 90 percent of the drugs got through, which was a more-than-acceptable loss. There were plenty more people who were prepared to take the risk of becoming a mule to pay off their debts, usually to the same people they were working for. The cost of what was lost bore little relationship to the market value of the goods. Therefore, the money to be lost was insignificant to the bosses in the drug trade. It was significant and a necessity to the mule. And there was the problem.

The CEOs of the drug business had people who monitored the others, rather like Harold's new role in the OIG at the CIA. Except that these particular people had different rules. They could, and did, ruthlessly enforce a code of practice that did not tolerate either disloyalty or error. And they did not need to worry too much if their enforcement occasionally made an error of judgment—beat up the wrong man or killed the innocent helper. There were plenty more people who would take their place, usually oblivious to who they were replacing. This brought a whole new meaning to the practice of risk management.

But the reality was that the people at the very top of the chain were only in it for the money. Significantly few drug bosses were drug users. And very few drug deals were done on credit. Sure, the larger the agreement, the greater the chance of getting short-term credit, but the concise term, and never more than a small percentage. People who owed money for drugs did not owe it for long or did not live long. And so, the DEA, the FBI, the CIA, and anyone else who sought to peek into the murky world of drugs and dealers had to resort to the careful, thorough, and often fruitless monitoring of millions of seemingly unrelated and irrelevant bits of information, just looking for clues.

Looking for hooks into organizations that were exceedingly difficult to track and trace.

The people who ran these organizations were chameleons.

'**The Drug** Enforcement Administration has the same problem as the CIA!' Taylor mused. Everybody is an expert when armed with the facts and when those facts are put into context. At the CIA, we get millions of bits of data every day, and we have teams of analysts pouring over that data, trying to find links. But they rarely recognize all the links, and without the critical link, we could go off in the wrong direction. At times, we leave things alone and see what else develops.'

'Like?' Marshall asked.

'Well, if I can speak off the record. There are often different views on how to tackle a problem. You only need to recall what happened as far back as the Kennedy administration to see what chaos can be caused when bureaucrats and politicians cannot agree on methods and the end objective. It was postulated that the CIA had a plan to have the Mafia kill Castro. The Mafia had plenty of motivation. They used to make plenty of money running the casinos in Havana. The problem was that the CIA involvement was so covert that the CIA did not bother to tell either their political masters in the White House or their military associates at the Pentagon. The result was the Bay of Pigs fiasco and, some say, ultimately, the assassination of President John Kennedy. Others say that the CIA or the Mafia may have been responsible for Kennedy's death. There are all kinds of conspiracy theories, most of which can be discarded as rubbish, but in the end, you will still never hear the actual truth, and conspiracy theories will go on forever.'

Taylor paused for effect. For some reason, it was important that Karen Marshall should be impressed. What that had to do with Harold's original plan was a moot point.

Probably Harold was beginning to think with his dick rather than his head. That may have been caused by too much wine. It was more likely caused by the fact that he hadn't had sex with anybody for as long as he could remember. He continued, satisfied that he was indeed making an impression on this young lady.

'Of more recent events, I was never happy with how the aftermath of New York 9/11 version 2 was handled, and I do not think we got to the truth of what exactly was behind that. I have reason to believe that other people were involved in the CIA. And I believe that involvement has its origins in the drug business rather than with any terrorists. There can be no other explanation based on the information I have access to.'

Harold paused, again more for effect than anything else. He was close. He was drawing Karen Marshall into the web.

'My problem is now. How do I go about finding out if my suspicions are correct? Being so new at this job, I do not yet know sufficiently well the people who work for me. From what I can gather, they are mostly ex-CIA personnel, and I should be able to trust them, but I cannot be certain in the circumstances. I do not yet really know them. The FBI Internal Affairs Office, or Office of Professional Responsibility, could, on my behalf, undertake a covert investigation, but they suffer from the same problem that I do. That office is staffed by ex-FBI personnel, and I believe that the drug problem has also infiltrated their organization. The OPR is respected, but certainly not loved, across all agencies, and the slightest hint of their involvement in investigating the problem could cause all evidence to evaporate. Worse case, ex-CIA and ex-FBI people talking to each other about an investigation into a business involved, it would be a disaster!'

Harold was now waiting for a reaction.

And he got one.

'You would like me to make some discreet inquiries?' asked Karen with a conspiratorial air and a mischievous smile.

'It would help if you could,' replied Harold. 'But not if there is a risk of it getting back to anyone at the CIA or the FBI, at any level.'

'That bad, huh?'

Chapter 7

The Russians

Evgeny Andreyevich Ovsyannikov was due to retire in a year after serving for over forty years in the diplomatic service of initially the Soviet Union and now his beloved Russia. He had been at his present posting in Washington DC for the last five of those years. He was regarded in the circles he travelled—commonly known as the cocktail circuit—as a pleasant and quiet member of the diplomatic community who said little. He mostly listened to the somewhat inane and tireless conversations his job involved. He sometimes liked to listen to diplomats speaking hour upon hour of blather, saying nothing of even the remotest beneficial interest but delivering it with such finesse! But his interest was in gathering information. And it was often what was not said that could be the most interesting.

Ovsyannikov looked much older than his fifty-nine years. A bald man of about five feet ten and slightly overweight, he wore a rumbled grey suit and a grey shirt that matched his featureless gaunt face.

The office where he worked, such as it was, lacked the comforts and views afforded the diplomats in Wisconsin

Avenue, which housed the Washington Embassy of the Russian Federation. Instead, he was accommodated in the Russian Cultural Center in Phelps Place. That was because he was a cultural attaché.

At least that was the description on his diplomatic passport.

Ovsyannikov still preferred to regard himself as a member of the Soviet KGB. So much had changed under the new order.

The Russians had reorganized their intelligence services in 1991, and the KGB was now the foreign intelligence service under the acronym of SVR. Much of the bite had gone out of the service since that change, mainly affecting how the security services operated within Russia. They were still playing the same games on the international scene, so why change? He was one of the many people in his profession, from both Russia and other countries, who nostalgically wished they were back in the days of the Cold War between the United States and the Soviet Union.

Now that had been fun!

Most people regarded a job in his country's intelligence and security service as clandestine, secret, and exciting, whereas it was extremely open, repetitive, and dull. The area of concern to Ovsyannikov was the CIA, and he was aided in this by about a dozen or so other 'cultural attaches,' a handful of paid informants, and the ever-useful Internet. Thanks to the latter, he sometimes thought that the world would see the end of intelligence gathering as he knew it. Just read up, plagiarise appropriate bits, forward your report, and have another vodka martini shaken, not stirred.

Ovsyannikov was probably the only Russian assigned to Washington who knew the identity of their primary source of information within the US government services. This source had to be used with care out of fear that its information could reveal *who, where,* or *what* it was. The source was also helpful in feeding misinformation to the government, although other assets usually handled that for similar reasons.

Apart from this, like any other intelligence-gathering function, the work for Ovsyannikov consisted of reading through screeds of paperwork to achieve very little. Sure, things had moved on so that it was all digitized, but you still had to read it. Only very occasionally did something juicy bubble to the surface.

And one such something had recently got the attention of his masters in Moscow. And he was tasked with finding out as much as he could about this intrigue.

The CIA had recently been badly shaken up by a drug case. It was not the mere taking of drugs that caused the Russian interest. The CIA had a long history of involvement in the drug business, so there was nothing new in that. If people who worked for the CIA, or any other part of the complex world of intelligence and counterintelligence, wanted to screw their brains with drugs, then that was their problem.

What was more of interest to the Russians was *who* was involved?

Several quite senior-ranking officials within the CIA and the FBI had recently been caught aiding and abetting the supply of drugs, and they had been very quickly and very quietly removed from their posts. These criminals would spend a long time incarcerated in federal prisons and would be useless to the SVR, or anybody else, when or *if* they ever emerged.

The Russians had long since given up trying to get people inside the United States penal system, pumping such disgruntled people for information. There was always a problem dealing with American criminals. You could not trust them. At least in the old Soviet Union, you could torture people, which was a far more efficient way of extracting information! Give people the option of talking or dying. They usually chose the former of the two alternatives. Not that it did them much good. They usually talked, and from that point, they may as well have been dead,

The Russians had a much higher probability of success out in the field. The massive number of people employed in the US security and intelligence services made it inevitable that someone would eventually talk. It was a bureaucracy, after all, with all the quirks and idiosyncrasies that bedevilled all sides.

As regards the recently revealed drug business going on within the US security service, if all the people that were involved in this drug trafficking had been swept up, then that left an opportunity for someone else to step in, drug users being what they were—parasites and creatures of habit. On the other hand, who was now doing the business if they had not all been swept up?

If they had not been caught in the initial sweep, where were they hiding?

And of paramount significance from the initial Russian analysis was that they would have to be at an extremely prominent level to have escaped the original purge. The case had gone cold, but it was not yet dead.

However, the Russians' information had now acquired had come as quite a shock. Whether or not it was true, it was too early to tell. But if it was true, here was an opportunity to do considerable damage to the whole security and intelligence network of the United States. Thus far, the entire business had been kept remarkably quiet. But the Russians had enough information that they could reveal the sordid truth and at least cause considerable embarrassment.

The best way to do this was to use the US media. The Americans would never learn, would they? Their media loved nothing more than to embarrass their government, politicians, or servants. In the Russian view, there was absolutely nothing wrong with taking steps to stop journalists from reporting on matters that their political masters regarded as inappropriate, not so in Washington. It was almost as though American journalists had a right and a duty to report anything.

And it did not seem to matter whether the story they told was true or false.

The alternative to having the media crawling all over the story was to use the knowledge to gain access to informants at the highest possible level.

Simply threatening to unmask the criminals should do it.

The Russian source had provided enough information to start the ball rolling. The story thus far was that an assistant deputy director of the CIA, who went by the name of Stephen Rodriguez, had become a person of interest. According to information that the Russians had received, Rodriguez had been instrumental in sorting out the original mess in the drug case and was therefore seen by the CIA and others within the sizeable bureaucratic structure as one of the good guys.

But the Russians also had information that suggested otherwise. That information indicated that Rodriguez was an organizer behind a drug network that made the few who had been caught looking like chicken feed. Rodriguez had been in a unique position when sorting out the mess. Sure, any of the people caught up by the initial sweep could have named Rodriguez as having been involved, even if he hadn't been involved in the matter. That seemed to be how things worked in a democratic and capitalist society. Sure, other factors at play could have marked those who were caught to everyone in the drug business as narks. And there are two things you do not want to be in a US prison. Firstly, noticed as part of the more comprehensive 'enforcement' network by the criminal fraternity—whether past or current did not matter—and in prison, the FBI did not carry the same weight as it did outside. Secondly, noticed as a *nark* by the drug fraternity.

It was early days, and Ovsyannikov was in no hurry. His sources had not indicated that Rodriguez reported to anyone higher in the CIA—that is, on drug-related matters. And they could not, or would not, say whether he was reporting to anyone else within the security and intelligence network. Indeed, it would suit the Russians if he were. The bigger and broader the scandal, then so much the better.

The Russians in Moscow preferred the broader political objective of maximizing the embarrassment for the Americans. Ovsyannikov preferred a behind-the-scenes approach which would add an unprecedented level to his pool of informants. In the good old days, that would be the approach that the KGB would have taken. However, the political dance was too hard to keep up with these days. In any case, such decisions were way beyond his pay grade.

Ovsyannikov conceded that there was a good chance that the CIA would eventually wake up and expose the scandal. There was only a remote chance that he could turn any of the players into informants. In a way, he felt sorry for the people in the CIA—after all, they were all in the same business as he was. And he would only reluctantly accede to the grander plan of his political masters.

He settled for following the case and seeing where it led for the time being.

One avenue of inquiry could be the inspectorate within the CIA because that is one organization in the vast and cumbersome intelligence network that could, and should, investigate such things. That avenue had both pluses and minuses.

The Office of the Inspector General was established in 1989 as an independent organization to worry about the three *e*'s of all bureaucracies: economy, efficiency, and effectiveness. And, of course, accountability. It also supposedly aims to detect and deter fraud, waste, abuse, and mismanagement, which means the Office of the Inspector General is like any other government auditor, at least in its stated objectives. But living and working under the same roof, could it be *independent*, and could it be trusted to act?

The CIA is such a vast organization that people in the 'independent' inspectorate would be expected to have some working knowledge of the organization it was to inspect. For this reason, the OIG had recently recruited as an assistant inspector from within the operations division of the CIA no less a person than the immediate past head of station in Wellington, New Zealand—Harold Taylor.

The appointment of Taylor to the position of OIG may have been coincidental. But Ovsyannikov had received information that Harold Taylor was involved in the original clean-out.

Or was he?

He had also received information that the son of Harold, Mark Taylor, had also been involved. Whether directly or indirectly, with the prior knowledge and approval of the Company, the Russians had no evidence either way. Information was slowly coming in and building a picture—that Mark Taylor was somehow involved in preventing, and failing to avoid, a September 11 'event' in New York City. How the junior Taylor came to be involved and what exactly he was doing was vague, but so far, this was as much the Russians knew.

Harold Taylor, the father, had recently become a very senior member of the hierarchy of the CIA. On the other hand, Mark Taylor, the son, had never been a member of that organization.

Or had he?

Mark Taylor had a distinguished military career—first as a marine and later in the United States Special Forces. He had 'retired' and, as far as the Russians could tell, he had done so with the full blessing of a grateful nation. That meant he had not been forced to retire. And there was no evidence of any continued clandestine or covert association with the United States military or their security services.

Taylor was now a businessman, which in America could mean anything. But, again, his business did not have any connection with any military, intelligence, or other government agencies, apart from the fact that his company was involved with computers and security. And that was puzzling to the Russians.

Informants had told Ovsyannikov after all the dust had settled that Taylor had been overseas immediately before the second 9/11 event. But apart from a brief visit to New Zealand, where else he had been, or why, remained a mystery.

On the family front, well, the son of the Taylors had no family except for his parents Harold and Elizabeth. Taylor had at one stage been married to Helen Cole, whose father was a military man. The Russians were aware of his background, which included a long history going back to the American civil war, but there was no future in pursuing that. And while Helen appeared to be a bit of a fruitcake and quite sexually active, that was a dead-end because Taylor and Cole had divorced.

Ovsyannikov made a *Note to themself*: find out some more about Mark Taylor. For example - did he go to New Zealand to see his family? Or was he away doing business on behalf of either the CIA or some other part of the complex United States intelligence community?

Understanding and following Harold Taylor in his new position was more straightforward. The Americans were so free with their information that it was not hard to find where Taylor worked and lived, and his duties were spelled out for all to see by a Google search. Ovsyannikov accepted that this information did not reveal precisely *how* the OIG worked. Finding out exactly what Taylor was investigating required more effective use of informants, but eventually, that information would be forthcoming. However, just doing his regular job led to yet another helpful coincidence.

By pure chance, Ovsyannikov had lunch in a restaurant that catered to government officials. Well, it was not really by chance. On many a quiet day, cultural attaches from various countries lunched at the same restaurant to catch up with friends. Or, more correctly, to see who else was catching up with whom. Who should be there lunching together but Harold Taylor, the newly appointed assistant inspector of the OIG, and Karen Marshall, the director of intelligence of the Drug Enforcement Administration?

Ovsyannikov had an excellent memory for faces, like all people in the diplomatic community. Being in the intelligence business, he also had excellent instincts.

If it were not for the stories about the CIA and drugs that were crossing his desk, Ovsyannikov would see this meeting as having had no significance in the grand scheme of things. But it did have value, if for no other reason than the intensity of the discussion, which could best be described as unusual in so public an arena.

Of course, it could have been that Harold Taylor just wanted to impress the lady. After all, rumour had it that Marshall was available and somewhat lonely. Or maybe Taylor just wanted to get into her pants. But heaven forbid! Taylors' wife, Elizabeth Taylor, was a pretty formidable lady but barely attractive, designed to drive any man to despair rather than attract him into her liar. Yet Taylor was so old school that a sexual motive seemed unlikely.

What seemed to be more likely was that they were discussing the same business that he was now investigating. Ovsyannikov watched as the restaurant emptied, and finally, both Taylor and Marshall took their leave. He sipped the last of his Merlot. A few glasses of red wine worked wonders for the imagination. Watch. What was to be the next step in this intriguing story?

In the quieter part of town in his office at Phelps Place, Ovsyannikov pondered what he had learned. He was beginning to make some progress. He had seen a senior official from the CIA—well, the Office of the Inspector General, which was the same thing—talking to a senior official from the DEA.

He had not been sufficiently close to the men to able to hear their conversations, but their body language said a lot. It would not be possible to bug the restaurant (the Americans were so paranoid they probably had the building regularly swept anyway), but next time, he would try to get closer and maybe lip-read.

The Russians, and many other people, had salivated at the thought of getting an informant on the restaurant staff; but all the waiters employed there were ex-US Navy stewards. Tangling with them could land you in a whole heap of trouble.

Ovsyannikov would report his conclusions to his masters, and, as with all reports of things past, he would have to include some comment on what he intended to do next.

Firstly, it was time to start putting tabs on Stephen Rodriguez. Or his family? According to the file, Rodriguez had a couple of daughters with his Latino wife, who was quite attractive if one liked an older woman, and quite fiery.

Secondly, he must try to follow the goings-on between the OIG and the DEA. He did not expect anything to come of his thoughts on the involvement of Mark Taylor, the son of Harold, in the earlier episode. So, he would not mention that unless it came to anything.

If it ever did.

Chapter 8

The Taylors

It was not that long since Mark Taylor, son of Harold Taylor and the owner of a computer software development company called Taylor Software had agreed to take on a new personal assistant in the form of one attractive lady named Debbie Peterson. Debbie was petite and shy. She was always looking to avoid the limelight, yet always ready to make anyone feel comfortable and welcome. She was ideal as a PA, and she was a lovely person.

Debbie had previously worked for one of the clients of Taylor Software, a finance and insurance organization called the Augem Group. She had come to Mark's company freely and with the full knowledge of the Augem chief executive officer and the general manager. Both gentlemen—Rob Augem, the CEO, and Matt Reynolds, the GM—had asked Mark to take her on rather than lose her entirely in the rat race that was New York City.

And that was quite understandable in the circumstances.

It was a complicated story.

The previous personal assistant at Taylor Software had been an equally attractive young lady called Annette Covic, who had immigrated from the chaos that had become of the previous country of Yugoslavia in the Adriatic to seek a better life in the United States. She came to work for Taylor Software on the recommendation of Matt Reynolds. At that time, Debbie Peterson had been the receptionist and secretary of the Augem Group, which in turn had been a client of Taylor Software.

Annette Covic had subsequently died—well, in fact, she had been murdered in cold blood by someone who should have known better, an agent of the FBI.

Shortly before Annette's death, the chief executive officer of the Augem Group had been a gentleman called John Dubois, not Rob Augem, as many would have expected to be in charge since the company was founded by and named after him. Dubois was arrogant and aggressive, characteristics that did not endear him to his peers or his minions. Consequently, there was not a great deal of sadness when John Dubois had also died—well, in fact, he had committed suicide by jumping off the roof of a sixteen-storied building where the Augem Group had its New York office.

This was all too much for Debbie Peterson, who blamed John Dubois for Annette Covic's death, even though the deaths had occurred in the order – first John Dubois and secondly Annette Covic. Peterson had said that she would have to leave the Augem Group given the drama. Rob Augem and Reynolds understood, but they were both somewhat mortified to see her go. Then Augem and Reynolds had an idea. They tried to convince Mark Taylor to take her on since he needed a new personal assistant.

Perhaps surprisingly, Mark Taylor agreed since his

last PA had come from the same source. And Debbie Peterson had joined Taylor Software.

And it was not so long afterward that Debbie realized that she was very much in love with her new boss.

This boss was quite different. Mark was tall, powerfully built, and extremely fit. He towered over his PA and most others, but not in a brutal way. Mark was quiet and gentle in how he went about things and dealt with other people. He had come from a military background, where he had been trained, and learned that patience and discipline were vital ingredients to success in his chosen career. And when he left the military, he found that those ingredients were equally applicable in the business world.

Mark Taylor was incredibly good at reading body language, yet he did not need to employ that skill to discover Debbie's feelings towards him. They had made love shortly after she had joined Taylor Software, and that had been initiated more out of loneliness on both their parts than from any other reason. Mark also realized that he was now very much in love with his new PA. But Debbie's body language told him that the relationship would need to change if their love and respect were to endure. Spending quality time together was important. But living and working together could, and would, cause issues somewhere down the track.

Mark had his own problems. He thought he had been in love with Annette Covic, but that relationship had ended almost before it started and before it could develop into something truly meaningful. He had to admit that his initial infatuation with this girl had been driven more by lust. But when he got to know Annette better, it was true love rather than animal instinct that caused them to fall into each other arms.

The fact that Mark had failed to take the bullet that had ended her life could be easily and logically explained by this rugged ex-United States Special Forces man. Mark was doing what his training had dictated that he had to do. He had gone for the gun and the person who was about to fire it at Annette rather than take the heroic and suicidal action which would have resulted in both of them being killed. Mark had been a split second too late in his dive to save the lady he loved. The sad result was that Annette was now dead, leaving Mark Taylor and various other people with a huge void to fill somehow.

Mark had seen his share of death. But never had he seen someone he loved shot down in cold blood before his eyes while he had valiantly but vainly tried to prevent it.

Mark would never forget that day.

Mark would never forgive the man who had pulled that trigger.

But he had to move on despite that moment's vivid and heart-breaking memory.

The problem with death is the feeling of hopelessness when a relationship suddenly ends when someone whose presence is taken for granted is no longer there. At the time of Annette's death, or at least when the hectic pace of his life at that time returned to near normal, Mark was overcome with grief. Yet his life had to go on. Like a body being swept downstream in a raging torrent of water, there were other things to worry about at the time than the reason for the predicament.

Try as you might. Wish as you might. There is no going back.

And there is no turning back the clock.

Another part of the problem was that despite being forced into believing that this episode in his life was at an end, he now knew that it was not. And how did he avoid the same fate being repeated for him, those he associated with, and those he loved?

Would that horrible moment in his life be forever in his mind, or could he genuinely move on?

In the peace of his apartment, one evening after a busy day at Taylor Software, Mark and Debbie were sitting down listening to some quiet music and enjoying each other's company when he raised the question that had been forming in his mind for some time. The words came out of his mouth in a rush fearing that he would stumble over what he wanted to say. He did not want to pressure this young lady. He knew that he had probably placed himself under enormous pressure by thinking about it too much. He knew what he wanted to say. The hard-nosed ex-military man, used to dealing with lowlife criminals and superior officers without hesitation, would stumble regarding delicate personal issues. He just did not know how to say it.

'How would you like to work from home?' Mark asked. Then he added, 'Be it from your apartment or ours?'

Because of asking that simple question, the hug he got initially confused him. He was a very shy person, especially with members of the opposite sex, and the ability to read body language did not necessarily extend to an ability to understand women. Body language was one thing. The logic behind what women thought and did was another thing entirely.

However, he needed not have worried. Debbie patiently explained to this thoughtful and endearing man.

He had said two things that pleased her, whereas Mark thought he had said only one thing.

Debbie had come to Taylor Software as a form of

escapism, fallen in love, or, rather, confirmed a passion that she had always felt for this shy brute of a man and then realized that it could be all a fairy tale. They each needed to have some space, and if they did not have that space, their relationship could and probably would end in disaster. Working and playing together was fine for a while. But many a relationship had floundered under the pressure of constantly being together and living through all the dramas that business and private life entails. Small, irrelevant questions became significant explosive issues. After all, Mark was the boss, and he made decisions based on a kaleidoscope of information that only he could know. Others viewed those decisions based on a different perspective and a limited perception. If he was *the* boss, that was no matter. If, or when, he made a mistake, *his* company bore the cost, and only he was accountable. However, different forces are at play when an issue becomes personal or other people are involved.

Mark needed not have worried. But, in the brief time that he and Debbie had been together, he could not know that.

Mark had said, 'work from home … And ours.'

She hugged him again and then asked in her excitement, 'You mean that you want me to live with you?'

The stammered reply of *'Of course I do … I did not think you would want to!'* resulted in a more passionate embrace. And that resulted in the need to begin removing some of their clothes. Before long, they were both completely naked as the passionate embrace continued.

Mark had never really understood women, but he was happy to go along with the unexpected digression.

They made love as passionately as Mark could ever remember, the reasons behind the interlude quickly becoming irrelevant.

But they are not forgotten.

The following day, Mark was alone in his office, trying to avoid letting his mind wander, shaking his head in sheer wonderment at what drove his lover to be so passionate about so small a matter, and contemplating a meeting with an assistant inspector general of the CIA.

The last time that Mark had left the office of Taylor Software for a meeting with the same gentleman had resulted in no end of trouble made him apprehensive. Sure, that meeting had taken place half a world away, in Wellington in New Zealand. And sure, the guy was his father. But his father, Harold Taylor, was still working for the CIA. That had Mark somewhat nervous, especially since Harold was now in a much more elevated position than he had been as a lowly station chief in far-off New Zealand.

Nonetheless, the meeting was to take place at the senior Taylors' residence, and, since it would be pretty normal behaviour for the son to visit his father at his parents' home, he did not expect any of the particular dramas that would have been associated with a more formal visit to the CIA headquarters at Langley. Mark would be taking Debbie along for dinner. He hoped that his mother would accept Debbie without the usual acrimonious scrutiny that mothers seemed to reserve for women who were distracting their boys' attention from their more worldly duties. And from their mothers.

Mark did not know that Harold Taylor was about to deliver some riveting news. Otherwise, he would have felt even more apprehensive. He had no idea why he had been summoned to a meeting, except for the fact that Mark had himself alerted Harold to the existence of a particular problem in the CIA concerning one who went by the name of Stephen Rodriguez, who was in no less a position than that of assistant deputy director of intelligence.

While issuing the invitation to come to Washington, Harold had gone out of his way to assure Mark that he just wanted to bring him up to date on how things were going. He had recently returned to Washington after a period as the CIA chief of station in Wellington. His peers would not have regarded that posting to Wellington in the spook world as riveting.

But Mark knew different.

And Harold did as well.

The events that had occurred because of that posting had led to Harold's promotion, albeit to a vastly different role in the organization to which Harold Taylor had dedicated much of his adult life.

Mark sighed as he looked at the paperwork on his desk. Most of it was the trivia that every business must deal with. Some of it was important, which concerned deals that took so much work that rested on the whim of some executive. Those 'business' decisions were not made entirely on the merits or otherwise of the presented relevant facts. They were often made based on who slept with whom, and they were often influenced by people who knew next to nothing about the factual issues involved.

Mark reflected on his experiences in his previous life with Delta Force. Life had been much easier in that life. The rewards were so much simpler. You won, or you lost. It was not your personal fight. And at the end of the day, the world would keep spinning. You trained long and hard to push the balance of each battle in your favour. You became so good and efficient at your job that you never lost a battle of your own accord. The only time you lost—or, to put it more correctly, you did not win—was when some other cretin fucked up, usually the result of poor intelligence or, more accurately, the flawed analysis of that intelligence, or when information vital to the outcome of the job was quite simply withheld on a need-to-know basis by some bureaucrat whose world revolved around paperclips.

Mark and Debbie left New York City at 5:30 am on Saturday for the long but pleasant drive to Washington DC. They could just as quickly have flown from New York to Washington, but they did not for a couple of reasons. Firstly, Mark did not like the hassle associated with air travel, particularly in the post-9/11 era. Secondly, he was reversing a trip he had done not that long ago, that time from Washington DC to New York City; and to him, it was a sort of finalization of all the brutal drama that that trip had involved. Besides this, he had Debbie to think about now.

Debbie was somewhat apprehensive—not about the trip, but about where they were going or, more correctly, the formidable people she would meet.

Mark had laughingly explained to her the peculiarities of the Taylor family. Still, with Debbie also being a shy person, she was wary of meeting a high-ranking government official and his somewhat overbearing wife in the spook business.

Debbie had met the senior members of the Taylor family once before.

At a funeral.

They did not act or look particularly friendly, which was understandable. Still, reading their body language, she did not expect that their attitude would change very much in the more informal environment of their family home. To Debbie, the Taylors were like a pair of marble statues, cold, and looked like people who were members of the same family in name only. The exact opposite of the man who now sat beside her.

By the time they had made it into the Washington suburb of Bethesda, where the Taylors had their current residence, Mark and Debbie were both relaxed and looking forward to a weekend without the stress of the big city. At least that would be the objective for Sunday.

The house was beside the park in Chevy Chase, Village, and although the trees had lost their foliage at the onset of winter, the view was still peaceful and pleasant. Whether the Taylor family could afford to live in so affluent a suburb as Chevy Chase, Mark did not know. But neither of the senior Taylors seemed to be affected by the apparent anomaly. He remembered overhearing some talk of money on his mother's side of the family, but such boring matters were never discussed openly when he was at home, so that was an end to that matter.

When they arrived, Mark's mother seemed quite pleased to see her son and went out of her way to make Debbie feel welcome and at home. His father, however, could not help himself. Harold was dressed as though for a more formal occasion in a white shirt and a tie, but he at least had tried to make an effort to impress his guests. Mark and Harold sat outside while Elizabeth insisted that they take tea. Eventually, Mark persuaded his father that they should have something a little more in keeping with the informality of the occasion, and they passed the late afternoon pleasantly enough, drinking beer and chatting about earlier times when they had acted like a more normal family.

But it could not last.

After a somewhat formal dinner, Harold invited Mark into his study while Elizabeth and Debbie talked girl talk while cleaning up the table.

Harold very quickly got down to business.

'Tell me again—why do you think I should investigate Stephen Rodriguez?' he began their official informal chat while he sipped on a glass of port, and Mark struggled with brandy that his mother had served in a giant glass.

'Father, I have already told you—Stephen Rodriguez was somehow involved in the original appointment of John Dubois as chief executive officer of the Augem Group,' replied Mark in exasperation. 'That alone should raise a red flag even for an organization such as the CIA!'

Indeed, Mark thought, he did not have to go through the whole sorry tale again!

Mark had been to hell and back due to the chaos caused by John Dubois. He had lost Annette Covic – the girl he loved. He had also lost his close friend, CIA agent Paul Williams who he had met while serving in the United States Special Forces. Dubois had been responsible for three explosions in New York City on the anniversary of September 11th, 2001.

In the aftermath of that debacle, Mark had got the truth out of Rob Augem – founder of the Augem Group. Stephen Rodriguez was the man who knew of Rob's earlier indiscretions during the share market troubles in the 1980s. Rodriguez had used that knowledge to get John Dubois appointed to the Augem Board to ultimately replace Rob as the head of the organization. He had used that knowledge to ensure that Rob Augem remained silent about John Dubois's evil plans.

But, as was not unusual with Harold Taylor, the older man had an ulterior motive for raising the subject the way he had. His face became grim.

'I think I may have a hook into Rodriguez, but from a most unexpected source because it has nothing to do with John Dubois and the earlier affair!' Harold waited and then added. 'At least directly!'

'You want to tell me about that?' Mark enquired, now suspecting that Harold did but never quite sure. After all, on a strictly need-to-know basis, it was hardly the subject for a Saturday-evening chat between father and son, the former an assistant inspector general at the CIA, and the latter merely the boss of a small computer software company. Sure, the father was the assistant inspector who was second in charge of one of the most feared organizations on the planet. Anyone who put the fear of God into people who worked for the CIA had to be important and powerful. And the son was the boss at Taylor Software, which specialized in security systems. He was an ex-Special Forces and Delta Force operator and, therefore, a person who knew all about security and intelligence.

And killing people.

But both knew all about keeping secrets, and once a secret was shared, it was no longer a secret.

'That is why we are talking here,' Harold said, trying hard not to talk conspiratorial and failing.

Harold continued, 'We now believe that someone in the CIA has drugs shipped into the United States from Southern Asia and is involved in their distribution. Our investigations cause us to believe that your friend Stephen Rodriguez could be involved.'

Mark looked at his father, but nothing registered.

'You don't look at all surprised!' Harold ventured.

'Should I be?' Mark responded.

Mark had done his fair share of chasing drug barons in various parts of the world in an earlier life, with varying degrees of success. The degree of success, or, on occasions, the lack of success, was not due to any shortcomings on Mark's part. They were due to either lousy information assumed to come via the CIA or atrocious decisions made at a higher level—maybe, maybe not, based on the same wrong information. In both situations, he could point the accusatory finger at the intelligence gathering community, and, since his missions were overseas, that meant the CIA. And the assistant deputy director of intelligence would have had something to do with that.

But worse than that, not so long ago, Mark had battled with some relatively senior members of the same community—from within both the CIA and the FBI—and he was left in little doubt that drugs had played a big part. Could the drug barons have influenced the flow of reliable information within the organizations that were supposed to be investigating them? It was not lousy information—it was disinformation or information diversion. And then to find out that the dirty tricks played both years before with Rob Augem and, more recently, with John Dubois, there could be ample reasons why Stephen Rodriguez should now be top of the list of suspects.

Mark needed to be careful that the hate he felt for Stephen Rodriguez did not affect his judgment. He had found the connection between Rodriguez and Dubois. Was that sufficient to accept that what his father now had to say about Rodriguez would necessarily be true?

'I suppose not,' Harold sighed, answering Mark's original question. He lowered his voice as he continued.

'The problem is that I do not get to see the original data apart from being very new to this job. Everything is analysed before it reaches my desk, and often, the origins are withheld. Now I understand that. Even though I may have the responsibility as a sort of resident executioner of the CIA, agents in the field still must protect their sources.

And the people who work for me are ex-agency so that they would have a divided loyalty, wouldn't they?' Harold rambled on for a few more minutes, most of which Mark could ignore, for he knew what was coming.

Well, almost.

The last time he had a similar conversation with his father, Mark went to parts of the world he had not heard of beforehand. And two of Mark's friends had died because of that, along with a few hundred residents of New York City. Neither Harold nor Mark could be blamed for that, but some members of the CIA and the FBI, the much-vaunted Federal Bureau of Investigation, had played a crucial and controversial role.

Although some of them had been caught in the wash-up of that little affair, others were still at large and were, in fact, still collecting their government pay packets and making a heap of money on the side. It was not unreasonable that Mark Taylor could view such goings-on as just not his problem, leaving the likes of his father in his role as an assistant inspector and the vast United States judicial system to sort them out. But then he had lost two friends, and at least one person should carry the ultimate blame, if for no other reason than that he had utterly fooled Mark, not to mention the entire United States judicial system. And that man was indeed likely to be the assistant deputy director of intelligence of the CIA—Stephen Rodriguez.

Mark eventually interrupted his father's ramblings.

'Father, you know Rob Augem and his reputation. Apart from that, he was in no condition to lie when he gave me that name. And what would he gain by doing so? Why not accept that as fact and move on? What *new* information have you come up with in your elevated *new* position?'

Harold could be a real pain up the ass at times, and

this was one of those times. But slowly, the gist of his thoughts began to come out, rather like getting blood out of a stone.

From previous experience, Mark surmised that Harold was struggling to justify some plot that he had only half worked out and that someone else would have to connect the dots. Or was Harold just, once again, playing at being a spook? Or had he already decided on a plan of action? Was he waiting for some indication from his son?

Mark took a sip from his brandy.

Harold was painting a picture.

'I had some people at the Drug Enforcement Administration do some digging for me. That digging shows that we believe there is a trail of drug trafficking and dealings that lead to someone in the CIA. Indications are that the drugs originate in Afghanistan. We do not know how the drugs are organized at the supply-and-production end, how they get the drugs smuggled across our borders, or how they distribute them when they get here. We know that there have recently been some interruptions to the flow of drugs out of Afghanistan that has affected the distribution here in the United States. All that we have been able to find out so far is weird. There are drug users in the CIA and the FBI—mostly recreational or social users, but users, nonetheless. What we cannot find out is where they buy their drugs from. And that led us to the thought that someone was being very clever. Someone in the CIA, or some other part of our government intelligence and security bureaucracy, is bringing in drugs for distribution only to the people in the same bureaucracy. You can imagine they have a huge body of potential users in organizations that are used to keeping secrets. As with all bureaucratic organizations, they protect their own, so it is hard for us to penetrate.'

Mark could hear noises coming from elsewhere in

the house that indicated that they were about to be joined by the ladies. But he had not factored in his mother's uncanny sense of knowing when not to interrupt her husband of many years.

With a sense of foreboding, Mark asked, 'You said for "us" to penetrate. Who are "us"?'

Harold laughed. 'I have been talking to someone high up in the DEA, their director of intelligence—off the record, of course. I have not yet got enough confidence in my own division to let them loose on my inquiries. She gave me a clue. You should meet Karen Marshall sometime. I am sure you would find her quite interesting,' Harold concluded with a chuckle in his voice and a twinkle in his eyes.

Mark was somewhat shocked. Did he detect that his father had taken a liking to another woman? He hoped his body language was giving nothing away as he tried to stay on the principal subject.

'So, how does this tie in with Stephen Rodriguez?'

'Well, it does not really,' Harold began. 'Except for two points. Firstly, the DEA is certain that the origin of the drugs is somewhere in Afghanistan. Through the FBI they have picked up small samples of heroin being used by government people that they say they can trace to Pakistan, and that probably means that it has been refined into heroin from Afghanistan opiates. And the people who they relieved of the heroin are known to be close associates of some people in the CIA. Secondly, I have access to information that tells me that your friend Stephen Rodriguez is due to go on a covert overseas trip very soon. And that trip is to visit the various CIA groups who are assisting United States forces and the ISI in the northern border country of Pakistan and, you guessed it, in Afghanistan.'

'That is not exactly riveting evidence, is it?'

Mark had to ask despite his father's body language that exuded a fair degree of confidence.

But Harold did concede, if not in his body language, at least in his words.

'No, it is not. Stephen's visit could have something to do with the Government's concerns about the alleged links between the Pakistani ISI and the various militant terrorist groups in that part of the world, including the Taliban, al-Qaeda, and a few others. We have ample evidence that some Pakistani intelligence people are tipping off militants in the tribal areas whenever we, or even they, are about to strike at them. The situation is bad enough in Afghanistan without us having to worry about what happens in Pakistan. We are funding Pakistan to the tune of billions of dollars, and I am not sure that the money is well spent, but that is another story.'

Harold paused for a moment, lost in thought. The Pakistan issue was a much more significant problem than anyone in the CIA cared to admit. Of concern to Harold and others was that it was beginning to impact their own people in ways that could affect how this thing played out. Better not to tell Mark about those matters. Better that he believed that the CIA had things under control!

'To return to your question,' Harold continued. 'If the CIA, or our government, wanted to press home our concerns to the governments of either Afghanistan or Pakistan, I would expect that to occur at a political level, a much higher level than the intelligence and security bureaucracy. That is because decisions in Pakistan are also made at a political level. In any case, who could you trust in the ISI? So, the ADDI's visit would be on operational matters. Now, on another subject, we are hearing rumours that there has recently been some interruption to the flow of drugs which involves both countries. My theory is this: someone is interfering in the smooth shipment of drugs from Pakistan or Afghanistan. Someone has alerted the people at the United States distribution end of this pipeline, so someone must go and sort it out. Therefore, logic says someone will go, and soon. Stephen Rodriguez has plans to go to Afghanistan sooner rather than later. The timing is too convenient to be a mere coincidence. And you know what the CIA thinks of coincidence?'

'That is quite a leap in logic!' Mark retorted. 'And you also know what intelligence people think of assumptions! It could just be that Stephen wants to visit his people on the ground, who I must assume are under a certain amount of pressure, given the complex situation they are in and the crazy people they have to deal with. Rodriguez could just want to find out the situation before he recommends committing more resources to his masters in the CIA. He does, after all, have the responsibility to advise his superiors on such matters, and he can best do that by going and taking a first-hand look.'

Harold sighed. Why did Mark always have to be so logical? But then, after Mark had spent some years working with the United States Special Forces and Delta Force, he was trained to think. This meant that Harold's attempt to get Mark to go along with his plans was not going as well as he had expected. And Harold had already committed himself to a course of action that involved Mark Taylor.

It was probably a case of 'like father, like son.'

In discussions with his newfound friend, Karen Marshall, at the DEA, Harold had conceived of a plan dependent on the cooperation of two more people, and as far as Harold was concerned, the deal was done.

The first person that the plan depended on was a DEA agent, who went by the unlikely name of De Lawrence Darrington, otherwise known as Del, to people who knew him well and as Lawrence to people who he met for the first time or who lacked the desire to be relatively so informal. Del was reputed to be a specialist in chasing down drug suppliers. The second was a person that Harold had said had all the necessary qualifications to take part in a covert operation in the Indian subcontinent. That operation was intended to track the ADDI, Stephen Rodriguez, on his forthcoming trip to Afghanistan and find out if there were any links to the drug trade.

Finding an operator or an agent who had all the necessary qualifications and would be able to participate in so covert an operation was problematic. Del was described as a robust, no-nonsense agent who would worry a problem to death, which was fine. Karen Marshall had selected Del because of his previous record, and because he was single, he would not be missed if he disappeared for a few weeks. But Del was neither trained nor would he be inclined to get involved in a firefight. And this job could well involve such action. Del needed someone to look after him and watch his back while he went about his job of tracking drugs and whoever was trafficking them. And the best person to do just that was someone with a wealth of provable experience and expertise in the hard-nosed business of covert operations.

That person was Harold Taylor's one and only son —Mark Taylor. It was not a case of nepotism; Mark was authentic.

Mark should have known what was coming based on their previous experience with his father.

Harold certainly had a way of twisting any argument to fit his purpose.

He was a very experienced spook.

'Mark, I know it is quite a stretch, but we still need to check it out. We have a man in the DEA who is ideally suited to check out what is happening in the subcontinent.

He should be able to identify where the heroin is being refined and where the opiates are sourced, and that is good. But we want to follow the ADDI at the same time and find any links between the drugs and the CIA. We have lost nothing if nothing comes out of it, provided our operation remains covert. If something does come out of it, we must be sure that we can do something about it. The ADDI trip is scheduled to take seven days, so that should be as long as we must reach some conclusion. We need someone to follow the ADDI while the DEA agent is doing his job. We thought that the best person to accompany him on the trip was you.'

Mark exploded. 'Why me? I am not part of your organization. What makes you think you can just call on me to drop everything, go to the other side of the world to do your bidding? I have a company to run—or have you forgotten that some people in the world have to work for a living?'

It was now Harold's turn to show some emotion.

'It is not a sanctioned mission unless you would like a job with the DEA. But more to the point, we do not know how wide or deep the problem is. We cannot use any CIA resources for the obvious reason that we would, or could, immediately alert the very people that we want to investigate. And you know the problems we have with the FBI—they would just love the chance to take someone in our organization down, and the CIA cannot afford that, particularly after the other recent episode. The DEA would be fine, except that the Pentagon is supporting their operations in Afghanistan. And on drug-related matters, as with other matters, that place leaks like a sieve. So, the fact is, we are on our own, and we must be undercover and covert, even from our military and civilian forces.'

And then he added what he hoped would be the clincher: 'And it is personal.'

And he was not wrong.

Harold knew that Mark would always argue against what he proposed in the quirky relationships between fathers and sons. But Harold also knew that the subliminal message he had just delivered would win Mark over.

Mark had a fleeting thought that he should get up and walk away. But he knew that he was hooked. First, he would have just one more attempt to reason with his father, then ...

'OK, just assume for the moment that I agree to your crazy plan. What makes you think I can follow a very senior member of probably one of the most feared and ruthless organizations on the planet without being spotted on day one? I have been on an FBI course at Quantico in surveillance techniques. Amongst other things that I learned; three things were impressed upon us.

'Firstly, never underestimate the people you follow, especially if they are experienced professionals who have had the same training as their followers.

'Secondly, know your territory to adapt quickly to any sudden movements or change of plan by the person being observed. I have heard of Pakistan and Afghanistan, but my knowledge of those two countries ends there.

Thirdly, be prepared to constantly change your people and their methods to avoid being spotted or killed!

Let me remind you—I am known to Stephen Rodriguez. At the Special Forces training camps, people were repeatedly advised of such things so that we could be aware of the dangers. We were told very forcefully, "Do not try this on your own." Now, correct me if I am wrong here. You said that you had one man from the DEA. Where is the rest of our surveillance team?'

Harold appeared to be not the least bit concerned.

'I have every confidence in you, Mark.'

'You have to be joking!'

Surveillance is, at best, a haphazard affair. To follow someone 24/7 and not be spotted is tricky at best. More likely impossible. But and here is the issue, you had first to establish *normal behaviour,* and then you had to at least have a plan around that. If the followed person had a nine-to-five job and sat at home watching television the rest of the time, their surveillance was relatively simple. You had points of reference such that if you happened to lose track of the target for any one of a thousand possible reasons, you picked them up again at work or home, and their surveillance resumed. The purpose of the surveillance would be to determine whether the time when the target was 'lost' was significant. Since surveillance was usually to determine where the target went, what they were doing when they got there, who the target was meeting or anything that denoted *unusual* or *uncharacteristic* behaviour, then when contact was lost, it was at least significant. If none of these norms existed, such that there was no constant point of reference, then, usually, it was fatal.

In the case of Stephen Rodriguez, he was traveling halfway around the world, going to a country where there was a war going on. Rodriguez would undoubtedly be meeting a wide variety of people in various places, but they would all have one primary thing in common. They would all be fully trained in the art of surveillance and countersurveillance. And all of them, apart from Stephen himself, had a massive advantage over Mark Taylor and his 'team.'

They were playing their game in their territory.

Mother must have heard the outburst. As if on cue, the ladies came into the study armed with drinks: wine for

Debbie and Mother and glayva liquor for Mark and his father.

'Now you two have been talking long enough,' his mother remonstrated with them. 'Mark, you should not leave this delightful young lady on her own.'

Mark could only shake his head. No wonder he had never really understood the female side of the species.

They went into the living room, where the conversation drifted onto matters of far greater importance than what Mark and Harold had been discussing. The room needed redecorating, the window blinds needed modernization, and they needed to replace cushions. Nothing further was said concerning the CIA, drugs, or foreign places. It may have been that Harold did not perceive Debbie as having been cleared for such matters. Body language said to Mark that neither was Mother.

And that would be unusual. Maybe there were other reasons, but Mark was too tired to think about what they could be.

Eventually, using the excuse that they were tired from the journey from New York, combined with the food and drink, Mark and Debbie excused themselves and retired to their separate rooms. As they said good night, Debbie was concerned that Mark looked troubled about something but thought better of raising the issue out of deference to Mark's tired state. Neither of them seemed prepared to be the first to say good night, but finally, they went their separate ways with a kiss and a cuddle.

Mark could not sleep.

Nagging away in his mind were the thoughts of what was going on, particularly Stephen Rodriguez's role.

Not that long ago, Mark, along with a friend whom

he had barely known, had gone to Langley and had a meeting with Stephen Rodriguez in his office. That had eventually resulted in the exposure of a plot that involved both the CIA and the FBI in the murder of his two friends and indirectly in the senseless deaths of several hundred residents of New York City. Ignoring all the trouble that had happened, the primary cause behind the whole thing was clear.

Drugs.

Stephen Rodriguez had appeared to have not been a part of that plot. But now, there was some circumstantial evidence that he was involved with drugs. Could that mean that Rodriguez had always been engaged and had simply emerged from the mire of that debacle untouched, by chance, or by design? What if there was another scheme that even the people caught up in the earlier chaos knew nothing about? If that was the case, and Stephen Rodriguez was involved, Mark had some unfinished business. Whether by chance or by design, Stephen could have been involved in a situation that had cost the lives of two of Mark's dearest friends. Never mind the countless other people who had lost loved ones on that fateful day.

This was why Harold had said that this business was personal.

Then, moving on to Harold's plan, there was a very definite problem with the number in the team—if you could call two a team. There would certainly be no problem keeping it covert! But when it came to the activity of following someone, that would not be so smart. The FBI would probably start with a team of about twenty, even for the most mundane surveillance. In this case, Mark would be trying to track the movements of one of the most experienced people on the planet regarding surveillance and countersurveillance. If that wasn't bad enough, this whole exercise was to take place in Pakistan and Afghanistan, places where Mark had no experience, no knowledge, and no contacts. Worse still, there was a war going on out there! It wasn't exactly a war that abided by any form of convention.

Mark tried to think positively about that. They could not call on any resources from the CIA simply because the CIA was the subject of their effort. Any involvement of any other American assets—be they DEA, US Foreign Service, or any one of dozens of other quasi-security and quasi-intelligence organizations—would leap at the chance to help. And jump at the opportunity to talk about it; therefore, you could quickly forget being covert.

There would be little, if any, help from US allies apart from the British in Afghanistan. The United Kingdom had a long history in South-East Asia and was reputed still to have a significant presence of intelligence assets there. But would Mark want to involve the Brits in what would be a highly embarrassing matter for the United States and the CIA?

But two people! Still, it was only for a week.

At about 2:20 am, he tried to relax by switching his mind to other things, like Debbie. In fact, for one moment, he fantasized about going along to her room and making love to her in the same house in which his parents were sleeping. But he rapidly decided against it. Mark would not use Debbie just to get his mind off other things and would rather wait until he could give her what she deserved—his undivided attention.

Why his mother had decided to give them separate bedrooms, he could only hazard a guess. Mark was a grown man! Maybe, Mother did not want to embarrass anybody, so she had made them separate rooms but would quite understand if they decided to share. Somehow, he did not think so. Even when he was married to Helen and his parents had come to their place for an infrequent visit, he did not make love to Helen while they were in the house. Helen just made too much noise. Even then, and for as long as Mark could remember, his parents had slept in separate rooms. He often wondered, as kids do, about the goings-on in their parents' bedroom. He even wondered how on earth he was ever conceived!

He awoke with a start. It was 2:40 am.

Someone had crept into his room! Years of training in the US armed services and years of experience in the world's dark places had attuned his subconscious to awaken him just as the door opened. The slight breeze and change in the air caused by the silent opening and closing of the door was enough. Mark was instantly alert and tense. He was in his parents' home, and the middle of Washington DC was no cause to abandon all the training and the highly tuned instincts that had served him well over the years.

And had kept him alive.

He tried to focus in the near-complete darkness. He tried to make out the shape, slowly moving towards where he lay. He was ready for instant action when the intruder made a false move. Mark could sense that the movements were of someone unsure of where they were or what they would find. Weren't they in for a surprise?

There had been several break-ins in the local area recently, and a few ladies had been molested. Mark's blood turned to ice as he thought of the punishment he would inflict if he happened to catch such a perpetrator.

The person crept closer. Mark prepared to defend himself. He did not want to strike too early, but he would, and could, strike with lethal force.

And then the tension rapidly dissipated.

He realized it was Debbie.

How could Mark tell Debbie of the thoughts that naturally came to the mind of someone who had been trained to kill?

She snuggled up to him in bed and giggled, sensing the tension.

But not the reason.

'You could not sleep either?' Debbie whispered.

'Are you OK?' Mark enquired, holding her close, staring up into the eyes that were full of innocence and love.

She giggled again. 'I want you! Just because we are in your parents' house does not mean we have to behave!'

Her hand travelled down his broad, hairy chest, paused over his well-formed abs, and then crept under the band of his shorts. Mark was becoming aroused, and before long, he abandoned the thoughts that had been invading his mind for the last few hours.

Mark concentrated all his attention on satisfying the lady he was in love with. He kissed her passionately as his hands wandered over her body. The housecoat she had been wearing quickly slid off, revealing that she had nothing on underneath. Mark caressed her small breasts, not wanting to appear in any hurry. Debbie climbed on top of him. He moved slowly, fearful that they would make too much noise, and that just seemed to make her more excited until they finally exploded in the throes of their climax.

Debbie could perhaps have changed the unfortunate course of the events that were to follow if she had raised the issue of what other matters were on his mind.

But she did not.

She was too intent on making love to this man who had changed her life for the better.

Chapter 9

Decision Time

The following Sunday morning, the Taylors had a late breakfast and an early lunch. The need for both meals completely escaped Mark's sense of logic, but his mother insisted, so that was that. And then Mark and Debbie said their good-byes and made their way out of Bethesda, onto the Capital Beltway, and then onto Interstate 95 for their trip back north to New York. There was a sense of relief at having escaped from the stress of being around Mark's somewhat overbearing parents.

But there was something else going on that both Mark and Debbie needed to discuss away from the suffocating atmosphere of the Taylor household and out of earshot of anyone else.

Mark was not a moody person, but he was reticent this day. It was undoubtedly to do with his visit to his parents in Washington. His relationship with Debbie had not yet developed into one where they could automatically sense when one was struggling with matters as conflicting as the dilemma that Mark now faced.

And, as with most men, he held it inside.

Mark had a problem. He did not know how Debbie would react when he told her about it.

Mark had had a few words with Harold in the morning while Debbie was taking a shower. Those words were terse.

Whether Mark had made the correct decision during the long and mostly sleepless night, he could not know at this time. But he had made the decision. He would, just this one more time, accede to his father's wishes. Not out of patriotic duty to his country nor out of loyalty to his father. Mark would do it out of probably erroneous loyalty to his two dead friends and, if he dared to admit it, out of a determination to at least get even with the assistant deputy director of intelligence at the CIA—Stephen Rodriguez.

Mark had spent quite some time in his past life—first with the Marines, then with the United States Special Forces, and then on covert missions with the elite Delta Force—trying to get a modicum of control and sanity into the corrupt world of drugs. It had not always worked. But what Mark could not stand for were people in positions of trust in the country that he had worked so hard for, profiting from the very evil they were supposed to have a commitment and a duty to combat. Mark had done his absolute best despite the constant problems thrown in his way, often by the very people that were now the subject of this latest exercise. So, he would try once more, be it on behalf of his father or on behalf of the dear friends he had lost.

Mark had, of course, a condition.

When Mark had last travelled overseas on one of his father's previous errands, he had been accompanied by Brad Morgan. The latter had worked for the CIA Directorate of Science and Technology. Brad was a computer expert and was particularly adept at hacking into computers. On that trip, Brad's skills had been put to excellent use. So good that Brad now worked for Taylor Software, having quit the CIA in somewhat acrimonious circumstances. But those skills were not required this time. If Mark's reading of the situation was accurate, and from his understanding of the hostile environment they would be traveling, what would be needed on this trip would be brute force? And what better person to provide that from outside the current ranks of the United States military and intelligence networks than his friend Archibald Thomas Miller LLB, otherwise known to friends and foes alike as Dusty.

Dusty Miller was, like Mark's ex-Special Forces. They had met on several trips into places and to do things that were never acknowledged on any official records. The fact that Mark was officially an officer, and that Dusty formally was a sergeant had not distracted from the fact that they became remarkably close and firm friends. They had continued that friendship on into their civilian lives. Dusty was well over six feet in height and over 240 pounds in weight, making his Afro-American posture quite frightening even to those who knew him. The people who did not know him would remain frightened until Dusty had reason to let them relax. But apart from the image of intimidating and brutal strength that he projected, Dusty was good, with all kinds of weapons and someone you would want to have on your side in a fight.

There was, of course, no guarantee that things would end up requiring a person such as Dusty, but Mark was not one for taking any chances. And Mark had always been trained to work as a team, and he would be more comfortable if he had his trusty sergeant alongside him. The representative from the DEA that was to accompany them on their trip may well be a team player. But on the other side of the world, remote from the comforts of home, in a particularly hostile environment, was not the best place to find out whether or not he was.

Mark and Dusty had a variety of arrangements that suited their respective businesses, although Mark thought the arrangements were a little one-sided. Dusty, now a civilian, acted as the lawyer for Taylor Software, and he did that job with his usual brutal efficiency. Dusty also provided offsite backup facilities for Mark's software. That arrangement ensured that no one outside Mark's circle of close friends could ever get their hands on his source code and encryption algorithms. Dusty had also run Taylor Software while Mark was away doing other things. In truth, therefore, Mark owed Dusty big-time; but someone else would have to run the company on this occasion.

He needed Dusty for a pretty different role this time.

Mark had got his father to agree that Dusty would also be along for the trip, leaving Harold with the task of getting the agreement of his friend at the DEA, Karen Marshall, and leaving Mark with the much more challenging task of convincing Dusty that he should come on the trip.

Mark had two difficulties to overcome. The first one was to convince Dusty to make the trip. His chances of doing so were about even. The second one was to convince Debbie that he should go. His options here were also about even if only he could get out of his mind the grief, pain, and sorrow he had experienced as a direct consequence of his previous overseas trip. While Debbie could not know the full details of that escapade, she had still ultimately paid a high price, and Mark knew that she would not easily forget as a woman.

As they cruised northeast towards New York, Mark

finally decided to tell Debbie what was on his mind.

'My father wants me to go overseas for a few days,' Mark started, unsure what he would say next. That depended on how Debbie reacted. He had never envisaged that he would be placed in such a position. He felt guilty as hell at having to put the lady he loved in such a position.

'Oh! Where to?' Debbie asked. She sounded interested but not worried as she watched the traffic go by.

'Oh, just over to Pakistan, and maybe Afghanistan,' Mark replied, keeping the conversation light.

'He wants me to check up on some of his friends who will be there soon.'

Debbie did not react negatively. She was so trusting. No *'Why you?'* No *'What about me?'* No *'Who will run the business while you are away?'*

These were the kinds of questions his ex-wife, Helen, would have asked. As Mark later found out, Helen had her own reasons for asking such questions, which had little to do with Mark's travels and more to do with what she would get up to in his absence. But he was supremely confident that Debbie had no ulterior motives. Mark felt a lump rising in his throat, and he was glad that he was wearing his wraparound sunglasses.

'When do you need to leave?' she asked.

Now that was a tricky question. The ideal time to go was at about the same time that a particular CIA official did. But Rodriguez would not be traveling on American Airlines or any other commercial flight, would he? The typical method of travel for someone of assistant deputy director rank would be to travel on a Gulfstream V C-37A, a long-haul business jet, of which the CIA had quite a few —more of them than would be known to the general public. The distance between Washington Andrews Air Force Base and somewhere like Pakistan, where Mark said he was going, and Afghanistan, where he would ultimately end up going, was more than seven thousand miles. From Mark's previous experience of such things, the maximum range of the Gulfstream jet was about 6,500 miles. So - Rodriguez would need to stop somewhere to refuel. As far as the CIA and the ADDI would be concerned, that would be a simple arrangement with any number of choices of both military and civilian landing places. Friendly places, that is.

Not so for anybody, such as Mark and his team, attempting to follow Rodriguez. Mark and company would probably have to travel on a commercial flight, and that flight would not be landing anywhere except the places it was scheduled to.

Not the least of the problems was, even if someone knew when Rodriguez was leaving, they had the additional task of finding out precisely where he was going and then how to catch up with him before he was whisked away by as yet unknown friends or foes to God alone knows where.

The probability was that Rodriguez would end up in Kabul, the capital of Afghanistan, and the CIA would not be too keen on having a Gulfstream V C-37A providing target practice at any of the lesser landing areas in that country. It was bad enough in Kabul! But of equal probability was that he would also visit Pakistan. He would most likely visit the capital of Islamabad, where the airport, now known as the Benazir Bhutto International Airport, at least had a shared presence with the Pakistani Air Force.

However, one of the more obvious problems of making such a trip could be overcome relatively easily. The DEA also had access to the same type of long-haul business jets as did the CIA, and the good news was that the DEA had its own pilots and did not have to depend on others to help them get around. But they also had a couple of other problems. The operation, code-named Porto, that Harold Taylor and Karen Marshall were planning was so covert that even the people within the DEA itself would know nothing or extraordinarily little of what was intended. So how could they be sure that an appropriate means of transport would be available at short notice and then would, or could, follow another jet to an unknown destination on an undisclosed flight plan?

An alternative would have been to get agents in place at the likely arrival points of the ADDI in both Pakistan and Afghanistan as cover until the 'team' of natural agents arrived on site. Again, this, in turn, such a course of action presented its own set of additional logistical and other problems, not the least of which was that it would spread knowledge of what was going on way too far.

From this quagmire that was the Porto Plan, Harold had developed the typical bureaucratic decision: when Harold got the word that the ADDI was on the move, he would contact Karen Marshall. If a DEA aircraft were available, they would use it; otherwise, the three agents would fly by a commercial airline.

With all these imponderables in the mix, the Porto Plan could be effectively stuffed right from the start.

Debbie had asked the question *when*, and she was entitled to an answer, or rather, Mark needed to come up with one.

He answered her by simply saying, 'There are a few matters to be worked out first, probably within the next couple of weeks, I think,' and just left it at that.

It was amazing how Debbie took it.

Mark's mind drifted back to when he had been married to his then-wife, Helen, five or so years before. Helen would have nagged him until she found something much firmer than that. It took Mark a while to fathom this out. As it transpired, Helen had probably nagged him to give a specific date so that she could arrange her busy and almost entirely social schedule, which included numerous romantic encounters with other men. He still did not understand women, but he was beginning to appreciate the freedom, and the love, which came from Debbie in such a simple and uncomplicated way.

Debbie just leaned across the front seat, gave him a brief but warm kiss on the cheek, and said, 'Men get all the exciting things to do,' and just left it at that.

Maybe Dusty would be easy as well!

The following morning, Mark went into the office of Taylor Software, rang his lawyer, and invited him to lunch. Dusty was not too busy and seemed quite pleasant for a change.

His typical greeting so early in the morning would have been, 'What the fuck do you want?' At which no offense would be taken either by Mark or by anybody else using the four-letter word.

When Mark suggested that they go to the Quest Restaurant on Broadway on the upper west side of Manhattan, Dusty avoided his usual comment about Mark's current millionaire status. Dusty just asked, 'What time did you have in mind?' And in response to Mark's hesitation, he said, 'OK, I'll see you there at one o'clock,' and disconnected the call.

The Quest is one of the more fashionable restaurants in New York City, and Mark made an effort to dress smart. Mark arrived at the Quest before Dusty and watched from his table towards the back of the restaurant while Dusty made his way through the other guests, exchanging greetings, some friendly, some not so friendly. The big Afro-American guy smiled at them all; only Mark, with his ability to read his friends' and other peoples' body language, would have detected the subtle differences in his various reactions.

Dusty thrust out his huge right hand to Mark when he reached their table, then sat down and simply asked,

'OK, what's going on?'

Mark grinned. He knew that Dusty was just as content to have a sandwich at the local deli as come to a flash restaurant. But it would be assumed that Mark, or at least Taylor Software, would be paying, so that was that.

'I may have to go overseas again,' Mark began. And that is as far as he got.

'So, you want me to act as chief executive officer for Taylor Software again?' Dusty said while scanning the menu that seemed lacking in the basic burgers and fries.

'You don't need to invite me to a posh restaurant like this just to ask me that!'

'There is a little more to it than that,' Mark began again.

'Brad can run the office while I am away.'

That got the attention of Dusty. For one moment, he looked hurt. He looked up from the menu and simply said. 'So?'

Mark sighed. Why should it be so complicated? It was worse than asking a girl out on your first date, except that Dusty was hardly a girl, and they had both been on some frightening 'dates' to places in the past without seemingly a care in the world.

But Dusty had to know what they were up for, so Mark told him of the scheme that his father and his newfound girlfriend, Karen Marshall, of the DEA, had come up with, ending with, 'And he has agreed that the DEA guy and I should not go alone.'

Mark had no problem telling Dusty anything that required the utmost secrecy; everything that Mark had ever said about his business and personal affairs had stayed locked in Dusty's sharp mind, and they would stay there. But this time, Dusty rolled about in laughter, then composed himself, and then his eyes misted over as he recalled the last covert mission that he and Mark had been on in the mountains of Colombia. Due to an ill-conceived and poorly researched 'Executive Order,' they had achieved absolutely nothing.

Dusty did manage to say, 'So?'

It was now Mark's turn to smile. 'So, what do you think?'

Dusty studied his friend's face for a couple of minutes. The understanding between these two close friends was there. The respect was there. But at this moment, something was missing. And Dusty was on to it.

'You know that there are some rather nasty people out there in Pakistan and Afghanistan, on both sides of the conflict,' Dusty began. 'There is a war going on, and from what I hear, you can never be sure who is on which side. If you add the drug trade into that equation, you are talking about serious trouble. Having the motivation of nailing the assistant deputy director of intelligence of the CIA does not mean you should go rushing to get your ass blown off. Are you sure that you have thought this thing through?'

No. Mark was not sure.

In business matters, that is what lawyers were for. In cases involving emotions, lawyers were as useless as tits on bulls. But Dusty was not your average lawyer. Even if he had just ordered a grilled black forest ham and Swiss cheese sandwich with red onions and gaufrette potatoes, with little idea of what that was all about.

'Yes, I have thought it through.' Mark began, ordering the same as Dusty, not having read the menu.

'The problem for Harold and the director he is dealing

with in the DEA is that they know jack shit. My father has carried out a preliminary investigation into the affairs of Stephen Rodriguez and come up empty. There is nothing in the record of Stephen to suggest that he is anything but a dedicated public servant. But I know that something about the man is not right, as indicated by Rob Augem. And my father now has only a tenuous link between Rodriguez and drugs. However, the DEA speculates that someone in the CIA is somehow involved in drugs coming out of Afghanistan. They do not know precisely what drugs, but they assume that it is heroin. They don't know how the drugs are procured, where they are refined, how they are shipped, how they are imported, or how they are distributed. So that by anyone's language means that they know nothing. They think that Stephen Rodriguez could provide the missing link in this collection of unknowns, but they still know nothing.'

Mark was beginning to sound like Dusty.

Not that Dusty said very much. 'And?'

Mark could have done with a few more words from his friend, but none were forthcoming, so he continued.

'I don't believe that any of these things happen by coincidence. There are four things.' Mark began counting them off on his fingers.

'Firstly, the Drug Enforcement Administration has reports that say that someone, or something, is interfering with the flow of drugs out of Afghanistan and out of Pakistan. And that will influence the supply into the States.

'Secondly, the CIA assistant deputy director of intelligence, our friend Stephen Rodriguez, is taking off on a trip to Afghanistan, and he will be leaving sooner rather than later.

'Thirdly, as you know, we have just had a significant incident here in this city where drugs and some people within the CIA, the FBI, and only God knows who else were all involved. I am not at all sure that this was thoroughly investigated. It all seemed very convenient and quickly pushed under the carpet.

'Fourthly, Rob Augem told me the name of the CIA person that had threatened him on more than one occasion to stay away from what turned out to be a drug-related incident. That person was Stephen Rodriguez.'

'OK. Now what?' Dusty responded.

Mark nearly lost it. He had just made four statements to a lawyer that justified the course of action he intended to take at least at face value. No 'OK, good.' No 'OK, I agree.'

'Dusty, what is wrong with you? Can't you at least say something?'

Dusty smiled. 'Mark, you're the officer. I am just the sergeant. So, you told me how you decided to do something. Now tell me what you are going to do about it.'

Mark again sighed. 'The answers lie in Afghanistan. The fact that someone is interfering with the supply of drugs means that if he is involved, Rodriguez will try to find out *who, where,* and *how.* Then we follow the trail, and hopefully, that will ultimately lead us to a distribution network which now does not have anything to distribute.'

'And who pays for all of this?'

Mark paused for a moment. He knew how the CIA worked, and probably the DEA had similar arrangements. There would be accounts in various banks scattered throughout Afghanistan—in fact, throughout the world— many of which would probably never be used. Many of such funds would probably eventually find their way into some agents' retirement funds because keeping track of them was just too complex for even a bureaucracy the size of the CIA. While, in theory, anyone using these funds was supposed to, at least eventually, account for their use, *security considerations* usually overrode the need for the usual audit trails. Whether such concerns did or did not cover the situation adequately rested on the agents' honesty, but the CIA had long since given up on that.

Mark shrugged. 'You do not need to worry about that. The funds are there.'

'And my role in all of this is?' Dusty asked.

'Come on, if I am to go, I will need a sergeant to ensure that I do not step out of line. And as you said, Afghanistan is not exactly the safest place on the planet. I will need someone to do the heavy lifting and occasionally sort out disputes between the locals and visitors. I am sure everyone in that part of the world carries a gun, so we will just need a bigger one. So, you get to play.'

Dusty showed signs that he understood.

'Do I get to choose the rules of engagement?'

Mark could now smile because he knew he had his man.

'I hope it will not come down to that. But if it does, then sure, provided you don't shoot the ADDI. First, we will need to start growing beards, and you would need to get fit. I would not imagine that this will be an easy job.'

It wouldn't.

Chapter 10

Mice and Men

To say that Mark was a little disappointed when he first met De Lawrence Darrington was probably an understatement. But then, first impressions are not always correct.

Darrington was a man of little more than five feet seven and probably weighed in at little more than 140 pounds if dripping wet. He had an expression that said that the half of the world that he carried on his back was too heavy a burden. His glasses were large and thick-rimmed, and they seemed to distract attention from an ordinary face and a mess that was presumed to be his idea of a hairstyle. He had a bad case of acne, and he suffered from either a medical condition or a mental condition that caused him to have a bad case of body odour.

The file on Darrington had said that he was as dedicated and honest a special agent as the DEA could muster, and that would have to do for now. His demeanour and his body language said something entirely different. He lacked the confident swagger that Mark and Dusty were used to working with men who were part of a professional team, especially in the Special Forces. But more to the point, Darrington seemed nervous and scared.

Mark and Dusty decided to call De Lawrence by the name of Del, and he did not seem to object to that.

They met Del at what was assumed to be the DEA's equivalent of a safe house, which was innocuous and frugal like all safe houses. Mark was surprised to learn from Del that since Mark's earlier involvement with drugs, the DEA had developed a system of deploying overseas teams to assist in the war on drugs and deal with the drug traffickers and dealers in foreign places. In Afghanistan, they had two groups—the so-called FAST, standing for foreign-deployed advisory and support teams. Mark could only wonder why these teams had not stumbled upon the matter that his own unique and tiny group had been assigned to investigate.

Still, the DEA teams could not be everywhere, and two teams meant two more than none, didn't it? It was made clear to Mark and Dusty that these teams were primarily funded and supported by the Pentagon and that most of their training was provided by the FBI. These pieces of information were conveyed to them with a look and body language that said that at least one member of the DEA did not agree with this policy or this strategy. But it did not matter.

The small team that Mark was about to take into Afghanistan had no intention of using the FAST or anyone else in theatre on DEA business, no matter who funded and supported them, for anything.

Unless they got into some real trouble and desperately needed help in a hurry.

Their cover story for the mission was quite simple, if a little obtuse. Their stated job was to audit the two FAST roles in Afghanistan. They had to find out if the business of having the Pentagon support the FAST in theatre was working and how it was working before consideration could be given to operations of a similar nature at another time or in some other place elsewhere in the world. The use of an advisory and support team was a new concept. While the DEA staff could be expected to go about their duties unimpeded by the somewhat cumbersome administrative tail typical of anything that the Pentagon did, it was essential to know what happened in the field. This cover story required little or no research; it was plausible and typical of how inter-agency matters tended to work.

The reporting structure for the drug teams in the FAST meant that the Pentagon would also get to see what was transmitted to the DEA, and as was reasonable in any bureaucratic organization, that fact was a source of some resentment in the Arlington headquarters and some bickering at an operational level. Therefore, a team that was below the radar of both the DEA and the Pentagon was the obvious way to go about things, thereby avoiding being placed in a position of having to take sides in this particular argument between two organizations that were supposed to be on the same side.

Apart from this potential bureaucratic nightmare, the problem would be how Mark's team was to be managed, even if the team was doing nothing even remotely connected to their cover story.

Because Del was the only government employee on the team, he was the only one being paid a salary—and he worked directly for the DEA, he had assumed that he would be the one in charge. Mark did not think that he would be but said nothing. Dusty also did not think so either and said something.

Dusty's initial reaction was to get up and leave, but that mellowed somewhat when Del acceded that 'we are all in this together, and what we do when we get to Afghanistan would be governed by consensus.'

Which suited Mark and Dusty fine.

There were two of them and only one of him.

This bit of negotiation would indirectly filter back to Harold Taylor. He would be amused, annoyed, or apprehensive, depending on what had been agreed on earlier between the two organizations.

It would also directly filter back to the Directorate of Intelligence of the DEA and, therefore, to Karen Marshall, either through Del, or through Harold, or through both, where the results would be anyone's guess, depending on who she heard the story from first. After this little get-together, which Harold, or Karen, or both presumably arranged, Mark and Dusty decided to pay a visit to some old friends at Fort Bragg.

This decision was made without the knowledge of their DEA pal and without the prior agreement of either Harold Taylor or Karen Marshall.

Fort Bragg, located in North Carolina and named after the Confederate General Braxton Bragg, is the home and the training ground of some of the most elite soldiers on the planet. The training included participating in what could best be described as unconventional warfare, but apart from that, Fort Bragg was like any other Army base.

The training alone would kill most people. Members of the other services of government-trained, and hard in the cases of the CIA, the FBI, and the DEA, but nothing akin to what went on at Fort Bragg. The people at Fort Bragg were *unique*, and they knew it.

The world in which the United States Special Forces are selected, trained and where they operate is mainly unknown to the general public. Typically, military forces anywhere in the world are trained to religiously follow orders, salute anything that moves, and paint anything that doesn't.

The Special Forces are trained differently. They are trained to think and analyse everything constantly. Consequently, there is little place for rank in their organization, just the ability to get the job done quickly, ruthlessly, and efficiently. That was just bad news for whoever came up against them, and usually, those *whoever's* would not live or would not be free long enough to learn from the experience. In such a force, there must develop a comradeship that is like no other. And that comradeship usually spans the life of all who participate.

Mark and Dusty had, in a previous life, been a part of this fraternity. But they had never been in Pakistan or Afghanistan on combat or any other mission, so they needed to get up to date quickly.

And as it turned out, they got lucky.

From time to time, Fort Bragg hosts luncheons and dinners that have past or present leaders of the United States military forces as their guest speakers. If these leaders had been in places where the United States had been fighting, rather than warming their butts in some Pentagon desk job, then so much the better. And if these same leaders had been relieved of their commands (for various reasons, including allegations of gross incompetence); or that they could not, or would not, agree with what was proposed by the pukes who sat in a cosy office at the Pentagon or the White House; or had simply, and for whatever reasons (some disclosed, some not disclosed) had been prematurely retired, then that was even better.

The evening that Mark and Dusty had chosen to be at Fort Bragg was the day when the prematurely retired General Ian 'Mac' McKinley was to speak about his experiences in war-torn Afghanistan and, in particular, to explain at least some of his controversial views on how to deal with the Taliban.

The general had been the commander of the United States Forces in Afghanistan, and he had done a reasonable job. Mac did tend to grouse a little more than he should have about not being enough troops *in theatre,* but that was normal for a commander in the field. His more controversial views on what was happening, or was not happening, in this and other theatres were probably what got him relieved of his command. But being in the Army, and being a general, meant his views were cast in stone; and he was unlikely to be swayed from those views by people who had never experienced combat. And the troops would tend to support him and his opinions, contrary to the feelings or otherwise of the politicians' making decisions in Washington.

In press releases at Mac's retirement, it was stated that the job he had done was OK, but the battle against the Taliban needed to be redefined and redirected. For those who cared enough to think about it, this translated into the conclusion that it was not good enough for the people who now occupied the White House, the description of which may or may not have included the President, and so the decision was made that Mac had to go and be replaced by someone else, who would ultimately suffer the same fate. Generals do not take kindly to being told to do anything, and indeed not when they are told to vacate a prestigious military appointment.

So General Ian McKinley was an angry man.

Coming to Fort Bragg to deliver an address would have made most people in his position even more annoyed. There was an apparent dichotomy of having a 'retired' general, who was not exactly in tune with the current administration, address the elite forces he had previously been in command of. Even more of a dichotomy was that one of the reasons Mac had been given for his departure was that his replacement, Lieutenant General Roy

Spooner (with the nickname of Spike), was 'more in tune with the methods of the US Special Forces. With the hunt for Osama bin Laden not being exactly successful, it was thought that greater involvement of the Special Forces would be required. That was fine if it were not because the Special Forces had a different command structure, which did not usually involve the in-country *ground* commanders. And Spike was seriously junior to the man he was replacing. It could only be assumed that this was the American diplomacy system at work; the reasons given did not have to make sense. They just had to be delivered, leaving the media to make heads or tails of the story. And if the media pressed too hard, everything could be denied on the grounds of the risk of a breach in security.

Therefore, the speech was lively and interspersed with language that was not generally associated with a formal dinner but was widely associated with military men, and consequently, it was well-received.

And McKinley did have a dry sense of humour.

Mark Taylor was not interested in the politics that went on in the higher echelons of the United States government. Mark was more interested in getting a better feel for what life was really like on the ground in the troubled land. He could have watched CNN and got instant, up-to-date news on how the war was going, but that always gave a distorted picture. The cameras could focus on a fire in a forty-four-gallon drum while the voice-over would say that the Afghan capital city of Kabul was being burnt to the ground.

There were a few crazy reporters who accompanied the troops wherever they went, but their reports usually showed them ducking for cover. In contrast, the soldiers walked boldly down the middle of the road, the difference being one of perception. Mark could have read any number of newspaper and other media articles, whether they were actual news or simply background articles. Still, these reports were only produced when something of note —to the news media—happened.

And neither the CNN reporters, other media correspondents nor most of the United States troops ever went into places where they were not allowed to go, for several reasons (some valid, some not).

General McKinley did a reasonably decent job of stating the obvious. The United States forces in Afghanistan had to report progress; otherwise, what was the point of pouring billions of dollars into the conflict? The troops had set out to destroy the Taliban, and, at least initially, they appeared to have been successful.

The Taliban (the name comes from *Taleb*, the Arabic word for 'student') are Sunni Muslims, predominantly from the Afghan Pashtun tribe. To make things a little more complicated, the Pashtun tribes are not just from Afghanistan. More of them live in Pakistan than Afghanistan, and the odd million live in eastern Iran.

The Taliban are not very keen on democracy as a way of running a country and are not particularly tolerant of forms of Islam that differ from their own. The many tribes that make up the Pashtun people are also not exactly united, but the Taliban does provide a glue that can appear to hold them together. And it is hard to argue with a group of more than 42 million people when they embark on a conflict that involves disruption of the established order, and it is all done in the name of Allah.

The initial onslaught in October 2001, when the United States launched the military campaign called Enduring Freedom, aimed to remove the al-Qaeda group from Afghanistan. The Taliban just happened to be in the way. But since that time, two things, at least on the face of it and in the general's opinion, seemed to have occurred.

Firstly, claims were made that the Taliban no longer supported the al-Qaeda group, which is probably true.

Secondly, claims were being made that the Taliban were now stronger than ever, leading to speculation that they could never be wiped out, which was also probably true.

Whether the non-involvement of the Taliban with al-Qaeda was just a way for the United States security and intelligence services to avoid saying that they had no idea what had happened to Osama bin Laden and absolutely no idea where he was, did not matter; if you did not wear a turban and did not sport a beard, you were unlikely to survive for long in the border provinces of Afghanistan and Pakistan. The term now being used by the Pentagon and their friends at CIA headquarters in Langley, that the Taliban militants had 'regrouped' and had 'coalesced into a resilient insurgency, was just a polite way of saying that they were hard to find, difficult to contain, and impossible to count.

A more disquieting side effect of Operation Enduring Freedom was that it had seemed to encourage a few other Osama bin Laden wannabes both in the region of the present conflict and, in fact, throughout the Islamic world. Which led to the inevitable question, where was the next war going to be, and who would have to pick up the pieces? The United States had projected itself as the international policeman. It would be expected to get involved, but indeed there was a limit to what the American people, or more accurately the American taxpayer, would tolerate.

Still, the armed forces could only deal with what they had in front of them.

The more limited area that the general was particularly concerned about was the city of Peshawar in Pakistan, which had a population of close to 3 million and was only about ninety miles from the Pakistani capital of Islamabad. The city of Peshawar was also awfully close to the Afghanistan border, and Mac regarded it as vital to the American and NATO troop supply and support efforts. If that city fell under Taliban domination, that would be disastrous, not only for the allied forces but also for Pakistan. So, the fight against the Taliban presented the United States with a dilemma.

The Pakistan Army, although predominantly recruited from the Punjab, which was close enough to the region called Kashmir and its border with a nuclear-powered India to provide them with enough distractions, was still about 30 percent Pashtun. The Afghanistan National Army was a mixture of tribes and levels of illiteracy, which meant that some instructions were either simply not understood or ignored. Pashto is probably spoken by about sixty-five percent of the population but mostly from Pashtun-dominated areas in the country's south. Dari, the other 'official' language, is spoken by a similar percentage in the north. Consequently, most instructions were either not understood, misinterpreted, or inconsistently implemented.

Or that was the excuse for what followed.

Chaos.

The Afghan Army also suffered from other problems not generally associated with the fighting force of a sovereign state: gross inefficiency, widespread illiteracy, endemic corruption, lack of discipline, desertion, and theft, just to name a few. More significantly, and probably the main reason for most aforementioned characteristics, their training was poor or non-existent.

Most Afghanis were brave, resilient, and enthusiastic

enough. That was useless if the person was not appropriately trained.

The Pakistan Army and the Afghanistan National Army were supposed to help the United States and NATO forces overthrow Taliban resistance and bring a semblance of stability to the region. In the opinion of retired general Ian McKinley, there was a snowball's chance in hell of ever achieving that. With excellent reason, as it turned out.

It took the Pentagon hierarchy a long time to realize Afghanistan and Pakistan were duping them. And it would take them even longer to decide what to do about it.

In the opinion of McKinley, the close relationship between the Taliban and the Pakistan ISI was at the root of the problem. Unlike many of the world's intelligence organizations, the ISI was controlled by the military to the point that they may as well be the same organization. Many planned Pakistan attacks on Taliban or al-Qaeda positions were so well-publicized that the enemy was long gone by the time the Army turned up—if indeed they even bothered to turn up. The Taliban moved from one country to another with consummate ease, often under the eyes of the Pakistan Army. Even al-Qaeda operatives had the same freedoms except for monetary reasons (US aid to Pakistan, which ran into billions of dollars). Some low-level al-Qaeda or Taliban leaders had to be sacrificed to demonstrate Pakistan's commitment to their task.

The general had a point.

And as McKinley put it to those gathered at Fort Bragg from the greatest fighting force ever assembled on the planet to hear what he had to say,

'You are fucked before you start.'

After dinner, over a few beers in the mess, Mark talked with the people he had also come to see at Fort Bragg

—his old friends Mike Gilroy and Hamish O'Dea.

Mike and Hamish were both born and bred citizens of the good ole US of A, but they were also Irish if you went back just one generation. Both men were with Mark when he went to Colombia on a covert and cocked-up mission with the Delta Force.

They were among the few lucky ones to survive that little adventure.

The Irishmen had subsequently stayed on in the Special Forces, whereas Mark had had enough and got out. Both Mike and Hamish had done two tours of duty in Afghanistan, and as it transpired, they were about to embark on a third tour. Mark was not about to enlighten them on what was planned for him, but he could not help but smile as his two friends suggested that Mark would miss out on all the fun. There was the usual banter that usually follows an address by one of the most decorated generals in the US Army, and the remarks ranged from 'What would he know about what goes on?' to 'Wait until we get there!' depending on the experience or lack of understanding of the troops.

Soldiers are loyal to whoever gives them orders, but they are on the ground and come face-to-face with the enemy. While the general may have been right about some of his observations and conclusions, no one at Fort Bragg would be the least bit distracted from their task. There was a war to be fought, and some bad guys needed a kick up the ass. However, contrary to widely held belief, no one likes to go to war. Even the most bloody-minded soldiers were OK with the training but balked at having to get involved in a real fight. It has a habit of turning up the unexpected, and it was indiscriminate.

Mark tried to keep the conversation light.

'So, what is it really like on the ground in Afghanistan?'

Chapter 11

Jalalabad

The convoy made up of the ZIL-131 Truck, and the UAZ-469 four-wheel-drive vehicle had now made it to the vicinity of the city of Kabul.

Before entering Kabul, they had stopped for a rest just to the south of the city, four men sleeping while the other four kept watching for three or so hours. And then they changed over. But none of the men slept.

After the mind-numbing drive from Kandahar, always on the lookout for bandits and insurgents, constantly aware that a roadside device—well, a bomb—could be lurking around every corner, the group was tense, tired, and irritable. The UAZ-469 4WD, similar in design to a Jeep, was the lead vehicle so that, in the worst scenario, the Jeep would be the vehicle to get blown up first.

Now that, on the face of it, was not so bad. There were so many mines and other explosive devices scattered along this stretch of highway that they would be unlucky to strike a group of bandits—or, to give them the correct title, insurgents—at the same time as the Jeep was blown up. That is, provided they weren't targeted by a group that had a specific interest in what they were carrying. The loss of their leading vehicle would have had the advantage that it would mean that their cargo of drug opiates in the following ZIL truck would be intact. The probable loss of life of the driver and his gunner, was a factor, but after all, this was Afghanistan. However, the downside of this was that they would lose their lead vehicle, so the next time they encountered an improvised explosive device (IED), it would be the truck that took the hit. All that having been said, they felt relieved to have made it this far intact.

The place where they had chosen to rest was not exactly well hidden. They had just driven off the road in the middle of a narrow and barren plateau and stopped. The region just south of Kabul was five thousand feet above sea level, making it chilly. While the maps of Afghanistan showed a road, which went in a line between Kandahar and Kabul, really a curve, the reality of the situation was quite different. The road wound its way around gullies and ravines, up and down hills and mountains, and across bridges of varying quality, making the driving difficult and tiring.

The cold of the Afghan nights and the natural psyche of insurgents and others involved in the many varied conflicts in this country usually meant they should be pretty safe. That is, if the driver of the ZIL-131, a small rat of a man who went by the name of Faisal Ahmed, had not insisted that he take the opportunity to have a look at the gearbox. And to do that, Faisal needed light. Lights anywhere else in the world attract moths, and in most places, which was the only thing to worry about. But in Afghanistan, they would also attract the attention of any insurgents, or just straight criminals, who may also have been resting but would not be able to resist looking at the source of the light and maybe take advantage of the situation.

They again got lucky. No one seemed to care.

After a cursory examination, the driver, Faisal, said that he was not overly concerned by the problem. The truck had occasionally got jammed in gear, and a truck without a reliable gearbox on Afghanistan roads was not recommended, although it was pretty common. Faisal announced that he would nonetheless have it checked out by an 'expert' in Kabul. But the net result of this was that the men did not get much sleep.

Consequently, they were tense, tired, and irritable.

They finally got underway just as the sun rose to highlight the tops of the rugged mountain peaks to the north and east. In the years following the drama of the Enduring Freedom exercise, Kabul had become an extraordinary place. There were new buildings in some parts of the city, and money was being spent to the tune of many millions of dollars. Most of the *investment* was courtesy of the United States, but some were also from Japan and Saudi Arabia. New hotels were being built; the Safi Landmark in downtown Kabul was within easy walking distance of government ministries, the UN headquarters, and various embassies. Even Coca-Cola had opened a factory in Kabul to enable the residents of that city to experience the wonders of that Western beverage. Life was fairly good for much of the population, and it would have been hard to tell if there was a war going on.

But then there was the other side of Kabul. As in every city on the planet, there were parts of this town where sane men did not go, even in broad daylight. The problem was, in Kabul, there were just more such places, and you were unlikely to escape simply being robbed or with a mere mugging. And despite the arrival of truckloads of foreign money, new buildings, and new investment, parts of this city were occasionally subjected to bombs that could and did, make the place quite scary. The problem was that, to those who brought the bombs, it was of no concern which part of the city, new or old, they targeted.

The members of the small group who made up the convoy took all of this for granted. They had two business matters to attend to in Kabul, and the sooner they could get them done and be on their way to the east, then so much the better.

Firstly, they had to contact Martin Ellingham, who needed to keep track of their progress between Marjah and Peshawar. Martin could be found in the Kabul offices of the CIA, except that this little band of men was not too keen to ride up to the front door of that office. And so, the 4WD simply waited a short distance away, at the far side of the square that fronted the CIA compound, for Martin to come to them. It was no way to run a business, but the CIA was paying the bills, so they called all the shots.

The amount of money that each man would get paid for this trip far exceeded an average monthly pay even by Western standards, and it was also in US dollars. Therefore, waiting was not a problem. Not that the wait seemed worth it. When Martin finally walked out of the compound, he crossed the road, stopped by their vehicle to light a cigarette, muttered a few syllables, nodded his head in acknowledgment of the reply, and then walked back inside the compound, where he would send another innocuous e-mail to his masters in Washington. The whole 'meeting' had lasted no more than twenty seconds. The Jeep had been waiting for over an hour. Such was the arrogance of the Americans.

The second thing the group had to do while in Kabul was more technical. Faisal Ahmed had to take the ZIL-131 to another contact to have the gearbox checked out. Kabul—in fact, anywhere in Afghanistan—is not exactly the best place to have a gearbox, or any other piece of mechanical equipment, with problems. It was not as though you could drive up to the local agent for the surplus Soviet military vehicles and get some used parts. It was even more difficult, if not impossible, to get new ones.

Also, adherence to vehicles' maintenance schedules was not the norm outside of the military vehicles owned by the United States and allied forces.

In the case of the US forces, it was customary to have more support personnel than frontline personnel, varying from a rare ratio of one to one to a much more common ratio of twenty to one. The support personnel had to do something to keep themselves occupied, so they serviced, repaired, or rebuilt anything they could get their hands on. The time spent was already accounted for in whatever tour or mission they were assigned to, and any materials used were accounted for as a normal part of the operating costs of their unit. Since they were in a war zone, that was fair enough. Most military procurement systems scale up their re-ordering figures by some fictitious multiplier to cater to a 'wartime' environment, with the baseline of some theoretical 'peacetime' usage. But in the case of Afghanistan, the only available baseline figures were from the war zone, so the multiplier just got bigger.

Not so with commercial vehicles in the real world, where there were not unlimited funds that governments could provide. In the commercial case, there were only two types of vehicles: those that could run and those that could not run. Consequently, the roads of Afghanistan were littered with abandoned vehicles, some as a consequence of grievous bodily harm—well, bombs—and others whose life had merely expired being well past their use-by date, or vehicles that had simply run out of fuel and it was just not worth getting anymore. Close to the city of Kabul, all such abandoned vehicles were rapidly stripped of anything that could have a possible use ranging from genuine vehicle spare parts to bodywork being fabricated into cooking pots. Away from the city, no one dared go too far from civilization out of fear of being set upon by insurgents or criminals, who would get more from preying on the collectors than they would from what they were collecting. So, the abandoned and broken-down vehicles sat there like discarded space vehicles left on the moon.

The other problem that Faisal Ahmed, the driver of this truck, would encounter was far more practical but still technical. The 'expert' that Faisal went to see about the gearbox was not an expert. He knew next to nothing about the ZIL-131 and probably even less about gearboxes. He was chosen simply because he could be trusted and known to Faisal. Therefore, when Faisal expressed his opinion that the problem was a lack of oil, the expert eagerly agreed and supplied four gallons of oil that, according to the label on the drum, was specified for use in gearboxes.

The oil was not new, was not for gearboxes, and was probably a mixture of various used oil and multiple viscosities. But the container said that it was for gearboxes, so that was that. Not that it mattered.

The company that had built this ZIL-131 would have been mortified to learn of the use of oil of this consistency in their gearboxes.

When they came to top it up, the ZIL-131 had no oil left in the gearbox, and it was a miracle that the truck had made it this far. They filled the gearbox, and Faisal kept the remainder of the oil for future use. They checked for leaks. There were none. Faisal did not know it, but that was because all the sludges had conveniently filled the holes, and in the motor's current cold state and present thick consistency, nothing leaked—at least there was no sign of a leak now.

With the oil problem fixed and the CIA advised that the shipment was going ahead, they now had the simple matter of getting through, first to Jalalabad, through the Tora Bora region, over the border into Pakistan, and then on to their ultimate goal which was the city of Peshawar.

Like all roads in Afghanistan, the road to Jalalabad was littered with rocks as it wound down from Kabul, yet they were making excellent progress down the highway to Jalalabad.

The ZIL-131 approached the beginning of a long downhill section, and Faisal changed down a gear to use the engine power to assist his brakes. And the brakes certainly needed assistance, as they were well shot, so why take the risk?

But the gearshift had once again become stuck in top gear, and try as he might, he could not budge it. So busy was he concentrating on the shift that he almost ran off the road and would have done so had it not been for the steel barrier at the side.

He was again fortunate. There were no barriers virtually anywhere else on this stretch of road, and the truck would have plunged onto the riverbed that was some twenty yards down the bank. Not that there was any water in the riverbed or anything to distinguish that it was or had been a river in this barren and unforgiving, desolate country. There were no trees to slow the progress of a falling vehicle, and there was nothing to cushion the plunge when it reached the bottom of the steep bank. It would have indeed destroyed the truck and killed all the men inside.

Faisal gave up on the gearshift in fear and panic and hit the brakes to slow the truck's progress. This action had only limited success.

It is funny how men who have seen so much strife in their lives who have become resigned to anything fate could throw at them panic over such a minor matter. The co-driver, a small weasel of a man called Sitara, tried to assist by continuing to attempt to move the gearshift and seemed to think that screaming at it would somehow improve matters.

That resulted in the driver screaming; the net result was that two of the guards riding in the back abandoned the truck. The other four guards would have joined them had they not seen the fate of the first two—one impaled on a stump at the side of the road, while the other one simply bounced on the ground and then rolled over and plunged twenty or so meters down to the riverbed.

Finally, in a moment of sanity, the two incompetents in the truck cab decided on their only sensible plan of action. They steered the truck so that it scraped along the rocky bank on the left-hand side of the road, which slowed the truck sufficiently that the brakes could then have some effect. This worked, and they eventually brought the truck to a shuddering halt as it eased into a gravel area just off the right-hand side of the road.

The rocky outcrop that slowed them down was on the left side of the road, where traffic coming up the hill could well have expected to have the right of way was a minor consideration in the overall scheme of things. They were just lucky there was no traffic coming in either direction, so they had only the road to witness their embarrassment.

Sweat poured off the driver as he contemplated an earlier death than planned. The co-driver was not overly concerned about that. He was more concerned that this incompetent was the one who had assured them that the problem with the gearbox had been fixed, so Sitara continued to scream abuse at Faisal Ahmed. Things could quickly have turned nasty were it not for the timely intervention of the driver of the 4WD, who had witnessed the whole terrifying exercise in his rear-view mirror.

Initially, in the true spirit of comradeship and cooperation, Rashid Amin had driven faster to avoid being hit from behind. Still, seeing the truck brought to a halt, he turned his Jeep around and came back up the slope to see what the problem was. He was equally annoyed at the driver, but he still had a more practical problem. How to get their cargo to Peshawar?

Eventually, sanity prevailed once more, the screaming stopped, and they took stock of their situation.

It was then that they realized they were two men short. While the driver of the 4WD went back up the road to find them, Faisal examined the truck gearbox. This time, the result of his diagnosis was a little less scientific.

The gearbox was useless.

The options now were to get a replacement gearbox or a replacement truck and judging by the condition of the left side of the truck body that had scraped along the rocks and the inept braking system, they very much favoured the latter. This meant that someone had to return to Kabul, get a replacement, and, at the same time, tell Martin Ellingham that they would be later than expected arriving in Peshawar. Still, money was hardly an issue, and they would only be a day late, so this was relatively straightforward. The only minor problem now would be guarding the disabled truck and its cargo in this hostile country.

The 4WD returned from up the road with a gravely injured comrade and some more bad news. Of the two men who had exited the truck, one was dead at the bottom of the bank. The other one was severely injured and had lost a lot of blood. Whether he would survive or die, depending on how quickly they got him to a doctor, he would be no further use to this little band of men.

Now their options were virtually dictated to them. The 4WD would need to return to Kabul with the wounded man. Faisal would need to go because he was the only member of the team who could either ensure that the replacement gearbox would be compatible or drive the replacement truck. Rashid, the original driver of the 4WD, would need to go because he was the only one who knew how to get in touch with Martin of the CIA or whatever organization he represented in the chaos that was the remnants of the exercise called Enduring Freedom. That left just four men to guard the truck—Sitara, Qateb Saleh, and his two brothers, Ahmed, and Amir.

Well, shit happens, so that was the way it was.

The 4WD made its way back into Kabul in the early evening of that day. They dumped their sick comrade at the mechanic's home after narrowly avoiding a major confrontation over his earlier diagnosis of the problem with the gearbox. Then they left and went off to find Martin. That was not an easy task, but the men were in no mood for subtlety with what had already transpired down the road.

Uncharacteristically, they walked directly up to the compound's gates and demanded to see Martin. That caused a fright for the Marines, whose job was to ensure that no suspicious characters could gain entry or otherwise cause trouble. Even if the Marine had been able to speak the language, he would have had difficulty understanding what was being screamed at him, so he did what his training said he should do. He drew his weapon on the screaming lunatics and forced them to lie prone on the ground while getting two of his colleagues to spread the Afghanis' arms and legs and ensure that they were not carrying a bomb.

Some months earlier, an informer who was supposedly on the CIA payroll had walked into the place and blown himself and seven CIA agents, including the station chief of Kabul, into the next world. The security had improved somewhat since then—it was, in fact, quite draconian. It was not that the two men looked particularly suspicious or threatening. It was just that they would not explain their reasons for wanting to see the agent named Martin, whose second name they did not know, other than to point a rather oil-stained hand in the general direction of the east and shout, which is not a practice limited to more civilized Western people trying to communicate with the local natives.

Finally, after they had agreed to be searched to confirm they were not hiding anything which might interest the Marines, like a suicide vest, they were unceremoniously dispatched to the far side of the square and told to wait there. The Marine undertook to locate someone named Martin, and if he found someone of that name and he was interested in talking to these weirdos, he would arrange to meet with them, but away from CIA headquarters.

Martin Ellingham was a practical man. He had been in the CIA in various parts of the world for much of the past twenty-odd years and had established a reputation as a Mr. Fix-It. That was until three years previous, while on a mission in Iraq, he received a 'Dear John' letter from his loving wife telling him that she was seeing someone else. Ellingham temporarily lost the plot and took to drugs. Because of that, he was recalled to Washington, where he faced the inevitable sacking and no prospect but a life on the streets. However, he was fortunate that he met the right people.

He had been given a lifeline—well, more an ultimatum

—by a very senior official. In this case, return to the field to Kabul in Afghanistan and continue to do his work, with a small additional task: look after the drug trade. His initial reaction had been one of shock. But then he looked at the practical side and decided the answer was easy. He decided that he could do that, and so he had returned into the field, in this case to Kabul, with additional duties.

His masters back in the United States would have been unimpressed when he had to report this latest delay, even though it was hardly any fault of his. However, he could demonstrate his efficiency by resolving this issue and getting the shipment underway. It was too late in the day to contact the people who could help him now, but he would send a quick and innocuous message advising that everything was under control.

He told the two Afghani gentlemen to return to pick up a replacement truck in the morning. Martin quickly and correctly decided that there was little point in trying to find a gearbox for a Russian ZIL-131—at least a gearbox that worked. Trucks were easy to find. The only 'not so easy bit' would be to find one that could not be traced to the CIA. That was where his reputation for fixing things would come in handy, and he was pretty confident that this could be achieved. Finding reliable drivers was another issue entirely.

Even Martin and the CIA could not work miracles.

Initially, Rashid and Faisal were a little miffed at having to wait until morning; but as Martin reasonably pointed out, it was not his problem, so they were welcome to go elsewhere to find another truck if they wished. While Martin was keen to get the shipment moving, there was only so much he could do, and what was another day in this never-ending saga. The people in Washington may also be miffed, but they were half a world away and had no real idea what life was like on this side of the world.

Having been assured that things were under control, the Afghanis returned to their mechanic friend's house to get some food, rest, and receive the news they had expected. Their man was dead—not necessarily as a direct consequence of his injuries but, instead, from them not being attended to in an efficient and timely manner. After all, the man with whom the men had left their badly injured friend was a mechanic, not a doctor.

And they had ample proof that he was not even a particularly good mechanic.

The following morning, Faisal and Rashid returned to the square to collect their new truck. Well, it was not exactly new. All the markings that could have indicated where it had come from and what it had been used for in the past were obliterated. But to the trained eye of the Afghani driver, Faisal could see that it was another ex-Soviet vehicle. And it was ancient. It was precisely what the CIA would be expected to provide. They would do anything to place themselves in a position of deniability, and an ex-Soviet military vehicle was the preferred mode of transport for the anyone on the other side. And it was untraceable.

Faisal did not know of or care about such matters. He knew that the motor turned over instantly and sounded like it was in excellent mechanical order.

He could not get out of Kabul and onto the road east towards Jalalabad fast enough.

They made excellent progress. The truck was a significant improvement over the ZIL-131, which it had replaced, and the gearbox was smooth and true. Their only problem was that Faisal and Rashid were now alone in their respective vehicles and had no means of communicating with each other. The CIA had not thought to ensure that they had a CB radio in their new truck. Because of this, it took quite some time for them to realize that they had driven past where they had left the original truck. This was reasonable since there was no practical way that the truck could have been moved, and therefore that would have been the trigger that told them that they had arrived at the correct location.

Rashid, who was driving the 4WD, initially went well past the place where the ZIL-131 truck had been parked simply because the place they were aiming for should have been obvious. He had failed to take note of any landmarks that would have made the task much easier, but in the mad panic of their departure the previous day, the indiscretion could be overlooked. Faisal was too tired to care and simply followed blindly behind the 4WD. When Rashid realized his mistake, they stopped to discuss the issue and then turned around and headed back up the hill until they eventually located the gravel area where they believed they had left the ZIL-131.

Once there, they first looked up and down the road in bewilderment. How could a vehicle with a crippled gearbox and four armed guards have just driven off? Where had it gone?

But then Faisal looked over the bank and down to the riverbed. And there it was in a much worse condition than it originally had been from an unscheduled and uncontrolled trip down the bank.

But where were the men who had been left to guard it?

At about this time, Faisal and Rashid began to feel scared.

No one appeared to be in the region. But someone had managed to push or drive the truck over the bank, and therefore they had to have overcome the four men who had been left to guard it.

Or were the guards themselves responsible for the current fiasco?

Rashid just shrugged. It was no use trying to second-guess what had happened. He had to find out where the drug opiates were, and the only practical thing to do before he contemplated his next step, which may well have involved committing suicide, was to check the truck's contents down on the riverbed.

Leaving Faisal to now guard the 4WD and their new truck, he set off down the steep bank, stepping carefully to avoid setting off a landslide on the rock-strewn surface of the bank. It was not particularly steep, but the footing was treacherous, and there was no vegetation of any kind to stabilize the rocks or assist his descent.

He avoided succumbing to panic and took his time. He was little more than halfway down when he spotted blood, and then he found it wedged between two rocks, at least one of the guards. The body was crushed, and it had either been hit by the truck on its way down, run over, or thrown from the moving vehicle and carried down the bank. The man's dull, lifeless eyes were staring into space, but the expression that was frozen on the man's face was what caught the attention of Rashid. It was one of sheer terror.

Rashid was petrified of what else he might find when he got to the bottom of the bank. The only thing that kept him going was the thought that if the drugs were still in the truck, he could recover them from this seemingly hopeless position. He had not thought of how they could get the packages back to the top of the bank if they were there, but he could only deal with one thing at a time.

At the back of his mind was also the thought of the money. With three guards now dead, his share of the money had almost doubled! Still, it did not pay to get too far ahead of himself.

'One thing at a time!' he kept muttering as he scrambled farther down the bank.

He finally reached the truck. It lay wrecked and mangled on the riverbed. The truck body was largely intact but lying on its right-hand side. There was no sign of the other three guards, either dead or alive. Having rolled several times on its brief but shattering trip down the bank, the back of the truck was mangled out of shape, and the rear door was severely damaged and compressed. Try as Rashid might, he could not budge the door.

There was no way into the rear part of the truck from the driver's cab because, in the design of the ZIL-131, that was a separate and self-contained unit. He climbed up onto the left-hand side of the vehicle, where there was a window that had miraculously survived the unscheduled trip down the bank. The windows were supposed to withstand at least a 7.62mm cartridge traveling at 2,400 feet per second, so that was reasonable. He tried to peer through the window but rapidly gave up on that plan. The windows had not been cleaned in living memory, on either the inside or the outside, and in any case, the sun's angle made the task of looking in tricky, if not impossible. But then he felt relieved when he realized his luck had changed for the better. There were two pieces of good luck.

Firstly, the toolbox, an essential piece of traveling kit on any vehicle in Afghanistan, had been thrown out of the cab in the tumble down the bank. Although tools were scattered around a wide area, he was able to quickly retrieve some of the spanners and wrenches.

Secondly, the windows were bolted on from outside the rear unit for reasons probably only known to the now long-dead designer of the Russian truck.

However, Rashid was not so lucky when he came to undo the bolts that held the windows in place. Since the vehicle was first assembled in the early 1970s, no one had thought to remove the bolts. But they had painted them in the truck's earlier years as a military vehicle. Rashid yelled up the bank to Faisal that he had a problem, but neither getting nor expecting any reply or help, he began the painstaking task of chipping away at the paint.

Finally, after over three hours of hard labour, chipping off the paint and then using all his strength on the end of a spanner, the window fell to one side, and he peered inside.

A sudden cold chill gripped him, and Rashid turned to one side and vomited. Although it was difficult to tell one man from the other—such was the tangle of bodies thrown around as though in a washing machine—it is evident that they were all dead. One of the men seemed to stare accusingly up at him through dull, lifeless eyes, the hole in the centre of his forehead the only thing that suggested that he had died by the gun before the brief but violent trip down the side of the road.

Worse than that, there was no sign of the twelve packages that had been the cargo of this ill-fated trip. They had been removed before the truck was sent on its final and fateful journey.

But by who?

Rashid looked around the rugged landscape, searching for answers. There was just nothing to be seen except the barren and desolate land. Fear gripped his entire body as he fought the anguish and the dread of reporting back to the Americans that yet another of their cargoes had been lost. Rashid's far more critical concern was that he realized that there would now be no money.

He started to crawl back up to the road as tears of frustration streamed down his face while the unpalatable truth drained what was left of his energy from his tired body. He was not so concerned about the dead bodies on the bank and in the truck, for they were replaceable; this was a complex country, and there was a war going on, so you took your chance. He was more concerned about how he would explain to Martin what had happened. Yet another shipment of their precious drugs had gone walkabout, and Rashid could not explain it. And there would be no money coming to Rashid despite all the effort he had put into this trip. Also, he had been so engrossed in getting into the truck that he had not realized how much time it had taken—and then, he had mulled over the unwelcome news that he would have to deliver. While he struggled to get back up the bank, he had not had time to worry about other things, like, what had been going on back on the road during his absence?

At first, as he reached the top of the bank, he stared in disbelief. While he was lucky, Faisal was still here, if you could call it luck.

However, the shocking news was that their new truck was nowhere to be seen.

Faisal, who had been left to guard it, appeared to be asleep at the wheel of the 4WD. Rashid was, at the same time, both fearful and angry. He and the others were paid good money to deliver this cargo. Even if they did not know where the shipment was now, they still had responsibilities to report to their masters, and it was not too much to ask a guard to at least stay awake while Rashid did all the hard work. And now, not only had they lost the drugs and the truck, but they had also lost the replacement their client had provided.

Could anything else go wrong?

Yes, it could.

Faisal was not asleep.

Faisal was dead, his throat neatly sliced by a knife.

Tears welled once more in Rashid's eyes, and his body began to shake uncontrollably. Not out of sorrow for the loss of Faisal and the rest of the guards, but out of plain unmitigated terror. He crouched behind the remaining vehicle, looking furtively around, his eyes moving in rapid quick-fire movements over which he seemed to have no control. There was no one and nothing to be seen. He was utterly alone in the silence broken only by the lone and distant cry of a vulture. In abject terror, he realized that this was the way that these things worked. He would be the next, and the last, to go.

No one had survived to tell the tale from the previous shipments that had gone missing. There was nothing to suggest that he should be the sole survivor from this one, was there?

But then, another terrifying thought entered his scrambled brain. Maybe he had been left alone for one sole purpose in mind. He was left so that he would be able to deliver a message. Tears streamed down his face as he sought to come to some rational explanation of what was going on. Through the blur of problems that filled his mind, he realized that the more he thought about things, the worse he would make it. The first thing he had to do was to get away.

In sheer panic, he looked around for a means of escape. The good news was that the 4WD was still intact. And Rashid was again lucky. The keys were still in the ignition.

This was not like New York—there was no NYPD or FBI. Even if he could find someone who was even the slightest bit interested in his plight, there was no point in reporting the various goings-on to the Afghan National Police—the dead bodies, the truck 'accident,' the missing new truck, the missing drugs. For all Rashid knew, the police may have known far more of the events than he did; but he could hardly report twelve packages of opiates as missing. He threw Faisal's body out of the vehicle, cringed in abject fear at the engine's noise as it roared into life, and then took off back up the road at breakneck speed, half expecting a bullet in the back of his head.

None came.

It was about 5:00 pm when Rashid made it back to Kabul and the CIA compound.

The Marine guards were this time amused. They were experienced enough to be able to recognize the man. The Afghani who had only the day before looked like the neater of the two Afghanis was now a mess. The smell was almost overpowering. And he was even less coherent than he had been on his earlier visit. But they got the gist of what he was raving on about and, anxious to get rid of this man, again dispatched him to the far side of the square and summoned the man called Martin.

When Ellingham eventually came out to see Rashid, their conversation did not last long.

Martin Ellingham's first message was to Marjah. The previous few shipments of opiate had all disappeared somewhere between Jalalabad and the border with Pakistan. Stolen or lost, he did not know. He did not know what had happened, and there was just no point in any further investigation—unless they got lucky, and someone talked. As was the way in this country, there was little chance of that, at least to the Americans.

The latest shipment had disappeared between Kabul and Jalalabad. At least the good news was that someone had survived to tell the tale. Martin sent his appraisal of the latest loss to Marjah: the drug opiates had gone missing due to the incompetence of the Afghans, albeit aided by some mechanical problems. Try again.

Which translated into an e-mail that quite simply read, 'Mechanical problem. On the road to Jalalabad.' All suitably encrypted, of course.

Ellingham would have been expecting to say that the shipment had been successful. There was just no point in saying that it wasn't. They would understand the message. The careful inclusion of a period after the word *problem* would convey the message they did not want to receive. Whether they would be surprised by it was debatable.

The message that he sent to Washington was different. It would only be short and to the point, but it was the hardest e-mail he had ever written. It did not matter whether they had a survivor to tell the tale or that there was at least some variation in the *how* and *where* this shipment had come unstuck. The fact was that there would be a severe shortage of drugs in the distribution chain. Either they fixed that, or their customers would be extremely annoyed.

Having a captive clientele did have its advantages. But eventually, they would still go elsewhere to get their drugs if the interruptions continued.

It did not matter whether or not you had a captive customer base in the drug trade. That customer base would disappear in a New York minute if the supply dried up and you failed to deliver.

Transmitting at 5:30 pm from Kabul would equate to about 8:30 am in Washington DC. That simple fact meant that his message would be instantly read. And when the recipient came down off the roof, he would be immediately looking for blood. Even though the message had to be very carefully phrased, the reaction would not be good. The fact that it was encrypted would only worsen when the final translation made it onto the screen.

No delivery this time. Further information will follow after the investigation.

Chapter 12

Messages

Martin Ellingham sat at his desk staring at the computer screen, deep in thought. He would need to think hard and carefully before sending a further message to Washington.

There was one thing that Martin had not said to Marjah, and he had not relayed it to Washington either. Unlike earlier events with these missing shipments, in the latest case, one man had survived.

Why was that?

The theory that Rashid had been more than a little animated about reporting back to Ellingham was that they were being given an unequivocal message. That may have been logical, but it did not make much sense to Martin in the cold light of day.

If the message were 'Do not try to ship drug opiates through this channel!' the message would eventually be heeded. There was simply no point in continuing, was there? And then they would simply use some other channel, albeit somewhat inconveniently and with a fair bit of annoying rearrangement. Was the message to stop shipping through this channel or stop sending opiates to Pakistan?

They certainly had a message. And they now had a messenger. But who was the message from?

And what precisely was the message?

The story that Rashid had told to Ellingham was that he had been down on the riverbed to inspect the original truck. He did not know what had happened to the new truck. He did not see why the 4WD was conveniently left behind, albeit with a dead body sitting inside it.

Rashid had speculated that it was probably a simple matter of there being no one who could drive the vehicle. This was, after all, Afghanistan, where it could not be guaranteed that everyone would be able to drive. If this was indeed the case, then Rashid's story was plausible. It did make sense for the guy to go to all the trouble of clambering down the bank to look for his precious cargo.

And that is what had probably saved his life!

Martin was beginning to develop another theory of what had occurred.

What say that Rashid was the cause of all their trouble?

Maybe the story had panned out just a little differently.

Rashid could have ensured that the ZIL-131 truck had gearbox problems. He did not need to be a rocket scientist to be able to disable a gearbox. Iron filings would do the trick much more quickly than a lack of oil. But even an incompetent automotive engineer could diagnose that as the source of the problem, so on balance, a lack of oil was the probable cause, simply because it would be far less noticeable.

The plan would then be that the truck would simply stop in the middle of *nowhere*—at least nowhere as far as his so-called colleagues were concerned. That is precisely what happened, and Rashid had conveniently left the truck and the guards to meet their fate while returning to Kabul to seek assistance. Faisal had come with him to Kabul to get another truck, which was only to be expected. Rashid's failure to find the original truck on their return to the breakdown scene could have been planned. Just drive on and leave it to Faisal to find it!

Rashid had not counted on the lack of a CB radio to communicate with Faisal, but that fact, and the fact that Faisal was dog-tired, only made his plan easier to implement. All he had to do was drive on, stop, and appear to consult with Faisal, and then reverse back to the actual site.

Then his remaining problem was getting rid of Faisal.

And that was quite easily done. Leave him at the roadside to guard the truck while he did three things.

Firstly, go down to the truck and ensure that all the drug opiates had been removed before it descended on its fateful plunge. He would be expected to do so by whoever was pulling his strings. And he would be expected to have checked by the disappointed customer. Even in a remote place, as he said, the wreck of the truck lay, there was always the chance that someone would find it. Rashid would know this, and he would have checked everything to ensure his story was watertight.

Secondly, make sure of the fate of all the guards. Again, he would be expected to do that irrespective of who he was working for, but with a slight difference in emphasis. One side would expect him to find out if the guard were alive, while the other would expect him to make sure they were all dead. At t amounted to the same thing.

Thirdly, make sure that he had an alibi while his associates disposed of Faisal—for one side so that his story sounded plausible, for the other side so that he did not know more than he needed to know.

Deniability.

To retain absolute plausibility in his story, Rashid had to report back to the CIA, and on the face of it, that was tactically sound. Rashid could hardly simply reappear anywhere else on planet earth at some later date and deny all knowledge of the whole affair. There was the risk that he could not adequately explain himself to the CIA, who was quite adept at reading body language and could generally spot a liar from a hundred miles away. But did that matter?

There was also one massive flaw in the story Rashid had to tell. Why would anyone in their right mind leave a perfectly good vehicle with the keys in the ignition so that he could return and report to Kabul?

Apart, that is, from the other obvious question: Why was Rashid still alive when the 'message' would have been clear with or without another body?

Martin had the answer. Rashid's story was a load of lies and deceit.

This whole episode had all the makings of a plot by someone, or some organization, which had all the resources and skills necessary to pull it off. Martin had to chuckle. It sounded exactly like the kind of plot that the CIA would set up to fool the Russians or any other country or group that had incurred their displeasure. But surely, even the CIA would not be reckless enough to do that to their own.

OK, they had been given a message. It did not matter how that message was delivered; the question was, What the hell was going on? Or, to put that question slightly differently, why were the shipments of opiates that had previously passed peacefully to their destination suddenly being intercepted, and by who? The opiates had to pass through one of the scariest places on the planet. They had done so with the aid of a network of *contacts*.

Ellingham's blood turned to ice as he contemplated yet another theory.

This one with a hollow ring of truth.

The authorities, in their wisdom, had stipulated two things. Firstly, the drugs would be processed through Peshawar in Pakistan. Secondly, drug opiates, rather than refined heroin, would be shipped from Afghanistan to Pakistan.

The first stipulation he accepted as fact—it was much easier to trust people in Pakistan than it was to trust people in Afghanistan. The latter was just too volatile, as was their production process. The second stipulation was more obtuse. The idea was that drug opiates were infinitely less attractive to would-be thieves than would be refined drugs. That decision had been made in a country where it would be challenging to transport heroin and extremely easy to transport bundles of what could easily be disguised as second-hand clothing. But this was Afghanistan, and things were quite different in this part of the world. Still, that was the decision that had been made.

The drug barons in southern Afghanistan were setting up a few laboratories to process the poppies into heroin. And with good reason.

Money.

Were the drug barons seeking to interrupt the shipments of opiates so that they could muscle in on the refining? In which case, the horrible truth was that someone on the inside had arranged this whole fiasco while making it look as though it was the result of random theft.

There were just too many coincidences.

Of the last four shipments, all had gone missing. The only variable was where they had gone missing. And it was not as though the shipments were particularly valuable. OK, Afghanistan was full of insurgents, and criminals. But why did they attack these shipments in particular?

Statistically, there was a one in forty chance that a roadside bomb could hit any shipment, more of an opportunity in some areas of the country, like the south of Kabul on the road to Kandahar, much less in others. There was a one in fifty-five chance that you would be attacked on the road by insurgents, more of an opportunity in some regions of the country, like east of Jalalabad, less in others.

'You do the mathematics!' Ellingham said to no one in particular.

Getting four of these shipments, which were all destined via Peshawar to satisfy the needs of the CIA in the States, consecutively intercepted was improbable. Statistically, it was almost impossible.

Therefore, someone had set them up.

That, someone had to be in the Marjah end of the operation because only they could have enough information on the timing and routing of each shipment.

But who?

If it was the Marjah CIA cell, that could mean Jacob Dutton.

But what would Dutton possibly hope to gain? And what did he stand to lose? The answer was that he stood to gain nothing, and he stood to lose everything. He would know extremely well the terrible retribution that would be meted out. Unless, that is, he was being blackmailed or threatened, a form of criminal activity that was becoming very popular in this part of the world. But that was unlikely.

Martin Ellingham knew Jacob Dutton very well. They had long since established coded signals that would indicate whether either of them was under external pressure.

Jacob's two associates in the Marjah cell, Glen Weiner, and Cindy Johnston, could be involved.

But could they do so without it becoming apparent to Dutton?

On balance, probably not. Weiner was not regarded as the sharpest knife in the drawer and would be unlikely to have the necessary contacts to pull off something like this. he may have suggested some action to higher authorities back in Washington. He was unlikely to take any action himself.

If the rumours were correct, Johnston, who was more interested in banging the boss, would be unlikely to have the necessary contacts. And she was just too inexperienced. But not naive enough to realize that she would be way out of her depth and heading into big trouble if she got involved.

Dutton was an experienced operator, and he could smell trouble from miles away. In the unlikely event that he was involved in some plan to disrupt the supply of drugs, he would indeed have organized that in a more professional way and without dependence on idiots like this Rashid character. And he had not indicated that there were any external problems, so that was that.

It could be the drug barons in Kandahar, which would mean Ahmed Wali Karzai's involvement. And what would he stand to gain or lose? From all reports that Ellingham had seen, Ahmed was a chameleon. He was always keen; some would say highly and unreasonably too keen, to help the allied forces in any way he could to fight corruption. But why? Ahmed may well be offering to help the allies, but he was also probably one of the most corrupt people! And did anyone, including his brother, who was, after all, the President of this country, really trust him?

The answer to this latter question was, he did not!

And what did Ahmed stand to gain from disrupting supply?

Drug dealing and drug trafficking are just like any other business. It is competitive. And in a free market, you take your chance. The only problem for the drug trade is that you cannot advertise—well, not strictly speaking—and so you must adopt other means of gaining customers at someone else's expense. Reports had filtered through of *competition* between Kandahar and other areas in the Helmand province, which meant competition between Ahmed Karzai and Wakil Hekmatyar. The small amount of trade that the CIA was worried about might have simply gotten caught up in the resulting war.

On balance, what did Ahmed stand to lose?

Nothing really, so it seemed unlikely that he was the source of their problems.

Therefore, it was more likely to be the people who the CIA purchased their opiates, meaning Wakil Hekmatyar. That man was a nasty piece of shit, and why someone hadn't disposed of him a long time ago, Ellingham could only speculate.

What did Hekmatyar stand to gain or lose?

While Ellingham did not know all that there was to know about that gentleman, he knew that Hekmatyar regarded himself as the kingpin in the drug trade in the country's south. Ellingham also knew that several drug laboratories had been set up in the district of Marjah, and it was inconceivable that Wakil was not involved in them. Sure, some of them had been 'raided' by the Afghani Police and closed, but the laboratories simply reappeared somewhere else. This was typical of the drug business everywhere in the world; the more rugged, remote, and corrupt the country was, then the more likely that this would occur. Afghanistan qualified on all counts.

Then the issue to consider was - Which laboratories were closed and which were able to continue with or without the attention of the police?

Ellingham had received no information suggesting that Hekmatyar had been under more pressure, which was unusual. It would be typical of Hekmatyar to squeal to the CIA if the local police, or anyone else, put pressure on him and made it difficult for him to provide the service to which certain elements in the CIA had become accustomed. Therefore, it seemed likely that others were being hit while Wakil Hekmatyar continued.

So, Wakil stood to gain the processing of the orders rather than just the shipment of the raw material. And the reason? Influence? Money? Probably both.

What did Wakil stand to lose? He could lose what had been a lucrative trade should the CIA get really annoyed and take their trade somewhere else. But if Wakil did fail, then what would be the repercussions?

Ellingham hesitated. The more he thought through the options, the more complicated it became. This was a matter that was way beyond his pay scale. There were just so many imponderables, and it was not his position to suggest what they were. His problem was that his training at the Farm all those years before had taught him that if you presented options, you had to justify each one and then recommend which one you preferred. If he had stated the options and pointed to the most likely one, things could have turned out very differently.

But he didn't.

He started to send another e-mail to the powers in Washington DC.

I think we may have a problem....

Chapter 13

Plans

The atmosphere in the Langley office of Stephen Rodriguez, the assistant deputy director of intelligence, was not good. He had expected to receive a message to inform him that the goods had been delivered to Peshawar as planned and that regular service would now resume.

Many man-hours had been spent meticulously building a system that was now as nearly perfect as anyone could imagine. Their customers could now simply order goods as easily as they could order a book or a magazine. They paid for their goods via an unrelated credit card transaction before delivery. The goods were delivered promptly and efficiently to their nominated address. The security of the demand and supply in this system was immaculate. On the demand side, only carefully selected and authorized people could access the system, and these people were meticulously, continuously checked, and verified. Nothing escaped the intense scrutiny in one of the world's most security-conscious organizations, and absolutely nothing was left to chance.

Any threat to the system was thoroughly investigated and eliminated when it became apparent. Entry into the system was ruthlessly controlled. Only specific methods of payment were authorized, and these payment records were continuously screened to make sure that nothing untoward could be found in the vast audit trails that financial transactions created; after all, another division of the CIA was tasked with doing the very same thing, if slightly more randomly, than was this case. Only predetermined and approved delivery addresses were allowed, and any changes would result in delivery being withheld until they had been thoroughly and adequately checked and verified.

No matter how trivial, and whether by accident or design, any attempt to mess with these arrangements was dealt with ruthlessly. The people involved in such transgressions had their access to the system instantly withdrawn. The system itself was immediately reconfigured. The people were put on notice that their jobs, and indeed their lives, were at risk.

Recruits into the scheme were very carefully vetted before they gained entry. That meant that they had to, first, obtain their goods via someone who was already a member, and that was subject to meticulous scrutiny of what they did with the goods they acquired. And the whole scheme was working within an organization that was probably the best equipped to deal with any minor interruptions or indiscretions with permanent and lethal efficiency. It was inconceivable that a system could be designed to be more fool proof.

At least that had been the intention when Stephen had set up the scheme

Now the *supply* side had turned pear-shaped.

All such schemes were, of course, dependent on mere mortals to implement. Now that there was a problem with the supply, the entire system was rendered impotent.

However, of much more concern was the latest message that Rodriguez had received from Martin Ellingham, one of his agents in Afghanistan. After years of careful and thoughtful planning, Ellingham had implied that someone was trying to muscle in on the scheme and disturb the elegant system he had established. That was understandable, given the nature of the drug trade and the people involved. Although the world was flush with the billions of dollars generated by the drug business, there was always someone who would want a larger slice of the pie. That had to be at the expense of someone else.

But the whole scheme that Rodriguez was involved in was based on trust. And if there was one thing that the assistant deputy director of intelligence could not stand for, it was people who could not be trusted.

Trust should work both ways.

In the view of the ADDI, trust was, of course, a thing that applied only to others. The fact that Rodriguez would change any arrangement instantly and without consulting the others involved if it suited him was beside the point. As an assistant director of the CIA, he was entitled to do that, wasn't he?

With power came privileges. With such benefit came arrogance. With arrogance came the view that everyone should and would do his bidding. And there were other powers—the power to punish.

He would find out who had been so audacious to interfere in his little scheme. But first things first: He had to do something about the disruption to his supply and have it restored.

Before that, Rodriguez would first have to get an agreement from his director to travel. Then he would personally find and beat the living crap out of the son of a bitch who had chosen to interfere. And it should be pretty simple to get the agreement of his director to the travel that he envisaged. His boss was too involved in politics, or rather, too engaged with politicians, to worry about the odd overseas trip that his assistant deputy was planning to take.

Even if that trip was to Afghanistan and was at the expense of the American taxpayer.

Stephen Rodriguez was a man who had climbed through the ranks with barely a thought for the welfare of his fellow workers. This was a cutthroat world. The CIA was involved at the sharp end of one of the most ruthless dog-eat-dog businesses on the planet, so a hard-nosed approach was the norm for anyone who wanted to get ahead. It was a case of each to his own within the CIA. He had risen to the position of assistant director, and as such, he sat between the political appointees in higher positions and the professionals in the lower ranks. He was just under five feet eleven and a muscle-bound 180 pounds. He rarely bothered with a jacket and often had his tie loose and shirt open at the collar. But his informal attire, or his sour expression, did not fool anyone. He was one of the most ruthless men in the organization.

Except for this morning. He was correctly dressed in a dark-blue suit and contrasting red tie, with his white shirt buttoned to the top and a relaxed and confident expression.

He had an important meeting to attend, which accounted for his dress. And he knew how to play the bureaucratic game, which accounted for his expression.

The ADDI wandered up the corridor on the seventh floor of the CIA's Langley headquarters for his usual early-morning briefing session with his director.

The director of intelligence, James Schlesinger, who had himself been a field intelligence agent many years before his elevation to almost, but not entirely, the very top of the organization, was quite used to the mood swings of his underlings.

He smiled as Rodriguez walked in, looking quite formal for a change.

What does he want this time? Schlesinger wondered.

It was, in fact, quite unusual to have a man in the position of director that had any experience in the trade. Usually, someone got appointed by politicians, which meant that ability, experience, and practical knowledge were not high on the list of attributes they usually looked for. He had somehow slipped through that selection process. Consequently, his relationship with the men who did some work was good. And, at least most of the time, they talked in the same language and understood each other.

This morning, he could tell that something was especially wrong with Stephen Rodriguez.

Schlesinger smiled a morning greeting, waved his hand towards the more comfortable living room chairs, and came out with the boring but traditional, if cynical, greeting in intelligence circles.

'So, what's new?'

The ADDI waffled on for several minutes, going over matters that Rodriguez felt confident his director was already aware of. Briefings of this nature had to be tolerated by both sides. This was the bureaucracy at work. The director had to be briefed, and the assistant director had to provide the briefing. Hopefully, one or other of them would gain something from it, as the ADDI droned on, thinking of other things. The director only occasionally interrupted to indicate that he was listening or remaining awake.

Of course, any briefing of this nature had to be backed up by a written transcript of what the ADDI had to say. Or at least what he intended to say. The director had already been provided with the written version of the ADDI's report, which lay undisturbed on his desk. Schlesinger would, in turn, take the content of that briefing to another and higher-level meeting. At that next level, the same process would be repeated, albeit less detailed, and for security reasons, with parts redacted or omitted. But at that level, Schlesinger would be in a different role. He would be the one touching his forelock. At least, the higher the level of the discussion, the more likely the participants were to talk about their political interests rather than the facts being presented by the intelligence gatherers.

For this reason, the personal 'briefing' usually focused on whatever their political masters were currently babbling about just in case some questions may be asked at the next level up the chain. Right now, the media was doing a beat-up on human rights issues. So, at least for today, that would be the subject most likely to be discussed at all briefings.

Whether the CIA realized it or not, it was heavily involved in significant problems of the Government's own making. Since 9/11, the United States had favoured those foreign governments, which had a policy, or said they had an approach akin to that of the United States. That was to deny the al-Qaeda group, or whichever other terrorist groups were making headlines, a haven in *their* territories. In return, those governments, or at least some of them, did not have to worry too much about other matters that the United States government usually frowned upon, like the abuse of human rights. This could, of course, be self-defeating, primarily if the delicate balance required by such a foreign policy could not be maintained.

If people are unhappy, as they would be if denied fundamental human rights, they tend to get incredibly angry with their lot. And their communities become an excellent recruiting ground for organizations looking for people who are both disgruntled and have nothing better to do than to look for any form of employment in which they could vent their anger. And so, they did just that.

Apart from the more apparent conflicts in which the United States was involved in Afghanistan, Pakistan, and Iraq, they also had to deal with problems throughout the world, including Yemen, Lebanon, Palestine, Syria, Sudan, Eritrea, and Somalia—and the list goes on. All these countries were required to be monitored by the international intelligence and security services, which primarily meant the CIA in the case of the United States. And all these countries were required to be reported on in these endless briefings, whether or not there was anything new happening there.

Whether or not any politician in either the United States or the other countries saw the big picture, it was hard to tell.

On balance?

Probably not.

Eventually, the ADDI turned his attention to the small matter of the battles raging on in Afghanistan and related issues that, for him, were the primary purpose of the meeting with his director.

'Well, we seem to have problems in Afghanistan still. Information seems to have slowed again, and it is hard to get a handle on what is happening on the ground. There is still evidence of a leak of intelligence somewhere in the organization. The Taliban seem to know what our military will do even before they do. That points to the leak being in the country. We do not know from which intelligence unit the leaks are coming from, be it the CIA or the Army Intelligence and Security Command (INSCOM). I think it is about time I went and had a look. And I think I should be there when the Karzai event goes down.'

That was the polite way of putting to the chief two reasons, such that he would have no choice but to approve the trip. One of the reasons involved a fair amount of deception by the ADDI did not matter. Neither of these two reasons had much to do with the trip's real purpose did matter.

The facts were that the existence of a leak would be handled politically at the highest level, at least until someone had something concrete to go on. The CIA would point to INSCOM, and INSCOM would point to the CIA. That meant that any internal investigation by either group would focus entirely on the other. Meanwhile, nothing constructive would happen. However, the Director needed protection if things turned pear-shaped, and it would be incumbent on his assistant directors to provide that. Therefore, the trip would be approved on that basis alone.

Rodriguez also knew that the life or death of Karzai would be discussed at the following levels if for no other reason than it had been raised before.

And Karzai was still alive.

Schlesinger would be under pressure to be seen to have a handle on that situation. It was also a timely distraction from the issues mentioned earlier.

The President of Afghanistan, Hamid Karzai, presented the government of the United States with an embarrassing problem that was also really of its own making.

Like on many occasions in the past, when dealing with the changing governments in foreign lands, the United States had supported Hamid in his bid for power in Afghanistan, only to be let down by yet another, and almost-inevitable, problem.

Corruption.

But what could the CIA or the US government do?

They could do nothing because the world—or, instead, the media, perceived as the same thing—was watching and reporting.

On the issue of what they should do about Hamid Karzai, the CIA had appeared to get lucky. Their intelligence services in Afghanistan had uncovered an obscure group in the south of Afghanistan that had links with another group of exiles in Pakistan who wanted to get rid of the President of Afghanistan.

Well, more than just get rid of him.

They had the plot to kill him.

This time, if it was to support such a plot, the CIA was on safer ground than in the past. The group wanted to get rid of Karzai because he was looking to do a deal with the Taliban. If that were so, there would be no conflict of interest on that count as far as the Government of the United States or the CIA was concerned. The main aim of US operations had been to get rid of al-Qaeda; the Taliban is, at least initially, a secondary consideration. The Taliban had merely provided the environment where al-Qaeda had flourished, so they had to be removed. However, if Hamid did a deal with the Taliban, it would not be long before the Taliban got rid of Hamid, and the United States would be right back where it all started.

The CIA plan from this point on was quite simple. Encourage the people attempting to get rid of Hamid Karzai but leave no trace of any official, or otherwise, CIA or United States involvement in the attempt. Because the CIA, like every other organization in Washington, wanted to cover its ass, the final decision had to be made at a higher 'executive' level. The CIA is the only government organization that could legally carry out covert or clandestine missions on foreign soil. There would be no CIA mission, so no cover-up, and no risk that there could be a leak at some future date.

But the CIA still had to get approval since the immediate objective of the exercise was to remove the leader of a foreign power. Not that the removal itself would be the highest priority. That priority would be to deny all knowledge of any involvement.

And so, the CIA *did* get approval *both* for the removal and for deniability.

The CIA's answer to a simple 'Yes' or 'No' question from whoever was making decisions that day was, 'We do not want to know anything about it!' Which, of course, did not mean *no* since the word was not mentioned. It meant 'Yes, please, but we also will deny any knowledge of the event, especially if the plot should turn pear-shaped.' So, the CIA would need to have a body on-site when an attempt was made on Karzai. The person would be suitably armed. That person's task would be to make sure that the effort turned out the way the then-current thinking was leaning—rather like the days of old when the emperor gave the thumb up or down to seal the fate of the unfortunate target. Or the alleged assassin. Or both.

Jim Schlesinger waited for his assistant deputy to continue, and there followed a pregnant pause while two of the most powerful spooks on the planet waited for the other one to continue. But Stephen remained silent, obviously lost in thought, playing a mental game of chicken and egg, hiding-and-seek, or waiting to see what came next.

So, Jim commented, 'This Karzai business has unofficial blessing, provided we can ensure deniability. You are confident that there is no chance of any direct, or even indirect, CIA or United States Government involvement in the actual plot?'

Stephen looked up, somewhat surprised that the question had even been raised. 'Yes, we can have absolute confidence in that. We have had no direct dealings with the group, and none of our personnel will be directly involved.'

Stephen had every right to be confident. He guessed that one of Jim's worries was that the same source passing intelligence information to the Taliban could also pass on information about the CIA's involvement in the Karzai business. And that would, indeed, be embarrassing. Fortunately, Jim did not know that Stephen could control that.

Rodriguez had told Schlesinger everything that there was to know about the Tajiks. It was always best to tell the complete story with all the background information intact when talking to his superiors. That left his director free to interrupt, while it ensured that Stephen could demonstrate his knowledge of the subject in question. It also meant that Stephen could point to this briefing to show that ultimate responsibility would not end up on the desk of the ADDI.

Rodriguez certainly hoped it would not come to apportioning blame if something should go wrong, as it usually did.

Both men would, of course, make notes of their discussions this day as an appendix to the formal briefing notes. These sets of additional notes would be similar in their content. It was unlikely that either set would include the name *Hamid Karzai*—at least in the context in which the name had been raised.

On slow days, like today, the director let Stephen ramble on, either oblivious to or accepting of his own complicity.

'They are Tajiks!' Stephen opined. 'They do not like any form of central control, so we do not expect them to have any plans beyond their immediate aim of getting rid of Karzai. We do not know what motivates the Tajiks other than that they seem to blame Hamid for all their current and past problems. Hamid Karzai is a Pashtun, born just outside of Kandahar, where, as you are aware, the Taliban originated. Hamid Karzai originally supported the Taliban but then changed his mind and went off into exile in Quetta in Pakistan.'

'Whether Hamid met up with some Tajiks and upset them, or whether the Tajiks suspect that Hamid may have a cunning long-term plan to get the Taliban back into power, we do not exactly know. We also do not know if the Tajiks have enough resources to pull it off, but that does not matter. If they succeed in carrying out their plot, they will claim a victory, and we will, of course, deny all knowledge of any involvement. They are very unlikely to claim that they had any help in the circumstances. If they fail, and if they live to talk about it, they will attempt to blame someone else for their misfortune. Possibly, but unlikely, they may blame the US of the CIA. They will likely blame the Taliban, and we can at least support that attempt to blame the Taliban. The Taliban will, of course, blame us. There is nothing new about that.'

'So, we are in a win-win situation here. Either way, if I am in the country at the time, succeed or fail, I can activate our network to make a credible attempt at assisting the Afghani intelligence to investigate the attempt, or the death, of their President. Since we already know part of the plan and who is behind it, we should be able to influence what happens next. We cannot push too hard, but we can get the wheels turning so that the next man in power is not so troublesome.'

'The Carpet Maker?' the director interrupted, eager to demonstrate to his underling his vast knowledge of all the plots and counterplots, even down to knowing the participants' occupations.

'Yes. Delbar Jan Arman. He seems to be the logical choice,' Stephen answered, not knowing where this conversation would lead. He was fed up with the many changes that had occurred in the *preferred* leader stakes, at least in the eyes of the Executive, since the Hamid debacle had unravelled. And did it matter? These leaders were all the same. It did not matter which side of the political fence they sat on. As exercised in the United States and other Western democracies, politics was complicated enough, trying to drag fifty percent of the population, plus one body, along for the ride. But politics could be an entirely different ball game in other parts of the world.

Rigging the voting system—or rather, rigging the vote-counting system—or simply killing or putting the fear of God into your rivals often proved to be the far more straightforward methods of resolving the issues in less sophisticated democracies.

Once the politicians had the power to direct vast amounts of money, everything else that was even remotely connected to ethics and principles went out of the window. According to the respected Sir John Dalberg-Acton back in the nineteenth century, *Power tends to corrupt, and absolute power corrupts absolutely.*

But the Afghanis had taken corruption to a whole new level. And the policy of the United States seemed to be to let that happen in the interests of much more critical issues. The ADDI did not know what all those issues were.

Everyone above his level talked as though they knew what these issues were, whereas the ADDI felt that they knew nothing.

For having the ability and the foresight to form and maintain such opinions, Stephen could thank the organization he worked for. But that did not mean that he understood how that worked.

It sure was a funny world!

On the other hand, the director had to wonder if the United States' fundamental policy objectives in the subcontinent of Asia had filtered down as far as his assistant director. He even wondered whether there were some other policy issues that, in turn, had not filtered down, or sideways, to his level, but he could not worry too much about that.

The world was a complex place. No one could have all the answers—even in the CIA.

Although the United States had supported Pakistan and encouraged that country through financial and other inducements to fight the al-Qaeda and Taliban, the United States had quite a different plan in the longer term.

The United States had India to consider. And economically and perhaps strategically, India was far more important than Pakistan.

Not that the involvement of India in the present conflicts would necessarily improve things on the subcontinent as the Indians had problems of their own. There was such a thing as the Indian Mujahideen Islamist terrorist group that occasionally reared its ugly head. The Indian authorities remained clueless concerning its whereabouts, who led it, or even its plans. Add to this the Maoist terrorists causing trouble in the north of India and the remnants of an al-Qaeda–led group raising all sorts of strife in Kashmir, and you have potential problems. And in a country, albeit claiming to be the largest (which is debatable) democratic (which is also debatable) country in the world, with a corruption-riddled bureaucracy, it was hard to see a solution coming from this source anytime soon. The politicians would probably be the last group of people to know this reality, but at least for the time being, they were keeping quiet about India.

While nothing was said in public, the CIA, the Indian intelligence agency RAW (the Research and Analysis Wing of the Prime Minister's secretariat); the Indian Defense Intelligence Agency (DIA); the Afghan Intelligence Agency, or RAMA; and the Israeli organization with the impressive title of the Institute for Intelligence and Special Operations—the much-feared Mossad—and others, were all lined up to achieve a straightforward thing.

The destabilization of Pakistan.

That would require someone who was not aligned with Pakistan—or, correctly, someone who was not aligned with the Pakistan ISI—to be in charge of neighbouring Afghanistan. Recent intelligence gathered by the National Security Agency through electronic surveillance had suggested that Delbar Jan Arman was becoming more pro-Pakistan. Opinions within the US administration had somewhat changed in the last few days. Whether that change had filtered to a level that mattered would be critical to avoiding, or causing, yet another cock-up.

That was the trouble with intelligence. Someone had to present it, and someone had to react to it. On a particularly busy day, the offhand comment by the director about Delbar Jan Arman and his own minor political agenda may have gone unnoticed. But it hadn't. So now, maybe, they had to look to someone else.

To know where to look for someone else, the US politicians or executives needed advice from the foreign affairs people at Foggy Bottom. So as not to alert or alarm the diplomats too much, the question needed to be asked in the nicest conceivable way. The problem here was, who should ask the question? So, it would take time. In the meantime, it would probably get the wrong man into the job again.

Schlesinger sighed.

Instead of further confusing the issue, the director simply said, 'As long as we can ensure deniability' and left it at that. He then went on to say the words that the ADDI had been patiently waiting for.

'We scheduled a trip for you. It was over to you to confirm the dates—you already have all the authorization you need, so there is no reason you cannot go. Nothing is happening here to hold you back, is there?'

'No, I suppose not,' the ADDI replied. 'Things appear to be fairly quiet here after all that trouble in New York. The Brits seem to have a handle on our friends in Moscow. Locally, the Russians appear to be behaving themselves. And I could do with a break from all this bureaucratic crap and get out into the field again.' This said with a grin that only someone Washington had corralled after a life in the murkier world of spook-craft could appreciate the true significance.

'And it might not be a bad idea to take someone from the FBI along with me. That way, we can ensure that we can defuse any suggestion of CIA involvement should the plan to kill Karzai succeed, and I could use some assistance in profiling—get to the bottom of the trouble we may have with staffing.'

Schlesinger almost choked.

Only with extreme self-control, learned first as an agent and improved in the latter years as a quasi-politician, was he able to maintain his deadpan expression. After the recent events in New York, the somewhat brittle relationship that had existed for years between the CIA and the FBI had not exactly mellowed. But, on the other hand, both Jim and Stephen knew how these games were played. This was an opportunity to use their sister organization for their purpose while being seen to be cooperating. Fair call!

'OK, why don't you do that?'

And that was that.

In the way that only bureaucracy can do, the decision that Stephen Rodriguez, the assistant deputy director of intelligence, should go to Afghanistan at this time was made by the director. It would be recorded in the diary and on all the necessary authorization forms, which would litter the paper trail, as would the decision that an FBI agent should accompany him. That was a real coup. Primarily since the director had not raised the issue of who that person should be, thereby leaving the initiative to his assistant.

That suited Stephen fine.

Of course, the ADDI would need to show some constraint and leave a prudent amount of time before his actual departure. But he would need to go sooner rather than later. There was always the danger that something seen to be more critical would *crop up* to prevent him from going. Then some people who were waiting for delivery of their goods to be delivered would begin to get really annoyed.

Having a scheme that delivered goods with total impunity and without fear of anyone ever discovering what was happening was one thing.

Being unable to deliver drugs to habitual users was another thing entirely.

Rodriguez returned to his office and scanned through his current to-do list. He decided that nothing was that important, that it could not wait, or that could not be delegated to one of his minions. Then he sat back in his chair and contemplated other things that he needed to do. Something that could not be committed to paper. Again, nothing jumped out at him. Except, he must get up-to-date files of the people who worked for his organization and the other organizations he was interested in.

While he was in a very senior position in the vast and unwieldy organization, getting that sort of information was not as simple as some would imagine. Even the CIA was challenging enough! On the other hand, the FBI was not so hard. They seemed to take great pride in announcing who was who in their organization. However, the likes of the DEA and some of the other organizations in the complex security network were distinctly paranoiac about the identity of their employees. Stephen had been good at playing chess, but the number of moves that he would need to make, and the timing of those moves, made his head spin. He had initially been given the means of access to the files by one of his colleagues in the Directorate of Science and Technology. That means providing a *one-time* access code that just disappeared once he used it. It had to be continuously changed and updated each time he wanted to gain the access he needed.

This process was necessary for pretty obvious security reasons, and Stephen accepted that. But it was still a pain up the ass. The technocrats explained that it was dependent on several factors being in line, and because the assistant deputy director of intelligence was not supposed to have such information as the files would provide, it would always be difficult. What worried Stephen was that some lowly technician somewhere in the bowels of the US security systems could gain access to such highly classified data with apparent impunity, whereas he could not.

Why did computers have to make things so complicated?

Stephen Rodriguez made a mental note. As soon as he returned from Afghanistan, he would get the latest personnel lists to the appropriate people.

If the ADDI had done this before leaving for Afghanistan, things could have turned out quite differently.

But he didn't.

So, they didn't.

Chapter 14

The Second Bottle

Since his return to Washington DC, Harold Taylor had become more impatient than he could ever remember while he was the head of the spook department out in peaceful Wellington in New Zealand. It may have been the claustrophobic atmosphere of the bureaucratic jungle that he now found himself to be a part of.

But there was something more that was bothering him.

Quite possibly, a part of the problem was the feeling that this position of an assistant inspector in the Office of the Inspector General would be his last posting before he had to retire.

And that scared him as he contemplated his future. It is a phenomenon that most people are confronted with at some stage in their working lives. And it is not something that creeps up on a person. It usually hits them suddenly—rather like being hit by a bus.

While out in the field, Taylor had been the man in charge and very much dependent on his initiative to get things done. And while he had only a small part to play in the grand scheme of things, he had at least felt there was a purpose to it all. In that role, he needed his wife, Elizabeth, to act both as a barrier and as an escort so that he could attend all the diplomatic functions without fear that some inane throwaway comment would break his cover in some unguarded moment. And in that regard, his wife of many years had appeared to be his rock in an otherwise troubled and unstable world. Elizabeth seemed to thrive on being married to a spook. She enjoyed the intrigue of talking to people who thought Harold was something to do with cultural things and, consequently, unimportant. However, his posting to Washington DC had changed everything in a most sinister way. Now Elizabeth wanted to become more involved.

Whereas in his past roles, she had, quite rightly, left him to get on with his job of being a spook, she now began questioning what he did and why he did it. It seemed to Taylor that because he was now merely a bureaucrat, Elizabeth assumed that he could, and should, talk about it. Moreover, the more she questioned him, the more agitated they both became, resulting in lengthy periods of silence where they may as well have been on different planets. It was a classic case of one partner assuming that they knew as much as the other partner simply by their long association. That was not the case in practice, but there was little point in seeking arbitration to resolve the issue.

The fact that there was also the minor matter of their respective levels of security clearance seemed to escape Elizabeth. There was a simple dichotomy of the trust between husband and wife and the belief that the CIA would allow people to share with their loved ones. Consequently, the tension between Harold and Elizabeth had reached the point where it was now insurmountable.

Now the reality of the situation was beginning to set in. And retirement would not ease that confrontation. If Taylor were to retire while in Washington, that would mean that he would have nothing to do. He would no longer have the distraction of getting up each morning with a real job to do. He would then have to look forward to a life that offered few pleasures and none of the excitement that he had been used to.

He could write his memoirs! But then, they could not be published for fifty years! And that would merely be a repetition of his past life that he had not previously contemplated. And when that was finished, what next? In any case, Elizabeth would want to have a say in everything that he wrote, and that would defeat the whole purpose of the exercise!

There had to be something romantic in the life of a spy. But he could hardly see that coming out in writings, despite any poetic license he might employ, especially since that was to be vetted by a wife he had long since ceased to love.

The Taylors' house in Bethesda was one that they simply could not afford. Elizabeth, however, was so used to getting her way that Harold's objections had been brushed aside without even a second thought, and it became clear to him that this was the stark reality of his situation.

At home, he was becoming irrelevant.

Elizabeth had a big say in his life and work, but that was a one-way street. Harold had no say whatsoever in her life, and *her life* translated into 'their life' as far as the private life of the Taylors was concerned. There had never been much love, at least not in the traditional sense, in the Taylor family, and now the horrible truth of the lie that he had been living for so long was coming home to roost.

Harold had become irrelevant.

And that hurt the man who had done nothing to deserve such irrelevance. He now desperately needed more from his life. He needed a life and an interest outside the home. And, if he cared to think about it, he needed a life outside the claustrophobic rat race that he had become an integral part of to which he had become accustomed.

And recently, he had found something more interesting. Another interest in life. And another purpose.

Karen Marshall.

Not once in his forty-plus years of marriage had Harold Taylor ever thought of being involved with another woman. He had always had his job to do, which involved serving his country to the best of his ability. He had no time for playing around, and his strict and disciplined upbringing meant that the mere thought of being unfaithful to Elizabeth simply never occurred to him. For years he had frowned disapprovingly upon the antics of many of his peers who thought that their CIA status gave them the right to act like the fictitious playboy James Bond. He could never understand what caused men, having made the ultimate lifelong commitment to one woman, to look for other female company. It was not that he was bonded to any strictly moral beliefs or any religion. If he cared to think about that, he was an agnostic. But in his upbringing and his life, there were such things as ethics, trust, and principles; and they overrode everything else, so that was that.

But then, against the background of a deteriorating situation at home, the lives of Karen Marshall and Harold Taylor had crossed paths.

He had never felt quite this way about anyone before, and just thinking about Karen made him giddy. She was so different. During the few times they had met, he felt the urgent need to get close to her and touch her. She mesmerized him with her warm smile, and he was captivated as he watched the expressions play across that beautiful face. There was an openness there that held his attention. There was an uncomplicated, undemanding style. At the same time, there was intelligence and humour. She carried herself with confidence, but no arrogance or hardness usually besotted women who had risen through the ranks of government bureaucracy in the bitter struggle—women against men, women against women, women against the system. She made no demands. She accepted Harold for what he was, and she did not attempt to mould him into something he was not. She listened to what he had to say and accepted that without challenge. And then she came up with a different view, maybe opposed to what he had said, but told in such a way that it was the mere representation of something different to be considered, without any prejudice, pretence, or imposition.

And then there was her body!

Harold got a hard-on just thinking about her, and his imagination ran riot as he sat all alone in his office dreaming of what might be.

The contrast was stark. He had not made love to Elizabeth for more years than he cared to remember. The desire was gone; their marriage had become one of convenience, their life together more like a business relationship. They still, on occasions, kissed to say goodbye or to say hello, but that was a functional thing rather than one being driven by passion.

Karen, on the other hand, was so vibrant and so alive. And he *wanted* to kiss her! Nothing he had said to her seemed to belie the disarming and caring smile. And it was easy to transfer those looks, and his infatuation with her, from their business lunch table into his bedroom. He envisaged running his hands over her beautiful warm body, feeling the smooth curves, resting his hands a little longer over her pleasure zones as he gazed into those sparkling eyes. She would be imploring him to come into her world, and into that world, he would willingly go without even a moment's hesitation.

Harold knew that look. Karen would accept him.

As his hands lingered over certain places, her mouth would open provocatively in anticipation, encouraging him to go farther, imploring him to taste her. The fact that he now envisaged her body covered in soft silk and how the silk rippled showed that she had nothing on underneath made his experience even more erotic. Her breasts invited him to touch them as the nipples protruded proudly through the silk. Harold could now hardly control the urges that his body had not experienced for longer than he cared to remember.

And then their roles were suddenly changed. He lay on his back and moaned in anticipation of the pleasures he vaguely remembered from years ago that he knew were coming. Now Karen was the one taking the initiative. Their lips brushed together as her hand stroked the inside of his leg. He could barely contain himself.

They rapidly peeled off their remaining covering until they were both completely naked. They were in no hurry as they gazed at the other with wanton pleasure. They played with each other and explored the other's body, enjoying love and freedom, like teenagers experiencing sex for the first time. And then, unable to wait any longer, she took him inside her, and tears of joy burst from them both as they erupted in a beautiful and mutual orgasmic climax.

His telephone rang, startling him and shattering his daydreaming. Taylor was instantly dragged back into the real world.

He looked rapidly and nervously around his office, an all-consuming feeling of guilt causing his cheeks to flush with embarrassment.

Fortunately, there was no one there!

He answered the telephone in his usual formal way:

'Good morning. Harold Taylor speaking.'

The caller did not identify himself.

He did not need to.

'A Gulfstream V C-37A is scheduled to leave Andrews at 9:00 am Thursday. Destination Kabul, Afghanistan via England, Tel Aviv, and Peshawar. Your man will be on board.'

The call was terminated without the caller waiting for any form of acknowledgment.

Taylor expelled a deep breath, and he felt the surge of another kind of excitement flow through his body. All the planning and scheming that had gone on was now brought into sharp focus.

At last, the Porto Plan could get underway.

And the good news from the call was that he would subsequently need to make urgent contact with the director at the DEA, Karen Marshall—this time for a legitimate business reason.

For the second time in under a year, Harold Taylor was asking his one and only son, Mark Taylor, to go into harm's way; and right here and now was the only time that Harold could change his mind. But that would mean that he would need to renege on an arrangement he had made with the DEA. That was no small matter. What would matter more was that he believed that he had impressed the representative of the DEA, not only with his grasp of this complex problem and his ability to assemble the required resources to deal with it but also with the dynamics and audacity of his solution.

So that was that. He was committed.

He would not convey any doubts to the Karen Marshall of the DEA.

He would not convey anything to his wife, Elizabeth.

Harold Taylor was quite excited as he picked up the telephone and called the director of intelligence of the DEA.

May as well discuss it over lunch, he thought.

Karen Marshall concurred.

Now that all the plans had been set down and the people involved had all met, there was not much to discuss. Of course, there was one problem that Harold should have been more aware of, and that was the dichotomy that existed both within and without their respective organizations. Karen was the DEA director of intelligence, and that, of course, was quite different from the director of operations. However, both directors did, in fact, report to the same deputy administrator. Her role was to analyse intelligence information, which was quite different from gathering intelligence information. Consequently, the Porto Plan was a little beyond her usual sphere of jurisdiction, and the person she had chosen to use had been seconded from the other division.

On the other hand, Taylor had a background that was almost exclusively in operations. That would suit the present setup. Except that he would need to gather and analyse any information because he would not be passing it on to a team of analysts as had been the case on all his previous missions in the field. In the case of the Porto Plan, he had elected not to use any CIA people at all. Instead, he had elected to use his own son. The one previous occasion he had adopted this strategy had not exactly turned into a success. Still, the plan involved only the simple task of following a guy on an overseas trip, which should not be too hard.

Both Harold and Karen had a Caesar salad for lunch, washed down with a cold light Chardonnay. They sat in a small cubicle, seemingly remote from the other people in the restaurant. Harold liked to sit with his back to a wall—old habits die hard in the spook business—where he could see everything around him and see what other people were looking at—or pretending not to look at. Several people in the restaurant were known to and known by both Harold and Karen. Most people would understand that they held important positions in their respective government offices. Like them, they would be discussing matters that would later impact the lives of all the people of this great land and possibly beyond. Well, most of them would be discussing crucial issues. Others may be concerned with more personal matters.

Karen had lost her husband some eight years ago. Eddie Marshall had not been a heavy user of drugs, just an occasional social user. But Karen was trying to make her way up the ladder in the DEA and had put aside having a family to do so. She was, therefore, not too enamoured with her husband's social activities. And she said so.

After a night of heavy drinking, to add to the odd snort that he had had during the day, they had an argument, he left, killed himself when he crashed his car, and that was the end of that.

Having gotten over the initial shock of the death and

gone through the grieving process, Karen had found that she was not overly upset. She had avoided having anything to do with men since that time. It was not that she had lost her libido—it was just that she could not trust men anymore. Men were too unreliable, unpredictable, and worse, they had inconsistent values. It was pretty OK for them to use the combined resources of the husband and wife for whatever reason that caught their fancy. The Marshalls had rules which laid out how they were to conduct themselves as a mature, grown-up couple so that all the bills got paid. But her man had sought to control everything that he thought would affect their lives and used that as justification for trying to control his woman. But when there was no money, it was her fault because he had wasted it all. So, no, Karen had had enough of such duplicity. Men were off her radar despite knowing that she was an extremely attractive lady and still relatively young.

Off her radar. That is, until recently.

Harold Taylor was a strange man, almost a Jekyll-and-Hyde type of character, but lovingly unaware of the dichotomy. He appeared deeply committed to his job, the CIA, and the government. He was also clever, astute, and good-humoured in his quiet way.

At the same time, he appeared to be desperately unhappy and lonely.

Body language said that she could, and should, do something about that. As a matter of long-held principle, she hated the thought of interfering in another man's marriage. But when the reason for that marriage was so obviously dead, the softer side to her nature took over, and she felt obliged to do something!

And she had been alone for eight years!

But after talking for fully an hour during their lunchtime meeting on matters that had little to do with either the CIA or the DEA, they had to talk about work sometime to justify their lunch expense.

'Is everything set?' asked Harold, blissfully unaware of others who had used almost the same terminology.

'I have set things up as best I can in the circumstances,' Karen replied. 'There is a man in Kabul who will take care of the local arrangements—transport, any accommodation, and other logistics. They will be on their own, but Owen Squires knows Afghanistan and the people like a native. Mark should find him useful.'

'Does this Owen work for the DEA?'

'Oh no!' Karen laughed in reply. 'He is what you people would call a sleeper. One of our FAST coordinators recommended him based on his ability to fix things. We have used him a couple of times in the past. He is extremely reliable and can be trusted. It is over to Mark, but he is there if needed.'

'I am sure he will. Mark would need all the help he could get. And has your man Del accepted that Mark will run the show?' Harold asked.

Karen just shrugged. Del was not a big worry to her.

'Del is a little unhappy with the arrangements, but I have told him to go along with it for now.' Karen replied, again laughing.

She continued. 'We have agreed to run this as a DEA operation, but we will not make any direct contact with our FAST people either in Washington or in theatre. The cover will be maintained unless things should turn pear-shaped.'

That certainly sounded impressive and should have the desired effect on her lunchtime companion.

And Harold was duly impressed.

He smiled.

'Let me guess—Del was supposed to be in charge, but Mark and Dusty had a different view—is that about it?'

Karen smiled. 'Yeah, that about sums it up,' she replied. 'Your son Mark sounds like an interesting guy. Maybe I could meet him when this is all over.'

'Oh, I am sure you will!' Harold replied.

'Now, how about another bottle of that Chardonnay. I thought that first one was rather nice.'

And so was the second.

Chapter 15

Preparation

Mark Taylor was not having the best of days. He had got out of bed early without disturbing Debbie. She looked so calm and at peace as she lay snuggled into her pillow, the hint of a smile on her face as her dreams meandered on, blissfully unaware of the problems that were to come.

Mark rushed off to the gym for a quick workout and then back to his apartment—well, *their* apartment, as it now was. After a quick shower and a hurried breakfast with Debbie, he was then off to the office at Taylor Software for just another day in the life of a New York businessman.

About midmorning, a client from uptown had got confused about some perceived problem and insisted that the manager immediately drop everything and come and sort it out. So, to keep the peace, Mark had gone to calm the client down. Of course, there were other reasons why Mark went. This client, the CEO of the Styris Group, was considering a proposal from Taylor Software for a significant upgrade to their software worth millions of dollars. Sure, there was competition, and who knew *where* or *when* a decision would be made and in whose favour? But this call had allowed Mark to chat with one of the decision-makers. That chief executive officer of the Styris Group was annoyed. But very soon, he would not be. He would be embarrassed. However, it was important that the situation is handled diplomatically, and that the client should not be portrayed as a complete dick. Advantage Taylor.

As Mark had predicted, the problem had been so trivial that the embarrassed client had invited Mark to have lunch. And again, to keep the peace and not to want to get involved in any real work with so much on his mind, Mark had acquiesced.

When he finally got back to his office, it was 3:20 pm, and there was now a mountain of other things that required his attention. It was a little hard to concentrate with the prospect of a multimillion-dollar deal seemingly much closer, and Mark had undoubtedly got the hint that Taylor Software was the most favoured. The next meeting of the Styris board was coming up shortly, and the nod and the wink over the client's third glass of Pino Noir seemed to mean the deal was as good as done.

Still, other things had to be done, and it would have been a mistake for Mark to get too far ahead of himself.

Among the *things* was a message to call his father on his direct-dial number, and that message was only ten minutes old. Mark's initial reaction was to leave it until tomorrow. But then he realized that the message might have something to do with the Stephen Rodriguez affair.

Mark returned the call using his satellite telephone that had all the security features that modern technology could muster, plus a few others unique to Taylor Software. Connection with Harold's telephone took longer than average while also going through an almost comical encryption routine. But eventually, they were able to carry on a normal conversation.

'Hello, Father. How is your day?'

Mark could not recall ever knowing Harold drinking during business hours in the many years his father had been working for the government. But he was sure from the slightly higher pitch of Harold's voice and the careful way he pronounced his words that he had been drinking.

It was pretty standard in the police departments, and to a lesser extent in the federal authorities, for people to take the odd tipple, either to stay awake, drown out the boredom, or just to deal with the terror of what they had to do or had witnessed. But while the job of assistant inspector general of the CIA probably had its moments, it should not require a bottle of whiskey, or whatever tickled his fancy, to get him through a day.

Harold Taylor had plenty of minions who could do all that kind of worrying for him.

'Father! Have you been drinking?' Mark asked with a laugh, but he would not have been able to avoid the incredulous tone in which the question was asked.

There was an embarrassed silence, and then Harold replied, 'Well, yes, I had a luncheon appointment that got a little out of hand.'

Harold also laughed and then got serious.

'But down to business. Our friend is leaving from Andrews on Thursday morning—destination Afghanistan via England, Israel, and Pakistan. You still want to go?'

Of course, I still want to go! Mark did not say. Nor did he say, no, I'd much rather stay in the relative safety of New York City, among friends, doing what I am supposed to be doing and running a computer software business. Going home at night to Debbie—the lady that I love! —instead of running around the world on another covert mission that the CIA, with all its vast personnel and financial resources, seems unable to handle!

Instead, Mark simply said, 'Yeah. What's the deal?'

'OK, your cover is, while you are stateside, you will be officers of the DEA. They will provide you with all the gear you need and kit you out at Andrews Air Force Base. That will include a uniform, which you don't have to wear, but from all accounts, you better had—at least while you are at Andrews—to give you some authority and save the wear and tear on your clothes. The gear should include light arms—I believe the DEA uses the Glock—but I cannot be sure. The aircraft you are to travel on will be a DEA Gulfstream jet. It will leave shortly after the CIA plane takes off and copy its flight plan. You should initially end up in Pakistan, but you will just have to play along with whatever happens after that. When you eventually get to Kabul, Afghanistan, you should be met by a guy called Owen Squires, who will have transport for you and will take you wherever you want to go. De Lawrence will arrange your hotel bookings when and where you need them. Other than that, I think we have thought of most things.'

'And who are *we*?' Mark asked innocently.

Mark could sense his father stiffen in his chair before Harold answered.

'This is a joint operation, but the operation is not being run out of my office for security reasons. Officially, it is to be run out of the office of the director of intelligence at the DEA—Karen Marshall. A mobile phone number will be sent to your personal e-mail account for communications. A separate and secure e-mail account will also send a verification password. Brad will explain how that works. The contact's name will be *Michelle*, but we will not use any other names, only codes.'

Mark could only smile.

The CIA had a myriad of methods of communication, and those required a way of verifying who was communicating with whom. The password was irrelevant—it just needed someone to speak so that the voice could, or could not, be recognized by a computer. If the voice was not identified, the game was to keep the caller on the line for as long as possible while another search computer system took over. That computer was supposed to track who was calling and from where, but that rarely, if ever, worked. But the system using mobile phones was almost fool proof from a security point of view. If a contact failed for whatever reason, the number and the phone could be dumped, which was the end. Apart from being able to track and pin a call to the nearest tower, if you were fortunate, that did not tell you much. Based on his training with the CIA's technology department, Brad's role would be to explain how simple the system was. 'Michelle' would probably be a personal assistant who worked close to Karen Marshall and probably one of many incorruptible ladies or gentlemen employed by the security and other government organizations who spent their lives keeping secrets. This one would not, of course, be named Michelle, but you had to call them something! This was old hat to Mark, and he would let things take their course. The real intrigue for Mark was that his old man seemed to have finally found someone with whom he could exercise his manly instincts!

As the only son of Harold and Elizabeth Taylor, Mark loved his father and his mother in the traditional sense. But his mother was not the lovable type, and he felt sorry for his father. In the house at Bethesda, he had noticed that they not only slept in separate rooms, as indeed they had in their less grand place that they occupied in Wellington in New Zealand, but they were now at opposite ends of the quite-large house.

His mother's deportment would not exactly encourage anyone to pay her a night-time visit for the occasional romp around her bed. And even his mother could not just command Harold to get a hard-on. No, like all sons that had ever been born, Mark wondered about the sex life of his parents and reached the only conclusion that he could.

Mark concluded that there was none.

Now that his father seemed interested in this Karen Marshall lady, things would become complicated, but that was fine. Mark had been involved, in an earlier life, with matters of life and death, where there were more significant issues to be concerned about than playing around with the opposite sex. You could not allow affairs of the dick to interfere with matters that could see people get killed; but at the end of the day, people had to get on with their own lives.

Even presidents had their moments, so heaven alone knows what goes on at the administration's lower, and therefore less visible, levels.

Mark cautiously asked, 'You mean Karen Marshall is organizing the whole thing?'

He had to give the older man full marks for his stoicism as he answered with the full authority of an assistant inspector.

'Mark, you must understand that we cannot run the operation from within the CIA or the OIG. My office is too close to the real CIA, and most of my staff is ex-CIA. I would like to believe that we are all on the same side, but I do not know who I can rely on at this early stage in my appointment. It's just too risky. The director of intelligence, Karen Marshall, has agreed to run the show as a DEA operation, and there is watertight security on all aspects of the case. Very few DEA staff know that the operation even exists. It is what you people would call a black op—only this time, even the players don't know where they are going.' And he laughed.

Mark thought he would have just one more go at tweaking the older man's tail. 'So, how many bottles of wine did you and Karen have for lunch?'

Harold stood up well to Mark's jibe.

'Only a couple. You two should meet when you get back.'

Oh shit!

This was getting serious!

Now that the date was set, Mark had two days to get himself sorted.

He had read the first e-mail from his father, memorized the mobile phone number, and then deleted all traces of it from his computer. He then looked at the second e-mail and took note of his password. It was a ten-digit number that did not need a rocket scientist to determine where it came from. The first four digits—6275—were simply the *phone* word for Mark, and the remaining six digits were today's date in year-month-day format. A quick chat with Brad confirmed how the system worked: you simply stated your code as the first four digits, followed by today's date, and you were done. It was tricky to call from another time zone, but the idea was sound, and it could not have been simpler. How the speech recognition software dealt with the voice was for someone else to worry about, but Mark was aware of improvements in that area of computing in recent years.

He then rang Dusty to give him the good news and was surprised at the positive way he responded. 'Great! So, when, and where are we going, and where do we leave from?'

Dusty had never been one to leave a four-letter word,

particularly one beginning with the letter f, out of any sentence. But that was misleading. He was, in fact, a highly educated man, running his own law firm, and at times even running Taylor Software when Mark had been otherwise occupied. But deep down, Dusty longed for the days when they had been in the Special Forces together, crawling on their bellies through jungles and other remote and inhospitable places, covered in shit, dirty and unkempt, and loving every minute of it, doing things that others could only read or dream about or watch the unrealistic dramatizations of in the movies or on television.

Neither the press nor Hollywood would ever get that right—the press because there was just nothing to report. Hollywood because their representation was so seriously flawed as to make it ridiculous. Getting 'wet' was the in-house term used in the Special Forces when they got down to some genuine business, although for practical purposes, the men never showered or bathed while out on a mission. Of course, Dusty was not as young as he had been, but he was still a very powerful man, and certainly, he was someone who you would want to have on your side if it came to a fight, with or without the M-4 carbine assault rifle that he used to carry like a toy in his massive hands.

'We leave from Andrews on Thursday morning. I have arranged for us to drive down to Washington on Wednesday afternoon. We will be covered as DEA officers and will be kitted out down there. I am assured that they have the necessary sizes to fit your frame, even if you are a little overweight.'

Dusty did not appear to flinch. 'I have been going to the Gym!' he laughed. 'But you don't need to worry about me. Now, how about you? How are you going to tell Debbie about this little adventure?'

And that was what was worrying Mark now that the time had been set.

Mark remembered extremely well the chaos that had preceded and followed his last overseas *adventure* courtesy of his father and the CIA. Although he was confident that Debbie would not be tied up with anything like the nonsense that had gone on before, Mark was still concerned about having to leave her behind and out of his sight.

But Mark also knew that he could not take Debbie with him.

It was just too dangerous in the part of the world that would be his destination.

Maybe Mark should have taken her with him—had he known how things would pan out.

Chapter 16

Peshawar, Pakistan

The accommodation provided for them in Washington was not what or how they would have expected. They were very quickly locked into a cocoon, and it was clear that the security on their mission had been well planned and strictly enforced.

Mark had been told to call a telephone number when they arrived in town, which he duly did at about 7:30 pm on Wednesday.

A computer answered the call: 'State your code.' Mark rattled off the ten-digit code, which was greeted with a 'Please wait.' The tone changed after a few seconds, and he finally heard a human voice: 'Good evening. Michelle speaking.' Since his father had said no names were to be mentioned, he did not say who he was but assumed it was OK to call 'Michelle' by the name given.

'Hi, Michelle. We have arrived in Washington.'

Michelle seemed to know who we were.

The next set of instructions was delivered in a simple and unemotional monologue. And then 'Michelle' wished him 'Good luck!' and terminated the call.

Mark was given directions to go straight to the Andrews

Air Force Base, now known under the more cumbersome title of Joint Base Andrews – Naval Air Facility, in Prince George's County in Maryland, about eight miles to the south-east of the city. Mark was aware of where that was from his previous life in the Special Forces, and they soon presented themselves at the gate. Mark and Dusty were expected by the Air Force guards. After a brief perusal of their papers, they were quickly whisked through all the security checks and then into an accommodation block that belonged to the Eleventh Wing of the United States Air Force. That Air Force unit (which did not fly) was responsible for matters of critical national importance, so it was apparent that someone was either taking this matter seriously or could pull some particularly important strings.

Whatever the case, no one spoke to them, or of them, by name, and no one questioned why they were there.

A meal was laid out for them in the Officer's Club, and then they were invited to have a drink at the club's bar. No one asked them what they were doing there, which meant that everyone knew at least enough about them to stay out of their way. They exchanged friendly nods with others who may or may not have been on their own covert missions and were left alone.

At 9:30 pm, a United States Air Force sergeant came to see them and politely asked them to accompany him to where they could pick up their gear.

No one had mentioned the kind of adventure they were destined for. The amount of clothing and equipment that they each had allocated to them would have kept a whole platoon of soldiers kitted out for months. While the Pentagon procurement system was seemingly designed to prevent anything from being purchased, once they eventually had the channels of supply organized, there were few limits on what could be done. The pieces of equipment that Mark was most pleased to see were the two satellite telephones. Having been on previous trips to places like Rabaul in Papua New Guinea, which was both remote and lacking infrastructure that even the local telephone landlines rarely worked, a satellite phone was a welcome relief after that little episode in his life—and having two telephones, instead of the one that would have been allocated by their friends from up the road at Langley, made perfect sense. It was not much fun being in the middle of nowhere, having a means of communication but no one to communicate with other than to report back to someone on the other side of the world.

In addition to the satellite telephones, they were each issued personal communicators of a type which Mark had not seen before—well, some years had passed since he had been on covert missions, and the technology had changed, maybe improved, but certainly further miniaturized. And the DEA would have access to the latest technology. With this gear, they would be able to creep around and talk to each other or listen to each other with not too much risk of being discovered or overheard.

They were also issued with miniature recorders, which were the same size and shape as the flash drives that Mark was used to carrying around in his pocket, a small camera, and a standard-issue DEA Glock 19 handgun. Whoever was driving this mission had thought it through and took no chances. They were issued digital watches that were both fire-resistant and waterproof, which would probably survive long after the wearer was burned alive, drowned, or otherwise dead. And it was as covert as the bureaucrats could make it—no signatures were required—a situation virtually unheard of in the chronic bureaucracy that stifled the CIA, DEA, and every other government institution. Which meant that the supplies had been written off, and there was no evidence of a paper trail that could lead back to Mark and his small team. Significantly, there would be no evidence of their very existence and nothing to link them to the DEA or the CIA. No paper trail of evidence of the kind on which many a supposedly covert operation had faltered in the past.

If Karen Marshall had organized the kitting out, she went up a notch in Mark's estimation, even though he had yet to meet the lady.

But Mark was sure that, with this attention to detail, it was not Harold Taylor who was organizing and provisioning this trip, which Mark thought was good news, for some reason or another.

Mark and Dusty finally bunkered down for the night, having been assured by the Air Force sergeant that breakfast would be at 6:00 am and that they would board their flight shortly before seven o'clock the following morning. Mark did not ask him *what* flight, *how* he knew, or *why*, and the sergeant did not volunteer any further information. But it was not too hard to work out what was going on and that they were being kept well out of the way of any prying CIA spooks.

This explained why they had been told to use a nondescript rental car for the trip from New York and why the name *Archibald Miller* appeared on the rental papers rather than the name of *Mark Taylor*. It was a simple ruse and one that would work because of its simplicity if anyone bothered to check.

The chances were that the CIA would only find out long after the event. Mark and Dusty would also be aboard the DEA Gulfstream long before the CIA's assistant deputy director of intelligence appeared to board his aircraft.

The apparent farce of having two awfully expensive and sophisticated Gulfstream V C-37A long-haul business jets, both owned and operated by the Government of the United States, and both going to the same place some seven thousand miles away to the east, and departing almost simultaneously, did not appear to raise any eyebrows.

At least not in their company.

Mark could not sleep.

There was just too much to think about.

He thought of ringing Debbie but reluctantly discounted that thought. He had said that he would call her when they arrived in Pakistan, so that was what he would do. To contact her any earlier would only have caused her to worry.

He thought of ringing Harold Taylor! He discounted that thought as well. They had nothing to discuss—at least not at present.

He thought of ringing Karen Marshall—now, wouldn't that be a hoot. But no, he had a faint suspicion that Harold would want to introduce them when, or *if*, they returned to Washington from Afghanistan.

He thought of calling 'Michelle.' She sounded charming and competent despite sounding like a robot, but it was not as though they were friends!

At least not yet.

They had not seen anything of the DEA agent and their partner, De Lawrence Darrington, so where was he? Maybe Del had taken the huff and decided against making the trip! Or maybe Del was already somewhere out in bandit country! Probably not. But it did seem strange that he had failed to show. Possibly, Karen Marshall wanted to keep the involvement of the two ex-Special Forces men away from the prying eyes of other DEA staff who may be passing through Andrews on their own covert or clandestine missions. If so, that was a good call, or so Mark thought. Maybe he was just getting paranoid. Perhaps no one was the least bit interested in Mark and his team. Maybe they had worries of their own.

In the end, Mark did drift off into a fitful sleep, none the wiser about any of the random thoughts racing through his mind.

Seemingly seconds after drifting off, he was awoken by an alarm at 5:00 am on Thursday; the alarm was so loud and penetrating that it scared him shitless. It took him several minutes to orientate himself and work out where and what he was doing here.

And then reality set in.

They were going to Afghanistan.

They were taken to their aircraft in the murky haze of smog that heralded a new dawn in Washington. They climbed on board, and there was Del. He was now dressed in the same uniform that Mark and Dusty had been issued with, but that did not improve his appearance much. To Mark's highly trained senses, he looked and was entirely out of his depth. Mark and Dusty had half the uniform on but opted to wear a T-shirt until they arrived wherever they were going. While the Gulfstream was used to carrying people, who were more accustomed to the finer points of life, they had no one to impress on this flight.

And they had a long way to go.

Since the wind was from the north, their Gulfstream had been taxied to a parking area to the south of Andrews, and there it sat.

And then it was just a matter of waiting.

Now that all the decisions had been made, and he was cleared to travel to Afghanistan, Stephen Rodriguez was becoming impatient.

The tasks that he had to achieve on this trip could simply be divided into three areas, only one of which had anything to do with the CIA. All three areas *had* something to do with the CI, but would he be reporting back to his director, Jim Schlesinger, on only one of these.

Officially, the task of the ADDI was to review the performance of the CIA units in Afghanistan and Pakistan and try to shed some light on how the Taliban were getting information before the allies. Having done that, Rodriguez would need to make recommendations about how things might be improved. That would be relatively simple to do. There were problems *in theatre* that would be easily identified, and the bureaucracy had a straightforward way of dealing with them. They would just move people around so that the problems, at least temporarily, went away. In a couple of cases, particularly the Marjah cell, some people needed to be moved out completely; but that was also easily achieved.

In his mind, Rodriguez had already written up his report to his director. He would need to spice it up with *some* 'local knowledge' obtained in the field because Jim was not dumb. If he did not, the director could reach a reasonably rapid conclusion that the report's substance would not have required a trip overseas to reach any meaningful conclusion.

Then there was Stephen's real reason for currently taking the trip. Somebody was trying to move in on *his* drug network. He could not rely on his people on the ground to deal with it; otherwise, why was the problem persisting? No, that was not quite right. It was unfair to leave it to his people to deal with; the problem could be created at a much higher level than they would have access to. And there was just too much at stake. If someone had to be killed in order to sort out the mess, it was better than Stephen himself being there. That would also clearly demonstrate to all involved that he was not a person to cross. While at least half of the people involved were fully paid-up members of the Company, this subject would not be mentioned in any report that Stephen would submit to his superiors.

And then there was his third task—sorting out any issues that may arise from the death of the President of Afghanistan, should that occur while Stephen was in the country. Sure, this could be mentioned in his report if the actual death did occur. But he felt that the chances of such an occurrence were remote. The Tajiks were a disorganized rabble, and, with or without assistance from the CIA, their chances of killing anybody were nil in Stephen's estimation. The Tajiks were just a helpful distraction.

So why had the ADDI suggested that he needed FBI assistance on his trip? The answer was that Stephen did not *need* someone for technical reasons. Deep down, the truth was that he wanted some personal company. Ideally, it would be from someone involved in the same business as Rodriguez and therefore had a personal stake in the drug business. It would be a difficult trip, and he felt entitled to some comforts.

And, as it transpired, he could get *that* someone who met all the criteria. It would be from someone whom Stephen Rodriguez had fallen in love with.

That was the real reason why Stephen was becoming impatient. The FBI had sent *his* agent, a gentleman by the name of Edward Hennessey, on a wild goose chase at entirely the wrong time. Another agent was subsequently offered to take Edward's place on the trip to Afghanistan, but the ADDI had politely declined that offer. Stephen had learned that another agent had offered to take Hennessey's place on the wild goose chase.

The FBI had also declined that offer; no reason was

given.

The dichotomy in these two events should have raised a red flag, but either they did not, or Stephen thought it irrelevant, or he just did not care.

Whatever the thinking, Stephen's view was that the departure of the Gulfstream would just have to wait until Edward reappeared.

The planned time for the departure of the CIA flight of nine-thirty in the morning came and went. By twelve noon, one of the two DEA pilots came down from the cockpit to chat with Mark. Not that the pilot could provide much in the way of enlightenment. He reported that the passengers who were to fly on the CIA-sponsored flight had been delayed—they were waiting for someone to join them, and they had to come down from New York, so the flight was now scheduled for one thirty in the afternoon. The pilots heard this information listening to the Andrews air traffic controllers. They were not supposed to listen to other communication traffic, so they could not very well request further information, even if they were interested. Which they were.

But who was the person coming from New York? Were they tied up with the matter that the DEA and the assistant inspector of the CIA were trying to investigate, or were they just getting a lift? If they were *just* getting a ride, they must be an important person. If they were *not* just getting a ride, then it did not matter whether or not they were a vital passenger—the sooner Mark found out about who they were, the better.

Mark again thought of calling his father, or the delightful Karen Marshall, to see what they could find out about the delay or the unexpected guest, but that would have been presumptuous. Indeed, they would be on to that of their own volition, and they did not need any prompting from a mere civilian.

Del did not seem overly concerned, but then Del was Del.

Their pilot at least confirmed a flight plan of sorts. They were going to fly to RAF Fairford in England, on to Tel Aviv, and then on to Peshawar. There was no mention of Kabul or Afghanistan in the flight plan. There was no apparent reason other than for fuel why they should go to England. The stated reason for the stop at Tel Aviv was for fuel, but knowing the CIA, it may be for some other purpose. Going into Pakistan before Afghanistan made sense. After all, there was a war going on in Afghanistan. From reports coming out of Asia, it was hard to tell where exactly that war started and where it ended. The western border provinces of Pakistan sounded like a place where you would not want to go, even with the backing of the US military.

Mark and Dusty could only wait and see what happened.

At least the Gulfstream had a good coffee machine.

Mark read all there was to know about the aircraft and what they should do in an emergency. The emergency was the easy part because Mark could do nothing about that other than pray to the God that he did not believe in. The aircraft was another matter. It was a Gulfstream V C-37A manufactured by the Gulfstream Aerospace Corporation in Savannah in, Georgia.

As with most United States-based aviation industrial companies, Gulfstream Aerospace had had various owners over the years that it had been in business. It was currently a subsidiary of General Dynamics. Why the aircraft made in America had to have a couple of Rolls-

Royce Deutschland BR710A1-10 high bypass ratio turbofan engines of English design but had been made in Germany was not stated. And Mark could only speculate. It would have been further modified from its original design as a commercial executive jet for use by the CIA and probably by the FBI and DEA. With the spread of ground-to-air missiles through both legitimate and illegitimate channels, there was a natural fear that terrorists would use them. In anticipation of this threat, the Gulfstream was fitted with a sophisticated jamming device. Such devices did not always work for a variety of reasons. There was no evidence that it either worked or it did not. In the case of this airplane, it had either worked, or it had simply not been tried. At least the jamming device provided some comfort to the pilots.

The distance from Andrews to Tel Aviv was about 5,700 miles, and the range of the aircraft was 6,300 miles. So, without the stopover in England, they could be cutting it fine, depending on the weather, the wind direction, and various other factors that Mark knew even less about. At least on this trip, if the CIA aircraft ran out of fuel, then so would the other one!

The Gulfstream could fly at an altitude up to 51,000 feet and travel at up to 630 miles per hour, although their speed on this trip would be determined by other factors, among them how fast the identical jet that they were to follow went—if it ever got off the ground!

In the end, Mark curled up in the seat and dozed, an occupation that Dusty had adopted from the moment that they had climbed on board the aircraft.

Mark was roused from his slumber by the second pilot, a gentleman who simply introduced himself as Simmons. They did not need any stewards on this flight. They were going!

Mark looked at his watch: it was now three forty-five

in the afternoon. They had been on board the aircraft longer than the length of time it would take to complete the first stage of their journey, and thus far, they had travelled about half the length of the Andrews main runway. Mark speculated that there was some rule that said that the crew had to change because of the hours that they had been on duty. But no one else seemed to react other than to be pleased to be going somewhere, even if they were unsure who they were following or where they would end up.

The CIA Gulfstream smoothly gathered pace down the western runway, taking off gracefully into the air and turning north-east to link up with the standard commercial air corridor that would take them across the Atlantic Ocean. About five minutes later, the DEA Gulfstream did the same thing. It was a unique experience. The pilot chatter with the Andrews controller was relayed over the aircraft communications system so that they were all fully informed of what was going on. Not that it meant very much.

Evgeny Ovsyannikov put his binoculars back in their case, started up the motor, and drove back towards the city.

It had been a long day. To achieve what?

His target had planned to leave about eight hours earlier, and he had wasted virtually the whole day waiting for the CIA aircraft to take off. All that he could now report was that it had taken off and was presumably now on its way east. And his target was still on board.

Like anyone with Ovsyannikov's knowledge and training or who had access to a computer (which was not necessarily the same thing), he knew the aircraft's specifications and would need to refuel on its way to the intended destination.

The Russian intelligence told him, correctly, that it would probably go via England and Israel, and the assistant deputy director of intelligence would no doubt take the opportunity to meet up with his friends from MI6 in England and Mossad in Israel, but that did not matter. The *matter* was what would happen when it got to where it was ultimately headed.

The Russians had informants in place at all the possible landing points and via the aircraft's registration number, and with access to flight controller information at most of them, they were in a unique position to follow it through to the next stage in this intriguing saga.

The second aircraft that had taken off from Andrews at about the same time as the CIA aircraft was not of any interest to Ovsyannikov. That was a DEA aircraft, undoubtedly on some pointless mission in the doomed US crusade to rid the world of drugs. The Americans were stupid. They could fix the problem quickly—round up the users in their own country and send them off to the American equivalent of Siberia. But no! Too many people in high places either took drugs or were inordinately influenced by people who did.

Ovsyannikov shrugged and smiled to himself. Involvement in the drug trade by people in high places of the US government meant that he had more potential recruits. The higher, the better. And for a variety of reasons, the ADDI of the CIA was as good a target as any.

There can be some variation in positioning in an air corridor, particularly in altitude; the DEA airplane pilot elected about 3,000 feet higher than the CIA airplane. That gave Mark a clue about the history of at least one of the pilots: he would have been trained in the military, probably the Navy, and probably on a carrier-borne fighter aircraft. The CIA airplane would possibly be aware of the tailing aircraft, but probably not its purpose, and probably not aware that it was tailing. Other than that, the plane was supposed to be friendly—at least they were supposed to be on the same side, which both the transponders indicated.

Eventually, Dusty and Del dozed off. Simmons joined them. But, again, Mark could not sleep. He went forward towards the cockpit, and the pilot invited him in. There was not much to see because it was rapidly becoming dark as they raced to the east while the sun settled behind them. Not that any light would have made that much difference. There was nothing to see other than a carpet of clouds in all directions, the only variety caused by the sun setting behind them and casting red and orange shadows that were forever changing in shape and density. It was all very peaceful and incredibly beautiful.

'Our friend is about fifty miles ahead and slightly below,' the pilot said in the matter-of-fact way that all pilots talk.

'You can track him?' Mark enquired, not because he did not believe the pilot but because he had a genuine interest.

'Oh yes, we can. To hell and back if we need to.' The pilot laughed and then added a question of his own. 'And what has the CIA done to earn your displeasure?'

That question placed Mark on the spot. How much did the pilot and his co-pilot know about this little mission? Probably nothing was the first guess., If this mission was so covert that the DEA people playing a supporting role did not know what they were supporting. On the other hand, the DEA was an organization that was quite used to keeping secrets and gleaning information from others. So that usually meant that everyone would know that they were part of a secret mission. Curiosity would then take care of the rest.

Now, to Mark, who had been on his share of covert missions in his earlier life in the United States Special Forces and had seen what happens when people are not adequately informed, this was untenable. Mark had to be aware that his father had organized this mission, and his father was a man in an enormously powerful position. Yet his old man had not delivered formal or informal instructions to Mark and Dusty about who they were to tell or not to tell. In the confines of an aircraft cockpit, high above the Atlantic Ocean, it seemed reasonable that the driver should be informed of what the hell was going on.

It seemed pointless to talk about a mission to check on the rights or wrongs of working to control an operational group established by the DEA and follow a CIA aircraft, but sillier things have happened! A covert mission, where you kept as much as possible hidden from the enemy, was one thing. Lying to the pilot you depended on to get you to where you needed to go was stupid.

Mark briefly thought about having a chat with Del about the subject but discounted that thought because, first, it would give Del a feeling of importance and the impression that he had to be consulted. Secondly, he felt that Del was next to useless and, being a public servant, would err on the side of caution—to do nothing.

He answered the pilot's questions with three of his own.

'How much do you already know about our mission? How much do you need to know? And what is your background? Apart from the obvious: you were trained in the military—and let me guess, Navy, right?'

The pilot again laughed. There was no hurry. He had many hours to kill while he went through the mind-numbing drill of watching a computer system drive the aircraft, including taking off and landing and watching the instrument panels for any warning lights that might indicate that something needed fixing. With the way the Gulfstream jets had been built, providing several levels of redundancy into everything except the coffee machine, which was most unlikely. In any case, the computers were programmed to sound a warning at the same time as indicating warning lights that showed on the dashboard. But the human brain is programmed to record and react to movement, so they watched anyway.

The pilot's name was Brian McKinley, referred to as Griz by his peers, friends, and foes alike. The nickname had been given to him, for reasons that he just did not know, in the days long before he was bouncing fighter planes, EA-18G Growlers, off the flight deck of the carrier USS *John C. Stennis*.

That had all come to a halt when the aircraft carrier was in dry-dock for a year for what the United States Navy referred to as a DPIA, which translated into the unlikely 'dry-docking planned incremental availability.'

Whatever that term meant, it did mean that there was no flying to do for some time, so Griz had accepted a job with the DEA flying their fixed-wing aircraft into interesting places. Not as exciting as flying fighter jets off, and hopefully back on to, aircraft carriers. But he got to see much more of the world and got a wildly different understanding of how men spent money trying to kill themselves and others.

As for how much Griz had been told about this journey, the answer was that he had been told nothing.

As for how much he needed to know, following another aircraft with today's electronics did not exactly test the brain. Still, it would have been nice to know, especially since, for a change, the other aircraft was supposed to be friendly, and so were its passengers. At least the last time anybody checked, the CIA and the DEA flying their fixed-wing aircraft into interesting places. Not as exciting as flying fighter jets off, and hopefully back on to, aircraft carriers. But he got to see much more of the world and got a wildly different understanding of how men spent money trying to kill themselves and others.

As for how much Griz had been told about this journey, the answer was that he had been told nothing.

As for how much he needed to know, following another aircraft with today's electronics did not exactly test the brain. Still, it would have been nice to know, especially since, for a change, the other aircraft was supposed to be friendly, and so were its passengers. At least the last time anybody checked, the CIA and the DEA were on the same side!

From the flight plan Griz had already filed and the flight instructions he had received from his boss in the DEA, it looked like it would not be long before things turned pear-shaped. They were heading into territory where there was a war going on, and in that territory, no one could be certain who was on which side. There was the added problem that a comparable situation could develop with his own people.

As seen by Mark, the problem was that the less the pilot knew, the less he would be able to react instinctively in a situation that demanded his attention and commitment. The less the pilot was told, the more he depended on his passengers. And this strange mixture of passengers had not exactly talked about who they were, where they were going, and what they were going to do when they got there.

These things aside, the bureaucrats saw the pilot's job as just to fly the airplane.

Mark had to laugh as well. It seemed that all the various departments of state, particularly those who had security as an issue by their very responsibilities, could not work out how to use information.

There had been many examples in history where information was known and available, but it was not passed on to those who needed it, supposedly out of fear that they could reveal their sources. Or it could have been that the same information may make its source evident to someone. It could, of course, have been simply out of ignorance. That resulted in people dying, like at Pearl Harbour on the morning of 7 December 1941. And this particular mission could well flare up similarly because the only people who knew about it were Harold Taylor; his girlfriend, Karen Marshall; Del, who would have been better named Dill; Mark; Dusty; and someone who went by the name of Michelle. This group of people was unlikely to be involved in anything like the mayhem caused at Pearl Harbour. But it could just as easily go off like a bomb or a rocket, and none of the 'team' that Mark was leading would be heard from again.

Mark told this likable pilot the simple facts.

'That CIA airplane that we are following has onboard a gentleman we believe responsible for bringing drugs into the United States. We intend to follow him wherever he goes and hopes to discover how he is doing that and how his distribution system works.'

That about summed it up, Mark thought.

Griz held Mark's eyes for a few seconds, a knowing look on his face.

'But you and your friend Dusty are not DEA. So, who are you?'

'We are officially DEA, but no, we are not. And we are not CIA either,' Mark replied, before leaving some mystery that he hoped would raise no further questions.

'Dusty Miller and I have been on a few operations of a similar nature in various parts of the world. We are civilians now, but we both have a history in the Delta Force.'

'You don't want me to bug the other aircraft so you can listen in, do you?' Griz asked in a conspiratorial tone, though the body language partially said he was joking. 'We often bug airplanes. It's tough to do, though, with all the extraneous noise in-flight, and you can't test it on the ground. Still, it's amazing what people talk about in the confines of an aircraft cabin!'

Tell me about it! Mark thought. What was he doing at precisely this moment but talking about things that were better left unsaid?

'Wouldn't the CIA have the sense to sweep the aircraft for bugs occasionally?' Mark countered.

Griz sighed and then laughed. 'Yeah. That's the problem with you guys. You're too paranoid!'

'I hope you're not putting me in the same boat as the CIA!' Mark responded with feigned indignity.

The comment just brought a smile from Griz as he asked another question of a type that came as no surprise. 'No offense intended or implied. What are you two doing with that idiot for company?'

'I presume you mean De Lawrence?' Mark asked, surprised that Griz should ask such a question about a fellow DEA officer rather than by what he asked.

For the first time in their brief conversation, Griz looked worried.

'Yes, well, I know De Lawrence from other operations. He has been with the DEA for quite some time. I would not describe him as the sharpest knife in the drawer,' he observed.

Mark just shrugged.

'It should not matter.'

It did. But it was too late to do anything about it.

The Royal Air Force Station Fairford was not precisely

the busiest airfield in the United Kingdom or indeed in the county of Gloucestershire. If it were not for the US Air Force taking up residence by establishing a Combat Support Wing for their GSUs (Geographically Separated Units), there would be little or no activity at all. Being in the southwest of England, it was remote by UK standards, so it was nonetheless a useful place for aircraft from the intelligence services to call without causing too much of a stir. At least in the general public. It was a focus of much attention to those in the security business.

When the first of the two US Gulfstream jets landed, the assistant deputy director of intelligence was met by a couple of innocuous-looking characters and hustled off for a cup of tea. When the DEA Gulfstream landed, co-pilot Simmons took off to meet someone from the UK police who was presumably had something to do with drug enforcement in their country. Besides the respective pilots overseeing the refuelling, everyone else was disembarked and ushered into two separate transfer lounges.

Mark thought that the arrangement was rather odd but said nothing. He could not know whether it was an inter-agency thing, the Brits playing cute, or whatever. Nevertheless, the arrangement suited Mark fine. The three DEA visitors settled in in the not-very-comfortable civil service prescribed chairs. They accepted the drink and biscuits provided by a pleasant and attractive female RAF warrant officer, who, having no one else to attend to, they sat down and passed the time in idle conversation.

The warrant officer said that she was from the northwest of England, which would have been very evident from her accent had any of them had enough knowledge of England and the peculiarities of speech in that country to recognize her accent. She claimed to have been in *the service* for about six years and said she was looking forward to an overseas posting when the opportunity arose. Mark restricted his conversation to the weather, apart from an admission that they were with the DEA. Which the not-really-RAF-warrant-officer Bridgette Shaw said that she found quite interesting. Bridgette was her given name, but *Shaw* was an adopted name, at least in front of the present company.

The British Secret Intelligence Service, or MI6 as it is commonly known, does not normally mount operations in the United Kingdom. Like the CIA for the United States, it is a foreign intelligence service. The UK domestic intelligence and security is provided by the Security Service, otherwise known as MI5, which, in turn, does not typically mount operations outside of the UK.

But there are more practical considerations than bureaucratic demarcation when matters of international concern are involved. There would no doubt be a dispute over whose area of jurisdiction the present issue was in, but for the present, the Brits would try to find out what the hell their so-called allies were up to and sort out the turf war later.

With two US 'official' Gulfstream aircraft visiting England simultaneously, MI6 had some suspicions, which would have explained why the CIA and DEA visitors were being kept apart. After all, that was the arrangement that had been asked for by the DEA, and that just did not make any sense to their MI6 and MI5 hosts.

The visitors presented MI6 with something of a dilemma. The Brits had requested brief details of who was on board the CIA aircraft to be signalled ahead so that the customs issues could be dispensed with. They had asked for similar information from the DEA flight, which was complied with, keeping UK customs happy and presenting MI5 with all the facts. And MI6 with all the worries.

The CIA information provided to *customs* was valid,

as was the information from the DEA aircraft. What did not make sense to MI6 was why Mark Taylor had suddenly joined the DEA? Had this got anything to do with the recent appointment of his father, Harold Taylor, to the assistant inspector at the OIG? And what was the point of two identical aircraft with the same flight plans, with each aircraft having the ability to carry the whole lot in one load? While this could, of course, have something to do with as-yet-unfiled flight plans, which could take their passengers to entirely different destinations, the provisional plans filed back in the States said that both of the aircraft had at least *similar* intentions and would, at the proper time, return from whence they came.

The ADDI had advised the UK government of his impending visit and asked for a brief meeting with the heads of two sections dealing with the Middle East and Southeast Asia. That request was, of course, granted, and the British attendees would be picked and briefed based on their knowledge of the subjects, the personnel involved, and their expectations of where these discussions might lead. The MI6 expected the meeting to discuss matters of mutual interest of a security and intelligence nature. They did not expect that the talks would touch on the subject that they were apprehensive about—namely, the suspected involvement of Stephen Rodriguez in the drug trade. But there was always hope.

An RAF warrant officer was also assigned to serve refreshments for the CIA contingent and generally provide the same services as Bridgette did for the DEA people. This time a male officer was provided because MI6 also had suspicions about the sexual orientation of the ADDI. And the gentleman by the name of Richard Barnaby, who was also not a warrant officer, was a senior officer from MI6; therefore, both his first name and surname were fictitious.

The Brits did not expect to find anything useful from the two discussions. None of their concerns had anything to do with MI6, who was not into the drug business. That was left to the UK police. However, spooks being spooks, they took the opportunity to try to complete some bits of the jigsaw.

MI6 knew about De Lawrence of the DEA contingent, and there were no concerns there. They had no idea who Archibald Miller was, and they were scrambling to fill that gap in their knowledge. But it was known to the Brits that Mark Taylor did not belong to the DEA. Some months earlier, they had received information from the Australian Secret Intelligence Service that a Mark Taylor, son of Harold Taylor. at that time, known to be the CIA head of station in Wellington in New Zealand, had wandered into Australian territory. Investigation of that incursion had eventually revealed that Mark was doing something covert on behalf of his father. Since then, the fact that Harold had recently been appointed as an assistant inspector at CIA headquarters in Langley meant that MI6 had a watching brief on how that turned out. Therefore, the arrival of Mark Taylor at Fairford immediately after the arrival of the CIA ADDI raised several flags. And it did not involve any rocket science to arrive at a reasonable assumption of what was going on now.

Of course, MI6 would not rely on any assumptions. And since the US and UK intelligence and security networks were in bed together on most things, any conclusions reached would need to be shared. The issue was *when* and with *whom*? And then, of course, there was still the issue of a *need-to-know basis,* even among the absolute best friends.

Within an hour of their landing, the two Gulfstream jets left Fairford and headed east, leaving MI6 composing messages which raised more questions than answers to be distributed to their assets.

Most of which were also headed east.

After just over four hours' flight time, the aircraft started a slow descent into Ben Gurion Airport, the main airport in the state of Israel and located ten or so miles to the southeast of Tel Aviv. Strange as it may seem, the CIA Gulfstream did not head for an Israeli Air Force base, of which there were many in this country, where the security would have been at a much higher level. That probably had more to do with politics since the United States and Israel were currently involved in a diplomatic scrap over the use of Israeli forces in Gaza. Still, an argument between diplomats had nothing to do with the security organizations.

Griz had woken his passengers with coffee and sandwiches about an hour earlier and suggested that they adjust their watches to local time, which was about seven o'clock in the morning. Griz told Mark that the 'target' aircraft was also descending and that they would be on the ground at about nine o'clock, depending on other traffic.

According to Mark's calculations, the CIA airplane would have had enough fuel onboard to make it to Pakistan. Mark was anxious to get to their ultimate destination but accepted that was not his call. Griz also asked Mark what his plans were once they were on the ground in Israel and nodded his head in agreement as Mark outlined what he intended to do.

Del and Dusty would observe and find out what they could about the CIA people. Mark would stay with the aircraft. The problem still was that Mark was known to the assistant deputy director of intelligence, whereas the other two were not. Mark could not risk being seen, at least not until his beard was presentable. While the Ben Gurion Airport was a busy place, especially at this time in the morning, it was not so busy that a guy of Mark's height and stature would not stand out. Although the risk of Mark being seen and recognized by anyone was small, it was a risk that was just not worth taking.

In any case, the ADDI was not expected to do much other than to take a leak and perhaps exchange pleasantries with his local Mossad contacts—members of the much-feared-by-some and well-respected-by-others Israeli intelligence service. Mark felt that it was unlikely that the visit to Israel had anything to do with the reason for their trip. The problem was that he could not know for sure.

Dusty and Del's surveillance was merely a precaution, and they would not risk being conspicuous to any of the many security personnel who seemed to be everywhere around Ben Gurion.

Surveillance of any kind was always a problem for both sides. Those being followed or observed would be on the lookout for any abnormal behaviour of those around them, as was expected by people in the security business. Those doing the following or observing would want to be invisible and blend into their surroundings. So those who were being followed would each have a plan that involved doing something to draw out anyone who was tailing them from the crowd. It was simply a game that could have deadly consequences for anyone who did not know or did not follow the rules.

The travellers were quite used to the increased security at airports, particularly in the post 9/11 era, but security at Ben Gurion took that to a whole new level. The atmosphere was extremely tense. Ordinary people seemed to be constantly looking around, anticipating, expecting, and fearing that something would happen. There was not the usual casual wandering around that people do while waiting for their flights to depart or waiting for their loved ones to arrive. It was an atmosphere that came from living a life close to the edge; in a country where people claimed a right to exist in this 'promised land,' they lived in fear of any kind of reaction from other people who had the same claims but a quite different view of their rights.

Dusty returned to the aircraft about an hour after leaving it. He had nothing of interest to report other than that the ADDI and another man had been met by a short military-looking gentleman and whisked away in an official-looking but unmarked car. Dusty was sure that he had seen the other man somewhere before but could not get a close-enough look through the crowds. He called it quits since there was nothing to gain from drawing more attention to himself than his massive frame allowed.

In the meantime, Del had met up with one of his colleagues from the Israel Anti-Drugs Authority—naturally known by its acronym as the ADA—and was having coffee with him while keeping an eye out for the friendly spooks.

This was the first time since they had left Washington that Mark had had the opportunity to talk to Dusty alone, so he brought him up to date on his earlier conversation with their pilot. Dusty just nodded and allowed his body language to do the rest, not for the first time since they had been involved in this mission.

Their visit to Israel was unlikely to reveal any information to assist them in their purpose. They just bided their time, waiting in frustration for something to happen.

But nothing happened.

Their aircraft was fuelled, serviced, and ready to leave at a moment's notice, but the CIA airplane showed no signs of going anywhere until well into the afternoon. The inactivity, boredom, and tiredness caused Mark's mind to play mental gymnastics.

What if his father and his associate in the DEA had got it all wrong?

What if the assistant deputy director of intelligence was just off on a government-sponsored junket, and there was no drug dealing or trafficking in any of this?

On the more positive side of this mental debate, what had they to lose?

And the answer to that was nothing, except perhaps the chance to sort out what had been festering in Mark's mind for some time—getting even with the ADDI. Stephen Rodriguez was somehow tied in with the debacle that was the second 9/11. Therefore, Rodriguez was somehow involved in the deaths of Mark's two friends.

But *how?*

It was frustrating waiting around with nothing happening, but there was nothing that Mark could do about that. He could do nothing about Rodriguez for the time being, at least not until they reached Pakistan. And then what?

At least he had the opportunity to call home.

Mark waited until 1:00 pm so that he did not call while Debbie was asleep. It was 6:00 am in New York, and she should be well awake and into it!

The beauty of satellite telephone technology is that it does not require any local network: your device that is defined as a terminal but looks a little different from an oversized cellular phone—it just bounced the signal off the nearest available satellite rather than a cell tower, except that the satellite was much farther away. And although there was a slight delay while the voice travelled many tens of thousands of miles out of and then back into the earth's atmosphere, the sound quality was second to none.

The other advantage of the technology was that the person being called would have no idea from *whom* and from *where* the call had originated.

'Good morning, Debbie. I hope I did not ring too early!'

Despite the hour in New York, Debbie seemed happy to hear from Mark, even though standing in the eighty-six degrees of the heat of Tel Aviv was hard to convey to someone shivering in the cold, near-freezing temperature of New York City.

'Hi, honey. So, you have arrived in Pakistan?'

Mark groaned into the phone.

'No. We are still in Tel Aviv, Israel, but we should be on our way to Pakistan soon. Is everything OK?'

'Yeah, we are fine. I miss you already. Please take care.'

She chatted for a few minutes, and Mark let her go on. It wasn't his phone, and someone else was picking up this tab. He presumed that *we* to whom Debbie had referred was her and Fridge, Mark's cat. He assumed that the 'someone else' that was picking up the tab was either the CIA or the DEA or some combination of both, and that was fine.

It seemed strange to be off on a covert operation and having a chat with his girlfriend without a care in the world. No! She was *more* than his girlfriend. Debbie had become much more than that. She was so loving, so kind, and so understanding. But in the end, he had to terminate the call. There was work that had to be done. He saw Del wandering across the tarmac towards the aircraft without a care in the world. And that was one of the things that he would need to work on.

'OK. I love you. I will call you when we get to Pakistan. Bye.' And that was the end of that.

Except it was not.

Mark then called Michelle.

He went through the usual security, and finally, she spoke. 'Good morning. Michelle speaking—how can I help you?'

'Hi, Michelle. Could you do something for me? An extra guy is traveling on the CIA airplane. I need to find out who he is.'

There was a pregnant pause, and Mark was sure someone else was in on this conversation. Then a somewhat hesitant Michelle came back on the phone. 'I do not think I can do that.' She replied.

Mark persisted. 'Well, who can tell me? I need to know!'

Again, there was a pause, then Michelle returned. 'I will make some inquiries. If you call me back in, say, two hours, I should have some further information.' At least she did not ask if there was anything else that she could help with, as is the way with other helpdesk operators.

Mark just said 'OK' and then disconnected the call.

Mark called his father.

The reception he got on this call was somewhat different, but that was expected. His father was concerned that Mark had broken protocol, but Mark bulldozed through that argument.

'We are in on the way. I have just finished talking to 'Michelle' as instructed, and I am not impressed. I need someone to do something for me. Find out who the guy is accompanying the ADDI on this trip, and what is he doing on that airplane?'

The question seemed quite simple, but it was early in the morning, so his father responded with his own question.

'What guy?'

Mark could afford to be patient. He would, after all, eventually be paid for making this trip, and they were not exactly under any pressure at this point. He avoided the obvious answer of '*I asked you that question*' and simply explained the delay at Andrews Air Force Base and the apparent reason for it.

Harold's response was typically vague.

'I did not know of that. Is it significant?'

Patience does have its limits.

'Father! How should I know? We are going to start following a man who now has an assistant. So, to answer your question, yes, it could be significant. I am asking you to find out who the guy is. My theory, such as it is, is that if it was worth waiting nearly an entire day for the guy to turn up, then he must be significant. The guy boarded one of your aircraft, so it does not require a rocket scientist to work out that he is also probably CIA. Can you or the DEA do something about finding out who and what he is? Yes, or no? Or is that question too hard for you?'

Mark disconnected the call without waiting for an answer.

The team sat down in the airplane and ate the food that Del had thoughtfully arranged for one of the airline caterers to bring on board. Del did have his uses, although there was a certain tension in the atmosphere. Perhaps it was from the expectations of what might happen on the next leg of the journey.

The assistant deputy director of intelligence had a thing about leaving airports around late afternoon. Finally, at 4:00 pm, Griz popped out of the cockpit to say they were once more on their way. They went through the usual rigmarole of waiting until the CIA Gulfstream was in the air and well clear of Ben Gurion Airport and had turned and climbed to the east. Then the DEA Gulfstream also took to the skies and headed east, like a puppy dog following its master.

Mark did not ask how they had arranged their flight plan in the apparent chaos of the afternoon, but they did, and that was all he cared about. Again, the traffic controller chit-chat was fed through the speakers so that they all knew what was going on.

Nothing was going on.

They were on their way to Peshawar, which was over 2,000 miles to the east as the crow flies but would be a little bit farther as they zigzagged their way through or around the odd country that it was not advisable for a CIA flight or in some cases any United States flight, to travel over. Still, that was not something that Mark should concern himself with. Wherever the first airplane went, the second airplane would follow. And that was that.

The only concern for Mark was that they were expected to land in Peshawar at about 11:15 pm. While arriving in darkness when the airport would be quiet suited the secretive nature of their mission fine, it did nothing for their objective: to find out where the people on the CIA airplane were going.

There was the usual apprehension as their flight came to land. Although Peshawar was relatively safe (it was not unknown for bombs to go off or for terrorists to have a go at anything that may have links to the United States Government, security services, or military services, or links to anyone or anywhere else), none of the three members of the DEA team had any experience of Peshawar or Pakistan.

But Griz did.

Chapter 17

The War Zone

The arrival of the two Gulfstream V C-37A aircraft, almost simultaneously, did not attract much attention at the Bacha Khan International Airport in Peshawar. Except, that is, in the control tower, where members of the Pakistani ISI woke up.

While the DEA and the CIA could more or less control what went on in the United States and particularly at the Andrews Air Force base, both organizations could have confidence in the clinical efficiency of the air traffic controllers. Even to a certain extent, at the Ben Gurion Airport—they could have no such faith in the people who ran the Peshawar airport. Or, for that matter, the people who ran anything anywhere in Pakistan.

The airport was used for both civilian and military traffic. Although the two Gulfstream aircraft represented US civilian administrations, or at least were recognized as such in the United States, in Pakistan, it was assumed that the Government-owned aircraft were there for military purposes. The Pakistani ISI took a quick note of the arrival and would watch with interest to see what, if anything, transpired.

Not that there was anything wrong with that.

Whether friendly or not so friendly, all nations had to know what foreigners were doing within their borders. The problem was that the information tended to leak out of Pakistani government organizations rather more than you would reasonably expect of a sovereign power.

At this stage, it was doubtful that the Pakistani ISI could have even the remotest idea of what was going on, which meant that they would be more eager to find out. Had the Pakistanis spent the same amount of time tracking Osama bin Laden that they did following what their so-called allies were doing, there could have been a different outcome.

But they didn't.

And there wasn't.

Shortly after the DEA aircraft had arrived at their appointed parking area, Griz came to see Mark for a chat. Whether Del was concerned at the apparent snub, he did not show any outward signs that he cared. Dusty busied himself, changing into his DEA uniform, and listened to the conversation.

'I believe your two CIA friends are booked into the Pearl-Continental Hotel for two nights—must be planning on playing a game of golf—that is right alongside the Peshawar Golf Club! They will fly to Kabul on Sunday, the day after tomorrow. What do you want to do?' Griz asked.

'Is that not the hotel that someone tried to blow up a few months ago?' Mark asked in return, sounding concerned, if not a little scared.

Griz just laughed. 'It does not matter where you go in this part of the world. This is Peshawar, Pakistan—not New York City or Washington in the USA. The terrorists that used to be all over Afghanistan are now settled mostly in the western provinces of Pakistan, where they are not exactly welcome. It does not matter where you go in this city. There is always some nut likely to blow himself and anyone else into the next world. I suggest you book in the same hotel—that way; we can keep an eye on what your friends do and where they go. I will join you later. Just have a few things to do here first.'

Mark looked at Dusty and just got a nod in the affirmative.

Mark looked at Del and got no reaction at all. So, he replied, 'I think so. Can you arrange that from here?'

Without a doubt, Mark detected a look of irritation on the face of his new friend, Brian McKinley, otherwise known as Griz. When Griz just answered 'Yes' to his question and turned to go back into the cockpit, Mark followed him.

'What is going on?' Mark asked, not sure whether he wanted to hear the answer.

'Who sent that dickhead Del with you?' Griz fired back, clearly irritated.

'It is his job to make all arrangements once you are on the ground. But he is scared witless. Can't you get him replaced by someone a little more reliable before he becomes a real embarrassment?'

Mark did not know what to say. He certainly had serious doubts about the representative of the Drug Enforcement Administration when they had first met back in Washington. He was being told by another member of that same organization that the guy was as useless as tits on a bull. And Del was initially supposed to be the one in charge! They had only been on a joyride so far, but they were about to get involved in some real covert work. And now this. Mark had to admit that he could blame no one but himself. He was supposed to be incredibly good at reading body language.

But he had not read this one, or at least not reacted to it, and the price could be high.

'I will need to talk to your director. What time is it in Washington?' Mark asked.

At least it would be around three o'clock in the afternoon in Washington. And, of course, Mark would not be talking to any director at the DEA. At the very least, he could talk to Michelle.

And if that did not work, at least Harold should be back from lunch.

For Griz, the situation was a little tricky.

His job was to fly the aircraft from point A to point B. Because the DEA employed him, there were differences from the position of a typical commercial pilot. The two significant differences were, firstly, that he would be aware of the confidential nature of some of the missions, and therefore, secondly, that he could not talk openly with anyone about where he was going or why.

He now found himself in a contradictory situation where the people he worked for may not even know what was happening.

The DEA was a bureaucracy. As part of such an organization, Griz had a dual responsibility to respect the confidential nature of his work and report to the authorities his time spent on the job.

It would be impractical not to report where he was.

And to not report who was onboard his aircraft.

Chapter 18

Jigsaw Pieces

Mark's team got to the Pearl-Continental Hotel well after midnight, although nothing that the visiting Americans seemed to do fazed the receptionist. It was difficult for Mark to read whether he was just pleased to see Americans or whether he had been trained that way. He was originally from California and was bending over backward to be of assistance.

As visitors to this strange country, he knew that his team would need to be careful. They could not trust anybody, including the zealous receptionist. They would be recognized as Americans, but unlike most Americans abroad, they would need to stay below everyone's radar, including that of other Americans. The city of Peshawar had more than its fair share of conflict and bombings. While these were usually a result of arguments between local groups, the Americans and their allies were never far from the troubles.

The fact was that Peshawar was one of the most unstable cities on the planet.

It was strange. Here they were, in a foreign city, supposed to be following people who were experts both at surveillance and countersurveillance. And the odds were not all that great for Mark's team to successfully follow their CIA friend while remaining covert. The only person who seemed capable of helping them was supposed to pilot the airplane and could not be expected to do much else. De Lawrence, the only person who was officially on their team, who should have had contacts, and who should have been able to point them in the right direction, was a fruitcake.

On the positive side, at least the beards that all three had grown since they were first assigned to this mission began to take shape. That is, apart from Del, whose beard defied description. It was awful. This meant that Mark could soon start to move around with some degree of impunity, but not yet. That was if his height—six feet four—did not give him away. Dusty was fine: although big, he was about the same colouring as most of the residents of Pakistan and the residents of surrounding countries. And a critical factor was that Dusty was not known to the CIA's assistant deputy director of intelligence. As far as Mark was aware, Del was also not known to the ADDI. That would have also been a benefit if Del had not been so inept. Or, rather, if Del had been able to gain the respect of his fellow travellers.

When they had first arrived at the Pearl-Continental, Mark and Del waited outside of the hotel in the taxi while Dusty went inside to check them in and, more importantly, to check out who was around.

No one appeared to be around.

The inquiry from the reception desk as to what all the late-night activity was about just brought a smile to Dusty. His smile broadened as he read the other bookings for Stephen Rodriguez and the man named Hennessey who was accompanying him happened to be on the same floor as Mark and the team. In this hotel, they thought that the foreigners should be kept together! Dusty signed all four of them in and then left a message for Griz before whisking the other two in through the main door and then up the stairs to the fourth floor.

Mark and Dusty shared a room, while Del and Griz had separate rooms.

Dusty was not as good as Mark at reading body language, but you did not need to be a rocket scientist to prove that something was wrong.

'So, what is wrong with Del?' he asked Mark when they were safely ensconced in their room.

Mark shrugged.

'I talked to the pilot. His reading of Del is that he is scared. If Griz is right, and at this stage, I believe that he is, we have only got as far as Peshawar. What will he be like when he gets to Kabul in Afghanistan?' Mark asked the ceiling.

'And you intend to do what about it?' Dusty enquired.

'How the hell should I know? But I am going to do one thing.'

Mark went out onto the balcony, taking the satellite phone with him. He paused for a moment, deciding who he should call first. But that decision was quite simple.

After talking to Michelle and then talking to his father, Mark would probably get frustrated, get involved in another argument, and consequently be irritated.

He called Debbie first.

'Hi. We just got into our hotel in Peshawar. How was your day?'

Debbie was fine, but it was good to hear her voice.

Mark was missing her in a way that he had never experienced before. When he had been married to that sex maniac called Helen, he never felt this way. He could have felt this way in a later and very brief relationship with his PA, Annette Covic, but in that case, he had not had the time; such had been the hectic pace of his life.

And then Annette was gone—killed in cold blood, right in front of his eyes—and Mark had been unable to do anything about it.

The man who had fired the shot that killed her had been a member of the FBI. He was locked away in a federal prison and would remain locked away for a long time. His sentence was not solely for the murder of Annette. His sentence was not really for murder at all. His legal team had argued, well out of the public spotlight, that he was reacting in self-defence, acting in his official capacity as an officer of the law. Annette was, after all, meant to be the third suicide bomber in the second 9/11, and she was the one who presented a *clear and present danger*.

So, that was that. Ignoring the fact that the innocent twenty-three-year-old girl was already being held at gunpoint by one of his partners in crime and presented no danger to anyone. It was a little more challenging to explain the FBI agents' later actions, which was why he had been locked away. Justice was not exactly fair, but at least, in this case, the system managed to lock up the right man, albeit for the wrong reasons.

Mark was determined that Debbie would be safe and not get embroiled in such nonsense. He just had to get this job done and return to the United States and Debbie.

Meanwhile, there was this little job to complete.

They exchanged 'I love you,' and then she was gone.

Then he rang Michelle via the DEA voice identification

system.

'Hi, Michelle, have you made any progress in identifying the guy on the airplane?' was the most straightforward question that Mark could devise.

Again, the pause. Furthermore, the feeling that someone else was involved in the conversation. Then she replied.

'Yes, we have made some progress. However, we understand that your other contact would be better explaining.'

'Michelle' then disconnected the call without waiting for an answer.

Mark rang Harold Taylor.

'Hi, Father. We have arrived in Peshawar—a little later than we expected, but safe.'

'Yes, I heard you had arrived,' his father began. Harold did not say how he had heard that, but the assumption could be made that the DEA and the CIA were still talking to each other. At least the OIG, in the form of Harold Taylor, was still talking to the DEA, in the form of Karen Marshall. And presumably, Del was talking to his director. Or did Del have to go through another calling option? Or the same—Michelle?

'Father, I think we have a problem. You can say that I am just keeping you in the picture, but we need to do something about Del.'

Mark was sure he could sense Harold's shoulders droop, and there was more than the delay typically associated with satellite phone technology. At least, Harold did not start accusing Mark of any wrongdoing, as is the norm in father-son relationships. Mark was surprised by his answer.

'Yes, I think we made a mistake with De Lawrence. Karen rang a few minutes ago, and she said the same thing. She is genuinely concerned about his state of mind. She is genuinely concerned about his state of mind. She did not anticipate his reaction to being so close to a war zone. However, it is too late to do anything about him now. You will just have to do the best you can.'

Mark was about to sound off at the casual way his father left that subject.

Once again, the troops in the field had to carry the can for an inept bureaucratic decision, but Harold got in first.

'Now, about the gentleman who is on the airplane with Rodriguez. The official story goes, the ADDI required someone from the FBI to accompany him to do some research on the CIA staff in Afghanistan. Something about profiling. There has been evidence of a leak, or several leaks, of information, so I can understand that the CIA personnel are under suspicion. I do not yet know the background of this FBI guy, but I have someone checking into him and should have more information soon. His name is Edward Hennessey if that helps. And I suspect that something else is going down. It is most unusual for the two organizations to be so cooperative! If the objective is to investigate the leaks—or, rather, to investigate the people who are likely to be involved in any leaks—it is unheard of for the CIA to involve the FBI before they have at least got a strong suspicion of who is responsible. I have heard nothing on that front, but it should have been referred to my office as routine. My conclusion would be that the CIA knows where the leak is. Otherwise, why involve the FBI? And the leak could be at such a level that they are not following normal protocol.'

His father talked for a few more minutes, but most of it went over Mark's head. Mark was quite used to the CIA fouling things up: if they could not identify someone from their sister organization, the FBI in Washington DC, they were in real trouble. But if the ADDI needed a profiler on this tour, and if there was a leak in Afghanistan, then so be it. Far more important was the representative of the DEA that Mark would need to contend with! Maybe they could borrow the FBI to do a profile on Del!

Whatever else happened, Del would come with them to Kabul, whether Del liked it. Owen Squires was to be their first contact in Kabul, and Del was the only one who knew him or at least knew of him.

Mark just had to hope that the mysterious Owen Squires was an improvement on the personnel that the DEA had to offer so far.

Mark said 'OK' to the assistant inspector and terminated the call.

Mark could not think of anything else to say.

There was a knock on the door as he returned to join a bemused Dusty, who had heard at least one end of the three brief conversations. They both exchanged looks in response to the knock and dropped into the roles they had trained for in Delta Force. Even though their presence in Peshawar did not seem to have got anyone overly excited, they were taking no chances.

Dusty picked up his Glock handgun, chambered a round, went to the door, and peered through the spyhole, while Mark took up a station, not in the firing line, should anyone be inclined to fire through the door. Although Mark had heard that bandits and other criminals in this part of the world were more likely to shoot themselves than their target, there was no point in allowing them to demonstrate their incompetence.

Mark also chambered a round, eased his Glock into a firing position, and exchanged another look with Dusty, who opened the door.

It was Griz.

They all laughed at the display of firearms. Mark noted that the reaction from Griz was one of calm acceptance.

Mark did not know if that was a good or a bad thing.

They each took their choice of drinks from the minibar—an unusual facility in this part of the world. Mark because he needed one, Griz because he was not flying anywhere for at least twenty-four hours, and Dusty because it was there.

Mark told them about his conversation with Harold Taylor, at which both the listeners merely shrugged, and then they got down to discuss their plans for the next day. It was well after 2:00 am when they finally turned in. It had been a long day.

To Dusty, sleeping was not an issue.

To Mark, it was.

The morning turned out to be hectic. It took some time to convince Del that it was inappropriate for him to wear his DEA uniform. There just did not seem any point in advertising that they were Americans in so hostile an environment. In the end, Dusty told him to 'get real or get fucked,' and that piece of advice seemed to work.

Del was tasked early in the morning with two things: firstly, making sure that their communicators were working, and secondly, getting them some mode of transport. The original attitude that Del had displayed in Washington of intending to lead the group on this covert mission had been replaced with one of sullen subservience. Maybe it was acceptance of his lot. Or perhaps it was a sign of something else going on.

Maybe Karen Marshall had put a flea in his ear.

Mark had not mentioned to Del that he was aware of his contact with the people back in the United States, so it was probably the short speech Dusty had made that finally got the message through to Del that he would not be in charge.

The first task was completed efficiently enough when Del went for a wander outside to test the communicators for range and reliability. Their equipment had a range of about 500 yards, which was good enough for what they needed. Del returned from his trip, gave Dusty the keys to a Toyota Camry sedan, and then took a seat in the reception area to watch and wait.

Mark had his breakfast in his room while keeping an eye out for any movement from the adjacent rooms, which housed the assistant deputy director of intelligence and his FBI accomplice. When the ADDI eventually did come out of his room, he was alone. Stephen Rodriguez went to the elevator, and Mark just broadcast an appropriate message over his communicator, hoping that only three people were listening in to what he had to say.

Dusty went through the regular hotel routine of having breakfast in the dining room, and Griz joined him. They watched as Stephen Rodriguez came into the dining area, where he met a Pakistani gentleman. From the body language of both men, they had obviously met somewhere before. Not that their meeting seemed particularly friendly. They ordered something to eat and drink but continued an animated discussion throughout their meal.

Dusty watched, ate, waited, and occasionally kept Mark informed. They were sitting around having coffee when things started to happen. Now the group would find out if their plans would work. Dusty had to follow the ADDI, and he had to be accompanied by Del as their resident expert on matters that concerned drugs, and in case one of them had to follow on foot. They were gambling that Dusty could find his way around Peshawar and that Del would concentrate on his job and stop worrying about being blown up. In his own way, Dusty thought that he had the latter issue settled by politely informing Del, 'Don't fuck this up, or you will have me to deal with!'

Mark was frustrated, but what else could he do? He did not yet have enough confidence that he could afford to be seen by Stephen Rodriguez, and it was better to err on the side of caution. The city of Peshawar had a population of over three million, so it should have been easy to hide. And the city was a significant feeder point for allied troops traveling to and from Afghanistan, so there were plenty of Western and other military people around, most of them in uniform. But the intention was to follow the ADDI, which meant getting close. This, in turn, meant that Mark could not be part of the following team, at least not yet. Griz had nothing else to do, so he kept watch in and around the hotel while Mark sat in his room, his only knowledge of what was going on being the occasional chatter on his communicator. It was not until much later in the evening that Del and Dusty returned to provide a thorough, if essentially meaningless, report of the day's activity. Except Dusty had some news that meant they were on the right track.

Dusty had established a clear connection between Stephen Rodriguez and drugs. But at this early stage, it was not solid enough to take it to the bank.

Stephen Rodriguez had shaken hands with his Pakistani friend on leaving the hotel and was then picked up by a car with consular registration plates. It was evidently from the United States Embassy. In the chaos that was the city of Peshawar, where traffic flow is determined by the rule of brute force and not much else, Dusty and Del had a difficult job following the vehicle. However, the Toyota that Dusty was driving was not exactly in pristine condition. Hence, his chances of being spotted by either the senior representative of the United States spook business or his driver, who was also no doubt well versed in such matters, seemed remote. You could add to that the other cars around, which seemed to appear with regular monotony wherever Stephen Rodriguez went. These cars probably belonged to the Pakistani ISI, and apparently,

Rodriguez and his driver ignored them. This translated into two facts. Firstly, the Pakistani ISI was expected to follow the assistant deputy director of intelligence wherever he went—at least until they got bored and found something more useful to do. Secondly, the CIA was fully aware of their presence.

And that they were either harmless, incompetent, or both.

A person who believes that they are being followed can take various steps. They can take the passive view that as long as they know what is going on, they do not need to do anything, and that is fine so long as they are not going anywhere or doing anything other than going about their reasonable and regular business. However, they could take a more active role if they have reason to object to being followed. That could be either fun (just trying to lose the tail) or a deadly game of hide-and-seek. The outcome of this game would depend on whether those being followed could recognize all the people or vehicles engaged in the exercise of surveillance. There are many techniques involved in surveillance and countersurveillance. But at the end of the day, there is a large chunk of luck involved.

As far as the ADDI was concerned, he knew where he was going and did not care who else knew. It was good fieldcraft to check who was following and look for signs of new or different techniques. But if you do not care, then there is no point in revealing that you are even aware of their presence.

So, he didn't.

The ADDI ended up at the United States Consulate on

Hospital Road. Barriers were in place, so Dusty and Del had to watch from a distance as the consular car entered the gates to what was a secure compound. The vehicles they assumed belonged to the ISI took up positions some distance away but without any apparent concealment. They could all see through the wrought iron gates what was going on in the compound, particularly *who* and *what* came out of it. For his part, Dusty parked the car and then sat on the vehicle's bonnet from where he could get a better view of the street-side chaos.

And waited.

They did not have to wait long. Within half an hour, the consular car, with Stephen and the driver the only occupants, came out and took off in a south-easterly direction, with the usual flotilla of ISI vehicles scrambling in their wake. Since Dusty was not familiar with the city's geography, he simply followed the ADDI vehicle at a discreet distance. He was pleased that the phasing in and out of ISI surveillance made his job relatively easy.

This time, they eventually ended up at the south-eastern end of the international airport, in an area that was some kind of military establishment. Peshawar airport is shared between the Pakistani military forces and the civilian authorities, so this was no real surprise. The consular car simply pulled up at the security gate and, after no more than a cursory exchange of greetings and a casual examination of some paperwork, proceeded inside. That caused Dusty to panic temporarily. While they drove on before turning to park some distance from the gate, he could see the two Gulfstream jets parked up, and one of them was not too far away. If the ADDI had changed his plans and headed to his jet, the operation codenamed Porto could be in big trouble.

A quick exchange of words via his satellite phone got Mark to check on what was going on at the airport. Within a few minutes of this call, Griz checked with the airport control tower. They were aware of no immediate plans for the Gulfstream to take off anytime soon, but that did not mean much. Mark managed to calm Dusty down, having gleaned some information that the central CIA cell in Peshawar was located at the airport. But that also did not mean much either. Most of the activities of the CIA and the military security people occurred away from their official residences, so the odds were that it was just a routine visit. In any case, there was nothing that Dust or anyone else could do.

Except, wait.

There followed a two-hour wait while absolutely nothing happened. And then the limo, complete with its passenger, came back out of the gate, turned left, and headed straight back to the Pearl-Continental Hotel. Once there, the ADDI was dropped off, which was the end of that.

The whole trip had been a complete and utter waste of time. Or so it appeared to Dusty. Nonetheless, he sent Del off to find another vehicle. Any kind, so long as it was a different colour.

Del managed to achieve the task quickly and efficiently.

Dusty communicated these useless bits of information to Mark when Stephen Rodriguez reappeared at the hotel entrance with another man. And this one looked like the guy who had joined the ADDI at Andrews back in Washington and who he had been with on their brief visit to Tel Aviv. Stephen then raised his hand to a passing taxi, which stopped at the hotel, and the two men got in.

It could not have been a passing taxi. The driver looked like the same Pakistani man Stephen Rodriguez had breakfast with at the hotel earlier in the morning.

Dusty had no idea what they were doing or where they were going, but he doubted that they would repeat their visit to the military side of the airport. He followed once more, taking care to stay well back from the vehicle they were following. Apparently, this trip was of no interest to the ISI because Dusty could not detect any of the cars accompanying the ADDI on his earlier travels. This made his decision to switch cars a good one, as he did not feel quite so vulnerable in the new *disguise*. Although following a taxi, as opposed to a consular vehicle, was a bit of a mission, the problem eased as they sped off and away from the hotel area.

Dusty began to think that he had it all wrong for a while. They were heading back down the Saddar Road that led to the southern end of the Peshawar airport. However, when they got to the airport, the ADDI car turned left into Bara Road and drove southwest, which seemed to be leading them nowhere. That caused Del to panic again and Dusty to feel a little concerned. Following people through the jungles of Colombia was one thing; following people around the roads and streets of Peshawar was quite another.

'We will find it difficult to follow them if the traffic gets much lighter. Do you think it best to return to the hotel and leave your heroics until we get to Kabul?' Del asked, having sensed the tenseness in his Afro-American friend.

The reply he got from Dusty would have left little doubt of what he thought—not of the comment about heroics, but Del.

Dusty merely said, 'Shut the fuck up!' and drove on.

Dusty had studied a map of Peshawar and the surrounding area and racked his brain to second-guess where the people he was following were going. The last thing he needed was a wimpfor a companion while concentrating on where they were headed and where they might end up.

Mark also had a map back at the hotel, and he tried following their progress, but neither of the two could see any logic in the direction the ADDI was headed. The only thing looming on the map was the Badhaber refugee camp, but why on earth would the ADDI want to go there?

While United States people might be at least tolerated, the military and the CIA would be loathed by most people who were rendered homeless by a war seemingly without an end and where the United States was quite simply the latest and obvious target for all their pent-up anger.

Just when Mark and Dusty were about to give up trying to guess where the ADDI's car may be headed, the taxi turned right onto the Hayatabad Road and headed north. Their conclusion? Either the driver did not know his way around Peshawar or excellent reason to avoid the more direct and infinitely shorter route. The car had travelled in a massive U-shaped journey. Whatever the reason, they ended up in an industrial estate, and the taxi pulled into the parking area outside one of the buildings.

It was a textile factory, which, according to the decal of the roller door, belonged to the Aziar Group of companies.

The industrial area had only recently been built. There were rows of buildings, all of the same size and shape. The residents did not expect any retail foot traffic in this part of Peshawar because, apart from the fact that there was none, the buildings were not exactly inviting. There were very few signs to indicate who was in residence. On the edge of each section nearest to the road, every building had a series of carparks with positions marked at regimented right angles to the road. There must have been thirty parks to each building, yet there was not a single vehicle occupying them as far as the eye could see.

It was the same problem worldwide: developers built industrial parks to a specification that some brain-dead architects assumed that people would want in the fantasy land that was their dreams. Only a couple of industries in this part of the industrial estate were prepared to state who they were—the textile factory and a children's toy factory next door, which seemed by the colouring and style of the signage to be owned by the same group. Maybe the ADDI wanted to buy some clothing or curtaining materials for his wife, or some toys for his kids! Whatever his interest in the Aziar company, Stephen certainly had a strange way of getting there. It did seem overly odd that he should delay a flight out of Washington to ensure that his mystery guest from New York could accompany him to this remote location. Dusty smiled at the thought of wasted taxpayer dollars but thought better of sharing that thought with Del, who was part of the same bureaucratic jungle.

The three men in the taxi, including the driver, got out and, after a brief and animated discussion, disappeared inside the Aziar building.

Dusty got on the satellite phone to talk to Mark about this new situation. They had to find out, if they could, why the ADDI had come all this way to visit—what? The course of action that Dusty recommended was to wait until Stephen, and his friend had left the area before taking a closer look at the factory, with or without Del.

The decision made by Mark was that Del should follow the ADDI when he and his fellow travellers left the building, and that Dusty would stay behind to watch the factory or whatever it was. They would worry about how Dusty got back to the hotel later.

And Dusty was quite OK with that.

However, the arrangement was not OK with Del, and he started to argue with Dusty.

'I am the expert on drugs, and I am the one best equipped to handle this!' was his opening statement.

At first, Dusty was going to say that Mark had made the decision, and that was that. But then he thought of the state of mind of this representative of the DEA, and so he smiled and simply said, 'OK, so I will follow the ADDI, and you remain here to watch the factory. We will arrange to pick you up later, or better still, just go straight to the airport, and we will meet up with you in the morning.'

Dusty did not even swear. He just watched as the message was received, analysed, and then understood in all its stark reality.

'But you will have to stay with me!' Del blurted out. 'You Special Forces guys always do things in pairs!' he added to emphasize the logic of what he had just said.

Dusty tried to stay calm and relied on his overpowering size to get the message finally across to this blubbering idiot. They had time on their side because there was no sign of any activity at the factory, and the taxi was still parked out front.

'Listen to me carefully because I will not repeat myself. You, Del, will drive this car and follow that taxi to wherever it might go when it leaves here. I have seen more drugs than you have ever seen from all sides, so don't give me that shit about who the expert is here. There are only two of us, and two jobs are to be done. The decision has been made. Now live with it or get out of here right now.'

And that was that.

It was nearly 5:30 pm and beginning to get dark when two of the men came out of the factory—Stephen Rodriguez and the Pakistani. The mystery man that the ADDI had brought from New York was still in the building. The Pakistani was still talking and waving his arms around as they got into their taxi. Then they drove off in the direction they had come, with a very tense and ultra-cautious well, scared—Del on their tail.

FBI agent Edward Hennessey could not believe his luck. Stephen Rodriguez had left him to oversee the goings-on at the factory. It appeared that Rodriguez had absolute faith in him. And that was fair enough, given the pace at which their relationship had developed.

Although it is an Irish name, *Hennessey* is usually associated with brandy and the French. Edward Hennessey was a third-generation American and had few traits of his Irish ancestry.

Despite the name and the fact that he was still a Catholic, the young man's life in the FBI had been difficult. He was very bright, attractive, and intelligent. He had finished all the courses in the top 2 or 3 in the classes that his entry into this chosen career had entailed. Hennessey had an aptitude for profiling because he had an unusual affinity with people and an unusually accurate reading of the people he met. And it was this ability that had landed him this job.

Certainly, Rodriguez had recognized his talent when they had met by chance at an FBI short course at Quantico. The ADDI was unaware that their meeting had been intentional. He was also totally unaware that the FBI wanted a reading on Stephen Rodriguez.

There was one other factor that made life difficult for Hennessey in the service of his country. That factor he had tried to hide from his peers, but apparently, the experts in profiling had probably discovered what he was trying to hide very early in his career.

Edward Hennessey was gay.

The problem was not knowing whether his peers in the FBI would hold that against him. Edward was not living with anyone. He shared all the usual, if politically incorrect, jokes with the people he worked with. All of them seemed to treat him like any other bloke.

Then his boss at the FBI had asked him to meet Stephen Rodriguez, which did seem to be a little above his pay grade. They met, and Edward duly delivered his report to his masters. In brief, Rodriguez was an arrogant son of a bitch, focused on himself, unlikely to suffer fools easily, if at all, but dedicated to his country and his job. It then seemed a little strange that Edward had been summoned into the office of one of the assistant directors—Peyton Reed—and asked to attempt to get to know his friend Stephen a little better. No explanation of why. Just get to know him and report back.

What he found out was that Stephen Rodriguez was a very troubled man. And that Rodriguez would have been even more troubled had he known of the role that Edward Hennessey was tasked with playing.

Then came the move that escalated the task to a whole different level.

Rodriguez had asked Hennessey to accompany him on a trip overseas. The pretext was that Stephen would require some assistance from the FBI. Edward thought both the request and its transmission method to be rather strange and mentioned it to Peyton. The answer that he got was a wry smile and little else other than a 'Go with it.'

That was until the day of his planned departure on the trip to the east.

On his way to Andrews, Peyton Reed had taken Edward to one side and asked him if he was still happy to go to Afghanistan. The reason behind the question came from a chance snippet of information that the FBI had picked up at a presidential briefing. This indicated that the NSA, conspiring with the CIA, had been playing around with the internal communications of the US security services. In itself, that did not mean very much because the real aim of the NSA exercise was to compromise foreign communications, and they were only using 'friendly' communications to avoid any chance of detection by their eventual target. However, that target was the Russian setup in Afghanistan, so it was only a matter of time before they switched their attention to that area. One result of that could be the prospect of compromising any FBI overseas operations. They could not reveal what the FBI was doing because, while it was not strictly illegal, the NSA would frown upon it.

And would send the CIA into an apoplectic fit.

Eventually, it was agreed that Edward should continue with his mission because he was making excellent progress. It would be a shame to miss the opportunity to make further progress. It would, however, mean a few changes to standard procedures. Edward would still have access to a satellite phone but would not use it to report anything about his covert mission. Instead, he was rushed off to talk to the crypto people and get a crash course on how to record events using a less modern technique.

What he could not retain in his memory would be committed to paper.

This whole affair meant that Edward would be late for his flight. Peyton saw that as an opportunity to test his resolve by offering an alternative agent. But as per the profile that they had created, Stephen was adamant that Edward Hennessey would be the one to accompany him on the trip.

So, Stephen Rodriguez and the CIA airplane would just have to wait.

The fact that Del lost the taxi he was to follow, or at least he claimed that he had lost it, made trivial difference as it transpired. The cab simply went back to the Pearl-Continental Hotel and dropped Stephen Rodriguez at the entrance.

The only person that Del could find at the hotel when he turned up a half-hour later was Mark. Mark did not feel inclined to inform Del that Griz had gone back to the airport.

There seemed little point in overtaxing Del with too much information.

Dusty surveyed the buildings to see if there was a way to get in. He would need to get in undetected after the people still inside had left for the day. That is, if they left. Because the buildings in the vicinity were all the same size, shape, and configuration, he could make his assessment just as easily by looking at any of them. But that would mean having to move from his position, where he could watch the front door of the target building.

There were very few windows other than those along the front of the factory. Down the left-hand side of the building, there were two small windows of frosted glass, which Dusty took to be the toilets, possibly one for males and the other for females. It would not matter which of these windows he tried to break through. The window frames were just too small for a person the size of Archibald Miller, so that was an end to that matter. If Dusty had to go into the building, he would need to go through the front door.

At the factory, things were starting to get interesting. Shortly after the ADDI had left, most of the people from the two factories began to leave for the day. The people were all collected by cars, and as far as Dusty could tell, those cars seemed to be driven by people in uniform. There were still some lights on in the building, which indicated that someone, or some people, had stayed behind. At least the gentleman who had accompanied Stephen Rodriguez from Washington had still not left the building.

He was still there waiting for, or doing, what?

Dusty had learned, and learned very well, both on covert missions with the United States Special Forces and as a lawyer, to be patient. He just waited in the lengthening shadows. He was blending into the background. Silent and immobile.

It was much later in the evening when a truck arrived at the textile factory loading bay. It had no distinguishing marks to indicate where it was from or what it was carrying, except what may have been indicated by the driver and his three colleagues. They were all carrying AK-47 rifles, and it looked as though they knew how to use them. The truck reversed up to the door while two men stood looking towards the road, their rifles at the ready. As the factory roller door opened, the driver exited the vehicle and went inside. The fourth man then began issuing instructions as the driver now appeared with a forklift truck to offload the goods.

Dusty could not see what they were unloading from his position, hiding behind some bushes. They just looked like large packages of materials.

Dusty crept closer. He took great care that his massive frame was well hidden in the shadows. And that he always had an escape route if he should need it.

When the unloading of the truck was complete, the four men, together with the one man who was already at the factory loading bay, closed the doors, and then they all went inside.

Dusty paused for a moment. The reason for his being in this place at this time was to follow Stephen Rodriguez, who was alleged to be involved in the drug trade as a dealer or as a trafficker, or both. Maybe the big boss. If either of these scenarios turned out to be accurate, and the packages that Dusty had just witnessed being unloaded turned out to be drugs, then this could be a crucial piece of information. If it turned out to be just what it looked like, a shipment of textiles, then so be it. But he had to find out.

He crept up to the door and listened.

Whatever the men were talking about, they seemed to be in a good mood. What they were talking about, Dusty did not have a clue. But he did have a DEA-supplied recorder in his pocket. He switched it on and began recording, although he did not know how good the reception was or how good its reproduction would be.

Dusty checked his DEA-issue Glock 19 handgun. He would probably not need to use it, but it gave him some confidence since he was on his own with nothing and no one to back him up.

The men appeared to be in a room just to the left of the roller door of the loading bay, and from the clinking of cups, they were obviously in some form of refreshment area. There was an access door set into the right-hand side of the roller door, and this door opened outwards. That was where Dusty headed. There were no lights on the outside of the building, and in this part of town, there were no streetlights, so the chances were even that he would be able to open this and see what was going on inside. That is, of course, provided there was no one near the door, especially someone who was holding one of the AK-47s. Dusty had a standard Glock model 19 pistol, not his weapon of choice, but no match in range or firepower for an Avtomat Kalashnikov assault rifle.

Dusty opened the door slowly and carefully, just sufficiently so that he could peer inside.

The room that the men were in had a door, the top half of which was a window. As far as he could tell, they were all seated. Therefore, they would not be able to see him. They should still be able to see the partially open door, but the odds were in his favour from their angle. However, they seemed otherwise occupied now, so he crept farther inside, leaving the door open behind him. Now he could look at the rest of the area.

Immediately ahead of him were several packages stacked to about four meters and about one meter from the right-side wall. A passage to the left of them led to double swing doors that seemed to lead into another much large area of the factory. There was another door farther to his left. This was a different door type from that, enabling entry to the refreshment room. This door had no window and nothing to indicate what was inside. The only thing that attracted Dusty's attention was the rather large numeric pad that sat on the wall beside the door. That meant that someone would need to know a combination code to gain access through this door.

The decision of what to do next was made for him. A vehicle was approaching from the north. The front of the factory was well back from the road, and the door was hidden from the road by the truck that was parked there. The chances of the driver or passengers of the approaching vehicle either seeing or being the least bit interested in what Dusty was up to were remote. However, there was the chance that the vehicle was headed right here, based on his observation that the rest of the industrial estate seemed to be devoid of life!

Dusty slipped back to the door, allowing it to swing closed, and then stealthily moved to the right side of the stacked packages. And it was just as well that he did. The lights from the vehicle gave an outline to the roller door, and then they were extinguished as the driver parked alongside the other truck and killed the motor. There was an almost-timid tap on the access door and nothing for a few seconds. Suddenly the whole room was flooded with light, the door of the refreshment room opened, and a man in a business suit strode out to the access door. The Pakistani man was about the same size as Dusty, about forty years of age, with a long black moustache. He opened the access door and greeted the visitors with not exactly the friendliest greetings. The two visitors were also Pakistani, both of them older than the other man and wearing white coats. They looked to Dusty like pharmacists or doctors, but they could have been from anywhere and been anything. They greeted their host as Mr. Shafique. Then, without any further talk, the three men walked over to the door with the security lock.

Shafique entered the code to open it, ushered the two laboratory types inside, and closed the door behind them.

Shafique rushed back into the refreshment area and ushered the four men from the earlier truck out of the building. He then closed the access door and disappeared into the factory at the back of the loading bay through the double swing doors that Dusty had noted earlier.

Dusty did not have long to wait for something else to happen. It could only have been ten minutes later that another vehicle came up to the door. The vehicle lights were extinguished, and then there came another knock on the door. Shafique again came to open the door, and this time he greeted the visitor like a long-lost brother. The only problem was that this 'brother' was dressed in a uniform. The uniform was that of a Pakistani police officer, and judging by the insignia on his shoulder, he was quite a senior one. Dusty did not know enough about the Pakistani police force to know. But he did know enough to be worried. And his cause for worry was only increased by what happened next.

The gentleman called Shafique hugged the police officer,

whom he referred to as Shoaib, then left the building and drove away in the vehicle that the officer had arrived in. But not before he had introduced Shoaib to another visitor—Edward Hennessey, the man who had accompanied Stephen Rodriguez on the flight from Washington. While it was evident that they had not met before, it was equally apparent that they had something in common. What that something was, Dusty was about to find out.

Shoaib closed the access door, went to the refreshment area, and turned off the lights in the loading bay. Then the two men opened the next entry by entering the code. They left the door open and started a more amicable conversation with the two white-coated occupants. Again, Dusty could not understand what was being said. He still had the recorder running and hoped that someone who spoke or understood the language would make some sense of it later.

Of genuine concern to Dusty was the ease with which the police officer moved around the property. This was not the first time he had visited the building, and he appeared to be perfectly at home. As indeed did the American FBI officer, who seemed to immediately be accepted as part of the group while not familiar with the surroundings.

Of even greater interest to Dusty were the contents of the room. Dusty had made several trips to Colombia. There he had seen drug laboratories, and here was another one. All the memories of that trade came into focus.

The drug, also known as diamorphine, is synthesized from morphine, which in turn is derived from the opium poppy. It is a straightforward process to extract the opiates from the poppies and manufacture any number of drugs for which the opium poppy was the source.

It was easy with the correct equipment—and it did not require much, nor did it cost much. With the necessary skill, and it only needed one person with a reasonable understanding of basic chemistry, it was easy. With somewhere secure to do it, and with the Pakistani police riding shotgun, which was taken care of.

You had the means to produce the white powder.

Heroin.

Chapter 19

Dodge City

Included in the equipment that the DEA had supplied to them back in Washington, Dusty had a miniature camera. He had no way of knowing whether the pictures would be good or bad. However, with the obscene amounts of money that the DEA spent on acquiring the latest technology, he would expect the images to be excellent and the image definition superb. From that distance and given the angle he tried to keep hidden behind the bales of materials, he did not hold out much hope of getting the ideal definition of the men. But he took numerous photographs anyway.

A drug laboratory was, after all, just a drug laboratory. And with a bit more luck, Dusty may have been able to have got a clear shot of the participants working with the drugs, which happened to include the friend of Stephen Rodriguez.

Dusty decided that he had done enough for one day. He had the connection, and the sooner he communicated that to others, the better.

Dusty now had to worry about getting the hell out of the loading bay. And then he had to get back to the relative security of his friends who were waiting for him back at the hotel.

His extraction would require some careful planning. Had he been back in New York, it would just have been a matter of ringing the NYPD or the DEA or any number of other three- or four-letter acronyms and waiting for the shit to hit the fan.

But this was Peshawar in Pakistan, and Dusty was not sure that he would gain much at this early stage in their mission by causing that kind of chaos. In any case, the Pakistan police were already here, and they did not seem likely to be of much use in arresting any of the participants. He could contact Mark back at the Pearl-Continental and ask for his opinion. He had that capability via his satellite phone. But in the present circumstances, he did not have that as an option while he was within earshot of people involved in what was an illegal business anywhere else on the planet.

Patience was the only option that Dusty had.

Shoaib, and the person whom Mark had identified as an FBI agent, stayed talking to the two gentlemen in white coats. This conversation was conducted half in English and half in some other language which Dusty could not understand. The two gentlemen in the white coats did eventually reveal their names. The smaller and older of the two was called Ghulam. The taller and younger one was called Hafeez, or Hafiz. And the guess that Dusty had made about their day jobs was half correct. They were both pharmacists. What he could not have anticipated was who they worked for. They both worked for Pakistan's Combined Military Hospital right here in Peshawar. Whether the brigadier who oversaw that hospital had the faintest idea of what his subordinates got up to when their day jobs ended was not the point.

The point was - Who could you trust in this country?

Here was a high-ranking Pakistani police officer, talking with two gentlemen who worked for the Pakistani military in a heroin laboratory. The factory that housed the laboratory had recently been paid a visit by no less a person than the assistant deputy director of intelligence of the CIA. And now they were all amicably chatting with an FBI agent who had been flown into the country on a CIA Gulfstream jet courtesy of the US Government.

What chance did the drug enforcement cell of Pakistan customs have against such odds?

The answer was, not much.

After what seemed like an eternity, Shoaib came out of the drug laboratory and went into the refreshment room. From the noise he made, he was not too pleased with the previous occupants while carrying on a shouted conversation with Ghulam and Hafeez. Dusty had no idea what that conversation was about, but at least the shouting would have improved the take on his recorder. Shoaib came out of this room carrying a tray with something in a jug and four cups and returned to the laboratory. There followed another exchange of words. And then Shoaib simply closed the door.

This was the chance that Dusty had hoped for. The only risk was that someone would return from the back of the factory at an inopportune time, but the chances of that seemed remote, so the risk was acceptable.

And Dusty almost got this one right.

Dusty eased the access door open. He crept outside as silently as was possible. Then he quietly closed the door behind him.

There was nothing outside except for headlights coming down the road. He went to the left side of the factory and hid as best he could behind some withered bushes. It was not the best hiding place, but it was the only hiding place. And there he waited.

And it was just as well that he did.

The vehicle turned into the driveway of the factory, parked by the loading bay doors, and Shafique got out. For just a moment, Shafique hesitated as if listening for something that he had heard as he looked around. Dusty could only hope. If Shafique had seen some movement in his headlights or had discerned the shape of a man against the wall, this could have become embarrassing. Dusty had little doubt that he could handle the immediate situation by brute force, if necessary, but what would be the aftermath?

After what seemed like an eternity, Shafique shrugged, knocked on the access door, and eventually, Shoaib opened it. Shoaib stepped outside, and the two men became engrossed in a somewhat animated conversation. Dusty had no idea what that conversation was about, so he turned on the recorder again. It immediately sent out a beep that sounded about as quiet and subtle as a ship's foghorn blast in the stillness of the night. The machine was presumably and helpfully informing Dusty that the battery was running low. But it did not help the current situation.

The two men standing in the open immediately whipped around and stared directly at where Dusty was hiding and at the origin of the noise. Shafique drew a gun from under his jacket.

Behind the factory was a broad expanse of open space, and then on the far side of that space, there was a row of other buildings that could be factories or other office accommodations. Dusty now had the choice to stay and probably fight or flee.

Again, the decision was made for him.

While Shoaib rushed back into the loading bay, presumably

to get his weapon, Shafique went to the vehicle to switch on the headlights.

Dusty fled.

Even in the hands of an experienced professional, a pistol is not much use against a moving target and is useless at much less than a hundred feet. The glare from the lights would do nothing to improve the situation for the Pakistanis, firing from light into darkness. And yelling in a language that the person fleeing could not understand —well, yelling in any language—achieved nothing.

A couple of shots came from the direction of the loading bay, but they flew harmlessly overhead. Strangely, neither of the men came after him; long before Dusty had made it to the other buildings, the vehicle lights were extinguished.

Now Dusty had another problem.

Where was he?

Dusty decided to head to his left from memory of the map he and Del had in their car. That should take him north and eventually to the railroad and the Grand Trunk Road. Then it was simply a matter of flagging down a taxi and heading east back to the Pearl-Continental Hotel. That is, if there were any taxis in this part of the world other than taxis that were under the control of the police.

And that was a good plan had it not been for the police. This time they were in official police vehicles.

While they did not scream around in the same manner as the NYPD, two police cars came from opposite directions on the road where Dusty had been headed. They were slowly checking the buildings on either side. Across the space to the left of where Dusty was now, there was a distinct increase in traffic, and that traffic was flashing red and blue lights.

Dusty's decision was again the only one he could make. He thumbed his satellite phone to call for help. Fortunately, the police seemed disinclined to do anything other than drive, and no attempt was made to get out of their vehicles and track the intruder on foot. Dusty was unaware of the circumstances that gave rise to this situation, but he was thankful for them, whatever they were. He could have assumed that he had been mistaken for an opportunist burglar, although it did seem to be a strange place to find one. He would just have to wait and see.

Patience.

About thirty minutes later, another set of headlights came down the road from the north. At the same time, a police car came from the south and stopped the vehicle almost directly opposite the position where Dusty was hiding. The car was the same one Dusty had been in earlier that day. Whatever the driver said to the police, it seemed to work. There was a signal from the vehicle, and while the police car drove north, Dusty recognized the driver, ran to the car, and climbed on board.

The driver was Griz.

Within twenty minutes, they were back at the Pearl-Continental Hotel. Dusty was not surprised to find that Del had failed in his part of the mission. But he was more than pleased that Griz could understand at least part of the chatter that Dusty had recorded during his evening. It did not add much to what he had observed other than to confirm that they had discovered a heroin laboratory and that some high-powered people were involved.

Mark was pleased to see his old friend come back in one piece and was more than happy that he had decided that Dusty, rather than Del, was the one who stayed behind at the factory.

Griz, who had been talking to someone at the airbase, got off the telephone and delivered some other news.

'It looks like your friends will travel to Kabul in the morning aboard the United States Air Force Boeing C-17 Globemaster. They probably don't want their pretty executive jet to get shot at by the Taliban. If you wish, we can get to Kabul before they do. It should mean that you can be organized on the ground and waiting, rather than going through the rigmarole of shadowing them. The Globemaster is scheduled to leave Peshawar airbase at about 8:30 am, so what say I get us into the air before that?'

His question was directed at Mark, who merely nodded in agreement.

But he got a surprising reaction from Del.

'What do you mean? Why would the Taliban want to shoot at a Gulfstream and not at a Globemaster? And doesn't that mean we are at risk?'

Griz looked at Del and shook his head, and his reply probably was meant to frighten rather than appease him.

'Del, in case you have not read the papers recently, a war is going on over the border. Several wars are going on both sides of the border. Shooting at things, especially American things, is what the Taliban do. They have probably given up on the Globemaster because it can handle small arms fire. The Gulfstream might be quicker and can fly higher, but when landing, it is just another aircraft, and it does not handle small arms fire too well. The security around Kabul is not too bad, but accidents can happen. You're not scared, are you?'

Mark and Dusty watched the exchange with part amusement, part concern. They could not have cared less whether or not Del was frightened. To the two guys who had been on far more dangerous missions into far more dangerous places, this was a risk that they just accepted.

And Del would have to accept it, too, because they needed him in Kabul.

'Of course, I am scared! Who wouldn't be?' Del almost shouted. 'Shouldn't we go by a more secure form of transport?'

Griz was beginning to get annoyed but managed to keep his voice calm.

'Do you want to call the administrator, or shall I? Ask him if he could arrange to add the Globemaster to his inventory because one of his agents is a wimp! You can, of course, travel by road. I would say that your chances of getting over the border and then through the Tora Bora are about nil. Still, it's your call!'

Mark decided that this conversation had gone far enough.

'Look, we know the risks. We accepted those when we signed up. Now, can we order some food, have a drink, and calm down. Del, we are going into Afghanistan tomorrow, and like it or not, you are coming with us.'

Del started to protest.

Mark waved his hands in dismissal and addressed Del.

'We have come this far. Either you are with us, or you are not. Make the decision now to come with us, or you can take the next airplane back to the US. I need hardly tell you that your career with the DEA will be over.'

Chapter 20

Division

Mark's team left Peshawar at eight o'clock the following morning. As their Gulfstream V C-37A raced down the runway of the Peshawar International Airport, they passed three Globemaster types of transport sitting on the apron in various stages of loading up, at least one of which would follow them into Kabul.

Or so they thought.

Mark had felt the adrenaline start to pump while Dusty had told him about finding the heroin laboratory the evening before, but his enthusiasm had waned somewhat at the realization that this was only the start. They did not have any tangible evidence of CIA involvement and no clue how, or *if*, this laboratory was shipping the drugs to the United States.

Suspicion was akin to making assumptions. Gathering evidence was another matter entirely.

With the people they had been assigned to follow, absolute proof of their involvement in the drug trade would be needed.

Mark had called home at about two o'clock in the morning, local time, to catch Harold Taylor at the office at five o'clock in the afternoon and bring him up to date.

He was disappointed. Harold had a prior engagement and could not be contacted, so the ever-efficient secretary at the CIA Langley headquarters had informed him. Mark had little doubt that Del would have reported to the DEA, but he was unsure what Del would tell them and what Del would not tell them.

Mark also called Debbie.

She was concerned that Mark was going into Afghanistan. That afternoon, there had been news of explosions in Kabul, and the people who blew themselves, and several other innocent bystanders, into the next life. They did not differentiate between good guys or bad guys, foreigners or Afghanis, military or civilian, male, or female.

Mark tried to assure her that he would be all right, but that reduced Debbie to tears that would not stop. She loved him, and she wanted him home. He loved her too, but how could he turn his back on what he had committed to do?

The answer was no—he could not abandon the trip for reasons that Mark would have some difficulty explaining to this emotional young lady. In his view, while women generally had a remarkable sense of loyalty and trust, they could not seem to understand the bonds between men and their commitment to each other. Neither could they know or chose not to understand the commitment men could make to a mission and a cause. Usually, the females of the species hold grudges forever, but in the present case, Mark had an insatiable urge to put things right. That meant that he would not rest until he had finally established whether Stephen Rodriguez was a crook.

However, at the end of it all, the real problem was that Mark just did not understand women.

The distance between Peshawar and Kabul is a mere 140 miles or so as the crow flies, which means they were no sooner at cruising altitude than they began their descent. It would have made more sense to drive in any other place on earth, but for three minor considerations. Firstly, the distance by road was quite a bit longer than the distance by air due to the mountains. Secondly, that would involve going through a border control manned on one side by the Pakistanis and on the other side by Afghanis. Thirdly, it was probably the most inhospitable road on the planet, with a history of roadside bomb explosions and some very unsavoury inhabitants.

The Gulfstream is only a relatively small airplane. It got buffeted around, crossing over the mountainous border, and heading into a stiff westerly wind as they looked out of the windows at the cold reality of where they were headed.

Vast areas of nothing.

The border between Afghanistan and Pakistan is marked, at least on maps, by the Durand Line. It is doubtful whether Henry Mortimer Durand, the British Foreign Secretary for India in 1893, had even the remotest idea that his plans for a demarcation line between two nations would cause so much bickering over a hundred or so years later. Why anyone would want to dispute over vast tracks of nothing would have been a mystery. But still, the people of Pakistan and Afghanistan squabbled, even though their respective governments had little or no say in what went on, on the ground. There was no rule of law. This land, so rugged, remote, and inhospitable, was governed by tribal groups who did not recognize any authority. And they had no concept of a Durand Line or any other form of limitation on where they could or could not go.

The DEA Gulfstream did not fly into the Kabul International Airport. Instead, it passed into the United States military–controlled Bagram Air Base, which was about thirty miles to the northeast of the Afghan capital. This airbase was a military establishment, and the United States forces felt significantly safer landing there. It was, therefore, the place where the Globemaster would come, bringing with it the civilian ADDI and his entourage.

Not that landing at Bagram airport was for the fainthearted. The air was buzzing with activity. AH-64 Apache attack helicopters were constantly patrolling the surrounding areas looking for insurgents who were likely to fire on any aircraft crazy enough to want to land or take off from this place. The Apache was well equipped to deal with anyone who tried—after, the insurgents gave away their position by firing something. That meant that the target would need to cope as best it could to avoid the initial attack.

Military airplanes were reasonably well protected against small arms fire. Gulfstream business jets were not. The pilot seemed outwardly calm, but even Mark and Dusty held their breath as they came to land. As the airplane cruised onto the apron, there was a combined sigh of relief from the pilot and passengers alike.

In Washington, they had been told that they would be met by another undercover agent when they arrived in Afghanistan. Mark would have assumed they would have met up with the man once they got to Kabul. No one had said who this person was an agent for or how deep undercover he was. Mark had only been given a name: Owen Squires.

And neither Del nor Griz had met him before, nor did they know anything about him.

In the uneasy silence that occurs when engines are switched off, they now had to wait for someone to follow and someone who would help them do the following. Their target was still to arrive at Bagram, and once the ADDI got himself from Bagram Air Base to Kabul, he would unwittingly decide what they all did next.

A dust-covered Hummer arrived at the steps of the Gulfstream. A guy, who looked as though he had just stepped out of an advertising poster for an al-Qaeda recruitment campaign, got out.

He could not have been much over five feet six in height and 130 pounds. He had a full beard and a grey turban around his head. His clothes consisted of a blue or grey faded shirt that came down to his knees, a pair of baggy off-white pants, and a coat that was a darker grey than the shirt. He walked with a limp, and it was clear that the limp was permanent from how he carried himself.

It came as a surprise that this turban-headed individual turned out to be the gentleman by the name of Owen Squires.

Mark met him at the airplane door and introduced him to Dusty. Del introduced himself, holding out a limp hand and saying nothing other than his name. The grip in Owen's handshake was firm, and the smile friendly.

'What is the story? Who is the boss?' were his first two questions.

Mark answered both with a question of his own.

'How much do you know already?'

There seemed to be little point in repeating something if he already knew. There was less point in telling him anything he did not need to know. At least not yet.

Owen was not the least put out by Mark's caution. He smiled and replied.

'I was contacted by the director of intelligence at the DEA, and she instructed me to assist you as best I could. That is all I know. I often get asked by the DEA, sometimes the CIA, occasionally the military to do odd jobs. I have no idea why you guys are here. If you don't want to tell me, then that's fine. I assume you're the boss?'

Mark had to smile at that. 'No, not really. Dusty and I are not officially with the DEA. Del is with the DEA, so you could say that Del is the boss.'

Body language is a language all its own. It does not matter what age, race, sex, or creed. People who can efficiently and accurately read body language have a tremendous advantage over people who cannot. Some aspects of body language can be taught. But the actual reading is instinctive or intuitive and goes much deeper than anything that can be taught in a classroom.

Mark had always been adept at reading body language, and he was pleased to see that Owen was as well.

'OK, so what is the plan?' Owen then asked. His question was addressed to Mark. Owen ignored Del.

Mark told him.

'There is a gentleman who will arrive in Afghanistan shortly suspected of drug dealing or drug trafficking. Our job is to follow him wherever he goes and find out what he gets up to and who he meets. The suspicion is that he is arranging the shipment of drugs from Afghanistan into the United States. We do not know how he does that, how the drugs get shipped, and even who his users are. We do not know how the drugs get distributed. We know five-eighths of fuck all.'

Owen looked at Mark for a few seconds, wondering if he would continue. But he did not.

He asked the next obvious questions.

'So what? We know that drugs are shipped out of Afghanistan, and we know that the United States is where most of them end up. So why not leave this to the DEA? Why the special treatment? Who is this gentleman?'

Mark paused again. The answer would seem inappropriate.

'He is Stephen Rodriguez, the assistant deputy director of intelligence of the CIA.'

Owen looked suitably dumbfounded. 'Oh shit!'

Mark smiled grimly. 'Those are exactly my sentiments.'

The two men exchanged looks before Mark continued.

'Yes. "Oh shit" just about sums it up. What I want to do now is split into two teams. You and I make one team, Dusty and Del the other. If the assistant director leaves the airbase, we follow. Dusty and Del, stay put at the airbase for now just to cover our ass. We do not know where he is going, and we don't want to take any chances of losing him. And at the same time, we mustn't be seen.'

'OK, I'm happy with that,' Owen replied in an accent that Mark could not place. It was undoubtedly English, probably northwest, but with a mix of Gaelic or Celtic tones.

'How do we communicate with each other?' was Owen's next question.

Mark pulled his satellite phone out. 'We all have one of these—satellite phones. They are superior to cellular phones. We do not have the headache of getting consistent coverage as with cellular phones, and they are hard to trace. Have you got one, or can you get one?'

Owen shrugged and smiled. 'I can get one. Are you working on the DEA network, or is the coverage random?'

'No, we are not on the DEA's network.' replied Mark. 'We are covert. The DEA may have contacted you to arrange this little job, but apart from a select few, they do not know we are here, who we are, or what we are involved in. And unless we get into real trouble, I intend to keep it that way. You OK with that?'

'Yes, fine with me,' Owen replied with his characteristic shrug, and then he became all business again.

Mark did not understand the significance of the commentor the smile, but at least he was beginning to like this guy. The body language said it all. But then, Mark had been wrong before.

The Air Force Boeing C-17 Globemaster came into land. It looked so ugly, huge, and ponderous that it seemed like a miracle that it could fly at all. The engines appeared to drag the wings down towards the ground as the aircraft trundled its way along the runway, finally coming to a halt two hundred yards from where the DEA Gulfstream was parked up.

The base ground crew immediately began unloading the C-17, and neither they nor the aircraft crew appeared to have much time to attend to their passengers. But eventually, Rodriguez came down the steps and was met by a man who looked totally out of place in the busy military facility and even more out of place in the harsh reality of Afghanistan. He was obviously some minor official from the United States Embassy. He did not speak to the ADDI—waiting, as protocol demanded, for Rodriguez to talk first.

That was partly because Rodriguez had nothing to say to someone so low in the pecking order. Partly because the guy was new and wondered what all the fuss was about —he would have expected the CIA to pick up their ADDI even though his first call would be, again as protocol demanded, on the United States Ambassador in Kabul.

The FBI agent accompanying Rodriguez off the airplane looked scared, and he hurried along behind as if anxious to be somewhere else. Mark still had no idea who the guy was, and that was something else to worry about. The FBI gentleman gave the impression that he was a *nobody*, but that could mean anything. Apart from his very brief appearance in Peshawar and Dusty's experience at the factory, he had not done anything of note. And Mark did

Mark would need to contact Harold again. Something was going on out of the left field, and Mark knew he would like to find out what it was. Cooperation between the CIA and the FBI was unusual. And Stephen Rodriguez would be highly unlikely to encourage collaboration between the two organizations at the risk of exposing the underbelly of his organization to a mere profiler. That was unless Stephen Rodriguez was, in fact, innocent.

The ADDI, accompanied by the two men, rushed through the terminal, and the embassy guy waved to a black Hummer, which moved over, picked them up, and then headed southwest towards the city of Kabul. At least that was a clear intention. The vehicle went to a staging area, where it linked up with a convoy. No one travelled alone in this country.

Dimity Lebedev was a young agent of the Russian SVR. His job was to watch who came in and went out at the United States Bagram Air Base.

It was boring, but someone had to do it.

Lebedev watched as the aircraft landed and then waited to see what happened next. As was usual, he was disappointed. Nothing happened at Bagram other than the occasional visit by some bigwig, at least on his watch, but he had a job to do. However, on this day, things started to get interesting.

He had witnessed the arrival of the Gulfstream jet. That was unusual—even the Americans would not usually risk so vulnerable an aircraft in this part of the world. That usually meant the CIA or the DEA. And he noticed that no one exited the aircraft.

Now that was strange. They were either waiting for someone, or the aircraft had come just to pick someone up.

Lebedev had seen a local Afghani drive up to the Gulfstream, which was unusual but interesting. If that is what it was, the disguise did not fool the Russian. He was dressed almost identically. And driving a Hummer was the dead giveaway, apart from the fact that he must have had ready access to the base. Trying to find out who this guy was should not be too hard. But that would have to wait.

Lebedev had then witnessed the arrival of the Globemaster C17, and apart from the normal unloading of goods that went on, he noticed two people disembarked who looked non-military and important. At least they had been met by an embassy official, so that probably meant diplomats. But they were obviously under the watchful eyes of the people in the Gulfstream. He got interested when it looked as though the people in the Gulfstream were following the Globemaster's people. A large man exited the Gulfstream, joining the raghead in the Hummer, and set off.

He made a phone call. Then he wandered over to a nondescript vehicle, climbed inside, and discreetly followed the visitors. There was no hurry. The Americans treated the most minor thing as a major event, and they still insisted on using vehicles that stood out like dogs' balls, so by the time they got organized, he would be able to find the diplomats.

Mark and Owen pulled into the traffic, a discreet distance behind the black Hummer, and followed. There was no point in considering surveillance techniques as Owen explained life around Bagram and Kabul. Although it was only a short journey, traffic was marshalled into a convoy, and the convention was that you stayed in your allotted place. And that gave Mark an inkling of just how useful his new friend Owen could turn out to be, in this case, was an Afghan policeman, and although he conversed with most of the Americans in English, he automatically switched to either Pashto or Dari when he saw Owen behind the wheel. Mark was too new to Afghanistan to know the difference between the Pashto and Dari languages. But he could read body language.

'You understand the local language?' Mark asked.

Owen smiled. 'You soon pick up enough to get by. But I would not say that I am proficient. Anyway, we are not in school. I can understand what is being said. And I never let on that I know what the locals are talking about. That way, they usually let you know what they are thinking by talking among themselves—know what I mean?'

Yes, Mark did know.

He had plenty of experience dealing with languages. In the jungles of Colombia, it was helpful at times to converse in Spanish. That way, the surprised locals would delay a second or two before firing. And that was usually all the delay that was needed. Otherwise, Special Forces used hand signals to communicate with each other.

It could, of course, work both ways. Stephen Rodriguez had been in Afghanistan earlier in his CIA career. He would probably have a crude understanding of Pashto and Dari. And, being a career spook, he also would never let on that he had that understanding. Still, you cannot worry about everything, Mark mused. Right now, his job was to follow the ADDI.

Fortunately, it was doubtful if anyone had the wit to concern themselves with surveillance or counter-surveillance. The chaos that typified the traffic in and around Kabul simply added to the problems caused by the rock-strewn roads. The frequent passage of military vehicles had worn a well-used track, but such was the arid nature of the surrounding countryside that the roads were full of potholes. That did not stop the traffic from moving at insane speeds.

Eventually, they made it into Kabul as the convoy dispersed, and the Hummer carrying the assistant deputy director of intelligence found its way through the various obstructions that surrounded the United States Embassy gates on Great Massoud Road in the Wazir Akbar Khan neighbourhood. Then Mark and Owen just parked and waited a discreet distance away.

It was again a game of patience.

Owen had arranged accommodation at a guesthouse called B's Place in the suburb of Qala-e-Fatullah, just north of the city. He had chosen a guesthouse in preference to a hotel because there would be no registration, far less hassle, and less chance of their being observed. Owen explained that this guesthouse had been chosen for no other reason than that it was owned and run by an Australian, the significance of which completely escaped Mark.

The problems of covert surveillance operations in foreign cities are not well known to the general public. The mind-numbing boredom of staring at a specific point on the landscape in case the target emerged was only a part of the issue. Staying awake was one problem; staying focused was the other. But the real problem was checking on the counter-surveillance measures that may or may not have been in place.

While Mark would need to rely on the local knowledge and experience of Owen, at least for a while until he got used to the unfamiliar environment, he did not, and could not, know anything about the local CIA or about the many other organizations that plied their trade in this part of the world. Mark could only concentrate on when the person being followed was going to emerge and, at any time, could be whisked into a car and taken anywhere. That meant that there were no more than a few seconds to recognize the target and react. That was OK if the surveillance was well resourced, with plenty of people to share the staring and keep each other awake. But this time, there were only the two of them, and only one of them was familiar with who they were watching. Even the slightest change in his appearance and this whole exercise could be a complete waste of time. Still, they had to do it.

As Stephen Rodriguez showed no sign of movement, Mark called through to Dusty and arranged some relief. While Dusty had to wait for the next convoy to be formed, it did not take long for him and Del to join up with the rest of the team. The four cycled back and forth between the United States Embassy and their accommodation in Qala-e-Fatullah throughout the day and through the night. That meant that they did not get much sleep. By the early hours of the morning, they were all dog-tired.

As far as Mark could tell, Stephen Rodriguez had not left the embassy. He began to hallucinate as he fought to maintain some form of concentration. And while he worried about what the assistant deputy director of intelligence may be up to, he also had other things on his mind. Dusty he could rely on. But what of the other two? The reason Mark had split the group the way that he had was to cover for Del, who he thought was at best unreliable.

And then there was Owen to consider. He appeared to be OK, but the fear was that he would not have the commitment to their task that Mark thought was necessary. Only time would tell. As things stood, Mark would stay with his old maxim that two was the minimum in a team and therefore had to accept that they would have only two teams.

It would take only a few seconds for the man they were following to slip out, and he would be lost, probably never to be found again—at least on this side of the world. Their mission was seriously under-resourced.

If they lost track of Stephen Rodriguez now, they may pack up and go home. At the same time, Mark had to avoid their being spotted by either Stephen himself or any of the CIA personnel that would be surrounding him. They had to assume that the CIA would have counter-surveillance measures in place, so they would also have to compete with that.

It was all just getting too complicated.

Chapter 21

Marjah

The ADDI emerged from the United States Embassy, looking nervous and on edge the following day. He was dressed in Army fatigues, with no insignia to indicate his rank or the organization to which he belonged.

Rodriguez got into a Hummer along with three other men. One was a half colonel in some Special Forces group, and the other two were at least dressed as Marine lieutenants. There was no sign of Hennessey - the man who had accompanied the ADDI from Washington. The Hummer moved out of the compound and turned north.

It did not go far.

The relief felt by Mark at seeing the ADDI emerge from the embassy galvanized all four of them, and there seemed to be a new urgency in the small band. Some luck was on their side; all four of the team were in immediate proximity when he decided to move.

Mark and Owen trailed behind the Hummer, and Dusty and Del initially took a parallel route. The intention was that they would occasionally leapfrog each other to avoid the chances of their being spotted, but that was no easy task in the winding and haphazard streets of Kabul.

Fortunately, there was dust everywhere, and it would be tough for anyone to spot a specific vehicle, either ahead or behind. No sooner had the journey started than it ended abruptly. Rodriguez got out of the Hummer outside another compound, and then the Hummer just took off, leaving him standing alone on the side of the road.

The ADDI looked nervous as he waited.

Kabul was quite different from Washington, and although he may have been familiar with the surroundings, anywhere in Afghanistan was not the place for Americans to be standing around on the street alone. So that was probably why he had dressed without any outside means of identity. Still, he was identifiable as a foreigner and an infidel, which was usually enough to make him a target. But he did not have to wait for long.

A gentleman came out of the compound and met him on the street. He was also a foreigner and an infidel. The man was tall and skinny, blue-eyed, with an unruly crop of hair, and he had not shaved for a day or two. He was dressed in a very crumpled suit, his tie barely tied around the collar of a once-white shirt. He had the demeanour of someone who had not had much sleep recently.

Body language displayed deference that suggested this guy was from the same organization, the CIA. And secondly, he was seriously outranked.

He still managed to exchange some angry words with Rodriguez. Maybe he was just plain tired, but from the body language alone, he certainly was far from pleased. Mark could not hear what their argument was about—they were just too far away. All he could do was look through his binoculars and read the name tag that hung around his neck: Ellingham, Martin – Group B.

Mark turned to Owen with a questioning look, and Owen once again came up with the answer.

'That guy is CIA. Unlike elsewhere in the world where they just use numbers, they wear their names—don't ask me why. And I have no idea what Group B means. I doubt whether he does either. It is not a clever idea to advertise that you're a member of the CIA in this part of the world, so it is a kind of disinformation. Everyone knows about their purpose of being here.' Owen added, 'The only thing they can do is change groups from time to time, to add a little confusion to an already chaotic situation.'

Mark had to ask.

'So why would Stephen Rodriguez, who is probably the most senior CIA official ever to visit this part of the world, meet with the guy outside of the compound?'

Owen had no answer to that question.

Mark was even more confused when eventually, both men turned and walked into the compound.

It turned out to be the CIA headquarters in Kabul. That was quite reasonable, given that the ADDI had, at least officially, come to this part of the world to visit such places. The two men continued their argument as they got past the security and disappeared.

Martin Ellingham could be forgiven for becoming heated in his discussion with Stephen Rodriguez. The logic of his argument should have put him in line for a promotion. But as is the way with bureaucracy, it does not pay to argue even when you are right. Especially when you are seriously outranked. More so when, with a display of impatience, you describe the person who outranks you as an idiot.

Ellingham would be unlikely to get promoted anytime soon, and he realized this. But he thought he would try, just one more time, to talk some sense into the arrogant visitor from Washington. After all, it would not look good on the Ellingham curriculum vitae if that included overseeing the death of the ADDI, unless, of course, that death could occur before any mention was made of his involvement. The only thing that Martin had in his favour was that Stephen Rodriguez had personally recruited him, and he could always fall back on the threat to reveal to anyone who cared to listen why that had happened. That, of course, would land Martin Ellingham in an even more trouble!

'Sir! United States Army engineers may have built the road south between Kabul and Kandahar, but that does not make it like Interstate 95 that you people from Washington are so used to. And having got as far as Kandahar, the roads from that point onwards, for the most part, are little more than goat tracks. That is, if you get that far. We can arrange for you to travel by air—either on a helicopter or on a C-130 Hercules transport which travels up and down between Kandahar and other places to the south daily.'

That should have done it. A major mystery is why anyone with even half his faculties intact that had access to some other form of transport would want to travel by road anywhere in Afghanistan. Except for the ADDI.

Rodriguez replied with a shrug,

'I think you are exaggerating the risks.'

One of Ellingham's other significant problems was quite simply that the ADDI would expect someone to accompany him. And knowing his luck, he would be the one selected. He tried one more time.

'Travel by road in this country is hazardous at the best of times. If the Taliban, or any one of the many insurgent groups, get the word that there is someone of your rank and in your position traveling anywhere outside of Kabul or a military base, they will try to intercept you. Or, to put it bluntly, kill you.'

Stephen Rodriguez smiled. This dumb guy did not know that the ADDI had lived and worked in Afghanistan before.

'Well, you will just have to ensure they don't find out!'

There was just no point in continuing the argument. The good news for Ellingham was that the ADDI advised him that he did not want anyone from the Kabul CIA cell to accompany him on the trip south. The unwelcome news was that Ellingham would be the one who would have to report to his masters if another body were to be produced in this never-ending conflict.

Ellingham would have some shocking news to deliver.

But not reasonably what he would have expected.

The next argument between Rodriguez and Ellingham concerned Wakil Hekmatyar, their leading supplier of drugs in the district of Marjah.

It was not that Ellingham had any qualms about Hekmatyar being killed or anyone else being killed, for that matter. His objection to what Stephen had to say on the matter was twofold.

Ellingham was confident that if someone needed to be killed, Jacob Dutton could easily accomplish that task with minimal fuss and risk to the CIA. Also, he did not see any point in exposing someone of the rank of Stephen Rodriguez to a potential entrapment should everything turn pear-shaped. Sure, Hekmatyar would be no match for the might of the CIA should that organization decide to carry out his termination. But Wakil Hekmatyar was several hundred miles away in Marjah, and in that town, he was a man of considerable influence and power. That power was not comparable with that enjoyed by a senior official from Washington DC.

But this wasn't Washington DC.

This was Afghanistan.

The Helmand province was not exactly renowned for peaceful coexistence with the Americans— or anyone else, for that matter.

Over the last week, Ellingham had investigated and analysed what had been happening with the shipments of opiates sponsored by the CIA.

What had happened was that they had quite simply vanished, so he did not have a whole heap of evidence to go on. His conclusions were therefore based on assumptions. At the very least, that alone would have made his report suspect. To an ADDI of one of the major spook organizations on the planet, which would have made his report rubbish. However, Ellingham and Rodriguez were at least on the same page.

Wakil Hekmatyar, or someone close to him, or someone familiar with his organization, or someone aware of his dealings with the Americans, had to be the source of their troubles.

Whether Stephen Rodriguez did not trust anyone else to take care of this irritation, Ellingham simply did not know. All that he knew now was that Rodriguez was leaving for the south and that he was going to travel by road.

It was when Rodriguez came to leave the CIA headquarters that things started to turn pear-shaped. As the Hummer went out of the gate and turned left, a rattle of gunfire erupted from across the road and stopped the Hummer dead in its tracks. And then, a group of roughly clothed men carrying AK-47 rifles burst out from behind a truck and began sprinting towards the vehicle they had fired on.

Mark reacted as he had been trained to. One of the insurgents was brought down by Mark's first shot from his

Glock pistol. That caused the group to break stride and turn their attention toward this unexpected interference. Their hesitation gave enough time for the driver of the target vehicle to grab his automatic rifle and bring down two more of the attackers. That caused further hesitation by the attacking group. Mark shot another in the right leg, and he crumpled to the ground, yelling something, and waving his arms in the direction that the group had been headed.

However, the rest of the ragtag band realized their hopeless position, abandoned their fallen comrades, and rapidly disappeared back in the direction from which they had come. The whole event could not have lasted more than thirty seconds. By the time the attack was all over, the force from within the compound had reacted and spread out in the street, guns at the ready.

Unfortunately for Mark, their perimeter included the area where he was parked.

Four of the Marines cautiously approached the guy that Mark had shot, pointing their semiautomatic rifles directly at him. He was still mouthing off in what seemed like a tirade of abuse. One of the Marines turned to the other three and said *Taliban!* The Marine then turned back and shouted some instructions in what Owen said was a rough version of Pashto, and that seemed to do the trick.

The Taliban guy claimed that he had taken no part in the fight and now seemed to be saying that he was an innocent bystander. This seemed to anger the Marine. He clubbed him to the ground with the butt of his rifle and quickly wrestled him to a facedown position. He then sat on the man's back while one of the other Marines trussed him up, hands and feet, and then they dragged him by the arms, feet trailing on the ground, back inside the compound.

The still-angry Marine captain then approached the Hummer, and although his initial comments were friendly, his body language said otherwise.

'Thanks for your help. Now - who are you?'

Mark had to think quickly.

He could not afford this isolated incident to jeopardize their entire mission at any stage, let alone this early. He tried his 'official' cover story.

Mark shrugged and said,

'We are DEA. I just happened to be in the area when this happened.'

The captain looked suspicious.

'We don't normally expect DEA to come out shooting or reacting as you did.'

Mark grinned.

'Sorry about that. It is hard to forget where I was brought up. And I can't tell you that; otherwise, I may have to kill you too,' he said with a laugh.

The Marine did not look either impressed or entirely convinced. Still, he nodded in apparent understanding.

'We will need to talk to you later. We have been after that low life you shot for a while. Where do we find you?'

Owen came to the rescue. He smiled at the Marine, saying.

'Just liaise with Brett O'Hara. He will know where to find us. Just mention my name. Owen.'

Mark had no idea who Brett O'Hara was, but the name meant something to the Marine because he just raised his eyebrows and then rushed off to another part of the perimeter. He had other things on his mind. Mark hoped that he would forget the whole incident, but knowing the military as he did, his action would probably be recorded in some report.

'Who the hell is Brett?' Mark had to ask.

'He is the DEA link guy in the CIA. No problems because he knows me but does not know anything about where I am going or what I am doing.'

Mark felt a cold shiver go up his spine.

Were they getting too close to the in-theatre people?

He decided to say nothing at this stage. He had known other missions fail because people make connections, often for seemingly entirely innocent reasons. He would need to watch Owen.

The vehicle that had been the apparent target retreated into the compound, and gradually, the Marine force did the same thing. It did not look as though the ADDI would be venturing out again anytime soon.

It was another Russian who had observed the whole event. Pavel Ianovsky was new to this business and did not know why he had been told to report on the movements of this group of visitors from overseas. He did not react to the attack on the CIA vehicle; otherwise, he would have blown his cover. However, he observed a change in how the CIA provided security, which he thought was quite cute. They had the usual people surrounding and looking out for someone of this guy's rank. But they also had other people riding the familiar security blanket.

From his sources, Ianovsky has was informed that his target was heading south. However, he did not know if this incident might cause a change of plan. He panicked and rang the Russian Embassy. The person taking the call was unaware that there was even an operation running. However, recognizing the panic in the caller's voice, he escalated the call and put it through to the head of station —Yuri Alexseyev.

That should have calmed things down, but it did not.

'Call Oleg in Kandahar. Let him handle it,' he said and terminated the call.

Mark, Dusty, and Owen eventually left the city of Kabul the following morning. Del was left behind in the capital on the pretext that he was needed in Kabul. This decision came much to the relief of Del, who was scared of everything in this godforsaken hellhole. It also came to the relief of the other three. There was also a certain amount of logic to it. At least someone from their party would still be alive if the convoy heading south got attacked and wiped out. Mark also had a feeling that if there was a quasi-illegal CIA operation going on in Afghanistan, it had to be controlled from Kabul. Therefore, Del would have more than enough to do to keep him occupied.

Before leaving the Afghan capital, Mark had called his father more out of courtesy than anything else. He was somewhat surprised at Harold's attitude over his decision to leave Del behind. Harold was ambivalent about the whole business, and Mark was unsure whether or not he agreed. Harold did seem a little preoccupied. He had some news about the FBI agent accompanying Rodriguez, about which he was also suitably vague. Investigations that Harold had undertaken in Washington suggested that something else was going down in Kabul that the FBI would be better equipped to handle.

He had no idea what that was.

At least he said that he would find out what it was.

At first, Mark was also unsure of the ADDI's intentions. But it soon became apparent that Rodriguez was going south with a convoy that was being formed by a force that mainly consisted of Brits, with a smattering of other European personnel. Whether the allied forces cared much about having a senior member of the CIA in their midst, they gave no indication. There was just Rodriguez, his mysterious visitor from Washington, and a couple of jarheads who were presumably to drive and protect the ADDI's Hummer.

The convoy consisted of several light vehicles, a dozen or so trucks that seemed to carry an assortment of goods, and various personnel—some in civilian clothes, some in uniform. Owen somehow managed to get the agreement of the convoy's marshal that the Humvee with Mark and Dusty aboard could join without any more than a cursory explanation that they were headed somewhere to the south. At least, that is what Owen said that he had arranged.

Mark had no reason to doubt his word.

The convoy headed out of Kabul, traveling east along the Kabul/Jalalabad highway. It turned right onto the road that led south to Kandahar on the city's outskirts.

This was the first time that Mark and Dusty had travelled any distance in Afghanistan. While they were as curious as anyone new to this part world, they were appalled by the brutal reality of the bleakness of the countryside that they were heading into. The mountains seemed to press in as Kabul and its environs, and any semblance of civilization rapidly disappeared behind them, and they headed into the unknown.

The land was virtually devoid of anything growing, so there was nothing to break up the monotonous grey and the stifling dust. The road itself was pretty new, having been built at considerable expense by the US forces and their allies. Much of the money poured into that scheme had found its way into various other pockets, resulting in a less-than-satisfactory job. The road was rapidly showing the signs of quickly becoming worn out and inadequate. There also appeared to be a lack of maintenance and repairs.

There was tension throughout the convoy as they wound their way down the valley. The road had been built with United States money and local labour to ease the transport problems between the capital of Kabul and the troublesome southern provinces. But having a reasonable surface on which to travel after the goat track that had superseded it did not ease the minds of those who knew what the journey would have in store. The trip would be through one of the most inhospitable places on the planet, surrounded by mountains teeming with insurgents and other criminal groups.

The convoy was going to Kandahar, stopping at Ghazni, Surkhi, Kharjoy, and Shahi Kalay to drop off goods and occasionally drop off and pick up people. Apart from the town of Ghazni, no place would have made it onto any tourist map. The locals in such places just stood and stared at the convoy and its members as it passed, their faces registering nothing. They did not look either curious or interested, neither benign nor threatening. The sullen look of people resigned to their fate, who hated but accepted what was happening in this their land. What could be going on in their minds? Were they wondering who would be the next to die? Maybe they were planning who would be the next to die.

While traveling on the road, the coalition forces were constantly on the lookout and on the alert. On more than one occasion, the convoy had stopped before a bridge, or a bend, or a narrow point while some armed soldiers went ahead to check that they could proceed. Bandits, insurgents, land mines—any form of interruption to their intrepid journey—were routine in this country. The soldiers knew how to search and what to look for. The Taliban and their friends had learned by observation what the allied forces would do. So, the insurgents varied their strategies. The allied troops also knew this, so they varied their methods. The allied troops were looking for what was different. It was a constant game of cat-and-mouse.

The show of force by the NATO troops might be enough to frighten off any possible attackers. However, because the soldiers were constantly on the lookout, the tension was rapidly passed down among the members of the convoy.

Even the convoy did not assure that this was either a safe way to travel or a safe place to be in.

A journey that should have been concluded in less than a day turned out to take them the best part of two days. The convoy holed up for the night at a small military compound in the town of Shahi Kalay. The reasons for the delay were common in this part of the world. Just south of Ghazni, they came upon a smaller convoy that had been held up by a curious combination of events. A couple of trucks had suffered punctures, and when they stopped to fix the problem, they were attacked by a group of insurgents. It turned out that the initial problem had been caused by an IED that failed to explode, which just made the whole exercise more complicated.

The larger convoy, of which Mark and his team were a part, arrived on the site just in time to drive the insurgents away. More precisely, the insurgents merely retreated and disappeared into the surrounding hills in the face of forces that outnumbered them and had greater firepower. It took a couple of hours to sort out that mess before the two convoys proceeded south with greater caution than had previously been the case. They had also been delayed by various amounts of debris on the road, and the allied commander checked for roadside bombs wherever there were signs of recent activity. Mark did not have a clue about what those signs were, but they patiently waited in deference to the man's experience and watched.

Mark made a point of being about two vehicles behind that being used by the assistant deputy director of intelligence and his team. There seemed little point in coming all this way to find that Stephen Rodriguez had dropped off somewhere along the way when they got to wherever they were going.

It was explained to them that the convoy could not attempt to enter the city of Kandahar at night. Even with their superior arms, the risk was just too significant. The reason given was that Kandahar was the home of the Taliban.

Mark suspected that there was more to it than the troops would say.

When they did enter the outskirts of that city shortly after midday, the tension noticeably rose throughout the convoy, and what should have felt safe after the stresses of their journey turned out to be anything but.

Mark and his small band were aware that Kandahar was still a stronghold of the many insurgent groups and had a history of trouble, which would deter tourists, many of which would deter even the most heavily armed troops. Mark was quite relieved that their stay in this city would be very short-lived, and Stephen Rodriguez seemed intent on rushing on towards the district of Marjah. Although Kandahar is by far the largest city in this part of the world, the CIA had long since given up maintaining a base here, preferring instead to have satellite cells in the outer districts, where they were not so obviously a target.

About a half of the original convoy was also headed farther south, and Mark and his team were quite happy to tag along, especially since the soldiers who left the convoy in Kandahar were replaced with more heavily armed troops.

That had its downside. In this land of contradictions, 'more heavily armed' meant that there was more reason to be heavily armed. Paradoxically, this made their convoy a more obvious target for the local inhabitants, whose attitude seemed to have changed from sullen acceptance to open hostility. Of more concern was that many of the additional troops were from the Afghan Army, which did not exactly have a reputation for reliability.

The next city they entered was Lashkar Gah. With a population of around two hundred thousand, the place was remarkably peaceful after the stress of being in Kandahar. Although the surrounding country was barren and arid, the town was built between the Helmand and Arghandab rivers, and there was evidence that the locals had at least tried to make the city liveable. Trees were planted beside the road, and the city had an air about it that suggested someone cared.

The countryside did not appear to be quite so hospitable when they left Lashkar Gah and headed southwest towards Marjah.

The roads in and around Marjah were not paved, and had it not been for the ruts caused by the passage of heavy trucks, there would have been little to indicate that there were roads. The troopers advised that they should all remain alert, as there was still the constant threat of bandits and roadside bombs. At least the terrain was flatter than it had been during the long journey south from Kabul. So at least you would be able to see if anyone was about to attack. Also, because the road was ill-defined and the ground was so hard and barren, you would be unlucky to stray into the site of an IED. Maybe.

There was again tension in the air as the convoy rushed

on through the dusty terrain as though the troops were eager to get to their destination. When they finally entered the outskirts of Marjah, the air of achievement at having got this far unscathed was mixed with an air of bewilderment, especially for the people who were having their first experience of the town.

It was as though they had travelled back in time.

Marjah was a dump.

The truck carrying Rodriguez went straight into a compound that was the local headquarters of the allied forces. While Owen and Dusty went off searching for some accommodation, Mark, having changed into clothes resembling the local population's, found a rock to sit on where he could overlook the compound and its surroundings.

The area in front of the compound gates was barren and had been bulldozed to maintain a reasonable distance between it and any homes or other buildings. It looked as though the ground had been cleared to give the troops at the compound a clear view of anything and anyone coming near them. Mark tagged it as the killing field.

A small group of young lads was playing football— *soccer* was the local term—up close to the compound walls. They seemed oblivious to the fact that there was a war going on in their country. Although the guards from within the compound kept a close eye on what the boys were doing, it appeared that was simply because there was nothing else to do, rather than looking for, or expecting, any threat.

Off to the left of the gates, sitting on a rock also watching the game, was a boy. Mark judged the lad would have been about fifteen or sixteen years old, but it was hard to tell in this godforsaken country.

Children tended to be much smaller than their American counterparts with a poor diet. And the harsh environment also took its toll. Add to that the worry about and the simple experience of constant conflict that gave the lad a complexion that made him look far older than he was. The fact that he had only one leg, probably courtesy of a roadside bomb planted by one of his countrymen, spoke of the dramas that he had encountered in his short life.

Mark could only shake his head as he mused about the mindless carnage that war inflicted on the innocent.

Then things got interesting.

The compound gates had briefly opened, and a man came out into the killing field. In Mark's judgment, he was a man in his mid-forties, tall and probably overweight. He was casually dressed, but he had that air about him that suggested he was of some importance. Probably a civilian assigned to Afghanistan in some security detail, or maybe just a maintenance guy. Whatever else he was, he was a Caucasian, yet he seemed at home in the environment.

He casually surveyed his whereabouts as though looking for something or someone. He then strolled over towards the rock where the one-legged boy sat. The pair exchanged a few words, which could have only lasted a few seconds. Then the Caucasian male abruptly turned around and disappeared back inside the compound.

To Mark, the exchange had been both unusual and confronting. Mark was incredibly good at reading body language. Something about this very brief encounter did not sit well. While the man had been casual in his approach, when he exchanged a word or two with the boy, he had the attitude of a superior talking to an underling. And the content of their conversation appeared to be important.

Whatever words were exchanged, the answer he got from the boy was in the affirmative.

Again, Mark shook his head. He was getting paranoid! He had been away from his office for too long. He was expecting something when there was probably nothing there. He stood, took one last look around the killing field, and walked away towards where he had arranged to meet his two friends.

Mark had nothing to report.

If Mark only knew.

He had witnessed one event in a chain of communication that was part of the very reason why he was here in Afghanistan.

Chapter 22

Organization

Marjah was the place where Stephen Rodriguez could begin to make some progress.

This was where the whole business started so he would commence his investigation here. The ADDI was no fool. Whether bent or corrupt, you didn't get into his position in the CIA by taking any chances. His whole life was built around planning down to the smallest detail. In the present circumstance, with so much at stake, now was certainly not the time to relax those standards.

Rodriguez had spent many years carefully building up a network, which involved several essential elements.

Firstly, he had to identify and select a few people from within his own organization - the much-vaunted Central Intelligence Agency - which had similar principles and objectives to his own. Namely, they had to be drug users; otherwise, there was just insufficient motive. And they had to be dedicated. Not to the CIA but to 'the network.' They also needed to be single so that there was no risk of them coming under pressure from their loved ones. Or anyone who might seek to use their loved ones to apply pressure, like the FBI or the DEA, to mention two organizations that might seek 'information' in this way.

And like the drug barons on both sides of the world, who could be even more ruthless.

Getting people, and retaining them, was not a problem in Washington DC. If someone stepped out of line in Washington, they could be swiftly and permanently dealt with. However, getting people and retaining them was a problem in a lawless place like Afghanistan. If one of his chosen few made a mistake or deliberately turned against the network, any disciplinary action would probably be too late. But that would not stop some form of punishment from being meted out.

Secondly, he had to identify people in the United States diplomatic service who could be trusted. Here, he had the same problems as he had with his own CIA people. Plus, an additional one.

His network required a conduit for the movement of goods. The diplomatic courier service supplied that conduit. That same conduit was so simple that it beggared belief. But diplomats are a different breed of people, so the tactics in dealing with people in the diplomatic service needed to be slightly different. They had to be low-level. At a higher level, ambition could quite easily take over, and when the promise of power and position take over, people can do strange things, especially the people in the diplomatic service.

They had to be drug users—that was a given. But unlike the CIA people, these people had to have a family back in the USA. That way, Stephen could control them and quite easily put a brutal and permanent dampener on their diplomatic, political, or other ambitions. The good news was that such people would be unlikely to be threatened by any external bodies because their involvement would be extremely difficult to detect.

Thirdly, and the most difficult and the most important,

Stephen had to have a reliable and constant source of supplies. Here, he had to look for people who had one essential characteristic. Greed. That supplier would be controllable by the sheer dollar value that their clients would be prepared to pay for the goods. That would be tempered by the massive cost that they would suffer if they were to lose the account. And, of course, the ever-present threat they could, and probably would meet a premature end should they step out of line.

From his years as station chief of the CIA in Kabul, Stephen Rodriguez had at his disposal a vast amount of data that concerned the drug trade, both in Afghanistan and elsewhere in the world. The CIA had to keep 'abreast of developments in the drug world for the simple reason that drugs, and especially drug money, were an integral part of the life of the terrorist. Not because they needed the drugs, but because they needed the money.

Rodriguez had an endless supply of up-to-date data coming across his desk about the drugs, the dealers, the money, and their networks. Drug dealers are usually loyal to the people in their network and their own customers. Admittedly, the degree of loyalty, and the direction that it took, were heavily dependent on the other factor—money. If someone were to step out of line, they were usually dealt with swiftly and permanently—a brutal Darwinian process that keeps the system working efficiently and keeps the people honest. Or as honest as can be expected during what is essentially a criminal activity, and amid vast amounts of money that keeps that system lubricated.

In looking for a supplier, Stephen had initially narrowed the field down to two options: either the Kandahar-based Ahmed Karzai, the brother of the President of Afghanistan, Hamid Karzai, or the Marjah-based Wakil Hekmatyar. Stephen had a nagging suspicion that both men were, in fact, integral parts of the same organization, but it was difficult to get a precise read on this situation.

Among the known things that these two had in common was that they were both criminals.

Consequently, they both lied.

On the first examination of the facts presented to the ADDI, there were advantages in going with Ahmed Karzai.

Karzai had immense influence because of his brother being the President of Afghanistan. And apart from that influence that the younger Karzai had in the Kandahar region, his brother could always dig him out of a hole should he land himself in any trouble.

However, that could also be a disadvantage. Ahmed was a politician. And, by all accounts, one who could not be trusted to do anything other than what suited his, and only his, purpose. There was a risk that Ahmed would see more to be gained from using the contact with the CIA as part of some political agenda at the expense of the more routine drug trade. In other words, Ahmed had too many fingers in too many pies. When push came to shove, Ahmed would side with whoever suited his plans, and no amount of money would be enough to distract him.

On the other hand, Wakil Hekmatyar was a more normal criminal with none of the political baggage that Ahmed carried around with him. Hekmatyar controlled a vast distribution network that included a large and motley collection of crooks and the appropriate elements of the Afghan police force. His sole purpose in life seemed to be the supply and distribution of drugs. Well, he was making money by selling drugs, which may or may not have been the same thing.

Hekmatyar had a reputation for being a nasty piece of

work, but that was only to be expected in his business.

Rightly or wrongly, Rodriguez had elected to go with Wakil Hekmatyar.

Now his man in Afghanistan had concluded that Hekmatyar was playing games—and that may well be so. Before anything else happened, Rodriguez needed to be sure, and that was the reason why he had decided to come south to Marjah at the start of his investigation. Stephen was not one for taking chances, and there were other people to consider as possibly being implicated, and that was a real worry.

Like the people in the CIA who were not a part of the ADDI's little scheme.

Martin Ellingham: born 10 October 1964 in the city of Des Moines in Iowa, only son of Thomas Ellingham, lawyer, and Mary Ellingham (nee Brightside), a schoolteacher. The family moved to New York in 1974 while Martin was at the tender age of ten to further the Ellingham senior's career by joining a leading firm of barristers in Manhattan. That move enabled the junior Ellingham to be educated at the New York University, initially at the Leonard N. Stern School of Business, later switching to the Global Liberal Studies program to learn foreign languages and 'broaden his view of the world.'

Ellingham was recruited into the CIA in April 1989. His mother died of cancer in June 1993. His father fatally shot himself in an alcoholic stupor in December of the same year. Ellingham himself got married. But was now divorced. That is what got him involved in drugs. And that is what resulted in his being recruited by Rodriguez and sent to Kabul.

Whether married, single, or divorced, all CIA personnel must undergo periodic psychiatric assessments, and even Rodriguez had to respect their findings. Ellingham was assessed as conscientious but unstable. The psychiatrist felt that he was upset by the untimely deaths of both his parents and that his later divorce had further unhinged the young man. The overall conclusion of the head shrinks was *these events may affect his judgment.*

Well, they would, wouldn't they?

Rodriguez's assessment: Ellingham could be the weak link and may need to be replaced. However, the facts were that Ellingham did not have all the information that he would have needed to orchestrate the disappearance of four shipments of opiates. He had expressed the view that Hekmatyar should not be trusted.

Rodriguez believed that this might be just a ploy to distract attention away from Ellingham. And the other issue was, Could Ellingham be part of a more worrying scenario? Could he have an accomplice in a plot to unhinge the network? The rationale is that the occurrences of the last few weeks would, firstly, require the input of more than one man and, secondly, require an almost-intimate knowledge of the whole scheme.

Jacob Dutton—born 27 July 1965 in the city of Houston in Texas, only son of David Dutton, engineer, and Anita Dutton (nee Wassenaar), checkout operator. Dutton moved to Washington when his mother left home for another man who would pay her some attention after she had endured over twenty years of playing a secondary role to vintage cars. Since then, there has been no contact between Dutton and his biological parents. He was educated at Washington Strayer University, graduating with a degree in criminal justice in 1990, and recruited by the CIA the same year.

Latest psychiatric assessment: a bit of a loner, not a

team player, probably destined to remain where he was, in the lower echelons of the service. The basis for this assessment: nothing concrete other than field reports submitted by Jacob Dutton's boss in Marjah, Glen Weiner.

Rodriguez made a note to check on this Weiner character; he did not sound like the sharpest knife in the drawer.

Stephen Rodriguez's assessment: Dutton was precisely the type of person he needed in his network. However, Jacob did have access to all the information that would be necessary to arrange for the disruption of the shipments. And he could also have been an accomplice and was in just the correct position to orchestrate the whole crazy deal.

That left a couple more questions. Well, riddles. Why had Martin Ellingham not exchanged his view of Wakil Hekmatyar with Jacob Dutton? Or why had Jacob not mentioned those views in his reports? And why had Martin not informed Jacob that there was a survivor from the latest catastrophe?

Surely, the survivor, Rashid or whatever his name was, would find his way back to Marjah. Unless, of course, Martin had otherwise got rid of him. Since Martin had not informed the ADDI of any such execution, Stephen could only assume that Rashid was still alive. It, therefore, made sense that Jacob would eventually find out.

Martin and Jacob were both critical parts of the network. So, had there grown a lack of trust between the two men? If so, why? Or had they embarked on a scheme to take over the network?

Then there is another issue: if Jacob could find out that Rashid was still alive, so would Wakil Hekmatyar. And that was an area where it was difficult for Rodriguez to exercise any control.

What if Hekmatyar had teamed up with Dutton, Ellingham, or both? It did not make much sense, but in the complex world of drugs, where minds were easily twisted, and motivation was always masked by innumerable complications of which money was only the precursor, anything was possible.

The task Rodriguez now faced was to find out in all this mess was to answer a straightforward question.

What was going on?

Then he could decide who he had to terminate first.

Chapter 23

Ducks

The conversation would eventually get around to drugs. Official reasons aside, the sole purpose of Stephen Rodriguez coming to this hellhole was to find out the truth of what had happened to the previous shipments.

The only known fact was that the drugs had failed to arrive in Peshawar.

He had to make sure that the next shipment did get through. To get at that truth of what had happened, he had to have a serious talk with Jacob Dutton.

But before any of that, he had to go through the mind-numbing ritual of getting briefed on matters of far lesser importance by the whole team in the Marjah cell.

Marjah was not exactly the most prominent place on the planet. Although, to the three people who made up the Marjah cell of the CIA, it was the only place. Consequently, their view of the world suffered from a severe case of tunnel-vision.

None of the Marjah cell members would have expected to meet anyone as high up in the Central Intelligence Agency as the ADDI, so they were presented with a unique opportunity to impress and be heard.

Unfortunately, the bureaucratic system was several steps ahead of them. The ADDI would not be expected to have met the three people either. But he had access to all sorts of information—some based on facts, some based on opinions, some based on hearsay.

The ADDI knew that the head of station in Marjah was like a misfit who could not wait to return to the peace and tranquillity of home. Therefore, when Rodriguez returned to the United States, he would recommend that the employment of Glen Weiner as a station chief be terminated. And that he would spend the rest of his insignificant career straightening out bent paper clips. Not quite in those terms, of course. He would probably be promoted but out of harm's way to a desk job in Washington.

That would be a part of the ADDI's impressive official report, which would justify his trip to Afghanistan. And, it would add another notch so that he could say that they were making 'progress' in improving the flow of intelligence or some other such bureaucratic rubbish.

It would also be used to placate the people down the road at the Pentagon by demonstrating that the CIA could react to situations where their staff was not meeting the military's expectations. It is a sad fact, but that is how the bureaucratic system worked. It was *the system* that caused most of the problems. But it was always individuals who paid the price of failures. Not that the Pentagon would get to read his report. Director Schlesinger could let the odd snippet of information drop into a conversation the next time someone from the military side of things chose to have a dig at the CIA.

It could enable Rodriguez to suggest the promotion of Jacob Dutton, thereby making it easier for all concerned to conduct their business in this challenging and troubled country. Not official CIA business. Nonetheless – it was business. However, before he could do that, he would need to ensure that Dutton could still be trusted.

Rodriguez also needed to be sure of the loyalties of the rest of the Marjah cell. To the ADDI, Cindy Johnston was an enigma, both puzzling and contradictory. Operations Officer Johnston appeared to be the fulfilment of everyone's dreams. Well, at least the male members of the team. But you could never quite know in this enlightened and promiscuous age. She was good at her job, doing exactly what was required of a young field agent. She was pleasant to everyone, and there was no record of her having got on the wrong side of anyone. She had stunning looks that would brighten any office. However, she did get involved in asking questions related to her areas of responsibility that were embarrassing at times, at other times, stupid.

While the President of the United States may accept that having the CIA dealing in drugs was all part of a much grander plan, at the lower level, to one who was devoutly committed to her religion, it did not make any sense. Drugs were the work of the devil. However, it was only a matter of time before she stumbled upon the actual truth of what was going on. The involvement of her fellow workers in the same trade that she was trying to stop.

Consequently, Johnston would also be mentioned in the official report, strongly recommending an early transfer to somewhere else where there would be no conflict with the ADDI's plans. That was if Rodriguez could not find a valid reason. For example, the reasons given could be that it would not be much fun for a pretty girl in such a male-dominated environment as Afghanistan and other such nonsense. It was probably good for someone's morale in the cumbersome Human Resources Division of the CIA to show that the allocation of jobs ignored gender. But the reality was it was an easy decision. Director Jim was a field operative from way back, and he would still enjoy the dig at the administrative side of his organization.

In any case, so far, Johnston had been fortunate. She had managed to stay out of reach of the Taliban. The ADDI would assess that in the field, she was vulnerable, that her appointment to Afghanistan, and especially to the Helmand province, was inappropriate. She could not advance in the service stuck in this hellhole. Rodriguez could take the view that she was completely out of her depth, and that would be the end of that. But that would also involve conflict, or at least debate, with his HR department.

Rodriguez thought this transfer would also have to be a promotion to avoid any issues with Cindy Johnston not wanting such a move or prevent the accusation of gender bias. Such is the way that all bureaucracies work, although in this case, Johnston was quite clever, as well as good-looking.

Still, the FBI's Edward Hennessey should look at her case and see what reasons they could come up with for that transfer. And in Hennessey's case, there was no danger of any gender bias. Cindy Johnston could try to work her female magic without knowing that this guy brought a whole new meaning to the term *Getting into your pants!*

All of this ignored the real issue. What would the head of station have to say about the transfer of his girlfriend? Still – the ADDI's plan also included the removal of Weiner, so the issue would not arise – would it?

Edward Hennessey was here in Afghanistan to do several jobs. For the FBI, he was tasked with finding out whether the CIA team in Afghanistan was responsible for intelligence leaks to the Taliban. The Pentagon had asked for the FBI's involvement out of sheer frustration at the efforts of the CIA to provide an answer other than *'It is being looked into.'*

This translated into *'It is none of your business'* hence the frustration. Despite the bad feeling between the FBI and the CIA, the FBI director had been reluctant to get involved. That was until he was told by the NSA, in no uncertain terms, to butt out.

The NSA had raised the director's hackles even further with the advice that Stephen Rodriguez as ADDI was going to investigate. That meant the matter would be handled *in-house* by the CIA. Having recently crossed swords with Rodriguez and not being particularly impressed by him, that raised a flag. It raised several flags, not the least of which was the obvious question - How could the ADDI investigate his own organization without prejudice?

For this reason, the director had decided that FBI involvement was necessary. The honey trap that the FBI came up with to deal with the Rodriguez case was quite comical. They could not have asked for a better outcome. The FBI had simply said *'Yes'* to a request for assistance. And here was Edward Hennessey, at the request of Stephen Rodriguez, doing the job that the Pentagon had asked for.

As far as the CIA was concerned, Hennessey had been asked to provide profiles of the CIA people on the ground. The purpose had nothing to do with leaks, although that fact had not been communicated to Edward. It had more to do with competence, or rather, incompetence. Hennessey was tasked with providing information on whether

CIA operatives were suitable for the task—a task for which they had been selected and extensively trained at spy school. Therefore, any reasonable person would conclude that the people must be failing in handling information. It was doubtful that this did not involve passing it on to someone other than, or in addition to, the people they worked for.

This suggested that the CIA, Stephen Rodriguez, or both already knew where the leaks were occurring. If so, were they looking for other reasons to move the players, or the playing field, to avoid having to admit the failure of their organization?

Or were they looking to shift the blame?

And now, the task had taken another interesting twist. Edward Hennessey had no choice but to participate in social drugs to maintain his role in befriending Stephen Rodriguez. Heroin was Stephen's drug of choice. And the profilers of the FBI missed a trick – so it was with Edward!

The meeting finally ended, with everyone satisfied that they had dealt with all the issues.

None of the issues raised by Glen Weiner about the lack of resources to enable him to do the job properly would go any farther. Neither would Weiner.

The various issues raised by Jacob Dutton about the problems of recruiting agents—or to be more correct, retaining agents—would be filed under *Things we already know about life in Afghanistan.*

The issues raised by Cindy Johnston about the apparent impunity of the drug lords were important stuff because they included names and, therefore, would be entered in the files, at least for the ADDI's own reference. Rodriguez already knew the person's name that the CIA— or to be more correct, the CIA drug network—was dealing with, but you could never have too much information.

Nothing in the meeting would have drawn any attention to Wakil Hekmatyar, but Rodriguez began to form the view that he should be looking beyond his own organization. If Hekmatyar, not CIA people, were the root cause of Rodriguez's current problem, they would need someone else to take Hekmatyar's place. Considering the need-to-know basis of the operation, it was sure that Hekmatyar would need to have an accident to get him out of the loop.

Rodriguez was unsure how such things could be arranged in this part of the world. But he was sure that it could be. This minor side issue would not go into the report since it was not raised.

After the meeting, Jacob Dutton offered to show the ADDI around Marjah. And Glen Weiner was pleased to let him.

Both Rodriguez and Dutton were pleased to get out of there. And Weiner was happy to see them go. While Stephen Rodriguez was pleasant enough, the stress he brought to the table was too much. Johnston was pleased to meet so high-ranking a person in the CIA and was in awe of his clear understanding of the issues. But she cringed at the attitude of her boss. On the other hand, Jacob appeared to be just too dumb and subservient.

Rodriguez and Dutton got into a Humvee and left the compound. The relief both men felt was palpable.

But for different reasons.

Naeem made a mental note of the departure from the compound of two Western gentlemen. He knew Jacob. He had no idea who the other man was. He only knew that he was the senior of the two and that the man was aggravated about something.

Dutton drove out to the eastern outskirts of the area and finally stopped the vehicle a few hundred yards from the warehouse where Wakil Hekmatyar did his business. There he waited for the ADDI to break the silence.

'So, what is your take on Glen Weiner?'

Dutton thought for only a moment before replying.

'He is OK as a boss but hopelessly out of his depth. At least he still knows what his dick is really for, other than pissing through it,' Jacob added with a laugh. May as well spice things up now he was out of range of the 'office.'

'What are you saying?'

'Glen and Cindy are having it off. You can't keep a thing like that a secret in this place,' Jacob replied, knowing that bit of news had two reasons why Glen would be fast-tracked out of Marjah, probably closely followed by Cindy. But in opposite directions.

Rodriguez just nodded and picked up his sat phone. 'Weiner and Johnston, you started yet?

The answer he got was obviously No.

Dutton had no idea who he was talking to.

'OK. Just a heads up. They are an item. No moral issue, but a company issue. You know what you have to do.'

Then Stephen killed the call, and he just carried on talking.

'OK. It looks like we need a change of plan,' Stephen began. 'What do you know about Hekmatyar's operation?'

Dutton was not about to fall into the trap that the ADDI had planned. He did not know that Rodriguez had reason to suspect him of any wrongdoing. He was confident that there was no reason for the boss to suspect him of anything. However, he was smart enough to realize that there was a problem, and Rodriguez was here in Afghanistan to sort that out. That was not Jacob's job, and he wasn't on a pay scale that warranted him making executive decisions. So, his reply was non-committal.

'Wakil Hekmatyar is a small-time crook. But in this town, he calls most of the shots in the drug business. I believe that he gets his orders from Kandahar, and I also believe that he is tied up with Ahmed Wali Karzai.'

Now that was something that the ADDI did not know. He had suspected that Hekmatyar was not alone. But not that there was any link with Kandahar.

'When is the next shipment due to head north?' Stephen asked without indicating any concern at what Jacob had said. Or, more correctly, apparently oblivious to what the hell Jacob was talking about. Hekmatyar and Karzai were competitors! But there was another issue at play.

Ahmed Karzai was only the brother of the Afghanistan President!

People in the CIA are trained to hide what they already know. They are also trained to know when someone else is hiding something, but life can become too complicated if you overthink!

Jacob had got the message at this stage: Stephen did not know who he could trust.

'We were waiting for you to give the word on the next shipment,' Dutton replied with a shrug of the shoulders. 'I have tentatively planned for the shipment to be in a convoy which should leave in about two days—the same convoy that our friends the Tajiks should travel in. The timing is perfect, and we may as well keep them all together.'

The ADDI was thoughtful for a moment. The CIA was under pressure from several sources. The United States Government was committed to ending the drug trade in and from Afghanistan. But they had a snowball's chance in hell of ever achieving that. The DEA's efforts in this part of the world, while launched with much fanfare to the American public, were a token at best. And they were grossly under-resourced. The facts were that the CIA did most of the work on the ground, and everything that happened in Afghanistan and elsewhere eventually made it to Stephen's desk at Langley. So, there was pressure, but manageable pressure.

Rodriguez could not stop people from finding out about the workings of the drug trade and its distribution networks. Or stop them from coming up with plans to deal with them. And as the ADDI of one of the most feared spook organizations on the planet, he had to be seen to welcome those plans with as much enthusiasm as he could muster. That simply meant that he had to continually change how his own network operated. Stephen was leading a double life, and that duality brought complications.

The real pressure came from people who were in his drug network. Nothing had happened to stem the flow of massive quantities of drugs into the United States, where there was an insatiable appetite for anything that people could inhale or inject for a moment's escape. And there probably never would be. However, that was no concern to Stephen. What had happened was that someone had stopped the flow of *his* drugs.

So, who was it?

While he did not know yet who it was, it was clear that someone was targeting shipments, and he was caught up in that. But someone could be applying pressure. Was that pressure being applied by Wakil Hekmatyar? Could Hekmatyar be replaced by someone more reliable if that was the case?

Meanwhile, the Tajiks and their little scheme to terminate their president's life was a small matter that either worked or didn't. Stephen had much more important things to worry about than that.

'What are the chances of setting up a meeting with Wakil, with just you and I?' Stephen asked.

Dutton was surprised by the question.

'I am sure he would be extremely pleased to meet you. He must be smarting from not receiving full payment for the previously lost shipments. We have so far been treated as a special customer, but you know how the drug business works: no money, no drugs. We have reversed that to no drugs, no money. Consequently, our friend Wakil is pretty annoyed,' Jacob replied reasonably.

Stephen snarled, 'Who set up the shipments? Wakil did! The drugs fail to arrive, so he doesn't get paid. End of story!'

'I had better arrange a meeting,' Jacob offered.

There was no point in arguing about it. Jacob Dutton knew where this was leading. And either Wakil Hekmatyar or Stephen Rodriguez, or both, would be even more pissed, sooner rather than later.

While at one level in this crazy business, the significant players rarely, if ever, met, there could be few secrets at that level. The CIA, represented by Rodriguez, was the customer, and Hekmatyar was the supplier. If these two came to a disagreement, things could turn real nasty – and quickly.

hey drove farther down the road and then parked their Hummer by an intersection. Most Hummers do not have an ignition key. In the military, with all its precision and attention to detail, where everything had its place, they made an exception to the design of military vehicles. If you were in the middle of a battle and wanted to get the hell out of there, there was no time to worry about who had the keys. So, the vehicles typically had a red button.

Jacob's Hummer, however, was modified back to the original specifications, so he was able to lock it up.

They walked to the east, the equivalent of two blocks

down the road on the left of the intersection. It was not like Washington DC. It was not like anywhere else on Earth. Buildings were haphazardly located on sections of land with no apparent building standards to comply with and indeed minimal regard for architectural elegance. They finally came to a building that could have been anything in a past life. Now it was devoid of signs to say anything about its inhabitants or purpose. It was just a rectangular building with a heavily fortified door. There were no windows at a low enough level that anyone could peer inside. The whole place was badly in need of some maintenance.

If Dutton was intimidated by anything in this environment, he did not show it. He just walked up to the door and hammered on it. There was no reply. Rodriguez started to go down the side of the building, presumably looking for some other entrance or signs of life. Jacob let him waste his time. There was no point in him becoming the target of another outburst from his boss. By the time Stephen had circumnavigated the building, to no effect, Jacob had chalked a sign at the side of the door.

Then he shrugged.

'Wakil will contact us when he is ready.'

The two men shuffled back to their vehicle. One of them was content: Jacob was used to the pace of life in Afghanistan, and he was used to the paranoiac suspicions and the arrogance of drug dealers. The other was wild: Stephen was used to having things done when he said so and was used to the subservience of those who did his bidding, both CIA and non-CIA.

It was well into the evening when the call came through to Dutton. The whole conversation was conducted in Dari, with the odd smattering of English when names were used. Rodriguez did not mind. He could not remember whether he had told Dutton that he had a good command of the local languages and was not about to tell him. Jacob explained to Hekmatyar what was required, and there was no deviation from what he would be expected to say. Wakil agreed to meet with them at 9:00 pm later in the evening. But not at the usual warehouse. They would meet in a remote area northeast of the town on the road to Lashkar Gah. And Wakil would meet with them provided that three conditions were met: they came alone, they came unarmed, and there would be no surveillance from the air.

Dutton agreed to meet. But it would not be at the place or at the time suggested by Hekmatyar. They would meet at a place about five miles to the south of Marjah. Jacob agreed that there would only be the two of them, and he said they would meet the rest of the Wakil conditions.

In this part of the world, the term *armed* meant that you carried enough firepower on your person to start World War III. Handguns were a type of weapon that generally were not understood in Afghanistan, and therefore they did not count. After all, handguns were useless over a range of more than a few feet, and most people in Afghanistan would not dream of getting that close to anyone they wanted to kill.

Unless the plan was a suicide mission.

It had been the ADDI's idea to arrange the meeting at a different place and time because that was the way he had been trained to think: never give the other party the advantage of choosing *where* and *when* you met.

Dutton thought the idea was profoundly stupid but kept the thought to himself. Hekmatyar would turn up—there was potentially plenty of money at stake—but he would turn up about an hour later than the 10:00 pm that

Stephen had suggested. That was just the way business was done. And the person that Wakil was to meet was only an assistant and a deputy director. In any case, such titles did not mean much to those outside the bureaucratic jungle.

Rodriguez had another angle on what was going on. He was becoming more confident that he had found the guilty party. The manipulation of the time of the meeting would be just a distraction. The selection of the place was probably reasonable. Stephen could not know whether anyone would be following him or Jacob. Therefore, it would be a clever idea to be able to observe the observers, and a long, flat road would achieve that.

From Wakil's point of view, he would know that the CIA would know where he carried out his business. Then they could have quite simply met with him at his warehouse. But so would just about every man and his dog in the Helmand province know where Wakil operated. There would always be someone watching, so he would not want to be seen meeting with any of his clients and certainly not anywhere near his office.

Rodriguez and Dutton left the compound at 9:00 pm in a nondescript truck. They got to the intersection where they had earlier turned left to get to Wakil's warehouse, and there they turned right. They drove on an ill-defined track through land barely cultivated for about five miles, pulled over, and turned the truck around. Then they stopped at the side of the road near a gateway that must have provided access to a farming property. There was not much point in having a gate because there was just nothing else to distinguish the confines of the property that it provided access to. The gate straddled a rough track that disappeared into the distance, seemingly leading to nowhere. The land was flat and featureless. They had chosen the ideal spot for the meeting. No one could approach them from any direction without being seen. And anyone wishing them harm was unlikely to have a truck that could outrun or outgun their vehicle.

For now, they were pretty safe.

It was bitterly cold, and the truck had nothing in the way of a heating system, so as soon as Jacob turned the engine off, the coldness began to creep into the cabin. Initially, adrenaline offset the cold, but that would not last. There was nothing to the south of where they had parked, and it was most unlikely that any traffic would be on the track at this time of the night. Facing north, they would be able to see any vehicles coming from the Marjah area. If there were more than one such vehicle, they would abort the meeting.

There was still no sign of Wakil as 10:00 pm came and went.

Jacob sat there patiently waiting, getting colder and increasingly worried. Stephen became apoplectic as 10:30 pm passed.

'Is there any point in staying here?' Stephen asked in an accusatory tone. 'He is not going to turn up, is he?'

Dutton sighed.

'He will turn up. My guess is 11:00 pm.'

'Why?'

Jacob again sighed. 'You were the one who wanted me to change the time. So, I did. So now Wakil will want the final say. He will come but on his terms. Wakil is simply making a point.'

Stephen muttered under his breath but held his peace.

A little before 11:00 pm, lights could be seen coming

along the road. There was nothing on the road other than the one vehicle, and as it came closer, the headlights picked out the CIA truck parked up on the side. When it was 200 yards away, Jacob turned on his ignition and flashed his headlights twice.

The approaching vehicle flashed the lights once it cruised to a halt fifty yards away and switched off the engine.

And then waited.

Dutton alighted from the truck, telling Rodriguez to stay where he was, and moved towards what was a battered Toyota wagon. For once, Rodriguez kept quiet. This was the crucial piece in any negotiated meeting and the time when there was the greatest danger. That is what you had minions for, so Stephen waited tense and apprehensive as Jacob moved towards the other vehicle.

Stephen's hand was never far away from the Glock 19 pistol, which he would use to defend himself should things turn ugly. He may also have to use it to protect Jacob, but that, of course, was very much a secondary consideration. His primary consideration would be self-preservation.

The door of the Toyota opened, and a man got out dressed in Western clothes. This was probably Wakil Hekmatyar. He did not move towards Jacob other than to just rest on the hood of his vehicle.

Jacob walked up to him, and they shook hands, as is the American custom. Nothing even remotely suggesting friendship made it to the eyes of either of them. The reason Wakil showed no emotion was quite simply because Jacob was just another customer, and there were countless more who were equally disposable. The reason why Jacob showed no emotion was more frightening. Wakil had brought some friends who were hiding in plain sight in the back of the Toyota.

They were armed. And they looked likely to fire first and to ask questions afterward.

Jacob smiled because there was no other choice. He thought of speaking in Dari out of deference to Wakil's appalling English. But that was not a good idea, especially with the paranoid Stephen waiting nearby.

'I see that you have taken the usual precautions! There is no need for that. I understand your concerns, but unless your friends put their weapons away, then this meeting is over. The boss wants to talk about the next shipment. I am sure the discussions can be amicable. Are you prepared to talk, or do we take our business elsewhere?'

That got a reaction.

Hekmatyar looked around, and Jacob sensed, rather than saw, increased tension in the man leaning on the vehicle, and particularly in the men still seated.

'Where else would you go?' Wakil asked. His tone of voice gave away the fact that he was worried.
But there was an implied threat, which made Jacob cringe.

Jacob again smiled. Dealing with drug dealers was like singing from a hymn sheet. You say this; they say that. You do this; they do that. You upset them; they kill you.

But not before they have exhausted all means of screwing the last dollar out of you. A dollar that should not be allowed to go to anyone else.

'Come on, Wakil. Your last four shipments have not exactly gone according to plan. Therefore, my masters would want to look at alternative sources—unless, that is, we can sort out what has been, at least until now, a good and lucrative arrangement for both of us. So at least talk to the man!'

Wakil was in a tricky situation. He had arranged for

one shipment that was supposed to end up in Peshawar to be intercepted. He had to do that to meet his commitment to a new Chinese buyer, so that shipment had simply kept going north and had not taken a right turn at Kabul and made it over the border into Pakistan. That was supposed to have been an isolated incident that could always happen in this wild, corrupt country. Accept it and move on. But another shipment had been genuinely stolen due to the stupidity of his own people.

Even so - Why did the Americans want to make such a big deal out of it? This was a risky business, and mistakes happened! But then he had heard stories about the Americans - they did not like their arrangements to be interrupted. So, their next shipment would go through no matter what. In thinking his way through all the ramifications, it was far easier for the Americans to have Wakil refine the drugs in Marjah, and that would be the end of all this nonsense. And that, of course, would be ideal from his point of view, because he would make even more money. But the first thing that Wakil had to do was to save face.

He moved closer to Jacob and almost whispered.

'I can guarantee the next shipment. Cannot we just get the shipment underway? We will increase the number of guards and pass the word that it is not to be touched.'

It is always the eyes that give a clue. What was Hekmatyar not saying? What kind of guarantee could anyone give, especially after the previous shipments had simply vanished? An increase in the number of guards he could do. Passing the word that the shipment was not to be touched would make it about as far as the outskirts of Marjah. Therefore, it appeared that Wakil knew more about the earlier shipment going 'missing' than he was prepared to admit.

Maybe Stephen Rodriguez was more competent than

he looked.

Maybe Wakil Hekmatyar was double-dealing.

'Wakil, I think you need to talk to my boss and assure him of what can be done. Only he can give the word on the next shipment. Only he can release any money. He will not do so unless, or until, he has a meeting with you. You and I know each other, and I do believe you.'

Dutton hoped that the apparent lie was lost on Wakil. Jacob continued hoping that this little chat did not end in a firefight.

'My boss is from Washington, and he gets paranoid about committing to anything without first meeting those he is dealing with. So do us both a favour. Talk to the man, and we can put this behind us.'

It was inevitable. Wakil would take his time, save face, and appear to be considering what Jacob had suggested.

Eventually, Wakil agreed.

He turned to his guards and made a brief signal which caused them to at least conceal their weapons.

Jacob signalled to his truck, and the ADDI cautiously came to join them. Before exiting the truck, Rodriguez had secured his Glock inside his jacket, where he could instantly retrieve it. Not that it would do him much good. It was not as though he was adept in using firearms, And the CIA rarely got involved in a firefight. However, on this occasion, Stephen was not on CIA business – was he?

Rodriguez was a relatively small man who relied on his position in the CIA to impress. Out in the boondocks, on a cold night, in the middle of this war-torn country, which did not count for much.

He walked up to Hekmatyar, shook hands, and then waited. The two men eyed each other suspiciously. Neither seemed impressed.

Finally, Jacob grew tired of this posturing and simply commented.

'Wakil says that he can guarantee our next shipment will go through.'

Rodriguez held the gaze of the Afghani drug dealer. How many men had he stared down in his long and illustrious career? He looked straight into Wakil's eyes and read the body language better than most, despite their distinct cultures.

This guy was scared. But of what? Was he scared of losing the business? Or was he lying? And therefore, scared of being found out?

Rodriguez decided that there was no point in maintaining the apparent charade. He surprised both men as he spoke in fluent Dari.

'What say we pay you now for the shipment? The only other difference is that we take it ourselves to Peshawar. OK?'

It was now Jacob Dutton's turn to be apoplectic. This was not the United States. It was not as though they just had to link up with Interstate 95 and cruise through. There was some seriously hostile territory around Marjah. There was even more hostility around the major city of Kandahar, which was virtually under the control of the Taliban. If they got that far, the border territories between Afghanistan and Pakistan were worse. Unless the ADDI had some serious troops at his disposal, taking the drugs through without local help would be virtually impossible.

Stephen Rodriguez had not thought to bounce his plans off Jacob, which was a mistake.

It would have been an even bigger mistake for Dutton to contradict Rodriguez in front of this drug baron.

Jacob said nothing.

For Hekmatyar, he had been presented with an excellent opportunity. Wakil was fully aware of the severe risks that this American idiot was prepared to take. Yet, if Rodriguez was ready to pay upfront, why should Wakil care? His only concern was how he got the money and how much.

Wakil could not hide the relief, which Jacob noted. He had no idea if Stephen had noticed. In all probability, he had.

Hekmatyar simply nodded his agreement.

Rodriguez was all business.

'OK. We will transfer the funds tonight and collect the shipment tomorrow.' He then continued as though a response was not necessary.

'The usual conditions on the funds will apply. The bank will need authorization from me, which I will give them when we receive the goods.'

The United States controlled the bank that he was referring to through a complex web of shareholding held in any one of several holding companies. But that did not matter. They only dealt with money, and the rules were relatively simple and religiously enforced.

Money was transferred by one party and was held in trust on behalf of the other party until it could be released. If it was not released, it just sat there. The money was used to buy drugs did not matter either. The sums were too significant to worry about what they were being used for. Like with most things, when large sums of money were involved, there was an honour among the parties.

The two men shook hands, and Stephen and Jacob turned to go back to their truck. While they walked, Jacob could feel the hairs on the back of his neck rise, as though an electric shock had touched them. Any moment, he expected to hear the crack of a rifle; but all those years of of training and then dealing with these people demanded that he walk rather than run.

No shot came.

While the two Americans drove back the few miles to the compound, Jacob was tempted to ask if there was something more that he needed to know about the ADDI's plans.

Dutton thought better of it and held his peace.

Eventually, the boss would need to talk to him

Oleg Demidov watched as the two men drove away. But he did not follow. They appeared to have done a deal. Otherwise, why had the American shaken hands with that slimeball Wakil?

But right now, he was more interested in the other party.

That Jacob Dutton should arrange to meet Wakil Hekmatyar in the dusty outskirts of Marjah was typical of the CIA mindset. They needed to have these clandestine meetings in obscure places and at weird times of the night to justify their existence in the spook business.

As far as Demidov was concerned, this meeting could just as easily have taken place at the warehouse in town. This was not Washington DC or New York City! Being out in the middle of nowhere in the late evening was a sure sign that you were up to no good. And it did not need anyone to be particularly observant to be able to track them.

Demidov had been too far away to overhear the conversation that had taken place. But he was intrigued by the gentleman who had accompanied Jacob Dutton. That gentleman had been seen around the compound and around Marjah for the last day or so, and he appeared to be someone from the CIA, either from Kabul or elsewhere, just visiting. But now, he had come to a meeting with Wakil, which set off a whole new set of warning signs.

Who the hell was he?

Then there were the other two people who appeared to be following. They were an odd couple. One was a big guy, very fit and serious looking; the other was a small energetic man who dressed as though he were a local. But they were both white, and everything about them said that they were American or European.

What were they doing in this remote place?

Spying on the CIA?

Demidov could only speculate. What if some other branch of the unwieldy United States bureaucracy was investigating the goings-on in Marjah? Maybe it was someone from the DEA's counternarcotics division. Now wouldn't that be a hoot?

He did not know that much about how the DEA operated. The Americans had sent out a couple of teams to Afghanistan that some bright spark in the bureaucratic jungle had decided to refer to as foreign-deployed advisory and support teams, known by the acronym *FAST*; although which came first when the bureaucrats thought that one up, the acronym or the name, was anyone's guess.

The question was, Was the DEA taking an active interest in the CIA dabbling in the drug business?

He made a mental note to make some further inquiries. Although the DEA had abdicated its responsibility somewhat by letting the Pentagon control its resources, they were nonetheless a serious threat to anyone in the drug business. And how much did they know?

If they knew of Dutton's arrangements with Hekmatyar, then that could be the end of the matter. And maybe Ahmed Karzai should back off in his attempts to muscle in on this trade. After all, there were plenty of other opportunities.

He must mention that to Yuri the next time they meet. And he would also advise him about the surprise involvement of the Tajiks, which Demidov remembered he had promised himself that he would do. Still, there were other things to do first.

The following morning, Rodriguez and Dutton took the same truck to the warehouse they had visited the previous day. This time Hekmatyar was there, and they quickly transferred the required number of packages into the truck.

The financial transaction that Stephen had implemented overnight had been confirmed. It was a miracle that Wakil was able to get confirmation because he had shown no aptitude for using the electronic gadgetry that made such things possible. But he seemed more than happy to accommodate the American plan. He had been paid. And he did not worry about delivery.

It all seemed too good to be true. The Americans must have been desperate. And his longstanding arrangement was still intact.

But then things started to turn pear-shaped.

It was only a throwaway line that caused it.

Once again, they shook hands—more a formal gesture than indicating that the two men shared a friendship.

And then Stephen simply stated,

'We may be in touch about other shipments in the future.'

That statement was just a statement of fact. But the interpretation that Hekmatyar placed on it caused him to shudder with rage. Did the Americans plan this as the last shipment? While the arrangements he had made many months before had involved more than a few problems, it had been very profitable for Wakil. So lately, he had lost a shipment. And that was annoying. But Wakil was buying the opiates for next to nothing, so he had lost nothing. He would have lost face if he had been dealing with Afghanis, but the Americans had no worries about that kind of nonsense. On the other hand, his business with China was in its infancy, and face did matter.

The Chinese were much more business-like than the bumbling Americans, and *face* was a major issue with them. But they could and did, switch suppliers without any warning. And without any apparent reason. And they drove a much tougher bargain.

Therefore, it was crucial to Hekmatyar that this lucrative trade with the Americans be retained. He thought he knew how he could do that. He knew that Jacob worked for the US government. He knew where Jacob worked and knew who he worked with—that incompetent Glen Weiner and that interfering bitch Cindy Johnston—so it was not too difficult to work it out.

This Stephen Rodriguez, or whatever his real name was, was obviously Jacob's boss and equally obviously was carrying on in a manner that hardly reflected the stated policy of the United States Government.

So, the Americans were vulnerable.

A wicked sneer crossed Wakils' face as he posed a simple question.

'You are not planning on more shipments? I have fulfilled all of your requirements, have I not?'

The ADDI was anxious to get away from this horrible little man and was not in the best of moods. Usually, he would have left all these dealings to Dutton. But he had to get the goods flowing again. That was why he had taken control of the matter.

When he thought about it later, he would realize that he could have been more diplomatic in his response. As it was, his response was mild.

'Wakil, we have to make a business decision based on several factors. Jacob will contact you should we decide to continue our arrangement.' And he left it at that.

'I have a great deal of influence in this trade,' Wakil began. 'And I have friends in Kabul.' He sneered.

So, Wakil Hekmatyar had friends in Kabul!

Well, we have friends in Kabul too, and they just happen to be bigger than yours!

Rodriguez just waved at Wakil and indicated that their conversation was at an end.

Wakil's face turned ashen and then turned red as the anger welled up inside him. This arrogant American needed to be taught a lesson.

As they drove up the road, Rodriguez realized that he would not need to see Wakil Hekmatyar again.

The little weasel should know better than imply a threat to the Americans.

The decision was made.

Stephen Rodriguez would ensure that Wakil was silenced.

Chapter 24

The Wagon Train

Mark Taylor was perplexed by the latest movements of the people they were following.

Stephen Rodriguez and Jacob Dutton were heading in the direction of Kandahar. That was reasonable and was to be expected. They had gone to great lengths to ensure that they and the truck's contents were part of a well-protected convoy heading north. That was also reasonable given how people travelled in this country.

So why had they again gone to the Marjah warehouse?

That was unreasonable.

During the last couple of days, Mark, Dusty, and Owen had been watching the ADDI. They wanted to find out as much as they could about his movements, and they wanted to know who he had been meeting with. It would have been nice to have had someone on the inside to find out what was being talked about.

Just keeping track of Rodriguez was challenging work.

They were able to gain some access to the compound

in their role as DEA officers, but they had to be careful to maintain a low profile. Mark had been able to ascertain through observation and with a bit of help from loose tongues of people both within and without the compound, that there were three members of the CIA stationed in the Marjah compound.

Knowing how the CIA worked, they probably had some other people working in the area. But they would be covert and beyond Mark's means to identify them. Such agents could have been recruited locally, but they were probably just Americans who would be working covertly.

While anywhere in Afghanistan would be bad, the Helmand province was probably the worst place in a country to be operating. The area was not exactly peaceful. And there was the ever-present problem of infiltration by the bad guys. Infiltration into the Afghanistan Armed Forces. Infiltration into the Afghanistan police. More significantly, infiltration into all forms of local governance. There was even a suggestion that there could be infiltration into the allied forces. That one was just too difficult to even think about.

And then there was the question of why.

At the level of governance, infiltration would involve the Taliban and an attempt to grab power. At the level of Marjah and the individuals involved, infiltration could mean many things, the paramount one being corruption.

At least the CIA was doing a reasonable job of making life difficult for the Taliban and the countless other insurgents, or just straight criminals, who sought to upset the best-laid plans of the officials who thought that they were in charge. And to do that, they had to be undercover. Whether the ADDI used such resources, Mark had neither the time nor the means to find out. All that he did know was that he and his small team were seriously outnumbered and keeping track of what was going on was difficult.

Against this background, following Stephen was not so bad.

Everything about Marjah was chaotic by Western standards. And because there was no normality or pattern, Mark and his team could hide in the chaos. Still, they needed to be careful. The three of them had changed roles at irregular intervals, hoping that there would be no pattern that would distinguish them from everyone else.

Mark thought he had worked out who one of the chief sources of local and immediate intelligence was. A one-legged teenage boy seemed to spend most of the day, and every day, sitting outside the compound and not doing much else. Except, he would occasionally talk to one of the members of CIA's Marjah cell—a Jacob Dutton. Indeed, their body language indicated that they were not discussing the weather.

The one-legged teenager also communicated with a much older man who was a local—it could be Taliban, but frankly could be anything. The body language again suggested that these two were not exactly friends.

So why did they speak, and what did they talk about?

Mark quickly concluded that following one of the CIA field operatives called Cindy Johnston to find out what she did and where she went, while that was an attractive proposition, was a complete waste of time. Following the head of this cell, Glen Weiner, also turned out to be a waste of time. They only found that out after their surveillance had wasted a considerable amount of time and effort. The fact that Glen appeared to be screwing Cindy at every opportunity at least minimized the damage.

It became apparent that the third man, Jacob Dutton, the man who was neither the chief nor the person assigned to spy on the drug trade, was the man who Stephen Rodriguez spent most of his time with.

The FBI man continued to be a bit of a mystery. He followed Stephen around like a sheepdog, yet he never seemed to communicate with anyone else. Not knowing what his role was made it difficult. Whether the FBI man had an official position would be difficult to tell. One of his unofficial roles seemed to be keeping Stephen Rodriguez company when neither of them was working, and that fact certainly spiced up otherwise-routine surveillance.

Dusty Miller was following the ADDI when Rodriguez and Jacob inexplicably left their vehicle at an obscure intersection. They then walked for two blocks and did nothing other than walk around and hammer on the door of a rundown warehouse. Then they returned to their vehicle.

It did not seem to be a particularly obvious function for a high official of the United States senior spook agency on an overseas visit. Still, Dusty had seen stranger things in his time.

Dusty noticed that Jacob had scribbled something on the warehouse door before leaving. He had called up Mark on his satellite phone and got his agreement to stay by the warehouse rather than continue to follow Stephen Rodriguez. He would stay and observe the warehouse. His objective was to find out if anybody reacted to whatever Jacob had scrawled on the building.

It was a flag written in Dari. It was, therefore, meaningless to Dusty.

But it was a flag.

A man came along with the body language of someone

who had not a care in the world. And someone who would not be the least bit interested in some meaningless letters scrawled on a building. Dusty had seen it all before. Just the casual glance. Then the double-take. And then the increased pace.

Other than the residents of the building, someone else was interested in the scrawled message.

But *what* did it mean?

Both Mark and Owen had to scramble to pick up the departing ADDI. As things turned out, that did not present too much of an issue because as Mark set off to try to find out where they were going next, they passed him returning to the compound. Since Owen was still watching the compound, Mark warned Owen of Rodriguez's movement and then continued to join Dusty near the warehouse.

If body language could converse in four-letter words, the person who read the message that Jacob had scrawled would have said *Fuck!* and other unprintable words in his native language. This left Mark with something of a dilemma. This was a person of interest and, based on their previous experiences in other parts of the world tracking down druggies, they could well be, at last, on the trail of something significant. The man was dressed in western clothes, but he was a local from his colouring and physical appearance.

So now the choice was to follow this man and abandon their surveillance of the CIA agents other than Stephen and Jacob. Mark decided that they were better employed doing just that, and, as it turned out, the shifting of their minimal resources from Glen and Cindy to this evil-looking man was an excellent choice. Mark left Dusty to continue watching the man and his warehouse and

and returned to the compound, little suspecting that they would soon meet again on another side of town.

Nothing much happened for the rest of the afternoon. On into the evening, Mark began thinking that they had misinterpreted the man's reactions at the warehouse. But what could he do about that? Jacob had left a message, and the Afghani had reacted. They now had to wait for something else to happen.

So, they waited.

Finally, there was some movement in the compound. At nine o'clock in the evening, Jacob and Stephen emerged from one of the buildings, climbed into a truck, and left the compound. The vehicle first headed east towards where they had been earlier in the day and then inexplicably turned south. That was a concern to Mark and Owen, but again, they could do nothing but follow—to where? Marjah had become something of a ghost town in areas previously occupied by the Taliban, at least during daylight hours, and very few people were around. South of the region called Marjah, there was just nothing, and little, if any, a sign of habitation. Owen, who was driving their vehicle, extinguished the driving lights and followed, staying a discreet distance behind the CIA truck.

The vehicle that they were following finally pulled to a halt. And then, for some inexplicable reason, it turned around and headed back towards Marjah. There was a moment of panic in the following vehicle as Mark and Owen contemplated being discovered. While the CIA was unlikely to concern themselves with the driving habits of the locals, Mark did not wish to alert them in any way. The vehicle that Owen was driving had seen better days, but it was a Hummer, and such vehicles were only used by allied forces; and, more importantly, by the remnants of the Drug Enforcement Administration. The DEA was scarce in this part of the world. One logical conclusion that the CIA officers could come to was that they were being followed. That it was by someone who they did not want was a given. That assumed that they were in the drug business, in which case they would assume the worst, despite their training and all that it said about making assumptions.

Mark's plan, made spontaneously and instinctively rather than based on any assumptions, was to just drive off the road and avoid being seen. The ground sloped away to the right, but they had to travel some distance until the undulations in the terrain would have managed to hide their vehicle from the road. This they did but were saved from taking any more drastic action when the vehicle that had been rapidly approaching them suddenly pulled off the road and parked up in a small area that appeared to be an access track. That meant that Mark and Owen had to get out of the warmth of their vehicle and creep behind some bushes. They provided only scant cover, so they spread-eagled themselves on the ground. They had a reasonable view of the road and the CIA truck from this position.

That vehicle and its occupants just stayed there and did nothing. Mark and Owen waited. And did nothing.

Another vehicle came along the road several minutes after their arrival. It just drove on into the night, the engine's noise slowly fading away. And then there was silence once more.

It was becoming colder, and the inactivity began to fray their already-shattered nerves. Mark had been involved in following, well, stalking, people as part of the United States Special Forces and Delta Force in many unusual places. In those missions, he had been well prepared and well resourced. On this mission, they were ill-prepared and lacking in resources. And they did not know what they were doing.

Mark could only hazard a guess at what Stephen and Jacob were up to now. He rightly guessed that their business being out in the middle of nowhere was not exactly regular CIA business. Obviously, their operation was covert; otherwise, he could see no reason why someone with the rank of assistant deputy director of intelligence of the CIA would be out on this cold night with no adequate protection. It was, therefore, also apparent that their mission was illegal, and had nothing whatsoever to do with the CIA.

There was nothing illegal about parking a vehicle on the side of a road and sitting there. But doing that for more than two hours was rather strange unless Stephen and Jacob were having an affair! Was Stephen being unfaithful to his other friend?

But at last, there was some action.

Away in the distance, a vehicle was approaching from the direction of Marjah. They watched as the vehicle got closer, fully expecting it to drive by. But it did not. The road was not exactly in pristine condition, causing the approaching vehicle to sway, but Mark was sure he detected a flash of lights on full beam, and that was answered by a flash of lights from the CIA. Now they might see some action!

They were not disappointed.

The new vehicle stopped some distance away from the CIA, and they watched as a man got out and just waited. Then they saw a man coming from the CIA vehicle, and from his height and demeanour, they judged him to be Jacob Dutton. They would have loved to have a means of listening in on the conversation but getting close enough to do that meant a risk that Mark was not prepared to take. But body language is still the same, no matter what time of day or night, no matter what country, no matter the subject. The visitor was annoyed.

Jacob was just doing his job. Stephen, when he eventually emerged, was the boss.

Mark was extremely pleased when they finally stopped playing charades, returned to their respective vehicles, and took off in the direction of Marjah. Mark and his team had spent many additional hours following, watching, and waiting. And they were learning absolutely nothing.

Rodriguez returned to his quarters tired and more than a little annoyed with the night's work. He would have to have a shot of heroin, but he had other things on his mind that needed to be attended to first. He wandered along the corridor and tapped on the door of Edward's room. The door was opened as though he was expected, and a grinning Edward met him.

'Started without me, huh?' he said as he kissed Edward.

'Oh, I thought you had gone out with Jacob,' Edward replied, busy closing and locking the door behind Stephen.

'Yeah. What a shit of a day! Got any painkillers?'

They both laughed. It was their private joke. It did not pay to use the correct name for their drug of choice around the people that they were usually associated with. Heroin was frowned upon by the FBI and the CIA. At least officially.

Edward skipped to his cupboard and produced a small plastic bag.

'I only have one shot, but you can have it!' Edward gushed.

'OK, let me at it!' He busied himself preparing the drug for inhaling.

Suddenly, Stephen turned to Edward as though he

had a sudden thought. 'I'll tell you what—I have a sample from a new batch,' he said as he reached into his back pocket and pulled out another small plastic bag, tossing it to Edward. 'Let's get these into us, and then we can have a quiet evening together,' he said with a grin.

It did not take long. They sat side by side on a couch, both waiting for the drugs to have their full effect before they got down to business. Edward was the first to be fully affected. He passed out. He had a huge dose of ketamine in his body, and on top of the heroin he had already consumed earlier in the evening, it was lucky the amount hadn't killed him. Stephen, on the other hand, was fine. It was a waste of heroin to blow rather than inhale, but he could get plenty more.

Rodriguez quickly went about his business. There had to be something that would confirm his suspicions that all was not well in this relationship. And it did not take him long to find it. A small book was hidden under the mattress and had notes written in some cryptic code. Meaningless to Stephen. Meaningful to someone who had the key to the code. The only thing that registered in any meaningful form was time and date notations. The rest was gibberish without a code breaker, but the damage was done. Why would a guy from the FBI, who chose not to use his sat phone, have coded notes? The answer to someone as paranoid as Stephen was that Edward was up to mischief. And who was the likely target? Could the target be Stephen?

Stephen cried. He had grown extremely attached to Edward, and although he felt that he had now confirmed his suspicions, he was still shocked by the realization that he was being betrayed. And then there was only one word that escaped his lips. 'Bitch!'

Rodriguez carefully replaced the book precisely as he had found it, and then made to take his leave. He cried again as he stripped Edward's clothes off and scattered them on the floor, before laying him on the couch in a relaxed pose. He hesitated and took one more look at his friend. Edward would have to die.

Sobbing, he exited the room without locking the door.

The following day, Mark and Dusty would begin to see for the first time that their trip into this hellhole was not a complete waste of time. Mark had had nothing to report to Harold Taylor back in Washington the previous night, and that was perhaps just as well. His old man sounded preoccupied with something and seemed neither surprised nor upset, which Mark thought was a little out of character.

Mark's disappointment at their lack of progress must have been transmitted across the globe when he spoke to Debbie. She asked when they would be home. Mark replied that he did not know. And that left unanswered a couple of questions in Debbie's mind. She still did not know exactly why Mark was placing himself in danger. She did not understand why he sounded so calm yet remote. And their whole conversation, normally so warm and understanding, drifted to a logical conclusion. Neither of them wanted to end their chat, but neither of them had anything more to say as their conversation drifted into an awkward silence.

Except to say, 'I love you!' before they terminated the call, which would have to do for now.

Mark had not told Debbie was the gist of this morning's conversation with Owen and Dusty. The next stage of their trip would be to return to Kabul, and Mark did not see that they could do so without some form of arms. Mark was an ex-soldier and felt that he was no use if he did not have something a little more persuasive than a pistol. Especially given his observation of life in Afghanistan. He had asked Owen if he could do something about that. About thirty minutes later, Owen had turned up with three AK-47s. While Mark would have preferred the US Army M16 rifle, he accepted that anything was better than nothing. And Owen had produced enough ammunition to start World War III. Mark did not expect to have to use the rifles, but he did notice a lift in the morale of his small team.

Dusty watched the compound and was surprised to see Stephen and Jacob commandeer a truck and head out to the east once again. Since both Mark and Owen had been out late the previous night, Dusty decided to follow them on his own. While this was breaking the protocol they had adhered to throughout the trip, Dusty reasoned that the risk of not knowing where they were heading was the worst-case scenario. And he was right. Unsurprisingly, the truck went to the warehouse, and the men did not waste much time loading up the truck with packages that looked suspiciously like textiles, but which were more likely to be opiates. By the time Dusty had realized what was going on, it was too late to get Mark or Owen to come down and confirm it. Dusty had seen more than his share of drug operations and was sure they were at last on to something. The question now was, what would they do with the opiates? Even Dusty could not perceive a man of Stephen's rank involving himself in shifting cargo of this kind.

But stranger things have happened.

When the convoy finally left the Marjah compound heading east, it was a strange combination of people and vehicles. During the assembling process, Owen had managed to find out that the convoy was headed for the United States military base outside of Kandahar and that it would then make the run north to Kabul the following day.

There was an amazing amount of knowledge freely available for what seemed like it should have been planned as a carefully controlled and secure mission. Some of it was pure speculation, of course, and the expectation of the participants would depend on who they spoke to last. In any case, the fact that many various elements were permitted to join the convoy was the end of any secrecy.

As a group linked to the DEA, Owen had no difficulty getting agreement from the marshals to join this convoy. The marshals were more worried about the Taliban than they were about a one-legged Welshman who worked with the DEA. Owen did not know the route they would take, except that it would end up in Kandahar. This was because the people running the convoy would take whatever way would help them avoid the latest presumed whereabouts of insurgents. That depended on the latest intelligence reports. Where they came from was anyone's guess, and the marshals either did not know or had other more important things to worry about or simply did not care.

For the security of their own covert mission, Mark had decided that they would link up with the convoy on the outskirts of Marjah, and it seemed as though they were not the only group with this plan. Stephen and Jacob left the compound at the same time as the convoy, still driving the truck, but this time accompanied by a Hummer with six Afghani soldiers and two other Hummers, each manned by a couple of US Marines. They went east again and then turned off towards the warehouse, where they parked and watched as the soldiers dismounted. This time there was no polite knock on the door. There was no door by the time the Hummer had driven straight into it. There followed a brief skirmish, during which several shots were fired, and then the soldiers emerged from the warehouse once more, this time carrying the body of a savagely beaten man in Western clothes.

From the way that sick man was being treated by the Afghan troops, it was extremely doubtful that the man would see another sunrise. At least not in this world.

One of the Afghan soldiers handed a rifle case through the window of the CIA vehicle and wandered off after his colleagues. Seemingly satisfied with what they had just received and witnessed, the three CIA vehicles with Stephen, Jacob, and their FBI friend on board headed out east to join the rest of the convoy.

A perplexed Mark and his team did the same thing. They did not know what had just happened, but they did know that one man appeared to be no longer part of the plan.

So that source of information was effectively, and probably literally, dead.

An equally perplexed Oleg Demidov did not know what to do. He had witnessed the whole event from the back seat of a nondescript vehicle in which he had just been following Jacob, off on another of his many trips. He carried with him a Japanese video camera, and he filmed the goings-on at the warehouse. How else was anyone going to believe this story?

Jacob, and whoever his consort was, was taking a significant risk. Demidov had witnessed the earlier events at the warehouse, and he knew that the CIA was carrying drugs! This was a complete change in strategy for the CIA. They usually employed locals to do all their dirty work and

leaving themselves always able to deny any involvement.
    But not now.
    And sanctioning murder as well!

Chapter 25

Strings

In Kandahar, the coalition troops were tense and on the highest alert. Their local intelligence had revealed a likelihood of some Taliban activity to the north. While that was not exactly unusual, there was ample evidence that the troops were getting twitchy. As with all such intelligence reports, they did not exactly reveal *where, when, or how.* The troops were on edge, and they were intensely concerned about who was forming up to join this convoy. They were also worried about what the participants would carry on this trip north.

The convoy that had originated in Marjah had travelled the ninety or so miles into Kandahar without any fuss. This was probably because it had been escorted by Afghani troops and was therefore of little interest to the Taliban.

The road from Kandahar to Kabul would be a different story.

The convoy would now be under the command of United States forces, and it would be expected to attract some attention. The initial threat would be from within the convoy itself, which had to be sorted out first. They would worry about what would happen on the road later.

It would have been much easier for the security forces to carry out their functions had they been at an airport or a railway station, preferably in another, more peaceful, country. There they could simply ban anything that remotely looked like an explosive device or a means of projecting such a device, or anything that looked even remotely like a gun or a knife; arrest the person who was carrying it, and that would have been an end to the matter.

Everyone carried a gun in Afghanistan.

The first vehicle that drew the attention of the forces checking the convoy contained a group of four men. All four appeared to be locals, and only one of them spoke any English. At least only one of them admitted to speaking any English. Which may or may not have meant the same thing.

This man, who introduced himself formally as Abdul Hadi Arghandiwal, which may or may not have been his real name, proudly stated that he was a Tajik. He pointed to a younger man sitting alongside him, who he said was his brother Zalmay, and waved a hand at the other two men as one would at the hired help. All four of the men quietly allowed themselves to be subjected to a frisk search, which revealed nothing abnormal, while leaning their ancient AK-47 rifles against the side of their dilapidated vehicle.

Their papers were examined with little more than a cursory look. The stated purpose of the trip was to attend a meeting of their sub-tribe, which, this year, was to be held in the capital city of Kabul. The marine who was carrying out the checks just smiled. It made a change from the explanation of visiting a dying relative; he had lost track of the number of times that story had been used! Some people would say anything just to get the protection afforded by a convoy for their journey. In any case, if they wished to go to Kabul to do something outrageous like kill the President, they were hardly likely to say so. Still, they had a note signed by the marshal at Marjah and countersigned by someone from the CIA, which was good enough for the marine.

A few vehicles later, the marshals came to the first group of Americans. These people looked serious. Dusty Miller threw out a hand, which was grabbed by the Afro-American marine, and they greeted each other like long-lost friends. Dusty and Shorty chatted for a few minutes before he referred his six-foot-seven friend to the rest of the group. That introduction should have made any further explanations unnecessary. Nonetheless, Mark stuck to their cover story as far as was necessary. They were on a fact-finding mission with the DEA, returning to Kabul, and then returning to the United States.

The marine showed some interest in the driver, who was dressed as a native until he was introduced as Owen. He responded in a language and an accent that no amount of training could ever disguise. Owen was from the British Isles, and the marine guessed, correctly, that he was from Wales.

The third member of this group was the one who made them look serious in military parlance. He had an almost-casual air about him, but the strength and confidence of the man were obvious. He had the look of someone who had done time as a marine—it takes one to know one. Mark just shrugged at the look of respect from the junior. The marine would grow up to be someone someday if only he got over doing traffic control in this godforsaken place. What impressed Mark was that he had been able to place Owen as a Welshman since, for most of his life, Owen had lived in England, then the United States, and then Afghanistan and Pakistan.

'Just a couple more groups to check out, then you can be on your way,' Shorty said as he headed towards the vehicle containing Stephen Rodriguez.

'Good luck!' Dusty called to his friend.

Shorty, the marine that Dusty had spoken to, was new to this job and had still to adjust to life as a full-fledged man in uniform. Born in Cicero in Chicago, life was rough and tough. He got out of Chicago to better himself and joined the Marines but never quite managed to shake off the inferiority complex of people from the bottom rungs of society. Shorty was therefore intimidated by the man who had just introduced himself as Rodriguez of the CIA.

His question 'What is in the truck?' was greeted with 'You do not need to know that!' The arrogant attitude of the other three people who made up this contingent did little to improve the situation. There was Jacob, who was also CIA, and who seemed to have the view that the whole exercise was something of a joke. There was a serious-faced prissy little man accompanying Rodriguez in an older military vehicle that had been discarded by frontline troops as just too dangerous, but which was OK for this journey. The last of the four was the driver of the truck, who would have looked more at home in the back seat of an Alfa Romeo—and he was scared.

The marine persisted for just a moment longer than was wise, which resulted in his senior officer being summoned. After a moment or two of brittle words, the truck was overlooked, and the marines settled for an assurance from the CIA contingent that all was well.

The marine wandered off towards the next group while making a note to have a word with the people accompanying the convoy. The CIA was not exactly popular with the military, either in Afghanistan or in Washington DC. At the marine level, it was no different. He would make sure that Mr. Rodriguez, or whatever his name was, would get no preferential treatment on this trip.

The next truck contained people who were much more pleasant.

'That guy, he gives you grief?' Demidov asked with a ready smile.

The marine was suspicious. Although the days of the Cold War were long since gone, Americans were still fed a diet of the evils of Communism, the Soviets, and all the other claptrap from a bygone age of political dramas. If this guy had a strange accent, and it sounded Russian, then he probably was Russian. If it quacks like a duck, waddles like a duck, then it is a fucking duck.

'Could you please state the purpose of your trip?' the marine asked, deadpan ignoring Oleg's question.

Again, the Russian smiled. 'I work on the security detail for Ahmed Karzai, the brother of the Afghan President, Hamid Karzai. We are going to Kabul for a speech. Ahmed flies by military helicopter. We peasants travel by road!' Oleg laughed. He was paid at a rate of more than $1,000 a day, and he got paid whether Ahmed was there or not.

In this case, not.

Ahmed Karzai had far more important matters to attend to in Kandahar than to waste his time going to Kabul, and especially listening to another political speech by his brother. The problem for the lowly US marine was, how did he check that out? Ahmed would not have to leave until tomorrow if he was to go. Flight time in a Bell Huey: under three hours. The marine could hardly call his office and ask about his flight plans of Karzai. The story seemed genuine. He knew of Ahmed and his relationship with the President. He knew all about his security detail, except that he did not know Oleg's position, but it had to be relatively senior. All the people who were anybody in this country understood the value of security, and they also learned the value of the Russians. It sounded insane. After all the stress that the nation of Afghanistan had been put through mainly because of the Russians, they still wanted to employ them for their own security. The world was insane. He had been humbled by the arrogant Americans and was now treated passively, if patronizingly, by Russians. What did it matter? They were not the Enemy.

The marine checked the two vehicles that Oleg and his team would be using. Then, with the same serious look on his face, he went off in search of the US military personnel who had the unenviable task of escorting this motley collection of individuals to Kabul.

The marine would have little to report other than the obnoxious CIA contingent. He probably wouldn't bother.

Why state the obvious?

For Oleg Demidov, this trip would be one hell of a laugh. Ahmed knew where Oleg was, where he was going, and why. Had the marine marshal bothered to check with Ahmed's office, he would have been told, yes, Ahmed was going to Kabul. Yes, Ahmed's brother, the President, was giving an important speech. And, just for a laugh at Oleg's expense, Oleg had to travel by road because he was scared of flying by helicopter. What he would not say was the real reason why Oleg was traveling by road.

From Ahmed's point of view, there was a unique opportunity. Ahmed had been trying to get the CIA—or, rather, he assumed the renegade elements in the CIA—who were buying drugs from his competitors to both change their supplier and have the drugs refined locally. At first, his plan seemed to be failing. Now it seemed to have succeeded for all the wrong reasons. Why the man had decided to dispense with Wakil Hekmatyar was unbelievable! So now he had him. Let him get away from Kandahar and up to Kabul, where he would feel safe and confident—all the trials and tribulations of Marjah far behind him. And then pounce. Put to him a straightforward and simple proposition. Change your supplier and method of operations, or we will reveal it all to the appropriate authorities.

Ahmed could chuckle to himself. Where did he start? While the murder of Wakil would not cause anyone to shed tears, it was nonetheless murder; so, he could pass the word to the Afghan police. That was the easiest and simplest way; he had plenty of their forces on his payroll, and it would attract the attention of the media. He could have much more fun if he simply released a statement to the press saying that the much-vaunted CIA was once again playing games in the drug trade and leaving them to sort out the embarrassment. The media would have a field day, the CIA would be shooting themselves in the foot no matter how they responded, and Ahmed's position would be secure. Brother Hamid had been under pressure from the United States, particularly the CIA, to get the drug trade under control. Now, in addition to telling the Americans to bring their own house in order, and cut down on demand for drugs, he could say to them that they had been caught with their hands in the cookie jar. The entire business was of their own making. Eureka!

Of course, no such thing would eventuate. Ahmed was

supremely confident that the infidels would bend to the inevitable. He could take control of another channel. He would also have essential contacts in the CIA who were now vulnerable to accede to any minor request for assistance that Ahmed may make. Or face the consequences.

Ahmed was not worried about Olezhka Demidov. He was as sure as he could be that Oleg was a fully paid-up member of the Russian SVR.

But - so what?

Demidov could not remember, in all the years that he had spent, first, with the KGB, and then later as an undercover operator working in security services, and latterly working undercover for the Russian SVR, an opportunity like this one.

As far as his immediate boss was concerned, he had explained the position as a win-win situation for Ahmed Karzai. The mess the Americans had got themselves into, not for the first time, could only benefit Ahmed. And the Russians were always on the lookout for CIA blunders, and this one was a doozy. So, it was a win-win situation all around.

Sure, his *job* was to keep track of CIA operations in Afghanistan, and that he was doing. But this was unique. What he had regarded as a low-level operation had suddenly blossomed out. There was nothing wrong with the CIA dabbling in drugs, but the people concerned had introduced someone from a much higher level. And that person had been responsible for the brutal murder of one of the players. Murder was not normal. The murder of people was not something that the CIA, or any other national intelligence agency, ever got involved in. People of their nature were in the business of collecting intelligence, and the last thing they wanted to do was to draw attention to themselves in so crude a manner. Unless that involved the killing of a head of state—but that was politics, not murder!

Oleg had concluded that there was trouble in the CIA ranks and that the SVR could take full advantage.

In the best interests of international harmony, of course.

But before that, the now-dead man had obviously incurred someone else's displeasure in the United States hierarchy. Whether it was the CIA, DEA, FBI, or any other acronyms, the people looked serious, professional, and covert. That meant that some members of the CIA were in some serious trouble. Certainly, someone was showing a distinct interest, and he guessed that, that someone knew more than Oleg did about who he was. And that was good news as well.

But before that, Jacob Dutton had done an extraordinary thing. He had met with a group of Tajiks. They may be many things, but involved in spying or spook-craft? Very unlikely. Had that meeting had something to do with the mysterious visitor? On first assessment, it seemed unlikely.

But now, the game had changed.

All the aforesaid were now in the same convoy headed for Kabul.

Forget about making assumptions.

There were just too many coincidences.

Chapter 26

The Battle of Ghazni

The convoy trundled northwards. It would be a long and slow journey. To the immediate east, which was to the convoy's right, were the mountains. Further to the east was the border with Pakistan. Not that anybody would want to go there. The terrain was too rugged, and there was just nothing there anyway. On the left of the convoy, to the west were the rugged and desolate mountains that made up the bulk of the Afghanistan interior once they had left the relative flatlands around and south of Kandahar. And there was nothing there either.

All the surrounding mountains, both to the east and west of this road, harboured the Taliban, al-Qaeda, and other insurgent groups. Many of them could, and did, pass as ordinary citizens when they chose to do so. Hence, this was a land where nothing could be taken for granted. This was a land of never-ending conflicts.

The length of the convoy, its diverse and fractured nature, and the lack of communication devices in all vehicles made it necessary for careful and constant monitoring by the US and Afghan escorts. The monitoring was particularly rigid as they passed through various towns and settlements along the way. Although most maps of the country show only the town of Qalat on the road between Kandahar and Ghazni, the one town that can claim to be of city size, there were many smaller towns, villages, and settlements. All with their share of Taliban sympathizers and other groups who did not take too kindly to the foreign troops in their midst.

It was, in fact, a nightmare both to keep the convoy intact, to prevent anyone from joining it, and to deal with anyone who tried to attack it. There was no point in having all the security checks when the convoy was first formed up in Kandahar if they were not to maintain security as they travelled through this inhospitable country.

By the time the convoy reached Ghazni, the American escorts were tired and irritable. There was tension for all see and feel, which spread through the entire convoy. A brief stop outside the military compound that housed the US and coalition troops provided some relief. Pleasantries were exchanged. Some people had reached their destination and left the convoy to its fate. Others joined the convoy for the brief run into Kabul. This convoy was not allowed inside the compound except for a few carefully selected vehicles. Mark and his small team stayed outside but took the opportunity to stretch their legs while checking on the movements of the others. The truck carrying the ADDI was one of the vehicles that could go into the compound. However, Mark was not worried that Rodriguez would choose to stay in Ghazni.

It was another shithole in a land of many.

The convoy was finally reassembled, and they made their way out of the city of Ghazni at about 3:00 pm, without incident. Not that there was much to see in that town either.

Ghazni had long since lost the aura of its former grandeur. The city, and a population of around one hundred forty thousand, survived as a strategic place in the middle of nowhere. The Taliban tended to stay outside the city, preferring instead to control most of the surrounding rural areas probably because many of the residents of this city were Tajiks rather than Pashtuns.

That did not stop the Taliban from continually harassing the residents and the foreign military. Life was not particularly pleasant in this arid and remote place.

It was cold and getting colder. Flurries of snow were beginning to whirl around. But no one seemed to care. That was regarded as the very least of their worries. They pressed on, anxious to get to the relative safety of their immediate target—the city of Kabul.

The city of Ghazni would be their last stop on the journey north.

The vehicles were now more widely spaced out. The drivers probably felt that they were now in much safer territory. They were far away from the Taliban-dominated south. The tension began to ease slowly. The convoy had just over two hours' travel time to Kabul, and then they could rest. The constant jolting of the vehicle eased as the road surface, while not ideal, began to even out.

They were almost there.

Rodriguez had handed the driving over to Hennessey, and he settled down in the back seat for a snooze. There would be a whole heap of trouble to handle once they got to Kabul. This was the last opportunity for him to have a break.

Mark began to plan their next moves. They now had a truckload of 'stuff' to keep an eye on, and there was a glimmer of hope that they were beginning to piece together a story.

Owen was driving, Dusty dozed, and Mark planned.

And then it happened.

And without any warning.

From their position towards the rear of the convoy, the noise from the engine of their Humvee prevented Mark and Dusty from hearing anything. But they saw the leading vehicle suddenly cartwheel end over end in a massive cloud of dust and smoke. The truck behind the leading vehicle, blinded by the smoke, careened into the wreckage. And then it ploughed forward as the soldiers and bodies were scattered on both sides of the road. The driver of the third vehicle braked violently and desperately flung the wheel away to the right and away from the debris that the earlier crash had created. His reactions were good, but that could not prevent the truck from flipping over. His passenger was flung out of the window and was probably dead as he landed on the side of the road. The vehicle came to rest on its side, effectively blocking the road.

Before anyone could recover from the initial shock, four or five rocket-propelled grenades, or RPGs, were fired from up ahead, landing mostly among the carnage in the front of the convoy. The RPGs caused little in the way of new physical damage but shattered the nerves of those who had witnessed the mess. It had to be assumed that the people in the leading vehicles were already dead. One of the RPGs punctured a fuel tank, and an explosion caused further devastation. This was followed by a massive plume of black smoke, which rose into the air.

Not content with the damage caused to the convoy, the RPGs were followed up with machine-gun fire, which seemed to come from all sides. The bullets pinged off the vehicles, scattering in all directions. Fortunately, the firing did not appear to be particularly well-directed or consistent.

At the instant of the first attack, it would have taken only the concentrated aim of more RPGs or some other form of explosive projectiles to destroy the convoy and most of its defenders. Fortunately for the convoy, the insurgents attacking them did not have any howitzers. It was more likely that they had simply used up their precious RPG supply.

Edward Hennessey, who was driving at the time of the attack, turned to Stephen Rodriguez, who was sitting in the rear passenger seat, fear on his face. Edward was about to speak when he saw the AK-47 rifle pointed straight at him. It had a suppressor fitted over the end of the barrel. Stephen just uttered the word 'bitch' and pulled the trigger.

The round shattered the right side of Edward's skull.

His dead body slumped at the wheel as the truck ground to a halt.

The first people to react positively were the allied marines traveling in the middle of the convoy. They immediately ran forward, weapons at the ready. They had trained for this situation and were trained to expect trouble. But even then, they could not have anticipated the withering burst of submachine gunfire that erupted from up ahead. It was only the truck that had overturned on the road that saved some of the men.

The two sections, each of two men who were in the leading group towards the front, despite all their training and discipline, were cut down as they ran forward and would have been dead before they had any chance at retaliation. The rest of the team scattered behind rocks on either side of the road, accompanied by the confused yelling of instructions and questions that typically accompany events of this nature.

Almost simultaneously, the others to react were Mark, Dusty, and Owen. Their training also spurred them into action. It was clear that the threat was coming directly down the road towards them, so they grabbed helmets and weapons, and that was where they headed. Owen jumped out to join Mark and Dusty and had the common sense to yell orders to the other drivers to get away from their trucks and into the rocks on the roadside to take cover as best they could.

As Mark's small team crouched and moved towards where they believed the action to be, Dusty suddenly lurched forward, knocking Owen to the ground—in the same movement, firing to his left. Whoever had set up the roadside bomb, an improvised explosive device, which had disabled the lead vehicle, had worked out what would happen. The convoy would be vulnerable from the sides as people moved forward to inspect the carnage and render whatever assistance they could.

Dusty knew what was happening and killed two men with that burst of gunfire. In doing so, he probably saved Owen's life. For the time being, at least.

Mark was oblivious to that. He now had other things on his mind. He grabbed Owen and another driver who looked more than capable of looking after himself and directed them to cover the right while he and Dusty covered the left.

It was a stalemate.

There was no command structure in place, probably because the person who was to take charge had been killed in the initial strike.

From the back of the convoy, the truck that was carrying Afghan troops was probably the slowest to react. They just did not know what to do, and no instructions were forthcoming from their commanding officer.

Dusty got mad and yelled out some orders of his own.

Whether the Afghans understood the instruction to 'get the down here and protect our flanks,' or whether they finally reacted to Dusty's body language, they did get out of their trucks and started to make their way forward into a defensive position, crawling on their stomachs.

Owen intervened before Dusty went completely off his trolley, splitting the men on either side of the road. Whether the Afghans would use, or could even fire or aim, their weapons, they did not know.

An eerie silence momentarily settled over the convoy as they stayed undercover. Sniper shots pinged off the trucks as the insurgents sought out new targets. In the absence of continuous fire, it was difficult to tell just where the enemy was located, except that they appeared to be well-positioned.

At least for now, they did not appear to be closing in.

That could not last.

Mark was unfamiliar with the fighting protocols in this part of the world. However, he doubted that the enemy would wait until dark before making a move. The United States and allied forces would always be at a massive advantage fighting at night. Therefore, if the insurgents had any sense, they would maintain a steady stream of fire at the convoy. That would enable them to assess the relative strength of the defending forces by observing where the returning fire was originating from. Then they would launch their final attack.

The security of the convoy was not Mark's problem. But he had to do something!

The relative inactivity that Mark had endured following Stephen Rodriguez on his travels and, frankly, achieving little had not dulled his instincts. To get some action finally spurred him on.

But Mark was puzzled.

He had been only two trucks behind the vehicles in

which Stephen Rodriguez and his friends were traveling. He was now virtually alongside the second vehicle that contained Rodriguez and Hennessey. There had been no sign of anyone exiting the vehicle. Getting to the door was not the issue. Standing up to open the door was. So, he called out.

'Is everyone OK in there?'

The reply that he got was a burst of machine-gun fire from out in the rocks to his left. From within the truck, all he heard was a stifled sob. He exchanged looks with Dusty and made a couple of hand signals. Dusty let loose a burst of fire in the direction of the earlier blast while Mark scrambled under the truck and around to the right-hand side. There were signs of further insurgent activity on that side as Owen pointed to the rocks and made a hand signal that suggested Mark stay down.

The problem of leaving people in their vehicles in the middle of a firefight was twofold: firstly, they were too simple a target if they as much as raised a hand, and therefore, secondly, they were not providing assistance to the rest of a seemingly vastly outnumbered defending force.

Mark was about to give up and move on when the truck door opened, and out tumbled Stephen Rodriguez.

He immediately scrambled under the truck. He was covered in blood, and his body language said he was scared. It also looked as though he had been crying.

'Is there anyone else in there?' Mark barked at the figure cowering under the truck. The answer he got was not what he would have expected from an ADDI of an organization of the likes of the CIA.

He assumed the response was negative.

All that Mark could hear was a whimper.

The truck that Stephen was in had a double cab, and he had been in the back seats. When their convoy had come to a sudden halt, and it was obvious that they were being attacked, he seized the moment.

He had been mulling over the previous few days in which he had observed the activity of the man who he had assumed was his friend. Well, more than a friend. The ability to read body language was not confined to people at the FBI, and Rodriguez was probably better than most.

Be it in the way Hennessey looked at him when he had assumed that Stephen was concentrating on something else or how Hennessey reacted to various events that had occurred. It was as though he was cataloguing in his mind everything that happened and why it happened. But what struck Stephen as odd was that the guy did not seem to communicate with anyone else in his organization. Most of the FBI agents that Stephen had been associated with, depending on which time zone they were in, reported to *someone* at least once a day. No FBI agent could be anywhere without having a mission. But Edward seemed to be the exception.

So, what was his mission?

There could only be one logical conclusion.

The ADDI had been set up.

It was Rodriguez who thought that he had initiated this trip around the world to be with his *friend.*

The FBI saw it differently. Stephen Rodriguez had been conned into trusting Edward, and the very same man was simply doing a job—as a spy, gathering evidence of what Stephen was up to while trying to maintain the illusion that everything was sweet and rosy in their relationship.

In the few seconds of confusion and chaos that had erupted in the convoy, Stephen opened the bag that contained an AK-47 rifle and fitted the primitive suppressor to the barrel. He then called out to Edward, who was still straining to see through the windscreen to find the source of their problem. As Edward turned around, he faced the barrel of the rifle. He had time to open his mouth to let out a cry, but the cry never made it to his lips. The suppressor did its job. There was a soft *pop* from the rifle.

The bullet travelled a few feet to reach its target. Edward was shot through the head.

The second shot gave more of a crack, and the windscreen was shattered.

And then the horrific nature of what Stephen had just done descended on him. He threw the rifle out of the window and sat there, tears streaming down his face. Tears of frustration. Tears of anger.

Even a sense of self-preservation deserted him as he stared at the man's body who he thought had been his friend.

Mark could not have cared less about what was worrying the ADDI. He had more critical issues to deal with.

He realized that he had to contact the remaining marines who had gone forward. Otherwise, they were all screwed. They could not provide any assistance to anyone if they were not organized.

Although Mark and his two men were not officially part of the defending force, he was probably equally, if not more, experienced at dealing with this kind of thing. And right now, he knew nothing of the plan, if indeed there was one. He also did not know if any of the marines had survived. There was still sporadic fire coming from up ahead, but he had no way of knowing who it was coming from or who, or what, it was aimed at.

What he did know was that no one was returning fire.

Mark knew from his training in a previous life and practical experience that it was no use staying in one place; otherwise, whoever was out there would simply manipulate their position around them. He also knew that he had to maintain a clear view of his field of fire while keeping his back covered. That presupposed that Mark knew what he was firing at and where the enemy was located. He also knew that despite the years that had elapsed since his time in Delta Forces with the United States Special Forces, he was probably as qualified as anyone to try to dig their way out of this hellhole.

Dusty had been with him on several such operations. Mark had been the officer. Dusty had been the sergeant. But rank did not count for much when you were up to your ass in alligators, trying to drain the swamp.

'I will move forward to try to link up with the other group. Cover me and watch my back,' was all Mark had to say.

Dusty understood and just nodded.

'You sure you don't want me to go? Sergeants are expendable!'

They both laughed at that.

Mark went forward.

To the west side of the convoy's position was an upwards slope that gradually got steeper until it climbed into sheer cliffs. On the east side of the road, the ground gently sloped away for a couple of miles towards what was a riverbed; then the ground rose to the mountains. Up ahead of the convoy, the road was flat and curved to the east before what appeared to be a sharp rise to the west. It appeared that there were no insurgents on the eastern flank because there was no cover, but the curve in the road meant that from their position in front, they could cover any movement on either side of the convoy.

The enemy forces had done their homework. Mark

gave a wry smile. These guys were not dumb.

Mark crawled rather than walked, keeping to the right of the trucks. Bullets were still fizzing overhead and coming from up ahead of the convoy. The flanks of what remained of the convoy were well covered by defending forces, at least in terms of the number of men, if not in their quality. Occasional shots were being fired from somewhere in the distance, which was suddenly silenced by a volley of fire from the defenders up ahead. It struck Mark as a little weird and not quite how he would have set up an ambush.

He had heard from soldiers who had experience in this country. Stories that said many Afghans were a little reluctant to fight in close. They preferred to kill from afar and wait until there was no one left. Or, if they could not see much future in pressing on with their attack, they would simply disappear. They were fighting a guerrilla war. They were like vultures, just waiting to clean up the scraps.

He had also heard that many were as likely to shoot themselves in the foot as hit anything they were supposed to be aiming at. But he also knew that there was another side to these soldiers' tales.

How come, after all the billions of dollars that the United States and their allies had spent on this mission in Afghanistan, the Taliban were still out there. Still able to cause chaos. And still, getting stronger rather than weaker?

The place of this attack had been chosen well. McKinley's talk at Fort Bragg, which seemed a long time ago and a long way away, had been right. The Taliban were not the fools that the people at the Pentagon took them to be.

The good news might be that this ambush, if that was what it was, may have been set up by one of the many other insurgent groups that existed in this lawless land. It may be just an attempt by an isolated group to rape and pillage. If the fight became too tough or ran out of ammunition, they would just fade away into this rock-strewn barren country. Back to being just another group of inhabitants living off scraps or handouts and waiting for another opportunity to have a snipe at the infidels.

Mark eventually made it to what he took to be the most forward position. The group of soldiers was well-positioned to the left and right of the still-smouldering ruins of what had been the three leading vehicles in the convoy. The uniforms were of US Marines, NATO forces, and the Afghan Army; and of those manning positions, he counted six United States, three SAS troops, and three Afghans.

From his position just short of the forward troops, Mark could see two men hunkered down behind the wrecks, but there was so much blood around that it was difficult to tell what nationality they were.

And whether they were dead or alive.

They certainly would be taking no further part in this little battle.

That meant that there were six men unaccounted for unless others were hidden in the rocks. He moved slowly and quietly farther to his left, and up ahead, he could see some bodies lying on the road. From the bloodstained uniforms, it was clear that some of them were Americans. At present, no one was firing. Just waiting to see what would happen next. And that could not last.

Mark's training kicked in again. He let out a low whistle, and he saw an arm partially raised in acknowledgment. Good. This was no time to be carrying on long-distance conversations. He made his way towards the position where the acknowledgment had come from.

For his trouble, someone out beyond the carnage must have seen the movement, and bullets whistled over his head. That was what everyone was waiting for. The replying burst of fire from the defenders was aimed directly at the point of origin, and no more fire was directed at Mark from that source. The incoming shots had seemed to come from a distance, and whoever was doing the shooting was not exactly accurate.

The returning fire had been accurate, but everything was relative. For the moment, the Taliban, or whoever they were, were too far away and too well hidden for any counter-fire to be effective.

In the earlier days, when the United States Army was busy trying to placate the Native American Indians, the Army had the advantage—the US Army had guns, and the Indians had bows and arrows. For the Indians, the degree of accuracy of an arrow would be measured in tens of feet, and that would be seriously affected by the wind and all manner of other factors, including riding on horseback while attempting to hit a moving target. The degree of accuracy with a rifle, other than a sniper rifle in the hands of a professional, would be measured in tens of yards, and over a short distance, the wind would not be a factor. But other things would be. So much for progress. The facts were that you would be, at least statistically, extremely unlucky to be hit even by a well-aimed shot.

Mark made it to the forward position and squeezed in behind the rocks protecting two marines.

'What are you doing here?' was the greeting that Mark directed at one of the marines.

Mike Gilroy had a face that could be recognized anywhere. Gilroy seemed always to have a crooked smile on his face. That problem had been caused by a bullet that had creased his left cheek in another long-forgotten skirmish, in another land, in the uniform of the United States Special Forces. The surgeon had done an excellent job of restoring his face to something resembling its original condition. That doctor could do nothing about fully fixing the nerves, but that did not impact the sense of humour of this likable Irishman.

Gilroy was, amongst other things, a very clever guy being proficient in as many as six languages, which he just naturally picked up. None of those skills were any use to him right now.

At first, Mike appeared not to recognize his visitor, which was not surprising, considering that Mark Taylor now had several days' worth of stubble that was rapidly turning into a full-grown beard.

Mark just grinned.

'You thought I was going to miss all the fun! Is this your idea of fun?'

The two men embraced as recognition lit up Mike's face. But then, just as quickly, they were back to being professional soldiers.

The fact that Mark was, and had been for over five years, back to being a civilian running a computer software company in New York City was forgotten. It was as though they were back in the jungles of Colombia, the only minor differences being that there was no jungle in this barren and inhospitable country, the snow flurries were getting more intense, and the temperature was approaching freezing.

Mike reported to his senior officer.

'This is Toby,' he said, indicating the marine sharing his position among the rocks. 'We have a force of about twenty insurgents up ahead and probably a few more on either side. The IED that has taken out a couple of our leading vehicles certainly wasn't here when the road was swept earlier today. The bad guys appear to be well-armed and well positioned, but they probably did not expect a convoy of quite this size. They are probably now having a quiet chat about what they do now. I guess they will wait for orders from the boss, which could take a while, knowing how their command structure works. The good news was that they were at about the maximum range of their guns, so they did not seem too keen on getting involved in an assault at this stage. I hope they are waiting until darkness falls before moving in or slipping away. And now, I don't think we can do much about that.'

'You think so? I would have thought they did not like to take us on at night with all the night vision gear we have,' Mark opined.

Mike just laughed.

'If we had the gear! That is all that was allocated to the troops in the provinces. There is little left for us who are just babysitting a routine convoy. And the insurgents seem to know that.'

'Well, we'll see about that,' Mark replied grimly.

'We have some gear. Who is in charge of this show?' he asked, looking at the smoking crippled vehicles, the bodies, and the blood, wondering whether he wanted an answer.

Mike nodded towards the mess that littered the road to Kabul.

'The major is among that lot—I do not know if he is dead or alive. We cannot get to them. We have tried slipping over while the other guys provide covering fire, but the opposition has got that covered from about half a dozen different angles, so we can't. To answer your question, I guess I'm in charge of this skirmish, at least until you showed up!'

'Come on, Mike. I retired from the service five years ago!' Mark replied.

But he knew how hard it was for Mike to be suddenly

left in charge of a hopeless situation. Mark had learned from his own experience in military service that you would give anything to pass the responsibility off to somebody, anybody, and Mike was no different in that regard.

'Where is Hamish?' Mark asked, knowing that the two men were virtually inseparable.

Mike bit his lip and nodded towards the road, which was littered with several bodies, none of them moving.

'He is up there on the road as well. You know Hamish—always has to be first! There is no protection there, so I cannot get to him either,' he concluded with a shrug.

'Have you been in touch with your HQ? I presume someone knows that we are under attack! I thought that all the major roads in Afghanistan were patrolled from the air. Does anyone know what is going on down here?' Mark asked, still unsure who was in charge.

Mike was bitter but still managed to smile, and this time the smile went to his eyes.

'They had an earlier problem up north, on the road between Kabul and Jalalabad. They will get to us as soon as they have got back, refuelled, and come down with a couple of choppers. We have also been in contact with the Brits. They have a Bell Huey chopper assigned to this area. That has also gone to refuel, and then they are coming on down. I just hope they make it before dark!'

'OK—and your contingency plans?' asked Mark.

'Take what trucks are still mobile and run back to Ghazni. But first, we have to get the wounded out of there.' he said, nodding his head towards the front of the convoy. 'We can check for other injuries as we go. What is the state back down the road?'

'We have about a dozen Afghanis spread around protecting the flanks. Dusty and our driver, Owen, have got that well organized. What happened to the other Americans in the convoy? I have no idea!'

'Do you have Dusty with you? Are you on holiday, sightseeing, or something?' Mike asked while still endlessly scanning the area ahead through the rifle scope.

'Well, not exactly,' replied Mark, unsure how or if to tell his friend why he and Dusty were in Afghanistan.

'I will tell you later,' Mark continued with a shrug. 'First, let's deal with this situation. I would guess that the insurgents have the road blocked farther to the north. Otherwise, there would be some traffic. And I would guess that they have subsequently sealed our retreat. Now we are on our own—is that a fair assumption?'

Mike was Irish by descent. He had heard all the military and other official theories about not making assumptions. When you don't know anything, you have to assume something. He smiled again.

'Well, that is what we would have done, but this is Afghanistan. I guess we should worry about that too,' he said with a shrug.

'Right now, first things first; someone must break this stalemate, or we're in big trouble!'
Mark was not Irish by birth—he was one generation removed from that—but Mike was right: one thing at a time.

'What are the rules of engagement?' Mark next asked and was relieved by the response that Mike gave him.

'The ROE, in this case, authorizes me to use whatever force is necessary to help get us and the people we are supposed to be guarding out of here and in one piece.'

The actual standard rules of engagement applicable to all US forces in Afghanistan have an out clause which says something like—nothing in these rules limits your right to take appropriate action to defend yourself and your unit. There was often disquiet among Special Ops forces about the conflicting rules, but now was not the time to get involved in all that. The ROE had a qualification that hostile fire may be returned. That was commonly interpreted to mean 'If somebody wants to mess with us, they will generally wish that they hadn't.' Mark had all the incentive he needed. That was apart from the fact that his most recent training had been with the Special Forces, and that was for very a different situation to that which they found themselves in now. There was nothing particularly fair about the way Delta Forces had trained. Just surprise the opposition and then silence them. If a fight lasted more than ten seconds, the mission would probably fail. But that rarely, if ever, happened.

'Let me talk to Dusty and see if we can do something about this.'

Mark crawled back down the line and away from the head of the convoy. The road's gravelly surface tore at the elbows and knees of his uniform, the occasional bullet pinging off the vehicles. It was a scenario that Mark was familiar with, but one where he was conscious of the fact that he had not done this kind of thing for years. Nonetheless, he knew that he was in his element, and plans started to form in his mind.

Mark thought he was again going to have to ask Dusty to do something that any sane person would laugh at and just walk away. He was pleasantly surprised. Dusty did laugh. Then he just yelled to Owen to take over his position, told him briefly what was going down, and then hurried after Mark with a huge grin.

Dusty liked action, which was better than sitting around waiting to get shot at. He was also in a similar position to Mark. He had been bored. The two of them could not be seen to be trying to take over, but Mike recognized that they could do what he could not do. Mike's job was to protect the convoy, so he had to stay put. If Mark and Dusty wanted to play cowboys and Indians, that was their choice. Mike could not know the reasons for their being in this hellhole, but they seemed quite at home.

When Mark returned to the forward position, they rehearsed their hand signals, and then he agreed with Mike on a rough plan. They each fired off a couple of rounds in the general direction of what they assumed to be the enemy position, not concerned if they inflicted any damage. It was better to waste a couple of rounds to ensure that their guns worked, and the first couple of shots would be wasted anyway. Shots fired down a cold barrel tended to miss their target and at the distance between them and their enemy, by quite a margin. Unless you were fortunate. It did not matter, because Mark did not intend to get into a serious firefight, but it was what he had been trained to do. He wanted to simply unsettle the people who were causing the problem. That was what Mark had been trained for all those years ago.

To react appropriately in any situation.

And to do so before the opposition could seize the initiative.

Mark was betting that the opposition had no such training and therefore hoping that the insurgents would do something stupid. Unsettled people, especially those without any training, do not fight very well. Mark certainly had enough ammunition. But he swapped the AK-47s for something more reliable.

Mark and Dusty crawled off the road to their left in a northwest direction with a couple of M16 rifles with M203 40mm launchers and an ample supply of grenades. They also had a set of communicators, which Mike had produced from his kit bag. The sun was beginning to get lower in the west, and the slope they headed up was already in shadow. They were still cautious as they moved up the hill. When they had put some distance between themselves and the road, they ran crouching and ducked from one cluster of rocks to the next. They were playing a dangerous game of hide-and-seek, but they had no other choice.

The plan worked well, and Mike was as good as his word. Just before they broke cover to cross open ground, there was an exchange of hand signals, and then a withering burst of fire was directed towards the insurgent positions. There was a certain amount of hope that at least some of their opponents were looking at the road and the defenders rather than up to their right.

But it could not last.

Mark and Dusty started to attract fire from farther up the hill and behind them. These insurgents were also firing from quite some distance. If they were in communication with the rest of their team, that could mean that Mark had been discovered earlier than he had intended.

Mark used his communicator.

'Mike, can you get a line on the guys who are trying to burn our ass?'

'Toby's on to that,' came the response. 'Just give us a minute. And stay where you are until I give you the Ok.'

Dusty, however, had other thoughts. He broke cover and ran farther up the hill. He could not be seen by the insurgents to the north. But he would be visible to any to the south-west.

He got the result that he wanted. The firing followed him. He ended up directly between the two groups. If it was not for the distance between the groups, it could have brought a whole new meaning to the phrase *killed by friendly fire*. Critically, it allowed Toby to get a direct and closer line on the insurgents up in the hills, and the exchange of fire enabled Dusty to get a good sighting on the insurgent position. With one more burst of fire from Toby, the firing from behind Mark and Dusty ceased.

Mark could see the remaining insurgents abandoning their foxhole and heading south from his position. That caused a whole cacophony of fire from the troops at the rear of the convoy, with mixed results.

Mark hurried up the slope, intent on chastising Dusty. It had been a foolish act—nothing like the patient build-up generally associated with a man as finely trained as he had been. But on arriving, body language told him to forget it, and he chose to ignore Dusty's greeting, something like *What took you so fucking long?* In any case, Mark had to remind himself that he would have been talking to his lawyer, not his sergeant.

Together, they pressed north, skirting around the rocks into a position where they had a direct line of sight on the insurgent positions to the north of the convoy. That told Mark what he needed to know. The insurgents appeared to have only primitive, if any, means of communication. Mark and Dusty took their time picking their targets, and the position was either quickly wiped out, or the insurgents fled. Then Mark and Dusty moved farther north to get a line and the next position.

That was where things started to go wrong.

They could no longer see where Mike and the defenders were holed up. And they were beginning to get farther into 'Indian' country, as Dusty described it. The dusk was also beginning to settle over the hillside, so visibility became an issue. The only advantage they had was that they were in the shadow of the hill, whereas the main insurgent force was out in the open. At least until the sun finally sets. But that did not stop stray bullets from heading their way from a position further to their left. They were also out of the line of sight of Mike and his team. They were effectively on their own.

Mark had to grudgingly acknowledge the skill of these insurgents and their organization. They had shuffled their forces to the north and west while Mark and Dusty had focused their concentration on the earlier and more obvious site. Now the insurgents were moving forward towards the isolated pair of ex-Special Forces men. Mark cursed as he realized he had been outsmarted by a bunch of barely trained part-time soldiers. He had been taught to *know your enemy*. But he had arrogantly assumed too much.

So much for soldiers talk. These insurgents were not so dumb after all. Now Mark had a fight on his hands that he probably could not win. They were now pinned down and under attack from three sides. Their only way out was to go back. That meant breaking cover. And the enemy knew exactly where they would be going.

Another crucial point became clear to Mark as he contemplated their fate. The insurgents had not committed all their ragtag army to the initial attack. Now they were moving their reserves forward and attacking the weakest point. Mark had to laugh as he realized the hopelessness of their position. The idea that the size of the convoy was bigger than they would have expected did not seem to faze the insurgents at all. It looked as though they were ready for a real fight. And as day moved to night, which Mark had again assumed would be in his favour, it appeared as though the insurgents were going to move in rather than fade away.

Mark called Mike on his communicator to let him know that they had encountered a far stronger force than they had envisaged. Mike was keen to come to their aid. But Mark would have none of that. Mike had to stay and defend the convoy as best he could. Mike's primary job was not to risk everything for a couple of his mates from way back.

Mark looked at Dusty, and the pair of them just laughed.

They had been in skirmishes together before. As they settled into defensive positions behind what little cover the rocks provided, they realized it was only a matter of time before their position was overrun. They would not go down without a fight, but their situation was hopeless. They would need to fight their way back to the convoy in the darkness.

If they lived that long.

They were contemplating their final move. Either dash the convoy and hope that the fading light would provide them with some cover or stay and fight with its inevitable conclusion.

Then they heard the steady *wup-wup-wup* of a helicopter. That was also coming from over the range to the west and out of the setting sun. Mark and Dusty hid as best they could among the rocks, hoping that the combination of fading light and their camouflage uniforms would keep them safe. A helicopter would always have a massive advantage. And if it were a military machine, night-vision equipment would only increase that advantage as night drew near.

However, whose helicopter, was it?

They had their answer very quickly. A shattering, if brief, burst of machine-gun fire silenced the guns on their left, and then the helicopter swooped on the positions being taken up by the insurgents immediately to the north. It was a Bell Huey bearing British Army markings.
Mark drew a deep breath.

As soon as the Huey started strafing the closest of the

insurgent positions, Mark could see the insurgents abandoning the rest of their positions and disappearing in a panic to the northeast. That was the break Mark and Dusty needed, and it was just in time.

They scampered back down the slope to the relative safety of Mike and his team of marines.

The Huey then came down to the forward position where Mike and his team were defending and delivered the news. The gunner, who had been handling the machine gun in the Bell, jumped down. The Bell did not land—a precaution that had become routine since the advent of IEDs. Mike was quite surprised that the gunner introduced itself as Wendy.

'Is this your command post?' she asked in a humorous tone, indicating the crude rocky outcrop they had been sheltering behind.

Mike grinned.

'Are we glad to see you? Yes. This is it. And thanks for clearing out ahead. Can we move out to recover the rest of our team?'

Although Wendy had as good a sense of humour as any of the guys, she did not return the grin.

'Better that you hop aboard and talk to the pilot. Eric has a better view of what is going down than I do. I only shoot people. But I would say that you have some serious problems. The quicker you get moving out of here, the better.'

Mark and Dusty stumbled back into the group, and then Mark and Mike went to talk to the pilot. The pilot looked remarkably cheerful for someone about to deliver some unwelcome news.

As a helicopter pilot, Eric had seen more than his fair share of conflicts while driving a variety of helicopters for the British Army. That gave him the confidence to assess the situation and ensure that the people he was talking to listened. And like all helicopter pilots the world over, he did not worry too much about rank.

Eric nodded his head towards a couple of headsets, which Mark and Mike quickly donned.

'You have a large force of insurgents moving down the road from the north. They are not as well dressed like you guys, but there are a lot of them! The leading group you walked smack into on your little reconnaissance trip,' he said, pointing to Mark. His body language indicated what he thought of that little excursion. However, he nodded some sort of approval.

'You were unlucky. Half an hour earlier, your plan would have worked. At their present rate of progress, their main body should be here in about twenty minutes. If you like, I can slow them down, but it is getting dark, and I don't have that much fuel. To your south, there is a small force deterring any would-be travellers coming north to join you, but we can deal with them. I do not know what your plans are, but my suggestion is we all go south and get back to Ghazni. I can clear the way.'

Mike looked to Mark, who just nodded. They were thinking the same. Mike was grateful for this straightforward Brit rather than one of the arrogant shits who would have been driving the helicopter had it been an American one. The American plan would have been an all-out assault, assuming a capacity that Mike's forces just did not possess. And when the pilots got low on fuel, they would simply leave the remnants of the convoy to fend for themselves.

Mike nodded his agreement.

'We have to check for wounded and evacuate them first if there are any. OK, we planned to fold back, recovering what we can, and, as you say, run back to Ghazni. There is quite a sizeable force there, and I don't think the insurgents will take us on once we get there. I plan to leave the remains of these trucks on the road—they are no use to us now. Could you hang on while we check for casualties?'

'OK, good plan,' Eric replied while never taking his eyes off the controls except for the occasional sweep of the terrain.

'I guess what you are saying is, if there are any casualties, you want us to take them. That would leave you unprotected without any aerial view of what is going on.'

Mike just shrugged.

His mind was already on the enormity of the task he had to undertake.

Eric accurately summed up the situation.

'OK, that is a big call. But it is your call.'

Mike and Mark nodded again.

'Let's do it!'

They stayed in the helicopter while Eric maneuvered the Huey over the chaos on the ground.

They found the major first. He had taken several rounds full in the face, and the shots had exploded out the back of his head. He would have been dead before his body hit the deck.

Close by was Hamish, who was severely injured and barely breathing.

There were four Afghani soldiers—two with signs of life, the other two very much dead. On the other side of the road, they found the bodies of the remaining two marines who had also been cut down in the initial action, either by the IED or by gunfire.

It was grim work loading the bodies and the injured into the helicopter. Wendy wanted to help, but Mark politely declined, primarily out of gallantry. He explained that someone needed to operate the gun—there was little point in the rescue party getting themselves killed. Wendy was well trained in attending to injuries on the field of battle. There was little that she had not already seen, particularly on the fields at another time and in a different war—around Kosovo in the Adriatic. But there would be plenty of time for her other skills to be put to effective use in attending to the injured once they had evacuated the area.

When all the dead and the injured had been cleared, Toby attached explosive devices to the wrecked vehicles. It would have been nice to have rigged them to explode when the insurgents arrived. However, one of the problems with explosives is that they are non-selective and could injure or kill any allied forces who happened by. Toby decided to just blow them up now. If nothing else, it would make for a spectacular sight and could delay the enemy force coming down the road. More importantly, it would leave nothing worth salvaging, as well as leaving no clues as to what casualties the convoy had suffered.

The four men—Mark, Dusty, Mike, and Toby—folded back through the convoy, convincing the drivers to turn their vehicles around. They loaded up the troops and started their journey back the way they had come.

An Afghan soldier had to drive the vehicle that Stephen Rodriguez had been hiding under. Rodriguez appeared to be still traumatized by the whole show and numbly crawled into his passenger seat and said nothing. They had to first remove the body of Hennessey, which was in the driver's seat and covered in his blood. They placed it in the back of the truck, wedging it between the bales of what looked like materials. A strange cargo to be taking on so hazardous a trip like this one, but you could never really understand Americans. To the Afghan soldier who had the task of driving, the occupant of the truck was just a scared American, probably part of the media group that, for some reason, insisted on following them everywhere and being a complete pain up the ass. Mark took over the vehicle that the Afghani had been driving, for two simple reasons: firstly, none of the other Afghanis knew how to drive, and secondly, it enabled him to follow close behind the ADDI.

The more obvious idea would have been for Mark to drive the ADDI's vehicle. But that may have been tempting fate a little too much. No one asked for an explanation, so none was given.

Dusty and Owen volunteered to be the lead vehicle of the returning convoy, and the remaining Afghanis took up the rear, with Mike and what remained of his US force safely tucked into the middle. Mark did observe that the number of Afghani troops seemed to have diminished by about a half from what he had earlier witnessed, and there was no sign of any other injured or dead Afghani bodies. He assumed that the losses were from desertion rather than from enemy fire.

At this stage, they had no actual body count for this exercise, but it was looking grim.

There was also the risk of more IEDs being on the road, but by the time they got underway, they were all just too tired to care.

The Bell Huey went ahead and managed a couple of blasts from its machine guns, which scattered the remnants of the insurgent group to the south. And then the helicopter hurried on towards the town of Ghazni with the cargo of the dead and wounded, the priority being to get the wounded attended to as quickly as possible.

As the helicopter pilot had inferred, the convoy was now vulnerable, with no air cover. At least it was now completely dark, and not the conditions that the enemy favoured. Still

Mark and his small band took the view that there was little that could be done about that now.

Any further fears that they might have had about the insurgents to the south were, however, quickly abated by the sudden arrival of two American AH-64 Apache attack helicopters. They made short work of any remaining insurgents as they escorted the convoy back down the road, and there were no further incidents as they made it back into Ghazni.

The battered convoy finally made it into the military compound after passing through the darkened streets of the city to the stares of an unsympathetic population.

Few of the people would have recognized the convoy as one that they had seen earlier on the same day.

To Mark and his small team, they had just experienced the harsh realities of life and death, in a land where this kind of conflict was an everyday occurrence.

Little did Mark know that things would get far worse.

Being shot by insurgents would be the very least of his worries.

Chapter 27

Wind Down

It was only when they were sitting down in the compound mess area enjoying a relaxing beer, courtesy of the Brits, that the adrenaline rush subsided, and he recalled why they were here in this godforsaken country.

Mark had not seen anything of Stephen Rodriguez or the body of his associate since their arrival back in Ghazni. He had been far too busy checking on the wounded and trying to get some semblance of order into the chaotic situation that had developed during the extraction.

Mike had gone off to report to his superiors, basically to find out if the major would be replaced, or if he was to assume command of his diminished force. It was doubtful if there would be any volunteers at the Ghazni base, but this was the US Army, and there was a protocol to follow.

Mark began to worry that, just maybe, they had lost Rodriguez in the chaos. Or maybe he had crawled off somewhere to use his position in authority to be flown to Kabul and out of this hellhole. It would be ironic if, having been involved in a firefight and all the adrenaline and excitement that caused, they had lost the whole reason for their being in Afghanistan in the first place.

Mark was confident that he had already saved the life of the ADDI, simply by getting him out of the truck and onto the ground. Their brief encounter had revealed nothing.

The demeanour of Rodriguez—one of sullen acceptance of his lot and no attempt to assume control of the tough situation—spoke volumes for the character of the man. Maybe Mark should have left him to his fate! But no. Mark had a job to do, and if he did it well, the US justice system would eventually bring Rodriguez to the fate that he truly deserved.

Now, where had he gone?

Mark need not have worried.

Stephen Rodriguez came into the mess dressed in US Army fatigues at the same time as Mike returned from his debriefing. Although Gilroy was anxious to be involved in a discussion with the medical staff Rodriguez simply interrupted him.

The ADDI looked as though he was beginning to recover his composure, but he still looked ashen, and very worried. He shook hands with Gilroy, and there was an exchange of information that caused Stephen to look in the direction of Mark. And then came the step that Mark did not want to see.

Gilroy nodded his head towards where Mark and Dusty were sitting talking with the Brits from the helicopter—Eric and Wendy. Rodriguez came over to Eric, said thanks, ignored Wendy, and thanked Mark and Dusty in a somewhat offhand way for *saving his ass*. He ignored Owen who was still dressed as a local, and then walked back out of the room without another word.

It did seem a lukewarm acknowledgment of the team that had probably saved the life of the most important guy they had ever met.

Rodriguez had virtually ignored the one man in the group of defenders who knew him and knew who he was. Sure, Mark had changed somewhat since the last time that they had met. That had been on September 13th. Just a day after Mark had lost two of his friends, and just two days after several hundred New York citizens had been slaughtered while going about their normal, routine lives. Mark had been in the office of the ADDI at Langley. That day, Mark had virtually no hair, his face had received a pounding from a variety of sources including a bullet that had shaved his temple, he wore glasses, and he was dressed in an immaculate dark-grey suit, courtesy of an Irish ex-CIA agent called Elliott Shannon.

Now Mark was much better presented.

Mark's hair was back to normal, although he could not remember when it had last been washed or combed. He had a full beard and a moustache. He was dirty and must have stunk from all the dust and sweat during his recent exertions. There was little water available in the compound to rectify that situation, and most of what clean water there was, was reserved for attending to the wounded. Mark was dressed in a uniform that made him look like any other United States Marine although his was probably dirtier and more ripped and torn than most of those around him. Crawling on your belly along a rock-strewn road, and then clambering over rocks, tends to do that. And Mark was simply too tired to change.

It was little wonder that the ADDI had failed to recognize him.

No one else knew of the thoughts that were going through Mark's mind at this time. Among them, while it would have been nice to be recognized as the one man who had been principally responsible for saving the life of Rodriguez, Mark was grateful that he had failed to recognize him.

The fact that Rodriguez had virtually ignored his team's efforts was what Mark had come to expect from this man. But the thought that they had been so close, yet there had not been even a hint of recognition, was very satisfying.

It was Wendy who summed up the feelings of the exhausted soldiers.

'Who the fuck does that asshole think he is?' she asked.

Mark had to think before replying. Apart from the fact that he was both surprised and amused at the crude way this *bloke* had asked the question, he would have liked to have stated the truth—that the guy was the ADDI of the CIA. Being only an assistant and only a deputy did not detract from the fact that he was an enormously powerful man. That should certainly impress the Brits that they were in the presence of the United States equivalent of royalty.

But Mark kept the identity of Rodriguez to himself.

Instead, he just said, 'Probably a bean counter,' and everybody laughed.

'A pity about his boyfriend!' Wendy commented to keep their conversation going.

Mark sat bolt upright.

'His what?'

Wendy shrugged.

'One of your guys was telling me that he lost a dear friend in the firefight, and he was pretty cut-up about it. At least that's who he said all the blood was from. Those two were an item!'

Holy shit! Mark thought.

So that was why Rodriguez had been so morose when Mark had first seen him back at the truck. While Mark and company had been trying to fathom who the mysterious person was who had accompanied Stephen Rodriguez on his trip to Afghanistan and had tried all sorts of theories of how he fitted into the scheme, they had never thought of that possibility.

Edward Hennessey was just a boyfriend!

Or was he?

The conversation continued, with the two Brits oblivious to this stunning revelation. How was Dusty going to react to that little snippet of information? There was nothing wrong with it. Men had their preferences, so be it. But Mark's team had wasted an awful amount of time to find out something that should have been obvious to someone with Mark's ability to read body language. And the result was significant for two reasons.

Firstly, how could a guy of ADDI rank have a homosexual affair without the assistant inspector of the CIA knowing about it? While some would regard sexual preference as a personal matter, the position that Rodriguez held in the CIA would, unfortunately, render that unconscionable. The security risk was just too great.

Secondly, if some mileage could have been made from this little snippet of information, that chance had died in the Battle of Ghazni.

It turned out that Mark and this crew had been involved in a little incident in Kosovo. Mark had then called a Colonel Tom Dean, who was part of the Kosovo Force (KFOR), by telephone. As a consequence of that call, Dean had gone off on a raid into Serbia to collect a general who had until then escaped the clutches of NATO and the legal team at The Hague. On that mission, Eric had been the pilot and Wendy the gunner of the helicopter that had done the extraction.

It was such a small world.

And now, because the Brits were short of pilots and crew in Afghanistan, these two had volunteered for a three-month stint in this hellhole. While Eric and Wendy rattled on about their experiences in many parts of the world, Mark would have loved to have filled in the gaps of what really went down that day in Kosovo and the terrible aftermath.

Mark had been trained to keep quiet and to keep things on a need-to-know basis. So, he did.

In any case, Mark was just too tired.

Chapter 28

Schemes

Stephen Rodriguez now had something else to worry about. He had lost a very dear friend, and if it were not for the fact that he had a mountain of other problems to deal with in this godforsaken country, it may well have overwhelmed him.

Rodriguez was, after all, a married man with two lovely daughters. Had it not been for a chance meeting with a male FBI agent in New York City in the period immediately after the second September 11 episode, he would never have known that he had any desire to be with another man. The FBI agent was so warm and beautiful. Admittedly, they were both high on drugs at the time, so that could have influenced his judgment. But the following day, his only desire was to be with Edward Hennessey again. And so, as that relationship grew, and his relationship with his wife of over twenty years declined, he began to plan another life.

The chance to take Hennessey away with him on an overseas trip appealed to him. It could not be justified, but it could be and would be, arranged. Rodriguez had discussed that possibility with Hennessey, and he had seemed quite excited. Then, in his discussions with Director Jim Schlesinger, Rodriguez had used the relatively lame excuse that FBI expertise would be useful in assisting in the follow-up to the assassination, or at least the attempted assassination, of the President. No one was supposed to know, or admit, anything about that; and a certain amount of secrecy was necessary. Therefore, the selection of an FBI agent to accompany him was left to Rodriguez.

Brilliant in its simplicity!

And now Edward Hennessey was dead. Killed, so the records would show, by a stray bullet in the battle of Ghazni - needlessly, so senselessly gone from Stephen's life. That left Stephen bitter, distraught, and very lonely.

The fact of the matter was that Stephen had fired the fatal bullet. It had all been a sham. Although he had no idea *how* or *why* Hennessey had been playing a double game. Edward had said that he loved Stephen. And Stephen had believed him. But Edward had been a setup.

What Rodriguez did not know was *why* and by *whom?* Was it the Russians trying a twenty-first-century honey trap to get at the CIA? Or, worse still, was it his own CIA friends trying to get a handle on his drug business? Or was it these cunning people in Afghanistan and beyond, trying to muscle in on his drug trade? Or was the infamous FBI trying their own form of entrapment?

Whatever the cause, and whatever the reason, Hennessey was not cut out for this type of life. The pressure of operating in a foreign country, especially one as remote and brutal as Afghanistan, had taken its toll. In a moment of erotic euphoria, Edward had let something slip. He wanted to get away from all this duplicity and just be with Stephen. Had the honey trap had been reversed? But Stephen had other information. Was Edward really playing another deadly game?

Much as he loved Edward, could he take the risk? Which

came first—love or business? Regrettably, in the middle of all the chaos on the road from Ghazni, when the IED exploded, Stephen had taken his chance and got rid of the problem.

That, at this moment, was not the problem that Stephen Rodriguez had to worry about.

It had all been so much easier when he was just a normal CIA field operative. In that role, he just waited for some orders to come down from on high, and then he just went about carrying them out as best, and as ruthlessly, as he could. Even when he had been the CIA station chief of station in Kabul, which now seemed like a lifetime ago but was only a few years ago, he still had to wait for instructions from higher up before he could do anything. Well, almost anything. Agents in the field must do something with their many, many hours of spare time, and they don't always wait for orders.

As a field agent, he had got together with a few of his friends who, like many in the service of their great country, were into recreational drugs. The problem with drugs was not the substances themselves. The problem was with the people who you had to deal with to get them. These people, or dealers, were not exactly law-abiding citizens. There had developed an obvious conflict of interest in the dealings with employees of the government. Stephen and his friends came up with a plan to circumvent this. They set up a drug network that bypassed all the usual criminals. And it was also brilliant in its simplicity and brilliant in its execution.

That was, of course, if only they could maintain a consistent and constant supply to meet an almost-insatiable demand.

This latest escapade with the supply chain had not

exactly gone according to plan. For the fourth time in as many shipments, someone had attempted to intercept it. And Rodriguez was not one to write that off as just a coincidence.

The last shipment had been interrupted by plain old bad luck. Well, coupled with the sheer incompetence on the part of the Afghans who were supposed to be experienced in making things happen in this chaotic country: a traffic accident and the way subsequent events unfolded allowed someone else. On reflection, the four shipments had been intercepted at quite different places and in vastly different circumstances, so there was no identifiable pattern. That, of course, did not mean that the same people were or were not involved.

The first shipment had gone missing somewhere close to the Pakistani border. And none of the people who were involved in that shipment, or any of the drugs, had been heard of or seen since.

The second shipment, according to intelligence sources in the drug trade, seemed to have headed north to the Chinese border and had also not been heard of or seen since.

On the third shipment, there had been at least one survivor who had revealed all the incompetence that had occurred on that trip in all its majestic glory. That had occurred on the road between Kabul and Jalalabad and appeared to have been due to mechanical problems, which just ballooned into an uncontrollable and complete mess.

But the result was the same.

No drugs.

The fourth shipment had been in a well-protected convoy and under the direct control of the ADDI. That was nonetheless attacked by insurgents well short of the city of Kabul. And it could be argued that the attack had nothing to do with drugs. Was that just a coincidence? Nonetheless, if this trend continued, the perpetrators may as well go into the fields south of Kandahar and pick their own poppies.

For the time being, this shipment was intact and safe, albeit a day late. But Rodriguez could not believe in coincidence. It was in his training, stamped indelibly into the very core of his thought process, drilled into the minds of all who went through the Farm in Williamsburg in Virginia.

He believed that someone, or some group, had managed to penetrate the organization. And he would have to find out who they were and deal with them—quickly, efficiently, and ruthlessly.

That was, however, not the problem that Stephen was worried about now.

As a part of his role as ADDI, Rodriguez had told his director that an assassination attempt would be made on the President of Afghanistan, Hamid Karzai. Stephen Rodriguez would be in the country to offer the full might of the United States forces, both covert and overt, to track down those responsible for this heinous crime. It did not matter to Rodriguez whether the attempt on the life of Hamid Karzai was successful or not. The kind of political thinking that decided whether it was good or bad for any or all countries was done at a level of his government where they had far less factual information, extraordinarily little emotion, and far too many spin doctors. But Stephen felt that his small contribution to the scheme so far had been brilliant in its simplicity. He had ensured that the group of Tajiks who were to carry out the assassination attempt were a part of the same convoy and would arrive in Kabul at the same time as the ADDI.

That would suit the CIA's purposes admirably. The

CIA would be close to the action. They would know who the people were. And they would know where they were. Therefore, they could quickly round up anyone involved who was not killed in the ensuing bloodbath. If anyone did survive and tried to escape, then they would be killed before they could be questioned and reveal even the slightest hint of any CIA involvement.

There was however one slight problem.

The convoy, with its weird collection of members, was now back in Ghazni. The President of Afghanistan was due to address a parade the following day in Kabul. All the media, both local and international, would be in attendance because the President had said that he was going to announce significant importance to the battle-weary citizens of his great country. In true political style, he had arranged a parade of the latest batch of the Afghan Army recruits who had completed but not necessarily passed, the first stage of their training. The fact that over half of the original recruits had simply disappeared back to wherever they had originally come from, complete with a new uniform and the latest weapons supplied courtesy of the allied forces, escaped no one.

The group of Tajiks who were intent on their plot to kill the President would now not make it to that parade, and they would need to make new plans. Rodriguez was confident, supported by intelligence gathered on behalf of the CIA in Marjah, that they would not scrap their original plans, having made it as far as they had. He would need to contact the CIA in Kabul and arrange for another opportunity. And that would need to happen fast if all the other plans that Stephen had on his plate were to come to fruition.

The problem was that he could not easily get in touch with the right people, and the odds were that he would need to wait until they arrived in Kabul. The road between Ghazni and Kabul was closed, and he could not know when it would be reopened. He could, of course, go to Kabul via one of the United States Apache helicopters, or via the British Bell Huey. But that would mean leaving behind both the drugs and the Tajiks, and he did not particularly want to do either of those two things. He certainly did not want to leave the body of his friend to be disposed of in the respectful but uncaring manner that is the way with the military embroiled in overseas conflicts, even if Edward had been a naughty boy.

That, however, was not the problem that Stephen was worried about now.

At present, Mark Taylor was the overriding problem that Stephen Rodriguez was worried about.

When Stephen had walked into the Ghazni rest area he had genuinely wanted to thank the people who had extracted them from what was a very tricky situation. He, of course, did not want to reveal who he was and why he was driving a beaten-up old truck full of rubbish.

Just so long as everyone knew that he was important.

But the sight of Mark Taylor sitting there had chilled him to the bone.

Rodriguez had not recognized the soldier who was so callously but efficiently barking out orders back up the road to Kabul. He had been in no condition to recognize anyone. Such was the stress he was under at that time. And such was his grief at the death of the man who was his lover.

But now he had recognized the one man who he had reason to be concerned about.

Why was the son of the CIA's OIG assistant inspector out here in Afghanistan? More particularly, why was Mark Taylor in Afghanistan at the same time as the ADDI?

Even more particularly - Why was he part of the same convoy as the one that was carrying opiates? And the convoy that was carrying the Tajiks?

How much, if anything, did Mark Taylor know? And what, if anything, was the relationship between Taylor and the late Edward Hennessey? It was hardly coincidental that Hennessey had been on an FBI mission and the son of Harold had turned up in the same place.

There were just too many coincidences.

The last time Stephen had seen Mark Taylor was in the ADDI's own office at Langley, and he had been reluctantly impressed with the guy's sense of justice and his dogged determination to see things through. Rodriguez had not been directly involved in the troubles that had resulted in their meeting, and during the aftermath of that meeting, he had been able to sit back and let matters take their natural course.

But now was different.

Why was Mark Taylor in Afghanistan?

Rodriguez had walked up to Taylor in Ghazni and shaken hands with him. Yet Taylor had shown no sign of recognition. Neither had Rodriguez indicated that he recognized Taylor.

Mark Taylor had a full head of hair, and a beard was dressed in fatigues and looked as though he had been dragged through a hedge backward. The last time they had met, Taylor was clean-shaven, wore glasses, and was dressed in a dark-grey business suit. So, there was a good reason why he could not be expected to recognize the man. But it was the eyes that Stephen had recognized. And he had almost shaken in fear without really knowing why.

Taylor had shown no sign that he recognized Rodriguez. And that was perfectly understandable. They had only met briefly, and Mark Taylor had been so stressed at that time that faces were not important. Actions were. And an ex-marine meeting a man so high up in the CIA hierarchy—Taylor could be excused for remembering the office rather than the person.

But *what* was he doing here now?

The odds were that he was on a covert mission.

But why? And with whom? And what was the mission?

Mark Taylor was the boss of a computer software company based in New York City. Those interests were as far removed from the goings-on in Afghanistan as chalk is from cheese.

However, there was another connection that Stephen had just cause to worry about. Mark Taylor's father was Harold Taylor, now the assistant inspector of the CIA. Harold had only recently taken up the position, and it was taking the business side of the CIA some time to get a handle on what his approach to the job would be. After all, the senior Taylor had been *one of them*. In fact, as station chief in Wellington in New Zealand, Taylor had reported to Stephen Rodriguez. Now he was on the other side—putting a ruler over his former friends and workmates!

The only thing that had been recently rumoured was that Harold Taylor had rapidly established a close working relationship with a certain Karen Marshall, who was director of intelligence at the DEA. And fair enough that he should. From all reports, the lady was attractive and available! Both of their respective organizations were tied up in anything and everything to do with drugs, drug dealers, and drug traffickers. Including their respective concerns about drug users both within and without their government organizations.

But how close was that relationship? And was there

a connection to the network that Stephen was involved with?

Or was this just another coincidence?

Stephen did not believe in coincidence. He did not like coincidences.

Now there was another coincidence that made his hair curl. Mark was the only son of a man who could make life difficult for someone in the CIA who was involved in drugs, or, for that matter, anything or anyone who had a hint of not meeting the high standards of that organization —Harold Taylor.

While head of station in Wellington in New Zealand, Taylor had taken the unusual step of using his son Mark to go on a covert mission, presumably because he did not know who he could trust in the CIA. Taylor had been proved correct in his judgment in that case.

Because of that little exercise, Harold Taylor was regarded as a mix between a maverick and a hero. That probably resulted in his promotion to the position as the CIA watchdog. It was not, therefore, unreasonable to expect Harold Taylor to employ some unusual methods, and some unusual people, in his new position.

The logical conclusion from all of this was that the appearance of Mark Taylor so far from home could be courtesy of his father.

Harold Taylor was an assistant inspector with the OIG. He would not logically be directly involved with overseas operations. However, Rodriguez had two areas of concern that he would not want any inspectors or their minions snooping around—his drug network, and the security considerations surrounding that. Stephen was confident that he had dealt with the security issues in Afghanistan by ridding himself of that sneak Wakil Hekmatyar.

But the drug network was a much wider issue and another matter entirely.

Then there was Karen Marshall to consider.

She was with a sister organization that, along with the CIA and the FBI, was trying to get a handle on the drug trade. While that was a never-ending battle, Rodriguez could control things within his own organization. But not so with the DEA and the FBI.

You did not need to be a rocket scientist to work out at least one plausible reason for the association between the DEA with the assistant inspector. Drug use in the CIA, FBI, DEA, and several other government organizations was on the increase, and someone would try to do something about that. The aspect that Stephen was having difficulty with was that it was now becoming personal. Marshall and Taylor were sharing information and could be focused on him!

But what had sparked their involvement?

As with all bureaucratic structures, a new broom usually attacked the obvious until that very system pummelled them into submission. Then, they went off to attack some other far less obvious, and far less important, offense. One that did not directly affect the bureaucrats.

But what if Harold Taylor had stumbled upon something, anything, that was linked to Stephen Rodriguez and either to drug use in the CIA or to information being passed to others? And once again, Harold had called on his son Mark Taylor to do some snooping.

Now that would be a genuine problem.

There were just too many coincidences.

To protect his network, Stephen would need to get rid of Mark Taylor. And what better place to do that than in Afghanistan where anything could and did, happen.

Rodriguez fired up his laptop, went into a hidden area of the hard drive, and pulled up his files on Afghanistan.

There was nothing particularly unusual about them, except that, unlike the official files, Stephen maintained the files himself. That meant there was no spin—simply hard facts.

He looked at the security arrangements for President Hamid Karzai.

Karzai had got a somewhat complex arrangement for his personal security, but it seemed to be under the control of the Russian SVR. He then looked through the role currently being played by the SVR—the Russian intelligence organization that had superseded the infamous KGB. He read through several papers that expressed various opinions on how these two were related, and then he looked back through some older files going back to the days when he was last stationed in Kabul. Eventually, he had a name.

He also had a telephone number, though it was doubtful if that number was still active. He should have remembered the direct line of the man that he needed to speak to, or he could just as easily have acquired the number through a Google search. Like all such organizations, they had two types of telephone numbers: available to the public and not available to the public. Neither of which was secret, and with modern technology, you could easily switch between the two, and no one would be any the wiser. The Russians were also getting quite good at recording and tracing calls. With these thoughts in his mind, he called the public number of the embassy of Russia in Kabul.

There did not seem to be much point in calling a Russian embassy in a place like Kabul and talking in English, so he spoke in fluent, if badly accented, Russian.

'Could I speak with Yuri Alekseyev?' Stephen asked the operator.

No, please. It would be very un-Russian to be calling

Yuri for any other reason than to give him information. And usually in exchange for money. In such circumstances, there was no need to be polite.

The person answering the embassy telephone was not the normal receptionist, one hoped because all he said by way of reception was 'Da.'

Yuri Alexseyev the call in a much friendlier manner.

He still said 'Da'—it just sounded better.

'Do you mind if we speak in English? It has been a long day, and I don't think I am up to trying to translate into your native language what I have to say. In any case, your English is near perfect, whereas my Russian is bloody pathetic.'

Rodriguez laughed, recalling earlier times when he had asked his then Soviet host, in Russian, where he could take a piss and was rewarded with another round of vodka.

'Who is speaking?'

'Where do I take a piss?' Stephen answered with another laugh. Alexseyev would remember that.

'Ah, Stefan! Where are you?'

Rodriguez could have done without the laughter. Yuri was a prick. However, for the moment, he was someone useful, and so, as is the way in all international relations, major or minor, he had to maintain the calm air of someone talking with a friend.

'At the moment, I am down in a shit of a place called Ghazni.'

There was no reaction to Stephen's plight, but Rodriguez could envisage the Russian being more than a little surprised.

He wasn't.

'What brings you back to this hellhole? I hear you have got a desk job at Langley—or have you been demoted?'

Yuri laughed as well.

Not that there was anything to be humorous about. The Russians would know exactly what position Stephen Rodriguez held in Washington. Their information was so good they would probably know before anyone else of any promotions, and any demotions, going on at the CIA. They probably also knew the brand of coffee being served out of the many machines that Western spooks like to have, which information, gathered at considerable cost to the SVR, was used simply to make the CIA feel uncomfortable —what other innermost secrets did they know? And being SVR, Yuri would never miss the opportunity to use the name *Langley* rather than the name *Washington* just to show he was part of the inner circle of the intelligence community.

Contrary to the belief pushed by Hollywood, and to a lesser extent by some of the media, relations between the various countries' spook organizations were more like a diplomatic courtship. Rarely, if ever, did they get involved in anything that could involve physical harm to either party. Verbal harm was another matter. Yuri Alexseyev was not like Stephen Rodriguez, and he knew that the name *Stefan* irritated him, so why not use it?

Rodriguez sighed. For one moment, he thought of asking Alexseyev for the latest CIA employee list. That would save time when he got back to Washington!

Stephen would have liked to have a dig at Yuri, but there was no difference in pronunciation between Yuri and Yuriy, and his command of the Russian language only told him that the literal meaning of *Yuriy* was 'farmer,' and there was no harm in that.

For the moment, he needed Alexseyev to do something for him. At the same time, he wanted it to appear as though Rodriguez was being helpful. He ignored the barb and got down to business.

'Yuri, we have a problem. No doubt you have heard rumours of a plot to assassinate President Hamid Karzai?'

'Oh, we have heard several rumours. This *is* Afghanistan, Stefan!' Yuri replied, his senses now immediately on the alert. Eventually, one of them would move on from this game of chess. But Alexseyev's antenna was raised. The Russians were aware that the United States President was not too happy with the Afghanistan President. It was therefore in Russia's best interest, at least at the moment, to keep Hamid Karzai alive.

The United States' position was probably, with the help of the CIA, to get rid of Karzai.

The old story in the ongoing diplomatic battle between two of the giants on the diplomatic scene—we don't know what position we should take, so we will settle for taking the opposite side to you, until we know some more or until the position becomes untenable.

Rodriguez continued.

'Yes, we know that. It is not unusual in this country to assassinate people rather than to discuss things amicably. It could be a matter of who gets Hamid Karzai first. An external plot organized by someone in Pakistan or one organized by his own supporters in Kabul!'

Never miss the chance to imply that the Pakistan Inter-Services Intelligence may be involved! The feeling in parts of the Washington intelligence community was that it was the Russians who were responsible for the trouble with Pakistan. But that issue would have to wait for another time and place. The immediate problem was, how was he to put this?

'Yuri, we have a particular problem. An obscure terrorist group, with the support of some United States mercenaries, is in Afghanistan now, and they intend to go for Hamid Karzai. We cannot be seen to interfere at this stage because we have no absolute proof, and you know what our media and legal systems are like. I thought I could call in one of my chips and get you to have a quiet word with them.'

Alexseyev had to think about that.

What chips?

In post-Taliban Afghanistan, the SVR seemed to be doing all the giving of favours to these arrogant Americans. They thought that the end of the Cold War was the end of the Soviet Union as they knew it. And they applied the same arrogant logic to mean the end of Russia. Well, who has the vast, largely unexplored regions of Siberia, which probably would, turn Russia once more into a major player on the world scene? Sure, Russia would need Western know-how to extract the vast resources, but the resources were Russian!   And this time, Russia had the business acumen to make sure that these greedy Americans would not be getting the biggest share of the cake. But now was not the time to get involved in semantics.

'When is the attempt to occur?' Alexseyev asked.

'Well, that's it,' replied Rodriguez. 'We believe that the plan was that they were to go to the parade tomorrow. Now they will not be able to. They are still headed for Kabul, but they will not make it by tomorrow. That means they will have to modify their plans. Therefore, we could intercept them before they can get reorganized.'

'You seem confident that they will not be here tomorrow. We had suspicions that an attempt would be made by some people from the south of Pakistan working with the Tajiks. Is this the same plot, or do you know something that we don't?' Alexseyev had to ask.

An icy shiver ran up the back of Rodriguez.

He immediately began to feel far less confident than he had at the beginning of their conversation. Maybe his elaborate plan was not so good after all. Had Alexseyev got wind of the Tajik plot? Hopefully, he did not know of the CIA's connection with it.

However, Yuri would be remiss if he did not suspect the involvement of others. The Tajiks were unlikely to be able to organize an event without help from some other party. The question was - Could Yuri be persuaded that the ADDI had better information?

The SVR intelligence was not so dumb! But what else could Rodriguez do? He had to persevere and maintain the impression that they were sharing information.

'We think they are part of the same group,' the ADDI continued.

'They got delayed traveling on the road to Kabul by an attack on their convoy just north of Ghazni. We have been following them. But there is now a risk that our cover will be blown. They are currently holed up in Ghazni, and it does not look as though the road north will be open before tomorrow afternoon at the earliest. Check it out yourself. I do not know if you have anyone in Ghazni, but the word should have filtered through to Kabul about the attack that occurred this afternoon. We do not know who was behind this attack—probably the Taliban.'

Yes - Yuri Alexseyev had heard about the attack. And that the road was closed.

No - it was not the Taliban. It was a more dangerous al-Qaeda affiliate group who had been trying to muscle in on Taliban territory. They were being quite successful, and certainly better organized.

And he had another bit of unwelcome news for the CIA, even if it was not true.

'No - we do not have anyone in Ghazni,' Yuri lied.

The SVR had a spook resident in Ghazni. He thought the CIA would almost certainly know of that. There were also a couple of Russian agents traveling in the same convoy! Which he thought the CIA would not know of.

Stephen Rodriguez felt relieved. His *friend* Yuri Alexseyev was lying. That gave him confidence that his story was being taken seriously.

'OK, this is what we can do. I will have one of our people contact you with the identities of these people. We should also be able to tell you where you can pick them up once they arrive in Kabul.'

Alexseyev had to ask.

'You do not normally hand us this kind of information, Stefan! And for our cooperation on this, you want what?'

Yuri had played such games before. He knew what the answer would be.

'Just trying to keep Karzai safe,' was the expected reply.

Now, why on earth would the CIA want to do that?

And why would the CIA be using an assistant director from one of the most senior positions in Washington to follow a couple of low-life Tajik rebels and their Western friends? That would indicate that there was far more to this business than had been implied.

Strange people, these Americans.

'OK, I will see what we can do,' and the call was terminated.

What was Alexseyev supposed to do now?

Yuri was aware of the arrogant nature of the CIA. They had information and would pass that information on to the SVR only when it suited their particular purpose. And heaven alone knew what they hoped to gain from it. Yuri was still unsure whether Stephen or the CIA in general, was aware that he worked for the GRU, the Russian military intelligence, rather than the SVR. And that difference was more than just a name. The GRU would approach any situation with a far more brutal attitude than their civilian counterparts.

Therefore, the CIA had virtually condemned some men to death.

Unless there was something far more sinister going on.

Yuri was far more senior in the Russian hierarchy than would normally be the case for the station chief in Kabul. That was because of the developing situation in Afghanistan. The Americans were having the very same problems that the Soviets had encountered during their occupation in the 1980s.

How do you tame so diverse a population in this landlocked country? While strategically Afghanistan may not have appeared important enough to care for, it was still surrounded by countries that were more likely to favour the Russians in the present political climate.

Well, except China. But you could not have everything you wanted! At least to the west, Iran would not be on any Americans' Christmas card list. To the east, there was Pakistan, where relations with Washington were brittle and getting worse.

Therefore, for the right, or wrong, reasons, the Russians had elevated their stake in Afghanistan.

There was also an ace that the Russians held, and of which Yuri was aware.

They had a mole deep inside the US intelligence service.

Chapter 29

More Ducks

The parade in Kabul was probably the biggest non-event in the long history of this war-torn nation.

The Afghanistan troops did a reasonable job of looking efficient and smart. They managed to avoid any overt display of boredom or incompetence. And they managed to present a reasonable turnout for their political masters.

President Hamid Karzai also managed to avoid any overt display of boredom. He performed his formal but cursory inspection, and then it was his time to address the troops.

Karzai's words were directed at the international media. And everyone would have been forgiven for failing to notice anything of significance in what he had to offer to the long-suffering and poverty-stricken residents of this land.

The President was not informed of any plot to assassinate him. Alexseyev did not see any point in alarming the man. It was just one more apparent attempt on his life, and it would probably come to nothing.

Why anyone would want to be a politician in Afghanistan,

where it was simpler to measure in months rather than years the survival time of almost anyone who had risen to a position in power, was a mystery to sanest observers. Possibly it had something to do with optimism. More likely, there was something in political animals that made them feel invincible despite the statistics. It possibly comes from a belief that they have the answer to all the nation's problems.

It probably comes from achieving the pinnacle of power at any cost, and to hell with the risks.

Or so Yuri Alexseyev thought as he watched the whole event as it unfolded. He had no interest in the speech. He had no interest in the Afghan troops. If he cared to think about it, he was not really concerned about whether Hamid Karzai lived or died. It was just a job.

In keeping with his responsibilities, he had men posted in all the building's surrounding the area where the parade occurred. Their focus of attention would be on the crowd. Their fingers would be on the triggers of their guns. The safety catches were off, and they were primed, ready to fire at the slightest hint of trouble.

Just because Alexseyev had received advice from the ADDI of the CIA that the infidels would not be here, was no reason to relax. There was something about the spook business. You could never know what was real or imagined, what was true or false, what was valuable information or bad information. And amidst all that, who knew what random nutcases were on the loose? And who knew what schemes were in the mind of Stefan, or the minds of the CIA? The perpetrators could already be in town!

Yuri had not told anyone that he had received any advice from that source, other than his masters in Moscow. It would be business as usual, and his men would be on maximum alert.

Only when the parade was over, and all the officials had been whisked away in their bulletproof cars, would Alexseyev relax.

Now he had another set of problems to worry about.

So maybe, the CIA had told him the truth. He was still perplexed by the call that he had received from his old adversary, but then, in this business, nothing surprised him anymore. Maybe the diplomatic balance had shifted yet again. But he found that hard to believe.

The CIA and the SVR could never be real friends, given the history of their respective countries and the countless years of conflict and aggression. Even in the more enlightened times that had followed the Cold War, there was still that underlying distrust. And the Russian paranoia and American arrogance were like mixing oil and water. Yuri shook his head.

The speech droned on until, to everyone's relief, it ended without incident. President Karzai was whisked away. Who knew whether there had been a plot, whether the CIA had been right or wrong, whether Yuri had done his job, or just got lucky?

At least President Hamid Karzai would be alive for another day.

In the Ghazni military mess, Mark and Dusty had both curled up in a corner, attempting to get some rest. There was nothing else to do.

The two Apache helicopters had taken off to the north to attend to yet another skirmish, and the British Bell Huey had also gone north to inspect the road and look for insurgents. A couple of heavily armed trucks had also headed north intending to clear the road.

Gilroy was off somewhere attending to Hamish O'Dea and another of his wounded troops and trying to get some organization and sanity into the day. They had not seen Stephen Rodriguez at all. Owen Squires was keeping an eye on the ADDI and would have let them know if he made a move. Total, utter boredom. They heard a helicopter land, and it sounded like a Bell Huey. That could mean that the British people had returned. But they were both too tired to care.

At last Eric and Wendy came into the mess with a cheerful grin on their faces. Not that this was unusual. They did not seem to care. They just wanted to fly their precious helicopter. They sat down and started to eat their lunch, prodding their two American friends to do the same.

'What is happening?' was the query from Mark, while Dusty simply expanded the question a little by adding a four-letter adjective.

'I suspect that you will be heading out in about half an hour,' said Wendy. 'Knowing the way that most US Army personnel work, you will be the last to know. I suggest you get some grub and go to the toilet. The plan is for the remains of your convoy to make a fast run-through once the road is clear. That is unless you would like a lift with us—our next stop is Kabul?'

Now there was a temptation. All the drivers in their convoy had two speeds—stopped and flat-out, and nothing in between. By the time they made it to Kabul—that is, if they made it to Kabul—they would feel like they had been through a mincer. The thought of a quick trip onboard the Bell helicopter was enticing. But there were other considerations.

The Brits could take off at a moment's notice and go anywhere that the exigencies of services demanded, while Mark and Dusty wanted to follow Stephen Rodriguez. Where he went, they went. While they knew that the ADDI must now be headed for Kabul, no one knew what would happen in between. Mark elected to take the conservative approach.

'Thanks for your help. Your offer is appreciated, but we have to go with the convoy.'

Wendy had another piece of information that she could not know the significance of. She had been talking to the clean-up crew, and they had been laughing about the insurgents getting more sophisticated. They had found an AK-47 rifle complete with a silencer and a carrying case beside the area where the battle of Ghazni had taken place.

Mark tensed. He thought that he knew where the items had come from. What he could not know for certain was who had fired the rifle, and who was at the receiving end of it. But Mark had his suspicions.

During all the chaos that had surrounded their unscheduled stay in Ghazni, Olezhka Demidov had just sat back and watched the scene unfold.

His suspicions about the experience of the team that had been showing extraordinary interest in Jacob Dutton and his friends had been correct. When faced with a problem that demanded brute force, they had reacted professionally, without a second thought. And in the course of such action, they had not been the least bit concerned about the people they had been watching. That caused Demidov to rethink.

What if they were just the heavies? They just trailed around waiting for any kind of trouble and were only following the guy from the CIA because he was someone important. Demidov would need to find out who this important guy was before he could make a judgement call.

And even that did not satisfactorily explain what had happened, did it?

Jacob Dutton and his friends had just been through

a quite harrowing experience. However, apart from the insipid-looking guy who always seemed to be wearing a black suit and a pink shirt getting himself killed, they appeared to be intact and still guarding their precious drugs. Nothing had changed there that was of any importance.

The Tajiks seemed the happiest of the three groups that Demidov had an interest in. They had contacted fellow Tajik friends in Ghazni, and since the convoy returned to that town, they had made those contacts again. It was difficult to tell whether there was any significance in that. They seemed calm and relaxed. That is, when they were not praying, which seemed to be their main occupation. He was beginning to wonder whether his enthusiasm was misplaced or born out of misguided paranoia.

Sure, he had heard rumours of plots to kill various big names in Kabul. And the Tajiks were as unbalanced as anyone in this crazy country, so it was extremely hard to predict what they might do. On balance, it seemed very unlikely that this pathetic bunch was even remotely involved in anything of that kind. And the CIA would not be so stupid as to get involved with anything like that, would they?

No contact had been made between any of these three groups other than the contact that you would expect during and after a fight. The leader of the group of heavies had barked commands at Dutton's friends, otherwise, they could have been on a different planet. And then the *friend* had made a half-assed attempt at thanking these men. But they did not appear to know each other. That was another confusing part of the riddle.

Or was that all an act? Were Jacob Dutton and the heavies all a part of the same group?

Oleg Demidov had decided that the time to make his

move on Dutton was when they got to Kabul. And that was still the plan. But maybe his contact with his boss Yuri Alexseyev would need to take a different tack. Having people in the CIA who were vulnerable because of their known involvement with drugs was a plus. Maybe that was all there was to it.

It required someone way above his pay scale to make such decisions. So, it would just have to wait until they got to Kabul. Then it would be Yuri's problem to worry about it.

It was a pity that the Americans had been clever in tracking and breaking the security on the Russians' somewhat crude communications; otherwise, he could have just got onto the telephone. Well, that was probably not true either. The Russians were masters at mathematics, so if their scientists could not come up with encryption algorithms that would defeat the Americans, then who could? But in this game, where the higher you went the more paranoia set in, someone had assumed that it was broken. That was one of the advantages of having a mole. However, the disadvantage was that a mole could be a double-agent, so just what could you believe?

At the very least, that paranoia had resulted in the orders that Oleg had received. So, the net result was that he and his information would have to wait.

While this whole business was not looking as clear-cut as Oleg had first thought, he would wait for a face-to-face meeting with Yuri. That was the only form of communication he could trust.

And there was no hurry – was there?

The convoy eventually made it into Kabul.

Although the trip was devoid of any of the drama that they had experienced the day before, everyone had been tense

Mark and his small band had to then find out where the ADDI was headed and what would happen to the packages that he was trucking. They would keep watching and waiting, looking for some clue of what Stephen Rodriguez would do next.

It all turned out to be singularly uninspiring.

The truck that was carrying the opiates was simply taken to the CIA compound and left there locked and secured under the watchful eyes of Jacob Dutton.

And the covert surveillance of Owen Squires.

The ADDI then called at the United States Embassy for little more than a few minutes. He then returned to the centre of the city and booked into the Kabul Serena Hotel.

Mark and Dusty were tired as they trundled into the hotel. They were dependent on De Lawrence to check them in and to find out which room the ADDI was in. Originally, Mark had planned to return to their original apartment but decided that they had to stay close to Rodriguez, given that they had received no indication that he was aware of them or their mission.

When they were eventually reunited with Del, he surprisingly seemed quite overwhelmed to see them. The decision Mark had made to abandon the original apartment, where Del had stayed, had been based on their current situation. They had to stay alert for any movement of their target, and they needed all the hands that they could muster.

This decision would turn out to be crucial in determining their fate.

Even if it would be for entirely the wrong reason.

The fact that Rodriguez had shaken hands with Mark back in Ghazni suggested some caution. The curiosity of the ADDI could become aroused by the appearance of Mark now appearing in the same hotel. Mark had also learned about coincidence. At the same time, they had to be aware that, even in this hellhole, Stephen Rodriguez was still a senior officer in the spook business and would still have people looking after him. And they would not be in plain sight.

That is why Owen's suggestion that they put a tail on the ADDI was met with a shaking of the head. You quite simply could not do that. All that they could do now was to act normally, and hope that in the process, they could gain enough information to maintain contact.

Rodriguez eventually came out of his room and went into the Silk Route Restaurant of the hotel. There he was, joined by another man who appeared to be an American. Del was the lucky one who was selected to keep an eye on the ADDI, and for the task, he was forced to order three courses while Stephen and his guest relaxed for a long evening meal. Del could not have known that this man was Jacob Dutton, the CIA agent from Marjah. Mark and Dusty got a buffet meal from another restaurant at the hotel—the Café Zarnegar—but were unable to see into the Silk Route.

Not that it would have told them much.

Before midnight, everything at the hotel settled down, and there was nothing to do except wait in frustration. Owen left the hotel to attend to other matters, leaving Mark, Dusty, and Del to draw up contingency plans for what could happen between Kabul and Peshawar.

They had been unable to control anything so far on this mission.

But having a plan was better than not having a plan at all.

That plan was doomed to failure anyway.

That failure had nothing to do with their surveillance methods.

Their fate was already planned by people who they had not yet even heard of.

Chapter 30

Deception

Mark had finally settled on at least a plan of action for communicating with the people back in the United States. He had thought that making his call to Debbie before calling Harold Taylor meant that he would be less uptight for the important business conversations. But then he found that he had been unable to sleep because of his discussions with his father. He realized his nerves just became more than a little frayed.

So, he reversed the plan and called Harold first.

Mark called Washington at about midnight Kabul time. That made it about 3:30 pm in Washington. His father sounded to be in a particularly good mood until Mark told him what had happened on the road from Ghazni, and then about his face-to-face meeting with Stephen Rodriguez.

How Mark could have avoided that meeting was beyond his comprehension; and how Harold, sitting in his plush and comfortable office in Langley, could even envision the events that had unfolded, Mark had no idea. But Harold still went ballistic. He managed to calm down when Mark explained what little had been said, but Harold was still a very worried man.

In Mark's opinion, his team had done an extraordinarily respectable job of keeping their trip around Afghanistan a secret from Stephen and the CIA for as long as they had. Still, Harold was paid to worry. Mark changed the subject to an issue that most concerned him.

'Father, we are no closer to discovering what the distribution network is if indeed there is one,' Mark patiently explained. 'We have seen some evidence that our original suspicion of the CIA being somehow involved with drugs in Afghanistan is correct. But just about everyone in the country must be involved in substance abuse or supply. Whether the CIA is involved in the local market or is involved in simply having its own sources as a means of influencing things in this godforsaken country or Pakistan is anyone's guess. You know the history of the CIA's involvement with drugs as well as anyone. My plan, for now, is to stay with our original intention of keeping an eye on Rodriguez. We keep following the assistant deputy director of intelligence as best we can until he returns to the United States, gathering as much information as we can. I am now sure that the eventual answer to the riddle will be found back in the States.'

Mark could almost sense Harold writing something down, although why he bothered was anyone's guess. All conversations into the CIA at Langley were automatically recorded irrespective of the origin of the call and irrespective of who received the call. Well, almost. When a call came in on a secure and independent telephone, as this one was, Harold would have to record the conversation on his own equipment. He would be very foolish not to. But then, Harold was from the old school, brought up in an age when everything was written down because recording devices were either non-existent or were too unreliable, or they could be tampered with, or the recordings could be stolen.

Harold cleared his throat. 'You are sure that you can go through with this? What if Stephen has worked out what we are up to?'

'Father, there is nothing to connect your office with Dusty and me—that is, unless someone in Washington has been talking. There is nothing to connect us with the CIA and drugs, or the DEA with an investigation involving the CIA. Provided we stay below the radar, we should be fine. However, I think we are going to have to stay well clear of De Lawrence from now on, other than for covert discussions, and we can handle that. Del is DEA, and we cannot risk Stephen making that connection. From this point, Del should fly back to Peshawar, Pakistan, and do whatever DEA guys do. Dusty and I will travel by road and follow the drugs. We are sure that they will end up in Peshawar.'

If that was meant to calm Harold down, it did not work. Was Harold starting to get sentimental in his old age?

'That is extremely dangerous!' he almost shouted into the telephone. 'If what you said the other day is true, somewhere between Kabul and the Pakistani border, or even on the other side of the border, the chances are that they, or you, could be attacked and killed.'

Mark sighed. 'Why did you ask me to come out here? Why do you think I said yes, provided I brought Dusty Miller along for the ride? This is what we do, what we are trained for. If we must go into harm's way, then so be it. We will handle it.'

Mark was beginning to sound like the Mark Taylor of old, back in the good old days of Delta Force, when going into harm's way was fun, something to look forward to rather than to avoid. Of course, then they had the authority to kill people—but you cannot have everything, can you?

'Karen will not be pleased with your intention to drop Del from your team!' was Harold's reply as he avoided the obvious.

What had keeping *Karen* pleased have anything got to do with the practicalities of life or death on the other side of the world? Mark thought about asking that question and in those precise words.

But he thought better of it. A more subtle approach was required where, Mark suspected, this affair that his father was involved in could be construed as involving the dick rather than the brain.

'Father, wait until tomorrow before you say anything to the DEA. We will have a discussion with Del in the morning and suggest a plan that keeps him involved. I am sure that any frailty in the plan will be more than offset by Del's natural desire to get the hell out of this place. Del will no doubt report to your friend Karen Marshall at the DEA when he arrives in Peshawar, by which time it will be too late to change things.'

'OK, it's your call,' was Harold's meek reply, before he became more business-like.

'I had one of my men enquiring into Edward Hennessey. He has come up with a story that someone wants to kill the President, and that may be the reason he is accompanying the ADDI. Have you heard anything to back that up?'

'How the hell would I know?' Mark responded. 'We are not exactly in a position to do much about that anyway, and the last I heard, the President is still in Washington!'

Harold laughed. 'We are not talking about our President. We are referring to President Hamid Karzai of Afghanistan.'

'But what has that got to do with Stephen Rodriguez?' Mark asked.

'Well, we must assume that Stephen is not involved. The more likely scenario is that he would want an FBI guy around to assist if anything should happen. Hamid's security is in the hands of the Russians, so I would assume we would leave it to them. But you never know. Treat it as just a heads-up for now and see what else transpires.'

'Well, I do have some news that complicates things,' Mark replied. 'Hennessey was killed back at Ghazni. And according to one source, his involvement with Stephen may be more personal.'
Harold jerked at that. 'What are you saying?'

'I am just passing on what was said. Treat it as hearsay at this stage, but it could be significant.'

'Oops! That is all we need!' was Harold's response.

What Mark did not know was that Harold was off to see Karen for a little more than a meal. And between the sheets, anything could, and usually did happen.

Mark terminated the call to Harold, and then he called Debbie.

His theory was correct—doing things in this order made him relax.

And he decided to tell her the truth. Well, almost the truth.

'We got involved in an incident on the way back up the road from the southern part of Afghanistan. I ran into some old friends from the Special Forces—it was good to catch up. That is why I could not call you yesterday. But never mind, we are back in Kabul now and just about on our way home.'

Mark could still not understand women, even the one that he loved; and he realized that the longer that he was away from her, the more he longed to be back with her.

She did not ask *when* he would be back or *when* he would be home. She just said to take care and told him that the business was running as smoothly as. She also told him that she loved him.

Mark relaxed and said he would see her soon, that he loved her too, then disconnected the call and fell asleep.

Mark was awakened by a tapping on the door. He glanced at his watch. In the early hours of the morning, he had difficulty focusing on the backlight figures. He was shocked to find it was 3:20 am, and it seemed as though he had only just put his head down.

Who could be tapping on the door at this late hour?

His first thought was that it was one of his team, but then why had they not used the *coded* knock that they had agreed upon? Unless that is, the person happened to be named Del, in which case all bets were off because he seemed devoid of any sense of the need for security.

He reached for his Glock which he had placed in the top drawer of the cabinet beside the bed.

Mark was still trying to orient himself to what was going on when the question was very quickly answered for him. The door burst open with a loud bang, and Mark froze.

He had witnessed and practiced the procedure, many times in an earlier life with the United States Special Forces.

Open the door quickly, and by brute force if necessary. While two men took up positions on either side of the doorway, aiming their semiautomatic rifles straight ahead, two other men, similarly armed, crouched, and then ran rapidly to the sides, one scanning to the left and the other to the right. As they moved farther to their respective sides, two more armed men, again crouched and similarly armed, rushed forward into the room. These two were the killers. If anyone had failed to die from fright at the demonstration of rapid, overwhelming, and brute force that had interrupted their sleep, their job was to nail those people at the slightest hint of resistance.

The execution was a little hesitant, indicating that the men had been suitably trained but they had not had much practice. The whole exercise could have been accomplished in a few seconds less time than it had taken, but overall, it was not too bad. The major difference was that the men did not speak.

But this was no exercise.

The force was an elite Afghan Army unit. However, the commander of the unit appeared to be a Russian. Not that it made that much difference. Mark was forcibly bundled out of the bed and spreadeagled facedown onto the floor long before he had the chance to even contemplate resistance or using his gun. The two soldiers pinning him down were not overly worried about his comfort as they roughly ripped his arms behind his back, tied them tightly with a plastic self-locking cord, and then, equally roughly, dragged him to his feet. He was about to ask what this was all about when his mouth was taped shut and he was marched quickly out of the door, along the hotel corridor, and into the elevator.

Not a single word was spoken by any of the soldiers, so Mark knew that this operation had been planned and executed down to the last detail.

Out in the hotel corridor, he was at least in the company of a friend.

Dusty Miller was similarly trussed up, and from the look on his face, and knowing Dusty as he did, he had not been taken as placidly as had been the case with Mark. Still, it was evident that whoever needed them to be captured, needed them to be kept alive.

The two friends exchanged a look that said several

things. The first almost-imperceptible nod of Mark's head said, *don't do anything stupid. Wait this out!* The second almost-imperceptible shake asked, *where is Del?* There was no chance of getting an answer. The tape was then bound over their eyes so that they could see nothing, and all they could then hear was the grunting and cursing of their captors as they struggled to force their guests in the direction that they wished them to go.

They were rushed out into the street, where they were bundled into the back of a Humvee and unceremoniously dumped on the floor.

The journey was not long before they were manhandled out of the Humvee, into a building where they were separated and each escorted into separate small, cold, and featureless cells.

The tape and shackles were crudely ripped off, and then Mark was propelled to the back of the cell, and the door was slammed shut.

The cell that Mark was in was a twelve-by-sixteen-foot space. It had a low wooden bench down one side, which was a lame excuse for a bed, with no mattress, no pillow, and no blankets. There was a can in the corner which may have been for rubbish, may have been a toilet. From the smell, it had certainly been used as the latter, and it had not been cleaned in the last century. There was a shit-covered rock in the bottom of the can, which suggested that some previous inhabitants of the cell had been Afghanis—no surprise there. The door was solid apart from a small opening that could only be accessed and opened from the outside. There was a bulb set high in the ceiling and surrounded by heavy wire that blazed down, filling the room with a harsh bright light. Blank yellowing walls with a variety of messages scratched haphazardly and with no meaning that Mark could make any sense of—the etched messages of the desperate or the condemned. No windows, giving no sense of night or day. The blank walls revealed nothing of where they were.

Mark had heard some horrific stories of the Pul-e-Charkhi prison in Kabul, where far more people went in than ever came out. Was that where he was? Or was he in some other containment area which, knowing the local customs, may be better but could not have been much worse?

They had taken his watch. They had taken his gold chain. At least they left him with the clothes that he was wearing, although they were the bare minimum. Then they had left him alone in the cold, bare room. There was no noise or movement, apart from the regular opening and closing of the inspection window and the occasional shuffling of boots, the occasional cough which indicated the presence of the guards on the other side of the featureless and immovable door.

Guards! Now that was a laugh. There was no way out, and the door was securely locked from the outside. There would be no rescue party on this mission for the simple reason that no one knew who they were, where they were, or what they were. So much for being covert! And Mark sure as hell did not know where they were, so even if he could have communicated with someone, he would have been unable to tell them anything.

Mark lay on the bench, trying to avoid staring up at the light.

For once in his life, Mark was scared.

With nothing else to do, Mark tried to rationalize his situation. He had been a fool, and he was not sure that he could handle that admission. Apart from Harold and Karen, the only person who could know that they were in Afghanistan was, in fact, the man they had been following, Stephen Rodriguez. And even the ADDI could not know why. And that was assuming he had recognized Mark at their brief meeting in Ghazni.

Or was it earlier? Had Stephen been aware of their presence long before that? The only other people who knew what they were up to in Afghanistan were his father and the DEA, and they were supposed to be on the same side. Apart from that, the only other person who knew that they were in the country was Mike Gilroy, who they had met at the Battle of Ghazni. Mike had no idea why they were really in the country, and Mark would trust Mike with his life. But there would be no cavalry coming to the rescue from that source.

Mark racked his brain, trying to think of how things could have gone so wrong. The only possible failure on his part had been in telling two members of the DEA what they were up to—Griz and Owen. And he had justified that, at least to his satisfaction, on a *need-to-know* basis.

No. It had to be Stephen Rodriguez. There was no other logical explanation of the predicament that they were now in. So, he could expect to be quizzed by the CIA or the Afghan intelligence, and they would be in no hurry.

And now anything could happen, and it would not be good.

At least Mark had that bit right.

Chapter 31

Terror

There was nothing to indicate what time day, or night, it was, and no one would tell him. There was nothing to indicate what had happened to his friend Dusty. Nothing at all to indicate what had happened to either Del or Owen. Nothing to indicate whether this would be their last *chat*, as the heavily accented English-speaking officer liked to put it. The interrogator was an officer, not local, probably a Russian officer—you could tell that from the way that he reacted to those around him. So much for Mark thinking that they had been taken in by the CIA. The good news was that the Russians would use their own interrogators. The bad news was that the Russians would have no respect for the niceties of inter-agency conversations.

Body language is the same no matter what the nationality—an arrogant disregard for both the prisoner he was talking to and the prison guards who lounged around, not sure whether to sneer at the prisoner or the tormentor. But the guards had done this before. They reacted to a nod or a wink and robotically shifted their prisoner as though he was just a piece of meat.

That was a problem the world over. You could have the most precious thing in the world or the most wanted prisoner in the world. It did not matter. You still had the lowest-paid guards watching over them.

It must have been the fourth time Mark had been dragged bound and shackled from his cell, along the corridor that had six similar cells on either side and into another room. This room was somewhat larger than the cell that Mark was being held in but had not much more in the way of creature comforts. There were no windows. There was no recording equipment—at least none that he could see. There were half a dozen plastic chairs, only three of which were ever used – the person being interviewed, the interviewer, and a guard. The fact that the guard had an M16 meant either that he had been trained by the US coalition forces, or that it had been traded for his normal AK-47, or that it was meant to put the interviewee at ease.

There was a table. It was made of wood and, at some stage in its life had probably been the dining table of a well-to-do family. Now it was stained with what looked like dried blood, covered in doodling by crazed people, and the obvious marks some made by blunt instruments, some made by knives. The legs were uneven in length so that they rocked as the officer scribbled on his pad, making an annoying creaking sound.

The interrogator made little marks on his papers as he wrote down the various answers to the inane questions that he asked repeatedly. A letter X probably meaning 'Wrong!' or 'Lying', a question mark meaning ask the question again and, in another way. The occasional tick meaning either that the interrogation was making some progress. Or that the question was just not worth pursuing.

It would have helped if Mark had been given any indication of what the hell this was all about.

But for the moment, and for the previous three interrogations that he had undergone, he had absolutely no idea.

His first interrogation, which had occurred shortly after their arrival, had been innocuous and relatively friendly. The officer had asked reasonable questions and appeared to accept the answers with a mixture of boredom, satisfaction, and arrogant disregard. After their talk, the interviewer just got out of his seat, nodded to the guards, and walked out, leaving his minions to drag Mark back to his cell.

After that, things started to turn ugly.

The next time Mark was roused from his cell, the guard placed a black sack over his head, and in the dim lights of the corridor, he could not see where he was being taken. He arrived in an interrogation room, where the black hood was removed, and he was told to strip. He did not understand the reason for doing so but was left in little doubt that this was required, and he had little choice but to comply. He was then securely lashed to the wooden bench and lay facing his interviewer. A crude but very bright light was then focused directly into his eyes. Then his interrogator pulled out a variety of instruments that he lay on the table one at a time, making sure that Mark was aware of what he was doing.

There were two types of pliers: long- and short-nosed—the long ones would be used for pulling teeth, and the short ones for crushing fingers and toes, and a hammer in case the bones needed a bit of extra persuasion. There were a variety of knives, used more to frighten the prisoner than for any practical purpose other than drawing blood and inflicting pain. There were a variety of wire contraptions, some delicate, more like those used by dental surgeons, and others that could be used to give unrestricted access to various orifices and other parts of the body. All designed to terrify the prisoner. And then there was the inevitable syringe with a bottle of colourless liquid in it.

The bottle probably contained sodium pentothal, which is a potential truth serum. It is used to make prisoners more compliant by reducing the higher brain functions—since lying is more complex than telling the truth—by making the prisoner more loquacious and cooperative, and therefore more likely to tell the truth. More likely, its use, in this case, would be to make the prisoners more compliant before administering some more lethal concoction.

None of these torture devices had so far been used on Mark, but the threat was there, and very real.

This was all standard procedure that Mark's training had told him to expect—knowledge that did not make his predicament any easier to take. He knew that at any time, the mode of interrogation could change. And the result would mean the end.

Mark was also not surprised when, first, a towel was placed over his head and then a bucket of cold water was slowly poured over the blanket, long enough to give the sensation of drowning and make Mark gulp for air—a process affectionately known as waterboarding in the Western world. Despite the position that he was in, Mark had to smile. Waterboarding was not a form of torture that was limited to the CIA. His tormentor made him aware that the process would be repeated if he didn't answer the questions truthfully, and it was, of course, the repetition that made this torture. Then followed the same meaningless questions—to find an answer to a riddle that, in Mark's view, neither he nor the interviewer knew the answer to.

The process was repeated.

Time seemed to stand still.

The same monotonous questions.

Mark had had no sleep since his abrupt arrival at this place. Sure, he could lie down on the bench in his cell. Sure, at some stage, they had thrown him a blanket, which he had pulled tightly around himself to try to retain some warmth in his body. The blanket stank and had not been washed in living memory. But it was all that he had.

The room temperature ranged from marginally above freezing to well below freezing, depending on the time of day or night. At least Mark assumed that was the case because he otherwise had absolutely no idea of the time of the day. He had nothing to eat or drink, and his body clock was telling him that he needed to do something about that, and soon. At least he did not have to use the 'toilet' for anything other than the occasional pee, so the smell in his cell was not too bad. He took the blanket with him when he went to the 'interview' room for the fourth time. No one seemed to object to that. Maybe they did not notice the smell.

Mark tried to be pleasant, greeting the officer with a 'Good morning, Yuri,' hoping that he at least might be corrected as to the time of the day or the name and bring some sanity back into his life. No such luck. Mark laughed at the thought that Yuri Alekseyev may not know the difference between the various forms of greeting, even though he seemed to have a reasonable command of the English language.

Yuri did not laugh. Like most Russians in this trade, he had that ability to look cold and to smile at the same time, without the smile ever reaching his eyes.

'What are you doing in Kabul?' Yuri started another round of questioning. Whether or not *Yuri* was his real name, Mark neither knew nor cared. That he was a member of the SVR, the organization that had taken over from the KGB in handling foreign intelligence matters for the Russians, was now not in doubt. What the hell Yuri was doing in Afghanistan interviewing an American 'prisoner' who appeared to have strong links to the CIA, the DEA, and Special Forces, and guarded by men who were part of the Afghan armed forces, was anyone's guess.

'I have already told you that. I am with the United States Drug Enforcement Administration. We are a small and covert unit checking on the performance of our administration's foreign-deployed advisory and support teams. They are supported by the Pentagon—that is, the US military headquarters in Washington, in case you did not know. Hence, we need to check from the DEA's view whether they are effective in that role or not. We are in Kabul because that is where our airplane is due to take us out of this godforsaken place. My role is to make sure that the DEA guy we are escorting does not get into any trouble. That's it. What do you not understand?'

It was as near to the truth as this bimbo needed to know, and it was also remarkably simple for Mark to remember, and therefore to repeat. It was their cover story, so that would be repeated by Dusty when he was interviewed. And by Del, if they had also taken him, prisoner. That is if Del had gone to a similar school on enemy interrogation techniques and the methods of coping with them.

'Why, then, have you not asked to see the United States Ambassador, or at least someone from your embassy? Surely that is the first thing you Americans do when you get into trouble in foreign places?' Yuri Alexseyev asked, showing little interest in Mark's reply to his earlier question.

Mark sighed. The same routine, the same questions, and the same answers. It was not as though Mark did not understand the techniques that were being employed. Keep asking the same questions until the prisoner changes his story. Act friendly, to begin with. Make the prisoner feel comfortable. Then turn up the heat no longer be friendly, maybe a little torture, certainly threaten. And then apologize. Go back to being nice. Act like a devoted friend. And when the prisoner begins to feel comfortable, take it all away again so that the prisoner doesn't know what is going on. Then pounce—worry the slightest change or inconsistency to death until you get to the truth.

Mark had been trained to deal with this kind of situation, and it all came back to him like riding a bicycle. When your hands were not tied behind your back, keep them on the table in front of you, steady, the fingers relaxed. Don't cross your arms. Don't scratch or rub your nose, eyes, chin, ass, or balls. Get your eyes steady and focused on the man asking the questions. Ignore the light. It was just a technique used the world over to get an advantage: always interview people with your back to the light, make it hard for them to make eye contact. The answer was to stare at the spot where the interviewer's eyes were supposed to be and smile. It did give the interviewer the impression that you were laughing at him because of the slight offset of the eyes and mouth, but what the hell? Don't do the slightest thing that would give the impression that you were trying to avoid the questions.

And do your absolute best, when or if you had to lie, to lie consistently.

Mark had only one real issue. When he was taught how to handle an interrogation, he was told that you had to avoid revealing something, anything, that would set the interrogator off on another tangent. But the problem Mark had here and now was that he had no idea why the Russian was interested in what was an internal issue for the

USA—the CIA investigating itself—and therefore he had no idea what this was all about.

Under training, and back in a much saner environment than this, it had been assumed that your interrogator had to find out something that you knew, and you had to avoid telling him what you knew, or even avoid leading him in the direction of the truth. But surely the truth, in this case, would be of extremely doubtful value to this Russian. So, Mark would continue with the story until the Russians revealed something else that might provide a clue. Mark tried to explain again, probably being a little bit more aggressively, but why not?

'Because we are, or we were, part of a covert operation,' Mark repeated. 'You do understand the word *covert*, do you? And I was not aware that I was in any trouble with Afghanistan or their Russian minders. But if you insist, our cover is probably blown now anyway. Would you please tell the Embassy of the United States of America that I need some help? Ask them to please collect a couple of their people from Charkhi prison, or wherever the hell we are. Tell them that they will find the people in the interview room having a friendly chat with the Russians.'

The next words from his tormentor would be the same: 'Later!'

And then Mark would receive another dousing with icy water.

Unbeknown to the interviewer, the water felt warmer than the freezing temperature of the room, and that made it easy to endure. And the water was cleaner than anything else in this festering place.

When he was eventually dragged back to his cell, Mark could rub himself vigorously with the blanket, then put his clothes back on, and he would feel cleaner for the experience.

But how much longer he could survive this insane ritual, he did not know.

Concentrate on small pleasures. Do not worry about things that you can do nothing about.

But this time, at last, Alexseyev introduced some variation.

'Tell me what you know about our President,' the Russian asked, leaning forward menacingly over the bench.

Mark was initially genuinely confused by this sudden change of tactics. The tactics being employed were by the book, and so was their effect. Mark recognized the slowness of his reaction and gritted his teeth to try to maintain his concentration.

'What? Vladimir Putin?'

Yuri sighed as a man might do when dealing with an errant child.

'No. I mean the President of Afghanistan.'

'What? Hamid Karzai? I have not met him. I have only read about him. What could I be expected to know?'

Mark was still confused, but the change in the subject was refreshing and enabled him to reassemble his thoughts, although his tired brain refused to make any sense of it all. Maybe they were getting somewhere, but where to was beyond the comprehension of at least one of them.

Alexseyev leaned farther forward. His eyes were focused intently on Mark's. His body language said he was about to reveal, or had revealed, something of importance. But what?

'Why would you want to kill him?' was the next question that Yuri asked.

'What? Kill Hamid Karzai!' asked an astounded Mark. 'You are insane! Why on earth would I want to do that?'

The expression on Alekseyev's face and his body language showed that it might be insane, but that he was deadly serious.

The interview ended on that note. Now there were two of them confused.

Yuri Alexseyev read body language like almost everyone in his trade. Mark's reaction had been genuine!

The hood was replaced on Mark's head, and he was roughly escorted back to his cell. He struggled to get as dry as was possible and then crept onto his bench and curled up, trying to maintain as much warmth as possible.

Mark knew that if this went on for much longer, his resistance would eventually be broken. He may be forced to reveal the real reason he was in Afghanistan.

What possible interest that was to the Russians, he had not the faintest idea.

The interrogation of Dusty followed a similar pattern to that of Mark, with no indication of time or place. With nothing in the cell to refer to, he just lay on the bench and drowsed, and waited for something to happen. Dusty had absolutely no idea what time of day or night it was, and, like Mark, he had lost complete track of how long he had been a guest in this establishment.

To state his role in Afghanistan to his Russian tormentors, Dusty took the view that he was quite simply hired to look after Mark Taylor and had no idea what Mark's mission was. That story did not go down too well with his interrogator, but the Russian had so far refrained from reverting to a more physical style of interrogation. Probably because this was the Russian's first experience of interrogating an Afro-American, and an exceptionally large and intimidating one.

Unlike Mark, there was no attempt to intimidate Dusty, no hiding behind lights, no drenching in cold water, just an amicable discussion between two grown men.

The guy doing the interrogation had reluctantly introduced himself as Sergey Drubich, and then only because Dusty had been insistent that if they were to have a polite conversation, he should at least know the guy's name. After all, Dusty had informed the guy of his full name—Archibald Miller—and spent quite some time patiently trying to explain to the humourless Russian, if you took Dusty's first name, or if the interviewer happened to be Ukrainian if you took his second name (how you got a nickname of *Dusty* out of a surname of *Miller*. It was perfectly logical to Dusty, as was Dusty's explanation delivered in a condescending voice.

But that did not seem to please his interviewer.

Finally, the Russian lost his patience.

'Who else is involved in this plot to murder the President?' he almost screamed.

Dusty was just as confused as Mark had been by a similar question.

'Why would I come to Afghanistan if I wanted to murder the President? Last I heard of him, he was sitting in the Oval Office. And that is on the other side of the world in Washington DC. I don't know what his plans are, but those plans probably do not involve him coming out to this hellhole anytime soon.'

In frustration, Sergey Petrov lashed out across the table, hitting Dusty with some force, having assumed that the guards would protect him. And Dusty's reaction was as would be expected of a man with his past association with violence. And given that he was probably twice the size of his tormentor.

Dusty instinctively launched himself at Petrov, grabbed him around the throat, and they both tumbled onto the floor. One of the two guards leaped to his feet and swung his rifle butt towards Dusty's head, which told Dusty an important piece of information. He was not about to die—at least not yet. The other guard was so petrified by the sudden and violent action that he did nothing.

For the first guard, unfortunately, the use of the semiautomatic AK-47 as a club created two problems— well, really one problem, which led to the other. His aim was hurried, and the bodies were moving, so he happened to connect with Petrov, knocking him unconscious. He instantly realized his mistake, so he then did what all enlisted men are taught to do: he fired his rifle. But again, he was hurried, and the bullet grazed Dusty and added to the statistics of Russians killed in foreign lands. This one was killed by friendly fire, although the 'friend' would have some explaining to do, both to the Russians and their hosts.

The other problem was that the guard could not speak any English. So, he yelled and fired again, this time, in his blind panic, missing and enabling Dusty to grab the rifle by the barrel and pummel the guy against the wall.

It ended there. Four other guards, who had heard the disturbance, rushed into the cell, and quickly rendered Dusty unconscious.

The guard who had fired the fatal shot did what any soldier would be expected to do in the circumstances.

He blamed Dusty.

The third member of the little group that made up the trio of prisoners was far more cooperative with their Russian friends, or at least he thought that he was. De Lawrence

Darrington had received some instruction from the FBI at their training facilities at Quantico. Therefore, he was supposed to know all about interrogation techniques that would be employed, and which he could be expected to endure, in the unlikely event that he was ever captured by the 'other' side.

But in the real world, drug bosses were not renowned for wasting their time in idle chitchat. They just disposed of whoever got in their way. Consequently, the FBI courses had not spent that much time teaching the DEA agents how to withstand the pressure that could be applied by people who wanted to get information out of them.

Add to that the fact that Del was scared.

Del would say that he was just being realistic to be cooperating—after all, this did not appear to be about drugs. But the confusion that he caused for his captors could lead to more serious problems down the line, which would affect Del more than the others.

The removal of Del from the hotel had been easily accomplished. He was just taking a stroll along the corridors because he could not sleep. He had noticed a couple of men in uniform, and so he abruptly about turned to return to his room. He never made it. Rather like a child cycling in mid-air, but without a bicycle, he had been carried between two soldiers and bundled down the stairs into a truck. As far as his scared mind could tell him, he appeared to be the only one of their little groups that had been taken. And to be fair to De Lawrence, he did take some responsibility for his predicament. He was in the wrong place at the wrong time.

What Del did not know was that he had been mistaken for someone else. It was quite coincidental that he looked nothing like Owen Squires, except in height. By virtue of this fact, the interrogators would expect that Del would know about what his friends had been up to on the road back from Kandahar. But he didn't. So, he couldn't tell.

But his interviewer did not know that he had the wrong man.

Because of this, there was chaos.

Del could not understand why, since he was telling the truth, nobody appeared to believe him. The very first interview had been undertaken by Boris Bosnan and had got nowhere, however, it did give the Russians a clue that they may have found the weak link in the group.

Yuri Alexseyev, who was the lead interrogator, had decided to talk to De Lawrence himself. He had taken to calling him Lawrence because he could not understand the *De* bit or the *Del* bit and decided to drop it. And Lawrence seemed to be quite OK with that.

Alexseyev was confused with this crazy American issue with calling people by some other name. He had heard the story with Dusty, and he laughed, more so because his colleague just did not get it than with the story itself. But Lawrence was different again. The thing that intrigued Yuri was that each time Del or Lawrence was interviewed, he added something to what he had already said earlier. And his story was so pathetic that it had to be a pack of lies.

He was also doing a very impressive job of pleading with his captors, and at times broke down sobbing in apparent terror.

While Yuri had trouble breaking through to Mark and Dusty, he had no such trouble with Lawrence and had, early in the piece, decided that this was the man who he could break. Mark and Dusty were hard men, and Yuri had not seen even a hint of fear in either man's eyes. It would require the use of mind-altering drugs to make any progress with those two. Drugs of this type cost money and had to be used sparingly and wisely. Yuri was from the old school, having been trained by the KGB. But he was a reasonable man. What was the point in turning men into vegetables when he could get the information from another source?

The technique of lying De Lawrence on his back on a wooden bench, shining a light directly into his eyes, having him repeatedly drenched in cold water had a quite remarkable effect. Lawrence was in tears and starting to blubber. And yet he remained resolute in telling the same story. The Russian began to think that Lawrence was, in fact, exceedingly clever. The Russian had thought that he had recognized the obvious signs that Lawrence would be the first to break, but the underlying consistency of his story made no sense.

'Tell me once again,' Yuri began in a kindly voice. 'What are you doing in Afghanistan?' And to make it appear that Yuri appreciated the effort, he set him up on a chair at the table and gave Lawrence a cup of coffee. Which Del proceeded to spill, being unable to keep his hands steady.

'I am with the United States Drug Enforcement Administration. I came to Afghanistan via Peshawar in Pakistan on a Gulfstream jet. The aircraft is still at Bagram airport waiting for me. I am following a senior official of the CIA who I believe is involved in drug trafficking. When I have enough evidence, I will return to the United States and begin proceedings against him. Several people in our country believe they are above the law. My job is to find out the facts and give the evidence to someone else.'

Lawrence droned on, but then added something else.

'All I want to do is complete the mission and then get home to my family. I do not understand what else I can say or do to help you.' He ended with an air of supplication.

The tears started to well up again. Did Yuri not understand that he was telling the truth? Yuri had not asked him any questions about drugs even though he had admitted working for the DEA. All he wanted to know was why they were in the country, and he had answered that.

Alexseyev tapped his pen on the table, looking into Lawrence's eyes, looking for the faintest hint of the truth. But all that he saw was fear. He opened a file, and after glancing at a couple of pages, he riveted his eyes on the prisoner.

'Tell me about your family.'

That made Lawrence blink, and he muttered something too difficult for Yuri to catch.

'I am sorry. I did not hear you. Repeat what you just said.' Yuri leaned forward onto his elbows. He had made a chink in the armour; Lawrence did not have any family. Yuri was therefore not surprised—just saddened, for a moment.

'I do not have a family.'

'OK. I already know that. What I do not know is, what other lies have you been telling us, and wasting our time?' Yuri asked, sitting forward and glaring. 'You would like another session with the water—*waterboarding* is, I believe, the term you Americans use.'

'I have told you the truth!' Lawrence shouted, and then emotion took over. 'I have no family.' He almost sobbed. 'My mother and father divorced when I was in my late teens, and neither of them was interested in me. I was an only child. By *family*, I meant my friends back in Washington.'

Even Russian interrogators, who tend to be less amicable than some of their Western counterparts, can read body language when it is so brazenly apparent. The guy was lying again. He had been down to the south of the country with Mark and Dusty. And still, he denied it. All he could talk about were his personal problems. And he appeared to be scared shitless.

Every American that he had ever interviewed seemed to think that the mere mention of DEA, CIA, FBI, or any one of several three-letter acronyms used by the Americans, was enough to explain the strange and arrogant behaviours they had to do was to keep on repeating the same thing and they would be safe.

However, Yuri was sure that Lawrence was close to cracking. He had seen many men suffering from post-traumatic stress disorder after they had been involved in the earlier wars in Afghanistan and witnessed the butchering of their colleagues and civilians, including women and children. Many of them would never recover and would be forever left with nightmares made worse by the fact that they had tried to bury their problems with drugs and alcohol. Also made worse by the fact that they had no, or little, support once the first signs of the stress that they were under began to emerge. Like Lawrence. He was almost suffering from TSD without the P! So now was the time to put the pressure on.

Alexseyev opened the file and flipped through it, reading occasionally.

'De Lawrence Winston Darrington. Born August 24, 1965, in Boston, Massachusetts. The only child of your father, Cyril Darrington, accountant. 'Mother: Elizabeth. Her prior name was Chapman. Housewife, after a brief career as a schoolteacher. Educated at Boston High. How am I doing so far?'

Yuri glanced up at a clearly shaken Del. He had got the basic information mostly from Facebook rather than from *official* sources, but what the hell. He had then followed that up with a little more information courtesy of a paid informer in the United States who had access to various databases and some FBI files.

'While you were at Boston High, your parents separated, and that was quite understandable: your father went to jail for fraud, your mother went into rehab to overcome her alcohol and drug problems. There she committed suicide. Some good came out of that, didn't it? It made you determined to join an organization that could fight against what your mother had been put through.'

Studied at the University of Columbia – New York – Barnard College.

Graduated with honours in Political Science 1992.

Joined the Drug Enforcement Administration in 1994.

Yuri leaned farther forward.

'From that point on, not exactly the most brilliant of careers, apparently passed over numerous times for promotion. Just the kind of person the United States would want to use on a mission of this type—a nobody. That is only a summation of the file we have on you. It is the gaps in the file that we are interested in filling in now. Like, what are you now doing in Afghanistan?'

Yuri briefly offered his notes to Lawrence and then pulled them away as if teasing him. His voice became a whisper.

'We can do this the easy way or the hard way. Your choice.'

'I want to speak to the US Ambassador!' Del shouted.

And that brought a smile to Yuri's face. He got up from behind the table and moved around so that he took a position in front of Del, leaning back against the table. He carried in his hand a small wooden-handled paperknife, which he twirled inches away from the face before him.

'All in good time. Just a few more questions,' he answered.

'Now, since you will not tell me what I want to know, let's play a little game. I will ask questions, to which your answers will be either Yes or No. Simple rules. No ambiguity. If you say that you do not know, or you refuse to answer, I may have to apply some persuasion. Now that's only fair, is it not?'

He prodded Lawrence playfully in the chest with the paper knife, insufficient to cause any serious damage. Enough to be uncomfortable. And to indicate that he could cause pain.

He saw the fear in Lawrence's eyes. Or was it defiance?

'So, are you ready to begin?' he asked.

'But I have already ...'

The Russian lashed Lawrence across the face with his paper knife, drawing blood in his left cheek, and awfully close to his left eye.

'Ah, I said "Yes" or "No" answers only. Do you want me to repeat the rules, or are you ready now to begin?' Yuri grinned.

'Yes,' came the whimpered response.

'Mark Taylor is your leader—is this correct?'

That question could have either a 'Yes' or a 'No' answer and they would both have been correct. Fortunately for Lawrence, he made the correct choice.

'Yes.'

'Good! We are getting along fine. Now, the gentleman who goes by the name of Dusty—he is employed as the minder, yes?'

That question was a hard one. Del had never met anyone as focused or as hard-nosed as Mark Taylor and could not imagine him needing a minder. But what the hell.

'Yes.'

'Now, both men have a history of violence, is that not so?'

'Yes.'

'Good! See, this game is easy! Now, you, Mark, and Dusty have just returned from the south of this country, no?'

It was an old interrogation technique. It had been in vogue since before the days when Fred Flintstone and Barney Rubble had first walked the earth, or so Joseph Barbera would have us believe. Suggest the answer that you know is wrong. Usually, by this stage of interrogation, the prisoner is so confused they copy the answer, hoping that their torment will cease, while unwittingly allowing the interrogator to apply more pressure.

To Yuri's surprise, Del answered, 'Yes.'

Maybe Lawrence was, at last, telling the truth! That caused Alexseyev to change the rules.

'OK, we will stop playing games. I now want two questions answered, and I want the truth. Firstly, who were you meeting in the south? Secondly, who were you meeting in Kabul?'

The two questions had Del confused. But not confused for the reasons that Yuri would have thought. Del was confused because he just did not know. That confusion caused a delay. That delay brought further pain. Yuri lashed out at Del, cutting his cheek again, and again close to the eye. At the same time, the guard started to pour cold water in a trickle over Del's head. Del gulped for air as the cold water took his breath away. The water mixed with the blood streaming from the cuts on his face and pooled on the floor.

'Put your hands on the table. Do it now,' Alexseyev instructed.

Del did as he was instructed, but not knowing the reason for the latest instruction, he was not watching very closely. Had he placed his hands flat, the damage to his fingers would not have been quite so bad? The hammer blow struck him just above the knuckle on the centre finger of his right hand and was delivered with such force that the finger instantly shattered.

His immediate reaction was to cry out and withdraw

the hand, but not before the hammer hit his left hand on the knuckle where the thumb joins the hand, causing excruciating pain and probably a fracture of the joint.

Del was trying to recover from nausea caused by the pain when a sickening blow hit him on the side of the head, and he tumbled onto the hard floor, still strapped to the chair.

Alexseyev mockingly admonished the guard.

'Come now—that is no way to treat our guest! He was just about to answer my questions! Weren't you, Lawrence?'

'Yes!'

As the chair and Del were lifted back up, Yuri hit him full in the face, and he crashed back down to the floor.

'Lawrence, I told you we had stopped playing games. Now I want an answer to my questions. I have not got the time for this!' He bent down to where Del lay whimpering on the floor. 'You may as well stay there. Now, my answers!'

'I don't know where they went or what they were doing. I was not with them. I was told to wait for them in Kabul, and that is all I know!' came the reply.

'You are lying again! Why would you want to do that when we were getting along fine?'

A boot hit Del in the stomach, and as he curled up in reaction, the next kick landed at the base of his left knee, shattering the patellar ligament, and ensuring that, should he survive this interrogation, he would walk with a permanent limp for the rest of his life.

Alexseyev immediately regretted the violence of his attack, but he was both angry and confused.

For the first time during all the interviews, the doubts started to bring some clarity into Yuri's thoughts. Had there been four men in this party? Had his roughnecks picked up the wrong man? If so, where was the other man? He calmed himself down. He would need to phrase his next question carefully.

'Lawrence! You said that they told you to wait in Kabul. Who told you?'

'Why? Mark Taylor—he told me,' Del whimpered.

'OK. So, the three of them took off and left you behind, is that right?' Yuri asked, already knowing, and fearing what the answer would be.

'Yes.'

'So, Mark, Dusty, and ... I'm sorry, I seem to have forgotten, the other gentleman's name was?'

'Owen. Owen Squires.'

That earned him a kick to the head. Not for getting the answer right or wrong. But out of sheer annoyance and frustration on the part of Alexseyev.

There was another man!

Unfortunately, as Lawrence turned reactively to see where the first kick had come from, the second kick caught him square on the temple. He was knocked out cold. Which, in the circumstances, was probably for the best.

Lawrence was a broken man.

Alexseyev was frustrated, but that could not be helped. He would try again later when, or *if*, Lawrence recovered from this session. For now, he had another, more significant, line of inquiry.

Who was Owen Squires?

More importantly, where was he?

Alexseyev had a couple of other issues to attend to, and in the meantime, his prisoners would not be going anywhere.

All he had to do was to confirm that President Hamid Karzai would survive this day. Then he would have all the circumstantial evidence that he needed. This evidence was hardly riveting, but it was good enough to earn him some respect from those who were forever questioning the need for his services. Usually from people who wanted Yuri out of the way so that they could implement their own devious plans. For now, all there was to do was to locate this, Owen Squires. Not that it mattered in the grand scheme of things.

The chances of this elusive man ever finding Mark Taylor and his team were about nil. Yuri was rapidly coming to the view that the three people that he had in custody would need to disappear.

But the Russians did not like any loose ends, so he would trace the fourth man.

Alexseyev dispatched two of his men to the hotel just in case the man Lawrence had referred to as Owen Squires turned up. They knew what to look for: a man dressed in grey, wearing a turban, small build about five feet six in height, beard, walked with a pronounced limp. They were looking for an Afghani, ignoring the deception that De Lawrence had attempted that would have them looking for a European. They were looking in a city of about 3 million people with about one-third of the population meeting that exact general description.

That is, apart from the limp, which reduced the odds by half. But the endgame would be quite simple because few would be looking in a hotel.

It was all a game of cat and mouse.

And the cat usually won.

Chapter 32

The Campus

The day turned out to be bitterly cold in the city of Kabul, and it was beginning to snow. The wind was blowing down from the mountains to the northeast, straight out of Tibet. Everyone was rugged up against the cold, and Yuri was not at all happy with that. It meant that anyone could easily conceal a weapon about their person in a city where there were more guns than people. It was difficult enough trying to deal with the threat of women wearing burkas, where only their eyes and their hands could be seen.

Alexseyev had no time for cultural intolerance, and he accepted in principle that people could wear whatever they wanted to. But in the security game that he was in, being able to recognize people was necessary; and in the case of people wearing the burka, by the time you were close enough to peer into their eyes, you could very well be dead. And the days were long gone when women, particularly the younger generation, just stayed in the kitchen.

And who was to say that men were not the wearers of the burkas?

For reasons only known to the politicians, President Hamid Karzai had been invited to address the students by the Chancellor of Kabul's University, Karim Khoram, before the students departed to all parts of the country for the end-of-year break. Not that there would be that many students. They had completed their exams, and the only people left on the campus were the teachers and the few dedicated students who were cramming in some extra study rather than returning to their inhospitable homes, or the few who just had nowhere else to go. That allowed Karzai to speak to a relatively small group of people without the riffraff that usually came to attend such an address.

Although Kabul University is one of the oldest tertiary institutes in Afghanistan, it has not had the greatest luck in meeting the educational requirements of the country. The ongoing wars have not exactly helped maintain a solid group of qualified teaching staff, and in that environment, it is hard to develop a culture. Nonetheless, as with all educational institutes the world over, the university has a vision that it will one day be internationally recognized as a seat of learning, research, and all the other functions that academics aspire to. Just not yet!

The group who would attend the Hamid speech would listen, and then quietly disperse, remembering nothing. They would be polite because Afghanis had not yet developed the confidence to challenge those in authority. But their main thought would be, *when are you going to fix our real problem—bring us peace, not words?* However, the group of teachers and students was still too large to be accommodated in one of the lecture halls, so the address was to occur outside on the sprawling campus.

That made President Hamid Karzai happy: there was more room, and therefore there would be more people. And he would not be shouted down by the unruly and rude media, which could occur in a more enclosed space.

That made Yuri Alekseyev very unhappy: outside there were more opportunities for the villains and many more vantage points from which they could aim. He did not have enough men to cover every vantage point. It would be difficult to search all the people in attendance. It was well-nigh impossible to search a bunch of students.

Not that it mattered, Yuri had surmised. He had three of the would-be assassins safely locked away and under interrogation. It was only a matter of time before he had them under control and got them to admit to the truth of why they were in Afghanistan. Admittedly, it was getting to the stage where he would need to start using drugs to get at the truth unless someone broke first. Of his three prisoners, Lawrence already seemed to be at breaking point, and if that peasant guard had not knocked Del out during the last interrogation, Yuri could well have got the truth. But in this game, you could never know. Mark was the planner and the one in charge. Dusty was the shooter, and he had proven his worth in that role by killing one of Yuri's associates. There would need to be retribution on that front, which would probably mean death for all three. Just a few loose ends to be tied up. He still had doubts about Lawrence—like what the hell was he doing with a team of professionals? And who was the mysterious Owen Squires? Probably just their driver. Possibly an enigma?

It seemed that the tip-off he had received from the CIA, courtesy of no less a person than Stephen Rodriguez, the assistant deputy director of intelligence, had been correct. The Russian was under no illusions: effective work at the CIA ended at the ADDI level. Anyone above that level was too busy playing politics and watching their own ass to worry about such mundane things as the assassination of a foreign president.

And what of the Tajiks? Admittedly, they were now getting clever—using Western mercenaries to do their killings. This was a new development, and he would need to come up with a new strategy to deal with it. The benefit to the Tajiks, and to anyone else that was in this business, was that the mercenaries would be trained to a far greater extent than would be normal for a typical suicide bomber. And they would focus on their target instead of indiscriminately blowing up half of the population to kill one man. It meant the game was changing once again. But to what extent?

Among the crowd, any crowd, there would be a mixture of people and a mixture of objectives—many wanting to cause trouble should the opportunity arise. Some focused on one man—the professional killers looking to assassinate their target. Some focused on just causing chaos, the terrorists, indiscriminately killing as many as possible. According to the people in the know, like the FBI, there are only two kinds of assassinations: functional and ideological. In the functional case, it is just a matter of convenience to get rid of the person who was the target. In the ideological case, there is more emotion involved: you must hate the guy who is the target, in which case it does not matter who else, including the assassin, gets killed. Combine the two—professional or terrorist, functional or ideological—and Yuri's problems of identifying threats just got that much harder. And having eliminated a known threat, he was back to square one—dealing with the unknown.

The problem could be simplified by treating all terrorists as plain criminals, which, of course, they are. But there is a difference: you can't always arrest them. Sure, you could overwhelm them with the brute force of manpower and arms, and then what do you say to them? 'Put down that bomb that you are about to explode, blowing yourself into the next life, or I will shoot you!'

There was still a job that had to be done. Yuri was still responsible for the security of the President, and that meant that he had to be aware of every risk. Locking up one group of assassins did not mean that there would not be others. Although he was confident that he had eliminated the main threat, he was still primed and ready for action. There was still the chance that the mysterious Owen Squires would turn up. Somehow, he did not think so. If he did exist at all, he had probably crawled off into the hole that he came out of, never to be seen again.

Yuri had tried to have the area covered for every possible eventuality. He had snipers hidden away on the roof of the buildings surrounding the university campus. He had people carefully checking the movement of people in and around the area. He had his officers constantly scanning the growing crowd, looking for someone or something that did not look quite right. All the little nuances—body language, demeanour, hand movements, who they talked to, and what about—had to be watched. And that was hard to do and got harder as the crowd grew, and the crowd became increasingly boisterous. And, of course, he had to be careful that he and his troops kept an extremely low profile. Students the world over were, well, students. And he was a foreigner in a land where the unexpected and the unpredictable were the norms, where the regard for human life was callously different from what even Alexseyev was used to.

Now that he had eliminated the specific threat posed by the Americans, that simply made his task that much more difficult. Politicians the world over were, well, politicians. You could not keep them in a cocoon. They had to be seen, and the more people that saw them, so much the better. In the state that Afghanistan was in, and had been for many years, it would have made sense to place a bulletproof shield around their President, or, indeed, any of their politicians. Even that would have negligible effect if someone decided to attack him with a truck loaded with explosives or with an RPG grenade launcher. Then economics and logic came into the equation. If you reversed all the logic, then you may as well not bother. If someone was going to kill him, then they would quite simply use whatever force was dictated by the conditions.

Sure, Alexseyev had a dual role. First, he was head of the SVR contingent in Kabul. Then the Russian Embassy had been asked by the Afghans to provide security services for their President, and what better cover could Yuri have? Instead of having to be forever tied up with the cultural people, who had the simplest task and had the simplest minds, he could now have a real job!

Having been appointed to oversee the security surrounding Hamid Karzai, Yuri saw his role as simply reducing the risk. You could never reduce the risk to zero. This was, after all, Afghanistan.

If he failed for whatever reason, and a successful attempt was made on the life of the Afghan President, then he would need to get out of Kabul, and in one hell of a hurry. Not so much as to avoid the finger-pointing that would ensue. He would need to avoid the bloodbath that would follow as the members of the Hamid Cabinet fought to decide who would be their next leader. They would be over the sorrow of losing Hamid in a New York minute. While they would not be overly concerned about who was responsible for the death, they would have to pay homage to the international press by taking it out on those whose security services had failed. It was just a fact: when one man left the scene, others had to follow.

It was a thankless task providing security for the President. But the pay was good.

Not that any of the money ended up in Yuri's pocket.

To the southeast of the campus was an older part of the university that had been damaged by fire some time ago. The first floor had subsequently been converted into a cafeteria. The second floor was used to provide reading rooms for students who had completed their studies and were now doing the research before deciding where to go next. The other two floors were too damaged to be of much use. They had been cluttered up with junk, and their access stairs had been blocked off and forgotten about. Except for one section of the fourth floor, which had a window with a perfect view of the stage where Hamid was due to appear.

At this window sat a sergeant in the uniform of the Afghan Army. He had an AK-47 rifle, like most of the other members of that force, but with a few extras. Fitted to the barrel was a rifle site manufactured by Smith & Wesson for the M&P15 rifle, and a suppressor also sourced from the same company. The sergeant also had a sat phone, which he held loosely in his hand as though expecting a call.

President Hamid Karzai finally made his appearance and raised his arms to the tumultuous, but not exactly enthusiastic, welcome from the crowd. He was backed up on the stage by some members of his government who stood there stony-faced and impassive, probably wondering whether this was the day they should make their move, not the least bit interested in what their leader had to say.

Alexseyev could not tell what the crowd was yelling about. He had a passable knowledge of the language, but chants in any language were hard to understand. He thought that at least some of the students were supportive of their leader. The look on Hamid's face would not have helped Yuri—after all, Hamid was a politician, and he was too far away to enable Yuri to look into his eyes and see the fear.

The crowd noise slowly abated, and Hamid began to speak. He did not have or need, the cue cards that many politicians in a more civilized part of the world would have employed. The speech followed the pattern of all such speeches: get the attention of the crowd and shout a few words that would appeal to them, then would follow a period in which he would actually deliver the message that he had intended, whatever that was, and then get the crowd aroused again by shouting more subliminal messages. Job done, back to the office.

The communicator that Yuri had attached to his ear crackled into life.

'To your right at your two o'clock, one hundred feet out, there is some movement. Do you read?'

Yuri scanned the crowd, and when he saw what one of his snipers had drawn his attention to. There were two men dressed like everyone else. But they were not listening to the speech. They were looking around and fumbling with something under their chapans. They looked too heavy to be flags.

They were guns!

'Got it! Who has a line of sight?' Yuri asked calmly of his troops.

'Four here. I have the one on your right in my crosshairs. I can take him out.'

'Eight here. The one on the left is obscured, but I have probably the best shot. There may be some collateral damage.'

'OK, wait,' Alexseyev cautioned.

They all waited. At least two of his snipers had the men firmly under control. Although Yuri had said to wait, they were trained to shoot if circumstances demanded it. If there was to be any collateral damage, it would only be a couple of students, so be it.

The speech continued until Hamid paused for the effect of what he had just said.

The Tajik Abdul Hadi Arghandiwal had been patiently waiting in the crowd—waiting for the right time, the right moment, where he could gain the best effect. And then Abdul saw the chance that he was waiting for. As Karzai raised his hands in mock acknowledgment of the din and the crowd noise subsided, Abdul and his brother theatrically drew their AK-47 rifles completely out from under their coats. They both shouted out a message of defiance that drew a collective gasp from the crowd who heard them—a stunned silence from the speaker, who could not hear the message, but certainly could see the guns.

There was a moment when the entire world seemed to stand still.

'Take them—now!' Yuri ordered. 'Try not to kill anyone else but get them down.'

A fusillade of shots rang out across the campus, and Abdul never had a chance to raise his rifle to a shooting position from which he could hit his intended target. But he did have his finger locked on the trigger as he went down, wounding or killing several of the students who were unfortunate to be in the random line of fire from Abdul's gun. Zalmay's first reaction was to attempt to hold his brother up, but that brought him more into the line of sight of the snipers, and he went down as well, but not before two more students to his left had been shot and killed. The result was absolute chaos.

Karzai was grabbed and unceremoniously dragged back into the building, while the crowd screamed and scattered, save for a few who had just seen their friends needlessly die, and remained paralyzed and weeping at the scene.

The danger was over. But no one could tell the panicked crowd as they rushed in all directions, trampling over anyone and anything that got in their way.

No call had come to the sat phone held by the Afghani sergeant. He removed the extras from his rifle and concealed them and the phone in the many pockets of his uniform. He then exited the building the way he had entered, mixing with the fleeing crowd and shouting instructions as he went. In due course, he would make his way back to his headquarters, in the Kabul CIA compound, where he would revert to his more natural identity—that of Martin Ellingham, and his more natural occupation as a field operative of the CIA.

There is a routine that all soldiers and security details follow in such circumstances. They had to check first that there is no secondary threat. That meant that the snipers and other security forces all stayed exactly where they were, overseeing the scene towards the front of the campus, which was awash with blood and littered with bodies, a few of them still alive. As the crowd rapidly dispersed, a deathly hush fell over the whole scene.

Alexseyev cautiously and meticulously checked with all his lookouts and snipers that everything was clear, after what seemed like a lifetime, but was only a few minutes, moved some of his men down onto the campus grounds. The rest maintained their positions, watchful, vigilant, guns at the ready.

The people who had stayed behind to attend to their friends were roughly spreadeagled on the ground, their hands tied behind their backs. Apologies could come later, if at all. The dead bodies of the two people who had initiated the event were rapidly identified and searched to make sure that they were not loaded with any other explosive device. There were none, but dead and injured alike, criminal and innocent alike, were roughly and very quickly rendered inert.

A couple of Afghan Army Humvees raced onto the campus. The dead were placed in one, the living placed in the other.

That is, except for Alexseyev.

He went with the dead.

Olezhka Demidov was getting frustrated from several perspectives, the main one being that he had been unable to locate Jacob Dutton. The other causes of frustration were his two bosses. One of these two could wait. Alexseyev had a more difficult role to maintain his cover, and it was understandable that he would be otherwise occupied. For his other boss, Demidov had been in almost-constant communications with Ahmed Karzai to keep him informed of his progress. But there was not much to report. That meant that Ahmed was getting frustrated, and that was not a good thing at all. He tried one more time to reach Jacob Dutton. And, at last, he was successful.

'Jacob! So nice to track you down! I wasn't aware that you had planned a trip to Kabul, otherwise things may have been easier!'

Demidov was a past master at distracting from the truth. Dutton would be easily fooled.

'Who is this?' Jacob asked.

Oleg laughed. 'You do not need to know that—at least

not yet. I have a message from Ahmed Karzai in Kandahar. You have heard of Ahmed?'

'Yes, I know Ahmed,' Jacob replied, still cautious and suspicious.

'Good. We are making some progress!' Oleg continued. 'He wants to offer you a deal. I understand you have had some problems getting supplies out of Marjah?'

Now Dutton felt a cold chill down his spine. Of course, he knew Ahmed. Of course, the CIA had previously chosen Wakil Hekmatyar of Ahmed Karzai to get their drug shipments. Of course, the drug world around Marjah would have a suspicion of what Hekmatyar had been up to. And, of course, the same drug world would know that Wakil was no longer around. The question was, what had this got to do with the Russians?

Jacob was scared, and scared men make all the wrong moves.

'Maybe we could meet and discuss the "deal" face-to-face,' he offered.

Demidov again laughed. He was enjoying hearing a representative of the CIA squirm. No, that wasn't it. This Jacob Dutton did not have a clue.

'No. That will not be necessary,' Oleg replied and then continued. 'I hear from my people in Marjah that your friend Wakil Hekmatyar met with an unfortunate accident.'

'I did not know! How did that happen?'

Come and watch the video, was the thought that resulted in the smile that erupted on the face of Demidov.

'Jacob, Jacob... Jacob! We both know what happened. Now let's stop playing games. Ahmed Karzai has a deal on the table. He is offering guaranteed shipments of anything that you want out of Marjah. Now take that to your boss for his approval. I will contact you at this time in twenty-four hours for your answer.'

Demidov disconnected the call.

The next person Oleg would need to talk to was his ultimate boss—Yuri Alexseyev.

Chapter 33

Next?

Before Alexseyev could talk to the CIA, he first had to talk to his prisoners. They may give him a clue and make his conversation with Stephen Rodriguez a little more amicable. He did not think so, but at least it would give him the time to gather his thoughts.

To take the simple version of his thinking so far, he had been well and truly conned.

The CIA had deliberately misled him into believing that these Americans were to attack President Karzai. The confidence trick had been confirmed by two simple facts. The Americans were captured and incarcerated. And, apart from the confusion that always arises in such cases, the Americans appeared clueless about any plot to kill his President. It had been confirmed when an attack did occur that it had not involved anything as robust as would have been planned by the Americans. Especially by someone with the obvious skills and experience of Mark Taylor and his small team.

Now Alexseyev had incontrovertible proof that the attack that had occurred had been carried out by Tajiks. It did not take a whole heap of logic to work out that the Tajiks had, indeed, been held up in Ghazni. That had been the reason why the original intelligence of their intended place and target had been skewed. But that did not explain why Alexseyev had been tricked into following the wrong group of men. Unless the delay in Ghazni had thrown the Tajik plans into disarray, the CIA had deliberately diverted attention away from them while they got reorganized.

What game was the CIA playing?

They had done some weird things in the past. But this was sheer lunacy! And to have involved the SVR in so simplistic a ruse was just inviting a conflict. Not only with the SVR, but with the Russians, and with their Afghan hosts. And with their own United States journalists and media who would have a field day feeding off yet another failure of their much vaunted, but heavily criticized, security and intelligence services.

Alexseyev now had a dilemma. He had to try to establish whether there was a link between the prisoners and the CIA. He also had to decide what he was to do with them.

There no longer seemed to be any point in threatening them with any physical harm. Extracting any further information from them may satisfy his curiosity. But it would not make his position any easier to deal with.

After the event on the campus, the first session that Alexseyev had was with Mark Taylor. Mark was a tough son of a bitch. At least his reading of the man was that Mark was honest. And Yuri would make the task a little easier.

First, he had allowed Mark to have a shower. Then he had supplied him with clean clothes and given him some food. Mark was then brought into the interrogation room looking far better than he had on previous occasions. And looking totally confused.

There was only a subdued overhead light. No sign of the water bucket. No sign of the drugs, shackles, knives, and other tools of the interrogation trade. No sign of the aggravation that had accompanied their earlier meetings.

'Are you feeling better? You are certainly looking better.' Alexseyev smiled as he asked the question. The smile still did not travel to his eyes.

For a few moments, Mark studied the man whom he had grown to hate. The body language of Alexseyev had changed. He was more relaxed with Mark. But he was still uptight about something else.

Mark had been taught to be wary of subtle changes in the mood swings of interrogators, changes in the way they treated their prey. After a lengthy period in the cold, without any comforts, without food or water, without any idea where he was, what day or time it was, the rules had suddenly changed. Caution was the order of the day.

When they returned him to his cell, would the situation revert to what he had endured previously? If Alexseyev was following established procedure, the plan would be to bring him up, let him feel just a glimmer of hope, then him down. Although the downs would be about the same, in the mind of the tormented, he would get lower and lower until eventually, he would break.

However, the confusion would ensure that Mark was not ready to give up. He still had no idea what this was all about. Had he been mistaken for someone else? Or was this just a game that the SVR was playing?

It would have been much worse in the bad old days of the Cold War and the infamous KGB. They would have gone straight in and bashed their prisoners into submission, irrespective of their guilt or innocence, and irrespective of their longer-term health. Today things were supposed to be much more civilized. But what was the purpose? And where, or when, would it end? The Russians still liked to amuse themselves, especially with Americans. But surely, word would eventually filter out. And the CIA and diplomatic intelligence would find out who they were holding and ask a simple question. Why?

Mark answered cautiously.

'It is nice to feel clean again, put on some clean and dry clothes, and to have something to eat and drink. I sincerely hope my friends are being treated the same way.'

Again, the smile. Alexseyev gave a display of almost being offended.

'Of course, they are! Why would we want to make them suffer while their leader is treated so kindly?'

Nothing had changed. Still, the subtle question that accompanied every statement. Mark could see a glimmer of hope but was still aware of the subtlety of the interrogator as he asked,

'Which leader? And the leader of what?' he asked. 'If you want to treat any of us kindly, you could begin by telling someone what the hell this is about.'

This time the smile on Yuri's face travelled to his eyes.

'I can tell you what this is all about shortly. In the meantime, I have some good news for you. Your plot failed. Then I have some unwelcome news for you. Your friends are dead.'

That news shattered Mark.

There was no disguising his body language. He stared at Alexseyev with intense hate in his eyes. Not so long ago, he had stood talking to a man who had been responsible for the deaths of his two friends—the innocent personal assistant Annette Covic and the CIA agent Paul Williams. And Mark vowed that if he ever got out of that situation alive, the guy responsible—Stephen Rodriguez— would suffer. Now the feelings that he had deep inside said that Yuri Alexseyev would be added to the list.

The problem was that Yuri had all the cards in the deck, and he wasn't even dealing. His loathing for the man who sat before him was absolute.

Mark asked in a whisper.

'Do you want to tell me how they died?'

'Sure. They were shot on the university campus, during a failed attempt on the life of the President. Now my job is to find out how you fit into the plan. And then we turn you and your associates over to the Afghan intelligence. What they will do with you, I do not know. But I would guess that you will never again see the light of day,' Yuri gloated.

Mark felt that it must have been the lack of sleep. His mind whirled around, making phantoms out of nothing. Yuri's words still did not make much sense. What the hell was Dusty doing at the university campus? Probably, he was not there at all! Mark knew the technique: keep the prisoner so confused that eventually, they would start to babble, and from the babble would come to the truth. Mark could deal with that, at least for the present. But who was the one who was getting confused? He looked at Alexseyev with a mixture of loathing and confusion, not sure how good his threat would be.

'If you are responsible for the death of my good friend Dusty, then either I or my friends will hunt you down, no matter where you may hide, and kill you as surely as the sun will rise tomorrow.' Mark's voice tapered down to a whisper as he stared into Yuri's eyes.

The message was a bit hollow, given that Mark had no means of escape and no means of contacting anyone. It was a surprise that he saw in those eyes more than a flicker of self-doubt.

'You may have just saved your life!' Alexseyev almost

muttered.

While he had been suspicious of the advice that he had been given by the CIA, maybe the three prisoners that he was holding were not a part of the plot at all. Maybe they were just fodder. His perception had been correct. What the hell did he do now?

'No, your friends Archibald and Lawrence are still alive. I was referring to your Tajik friends.'

And this time, it was Mark's eyes that were the focus of attention. And the reaction that Alexseyev saw, one of absolute relief, could not have been faked. Not unless the man was a machine programmed to hide his innermost feelings.

What Alexseyev could not know was the other reason for the relief that Mark displayed.
Yuri Alexseyev had failed to mention anything about Owen Squires.

Alexseyev went to the door, opened it, and issued some instructions to the guard standing outside. He then returned and sat across the table from Mark, lost in thought, saying nothing. Mark also said nothing. Never volunteer any information. Therefore, only speak when spoken to. Something was happening; Mark did not know what. He had been trained to be patient.

So, he waited.

The guard appeared moments later with coffee for Mark, tea for Yuri, and a plate that contained an assortment of biscuits and cakes, and then left.

Alexseyev indicated that Mark could help himself.

And then the interrogation started again.

'What do you know of the Tajiks? And do you know the Arghandiwal brothers, Abdul and Zalmay?' Alexseyev enquired. And he bit his lip when he saw the reaction that he had now come to expect.

Unless this American was incredibly well trained, he had not a clue what those names meant.

'I have heard of the Tajiks, but I cannot help you with those names,' Mark replied in all honesty.

'Have you ever heard of Stefan Rodriguez?' was the next question.

That surprised Mark, but horrible thoughts started to churn in his mind, and they chilled him to the bone.

Here was the connection. Mark recalled the conversation he had with his father Harold just a few days ago. Mark did not know of any plot to kill the Afghani President, but apparently, Stephen Rodriguez did. There were just too many coincidences. And now this Russian was on to something.

Could Alexseyev have discovered why Mark was really in Afghanistan? Or maybe Yuri was working for the CIA. Or worse still, for the assistant deputy director of intelligence.

Mark replied as calmly as he could.

'Stephen Rodriguez? He works for the CIA, as you well know.'

At times, body language can be a pain up the ass. At other times, it can be a godsend. At least Mark and Yuri seemed to agree on one thing: Stephen Rodriguez would be on neither man's Christmas card list.

Alexseyev now had three problems to deal with, and none of them pleased him.

Firstly, he urgently needed to speak to Stefan and find out why the American had sought to mislead the Russian. There may be a simple explanation: maybe the normally efficient United States intelligence services had just made yet another major stuff-up, and they would come limping along with profuse apologies, hoping to keep it all below the radar. Yuri did not think so. While he personally did not care whether President Hamid Karzai lived or died, he did not believe that the CIA would so underestimate the Russians. The CIA knew of the security surrounding the President of Afghanistan. They also knew that the President's greatest vulnerability was, in fact, from members of the very group that claimed to support him. Therefore, what mission was the Taylor faction on, and why had the CIA sought to distract them, or delay them, as seemed to be the case?

No matter how Yuri looked at this problem, he was coming to the view that it was personal. Could Lawrence have been telling the truth after all? Was Stefan really involved in the drug trade, and was the Mark Taylor team in Kabul to follow him? In that case, this business was very personal. And that was an extremely dangerous game for the CIA to play.

Secondly, he had the question of what to do with his prisoners. The normal procedure in a civilized world was to simply hand them back to the country from which they came. Since Yuri was with the SVR and had been in his previous life a member of the KGB, his instinct would have been to deliver them to the CIA. The reason for that was quite simple and easily understood. Anyone who had been interrogated by the 'other side' would then be interrogated by the 'friendly' side to find out what light could be shed on their intelligence.

The fact that this dual interrogation drove the poor victims insane was just the sacrifice we must pay for living in a civilized world. It was an accepted part of international relationships that neither side liked, but it was still pursued with ruthless efficiency.

Alexseyev was not a gambler. But if he had to place a bet, it would be on Mark Taylor not wanting to be released into the hands of the CIA and into the hands of Stephen Rodriguez. He already knew that Mark Taylor, ex-Marine, ex-Special Forces, ex-Delta Force, much-decorated ex-serviceman of the United States, was also the son of one Harold Taylor who had recently been appointed as an assistant inspector of the CIA.

Was it now possible that Mark Taylor could be tailing Rodriguez as a part of an investigation into some wrongdoing? Alexseyev knew that Stephen Rodriguez was not one of the people in the CIA that the Russians had managed to turn in that auspicious organization, but that was not to say someone else hadn't. And then there was the drug business, which would explain some of the information he had received from De Lawrence.
Alexseyev did not know how close to the truth his deduction had strayed.

The first two problems led to a third: how to avoid a diplomatic incident out of which there would be no winners, only losers. Pride was a serious part of international diplomacy. If Alexseyev had been conned, then, rightly, or wrongly, he would be the loser in this never-ending game of international chess. At least other people would see him as the loser, which amounted to the same thing.

The other part of that game was the American media. They would have a ball with the story that the CIA had managed to mislead the SVR. No matter that the life of the President of a country may have been at stake. The President had not died—at least not this time—so the media would focus their attention on the lead-up; and frankly, that did not look good. On balance, the loser could be the CIA. But if Mark and company were to tell their story and the Russians received a *please explain,* then Alexseyev's next posting would probably be to Somalia or some other shithole of the third world.

There was also another minor problem. One of Yuri's men was dead. He had been killed, at least according to two very unreliable witnesses, by one of the Americans. Now that story seemed rather far-fetched. How could one man overpower three armed men? And what could he have hoped to achieve by shooting a man dead before being overpowered? He had no means of escape. And Dusty seemed far too disciplined to have done anything that stupid. The problem was, how was Alexseyev ever going to prove it?

And the answer was, he wasn't.

Alexseyev sighed, gathered up his notes, and left the room without another word.

Mark was returned to his cell.

He had been allowed to take the biscuits.

'Olezhka! How good to see you again! And what brings you to Kabul?'

Alexseyev was pleased to see his old friend as he dragged himself back into the office to write up his report —which would not include where he had failed.

Demidov reached over and hugged the man. He had been surrounded by Afghans, and not much else, for over six months; and it was a relief to see one of his countrymen.

'I had to come to Kabul at short notice,' Demidov began.

'I won't bore you with all the details, just the important pieces. You may recall that I told you about the possible involvement of our friends at the CIA in the drug business?'

'Yes,' answered Alexseyev, looking for a pen to begin his report, wishing that Olezhka could find someone else to tell his story to. Demidov was a good friend and a conscientious worker, but he did tend to go on a bit. So, the CIA was involved in the drug trade! Does the bear shit in the forest? The CIA had been involved in drugs, one way or another, since their formation back in 1947, and that involvement would not end anytime soon! Whenever, and wherever, they did get involved, it appeared to result in a major cock-up. They never learned, these Americans!

'Ahmed Karzai has been dicking around with their arrangements, and now he wants me to offer them a deal so that Ahmed has control,' Oleg continued, not exactly oblivious to his boss's preoccupation with finding a pen.

That caused Yuri to look up.

'Why don't you do that? It would be in our interests, wouldn't it?'

At last, Oleg was getting the attention that all his hard work had demanded.

'Well, it certainly would give us the advantage. And I don't think the CIA will have any alternative. I have already talked to their man in Marjah, a guy who goes by the name of Jacob Dutton, who you may have heard of. He seemed to be quite amenable to the idea. He would just need to clear the arrangements with his masters. They arranged for their present supplier, Wakil Hekmatyar, who you may also have heard of, to be killed. Doesn't sound like the way to cement a long-term relationship.' Oleg laughed at his own joke.

Yuri had at last found a pen but felt that he had to contribute to this conversation. He laughed while lighting a cigarette and passing his precious packet of American Marlboros to his guest.

'Don't tell me! They got their Afghan friends to take him out, did they? And what did Hekmatyar do to earn their displeasure?' Yuri asked.

The atmosphere got conspiratorial.

'I presume that they felt that Wakil was responsible for what Ahmed was doing to them.' Oleg laughed. 'They brought some other guy in, and he made the decision. They had a couple of meetings, and then bang! No more Wakil. It all seemed so unexpected.'

'Who was the guy?' Yuri asked, leaning back in his chair, trying, and failing to blow smoke rings at the ceiling.

'We don't know, at least not yet.' Oleg continued, 'Fairly old guy, in his late fifties I would say, just under six feet tall, about 180 pounds. He had the agent Jacob Dutton running around like a flea in a fit, so he was someone senior—not that, that would be hard. The CIA only has three people in Marjah, and one of them is a woman!'

Oleg again laughed, but then stopped as though he had been hit by a bus. Yuri was staring at him and leaning forward in his chair as though he was about to leap across the desk.

'If I showed you a picture of this man—admittedly, it was taken about ten years ago—would you be able to recognize him?'

Oleg shrugged. That was a stupid question. All SVR agents, like comparative people in the CIA, were highly skilled in recognition techniques. They had to be. Their lives, the lives of the people they served, and the people who worked as their informants—strictly in that specific order, of course—depended on it. So what?

Fortunately, Yuri did not wait for an answer. He slapped a picture on the desk, almost challenging Oleg to deny him.

'Yes, that's the man,' Oleg replied and shrugged again. 'Who is he?'

Yuri thought about that. The Russians, although they had lightened up somewhat in the post–Cold War era were still paranoid about security. Worse than the CIA had ever been about the need-to-know basis. But, on balance, did it matter all that much?

'He is Stefan Rodriguez, the assistant deputy director of intelligence of the CIA.'

'Shit!'

'Yes, shit. Now tell me more about what has been going on in Marjah. Leave nothing out. We have got all night if needs be.'

And so, Demidov told Alexseyev.

About the equally confusing meeting that Jacob Dutton had earlier with the group of Tajiks. About the equally mysterious three men who had been following the CIA in and around Marjah. About the fact that all the three groups—the CIA, the Tajiks, and the three men—had been in the same convoy that had journeyed from Marjah to Kabul. Yuri let Oleg continue without interruption. It must have taken well over an hour before there was nothing more to tell.

In the end, the two Russians just sat there. The room had slowly filled with the smoke, mostly from Yuri's cigarettes, as he chain-smoked his way through the whole packet, and then rummaged in a drawer to find some Russian cigarettes, which would have made the air at Chernobyl seem pleasant. And then Yuri started.

'I have today, or was it yesterday,' he said, looking at his watch, 'prevented an attempt on the life of the Afghan President. The people who were responsible were a couple of Tajiks. They originally came from Pakistan, and we have yet to confirm, or rather, we had yet to confirm, how they got to be in Kabul. You now may have answered that question. They came to Kabul in the same convoy as the CIA. And it was the CIA who were involved in the plot to kill the President. What have they been playing at?'

Then his shoulders slouched. He continued staring into space.

'Now, the three men who were following our friends from the CIA. Fit men. American men. I believe I am holding them prisoners in this very building.' Yuri was talking to himself, but that did not stop Oleg from interrupting.

'Why are you holding them? Surely, you don't want to get into a diplomatic row with the Americans! What have they done?'

'We don't know. I guess the next stage of my interrogation is to find out why they were following the CIA. But let us speculate here. What say they are with the American Drug Enforcement Administration and following the CIA to find out what the CIA is up to in the drug trade? From what you tell me now, that seems quite likely.'

Oleg nodded. 'That was my assumption.'

'And you say the three were, one about six-four, one of comparable size and build but a black Afro-American, the third a small guy, quite thin?'

Oleg again nodded in the affirmative as Yuri continued.

'Well, it looks as though we may have to dispose of them, doesn't it? If you want to do a deal with the CIA, we cannot have this team reporting back to their masters in Washington now, can we?'

'I suppose not!' Oleg replied, not sure if he cared, one way or the other.

Neither man knew that the three men that Yuri had in custody were not the same three who Oleg thought they were.

Alexseyev was now convinced that there was a fourth man—the elusive Owen Squires.

This fellow could not know what had happened to the rest of his team.

And he never would.

Chapter 34

Intercession

The strange world that is inhabited by spooks did have some advantages. Although in the grand scheme of things, Stephen Rodriguez of the CIA outranked Yuri Alekseyev of the SVR by quite a margin, it was still possible to quickly track down where someone was in the opposing intelligence service. It did take some considerable effort on Yuri's part, starting with his station chief in Kabul, then through the Moscow headquarters of the SVR, then through the cultural attaché of the Russian Embassy in Washington DC, but Stephen Rodriguez was finally tracked down.

When he had called Yuri before, Stephen had said that he was in Ghazni, but he could, of course, be anywhere on the planet. Now Yuri had confirmation that he was right here in Kabul, and this time Yuri had a telephone number.

The circuitous route to find out this riveting piece of information did nothing to improve Yuri's mood.

'Stefan, it is Yuri. Just thought I would bring you up to date on that information you passed to me the other day.'

'Oh! So, you got it all sorted? Hamid is safe and well?' Stephen asked.

Stephen Rodriguez, of course, was well aware that Hamid Karzai was indeed safe and well, and Stephen also knew that Yuri would be aware that he knew. Such is the protocol used in international communications.

This was going to be difficult. Yuri tried not to sigh.

'Stefan, the information you gave to me was a little suspect. Unless you can help us, we can find no link between the three Americans we picked up and the plot to kill—'

Stephen interrupted Yuri in midsentence.

'You said three—who was the third?'

Alexseyev could not read body language over the telephone, but he could tell when someone went apoplectic.

'Yes, there were three,' Alexseyev replied.

'The two that you mentioned must have had a contact here in Kabul, so we picked him up as well.'

'So, who is he?' Rodriguez asked, the concern evident in his voice. If there were more people involved, then there were more loose ends to be tracked down. His plan could be coming apart. He could bluff his way out of the Alexseyev situation. But only if he had all the people in one place.

Who was the third man? What were his connections? And would someone else start poking around?

From Alexseyev's point of view, the situation was also getting messy. That the assistant deputy director of the CIA, in one scenario, had simply got things wrong, or in the second scenario had deliberately intended to mislead, was a major issue. That was quite simply not the way that things were supposed to work in the normally ordered world of international relations.

Even during the Cold War, there was some respect! But now that meant that to avoid a *situation*, the men would have to be made to disappear! But what else was going on?

Therefore, Alexseyev's only option was to make the situation messier.

'Why don't you come over and talk to them yourself? Thus far, we have very little information on any of them. Alternatively, how about you give us what you know, and that will give us the advantage in trying to find out more?'

Of course, Yuri knew what the answers would be.

No, I'm just about to leave. Or, no, we don't have any information on them. Alexseyev was almost right.

'Unfortunately, I am just about to leave. Otherwise, that could have been an interesting prospect,' Rodriguez began his evasion.

'Moreso because they are such a fringe group that we don't know much about them. It might be a better idea if you hand them over to us, and we will take it from there.'

Which, of course, Stephen knew would not happen. He was counting on it not happening. It would take some explaining at CIA HQ in Langley. It would also cause serious problems for the CIA station chief in Kabul, who was supposed to know what was happening on his own patch.

Alexseyev continued,

'Stefan, let me put this to you as plainly as I can. We can find no link between the three Americans and the Tajiks. The fact that the Afghan security forces shot two Tajiks on the university campus earlier today, that they were armed, and that the rifles that they were carrying seem to have come from the Afghan Army would seem to suggest there was a plot. The timing seems to fit with what is logical: they were delayed, so they took the next available opportunity. The role of the, shall we say, two Americans in all of this seems to be *nada* or nothing in your language. Therefore, this means that the information that you supplied to us was a load of rubbish, and we have spent many hours and a good deal of manpower getting nowhere. And my people in Marjah tell me that there was a meeting between the Tajiks and one of your local people, which seems to imply that you knew quite a lot more about this whole business than you have told me. Now let me speculate you supplied us with disinformation. Now what we need to know is, why? Why would you want to risk the lives of the Americans? Why would you want to risk the life of President Hamid Karzai? It just does not make any sense.'

There was a pregnant silence, and then Stephen changed tack, totally ignoring the observations made by the Russian.

'What do you intend to do with your American prisoners?'

There was another pregnant pause.

Alexseyev would enjoy the next part.

'In the circumstances, I think that we might need to pretend that we never had them. We do not want to be involved in an international incident, but our friends in Afghanistan security can soon take care of that. As they are aware that we have the prisoners, it would not look too good if we simply handed them over to the CIA, of all people. It is best for all concerned that they are made to disappear. Do you not agree?'

Stick that one up your ass, arrogant prick!

'Yes. You need to do what you think is best.'

And then the ADDI of the CIA simply disconnected the call.

Alexseyev was livid with both himself for taking the false lead (termed a dangle in the trade) and with Rodriguez. That action by the CIA had caused no end to the chaos, but the question remained. Why?

What on earth was it intended to achieve? Was it intended to embarrass the Russians as they tried to retain their status with the Afghan leadership, or was there some grander plan?

Alexseyev grabbed a secure line and called Washington.

Jacob Dutton had no idea who the person was that Rodriguez had been talking to, but he got the gist of the conversation. That would tie up one of the loose ends. There was one thing that you could rely on in Afghanistan —the ability to make someone disappear.

Now there was just one more.

'I had a call from a Russian ...,' Dutton began, but that was as far as he got.

'What Russian?'

'I don't know. He would not give me his name! Someone from Marjah,' Dutton blundered on.

It was not his fault! And Russians were everywhere in this godforsaken country. Of course, being in the spook business, Dutton was expected to know everything and everyone. But the Russian had said that he did not need to know who he was. Dutton was so apoplectic about the content of the call that there were other more critical issues to think about. Like how did he appear to know so much about the happenings in Marjah? In those circumstances, who cares about what his name was?

Rodriguez had visibly shrunk in his chair. And there was more bad news to come, and he knew it. He asked in almost a whisper,

'What did your Russian have to say?'

Jacob knew that he needed to be careful how he answered. 'He said that Ahmed Karzai was ready to offer a deal for shipments out of Marjah. Why he thought we would be interested in a deal, he did not say. He also said that he had heard that Wakil Hekmatyar had met with an accident.'

Dutton knew that his boss would not be pleased about this.

Rodriguez leaped from his chair, sending it crashing against the wall, and put his hands to his head as though fighting a massive headache. Then he screamed at Dutton.

'Why didn't you tell me this before?'

Now Dutton was confused. Before *when*? Before *what*? He just looked at Rodriguez and shrugged.

'I came from the CIA compound straight here. I did not think you would want to discuss this over the telephone.' He did not say, *you made the rules—I just do what I have been told to do, you arrogant piece of shit!*

But body language should do the trick.

For just a moment, Rodriguez looked at Dutton as though he was going to strike him. Then he shook his head, retrieved his chair from off the floor, and sat down again.

This was getting all too much! But Jacob was right. And what was more, Jacob was very much involved in this whole business, and he needed him. Such was the price of doing business.

It was not his fault that things were turning pear-shaped.

'I'm sorry,' Rodriguez said, although it was not obvious that he felt any such emotion.

'This Russian—can you describe his voice? Any accent?'

Fortunately for both men, part of CIA training is in voice recognition. Whereas most normal people would recognize a Russian accent and not much else, agents were better trained than that.

'Fairly smooth, quiet voice, St. Petersburg possibly —not Moscow. He had a very slight lisp, almost as though he couldn't finish a sentence before he started on the next one.'

Rodriguez was not listening. He played back a recorder and then turned up the volume. 'Yes, there were three. The two that you mentioned must have had a contact here in Kabul, so we picked him up as well,' said the voice from his earlier telephone conversation.

'Is that your man?'

'No, definitely not' Dutton concluded.

At least he was right on this one.

'So! Why is it that another Russian comes into the act?' Rodriguez asked, still talking to himself. Then he shifted his gaze to Dutton again and asked,

'You have definitely not heard him before?'

'No. Who is the man on the tape?'

'That is Yuri Alekseyev. We understand he is station chief of the SVR in this part of the world. He has got himself a part-time job as head of President Karzai's security detail. And now this Russian that called you says that he is somehow tied up with the President's brother. What a fucking mess!'

Dutton could see that it was. So, he asked.

'What am I to say to this guy when he calls me back?'

The whole thing was getting well beyond his means to comprehend. Fortunately, he had the man on the appropriate pay scale to make the decision.

'Do we have any choice in the matter?' Rodriguez asked the ceiling.

Chapter 35

Kidnapped

Would the Russian do what he had implied he would do?

Stephen Rodriguez mulled over what had happened, and what he thought would happen next. On balance, the Russians were ruthless, their Afghan friends even more so, if a little disorganized. If everything went according to plan, this would be the end of Mark Taylor and his cohorts. He considered the possibility of other people being involved but dismissed that as irrelevant.

Rodriguez had been involved in covert or clandestine operations himself, and it did look as though this was such an operation. However, it had been poorly organized, and grossly under-resourced. In that case, there would be so few people that knew what was going on that they would be unlikely to know what had gone wrong. And they certainly would not want to draw any attention to themselves or the operation. In the worst case, their first port of call would be to report the men as missing to the embassy, or to the CIA, DEA, FBI, or any of several other organizations that they may be associated with. In any event, they would find, as Yuri so aptly put it, nada.

But the problem was, could he trust the Russians?

He had a quiet laugh at that. Could he trust anyone? Could anyone trust anyone? Who knew what crafty little schemes the Russians could get up to? But in this instance, he could not see any mileage to be gained from playing their little games. And now the Russians seemed to want a piece of the drug trade. And control of Karzai.

Did that matter all that much? Afghanistan was fucked anyway. Rodriguez's scheme depended on supply, and drug suppliers were nothing if not loyal to their customers. Especially the ones that paid. On balance, the greater problem was on the other side of the world. If the information on his scheme remained on this side of the world, he was in the clear.

That left one main problem: the three men. They could survive, and that was an issue that he now had to worry about. There were just too many imponderables despite the assurances from the Russians and despite the Afghans' hard-won reputation for ruthless efficiency. Well, at least when it came to disposing of things.

Business was business. In the absence of assurance, he had to have some insurance. Just in case Mark Taylor reappeared on the scene, yet again!

Rodriguez rang his contacts in Washington. Not his official CIA contacts, but people on whom he could rely on to deliver what he wanted to be done. People who would deliver the necessary form of insurance. Too many things had been going wrong. Nothing major, nothing that could not be fixed. But now time was becoming the issue.

His major and all-consuming priority was that he had to get the supply lines up and operating again as quickly as was possible, or the whole house of cards could tumble down. He had a fair amount of money tucked away in places where the prying eyes of those vermin in the FBI would never dream of looking, and with money, he could buy whatever resources or identities he needed. If the house of cards did tumble, all that would leave behind was a vacant space. There was nothing to link him to the distribution network for the quite simple reason that it was hidden in plain sight for everyone to see, if only they could find it. The Internet and the world-wide-web had provided the intelligence community with the biggest headache of all. So why not use it themselves with no fear of ever being caught!

Within the next two years in the normal course of events, he would face the choice of staking a claim to go higher up in the CIA or taking early retirement. That was an easy decision. There was too much political crap and too much scrutiny if he stayed. The choice that he would make was to retire, and he would leave with the blessing of his government and their thanks for a job well done in the pursuit of a safe America, and the thankful blessing of the people who would seamlessly take over his networks. CIA networks. And drug networks.

Not necessarily the same thing. But that was being picky.

He needed some insurance just in case something untoward happened. He knew that Mark Taylor had an extraordinary knack both for surviving and for never giving up. It must have been a combination of Mark Taylor's training in the United States Special Forces and Delta Force, a dedication that was an indelible part of his character, and genes. His father, Harold Taylor, had a well-earned reputation for stubbornly worrying any problem to death, and for being virtually incorruptible.

Well, almost.

Rumours in Washington suggested that Harold Taylor was having an affair— although why anyone would want to have an affair with an old faggot like Harold, Stephen had some difficulty imagining. But the problem with that was, how could you get any leverage out of it? If he tried to influence Harold by saying, for instance, that he would reveal all to Mrs. Taylor, he knew exactly what the answer would be: 'Go ahead.' The elder Taylor would be very unlikely to place his personal position above that of his country.

Therefore, until he received confirmation of Mark Taylor's death, he would need to work on the younger of the two Taylors.

And Rodriguez knew exactly what kind of insurance he would need to hold.

Chapter 36

Insurance

The day had gone quickly for Debbie. While Mark was away on his covert mission, or just playing games, in Pakistan and Afghanistan, she went to the office of Taylor Software after lunch on most days. She went to just check on how things were going, check whether anything was needed, and to make sure everyone was happy and content. Her routine was that she collected the mail on her way to the office, discussed the events of the day over a coffee with Brad, dealt with any matters that required her attention, and then left for the apartment that she shared with Mark later in the afternoon before the traffic got too busy.

Today there was more mail than usual, more had happened in the last twenty-four hours, more people in the office, and more people to talk to. Consequently, she was later than usual returning to the peace and tranquillity of the apartment.

Mark had made a habit of calling her at about five o'clock in the evening, and although he did not call every day, she looked forward to hearing his voice. She had not heard from him for a couple of days, so it was probable that he would call today, and she could feel the excitement mounting as she made her way home.

Mark was a good man. Debbie had, for once in her short life, got something right. Mark would be home soon, but every conversation was precious, every moment that she could hear his voice made her feel good to be alive. Mark had become her rock in an otherwise uncertain world.

It was getting dark by the time she arrived at the apartment. The wind was starting to pick up and to turn around to the north. It would soon be bitterly cold. Debbie parked her car in her usual place in the basement garage and scurried to the access door, entered her code, and then went to the elevator. There was no one else in sight as she rode the car to the fourth floor and to their unit, where she could disappear into the warmth and comfort of her own little world.

The key to the apartment was on the same ring as her car keys, so she easily fed it into the lock, and then automatically stepped aside, looking for Fridge, the cat that Mark had adopted some time ago, expecting him to rush past. No time for greetings at this time of the day. It was time for food, and that would be the only priority for Fridge.

Except that there was no cat. And the door just eased open. Debbie realized that there was no necessity for a key. The door was already unlocked.

Like many people in this world, after an initial unease at the unexpected, Debbie thought nothing of either issue. She merely shrugged. Earlier in the day, before going into the office of Taylor Software, she had asked the manager of the building to arrange for someone to fix the catch on one of the windows. No big deal! When the wind blew from a northerly direction, the window rattled, so they should have it attended to before the winter really set in. The manager was old, but honest and reliable, except he occasionally forgot things, like locking doors, and probably never even noticed the cat sneak into the apartment. And leaving a door unlocked did not matter, really, because to gain access to the entire complex required everyone to use their access code, so everyone who was in the building had every right to be there. So, no damage done.

Debbie entered the apartment, took off her coat, and called out to Fridge, who she assumed had entered with the manager and would have made himself at home, probably on the couch in the lounge.

But Fridge was not on the couch.

She almost absentmindedly went into the kitchen, and there he was. Lying on the floor. He lay at full length, a circle of blood evident around his body. He did not move. Debbie raised her hand to her mouth to stifle a scream; fear of the unknown and the unexpected, crept into her previously ordered world.

Fridge was dead.

The silence of the room only added to the numbing realisation that one of the few things that she knew that Mark really cared about, and that Debbie could associate with Mark, was no more. Like Mark, Fridge was a loner. They had met by chance, chosen to live together by chance. The cat because Mark fed him. Mark, because Fridge was company. Both, because neither hassled the other, just accepted each other. Mark would be sad. Debbie was mortified.

Then she got the second fright of the night, and an involuntary scream almost escaped her lips but was choked off as the dryness of terror filled her throat.

'Do not scream, or I will kill you,' was all the man

said as he eased into the kitchen with his gun extended in front of him.

'Who are you? What do you want? What are you doing here?' The questions poured out as Debbie looked around for a means of escape. There was none.

The man gave no answers. He just motioned towards the door to Mark's bedroom, and another man appeared.

They did not look like robbers. Both men were dressed in charcoal-grey suits, white shirts, red ties, immaculately polished shoes. They had close-cropped hair and were clean-shaven. They were both slim and looked extremely fit. But it was their eyes. They both had cold grey eyes that seemed devoid of any life or any emotion, and they seemed confident in what they were doing.

The taller of the two men went back to the apartment door and checked the lock. This time it was locked. He then came back into the living room area and motioned a very scared Debbie Peterson into a seat. He sat down facing her. The same cold grey eyes stared at her across the coffee table. When he spoke, it was in a monotone—no feeling, no emotion, no anything!

'I am sorry about the cat!' was his first statement.

'Why did you need to kill him?' Debbie asked, the accusation and the bitterness apparent even though she was so scared.

The man smiled. 'We wanted to make a statement so that you would understand. It is only a cat. But things could get much worse!'

'What do you want?' Debbie whispered, absolute terror evident in her voice. She had heard stories of girls being raped and murdered in this city. But the men did not appear to be at all interested in such crude and despicable activity—they looked too professional. What did they want?

She did not have to wait for the answer, and that terrified her even more.

'You need to get a few things together. You are coming with us, just for a few days, provided Mr Taylor behaves himself,' the man replied, content that his implied message had been well understood.

Debbie had not had an easy life. In her earlier years, she had lived through a stormy relationship with her abusive father and her alcoholic mother down in Orlando, Florida. She had left Florida and come to the bright lights of New York City to seek a better life and get away from the abuse that she had witnessed, and away from the pain that she had felt. Once in New York, she had taken up a friendship with a guy she thought the world of. Tim Kirby was arrogant and abusive, but to Debbie, which was just how she expected men to behave. That is, until it became apparent that Tim was playing around with other women. After she found out about these affairs, and that she was by no means the only girl in his life, she slowly built up the courage to end their relationship.

Except that something got in the way. September 11, 2001.

Tim was on the ninety-second floor of the South Tower of the World Trade Centre when American Airlines flights 11 and 175 came to an abrupt and devastating halt, and so did the life of her apparent partner and friend, and many thousands of others. While she felt no particular sorrow at Tim's death, the traumatic effects of that day were etched in her memory for all time, and from that day, she had no desire to be with another man.

Then she had met Mark Taylor.

She never knew that a man could be so beautiful and caring. Mark was always so polite. He never raised his voice to her. Mark never got abusive to anyone. Debbie would ask him questions, and he would answer without evasion.

His every touch was one of affection. She loved him, and he loved her. Whatever it was that these two gentlemen wanted, there was absolutely no way that she would help them in any way to harm Mark. She sat and stared at the man, petrified but stoic. And then she rose to her feet.

'What do you mean? I have no idea what you are talking about, so would you please leave now.'

The man rose from his seat and towered over her. The blow to the left side of her face was so unexpected and was delivered with such speed, force, and accuracy that she did not have time even to blink. She crashed back down onto the couch, and it was only the fact that she rode the blow that further damage was not caused. Debbie's first reaction was one of shock, then of pain, then of the horrible realisation that, while she did not have a clue what was going on, it was pointless to resist.

And neither of the two men were about to enlighten her of what they intended to do.

'We will ask the questions,' the man stated in a calm but menacing voice. 'Now, when do you expect to hear from your friend Mark Taylor—and do not invite me to hit you again, because I will.' So cold, so callous, so matter of fact. The man waited for an answer.

'I don't know ... he calls when he can,' was Debbie's stuttering response between the tears.

The man looked at her patiently, and then with a sigh said, 'We can make this pleasant or unpleasant for you. it is your call. Now let us start again. I am sorry we have not had time for introductions. I am Karl, and my friend here is called Luke. You are called Debbie, and the person who we are all interested in is Mark Taylor. You are with me so far?'

The man called Karl paused, and Debbie simply nodded her head before he continued.

'Good, we are making some progress. Now Mark is overseas, is that correct?'

There was not a sound in the apartment, although Debbie's heart was racing, and she felt rather than heard the hammer blows. Her blood pressure must have been high and rising. She had a flashback to a time, not that long ago when the same Mark Taylor had come into her office at the Augem Group claiming to be a representative of the National Security Agency. He had a friend with him at the time called Paul Williams. Though she had never enquired into what all that was about, she did know that within a couple of hours of Mark's arrival at her office, her then-boss, John Dubois, had committed suicide. Not that John Dubois was any great loss to Debbie, or, indeed, the world. She also knew that Paul Williams and another friend of Mark's, Annette Covic, who was known to Debbie, had also died that very same day, and that Mark had been hurt.

It was obvious that somewhere in the past, Mark had acquired some very unsavoury friends. And now it appeared that Mark had some unfinished business in that regard.

The whole experience was frightening, and Debbie was frightened now. Was this something to do with Mark's past, and had it come back to haunt him? But what was it?

'I don't know where Mark is. He did not say where he was going,' Debbie defiantly replied. But her defiance was a waste of time. Karl could read body language. Debbie could too. But she did not have the experience to hide hers.

Karl again sighed and, surprisingly, showed immense patience. 'OK. I will tell you that he is currently in Afghanistan enjoying himself, but we are certain that he will be in touch. Now when do you expect to hear from him? He will come to no harm. We just need to know when he will call.'

The tears started to flow again, out of hopelessness, out of bitterness. Why did people not just get on with their own lives? Why did there always need to be all these twists and turns? If these two gentlemen knew where Mark was, then why did they need to know about his infrequent, personal, but innocent telephone calls with Debbie?

It was insane.

'He calls me when he can!' she sobbed. 'I just do not know when he will call, so I cannot answer your question. What is this all about?'

The patience that Karl had displayed until now was showing signs that it would not last.

But then the telephone rang.

The three of them stared at the telephone, as though frozen in time. At first, no one moved. Then Karl grabbed the telephone, switched it to Speaker, and handed it to Debbie with one hand, while nestling his gun threateningly in the other. He did not say, nor did he need to say, anything.

Debbie pressed the Talk button.

'Hello, Debbie speaking,' she said into the receiver.

'Hi, Ms Peterson, Joe here. Just letting you know that the guy to fix the window will be in on Monday.'

'OK. Thanks, Joe!' Debbie pressed the End button to terminate the call and handed the phone back to Karl with a shrug. 'Just the building manager,' she said as she sat down again.

Karl looked as though his blood pressure had also been going through the roof, but he rapidly calmed down. He was about to continue with his interrogation when the telephone rang again. The blood pressure rose again in all three of them.

'Be careful. Your boyfriend is too far away to protect

you now,' Karl said as he once again pushed the telephone receiver over to Debbie as she again stood up.

She pressed the Talk button and said, 'Hello, Debbie speaking.'

She was tense, but her shoulders sagged with relief when she realised who was calling this time. And she was strangely pleased that it was not Mark.

'Hi, Deb, it's Brad. Sorry to disturb you at home, but I have just had some great news and needed to share it with you. That deal we were working on with the Styris Group is going ahead. They just rang to say we have it in the bag. What I need to know from you is when you expect Mark to be back from his travels, so if you are talking to him, you could ask. They want him to sign the paperwork.'

Debbie bit her lip and stifled the tears. Everyone, friends, and foes, wanted to know when Mark would call, or when he would be back. She felt so helpless. 'Oh, that is good news,' she managed to say, fighting to stay in control. She paused, taking a deep breath. 'Err, I do not know when Mark will be back. When he calls, I will have to ask him.'

'Ah, well, please let me know. This deal is a biggie! Now, how about coming out to dinner tomorrow with me and Shania? Bit of a celebration, on the company. I am sure Mark would not mind—and you need to get out!'

The look from Karl said a very definite *No*. The body language of Debbie said *Yes*. So, she said, 'No, you go and enjoy yourself with Shania. You don't want me there, and I would not be very good company.'

'You sure?' Brad replied, and when he got no answer, he continued, 'OK. Well, if you change your mind, just let me know when I see you tomorrow. Sorry to have disturbed your evening. Bye!' And Brad just terminated the call.

Karl pushed Debbie back onto the couch and asked,

'Could I please have your mobile phone?'

When Debbie hesitated, things turned serious. 'Give me your fucking mobile phone—do it now!' And he moved towards her, threatening to hit her again.

She almost shrieked from panic. 'It is in my bag, over by the door. I'll get it.' She stood up but was immediately pushed back down by Karl. He went across to get the bag and threw it to her. She was scared, although she still had no idea what this was all about. There did not seem to be any point in resisting. They would do what they had to do. She retrieved the mobile phone but clung on to it as though it was her last link with reality.

'What is your mobile phone number?' Karl asked again, his tone menacing.

Debbie again hesitated. Not from a reluctance to cooperate, but out of fear. This man called Karl was getting mad, but he did not shout, did not even raise his voice. The threatening tone in his voice was more than enough.

'The number—now!'

She gave him the number.

He indicated to his partner, and Luke grabbed Debbie by one arm and escorted her to the master bedroom. 'You will need a small bag for your clothes. You could be with us for a week or so.' He stood by the door. Debbie explained that her things were in the other bedroom, which caused Luke to grimace with impatience, but he escorted her into the other room. She had no idea where they intended to take her. It did not seem to be anywhere either comfortable or friendly, so she just grabbed underwear, trousers, blouses, jerseys, and walking shoes, which she just stuffed into a bag. No makeup, no hairbrush. When she was done, Luke grabbed the bag and hustled her back into the living room, where Karl was on the landline.

He did not ask if he could use the telephone. He did

not say what he was going to do. He just keyed in a number from memory and started speaking to the person on the other end. With that completed, he then dialled another number. The mobile phone issued its catchy tune, he answered it, little more than grunted, and then killed both telephones. 'Right. Let's go!'

Karl suddenly pulled a spray canister out of his pocket and pointed it towards Debbie. She started to cry out, thinking that it was pepper spray or Mace; but she need not have worried. By the time that the first hint of her cry made it as far as the back of her throat, she was oblivious to anything else.

They manoeuvred the inert Debbie out of the door and locked it. They moved down the staircase rather than use the elevator, with Luke checking the rear, and exited onto the street and into an innocuous-looking black SUV, of the type and style used by FBI or the Secret Service. It would have struck Debbie as rather strange that Luke, who was in the front passenger seat, reached out and placed a red rotating light on the vehicle roof as they raced off into the night. All that she was aware of was a vague notion of movement, and not much else.

She would have no memory of where they were going.

Chapter 37

Worries

Brad Morgan was a very worried man.

Brad did not often worry because that was not in his nature, and he was a highly intelligent and practical man. He had been trained to analyse things carefully, thoroughly, and almost with detachment. But Brad sensed, rather than knew, that something was wrong when he had talked, briefly, with the boss's girlfriend.

Knowing that something was wrong meant nothing. Debbie had sounded tense, which was not normal, so his inquisitive mind said that he should find out more.

It was now nearly twenty-four hours since his last conversation with Debbie. Of itself, that was not an issue. Of more concern was that Debbie had not been into the office. Neither had she contacted Brad or anyone else at Taylor Software. And the Styris account should surely have generated some response, considering the immediate and longer-term effect on the finances of the company.

Maybe she was sick, but she seemed fine the previous day. She had no known relatives in this part of the world, so she would have nowhere else to go to. Brad would assume responsibility in the absence of the boss and find out.

He had heard nothing, so the place to start was the home.

Morgan had been working for Taylor Software for over two years. Well, that was not quite correct. Mark Taylor was particularly good at what he did—designed and wrote software for computer security systems. Over two years ago, Mark had got a contract to install a system for the Augem Group, a small but nonetheless successful player in the complex world of finance and funds management. Like many companies, their systems were occasionally looked at by the NSA and the FBI. The Augem Group did not know that, nor did they need to know that. It was just one of those things that needed to be done by the federal authorities in a free and democratic country to ensure that everyone played fair. Or, more correctly, everyone did not play *un*fairly. Or, of more interest to the federal authorities, did not get involved in activities such as money laundering, or supporting or encouraging terrorism, or got involved in other activities that would be frowned upon by their shareholders.

Taylor Software had developed a quite remarkable system that made it difficult for the NSA, FBI, and whoever else had a three-letter acronym for a name that gave them the right to spy on the citizens of the United States, and farther afield. Not that there was anything wrong with the software that Mark had developed. Nor was there anything illegal about a company securing its computer systems against some other party, government, or non-government.

So, the authorities came up with a scheme to deal with that situation. At the time, Brad Morgan was employed by the CIA in their Directorate of Science and Technology. Because government departments and the Agency do not exactly pay top dollar, it was assumed by anyone who cared to talk about it that the real brains were out in the free enterprise business world making some real money. But Brad was an exception. He just loved his computers. And there was not a computer system anywhere that Brad Morgan could not hack his way into.

When Taylor Software advertised for someone who had advanced skills in the telecommunications and computer business, the FBI and the CIA conspired to get Morgan into the company. The fact that Brad had subsequently left the CIA and now had a legitimate job with Taylor Software did not reduce the skills that he had acquired in his earlier occupation. And the ability to fiddle with computers was only a part of the story. He had been through the usual CIA training courses at the Farm, and he had other attributes and skills as well.

The fact that in the time that Brad was working for Taylor Software while also employed by the CIA he had been unable to find a way around the Taylor system spoke volumes about the skill that Mark had exercised in the software's development. Brad was certain that he could have *hacked* it given more time. And Brad was quite philosophical about that. That was the difference between private enterprise and government service. In private enterprise, he would have long ago given up as the effort was not worth the reward.

When Brad had spoken with Debbie, he was certain that something sounded different. She was hesitant, rather than her normal bubbly self, and, what? Scared? And her voice sounded remote. But why? Or maybe Brad was just assuming something that was not there. Maybe it was his reaction to her declining his invitation to dinner. Certainly, the reason she had given did not make much sense. Mark was away overseas, and, surely, Debbie would leap at the chance to have some company and to be with friends.

And Taylor Software would be paying for it.

Brad Morgan was an Afro-American, and proud of his heritage. Being in the world of spooks, where people, especially younger women, tend to be either aloof or complete nerds, he had simply not met any girls of a similar ethnicity or age. At least none that interested him or were sufficiently attractive as to arouse his basic male hormones. Out in the business world, he had met a few girls, and the nature of his work, not to mention a terrific sense of humour, meant that he could now engage in relationships.

And Shania was some relationship. They were only just getting to know each other, but Shania had been to the office, had met Mark and Debbie. Shania got along with Debbie, so well that at times it was Brad who felt like the odd one out. Shania was also Afro-American. Debbie did not have any prejudice whatsoever, so that could not be the reason why Brad's invitation last evening had been declined. And the deal which was to be struck with the Styris Group had massive implication for Taylor Software. So, her offhand reaction of 'Oh, that's good news' was so unlike the lady that he had come to know, had grown to respect, and had become part of the family.

Something was wrong, and it was not in Brad's nature to let the matter lie.

Among the things that Mark kept at the office were spare keys and the access codes to his apartment for use in emergencies. Brad was privy to this, and in Brad's view, this was an emergency.

He did not mind if, finally, he was made to look foolish. He just needed to be sure that Debbie was OK.

Brad called Shania and arranged to pick her up, locked his office, picked up a couple of bottles of wine, and was on his way. They would drive around to Mark's apartment on their way to dinner. If Debbie was there, he would try once more to get her to come with them. If Debbie was not there, dinner may have to wait while he found out where she was.

They entered the building and rode up in the elevator. They got out of the car on the fourth floor and walked hand in hand down the corridor to the door to Mark and Debbie's apartment. Brad knocked lightly and politely on the door.

No one answered.

They exchanged looks, and Brad knocked again, louder this time. A face appeared at the door behind them. The face was that of an elderly lady, the voice frail and frightened.

'There is no one in, has not been since last night. The lady went out with a couple of men. She didn't seem to be very happy!' the old lady concluded.

It is amazing how much crime could be resolved if only the police listened to old people who have nothing better to do than peer round their doors.

Brad smiled at the old lady and said thank you, and then added, 'We are relatives from out of town. She gave us a key, so we will just go in and make ourselves at home. Thank you.'

The incongruity of Brad's statement was totally lost on the old lady. And to be fair, it was totally lost on Brad. How two Afro-Americans could be relatives of the white American occupants of the apartment was unbelievable. But she just returned to her apartment and closed the door. That was when Brad pulled out a Beretta handgun. That was when Shania started to look worried.

Brad eased the key into the lock and squeezed the

door open. There was a strong and rather strange, repugnant smell that came from the apartment. Shania nearly jumped out of her skin when a cold hand touched her on the arm.

'I forgot to say—I haven't seen the cat!' The old lady had crept up on them again.

Brad smiled, but the smile did not travel to his eyes.

'Just go inside, and stay there until we give you the all-clear, OK?'

'No need to get huffy. Just forgot to mention it,' said the old lady as she was escorted back to her door by Shania.

Any chance of sneaking into the apartment was now gone, so Brad rushed in, telling Shania to stay by the door.

The first thing he found was the source of the smell. Fridge was still lying on the floor of the kitchen where he had been the day before. There was nothing to indicate what had happened to him. He was just dead, and flies were already starting their grizzly ritual around the body.

Brad twisted his face at the smell but pushed on into the apartment. He went, first, into Mark's bedroom. Then into Debbie's.

There was no one there.

It was so unlike Debbie! Brad felt the chill of fear as he contemplated what may have happened. She must be in trouble. But what?

Shania came into the room. She had a gun too, a Glock 19. Brad was more than a little surprised. Shania demurred and blushed. Then she recovered and kissed him lightly on the cheek.

'I should have told you before, but I guess I never got around to it. I work for the FBI,' she said with a grim look. 'Now, how do you want to handle this?'
Brad initially stared at Shania in disbelief.

He had assumed that she had an office job, because

that was where she went; and out of respect for her privacy, he never thought to enquire what she did when she got there. But then he had to smile. Having someone from the FBI personally involved could make some serious inroads into the bureaucratic nightmare that would normally be involved in reporting a missing person. There was no truth in the generally held view that people had to be missing for twenty-four hours. In fact, the FBI would prefer if people reported a missing person at the earliest opportunity.

Brad was unsure that anyone was missing.

Shania was better equipped to deal with that.

So, she did.

Chapter 38

Hypothermia

The first thing that Mark noticed of any activity in the corridor was when the look-through on the door had opened and abruptly closed again. And then his cell door had opened. The two men who entered were dressed in Afghan Army uniforms. They were carrying AK-47 rifles, and Mark was not about to test whether or not they knew how to use them. They obviously did not speak any English, but they certainly looked threatening. They motioned with their rifles that Mark should head towards the door.

Mark stepped out into the corridor. He was immediately grabbed from behind, and a hessian hood was placed over his head. A sticky tape was slapped around the base of the hood so that it was secure. A piece of rope was used to tie his hands together behind his back. From the noise coming from elsewhere in the corridor, he thought that the same fate was befalling some other residents of this block of cells.

After going around several corners, where Mark was simply manhandled in the direction that he was required to go, the party finally arrived outside the building. Mark knew this because of the bitter wind cutting through his clothing like a knife. It took his breath away. The temperature was well below freezing, and even the clothes that he now wore could not stop the bitter chill lancing through them. He stood for a moment, shivering in the cold while someone fiddled with a bunch of keys. Then he was pushed into a vehicle and onto a seat that had no form of cushioning and that simply intensified the cold. There his feet were none too gently bound with another piece of rope, and both his hands and feet were tethered to shackles so that he could not move.

Mark just sat there and waited. From the noises, cursing, and banging around the vehicle, he counted at least two other people being pushed onto the seats. From the grunting and gag-suppressed profanities coming from one of his fellow passengers, he was gratified to think that at least Dusty was one of them, and that he was still very much alive. And from the whining coming from another guest, he somewhat reluctantly had to accept that Del was there as well.

The team was back together.

And they would presumably share the same fate.

The vehicle started up. Mark could hear two other vehicles do the same thing. Lights briefly flashed over his hood, so at least he knew that it was night-time—but which side of midnight, he had absolutely no idea. The vehicles moved slowly at first, probably travelled little more than fifty yards, and then they stopped again. The driver exchanged comments with someone outside. Mark had no way of knowing what that was all about—they were speaking in Dari. But from the accent and above the noise of the engine, he would have concluded that it was Yuri Alekseyev giving the driver some final instructions. The conversation concluded in laughter, which did not bode well for Mark, and he assumed likewise for his other two colleagues.

Was this how it was to end? Mark had been in some strange places and faced numerous situations in which his life and that of his friends had been in danger. But, never had he felt so out of control. Never had he been faced with the prospect of leaving behind someone that he loved. Debbie would never know that he had simply passed away, many miles from home. And with no one knowing why?

Had he been able to understand Dari, he would have been pleased to at least learn that they were not about to be shot.

However, the rest of the conversation would have revealed the same ultimate result.

The vehicle started to move again, picked up speed, and, with the two other vehicles, the small convoy rushed out through the city streets and on into the barren wasteland that surrounded the city of Kabul. Mark tried to judge the direction they were taking, but having no idea where they were starting from, he very quickly gave up on that.

The vehicles droned on, the tires drumming on the road. Occasional pieces of blacktop gave them a smoother ride, but more commonly, the rough stone-strewn terrain tossed them around as the driver tried to keep the vehicle on track. Several times, Mark was simply unable to remain upright and crashed onto the metal floor, only to be roughly returned to his position by the guards who had the advantages that they could at least see what was happening, and that they were not retrained in the same way. And then the noise coming from the wheels slowly changed to a crunching sound, and the driver had to slow down. They were driving on snow.

The farther the vehicles went, the slower their progress

became. The vehicles appeared to be travelling up a long winding incline. Occasionally, the wheels lost traction where the snowdrifts had become deeper. The driver occasionally exchanged a comment with someone who was with him in the cabin, but none of it made any sense to their passengers. They were speaking in a language that Mark could only guess at. Where was Owen when you needed him? By the tone of the voices, Mark judged that this trip was not exactly going according to plan.

Finally, their vehicle lurched as it suddenly veered to the left and ground to a halt. Further discussions occurred between the driver and his accomplice, and then he heard the doors of the cab open and close. They did not switch off the engine or the lights.

When they opened the rear doors of the truck, Mark could feel the bitter cold as the blast of cold air through the door again took his breath away. It was already cold where they had been sitting on bare metal and with their backs against the metal frame, but that was nothing like the freezing cold that he felt now. He started to shiver despite his efforts to remain stoic while trying to retain some semblance of normality. And it would get worse.

They uncoupled his feet from the shackles but did not undo the rope that tied his feet together. He was roughly lifted by two men, one on either side, and dragged out of the back of the truck. Mark stumbled as his feet hit the ground. The snow would have been a foot deep, which saved him from injury. From the grip of the guards, it was obvious that these men were dressed for this kind of weather while Mark was dressed for indoors and was without gloves and without a windcheater that could have afforded him some protection from the elements.

Once he was clear of the protection of the truck, the wind and the cold hit him again, and now it was so cold that he had extreme difficulty breathing at all as they dragged him into the wind. He could feel the driving snowflakes being hammered into his face. The wind was so strong that the snowflakes stung. He had absolutely no idea where he was, or where they were going. He would be glad to get out of the storm. Any form of shelter would be better than where he was now.

After what must have been several hundred yards, the Afghanis left him standing there—really leaning into the wind.

Mark briefly thought about making a run for it. *Run* being a relative term. His feet were tied together. At best, he could move at a fast shuffle. Mark laughed as he envisaged a penguin hopping through the snow. The laugh earned him a vicious belt in the kidneys from what seemed like a rifle butt. So, what were they waiting for?

And in which direction would he *shuffle?* How many of them were there? Where were they? Were they still carrying the AK-47's that he had seen back at the prison or wherever the hell they had been holding him? Would they use the AK-47's? Maybe that was exactly what they wanted him to do. Get their prisoners to make a run for it, so that they would have something to laugh about. Mark wandering around in circles while they took pot-shots at him before he finally fell in a pool of blood, all alone and dead in a foreign land, miles from anyone or anywhere, and a long way from home and his loved ones!

Mark knew that he would only have one chance. From the grunting, cursing, and whimpering that was coming from behind him, he guessed that the soldiers were getting Dusty and Del out of the truck. If there were only two men against the three of them, there was at least a faint chance. But being blindfolded did present a few problems. Like, what if there were other men around just watching? And there would at least be the drivers of the other vehicles that had accompanied them out of Kabul, waiting for him to do something silly. What if those men were armed? What if they were standing at the top of a cliff, and his next step would be his last? He decided to give it one shot. If he could get Dusty to work with him—forget Del—they could still get out of this mess!

'Is that you, Dusty?' he asked into the wind.

He heard the start of the reply, and it was from Dusty. It was not Dusty who hit him. The blows were obviously with the stock of a rifle and were delivered with such force that had it been the base rather than the side of the rifle stock that hit him, knocking him to the ground, it would have been terminal. He again heard laughter. There were more than two of them. Mark would need to bide his time. Another opportunity would surely present itself, and that was all that he would need.

His arms were grabbed again, one man on either side, and they again started to drag him through the snow. They were moving farther away from the vehicles. He could tell this by the glare from the headlights that were no longer piercing his blindfold. The sound of the running motors faded away into the distance. Again, the grunting, the cursing, and the whimpering told him that Dusty and Del were being dragged along the same way. The noise of the motors gradually receded until they could barely be heard at all. All that he could hear now was the howling of the wind, and the grunts and groans of the men as they struggled forward through the snow. They must soon reach wherever they were headed.

Mark laughed. The two men who were dragging him to some other building, or wherever they were going, were beginning to tire from their exertion. Surely, it would have made much more sense to make their prisoners walk rather than drag them. The soldiers had all the advantages. They were armed. They could see where they were going. And they presumably knew where they were going. The prisoners were unarmed. Their eyes were covered, and their hands and feet securely tied. They had absolutely no idea where they had come from, never mind where they were going. Untying their prisoners' feet would have appeared to be a small price to pay. There was just no accounting for the stupidity of some soldiers!

While these thoughts were going through his mind, the soldiers suddenly just clubbed Mark on the back of his head, and he slumped to the ground, temporarily losing consciousness. He vaguely heard the muffled *thud* of what sounded like two other bodies being dumped into the snow. There were words exchanged in Dari. It seemed to be an argument between two of the men, and then nothing. Whatever the argument had been about, the one with the loudest voice seemed to win. Then Mark heard the crunch of footsteps through the snow slowly receding into the distance.

So, this was to be their fate.
There had been no place that they had been headed to.
They had just been left out in this wilderness.
To die.

In the background, Mark could just faintly hear the motors ticking over, but even that changed after a few minutes. The gears were engaged, one of the vehicles seemed to have a problem with slipping and sliding in the snow; and then gradually, it gained traction, and the noise faded away, swallowed up by the howling wind, the driving snow, and the night.

To be replaced with an absolute, deathly silence.

There was nothing to break the wind, so even that made no sound now that they lay on the ground. The snow was now over a foot deep and thickening by the minute.

It would not be long before they were completely covered.

There would be no sign that anyone had ever been there.

Wherever *there* was.

Mark had had an interesting life. He had been in some strange places, usually on behalf of his government, and usually in a relatively fair contest between good and evil. At the very least, the playing field had been level. In fact, the contest had usually been tilted in his favour by the weapons he carried, by the intelligence he had access to, and by his extensive training. He had been trained to deal with almost every conceivable contingency.

Mark had been trained to think.

So, what could he think and do now?

He commanded himself to go through the four basic procedures that had been repeatedly drilled into him all those years ago in training at Fort Bragg.

First, review what you did know so that you had a clear and concise base from which to start. Well, he knew nothing.

Second, review what manpower and other resources you have. Well, the three of them appeared to be together, but they did not have that many resources.

Third, study the terrain that you are in. Well, he knew that they were somewhere near Kabul, and the ground was covered in snow, and increasingly becoming more so. His eyesight was severely restricted by the hood, and his hands and feet were bound, so his chances of studying anything of his surroundings were about nil.

Fourth, and most important, know your enemy. Well, the enemy had just left; and apart from his initial view that they were Afghan soldiers armed with AK-47 rifles, there was not that much to know. Their real enemy now was the weather and the cold.

Mark struggled to focus his thought process but kept coming back to where he started. Their position was hopeless.

In training back at Fort Bragg and Fort Meade, they had been coached to make use of even the smallest advantage. Mark had been taught how to slip out of handcuffs and all manner of ties, the execution of which would make even Houdini envious. But this training had not factored in two important points. Firstly, the cold. Although it was only a matter of a few minutes ago that he had been dumped, his hands were already numb with the bitter cold, and there was just no feeling that would enable the dexterous manoeuvres that he had been taught. Secondly, the enemy. Whether Russian or Afghan, the American way of advertising, or bragging about, how good their techniques were simply made sure that in the real world, the enemy was well versed in countermeasures.

'Is that you, Dusty?' Mark called out.

The mumbled reply said that it was.

'I am trying to get these ties off my hands,' Dusty replied. 'They seem to get tighter the more I try!'

'Where is Del? Del, are you there?'

Silence.

The snow continued to fall. Fortunately, the wind was blowing above them, which suggested that they were in a hollow or were partially protected by rocks. Only occasionally, the wind eddied and reached down, trying to pluck from them what few clothes they had on. Then even the impact of the wind began to abate as they slowly got covered in more snow. At first, Mark had tried to move his body from side to side, tipping the snow off. Then the snow started to build up into drifts so that there was just nowhere for it to fall. In any case, the snow felt light and protected him from the wind, so he let it begin to cover his body like a protective shield.

'Have you got any idea where we are?' Mark asked.

At first, there was no reply, and a brief panic set in. *Don't tell me I am on my own!* Then he heard Dusty's voice.

'If these morons had any sense, we would be sitting outside the US Embassy. But I doubt that, so I have no idea,' Dusty said as gently as he could. 'I suggest we conserve our energy and wait until this storm abates. Maybe we need to wait until daylight. In this weather, we have no show!'

Why did Dusty always sound so calm and reasonable? Sure, just let the storm die out, as it would eventually. Wait until the sun comes up, as it must eventually. Wait until the tooth fairy comes and makes all my dreams come true. Wait until they were so frozen that the cold would numb them to sleep. A sleep from which they would never wake up.

Mark wound himself into a ball and then, with great difficulty, fed his arms over his feet so that his hands were now in front of him. A classic manoeuvre that he had been taught as a young marine. His hands were still tied together, but at least he could still use his fingers. Mark turned onto his side and brought his hands up to the hood over his face. He scratched at the hessian-like material, trying to rip a hole so that he could see, while removing the snow that had built up where he was breathing. His attempts to see were less than successful.

Maybe Dusty was right: wait until daylight. How long would that be?

Did not someone tell Dusty that the human body is not made to withstand this kind of treatment! Mark was tough. He had patience, and he could wait out most things. His patience had been proven in places like hiding in the waters of the Chesapeake Bay, to hiding in the festering jungles of Colombia, to hiding in the barren heat of the sand dunes (more like sand mountains) in Saudi Arabia, Iraq, and Somalia. In such places, the hiding was really a game where the benefits were measured in time, the costs measured in lives lost. But they were manageable places where Mark had gone of his own volition, and where he had access to resources. And he had access to his own faculties.

They were now in an impossible situation. In the beginning of an Afghanistan winter, they were exposed to the full fury of a snowstorm. The temperature was already well below freezing point and the wind-factor made it feel much worse. They were tied up and blindfolded. They had little in the way of clothing. Overall, their situation could hardly be described as manageable.

Mark was beginning to feel the first tingling in his feet. Yeah, he knew all the symptoms. Shivering was usually the first sign, and after that, things just got worse. As the body tries to retain its basic temperature of about 98 to 100 degrees Fahrenheit, something must give way. The essential bits keep working, so long as they have enough heat and energy to keep them going. The other non-essential bits like hands and arms, feet and legs, ears and nose will just have to do without or take care of themselves.

The body can cope with a small decrease in temperature and can adjust.

After that, things start to go wrong rather rapidly.

It creeps up on you.

And if you don't do something about it, then as surely as the sun must rise in the morning, you will die.

From hypothermia.

Chapter 39

Langley

The telephone rang. But it was not the call that Taylor was hoping for.

It was an internal call from his secretary.

'Yes, Helen, what is it?' Harold asked.

'Deputy Hazeldean is here to see you. Shall I show him in?'

'Sure. And, Helen, could you please bring me a coffee? I might need it!'

Ian Hazeldean was a political appointment to the position of deputy director of the CIA in the office of Corporate Resources. Why Hazeldean would want to speak to Harold was anyone's guess. All that had been said when he made the appointment was that he had something to convey to Harold that would be best done in person. Since he was a deputy director, and he was a political appointment, Harold Taylor had little choice than to agree to the meeting.

It was an unpleasant fact in Washington that such people could be dangerous to career officers. It was also a fact that they were often used to convey bad news where using the more conventional hierarchy command structures may prove embarrassing. Since the office of inspector was independent of the normal CIA organisation, Harold had nothing to fear. So why did he feel so uncomfortable in agreeing to meet with this insipid little man?

Hazeldean entered the room and glanced around as though inspecting a dirty toilet. His first comment was pleasant enough.

'So, this is where you keep all those nasty little secrets?' he commented as Harold ushered him into an armchair and sat down on the opposite side of the table.

'It is not what most people think,' Harold replied. 'Just routine stuff. The CIA runs a pretty polished operation.'

Helen knocked on the door and entered, carrying a tray that had a coffee urn, two cups, and a small plate with biscuits, which she placed on the table between them. She smiled at Harold's acknowledgement, just nodded at Hazeldean, and then took her leave. To a reader of body language, it would be obvious Helen did not like the man either.

When she had closed the door, Hazeldean began without being invited.

'Well, as I said on the phone, I have been asked to deliver a message. I have since received some further information. Apparently, there was an incident overnight in Afghanistan. We have three Americans missing, and we presume they are dead.'

Harold sat bolt upright in his chair. He dreaded what came next. It could explain the silence from the team in Afghanistan over the last few days. It could explain why Karen Marshall of the DEA had gone apoplectic, not having had her usual contact with her agent.

It did not explain why it had been left to a deputy director from an obscure branch of the CIA to deliver the message. Harold did not really understand all the technical jargon that Mark had tried so patiently to explain to him as regards their satellite communications. What bit he did understand was, Mark had used his computer magic to ensure that the phones were tamper-proof and could only be used by the person they were assigned to. If someone else tried to use them without a special security code, then the phones would simply become unusable for both sending and receiving.

Harold had hoped that the satellite phones had simply been lost or stolen. The next comment from Hazeldean suggested that things were not that simple.

'And one of the missing men is apparently your son, Mark Taylor.'

A cold shudder shook Harold he digested this last bit of information. He often wondered how he would take such news, but never, in his wildest dreams, had he imagined how it would feel in real time.

He looked at the impassive face of Hazeldean. There he could see no sign of sympathy, or even of any understanding or empathy. Hazeldean was a politician. He had never been out in the field and faced the ever-present dangers that men endured in the service of their country.

But he had to ask.

'How do *we* know this?'

Hazeldean merely shrugged.

'We have particularly reliable sources, as I am sure that you are aware. But more to the point, what was your son doing in Afghanistan in the first place?'

How to answer that question?

Harold could try the normal approach of *What control do any of us have over what our children get up to?* But he had a suspicion that it would not work. He could deny all knowledge, leaving someone else to figure it out. That would mean the issue would end up on Marshall's plate.

He could not, and he would not, do that.

'Well, I cannot tell you too much about that. As I understand it, he was on a covert mission, and you are not cleared for that. And he knew the risks!'

Hazeldean let his guard down for just a moment.

'You sure you were not playing cowboys and Indians again? You apparently have a reputation for being a bit of a maverick.'

Harold rose from his chair.

'Thank you for delivering the message, Mr Hazeldean. Now I think you can leave.'

'Sit down, Mr Taylor, if you please. I have not finished yet.'

Harold did as he was told. Being an 'independent' officer within the CIA did not mean much when it came down to personal matters. And this was going to get very personal, as well as political.

'You have a close relationship with the DEA, is that not true?'

'Yes, and—'

'To be more specific, with the head of their intelligence division—a Karen Marshall.'

'Yes, and—'

'Come on, Mr Taylor. We can talk as one man to another. How much does your long-suffering wife, Elizabeth, know of your liaison? Let me guess. Nothing.'

Harold remained calm, which surprised even him. He stared into the eyes of the politician. It would be pointless to try to appeal to the man's sense of fair play. Harold inwardly laughed. He had been naïve to think that Stephen Rodriguez was the most senior person involved in this drug scheme. And he had been naïve to take Mark's word that Rodriguez had not recognized him back in Ghazni. Now he knew why Hazeldean had come to his office.

Not to deliver a message.

To deliver a threat.

And in doing so he had revealed something else. Hazeldean must be delivering this threat on behalf of a group of people who would be concerned at whatever Mark and his team might have revealed about their trip to Afghanistan. That meant that he was associated with the ADDI. And that meant he had revealed how high up in the organization this corruption had travelled. Harold could now smile. The Office of the Inspector General now had a crucial piece of information. And maverick or not, Harold Taylor would use that and make Hazeldean pay.

'So, Hazeldean, you've come to deliver a threat. Well, I can tell you that it will not work. Thank you for delivering your message about my son. I will not thank you for the compassion you have shown, because there wasn't any. You can now leave, or do you want to be escorted out by armed guards?'

The deputy director merely shrugged and got to his feet. As he went to leave, he turned to Harold.

'You are a very foolish man.'

Harold held the gaze. 'We will see who is the foolish one,' he said and slammed the door behind the retreating figure.

Helen entered the room after a polite knock, but without waiting for any response, and looking quite flustered for once.

'Is everything OK, Mr Taylor?'

A thousand thoughts rushed through his mind in a kaleidoscope of emotions. *No, Helen, everything is not OK.*

I have probably just lost my only son. I will certainly lose a wife very soon. I probably have lost any chance of nailing Stephen Rodriguez, and probably lost any chance of retaining as a friend the one person that is making my miserable life liveable again.

But he could not say any such things to Helen.

For the time being, he would need to keep his emotions firmly under control. He said the first thing that came to his head.

'Sorry for slamming the door. That guy annoyed me, but I should have exercised more control. But nothing to worry about, Helen. However, it looks as though I will need to go away for a couple of days. Could you please check my diary and rearrange my appointments? Better make it for the next week.'

Helen now began to look quite scared.

'We cannot just rearrange them *all*, Mr Taylor!'

No one had spoken to Harold in that manner since his school days. And she continued in the same tone.

'You have a meeting with the director tomorrow, and the following day a meeting with the President's security advisory committee. You cannot get out of those unless you are ill!'

Harold smiled at that.

'OK, then I will be ill.'

Chapter 40

Rearrangements

If the CIA was excellent at anything, it was in blending into any environment and conducting all sorts of business with impunity. It could carry out almost any normal commercial transaction, whether legal or illegal, under both US rules and regulations and the rules of the host country. In fact, all nations had similar arrangements, and the host countries would, at least most of the time, ignore these goings-on in the interests of diplomacy. Afghanistan was no different. Except that in the Afghanistan case, most commercial transactions were made much easier by the fact that there was a war going on.

The first thing that Rodriguez and Dutton had to find out was, Did the CIA have a shadow company that could undertake charity work? The reporting requirements of charities are a little different from normal companies, in that they need to be able to show where their funds came from and, hopefully, where they went.

A straight charity or trust company was not the answer. Their search finally located a company that would suit the requirement—the articles of incorporation were sufficiently extensive, while sufficiently vague—Kabul Solutions.

Solutions to what was not specified, but the articles appeared to imply that it was a freight-forwarding corporation if it so chose to be.

That done, the next thing to deal with was, what freight it was forwarding, where this freight came from, where it was being forwarded, and how it was to get there.

Rodriguez realized that this was going to be time-consuming, so he had called his director and explained that he would require a few more days to sort out the mess. Not that the real mess had anything to do with official CIA business. But the sad loss of Hennessey in the battle of Ghazni was used as the reason for Rodriguez being delayed.

Jim Schlesinger did not sound really convinced. He was more concerned about the FBI reaction to the loss of one of their agents and any repercussions that may arise.

Well, that was tough. Edward Hennessey had been shot with an AK47 rifle, of which there were millions in Afghanistan. And this was a war zone, and some people just happened to get themselves killed. Rodriguez said that he was doing some follow-up on how Hennessey had been shot and that he was equally concerned about having lost a friend. He was also concerned that the loss would also further delay the job he was supposed to be doing, whatever that was.

In the end, Schlesinger agreed that since Stephen Rodriguez was the agent in theatre, he had best leave it to his minion to do what he thought was best.

Which was fine with Rodriguez. He had already effectively finished all his official work, so this was all the authority he needed to take his time to get *what, where, how, and when* sorted once and for all.

There was an urgent need to restructure the whole

method of transporting opiates from Marjah to Peshawar. Rodriguez was finished with the likes of Wakil Hekmatyar and his bunch of criminals. And he was certainly not going to do business with the Karzai brother.

The *what* part was easy. And that was why they needed an organization that could handle charity work. Shifting opiates from one part of Afghanistan to another was normally routine. Except that it tended to draw the attention of other people in the drug trade—to both the shifter and the people they were shifting to. So, in the future, their 'goods' would be marked as second-hand clothing and materials destined for the many refugee camps in Pakistan. There were several *charities* in Afghanistan that felt they had to contribute to the welfare of their colleagues across the border. Paradoxically, there were an equal number of charities in Pakistan that had the same good intentions, and so there was a regular flow of such goods crossing the border in both directions. This was only normal for any kind of business and would never change.

The involvement of the CIA in charity work was, at least officially, frowned upon. There had been several cases of note in the past, where the CIA, and indeed almost every other intelligence operative, had been involved in charity work as a cover for their none-charitable activities. The problem was the international uproar that was generated when their evil plans became public knowledge, so they tended to avoid such activities. However, this latest scheme was different in that they would be merely providing a distribution network and not actually participating in charitable work. In fact, the involvement of the CIA was so minimal that the matter would not be reported to anyone outside of those directly involved.

The *where from* part was a little more complex. Obviously, the opiates originated in the Helmand province, and using the current model, they would need to end up in Kabul. Therefore, Kabul Solutions would need to establish a presence in the south of the country and establish a collection point for donations. If this were sponsored by an international organization such as the CIA, then so much the better. That would make it legitimate for shipments of donated materials to be shipped via US- or coalition-protected convoys. The risks involved in previous shipments to Kabul would then be eliminated. Well, more or less, eliminated. Except in the case of a random event such as the battle of Ghazni, which no one could predict, and which was an acceptable risk.

The *where to* part was much simpler. The huge cost and reorganization involved in shifting the operation from Peshawar were beyond comprehension. It was the Peshawar operation that handled the refinement of the opiates, but more importantly, it got the product to a part of the organization that made it possible to ship it to the United States without risk. So, the answer to the *where to* question was Peshawar. The trick was in the how.

The US military had all sorts of logistical problems maintaining and supporting the presence of its forces in Afghanistan. To provide that support, it could, and at times did, use the Kabul International Airport. But it was the preferred option of military men to use the Bagram Air Base, about fifteen miles to the north. That was under US Air Force control. At Bagram, there was an almost-constant stream of the huge Globemaster aircraft landing and taking off. They came with a cargo of equipment and men to replace what was broken or injured and went back over the border to Pakistan with a cargo of extraordinarily little. The reason was that there seemed little point in returning damaged equipment for it only to be dumped. Consequently, there was plenty of space for any freight that happened to be available for the return trip. Provided, of course, that it had all the necessary paperwork, and that there was some organization at the destination who could take it off the military's hands.

Rodriguez already had a couple of companies in Peshawar that could receive the goods, companies that the CIA had established years before and had probably long since forgotten about: the Aziar Textile Company and the Aziar Toy Company. The fact that both organizations had excellent relations with the Pakistani police made the arrangements ideal.

There was, of course, the risk that an aircraft could be shot down; but that risk was mitigated by the facts that it rarely happened. And, if it did, there would be far more important things for the US military to worry about than a few packages of smouldering textiles. Add to that, by the time anyone arrived at a crash scene, any opiates that were still usable would have long since vanished. Any that were left on site would simply create a strange smell, which, coupled with the smell of death, would not raise any red flags.

Then the *when* would sort itself out. It would take a few days for Stephen to get the paperwork sorted out and to get a couple of trucks organized, and that would be that. A whole new method of shipping opiates, with none of the risks of their previous method, and no more dealings with the nasty people that they had dealt with in the past.

Now all that remained was to sort out the men down in Kandahar.

Rodriguez left that to Jacob Dutton.

'Good morning, Ahmed. I trust you are well?' Dutton addressed the man, who he had not actually met, in Dari.

Ahmed Wali Karzai had been expecting the call, and he was expecting that his plans had at last borne fruit.

'Ah, Jacob! Yes, I am well. And you are now ready for us to do a deal, no?'

'Good to hear you are well. But no, that is not the purpose of this call. I was calling to tell you that we are withdrawing from all our arrangements. It has just got too complicated, and with our failure to deliver goods over the last month or so, our clients have gone elsewhere.'

Dutton delivered this news in the tired voice of someone who had genuinely given up. In fact, he almost cried. But that was from trying to prevent himself from laughing as he envisioned the reaction at the other end of the telephone.

Ahmed could not believe what he was hearing and stumbled to respond.

'But that is not possible! Now that the criminal Hekmatyar is out of the way, I can guarantee delivery of everything that you need. Surely you can see that!'

Dutton could contain himself no longer.

'Sorry, that is it,' he said and terminated the call.

Chapter 41

Owen Squires

The Humvee was parked well off the road and hidden behind an outcrop of rocks. The time was well after sunset, and with the snow becoming thicker by the minute and rapidly covering the roof of the vehicle, there was not much chance of it being seen by any passing traffic.

In fact, there was no passing traffic. The weather had deterred even the hardiest of men from coming out on this bitter, miserable night. Except, that is, for the three Afghan Army vehicles and the Humvee that had followed them into the hills to the northwest of Kabul.

When the Afghan vehicles had turned around to return in the direction of the city of Kabul after disposing of their human cargo, their drivers and their guards would be nervous. At the same time, they would be relieved. But still, they would be on the lookout for anyone who had seen them on this deadly mission. There was a risk that they may see the vehicle that had followed them into the hills, and if they did, Owen would be in serious trouble. However, the weather conditions were continuing to deteriorate, and that one factor probably saved him.

Still, Owen Squires took no chances.

Owen had a job to do. And, unpleasant though that job maybe, he would do it as he had with every other task he had been given.

If his three American friends died, Owen had to know *how, where,* and *when.* It would also be nice to know *why,* but after all, this was Afghanistan, and rarely did anything have to make any sense.

What he would do next would be crucial. If someone was to take over the attempt to find out what Stephen Rodriguez, the ADDI of the CIA, was up to, Owen had to know what had happened to the original team.

Only then could he work out what he had to do next.

Hard though it may be, Owen would need to find out who Mark had contact with who Mark was working for, who Mark had trusted, and who Owen could trust.

Right now, he knew little, including one critical piece of information - whether the members of the team were alive or dead.

Owen had worked with Americans many times before, but he still did not fully understand their logic. The Americans took enormous pleasure in keeping secrets from their enemies. Paradoxically, they also took the same amount of pleasure in keeping secrets from one another. Their logic was based on the 'need to know.' And, right now, there was a definite need to know. But there was just no one to ask. Owen would need to find his way around that.

Owen Squires had not had the easiest of lives. He had left England at the tender age of eighteen and vowed that he would never return to the country that had given him so little. He was Welsh by birth, but his parents moved from the valleys of South Wales to Manchester in England when he was five years old. He was told by his parents that the reason for that move from the tranquillity of the Welsh hills into the rain, smog, and dirt that was industrial Manchester was to provide a better education for their son. That may well have been one of the reasons. The other reasons were far more significant. He was not told of the reasons, but it was not long before they became evident. The market was much bigger, and therefore they would get more clients, and they could make a lot more money.

Selling drugs.

After his father was incarcerated for his crimes, his mother tried to keep the business and the family together. However, under the combination of drug abuse and alcohol abuse, she also came to the attention of the authorities, and young Owen was subsequently placed in a variety of foster homes. There was no love lost in his relationship with his foster parents, and as soon as he had finished his education at Oldham Grammar School, he left his foster home behind to see the world. And as far away from his parents, foster parents, drugs, and the rain, smog, and grime of the England that he had come to know, and hate, as he could get.

Owen went to America, and like many young men who had had a tough upbringing, he ended up joining the United States Marines.

They say that military training can be character building, and it was. Owen was small, only five foot six and less than 140 pounds. And boys will be boys. One day, early on in their training, the much taller and heavier trainees thought they would have some fun at Boyo's expense. That turned out to be a bad move on their part. The following day, there were several of the young men who reported in sick. In fact, they were in hospital; and from that day onwards, Owen had no problems. At least not with the boys.

When he went to visit the boys in hospital to make sure they were all OK—well, as OK as they could be expected to be in the circumstances—he met one of the nurses. Gwen was also originally from Wales, and that started them talking, and the boys were forgotten.

Then there started a chapter of unfortunate events that no one should have to endure. His girlfriend, already his fiancée and soon to become his wife, went with some nursing friends on a visit to New York City. And when something happened and their skills were needed, they, without a second thought, gave it their all to try to help the victims of a terrorist act. It was just that they picked a dreadful day—September 11, 2001. The nurses were all killed when the Twin Towers collapsed, like many others on that day, bereft of any logical understanding of the reasons behind such a senseless and heinous act, or for the destruction of people's lives, loved ones, and property.

Despite his tragic loss and the mind-numbing sorrow that he felt, Owen was one of the first United States Marines to enter Afghanistan in the aftermath of 9/11 and Operation Enduring Freedom. Two years later, he went for a second tour—this time as a sergeant.

This time he was not so lucky.

He got caught up in an ambush, and although the United States forces managed to extricate themselves, Owen was gravely wounded. He was transferred, first, into Kabul Hospital, and then on the Peshawar Hospital. At Peshawar, there was a surgeon who had all the necessary skills to rebuild his shattered right leg. That surgeon was a small, dark-haired lady, Dr Safia Hassan, who had gained her incredible reputation looking after Afghan Refugees. And getting people who had had their legs blown off by IED's, or roadside bombs, back to walking again.

Whether it was the sensitive dark eyes or the sense of caring that she displayed during his convalescence, Owen became infatuated with the doctor. When he was finally able to get back on his feet again, and since his time with the United States forces was at an end, he went with Dr Hassan and became her assistant in the many Afghanistan refugee camps that had been established in Pakistan. It was a most unlikely combination—a Pakistani Muslim lady and a Welsh agnostic peasant—but they fell in love and became almost inseparable. It was during this time that Owen gained an understanding of the people, their culture, and their languages.

And then tragedy happened all over again.

Why the Taliban—why anyone would be insensitive enough to send a suicide bomber into a hospital, full of their own ethnic people, sick and unable to fend for themselves, is well beyond the comprehension of most sane people. But that is exactly what they did, and on one of the few occasions when Owen and Safia were not together, Dr Safia Hassan was killed.

Owen thought that he may as well end his own life. Such was his grief and abject sorrow. After the funeral, he went to have a few quiet drinks with some of his old friends—more or less to say one final goodbye before ending it all. And one of those friends recognized the signs and talked him into a slightly different course of action.

He would become an undercover agent for the DEA and assist in their never-ending battle in trying to eliminate, or at least control, the flow of drugs out of Afghanistan. This was the one and only area in which Owen and the Taliban would have been able to agree. Everything else that the Taliban stood for was an enigma. They were evil. Owen would bide his time. At some time in the future, he had no doubt that the opportunity would arise when he would get even with the Taliban. In particular, he would avenge the deaths of the two ladies who, in their own special ways, had captured his heart.

Owen's latest job had been to support this team from the United States DEA that had been sent to Afghanistan on some crazy scheme to find a link between the drugs and some of the officials of the CIA. His view was that the plan was a little loopy, but they had sent two very impressive people—Mark Taylor and Dusty Miller—who seemed to know what they were doing. He could not say the same thing for the incompetent De Lawrence, but two out of three was not bad for a team set up by the bureaucrats back in Washington DC.

Owen had done his job, which was to escort them around Afghanistan, try to steer them away from trouble, and assist in their mission as best he could. If Owen had any skill that was of benefit to the people he worked with, it was his ability to get anything that was needed. His knowledge of the locals and their customs, and the respect he was shown by the foreigners made it a simple matter to beg, borrow, or steal almost anything. Then it had all turned pear-shaped. Now his job was to find his people, and that involved quite a different set of abilities.

The three so-called DEA agents had checked in to the Kabul Serena Hotel, and they had not been expected to go anywhere until they had ascertained the movements of the gentleman from the CIA who they had been following. The assistant deputy director of intelligence, for his part, was not expected to move until the following morning, and so Owen had crawled off into one of his many hiding places to check on other matters that his job with the DEA involved him in, and to catch up on some much-needed sleep.

When, as arranged with Mark, he had returned to the

Serena Hotel at six o'clock the following morning, the people that he was supposed to be looking after had quite simply vanished from the face of the earth.

Before embarking on the task of finding out what had happened to his friends, he had to ensure one thing first: staying alive. He could not know where they were or where they had gone, but he had to assume the worst. And he was in grave danger, at least until such time as he had some answers. On the assumption that their disappearance had something to do with their mission, he could only speculate that the only reason why he was still wandering around was that he had not been at the Hotel Serena.

Therefore, it did not take a rocket scientist to work out that someone would now be looking for Owen Squires.

Fortunately, Owen was equipped to deal with that situation. Normally, Owen was dressed as a local. It was not that he had gone feral. It was just that he had come to realise the wisdom of wearing such clothes in a land that at times was ridiculously hot, at times was extremely cold. Add to that the dust, and he could see no sensible reason to wear Western-style clothes. Most of all, he could easily blend in with the locals. But now that would have to change.

He would wear his DEA-supplied uniform. Instead of the long shaggy beard, he would be neatly trimmed. He would dump his vehicle and get another one, more in keeping with *his* new image. The only thing that he could not change was the limp. Again, there was a *fortunate* aspect to this.

He was not the only one that had a limp in Afghanistan.

The first thing that Owen then did was to check out which of the original guests were still, at least officially, residents in the Serena Hotel. That check revealed that none of his three friends had checked out.

Neither had Stephen Rodriguez, nor the person who was accompanying him.

The hotel's internal telephone system, which simply allocated telephones the same number as the room, made checking easy. A simple call to the room that Stephen Rodriguez was occupying, with an apology delivered in Farsi for having disturbed him in error, was enough to confirm that at least the ADDI was still in residence.

So where had the others gone?

Owen tried calling Mark on his satellite phone and got no answer.

He did the same with Dusty, and then with Del, and he got the same thing.

No answer.

There was a number of possible explanations for this. They could have simply gone out for a jog and got lost. Going for a jog was a possibility with Mark and Dusty, even if it would have been ill-advised in downtown Kabul, but it did not seem likely in the case of Del. Even so, they were unlikely to have gone anywhere without their satellite phones. However, the arrangement made the previous evening was that the four of them would meet at six o'clock in the morning in Mark's room, and it was totally out of character for Mark to not be there, or to have a change of plans without letting Owen know.

One possibility that was difficult to discount was that the CIA had finally realized that their ADDI was being followed and had taken the three men in for questioning. But if that was the case, why wasn't Stephen Rodriguez involved? He was, after all, the one who was being followed. He was clearly the senior man present and would hardly be disinterested in the answers that interrogation of the three men might reveal. That would apply even more so if there was any truth in the theory that Rodriguez was a principal player in the drug business because he would not want others to find out the truth.

Another possibility for Owen to consider was that Mark and his team had been snatched by the Taliban, or some other insurgent or criminal group, for any one of many possible reasons. Kidnappings of Westerners was not exactly unknown in this part of the world, and money could be the objective. But in this case, that seemed most unlikely. There was just nothing to be gained. And Mark and Dusty were not exactly your average tourists. Maybe Del had been taken, maybe Mark and Dusty had been taken, but why all three? And it did not seem likely that insurgents would sneak into a fashionable hotel like the Serena and do a surgical extraction, as the CIA would term it, without anyone being aware that they had done so.

In any case, it was one thing to kidnap innocent tourists. It was quite another matter entirely to tangle with professionals.

Most hard-headed criminals would run for miles to avoid tangling with Mark Taylor and Archibald 'Dusty' Miller.

One other possibility was that they had been snatched by the Pakistani ISI. Certainly, it was looking as though whatever deal Mark and his team were investigating, there was some connection with Peshawar, and it was not unknown for the Pakistanis to interfere. But interfering on this side of the border was uncharacteristic and interfering with Americans very unlikely. Even so, the difficulty with that was which side would they interfere on?

Then there was a possibility of the Afghanistan intelligence agency being involved. Recently, the Afghanis were becoming more aggressive in asserting the authority of their fledgling security forces—basically trying to foot it with the big boys. But that aggression would have had to be tempered by other considerations, like *Don't upset the big boys.* Some of the older members of the Afghan service had received training from what was then the KGB, and more lately with the SVR, and still others had recently been trained by the CIA.

It was thought in United States security circles that Afghani forces could, and should, be used by the CIA when direct involvement of CIA personnel in any activity would not be seen to be in the best interests of the United States. Of course, the Afghanis would be advised that the activity was *in the best interest of Afghanistan,* but that would rarely, if ever, be the case.

Of all these, and other, possibilities, all things being considered, it seemed to Owen that there was a combination of these factors at work, but he had to start somewhere. So, he would place his money on the CIA using the Afghanis to do their dirty work, yet again.

He almost had it right.

The people who had been on the night desk at the Serena Hotel had gone off duty, shortly before Owen's arrival. He charmed his way past the objections of the girl at the desk and got a contact name and telephone number for the desk clerk from the previous shift.

When he eventually contacted the night staff, the gentleman was extremely eager to help. There was obviously some intrigue going on, and there did not seem to be any harm in telling the enquirer that three gentlemen of United States origin had indeed been removed from the hotel, in the early hours of the morning, by the security services of the Afghani President, Hamid Karzai.

That news made Owen's blood turn cold. This was related to one of the scenarios that he had envisaged. However, the mention of the President and his thugs complicated matters.

For reasons best known to the President or his advisors, Karzai had opted to appoint a Russian professional spook as the head of his security detail. It was thought in most circles that he probably did so because he did not have enough faith in either the CIA or the Pakistani ISI, or his own Afghani intelligence people. And given the recent, and not so recent, history of those organizations, who could blame him?

The truth of the matter could be that he just wanted to piss off the Americans.

Yuri Alekseyev, the Russian who had been appointed to head the President's security detail, was a fully paid-up member of the SVR, which had carried on in everything but the name where the infamous KGB had left off. In fact, the rumour in intelligence circles was that Alexseyev was also the head of the spook department at the Russian Embassy in Kabul. While the Russians were not quite the force or influence in Afghanistan that they once were, they still wielded quite considerable power and influence. And they were still up to their usual tricks of playing one side against the other.

And could they be trusted?

Probably not—at least not where American interests were concerned.

Still, Owen was not so much concerned with the politics of the situation. The involvement of the Russians was similar, but not the same as one of the scenarios that he had envisaged. He would now place his money on the SVR, the Russian foreign intelligence service, getting the

Afghanis to do their dirty work. But why involve the Americans?

This situation presented Owen with a serious dilemma. He felt that he should alert the CIA and the DEA. But what would he tell them? He was aware that Mark had intimated that they were noticeably short of manpower. Owen was also aware that their mission was supposed to be covert—so much so that their presence was unknown to other CIA and DEA assets in the country. Therefore, their mission should have been unknown to both the Afghanis and the Russians.

He did not contact either the Americans or the Russians, or the Afghanis.

Owen contacted the British Embassy. He knew a couple of people who worked with the British based at their embassy in Kabul. One of them, a gentleman called Mike Robinson, who, like Owen, had been brought up in the working-class area just to the east of the city of Manchester, was about fifty years old and worked as an 'assistant to an attaché.'

Mike had the well-worn look of a street sweeper or a rubbish collector. He was very amicable and certainly more approachable than many who were employed by the Brits. But he may not be the best person to contact. The other, a gentleman named Reginald Smith, had been educated in the British public school system—which meant that it was normally well out of the reach of the general public, and which therefore meant that Reggie came from a background of wealth and privilege. Reggie was listed as a cultural attaché. Owen had good reason to suspect that Reggie was a member of the British foreign intelligence service known as MI6 and would be more likely to be of some use if only he could break through the arrogant façade.

In the end, he settled with contacting Mike.

And in the end, as it transpired, it did not matter. Owen arranged to meet Mike at six o'clock in the evening in the Char Chata Lounge at the Serena Hotel. Whether Mike had a sixth sense, or it was pure coincidence, Reggie was there too. After the usual preliminary introductory and awkward exchanges, they got down to business.

'So, what are the DEA up to these days?' Mike asked while ignoring the signs that said No Smoking.

Owen knew how these games were played, but this was his first time when he was a player. Mike would ask the irrelevant questions. Reggie would sit there with a look of total indifference. Nothing would be volunteered. Owen was in another league, but he had to try!

'Well, just the usual boring stuff. Except that I have been escorting an investigation team around Afghanistan for a couple of days, and then they just vanished!'

That got Mike's attention.

'Vanished? Gone off on one of their *covert* operations that these Yanks seem to love?' Mike asked. But they were just words. Mike or Reggie knew something!

'I do not know.' Owen tried to choose his words carefully. 'I was to meet them in the morning. But they were not where they were supposed to be, and there was no message. Our communication was via sat phone. I tried to make contact but got nothing from any of them. It is quite out of character for Mark.'

Now that was a mistake. And Reggie seized on it. 'Who is Mark?'

'Oh, he is the leader of the team,' Owen answered with a shrug.

Mike and Reggie exchanged glances. There was an almost imperceptible nod of the head from the man who was obviously the boss. Mike asked the next obvious question.

'Have you been in touch with the DEA or the US Embassy?

'No. My understanding of their mission was that they were covert!' Owen answered with another almost-apologetic, shrug. 'I assumed that officially, they don't exist, so I am left with a bit of a dilemma.'

Again, the exchange of glances. Again, the nod of the head.

Mike sat forward in his chair. 'Can we talk off the record?' He got a nod from Owen. An imperceptible nod from Reggie, which said *Go ahead, but be careful.*

'Do you know that there is an assistant director from the CIA staying in this hotel?'

'Well, yes,' was all that Owen could say.

'And what do you know about the gentleman called Mark *from the DEA?*' Mike asked, with the obvious inference that he did not believe that Mark had anything to do with the DEA.

So that was it! Owen inwardly groaned. The Brits had made the connection. How much more did they know? Owen knew then that he was probably wasting his time trying to keep anything from them, so he had to try to learn what he could from them. They obviously knew who Owen was—otherwise, why were they even bothering to talk to him?

'I don't know all that much about Mark's background. But, yes, he was interested in who he referred to as the ADDI at the hotel. You understand, my job was the driver, but I knew enough to know that I could not contact either the DEA or the CIA. What I do not understand is, How the hell did you make the connection?'

Reggie now sat forward in his chair, a laconic smile on his face. 'Owen, it is what we do! If people come into our territory and start poking around, of course we are going to take an interest. Now, we know that your friends have been taken into *custody* by the Russians and Afghanis. We are trying to find out where they have been taken, but you do understand that it is not really our concern. We just like to keep abreast of what our other friends are up to, you understand. We do not know of any involvement by the CIA or your precious DEA. But knowing the way you Americans operate, we would not be surprised if there was. Now, what would you like us to do to help you?

Owen was in a tricky situation, and he knew it. And the Brits knew it as well. But Owen desperately needed help, and there was nowhere else he could turn to now. He was a little annoyed by the way Reggie grouped him in with the Americans, but he wrote that off as the arrogance of the Brits. Or was Reggie just deliberately winding him up?

Owen needed help. So - he asked, 'Ideally, I would like to know where the Russians or Afghanis have taken my friends. I would also like to know the movements of the ADDI and a gentleman called Jacob, who we believe is from the CIA Marjah cell.'

'We will try to find out what we can. We will also advise our American friends that they may have a problem —through a backchannel, of course. Stay in touch.'

And Reggie got up and left without another word. Mike had a look of sympathy on his face. He stood, shook hands with Owen, and repeated the message to stay in touch, and then he hurried out of the hotel.

Strangely, Owen felt very lonely.

But he could not wait for the Brits.

Owen's problem now was, where would they have taken the three men for questioning? And more to the point, what would they be questioning them about?

That is if the Russians or the Afghanis had not already disposed of them.

Owen had to take one thing at a time.

If the Russians were involved, there were two places that they could have taken the three men. They could be at the headquarters of the President's security service, which was hidden in the bowels of the Presidential Palace located in the central city overlooking the Kabul River. Alternatively, they could be in the Russian Embassy to the south of the city. Neither prospect held out much hope for the three men, although on balance, they might be slightly more humanely treated as guests of the Russians. The security detail at the Presidential Palace did not have a reputation for polite interrogation. After an initial chat, they just disposed of people whether or not what they had to say was useful. At least the Russians would talk first. But then, if their guests became an embarrassment, they would probably hand them over to the Afghanis for disposal, if the normal procedures in this complex country were to be followed.

Owen had a feeling of desperation. He had to make a guess where they had taken them, and if he guessed incorrectly, it would probably be too late for any attempt to rescue them.

Even then, it was not looking good.

On reflection, Owen guessed that they were unlikely to have taken the men into the Presidential Palace. Whatever the politics, the President and the Russians risked a serious diplomatic incident if they were caught with three Americans with DEA connections, no matter how tenuous. The Russian connection to the Afghanis was known so, at least initially, they would be unlikely to leave them to interrogation by so crude a body. It was only a guess, but Owen had to assume something. And on balance, it was a good guess.

Throughout the following day, Owen used every

available contact in his extensive network in Kabul to try to find out where the Americans had been taken. That did not result in any progress. Either no one knew, or no one would say.

By halfway through the second day, he was beginning to get desperate, and he was at the point where his only real option was to contact the DEA in Washington and report—what? And to whom? That he had lost their three agents? Agents that, if his understanding of the mission was accurate, they would know very little about. And that *little* was probably about as much as he knew.

The problem with clandestine missions was simple and obvious—the mission and the people involved were covert. Owen was employed merely to assist, so he would have a snowball's chance in hell of penetrating the wall that would be presented by the Washington bureaucracy. He knew how they worked. All would deny everything. Without the key point of contact, that avenue was closed.

He checked again with the Serena Hotel. None of his three friends had been seen again. Nor had they checked out.

He again called the three satellite phones' numbers.

Again, no one answered.

Then he had a stroke of luck.

What he was trying to do was to track the movements of the senior members of the President's security detail. He knew that the President was to address some student rally on the university campus that day. There, Owen got more than he had bargained for.

He was in the crowd on the university campus when shots were fired. The students scattered in all directions, the President was whisked away, and the Russian security detail came out to clean up the mess.

And there was Yuri Alekseyev of the Russian SVR and head of the President's security detail.

Call it a coincidence. While Owen was unconcerned with the politics of either the United States or the Russians, it was a remarkable coincidence that there was a leading executive of the CIA in town when there was an attempt on the life of the country's President. Owen had heard all the stories, and despite his pessimism about the thinking pushed out by the bureaucrats, especially about making assumptions, this was a chance that he should take. He had made one assumption that had so far not been disproved, so why not make another?

Owen decided to track the Russian.

Alexseyev went with a truck loaded with the dead bodies of the people who had been slain on the campus. The truck went to the Russian Embassy. The bodies were unloaded and bundled inside the Embassy through one of the rear doors, and then the vehicle left.

Owen stayed, waiting, and watching.

It must have been some time after 9:00 pm that there was some movement in the Russian compound. The gates to the compound were opened, and three Afghan Army vehicles entered. Although it was difficult for Owen to make out any details, three men—hooded, bound, and gagged—were trundled out of one of the rear doors and half pushed, half carried into the waiting truck. There was nothing definite about the identity of the three except that two of them were quite large. Not the average size for people in this part of the world. And they were certainly not the dead bodies that had arrived at the Embassy earlier in the day. They had to be the two Americans and their partner, Del.

This was too much of a coincidence.

But where were they going so late in the evening? It was hardly the time of day to be transferring them to another prison. But it was a time of the day when few people would venture onto the streets unless they were up to no good. Also, the weather was getting worse, adding another reason why people would not venture out. And fewer people out meant fewer witnesses.

As the truck, and what looked like two escort vehicles, exited the Russian compound, Owen followed at a discreet distance. The small convoy headed east. Rapidly all signs of habitation disappeared behind them. It then turned north and headed up the highway that would lead to Charikaz. Or it could have led them to Bagram. Although it was not the usual route, Owen began to have some hope that maybe they were transferring the prisoners back to the Americans, after all. But then they turned to the east again and into the hills. They were heading into what is one of the most desolate places on the planet.

He knew then that there was no fairy-tale ending to this trip. There was just nothing in the direction that they were now headed.

Owen switched off his lights—there was no point in advertising his presence, although that did make driving into a snow blizzard somewhat tricky. He just focused on the taillights of the vehicles he was following and concentrated hard on adjusting to the various twists and turns in the road from a half-mile back. He veered off the road on several occasions but fought his way back as driving conditions became increasingly hazardous. With the snow falling and settling, there was just nothing to indicate where the side of the road ended, and the loose rocks and dirt began. Fortunately, the leading truck had the worst driving conditions, so speed was not the issue. And in this extreme weather, they would, and, sooner rather than later, must stop because of the sheer impossibility of continuing.

The vehicles wound their way into the hills, which would soon become mountains, where there was just no identifiable destination. The prisoners up ahead may be believed that they were being transferred, but Owen knew from his knowledge of Kabul and the surrounding countryside—there was just nowhere to go.

His heart sinking, Owen made another assumption: it began to look as though they were going to kill the Americans and dispose of their bodies, in a place where no one would ever find them. At this time of the year, the snow cover could last for weeks, maybe months if they went far enough so that all that would be left to find would be skeletons.

Eventually, the convoy pulled off the road, and the three vehicles crunched to a halt. Whether it was where they had intended to be was hard to tell because the blizzard was now so fierce that it was difficult to see more than fifty yards in any direction.

Owen had no choice but to do the same thing, although he was quite some distance away. He parked his vehicle behind an outcrop of rocks, killed the motor, and proceeded to follow on foot. And he also had no choice but to wait and watch. One man against twelve heavily armed troops was an easy decision.

Among the equipment that Owen's Humvee carried around were night-vision gear and binoculars. His first thought was that he should use the night-vision equipment. That had good and bad angles. The good angle was that you could see at night, and with the amount of snow, there was plenty of ambient light to expect to get a fairly unobstructed view of what was going on. The bad angle, apart from the weight, and the fact that when he took the night-vision gear off he would take several minutes to refocus his natural night vision, was that there was so much snow blowing in from the east that he was virtually looking into a fog. He abandoned the night-vision gear and relied on his eyesight.

He watched the soldiers as they unloaded three men from the truck and trundled, whoever they were, quite some distance towards some rocks. He still did not know whether he was on a wild-goose chase, but he had to be sure—one way or the other. No shots were fired, but that did not tell him that much either.

He could understand that. Bullets were expensive, so why waste them? And the Americans were very adept at tracing bullets, so why take that risk? Most Afghanis were more adept at using knives rather than guns. And knives were much harder to trace than bullets or the rifles that fired them. They also made less noise than guns, although in this case, the noise did not really matter.

Whatever the soldiers were doing, they clearly had no intention of returning to Kabul with their prisoners. The only positive thought was that they could just leave them all tied up. In this weather, with the temperature well below freezing, anyone left in the open would last barely one hour. The snow was now coming in sheets, and while that meant that anything left on the ground would be covered by a cocoon of snow, all trace of the visitors and their vehicles would soon be gone.

It also meant that there would be little point in digging holes. Which was a good thing. In this rock-strewn environment, digging was not an option. Leaving any men above ground would have an equally adverse effect. They would die.

The combination of the snow and the cold would have a strange effect on the men. The body begins to shut down so that it can preserve as much energy and warmth as possible for essential services such as breathing. They would rapidly just get numbed into a deep sleep from which they would never wake up.

Owen could vaguely make out eight soldiers and three prisoners trudging through the snow—two for each prisoner and the other two walking point. Owen dared not follow for fear of being spotted by the soldiers who had stayed with the vehicles. However, he knew the direction that they were taking. He would rely on his instincts and memory. And the fact that in these conditions, the soldiers could not possibly go very far.

For once in his life, he just prayed that he would be able to find the bodies.

Finally, the soldiers came back to their vehicles laughing among themselves, probably glad to be rid of their prisoners. The drivers turned their vehicles around with some difficulty and headed back down the track the way they had come and back towards Kabul.

Owen was confident that they would not have seen him or his vehicle. They would be lucky enough to be able to see the road ahead of them. Such was the intensity of the storm. But just to be certain, he waited until their taillights had long disappeared into the distance. All sound was muffled, but he could hear the engines labouring as they struggled through the snow even though they were now traveling downhill. Until, very quickly, an eerie silence descended over the mountains.

He was alone.

Owen then had a choice. He could go back and retrieve his Humvee while he could find his way through the wind and the snow. Or he could go forward and find whatever the Afghanis had left behind them. While he sheltered behind the rocks, getting colder by the minute, he reluctantly admitted that he had only one simple choice. He had to retrieve his vehicle. Otherwise, whatever else happened, the prisoners would have no show, and they, and he, were all dead.

It was a difficult choice, but there was only one decision

that he could make. He would be dependent on his being able to judge where he was in relation to where the Afghanis had been. The lives of three men, assuming they were still alive, could be dependent on that judgement; and with the snowstorm gaining in intensity by the minute, he reluctantly accepted that the odds were not looking too flash.

Owen got back to his Hummer, and, although an atheist, he again prayed that the motor would kick in, as it strove to start in the chilly night air. Reluctantly, it did start on the third attempt. He drove his vehicle back onto and then along the track to where he could just make out what he assumed to be the ruts left by the Afghan Army vehicles and pulled to a halt.

He did not have the luxury of having someone remain with the vehicle. Leaving the lights on would be a complete waste of time because all that they would do was to reflect off the snow, at the same time as discharging the battery. He briefly thought of leaving the motor running to avoid the risk of it failing to fire but discounted that. If someone stole the vehicle while he searched for his friends, then he was as good as dead. The chances of someone finding the vehicle out in the middle of nowhere in this storm and at this time of night were remote, but it was still not a risk that Owen was prepared to take.

He put on a couple of spare coats and put three extra pairs of gloves in his pocket. They were all the spare clothes that he had. If he found the men, and they, or some of them, were still alive, they would need everything that he could give them. He got a ball of twine from the back of the Hummer, tied the end securely to the tow bar, and set off, following the tracks left by the Afghan soldiers, reeling out the twine behind him.

There was no reason that he could think of why the soldiers would not walk in a straight line to where they were going, so he followed the footprints at right angles to the way the trucks had parked. That worked well for about the first fifty yards or so, and then the tracks became more difficult to follow. And then they simply disappeared, buried under the deluge of freshly fallen snow.

Owen pressed on, trying to maintain his line, looking left and right. The wind from the northeast seemed to get stronger. There was no let-up in the density of the snowfall.

He eventually came to a gap between two huge rocks, and there Owen paused. Had he come too far? He stepped through the gap and did a brief semicircle around. There was just nothing. Stepping back between the rocks, he first went to his left, searching for any sign of activity. Then he retraced his steps and went right. There was still nothing. No sign, no sound. Even the rocky outcrop was slowly being buried in snow, and the whole area took on a surreal sense of peace.

There was no sign of anything.

Mark had felt terribly cold and could already feel his fingers and toes beginning to freeze. In frustration, he had tried to stumble to his feet, but all he could do was get up into a sitting position. And then the sheer force of the storm almost took his breath away. He called out to Dusty. There was no reply. He raised his voice and tried again.

This time he heard a mumbled reply.

'Where are you?'

That was Dusty! The voice seemed to come from far away, although Mark knew that it must be much closer.

'Sit up and say that again. In this weather, I cannot judge which direction your voice is coming from.'

'Which particular part of *where are you* did you not

understand?'

At least Dusty still had his sense of humour, although, in their present circumstances, it may have been misplaced.

Mark did not know how he was going to do it.

'OK, keep talking, and I will come to you.'

He had to laugh. Blind and with hands and feet hog-tied, he must have been a comical sight as he struggled to manoeuvre his body in the direction that he thought he should go. Fortunately, he crashed into the immovable object that was the bulky form of his friend.

'I thought we were going to wait for the storm to die down, or daylight, or for the tooth-fairy to turn up,' was the comment from Dusty, who tried to grin. But that was a waste of time since neither of them could see.

'Come on, Dusty, we wouldn't survive long in this. We need to get under cover, or we are all dead.'

'Where is Del?'

'I don't care where Del is. Come on! Back on the ground and try to get this tape off my head, and then I will do yours.'

The two friends struggled to claw at the tapes. Their hands were numb with the cold. Being unable to see made it even more difficult.

'Dusty, just rip it off!'

And he did. Probably removing a few chunks of hair and causing untold damage to the skin. Mark did not even flinch. He was now able to see! Mark removed the tape and the hessian cover from Dusty, and they were both then able to look at the ropes that bound their hands and feet. Again, they were lucky. The ropes were just about frozen solid. By carefully manipulating the bindings they slowly worked them loose. Although it seemed to take forever, they were now free of the shackles.

Together, they then searched for Del and finally stumbled over the body, which was no more than a small undulation in the snow. Mark ripped off the tape and tried to get some response from the body, while Dusty removed the ropes.

Mark gave up on trying to get a response from Del.

'He is alive—at least he still has a heartbeat. But he is unresponsive. We have to find somewhere to shelter,' said Mark as he looked around in desperation.

Before them, everything just looked like a white wall of snow. But in the eddies of the wind, they occasionally got a glimpse of a darker shade of grey off to the right. They grabbed the inert form of Del and half carried, half dragged, his body towards that patch. It turned out they were correct in their assumption. However, the grey form had been a mere crack in the rock face. They struggled on and were rewarded when the next grey shadow turned out to be more of a crevice. The hole in the rocks had barely enough room for all three of them, particularly since Del could only be laid down. Still, they crowded in the hole. At least they were sheltered from the wind. Now the temperature was merely five or six degrees below freezing, as opposed to being out in the open where the wind chill factor would have deducted another ten degrees from that temperature.

Owen glanced at his watch and pressed the button that lit the digital display. The display said that the time was 22:35. He had been searching for the best part of forty minutes, and it was now well over an hour since the Afghans had left the scene.

Where would he go next?

In the dense snow, he had lost all sense of time and space. Everything looked the same, except that the ragged shape of the rocks was slowly being replaced by the smooth, soft outline of snowdrifts. Within less than half an hour, there would be little point in continuing; and he would have to accept that the friends, who he had known so briefly, would be gone.

Sure, he could wait until the storm abated, or until the sun rose, whichever came first. Then he would have a better chance at locating them. But that would surely be too late. Owen was cold, and he was wearing three coats. From what he had seen, the prisoners had been wearing next to nothing when they had alighted from the convoy. And he could see no reason why the Afghan soldiers would have done anything about that.

Hypothermia does not differentiate between the good guys and the bad guys, the strong and the weak, the lucky and the unlucky. The fitter you are, the marginally greater your chances are of surviving, and that would certainly apply to Mark and Dusty. But there was a limit. And that limit was rapidly approaching. There was a fifty-fifty chance that Mark, Dusty, and Del had been alive when they were dumped in this wretched and isolated place; otherwise, why had the Afghanis not killed them when they first arrived? There was still a fifty-fifty chance that the Afghanis had slit their throats—that was just a part of the Afghani psyche. Whatever else had happened, there was a zero chance that they could have survived the cold for very much longer.

Owen tripped over the twine as he turned to retrace his steps, falling, and rolling into the snow. He hung on to the reel and pulled it. There was no tension. He pulled it again, and the end of his link hung loosely in his hand. How much bad luck did he have to take? Rising to his knees, he scrambled around, trying to find the twine that would lead him back to the road. Nothing. His journey through the gap in the rocks and his circling back and forth had relieved any tension that there had been on the twine, and it was now buried, probably until the next spring, under an ever-thickening blanket of snow.

He now had to think of other possibilities. The inevitable and ultimate plan was that Owen would carry on the investigation of Stephen Rodriguez in the place of the three men, once he had confirmed that they were all dead. But right now, he would be lucky if he got out of this with his own life.

The only guide Owen could rely on was the wind direction. He calculated that if he walked with the wind coming over his left shoulder since he had previously walked into it coming from his front right, he would eventually make it to the road. In this part of the country, the road, such as it was, twisted and turned up and down gullies, but his logic was OK. Provided, that is, the wind direction had not changed.

He set off, hoping that the buffeting he was getting from behind would not push him off track, and he compensated for that by moving slightly to his left so that when he got to the road, turning right would get him eventually back to where he had left his vehicle.

The snow was getting deeper, and Owen struggled to keep moving forward. His legs struggled to get released by the clinging snow so that his steps became shorter, and his breath became more laboured. He felt the energy begin to sap from his body as the initial adrenaline rush gave way to despair—partly due to exhaustion of his body, partly psychological.

He had failed.

The euphoria of having correctly guessed what had happened to his friends was replaced with the dejection of a lost cause. All that he could now hope for was that he would make it back alive. And now even that dream began to fade as his small frame on one good leg started to struggle against the elements.

Owen stumbled over something, cursing as he did so.

At least the snow was driving into the side of his head, which meant he was heading in the right direction. As he looked around to see what he had stumbled over, he got the full blast of the snow in his eyes. Then as he fought to clear his eyes, he stumbled again over something else, and this time he fell and landed in the soft snow.

He lay where he had fallen, and a sense of euphoria enveloped him. He was not going to make it, so why not stay where he was. Not so long ago, he had been going to take his own life. And now he was at peace, so why not stay? But then he was frightened back to reality.

He had found where one of the prisoners had been! He frantically scrambled around, checking to see what he had tripped over. And tears welled up in his eyes when he realized that he had found signs where there had at least been someone! He looked around. There were depressions in the snow, and scattered around were pieces of rope, hessian, and tape, which was evidence of human activity.

But where had they gone?

Owen almost screamed. 'Where are you?' he asked the storm. No reply.

Then he had an idea. He had a torch, which he switched on and shone around in circles. Over to his left were what looked like drag marks towards a rock wall. He crept towards it, always conscious of the direction he was taking relative to where he had originally been heading. Traveling along the rock face, he could see that there was no place anyone could have gone. But he moved a few more yards and then called out again.

He turned around to check on his location, and then turned dejectedly for one last look at the rocks before reversing to head back in the other direction.

And then the face of Dusty Miller emerged from the snow. Owen jumped from fright as the mouth barely moved and uttered words. They were not complimentary, but Owen felt more tears in his eyes from the absolute relief when Dusty spoke.

'What took you so fucking long?'

Owen was shocked at the state Dusty was in. His normal ebony skin condition had been replaced with an almost grey complexion. He was clearly suffering from frostbite, which was beginning to take its toll. Nevertheless, the mood of the pair had been raised at their meeting in this strange location. Although shivering uncontrollably, Dusty would not accept one of the spare coats that Owen offered. Instead, he grabbed Owen by the arm and propelled him towards the rocks and the place where the three men had been hiding. Once there, Owen found Mark desperately trying to keep Del as sheltered and as warm as possible using his own body. The look on Mark's face said that it was a forlorn effort since he was also cold and dressed in only flimsy attire. But he had tried.

Mark acknowledged Owen with a grim smile.

'Thank God, you found us. We would not have been able to survive much longer. Now, what can you do to get us out of here?

Owen could hardly hear a word above the howling wind, but he got the gist of what Mark had asked. He gave the spare gloves to the three men, although they were far too small for Dusty's big hands. He had only two spare jackets, and both were used to try to wrap around the inert body of Del. He appeared to be in a coma, barely breathing, and what breath there was came in ragged gasps, followed by a brief whimper. There were the tell-tale blotches of blood splattered over the skimpy clothes that Del had on, so he must have been in a hell of a state even before he had been dumped in this wilderness.

The euphoria of having been reunited with the team suddenly dissipated as Owen realized the more onerous task that he now faced: to somehow get the men back to Kabul, which he could only now regard as an alien environment, and into care.

Leaving Del for a moment, Mark, Dusty, and Owen huddled together to discuss the predicament. Whatever decisions were made now would decide their fate and the fate of their mission

Owen started their discussion by finally answering the question that Mark had asked him.

'I have a vehicle which is somewhere over there,' he said, waving his hand in the general direction that he thought was where the track was.

Mark nodded. 'Good lad. Do you think you can find it in this weather?'

The answer to that question was not so easy.

'Provided the wind has not changed direction, the answer to that question is, hopefully!' Owen replied, accompanied by a shrug of the shoulders.

Mark was the one in control. 'OK, we have to stick together. Dusty and I will carry Del. You lead the way.'

Owen started to protest. 'You guys haven't got the strength for that. You're almost in the same condition as Del!'

Mark brushed Owen aside. Mark was a big lad—six feet four and probably weighed in at an excess of 240 pounds. And Dusty was the same height as Mark and would have been at least forty pounds heavier.

'It cannot be that far!' Mark replied. 'And the longer we stand around here arguing about it could make your observation a reality. Come on, Dusty. Grab the top end and let's go. Owen, we owe you, but you going to have to wait. Get us out of here.'

They got Del out from between the rocks, and then Mark and Dusty took it in turns to carry Del using the fireman's carry. It was doubtful whether Del weighed much over 150 pounds, but they still struggled to cope with the deepening snow and the uneven surface that lay beneath. Owen could only watch as the two men doggedly, and without complaining, stumbled after him towards where he hoped they would reach the relative comfort of his Humvee.

They arrived at an area that, by its relatively smooth layout, was the track. There was no sign of Owen's vehicle.

Mark lowered Del into the snow and then collapsed alongside him. There had been no physical sign of life from Del, but Mark assured Dusty and Owen that he was still alive.

Dusty asked the obvious question.

'Well, what the fuck happens now?'

Owen could only apologize, but he tried to keep their spirits up. 'We must have come too far north, but I will sort that out. You three stay here, and I will go and find the Humvee'.

Dusty asked the obvious question, this time with more than a hint of sarcasm in his voice. 'How do you know we are *north* of where you left your Humvee? And I thought we had agreed that we should stay together?'

Mark could sense that things were getting rather tense, With Dusty being able to speak two whole sentences, neither of which contained his favourite word, meant that he was worried. He smiled at Dusty and nodded his head, trying to convey a message as they had done on many a covert mission in days gone by.

'OK, Owen. Do what you have to do. We are in no

condition to come with you. We will wait here. Don't be long.'

Initially, Owen was reluctant to go, and Dusty was split between staying and going with Owen to search for the Humvee. In the end, Mark nodded to Owen and sent him on his way, very soon disappearing in the snow. Dusty decided to stay with his friend and take his chance.

There was little chance that anyone would venture this far away from the city anytime soon, so Owen knew that their survival rested on his shoulders. Owen himself was also exhausted, and the only thing that kept him going now was the second burst of adrenaline. In the fuddled world of exhaustion and cold, Owen felt that his vehicle surely could not be far away.

Finding his three friends, and then making it to the road, had lifted his spirits. But it had done nothing for his physical condition. Owen was asking too much from his body. This was the first time since his injury, and the weeks spent in the hospital, that he had placed so much pressure on his body. Only now did he realize the toll that had been taken. Despite his handicap, Owen was supremely fit, but the last few hours had drained even his stamina, and he began to hallucinate as he limped and staggered rather than jogged along the road.

The stump that remained of his right leg was like a dead weight, and it became an even greater handicap as he dragged it along; every step seemed shorter than the last one. It was only a matter of time before he would have to give up the struggle and succumb to the bitter cold.

Such was his state of mind that he almost missed the Hummer as he trudged along. The truck was rapidly becoming buried under the snow, and the drifts had built up on the vehicle's left-hand side. He entered through the right-hand side, and tears again came into his eyes as the motor started after the fourth attempt. Getting back onto the road was not so easy as he struggled to ease the vehicle over and through drifts of snow. He eventually managed that and cautiously moved along what he thought was the road. He did not know how far he had to go. He just hoped that Mark or Dusty would see the lights and flag him down. But there was no Mark and no Dusty.

That was when he panicked.

Had he gone past where he had left the trio or had he still to go farther up the road? He wound down the window, despite the wind and the snow, and yelled at the top of his voice. He knew the effort was in vain, but he had to try something. His voice seemed to rebound off the snow. He was yelling, but no one would hear! Unless they were downwind, his voice would be lost in the wilderness.

The Hummer crept farther forward, the driver still unsure of whether to go forward or back. Tears of frustration welled in Owen's eyes as he peered through the windscreen. He was just about to make a fatal decision to go back when he saw on his left a vague outline of a snowman. At the end of one arm was a blue hand with the thumb stuck up in the air. He stopped the vehicle and rushed over to give Dusty a big hug: so pleased was he to find him again.

Dusty just shrugged but had a huge grin on his frozen face.

'What took you so fucking long?' he asked for the second time in the last few hours.

Chapter 42

Recovery

The three men should really have gone straight to the hospital. Del was in an even worse condition than he had been when Owen had first uncovered him out in the snow if that were possible. And Mark was not much better. Mark looked as though he was, in fact, just sleeping; but Owen knew that looks could be deceptive. Dusty was the better of the three—*better* being a relative term.

They did not go to the hospital.

Instead, they went to a sparsely furnished apartment that Owen had in the Char Qala district in the eastern side of Kabul. Char Qala was a densely populated slum district, where even heavily armed Afghan security forces would not dare to set foot, especially at night. But it was the place where Owen would feel the safest.

Once he got them through the door, Owen turned an oil heater on in the living room and made the three men, whom he had just rescued from certain death, as comfortable as possible. Dusty went into the tiny kitchen, boiled some water in a decrepit pan on an equally decrepit stove, and made some soup. Owen got on his satellite telephone and called a friend, who was a Doctor of Medicine.

He could not have been far away, because he arrived within fifteen minutes. He was introduced to Dusty as Dr Ghulam Qadir. The doctor just rushed past Dusty after a brief nod of the head, glanced at Mark, and then went immediately to Del.

The examination by the doctor took barely ten seconds. He turned to Owen and almost screamed in passable English.

'He needs to get to a hospital—now, or he will not live.'

Even though he was comatose, Del was shivering, his blood pressure had fallen to an unrealistic level, he was also having cardiac problems, and that was in addition to his wounds, suffered while he was held prisoner. There was no doubt that he was suffering from severe hypothermia, and probably pneumonia, and the normal re-warming of the body was simply not going to work.

The reason Owen had decided that they should not go to the hospital was quite a simple one. The hospitals in this part of the world were monitored, around the clock, by the Afghan police. And the reasons for that were also simple. One reason was that all the other official, and many more unofficial, organisations would also be watching the hospitals—after all, that was where the results of any trouble would end up. People with stab wounds or bullet holes tend to want to get them fixed, and they placed a higher priority, at least in the short term, on the fix rather than on what had been the cause. From the police perspective, they had the opposite view. And it was much easier to talk to people when there was some official-looking person wielding a knife, albeit threatening to save lives. Turning up at the hospital, with three half-frozen bodies was not in the same league, except for one thing. The bodies were those of people who were foreigners, now supposed to be dead; and the people who thought that they had arranged that were no less than the President's men. It would not take much more than a second or two for word to get out that the three Americans were still alive.

And a few more seconds for someone to react to that situation.

If the doctor insisted that one of them should go to the hospital, then that one would need to go as someone else. And the hospital would need to be under the control of the US military forces. Owen patiently explained to the doctor what had to happen now.

Owen would arrange things to keep the doctor happy and, hopefully, keep his friends alive. Making such arrangements for three would be difficult, but one was not a problem. Owen had all the required documents for his own use in his various clandestine operations with the DEA, and apart from the fact that Del was a bit taller than Owen, they were about the same age and shape. When lying down, everyone was the same height, so it would take a very sharp observer to spot the discrepancy of one inch. At least until such time as Del stood up. Thankfully, he would not be standing up in the near future. Equally thankfully, Dr Qadir offered to take Del, and after some very terse instructions on the care of the other two, they carried Del to the station wagon and sent him on his way.

Dr Qadir was taking *Henry Simons,* a freelance journalist, to the hospital. First, the doctor would take him to an emergency clinic that he had access to, to collect a thermal blanket, and then he would head north to the Bagram Air Base. There was just no point in taking Del to the Kabul Hospital for several reasons, among them, that, firstly, it would not be open at this time of the night, and secondly, there was a risk that it would not take the security people long to work out that there was something not quite right.

The next call that Owen made was to a number that he had not had to use before. It was his get-out-of-jail number that he had been given when he first signed up to his job at the DEA. The voice on the end of the line prompted him to leave a short message and a code. He left the name of Henry Simons, the name of the Bagram base military hospital, and the code UY674. Anyone who intercepted that code, if indeed anyone realized that it was a code, would go insane trying to work out what it meant. But it was quite simple. The first two letters were the code for Owen Squires, the next two numbers said how to get from 'UY' to 'OS' and the only one number in the sequence that meant anything of note was the 4. That meant 'extraction under duress,' and that would be enough to get both the medics and the military into action. Explanations would come later.

Dusty slept alongside Mark through the rest of the night and through the following day. Occasionally, Owen would slip a spoonful of soup through Mark's and Dusty's lips. A couple of times, Mark coughed; and at one time, he suddenly began to shake, but, according to Owen, which was to be expected. By the time daylight started to filter through the blinds well over thirty-six hours since they had arrived, Mark began to stir and opened his eyes.

The first thing that Mark noticed was the dog. It was large and black, of an unknown breed. It sat at his side, and as he stirred, the dog got excited, licked his face, and then appeared to look around for someone to share his news with.

All that Mark could see was Dusty sound asleep in a chair at his side, and Owen curled up on the floor and also sound asleep. The room was hot. He thrashed around, trying to get out of all the blankets that they had wrapped around him and tried to get some air. Mark stared at Dusty, then at Owen, and then asked of no one in particular, 'Where is Del?'

When he got no reply, he asked again.

'*Where* is Del?' Mark shouted.

That got a response. Dusty awakened with a start while Owen simply rolled over and grinned.

'So, the master awakes?'

'Where are we?' was the next question that came from Mark.

'We are in an old DEA dwelling—a safe house is what you Washington types call it.'

Mark was not so sure.

'And who is our new friend?' he asked, indicating the dog that looked as though he was more interested in resting his head on Mark's leg and licking his hand.

'Oh, Mo!' Owen replied with a grin. 'He belongs to the lady running the safe house. You will meet her later. She has gone to the market to get some supplies.'

Owen spent the next half hour explaining to the two ex-Special Forces men what had happened during the last couple of days. He had already explained this to Dusty, but Dusty listened again, adding nothing but a grim look on his face. Mark had little recollection of the events out in the snow, having acted for the most part on autopilot. Owen missed out on all the drama that had happened while he had traipsed through the snow in his seemingly forlorn attempt to find them and simply said that he had followed the Afghan convoy and retrieved them.

Mark and Dusty knew, however, that they had been extremely lucky to have survived; and it was all down to this one man. Judging by Owen's description of Del's condition, they must all have been extremely vulnerable, to say the least. But every story had its upside. It was doubtful that Del would take any further part in this mission.

They were still concerned about his safety and would continue to be until he was safely back in the hands of the DEA in the United States, but frankly, they were extremely glad that he was out of the way. The reason? He could no longer be trusted to keep their mission covert.

So, what of their mission?

Basically, it was shot to pieces.

The lady who entered the room a couple of hours later wore what looked like traditional Afghani clothes covered by a burka, which she dispensed with as she was introduced to Mark. Owen had a proud look on his face as he announced that her name was Halah, and then swept the little girl, who had also entered the room, off her feet and introduced her as Hayah. She must have been no more than four years old. There were a few noticeable things. Hayah was obviously the daughter of Halah—they were so alike. And they were both beautiful. And they both spoke faultless English. At least Mo was pleased to see them both, although the dog had decided that he would stay with Mark.

That was where most of the food seemed to be directed.

Halah immediately took Hayah off to the toilet, which gave Mark the opportunity to clarify this turn of events.

'Are you sure this is a clever idea, Owen?' he asked.

Owen looked a little confused, or embarrassed—it was hard for Mark to tell. The tone of his reply indicated that Owen was annoyed by the question.

'They come with the house! Have you got a problem with that?'

Mark held up his hands in defence. 'I am sorry. I did not mean to upset you, and I have no prejudice, if that is what you are thinking,' he began. How to explain to a man who had just saved his life, and he probably owed as much to the lady, whose life had no doubt been turned upside down by their sudden arrival on her doorstep.

'Owen, we are placing them in grave danger. I don't know as much as you do about this country, OK. But there is a war going on here, and like it or not, we are in the middle of it. Anyone wanting to do us harm simply has to grab Halah, and what do we do then? Or they just talk to Hayah—again, I don't know this country, but the CIA has a view that children should be kept out of situations like this. All they would need do is offer a block of chocolate for information. I have nothing against the kid, and I am sure she would not willingly talk to strangers, but she is a four-year-old child!'

'Thanks for your concern.'

The voice was calm and female.

Mark turned around to see the ladies had returned into the room.

'I do understand what you are saying.' Halah came to Mark and rested her hand on his arm.

'This is the life we have chosen. Our task is to get you and Dusty fit and on your way. If we get caught, that is the price we must pay. Anyway, there is always Mo to protect us!' she added as the dog came up to her for a pat.

Mark sighed and smiled.

'Call me old-fashioned, and I am no expert on modern women. But you must please understand where I am coming from. Dusty and I will not countenance your suffering because of our presence in your house.'

Mark had been slow to come out of the trancelike stupor that he had been in following his experience as a guest of the Russians, but then rapidly recovered as different parts of his body got the message that he was OK. The human body is a strange thing. When faced with overwhelming stress or cold, it simply shuts down non-essential services. Recovery can be quick for someone who is fit and strong. Not so for someone who is only one step short of being anaemic.

Within less than two days, Mark and Dusty had recovered sufficiently to begin to contemplate what they were to do next.

Halah raided the meagre stock of food that was in the pantry and made them a meal that mainly consisted of steamed rice with beans and raisins.

Then it was time to discuss where to go now.

The situation was that they had been out of contact with Stephen Rodriguez for several days, and their priority was to either re-establish contact or, at the worst, at least find out where he was. They had also been out of contact with Harold Taylor, and they presumed out of contact with Karen Marshall at the DEA. Mark's guess was that by now their mentors, sitting in their cosy offices in Washington, would be in a state of panic.

The other problem was that all the equipment that the DEA had provided for them was back at the Serena Hotel. That raised a question: Could they turn up at the hotel, tell a story that involved three people all losing their keys at the same time, and not having been seen for several days, and simply walk away with all their gear? That prospect seemed extremely unlikely. Owen patiently explained to Mark his reasoning for his change in appearance, and why it was unlikely that they could retrieve anything. At first, Mark was slow to comprehend, and then realised the sense of Owen's logic. And how lucky they had been so far, and how much they owed to this Welshman.

On the positive side, the storm of two nights ago was

still raging, and therefore no one would yet know of their survival. On the negative side, if Yuri Alekseyev was even half-competent at his job, someone would be watching to see who turned up to collect the gear from the Serena Hotel and follow them. Not because the Russians would expect the original owners to appear, but because there could be more intrigue involved in an already-baffling story. After all, Yuri was a Russian, the owners of the gear were Americans, and the Americans that had been involved thus far were apparently on two different sides. The Russians were, by nature, paranoid. And this was Afghanistan. The Russians would continue to watch and wait. Any little snippet of information that they could gather, they would.

Mark probably summed that situation up correctly: Stephen Rodriguez would use his position and influence to take ownership of what had been left behind at the hotel and try to gather what information he could from that source. The most obvious thing that he would discover was that Mark's team had been outfitted by the either the CIA, DEA, or FBI—such was the sophistication, albeit routine, of the stuff that they had in their possession. While that would not have pleased Rodriguez at all, he would assume that he could track what had been going on through analysis of the satellite phones. That would take time, and Mark hoped that his software security system would prevent that source, or at least render whatever information they gathered useless.

There would be no going back to the hotel by anyone in Mark's team to check. No one would until such time as the three of them were in another country, and then it would only be as an innocuous request from the United States Embassy to retrieve any gear left behind by the already-departed Americans. A brief call to the hotel asking them to close their account and store their personal belongings ready for collection was the best that they could be expected to do.

The one piece of equipment that Owen did possess was a satellite phone. The problem that Mark now faced was finding a number to dial.

The number for Harold Taylor had been on speed dial, and Mark could only vaguely recall some of the digits, which effectively meant he knew nothing. So, he called Debbie at home on their apartment landline. He knew that Debbie would be there—after all, it was almost 11:00 pm in New York City. She would, in fact, be sound asleep, but Mark was certain she would be pleased to hear from him despite the late hour. He would also be pleased to hear her voice, although he would not be telling her of his recent adventures in the cold and desolate mountains of this godforsaken country just yet. If ever.

But despite several attempts, Debbie did not answer.

Worldwide, there are a series of disparate telecommunications networks that manage to talk to each other. At least most of the time. And most of them have help-desks, although the term *help* is often a misnomer. Mark puzzled his way through various operators until he talked to someone in the mobile carrier firm that supplied his company's mobile phones in New York. Once connected, he asked for the mobile telephone number that had been allocated to Debbie. Why he had never bothered to find out the number before, he did not know. After all, Taylor Software was paying for it—it was just one of those things that happened automatically. However, the operator was not about to give out that information because Mark was 'not authorized to receive it.

In sheer frustration, he killed the contact.

Instead, he called Brad Morgan.

Brad was both relieved and surprised to hear from his boss, but the news that he had for Mark was all bad.

While Brad explained what had happened in New York, Mark did not know whether to be angry or to cry. It was all turning pear-shaped once again.

Brad had not seen Debbie for several days, and he had been unable to contact her on her cellular phone or by any other means. Brad's calls were answered, he asked who was calling, and then *click*—nothing. The good news was he knew her mobile phone number. Mark wrote that down, along with Harold's home telephone number. His last words to Brad were, 'Leave your telephone switched on and keep the battery charged. I will need to talk to you again.'

Brad did not bother to tell his boss about the Styris deal.
It just did not seem important enough.
Brad had correctly read that situation.

Although Mark had previously decided to talk to Debbie before calling Harold, he had little choice. He had a gut feeling that this would not be good. He could sense this black cloud about to descend on him and an already-bad mood would get worse. At least Harold Taylor was in a position where he should be able to do something about their current predicament. Exactly what Mark did not know, but the Porto Plan needed some urgent input from the person who had instigated it. The person who had been tasked with implementing it was rapidly turning his priorities to other matters.

Mark called the Taylor residence. It was now close to 11:45 pm, but that could not be helped. Covert operations on the other side of the world did not usually go by Washington office hours. And Harold should be used to it.

Mark's mother, Elizabeth, answered the phone.

Mark made a mental note to talk to his father about the rather surly response that someone calling a senior public servant on his home landline would get.

Not that she said very much.

'This is the Taylor residence.'

'Mother, this is Mark. How are you? Could I speak with Father?'

She did not say hello. She did not say how she was. She did not ask how her only darling son was. She did not exactly say either 'Yes' or 'No' to the question of whether Mark could speak to his father. What she said was, 'Your father is not here.'

His mother was beginning to sound like a help-desk operator.

'Mother, it is urgent that I contact Father. I have lost all my contact numbers. Where is he? And can you give me his mobile phone number?'

Mark got half an answer. 'He is not here!' his mother repeated and then said nothing.

Mark could almost visualize his mother glaring at the telephone. Mothers can be stubborn. And not easily understood, even by close relatives, and by men who were rarely on the same wavelength. But Elizabeth usually managed to maintain a professional attitude when dealing with her husband's affairs.

Not this time.

Mark took a deep breath. The senior members of the Taylor household had obviously had a disagreement about something, probably the floral arrangements for the dining room. But there was no time for Mark to take sides on any one of several issues that his parents may squabble about. At least he did not swear; otherwise, Mother would have just hung up.

'It is critical that I have Father's mobile phone number. If you didn't realize it, I am overseas and in a whole heap of trouble. I will call you tomorrow, and we can chat about other things. Please, Mother. It is important that you give me his cell number!'

That worked. She gave him Harold's mobile phone number, and then she just hung up. No good-bye. No *Well, how are you?* No *Where are you?* No concern that would have been triggered by her maternal instincts, like What kind of trouble are you in? Nothing!

Mark began to wonder whether *he* had done something wrong!

He called Harold Taylor's mobile phone number. It rang a few times, then cut to message service. *Sorry I cannot take your call. Leave a message after the tone, and I will get back to you as soon as possible.*

Mark called Debbie's mobile phone number.

The number rang for a while, and then he heard Debbie's voice just say 'Hello.' Her voice sounded strained and frightened—the voice of someone who was under extreme duress. It did not sound anything like the girl that he knew and loved. The whole connection sounded tinny, the kind of sound you get when a mobile phone is on speaker. There was a lump in Mark's throat as he cautiously answered.

'Hi, Debbie. It's Mark.'

Mark could have sworn that he caught the beginning of a response. But all he heard was a *click*.

And then the phone went dead.

Chapter 43

Panic

The panic that erupted in the safe house in New York was infectious. Karl could not contain himself as Debbie cowered in the bedroom, fearing for her life. He ranted at no one as he moved from room to room, searching for something. Eventually, he calmed down and rummaged through his pockets in a final attempt to find the scrap of paper on which he had written the number to call in an emergency. Karl had several telephone numbers to contact the man, but while that man was overseas, and while Karl was on this mission, only one of those numbers would he be able to use.

It had been stressed to him that he was not to make any contact that could be traced, and it was more than his life was worth to disobey that order. But the news that he had to deliver simply had to get through, even if it was already known by the man at the other end of the call. There was no choice. If it turned out that the man already knew, then so be it.

Karl had to be sure. Karl dialled the insecure mobile phone number.

'Hello.'

'Hi, it's Karl—'

'What are you doing calling me ...'

'I know ... but listen. Mark Taylor just rang.'

Stephen Rodriguez froze.

'But that is not possible!'

Karl took a deep breath. His job and his life were safe. For now.

'It was definitely him. We had the call on speaker. And Miss Peterson could not have been acting. She knew who it was, and it was him. What do we do now?'

Rodriguez's mind was on autopilot. 'Get out of that house now. Go to plan B. Destroy the phone. Keep the lady alive.'

Rodriguez threw the phone across the room, shattering it into small pieces and very effectively ending the call.

The anger welled up in Stephen Rodriguez. How the hell had this happened? He had been assured by the Russians that it had *all* been taken care of. The Afghanis had taken the bodies to a place so far remote, and in such atrocious weather conditions, that no one could possibly have survived. Those smart-assed Russians had cocked up again!

Rodriguez had said to them in the language of international speak, 'Make sure that Mark Taylor and his cohorts do not survive!'

But because no one wanted to take full responsibility, or to leave a trace that the interfering FBI could find, someone had decided that they simply could not shoot the prisoners. But since when was it that hard to make someone die or disappear? After all, they were in Afghanistan.

So why not just slit their throats instead of just *assuming* that they would die out in the cold. Knives were better than bullets. They could not be so easily traced. Give the FBI a bullet these days, and they could tell you the last time the shooter had a pee! But you must find the shooter first! On the other hand, there were so many bloodstained knives in Afghanistan that they could never realistically be traced. The FBI would have a snowflake show in hell of finding even the remotest trace. And now this!

Somehow Mark Taylor was alive. And therefore, Mark would now know that his girlfriend was in trouble. Not that Mark could do much about that, being on the other side of the world.

Rodriguez scratched his head. This was the very reason that he had a plan B, but he never thought he would need to use it. He had taken steps to have Debbie taken as a form of insurance, only to be released, with appropriate apologies, when he had confirmation that Mark Taylor was indeed out of the way. Now that the Russians had failed once again, things would need to be vastly different.

Did Mark know that Debbie was being held by the CIA?

Probably not.

Could Harold Taylor become involved? Probably not since less than 0.0001 percent of the CIA knew about what was going on. But Rodriguez could not afford any more slip-ups.

So, what did he do now?

Rodriguez had to believe that there was still a way out of this latest mess.

And Debbie Peterson would either have a role to play, or she would become collateral damage.

And he was OK with that.

Now the game would get messy.

Chapter 44

Revision

The three of them sat staring at the walls, and no one was prepared to break the silence that had descended on the group. The emotional thunder that had clouded Mark's face as he failed to talk to either of the two people that he had called had not dissipated. Dusty and Owen would not speak because they knew the mood that Mark was in. After Mark had told them what had happened in a very brief conversation with Debbie, Mark would not speak because he could not without losing his grip on his already-frayed nerves.

Mark just wanted to scream.

Now Mark had heard from Owen about the attempt on the life of the President of Afghanistan, just a day after they had been taken in for questioning. What, if anything, was the connection?

Finally, it was Dusty who broke the silence.

'Everyone for coffee?'

The other two just nodded.

Armed with a cup of strong coffee, Dusty looked at his friend and wondered how Mark must have been feeling. Mark had related the gist of each conversation to the other two, but only Dusty could have known the crushing burden that his friend had to carry once again.

Owen was just the driver and had known Mark only for a brief time. Owen may respect him, but he could not know him.

Dusty knew the signs. Dusty could not read body language as well as Mark could, but he knew that something was going to happen, and someone, somewhere would be deeply sorry.

'We need to plan,' Mark stated in a whisper. 'We need to find out what has happened to Stephen Rodriguez.' While in his mind he may well have been thinking of Debbie, he remained focused on what had to be done. Mark turned to Owen and asked, 'Where is Griz?'

'The last I heard, he was back in Peshawar,' Owen replied. 'I will check on both Griz and Stephen Rodriguez. Griz I can contact by telephone. As for your friend Stephen, I can either go out and do some checking, or I can contact the Brits.'

'Rodriguez is no friend of mine!' Mark shouted bitterly, but then shook his head and held up his hands in surrender, clearly thinking of something else. 'I'm sorry. Thanks, Owen. Could you do that?' he said without processing what Owen had said.

Mark then turned to Dusty. The ache behind his eyes and the bitterness in his voice was apparent.

'You remember back in Ghazni when the ADDI came over and thanked us for getting him out of a hole? I thought at the time that Stephen had failed to recognize me. In this game, they say *never* assume!' Mark added bitterly.

'I do not know whether he was involved in what has happened to us since we got back to Kabul, but just *assume* for a moment that he was. In that scenario, he must have been suspicious of why we were here in Afghanistan. Stephen used to be in Afghanistan with the CIA as head of station in Kabul. He would know how to contact the Russians, and more importantly, he would know *who* to contact. He could have contacted the Russians and passed on a tip. He could have suggested to them that we had nothing to do with CIA, DEA, or any other US government agency – that we were simply coming to Kabul to cause trouble. Maybe that is where Yuri got the impression that we had something to do with an attempt on President Hamid Karzai. Think about it.' Mark commanded his friend. But he still carried on talking.

'Getting the Russians involved achieves two things. Firstly, it gets us well out of Stephen's way. Secondly, Stephen knows how they treat people in this country. They usually kill people and ask questions afterward. According to Owen, there was an attempt made on the life of the President of Afghanistan the other day. The Russian, Yuri, asked me while I was being interviewed why we wanted to attack the President. Hell, I thought he was talking about *our* President at first. So, Rodriguez could have told the Russians that a couple of ex–Special Forces guys are in the country to do some mischief. We are not CIA, and not DEA, so it is simply perfect. There are just too many coincidences.'

Mark looked at Dusty and saw the look of horror on his face. They both knew that this story was beginning to make sense.

Mark continued. 'And now I cannot contact Debbie. I can contact Brad, and he says, try as he may, that he does not know where she is. Another coincidence? I don't think so. What say another part of the puzzle is that Stephen Rodriguez has arranged for Debbie to be held as a means of pressurising me in case we survived the other night? And like the idiot that I am, I try to contact Debbie, confirm to the entire world that I am still alive. And now Stephen can play his other card. There are just too many coincidences. We have been outmanoeuvred and out-thought! And it's all my fault! Thinking that I could outsmart someone from the CIA, with the experience and ruthlessness of an assistant director in the intelligence and operations unit. And now he has Debbie!'

Mark buried his head in his hands.

Dusty and Owen just looked on. What could they say? Dusty was aware of the last time a girl that Mark was close to had got involved, and the end to that story was not pretty. Owen was aware of the strong bond between these two friends, and there was something going on that he did not understand—and worse, he was powerless to do anything about.

They sat there in silence for what seemed like hours, but it was probably only a matter of minutes. It was not in the nature of someone like Dusty to say nothing in these circumstances, but what could he say without tipping his friend over the edge? In the circumstances outlined by Mark, and it seemed to be a reasonable assessment of the situation, it looked as though their whole mission was stuffed.

Mark eventually sat up and looked at the two men. Neither of them could hold his gaze.

'How do we find out what has happened to Rodriguez?' Mark asked, not really expecting an answer.

Owen did answer.

'I have contacted the Brits and am waiting for them to call me back. They may shed some light on what goes on!'

Mark looked more than a little shocked by Owen's observation. That seemed to come out of left field, even though Mark had not reacted at all to the earlier mention of the Brits.

'Why the British? You are talking to MI6?'

Owen told Mark what had transpired a couple of days

before when he had met with Mike and Reginald. And somewhat apologetically explained his reasons for that little diversion.

After a few moments, Mark nodded his head. 'Good move! I would not have thought of that, but I like it. What are the chances of meeting them again?'

'Well, they did say to keep in touch. So, I can try if you think that would help.'

Owen drove north-west along the Kabul–Paghman Road, cognizant of the fact that the last time he had driven in this direction, he had been on a vastly different, and scary, mission. Then, just before they entered the village of Paghman, he turned right onto the Sarak-e-koshkak trail that led up to the Qargha dam and the Kabul Golf Club. If anyone was following his vehicle or observing his progress, they would have assumed that Owen was alone. That was because Mark had simply curled up in the back of the Humvee and slept during what was to be a relatively short journey. Dusty was back at the safe house making sure that he had their back should something else go wrong.

The M16 man, Mike Robinson, met them in the golf club car park, such as it was. Robinson crammed them into a rough-looking golf buggy and headed off up the course. Eventually, they stopped overlooking the fifth fairway where a group of four were attempting to play towards the par 4 green. Not that there was anything *green* around the flag that marked the fifth hole. One of the players acknowledged a wave from Robinson, broke off from the other three men, and came over to join them.

His name was Reginald Smith.

They had spoken to Robinson earlier in the day, and that had led to their electing for this somewhat bizarre meeting place. Smith did not seem particularly concerned at the interruption to his game. He shook hands with Owen, and then reached his hand out to Mark.

'So, at last, we meet! Mark, the son of Harold!'

His voice sounded upper-class English, probably educated at Eton or Harrow, then later at Oxford or Cambridge University, as seemed to be the educational institutes where most of the senior British civil servants came from. But Reginald Smith was pleasant enough.

The two men eyed each other with a certain wariness, neither sure what to say. Surprisingly, Mark was the more relaxed of the two.

'Thank you for taking the time to see us,' Mark began. 'We won't take much of your time, and then you can get back to your game of golf. Owen has already spoken to you, but in case you need clarification, I will explain our situation. We are here in Afghanistan, courtesy of the Drug Enforcement Administration, to check on the activity of the assistant deputy director of intelligence of our CIA. We have recently had a few problems along the way, and we have lost all our gear. More importantly, we have lost track of our ADDI. So, in priority order: we need some gear, and we need to know the whereabouts of the man we were following. Can you, and will you, help us?'

Smith studied Mark for a few seconds, and his face broke into a smile. The smile did not travel to his eyes. Even so, Mark was having difficulty reading the gregarious Brit.

'You are saying that you cannot rely on your own CIA or DEA for support, and I do understand that. Looks like our profiling is accurate, for a change!' Smith responded smugly.

'It looks like the setup for your trip to Afghanistan was either extremely clever, or bloody stupid. Probably the latter. However, I like and appreciate your honesty. Yes, we will help you as much as we can. You will understand that we cannot interfere. After all, last time I checked with London, we are both on the same side. And you will understand that we will expect some form of reciprocation in due course,' Smith added with a twinkle in his eyes.

Mark stumbled with his reply to that.

'You understand that I am not officially a part of any Government organization. I cannot commit to anything specific! But since you seem to know of my father, I will advise him of your request.'

'Oh, there is no need to, as you say, commit to anything,' Smith replied.

'Just keep us informed as best you can. And I am sure you will have a chat with Harold at some stage. After all, the last we heard, he is still your father.'

The British MI6 chief seemed to find that rather funny, though no one else saw the humour. 'Anyway, we will work out the rest.'

Mark nodded. He was out of his depth. He knew it, and so did Smith. But Mark and his small team were in a desperate position. Mark would take whatever assistance he could get, leaving the *reciprocation*, and whatever form that may, or may not, take to the bureaucrats in Washington.

The Brit was still smiling. He gazed across the fairway to where his playing partners were still searching for a lost ball and shrugged. He looked down the golf course, towards the car park, and muttered something that did not sound overly polite and then turned his attention back to Mark.

'You could help us explain some of what goes on in Washington. My controller has started another conspiracy theory. He thinks that the CIA has a plan to take over the drug business. Your CIA is, of course, primarily interested in cutting off the funds for terrorists, but the intention would seem to be that it would make the supply of drugs to the US no longer financially worthwhile for criminals and terrorists. Would you like to comment on that?'

Mark was stunned.

This would mean that here he was, with his tiny team, taking on the might of the US Government, not just the ADDI and a couple of CIA agents, and the MI6 agent in place was speculating on exactly what Mark had been asked to find evidence of. But if the theory that Smith had proposed was even approaching the truth, surely the agencies such as the DEA and the OIG would be aware of it. Of even more importance, it could mean that the ADDI was involved in something that was quite legitimate. However, in Washington, anything could happen, and it was not something on which Mark could speculate. Mark had to choose his words carefully. He had only a vague idea of how these games were played, but he doubted that the Brit had told him the full story. In fact, the more likely scenario was that Smith had deliberately exaggerated his statement of position, in the hope that Mark would correct the misrepresentation.

'I would hope that such a theory would not get that much traction. It is not exactly logical, is it?' Mark asked. Smith laughed.

'No, not many people ascribe to it. Yet the CIA has been known to do some rather stupid things in the past. Just thought I would mention it! In any case, yes, we will replace your gear. Just give Mike a list of what you need. As for the whereabouts of your ADDI, we understand that he is still here in Kabul, holed up at CIA HQ, and has been so for several days. His next stop should be Peshawar, Pakistan. I am sure that we can let you know exactly when he leaves, but what he gets up to is anyone's guess. However, once you have gear, we can keep in touch by satellite phone.

Now I must get back to my game. It really is a struggle to keep losing to Sir Richard, but one must know one's place!'

He shook hands with Mark and turned to leave.

Mark held him back. 'Thank you!' he said, the sincerity evident in his words and body language.

'We will repay you somehow when we get better organized.'

'Oh, no need to worry about that, old boy. You obviously have more important things on your plate.' And then a wink. 'I will be interested to see how it turns out this time. Good luck.'

Mark watched the rear view of the MI6 officer retreat across the fairway. In the intelligence business, there was normally a trade-off where one good turn deserved another. In Mark's case, there was little real chance of that happening. The way things could work out, the British may get some kudos, which Mark supposed amounted to the same thing.

But what did Reginald Smith mean by *'turns out this time'*?

And just how much more did the British know of the mission that Mark was engaged in and its progress so far.

And what were they not saying?

Robinson drove them back to where they had left the Hummer in the car park. The golf course was mostly barren earth, and there was little to distinguish between tee, fairway, and green. The car park was much the same, and there was dust everywhere. Most of the recent dust had been caused by another Jeep-type vehicle that had just pulled in and parked alongside Owen's Humvee. The cart was dumped at the shop/office, and then Robinson went across to the jeep and exchanged words with the driver. He came back to where Mark and Owen were standing, carrying a small parcel, and gave them each a 9mm Browning pistol together with a spare for Dusty.

'We don't have the Glock yet, but these will do,' Robinson explained. 'Now tell me what else you need. We can pick it up back in Kabul, and then you can get on your way.'

Mark did not hesitate. 'Our immediate need is for clothes, satellite phones, cameras, and recorders. Anything else we can acquire as we go, especially when we get our people organized Stateside. That takes care of our practical needs. What we then need, desperately, is to find out the movements of Stephen Rodriguez, and based on the information so far, we have an obvious starting point. Who would have thought Rodriguez would be at the CIA compound!' Mark could not help but smile at the irony of it all.

Robinson was all business.

'Why don't we get back into town? The gear I can drop off at your place within a couple of hours. By that time, I should also be able to confirm the answer to your question.'

Again, Mark did not hesitate.

'No need for you to do that. One of us will meet you somewhere in town.'

By this time, Mark had about as much of the British hospitality as he could take. The Brits were good at what they did. Too good, in fact. Mark was not going to reveal the whereabouts of their safe house to add to their obviously vast knowledge of all things American. As he bitterly reflected, they may already know, although, on the other hand, it was a DEA house rather than the CIA's. But you can never be sure in the spook business. For all that he knew, Mike Robinson, with all his charm, and Reggie Smith, with all his arrogant swagger, maybe working in cahoots with the CIA.

At this stage, and with the state their mission was in,

it did not matter on which side.

The meeting with one of Mike's men was quick and efficient, apart from the fact that it had all the drama normally seen in the movies. With Owen behind the wheel, they drove into the centre of the city, past a certain intersection, at a prescribed time, and there, a man, dressed as a local, simply stepped up to their vehicle and handed them a key. He was a man of few words.

'At Kabul International, left luggage.' And without another word, he simply disappeared back into the crowd.

Mark had to smile. Robinson was probably, and correctly, a little miffed at having his plan to find out where the team was staying thwarted. They had no option other than to drive out to the Kabul airport, which was only about nine kilometres to the east of the city. Owen stayed with their Humvee, while Mark got out and went in search of the left luggage area. Under the gaze of a couple of Afghan policemen, Mark eventually found a locker that matched the key number. The locker contained a black backpack, which wasn't exactly the type and colour that Mark would have chosen in a place like Kabul. It looked just the type that a terrorist would use to carry a bomb, and Kabul had its fair share of bombings. He could do nothing about that, so Mark simply slung the bag over his shoulder, locked the door, and turned towards the exit.

The Afghan police stopped him.

With guns drawn, the first two were joined by three others who surrounded Mark and ushered him into the middle of a large empty space. Then a sergeant, also in the uniform of the Afghan police, appeared on the scene. None of the men came close.

'What is in the bag?' the sergeant asked in halting English.

Mark had to think quickly. He had no idea—just an assumption that the British had done what they said they would do.

'A couple of telephones, is all, plus a few other gadgets and some clothes.' Mark shrugged.

'Who are you?' the sergeant then asked.

Just a guy going about his business, picking up some luggage, Mark did not say.

The Afghan police were trigger-happy at the best of times. Being smart would not help. Especially given what could happen next, and especially if the Brits had added a few extras, like guns.

Mark decided to stay with the story that they had arrived in the country with. That would not go down too well, but it was better than lying.

'I am Major Mark Taylor with the US Drug Enforcement Administration,' he said, hoping that the use of his rank or the mention of federal authority would impress.

That either did not go down well or was simply not understood.

'Open the bag. And do it slowly.'

Mark did as he was told.

'Now, remove the contents and lay them on the ground. And slowly.'

Mark was impressed. The sergeant had obviously been trained by the Americans, and his English was excellent. It was anyone's guess about the rest of the policemen. Mark just hoped that they would not shoot unless instructed to.

Mark slowly withdrew the contents of the bag, one item at a time, and placed them on the ground. Mark felt relieved. There were no guns—just two satellite phones, a camera, a recorder, an odd collection of clothes, and a stuffed teddy bear.

Mark and the sergeant looked at each other for a moment, and then both grinned and shrugged. Mark wrote it off to British humour, although the joke escaped him. The sergeant pulled out a knife, and as Mark flinched, the toy was slashed apart. It revealed nothing.

'Why at the airport? Why not use Bagram?' the sergeant asked.

The answer to that was easier.

'I am on a covert mission. We must investigate our own military at times. It goes with the job,' Mark answered with another smile and a shrug.

Surprisingly, that seemed to work. The sergeant also smiled and nodded his head, apparently in total understanding of the situation.

'OK. You may go.'

Mark gathered up the contents of the bag, except that he dumped the toy into a waste bin. There was no point in carrying rubbish around, especially the remains of a teddy bear.

Once back in the Humvee, Mark told Owen what had happened. Owen expressed no surprise and just grinned. Owen did look surprised when Mark told him what they were going to do next.

'Do you know of an Internet café? One that will not ask too many questions?'

Owen did, and he headed there.

Once settled down at a workstation, Mark checked the time. It was now 4:30 p.m. That would make it about 7:00 a.m. in New York. Yes, Brad would be awake.

He called Brad on his mobile phone.

'Any news on Debbie?' Mark had to ask.

'Nothing. But we—,' Brad started to respond before Mark interrupted.

'OK, shut up and listen. Are you in the office?'

'Yes, but where are you?"

'Shut up and listen. I will fill you in later. Somewhere buried in my bits of software is a program called SatUtility and a date in the format that we use. Can you find it?'

Brad was confused, but at least he had something to do, and with computers. 'Sure. Do you want me to call you back?'

Mark retained his composure. 'No, I want you to find it now and download the compiled copy to me, but without the documentation.'

That brought a shrug from Brad. His boss was working on someone else's machine and did not want them to know what he was up to.

'OK, what is your address?'

Mark gave him the IP address of the machine and their location. A couple of minutes later, Brad came back on the satellite phone and said that it was done. Mark then asked him to read through the documentation that normally accompanied the program to check on the correct procedure for connecting a device. That was easy enough. The satellite phones each had a USB cable, normally used for charging the battery, but also used for downloading stuff from a computer. Mark connected the first device and quickly downloaded a couple of small files into the memory, and then told Brad to run the option to clear any malware, Trojans, or other odd routines from what was to Brad a remote device. They then repeated the process for the second device. Then Mark asked Brad to remove any trace of what he had downloaded and make certain that there was no trace that they had even been connected.

'OK. Done. Now can we have a quick chat about Debbie?'

Mark sensed that the news would not be good. Body language can be sensed over phone communication. But he tried to be positive.

'I hope you have some good news.'

Brad briefly explained what he had been able to find out from Mark's neighbours.

'Debbie has apparently been kidnapped by someone who has connections at a high level in Government. I think it is CIA, because when Shania tracked the report of a missing person, that inquiry led nowhere, and she was fobbed off.'

'Brad, you are not making any sense. What has your girlfriend got to do with anything?'

Brad laughed. 'Well, it turns out that Shania works for the FBI.'

Mark did not know whether to laugh or cry. 'OK, thanks, Brad. Talk to you later.' Mark terminated the call.

'What the hell was that about?'

The question came from the nerd who ran the Internet café.

Mark smiled. 'Just initializing these two phones. Thanks for your help.'

Mark paid the fee for the hour that they had used the machine and exited the Internet café.

Once they were back in the Humvee, it was Owen's turn.

'Well, what *was* that all about?'

'Just clearing any junk that the Brits would have conveniently left on the satellite phones,' Mark said with a grin. 'What I do in *real* life is to run a computer software company specializing in security systems.' Then he added, 'It is not that I don't trust our British friends. They are only doing what they must. But I do not want them to track us through the phone, and I am sure that is what they would have loaded on them. At least that is what I would have done. Anyway, now we have our own security.'

Owen just shook his head.

'I think we have another, more immediate, problem!

Someone is following us and has been for some time.'

Mark adjusted the passenger mirror to take a view out the back window but could not see anything that stood out. Owen suddenly turned right and slowed down. Shortly afterward, a Hummer turned into the same street and pulled to a halt on the right. Owen then accelerated, and the Hummer eased back out into the stream of traffic and continued to follow. 'OK. Got it. Can you lose him?'

'In this chaotic city? Anything can be done.' Owen turned left, and fastened his seat belt, motioning that Mark should do the same. They sped down the side street, made three further left turns until they were back on the original road. Then they turned left again, and then made a sharp right turn and continued in the direction that they had been headed. There was no sign of the Hummer.

The vehicle carrying Calvin Bonney came to a halt, as Calvin smiled to himself. Yes, they had successfully given him the slip. But also, yes, his mission had been successful. Now a few calls on his satellite phone, a quick call to pick up his passport, and he could get the hell out of this place.

Less than twenty-four hours prior to this, the archaeologist had boarded a United Airlines flight at Dulles International Airport bound for Islamabad, Pakistan. He had been a little worried about getting through passport control because the photo in the passport was of a man with a rough-looking beard and wearing a khaki shirt which had seen better days, which suited his occupation, whereas he was now clean-shaven and wearing business clothes. However, the officer at the desk had been quite happy to clear him through without a second glance. Once through immigration, he had gone to a clothing store and bought a set of casual clothes and discarded his business attire. It was an expensive exercise, but he just shrugged. There were higher priorities.

The departure official in Islamabad saw a tired and ashen Bonney and just smiled at his explanation of being beardless and passed him through the transit gate. It was only a quick change of aircraft at Islamabad and a quick hop over the mountains, and they landed in Kabul. The entry card said that Calvin was to visit the Mes Aynak archaeological site, about an hour's drive to the south of the city. That site, which had the remnants of Buddhist monasteries and other priceless artifacts, had been sold to the Chinese for more than 3 billion dollars.

The Chinese were not overly interested in Buddhism. They were interested in the copper-rich land, and it would not be long before the entire site was ruined forever. The arrivals immigration official was appropriately sympathetic to this quiet old man, and his hopeless cause. He waved him through.

Bonney had made it this far without any hitch.

Now came the question of what to do next. He could not contact his usual friends at the US Embassy. Instead, he called the British Embassy. Having gotten through to someone who could help him, he was told to leave a contact number and then to wait. The Embassy staff did not seem to be fazed by the fact that his phone number was obviously a satellite phone.

Bonney could not stay at his more normal accommodation, so he checked into a three-star motel, paying cash. He answered no questions other than muttering about the Mes Aynak site. He handed his passport to the receptionist, as was standard procedure for motels in this part of the world. It did not matter if he could not collect his passport at the end of his visit to Kabul. It was a relatively simple matter to arrange to get another one.

And there he rested and waited.

Then came the call from the Brits, and the old man was quite overcome with emotion, and cried with relief, at what the Brits had to say. Calvin was told to meet a Hummer at a discreet location not far from his motel, and he would be taken to a place some way out of town to observe what he had rushed halfway around the world to see.

Bonney had hoped to do more than just see. But there were other priorities. So, after observing the Brits and their co-conspirators do their business, and then following the co-conspirators back to Kabul, he was at least satisfied that things were returning to normal. The intention had been to find out where the co-conspirators were staying, but they had expertly given him the slip. And that brought a smile to the face of the archaeologist.

Mark Taylor would have made a superb agent in the field, if only he had followed in his father's footsteps!

Now he could get a series of flights that would eventually return him to Dulles in Washington DC. For the flights, Calvin would use two passports so that by the time he arrived back in the States, all references to Afghanistan and Pakistan would be lost.

And he could return to his original identity of Harold Taylor.

Owen drove toward the road where the safe house was located. Mark was still somewhat lost in Kabul, so he did not notice that Owen kept driving past. He did, however, sense that something was wrong.

'I think we have a problem,' Owen remarked as he pulled over and stopped at the side of the road. They both looked out the rear window to see a small group assembled outside the house, and a couple of vehicles were parked at odd angles to the road, which suggested they had stopped in a hurry. They both carried the insignia of the local police.

Owen restarted the Humvee and turned down the next side street before again pulling to a halt.

'I think it best if you stay here. I will go and investigate.'

Owen got out of the vehicle and rummaged around in the back before emerging with a change of clothes, which consisted of ragged shirt and trousers. He quickly pulled them on and then he limped off in the direction of the house, holding on to a cane and looking distinctly older than he had previously.

Mark got out of the vehicle and watched as Owen proceeded down the road. He did not know what to do other than heed Owen's instructions, so he stayed where he was, peering around the corner as Owen slowly approached the small crowd.

Owen then appeared to get involved in a casual conversation with the man who was apparently the leader of the group, then placed his right hand over his heart, bowed his head, muttered something, and then continued on his way before turning left, and disappearing from Mark's view.

Mark nearly jumped out of his skin when Owen suddenly appeared behind him. He looked worried.

'OK, the Sunni guy that I spoke to says that the police have taken a woman and a child away. When the police first arrived at the house, the neighbours heard a couple of shots and came out to see what was going on. That was all he could tell me. There is no sign of Dusty, and the police are still in the house. It looks as though your friend may have got involved in a fight and came off second best.'

Mark made to go towards the house but was retrained

by Owen. The anger in Mark was plain to see. 'What is the point?' Owen asked.

'I can't leave Dusty alone in that house! We have to do something!' Mark replied. Although he did get the message that Owen was trying to convey. There must have been at least a dozen police in the vicinity. Although they were probably poorly trained and lacked the dedication to duty that someone from the United States would expect, they were still all heavily armed. And they would show little interest in Mark's concern for his friend.

Just as they went to turn away, two of the Afghani police emerged from the house carrying a black plastic bag. Mark again took a step towards the house and again was retrained by Owen.

'That cannot be your friend Dusty in the bag. It is too small, and it would take more than two guys to carry him out. That must be Mo!'

Now it was Owen's turn to get upset. Tears came into the Welshman's eyes as he muttered under his breath.

'The bastards must have shot the dog! So where is Dusty?'

That question was answered almost immediately as a large man came around from one of the streets behind them. It was Dusty, drenched in sweat and puffing as though he had just run a marathon.

'Thank God you two are OK!'

'Where have you been? We thought you would have been in the house. What goes on? Mark asked his friend. Dusty was clearly also upset and could hardly get the words out.

'It was my fault! I decided to go for a run. Sitting in that house was a little claustrophobic, and Halah said she would be fine. I was coming back when I saw the police crawling all over the house, and they took the girls away before I could do anything about it. I didn't have a weapon, otherwise, I could have done something. I should never have gone!'

Mark put a hand on his arm.

'No! Don't blame yourself. There is nothing you could have done. What is important is what we do now.'

Owen bit his lip. Dusty was correct—he could have done nothing. But what had Mark said that very morning? He should not have taken the risk of placing Halah and Hayah in a position of danger, despite the calm assurance from Halah herself.

Mark sensed that this was getting out of hand.

'Owen, we do not know what has caused the police to come around. It may have nothing to do with us!'

'And I thought that people in your business did not believe in coincidence,' Owen replied bitterly.
Mark had to take that.

'OK, arguing about the rights and wrongs will get us nowhere. What is your procedure in cases where a safe house is burned?'

Owen took a couple of deep breaths. 'There is a plan B, which probably is the same all over the world. We would normally go to a designated house and wait there for instructions. In our case, we would expect the other people to assemble there too, but I doubt whether that will occur—either instruction or regrouping! What I recommend we do is go to the accommodation that we had in Qala-e-Fatullah. It is not the best, but it is in a part of town the even the police would be reluctant to venture into.'

Back at their apartment in Qala-e-Fatullah, Mark tried calling his father again. This time, Harold answered. Not that his father said much. 'Hello.'

'Father, it's Mark.'

'Mark, I told you I was out of town. Can this wait until I get back to the office? I have to go because my plane is on final call!'

'Shut up and listen!' replied Mark.

'We have a problem, which you are going to have to do something about. The safe house where we were staying has been raided, and the lady running the show and her daughter has been taken into custody. We are OK, but we need to do something about the ladies. Now, what can you do?'

At least Father was more talkative than Mother.

'You are going to have to bring me up to date with what is going on,' Harold replied.

'Father, we may have had our cover blown. Del is in hospital and looks unlikely to take any further part in this mission. We have, unfortunately, been guests of the Russian and Afghan intelligence people, and the upshot of that is that we have lost all our gear. Because of all this, we have at this moment got no idea where Stephen Rodriguez is. What we made arrangements to get some new gear, and then see what needs to be done this end. And I have just heard from Brad that Debbie has gone missing. So, we need some help with that one—and in a hurry.'

'What is wrong with Del? Does Karen know about this?' were the only questions that his father responded to.

And the truth dawned on Mark. He realized why his mother had been so terse.

Women always know. Be it body language. Be it attitude. Be it faint touches of perfume on the jackets and shirts that their men left for washing. They have a strange intuition that they often wished they did not have. Women know when their man has strayed. And consequently, it looked very much as though this whole mission was being driven by Harold's dick rather than by his brain.

Karen Marshall had been asking the questions, and

his father was too infatuated to see that his judgement was impaired by that. Rule number 1 in the covert operations business is - Keep emotion out of it. Rule number 2 is not what most people think (Don't get caught playing around) —it is much more subtle: Keep your dick in your pants.

Mark was already annoyed, having been through a kaleidoscope of almost-insurmountable problems and worries during the previous few days. Now he was plain mad. Little wonder that Mark's revelation about the relationship between Stephen Rodriguez and his FBI partner had seemed to fall on deaf ears! Harold Taylor was unlikely to pursue the matter when he himself was in no less a compromised position. What Mark said next, he would regret, but he would never apologise.

'Get real!' he started, talking in a tone that he could never recall having used before in conversations with his father.

'Del will eventually be OK, but for now, he is in a military hospital suffering from hypothermia, among other things. Last we saw of him, he was in a coma, but I say again—he should be OK. We are in a precarious position here, and we need some help. Now! I can leave Brad to follow up on the Debbie business, but if it turns out that she has been dragged into this business by any of your colleagues at the CIA, then they and you had better watch your backs. Our immediate problem is that we have lost all our gear and personal belongings. I need to get access to money. It does not matter whose, even if it's my own. I am sure it will eventually get reimbursed by someone sitting nice, warm, and cosy in Washington DC, but we have not got the time to wait around. And now we have lost two people who were helping us. They have been arrested by the Afghani police!'

'Well, I am not actually in Washington now, but I can get things moving. I will talk to Karen as soon as our conversation is over.'

And then it clicked with Mark.

'Father, you're at an airport! Where are you?'

His father was sounding quite flustered, which was unusual for the old man.

'I have to rush to catch my plane. We will get on to it as quickly as we can.'

Mark had had enough of the evasion.

'No, you need to talk to the Ambassador at the Kabul US Embassy now and get them moving to get the ladies released. The safe house we were using was run by the DEA, so they must be able to do something!' And that would certainly be of concern to his friend Karen Marshall, Mark did not add.

That seemed to get Harold's attention. Of course, involving the Ambassador would not seem like a good idea. At a US Embassy, there would be some senior official who would be the head of station for the CIA and responsible for other links to the US security services, and probably a different official who was responsible for DEA matters. Normally, an ambassador would be excluded from the finer points of the CIA head of station matters, but not so in Kabul. It was just too sensitive in this part of the world, and who knew—the Ambassador himself may be the CIA head of station. And that could be a major problem.

How was anyone going to explain to this Ambassador that the team who had been in Afghanistan following the ADDI of the same CIA and masquerading as a DEA team investigating the operations of the FAST groups under the control of the Pentagon—all without the Ambassador having any prior knowledge? And now that this team was in trouble, they wanted the Ambassador at incredibly short notice to try to influence the Afghani police to release two women who were not Americans and who were being held on unknown charges into his care? It would, of course, blow the whole game wide open, and most likely bring their investigation to a shuddering halt.

Harold Taylor appeared incredibly calm.

'Mark, you do realise what you are asking? The Ambassador has no knowledge of your mission!'

Mark was equally calm—at least he sounded so.

'And *you* do know what happens to young women who fall into the hands of the Afghani police? Halah was acting on behalf of the US operations in this godforsaken country, and you plan to do what? Nothing?'

Harold sighed. 'OK, I will see what I can do. The DEA will not be pleased at losing their safe house. I will go and see the Ambassador ... err ... I will call him and get back to you.'

Mark did not miss the meaning of what Harold had said. But he was beyond worrying about that now.

'Well, do something. I do not care whether your girlfriend is pleased or not!'

His father reacted like a spoilt child.

'What are you talking about? Karen and I are working this case together, and that is all!'

'Father, I did not mention any names—you did. I was recently talking with Mother, and she seems to be really upset about something. Now I know what it is. So, either get us some help here, or get lost!'

And he hit the kill switch on the satellite phone.

'Was that wise?' asked Dusty.

'No,' answered Mark. 'But it felt good!'

The US Ambassador in Kabul was a man named Quentin Armstrong. Prior to his appointment to Kabul, he had been the US Ambassador to New Zealand, and that was where he had first met Harold Taylor. Quentin was an energetic man with a reputation for getting things done, and that was probably why he had been selected to take over the difficult role in Afghanistan. His *energy* usually affected other parts of his life outside of his official capacity, and rumours had started to emerge that he was being unfaithful to his wife. Angela Armstrong had not accompanied her husband on his new posting, having had no desire to move from the peace and tranquillity of Wellington to the hellhole that was Kabul, and so she had returned to California.

All this information had recently passed through the desk of the OIG. After Harold's departure from Wellington, Quentin had temporarily assumed the role as CIA head of station, and was therefore now, and for the rest of his working life, a man of interest. Harold's view of the man was far from complimentary even before his latest dalliance, but he would need to put that aside in the present situation. He would need to resolve the current situation for two reasons: Firstly, he had the feeling that his son was displeased with his father, and he had to do something to placate Mark and get the Porto mission back on track. Secondly, and far more importantly than the first reason, he did not want to lose face with the lady whom he had fallen in love with. The irony of what Harold was proposing to do to achieve this failed to register.

'Quentin! It's Harold Taylor. How are you?' he said after getting through the drama of the embassy switchboard.

'Harold! To what do I owe the pleasure of this call? I hear you have had a promotion since you returned to Washington DC!'

'Yeah, not sure if it was a promotion!' Harold replied with a laugh. 'Well, I am currently in Kabul. I know that you are a busy man, but we have a situation that I need your help in resolving. Our Afghani friends have raided a safe house being used by the DEA and have taken away a couple of ladies. We want them returned. They have nothing to do with any covert mission, but it could result in an embarrassing situation for both of our countries if the problem is not resolved quickly and quietly.'

There was a pregnant pause before the Ambassador replied.

'I do not think that is something I want to get involved in, Harold. Your CIA ADDI from Washington is in Kabul at present, and he had said nothing about this. Maybe you need to talk to him. I am sure you know Stephen Rodriguez.'

Of course, Harold knew Stephen. And, of course, Stephen was the last person Harold wished to talk to. He wanted Quentin to act without the involvement of the CIA.

'Yeah, well, the situation is a little trickier than you would expect. We have a problem with our ADDI, and we also have other problems with our people in Kabul, as I am sure you are aware. It comes down to a matter of who we can trust, especially where the ladies are concerned, as I am sure you are also aware.'

So, do you get my drift? Harold thought.

Again, there was a pause and then a sigh.

'OK,' Quentin replied. 'I will try to use my influence to get the ladies released. You will owe me one for this.'

Harold had to laugh at that.

'Quentin, there will be no debt to repay. I am doing you a favour as an old friend. Now, if you do not secure their release, or if this conversation reaches the wrong quarters, then there will be repercussions. Do I make myself clear?'

'OK, Harold. Up to your old tricks again, I see!'

Chapter 45

Extraction

The weather in Kabul got worse rather than better. The chill wind was relentless as it continued to blow down from the north-east as the three men struggled to keep warm in the concourse at the United States air base at Bagram. They had achieved all that they could achieve in Afghanistan, which did not seem to be very much. They had had many exciting moments on the trail of Stephen Rodriguez, but at the end of it all, they had lost him. Rodriguez had boarded a Globemaster, presumably bound for Peshawar, and left. While Mark had strong suspicions about what the ADDI had been up to during their brief but event-filled sojourn to Afghanistan, it was hardly riveting evidence. All that they had witnessed could easily be explained by the organisation that made lying and coming up with cover stories an art form.

Mark and his team had eventually located Rodriguez at the Kabul CIA compound, only to then see him leave in a truck that seemed to contain the same packages that he had picked up in Marjah. Following the ADDI's truck was not particularly difficult because it joined a convoy heading to Bagram, so the Humvee just blended into the chaos.

The surprise came when they arrived at the Bagram Air Base. The CIA truck drove on to the base, and after only a cursory examination of some paperwork, went straight to the nearest Globemaster, which loaded the bundles. After a quick exchange with the driver of the truck, Rodriguez clambered on board the aircraft and was gone.

The latest turn of events caused a certain amount of panic for Mark's team. The only man that they had to monitor Rodriguez in Peshawar would be Griz, but he could not be in two places at once. And they needed him to come to Bagram to pick them up. And what would be his attitude when he realised that De Lawrence was no longer part of the team?

Mark's team had increased in size by two—at least the two girls had been released, thanks no doubt to the influence of the US Ambassador, and some profuse apologies, or possibly even something resembling the truth, delivered by Harold Taylor.

They had been delivered to Bagram Air Base courtesy of the CIA in Kabul, where they had been dropped off by a cultural attaché who went by the name of Martin Ellingham.

There was no future for the girls in Afghanistan, and so they had agreed to come with the team to Peshawar. The story, as best Halah could recount it, was that some local Sunni group had taken exception to the Arabs in their community running a house *of* ill-repute and had called the police. The fact that the dog, Mo, had been shot while trying to protect Hayah was the end of any association Halah would want with the scum, and she wanted out. Mark and his team would never know the truth, but they were just relieved to have the girls back safely.

As a consequence of Harold securing the release of the girls (although there was no proof that he had actually done anything other than speak to the Ambassador), Mark had reluctantly agreed that he would continue his mission at least as far as Peshawar and try to get some further evidence against Rodriguez. But Mark lacked the motivation, and his team was severely damaged. Mark still had no idea what had happened to Debbie, and he could do nothing about that unless he was back in the States. Dusty was still beating himself up about what had happened at the Kabul safe house and was now shadowing the two ladies as though his life, and their lives, depended on it. Owen said he was distraught over the loss of the dog Mo. At least that was what he said his problem was. It was either just a cover for his real worry that had arisen from Mark's earlier comment about exposing the girls to danger, or, as Mark had suspected, Halah meant more to Owen than he had revealed. Not that Mark could blame him. And, of course, Mark had no idea of the tragic history of Owen's relationships with women.

All this aside, what Mark now had to do was to quickly get back on the trail of the ADDI, but there had to be a period when no one would be watching Rodriguez, and that was of some concern. If Rodriguez had been organizing drug opiates to come out of Afghanistan to be processed into heroin in Peshawar, they could miss another crucial bit of evidence and would return home with nothing but theories. They were getting no help at all from Washington because, to the bureaucrats, covert meant covert: Mark and his few resources were not supposed to exist.

Reluctantly, Mark asked Owen to go to the military hospital where he understood that Del was being prepared for direct transfer to Washington DC Walter Reed Army Medical Center and offer to take him on the DEA Gulfstream.

It would not be the best for Del because he would not have the usual medevac facilities. But he was still officially part of the mission. And the decision would be for Del to make.

Owen returned sometime later with agreement that Del would go with the team. The medical staff had stipulated two conditions: Firstly, two specialised nurses would need to accompany Del, and secondly, the DEA, or whoever was picking up the tab, would need to arrange for the nurses to get back to the Bagram hospital. These conditions were way beyond his authority, but Mark agreed anyway. Someone else would need to worry about that.

Mark called Griz. It was against his better nature to have to lie, or to not quite tell the truth, but there were higher priorities.

'Hi, Griz. We need to get the hell out of Afghanistan, and we have a casualty to care about. Del is in a bad way, and the doctors want to get him to Walter Reed as quickly as possible. So, we are at Bagram and would appreciate a lift out.'

Griz sounded pleased to hear from Mark.

'What the hell happened to Del? And where is the CIA guy you were following?' he enquired.

'With Del. I can tell you the full story when we meet —sufficient for now to say he is injured and can no longer take part in our mission. But that is OK—we have a substitute. As for Rodriguez, he left Bagram in a Globemaster earlier today, and he should now be in Peshawar. We should be able to catch up with him when we get there. But that is not the priority. The point is, can you help?'

'OK,' was the response from Griz. 'I will need to refuel and file a flight plan. That should take about half an hour. See you in about a couple of hours or so!' And the call was terminated.

The fact that they were carrying with them a sick De Lawrence, and he was out of action for the near future, his loss did not really reduce the resources. However, while the loss of Del from the mission would not matter much 'in theatre,' it could make an enormous difference to the kind of support they would receive. Washington appeared to have lost interest.

Since Mark had told Harold where to go, no attempt had been made by anyone in Washington to contact them. The fact was that their mission to Afghanistan and to follow Stephen Rodriguez appeared to have failed, and in its inevitable way, the bureaucratic machine in Washington would ensure deniability and cut them off. At least that was something to which Mark could relate. Going off on a covert mission usually meant that the bureaucrats could quite simply deny that there was any such mission if everything turned pear-shaped.

The only piece of good news was that Owen had decided to make the trip to Peshawar, which restored the team to its original size. They bypassed the customs and other formalities at the air base due to a combination of DEA and Special Forces protocols, and the fact that they had a medevac person with them. There was some heated debate with Griz about the number of passengers and their positioning in the cabin. Although the number of people was well below the aircraft capacity, the medical team seemed to expect the entire cabin to themselves, and Del. Dusty sorted the argument with a few choice words.

The door was closed, and within minutes, they were airborne and turned east for their short flight across the border and back into Pakistan.

'We had a bit of a problem with the Russians in Kabul,' was Mark's opening remark to their versatile pilot.

'And that is how Del ended up in the state he is. In fact, if it wasn't for the intervention of Owen, all three of us would not have made it out alive. Now, I have had to commit to getting Del back to the US, and the nurses back to Bagram —bluntly, because I did not know how the DEA would react to extracting my team without Del on board, so I am sorry if I misled you.'

Griz shrugged.

'I haven't had much time to think about it. When we get to Peshawar, we should be able to get Del transferred to a military medevac aircraft, and the nurses can get a lift back to Bagram on a Globemaster. Just leave that to me. Similar things happen all the time, so the military are quite used to the rigors of a war environment. The more critical issue is - what are you and Dusty going to do?'

Mark had to think about that.

Personally, he wanted to get back to the US and find out what had happened to Debbie, and that was now his overriding priority. It was also important that he got back to the United States before Rodriguez. That was why he was pleased that Owen had agreed to come with them to Peshawar. Dusty he could rely on to continue to track the ADDI, and to find evidence of the drug trade. But Dusty could not do it all himself. Mark now had every confidence that Owen was the ideal man to assist. He was not so sure of Griz.

'As soon as we get Del organised, we will need to find out where Rodriguez has got to, and in doing so, we need to stay well out of sight. It is not so much that we need to follow him everywhere, as we did when we were last in Peshawar. We just need to know where he is, and we need to know if he makes any moves to leave Pakistan.'

Griz did not appear to detect any reluctance in Mark to share his actual plans. 'At the time of my leaving Peshawar earlier today, his Gulfstream was still at the airport, and the pilot had yet to file a flight plan out of there. Not that it means too much. Being CIA, he can leave at any time, and at short notice.'

Mark seemed satisfied with that. 'We had better not stay at the same hotel this time,' he mused. 'We cannot afford to be seen, and in view of what happened to us in Kabul, we will stay well out of the way.'

'Yeah, that was a bad business!' Griz mused. 'So how are you going to follow him now. That is, assuming you can find him?'

Mark wondered about that too. And he also wondered about how much Griz already knew of the goings-on in Kabul. Nothing whatsoever seemed to faze this amicable pilot, and he must have had tremendous connections and intelligence sources that kept him informed of almost everything that went on around him and beyond. Sure, as a DEA pilot, he had to have sources that provided him with all manner of bits of information that enabled him just to do his job.

In the shady unknown world of inter-pilot communications, they must have had many a laugh at the goings-on in high places, so to speak. The fact that during the original trip out from the United States Griz had been not only able to follow another Gulfstream, the flight plans of which the CIA should have been able to suppress but had also been able to find out *when* and to *where* they were going—that was very impressive. Or was it rather odd? And then the horrible truth hit Mark with the strength and impact of a catastrophic earthquake. He broke out into a cold sweat.

What if Brian McKinley, also known as Griz, was, in fact, working for the CIA? And if he was, the question was - which side was he on?

Mark cast his mind back to when they had first arrived in Peshawar. In their first serious discussion, Griz had suggested to Mark that he should get rid of Del. And his reasons? Del was useless! But where had he so quickly gleaned that piece of information? Maybe from the body language of the other members of the team. What if there were other reasons? What if Del had spotted something, or if Griz felt that Del may have spotted something that was not quite right? Griz knew that Mark was not happy with Del, so it was an easy game. Get rid of Del, and he could potentially significantly reduce their chances of tracking any drug deal.

Or was the problem that Mark was getting paranoid?

Mark surveyed the snow-covered mountain range to the north as they commenced their descent into Peshawar. He wondered how the beauty and grandeur of the sight spread out below him could also be the home of one of the most brutal and savage conflicts the world had ever seen. And he looked at the friendly and amicable pilot and wondered how, with all of his training and many years of experience of reading body language, he had failed to recognise what could be the obvious signs of deception. If this latest feeling had even the smallest element of truth, the plan that Mark had been forming for their recovery from an otherwise-failed trip was in shreds. He heard the words come out of his mouth - his mind was elsewhere.

'We will go straight back to the United States. I do not see any point in continuing with the mission.'

The reaction that he got from Griz neither confirmed nor denied the worst fears. Griz was either a superb actor, or he was one cool guy.

Mark could see the funny side. Everyone had a job to do, and everyone at this level worked for someone who controlled what was happening in their world. The US security service was a complex beast and was besotted with plot and counterplot. It was a wonder that people in the business knew which side they were on, or not on, from one day to the next. When on a mission, everyone sought to get that little advantage, or sought to push their barrow.

'I am sure we can track Rodriguez down. Don't you think it is worth one last attempt to do that?' Griz offered as he adjusted the flaps and raised the nose as he lined up the runway.

Mark spoke in a monotone.

'No, I don't. Thanks for all your help. I want to stop off in Europe on my way home, so we will not require the Gulfstream. I am sure the DEA will be pleased to have it back!'

And with that, Mark left the cockpit, tears of rage welling in his eyes.

Dusty sensed that something was wrong the moment Mark came back into the cabin. A casual nod of the head and an exchange of looks was all that was needed between the two old friends who knew each other like brothers. Looks exchanged on many missions where there was more at stake than on this one. Nothing more would be said until they were on the ground and out of earshot, and the prying eyes, of the others.

They were fortunate in having Owen to accompany them in Peshawar—at least they thought that they were. Mark and Dusty had not had the opportunity to talk, and their taxi taking them to an apartment sped through the traffic with such disregard for human life that the time did not quite seem appropriate. They clung to the seats, and only Owen seemed unconcerned. When they finally arrived at their apartment, the taxi sped off without charging them, to which odd event Owen simply responded that *the driver owed him.*

It was only when Owen took off to do some shopping that Mark and Dusty were finally alone.

Dusty immediately got to the point.

'What happened on the flight between you and Griz? You looked as though someone had a shit in your lunchbox!'

Mark consoled himself before replying. His plan now would be extremely dangerous, for himself, but more so for his friend Dusty.

'I have my doubts about Griz—a bit late in the piece, I admit, but nonetheless, I can no longer trust him.' He let the comment hang in the air while he thought of how to continue. Uncharacteristically, Dusty did not react, causing Mark to sigh. Was this going to be another case of the officer making decisions, the sergeant following orders?

Eventually, Dusty did react because Mark simply did not say anything further. 'And?'

Mark had been thinking the whole business through. He just had to trust someone. No one can go through life and hope to achieve anything on their own. Although Hollywood had produced countless examples of men, and sometimes women, single-handedly saving the world against incredible odds, the facts in the *real* world were that they would not stand a chance. Mark needed some help. And to get that help, he had to trust someone.

Dusty he could trust—they had been to hell and back on more than one occasion, and his trust in him was absolute. Mark was as certain as he could be that he could trust Owen. He had only briefly caught the gist of how the little Welshman had ended up where he was, and as he was, and that was enough for Mark. Especially since their near-death experience where, without Owen coming to their rescue, both Mark and Dusty would be consigned to history. For all his faults, Mark believed that he could trust Del—trust him to tell all to his minders back in Washington. He was only doing his job, and that did not have room for anything underhand. In any case, Del was now out of the picture. So that left Mark with just two people who he could call friends on this side of the world.

Then there was his father, Harold.

Basically, Harold was a good man whom everyone seemed to trust.

But what had happened?

Just because his son was on a covert mission, the plans for which had originated in Harold Taylor's own office, surely did not mean that Harold would relinquish any of his prior responsibilities to the people of the United States. If his son messed up, then he deserved to be cast adrift. However, had Harold let his dick get in the way? On balance, given the circumstances, his father would recover from his temporary dalliance, and normal service would resume. Yes, he could trust his father to do the right thing. But did he understand the exigencies of the service that occurred to men in the field? Harold had never been a soldier. He had always been tied up with deceit and lies, thinking of the greater good, oblivious to the short-term pain and anguish that occurred to those charged with making things happen.

That left Mark's other sponsor—Karen Marshall of the DEA. That must be some woman! To have dragged no less a person than Harold Taylor into her bed! If she was the instigator of such a move, then she must have been an extremely frustrated, or an extremely persuasive, woman. If Harold was the instigator, then he must have regarded Karen as an extremely attractive lady, and Harold must have been well and truly smitten.

What did that tell Mark?

It told him nothing.

He could speculate that Ms Marshall was resourceful—she would need to be just to have survived in an administration dominated by men. To have reached the level as the head of the intelligence division, she had probably trodden on the toes of a few contenders; but that was par for the course in the bureaucratic jungle that was Washington. But in order to have the trust of people like Mark Taylor, with many years of experience dangling on the end of threads of intelligence that dribbled down to the peasants, you had to earn it. Was the involvement of Karen Marshall just a ploy to try to impress Harold Taylor? Had she, in fact just built another house of cards that would tumble down at the slightest whiff of wind? And then what would be Karen's reaction? A shrug of the shoulders: 'It would have been nice if it had worked out differently. Now what should we have for dessert?' No, Mark had no reason to trust Karen Marshall. It could be for the quite simple reason that he had not met her. It could be that she must be one hard bitch! Perhaps dedicated to the job, to the extent that collateral damage was just the price that had to be paid.

Mark thought back to where this had all started, and with their visit to Fort Bragg. There they were all buddies and excited by the adventure of travelling overseas to play hide-and-seek in a foreign land.

Now it was a vastly different story.

Now it had become very personal.

The attempt to silence Mark and his friends was a serious risk that someone had taken. Mark had only theories as to how that had all eventuated. He had his suspicions. Now someone had decided to involve Debbie.

Sure, it was not an entirely dissimilar situation than that which involved Harold and Karen. It was a matter affecting relationships between a man and a woman. But Debbie was nothing to do with these people or the games that they played. She had become involved solely by being identified as Mark's weakest link. And once again, Mark faced the prospect of having someone that he loved paying the ultimate price for his involvement in a situation that was not of his making.

Mark needed to get back to the United States and get some more of his friends from an earlier life involved in the game—people that he had trusted with his life, and people that he knew he could trust now. The juggernauts that were the Central Intelligence Agency and the Drug Enforcement Administration could not cope with this problem. The people who had used their position of trust for their own gains would not be able to cope with the intense pressure that would be applied by the people Mark had in mind.

'OK. Here is what we plan to do.'

After half an hour, Dusty Miller was beginning to smile again.

Chapter 46

Friends

It was becoming something of a habit when Mark flew into Dulles International Airport, twenty-five miles to the west of downtown Washington DC. Well, the last time Mark had flown into Washington, he had come courtesy of the CIA, and then they had flown him into the Andrews Air Force Base. With the benefit of hindsight, Mark should have on that previous occasion flown directly into New York and rapidly got to the bottom of that whole sorry affair before it blew up in his face.

But that was history. He could not change anything then.

Hindsight is a wonderful thing that solves nothing.

Now there was just no point in flying into New York. There was apparently no Debbie to be found, and all the action that needed to take place would occur down here in Washington DC. This was where the CIA had its headquarters at Langley. This was where all the players would gather. This was where the matter would be settled one way or the other.

Mark had to have information, and that information would likely be found in Peshawar. Dusty was, first, Mark's best friend. But Dusty was a lawyer, not a detective. And while Debbie was critically important to Mark, his background and training drove him to a series of clinical decisions. He had to use what resources he had to the maximum. He would not be distracted. He would just have to manage several problems at once, and that meant he needed friends.

Giving Griz the slip had been the easy part. Mark had appeared to relent on his earlier comment that he would abandon the trail, and he had set out to track the CIA Gulfstream that was still sitting at the southern end of the Peshawar airport. Then he had quite simply walked from there to the International Terminal and boarded an Emirates commercial flight to Dubai. Having a healthy bank account always helped. He took the risk that he would be spotted but relied on a couple of simple facts. Firstly, the CIA could not be everywhere. And secondly, the relationship between the CIA and the Pakistan ISI was hardly cordial, meaning that even if he was spotted by an ISI agent, that piece of information would be unlikely to filter through.

After his arrival at Dubai, Mark was so impressed with the service that he had received that he stayed with that airline and flew non-stop all the way to Dulles. There would be no stopping off anywhere on this trip irrespective of what he had inferred in his discussions with Griz.

Now for the hard part.

His arrival at Dulles was a grind. All international travel post 9/11 is a problem for all passengers, especially for someone arriving from a place like Afghanistan on a commercial flight, while there was no actual record of their having left the country in the first place. However, it was unusual to be under scrutiny before reaching immigration control. Mark knew he was in trouble as he walked through the concourse. Most people would not notice, but then most people had not had the same intensive training as Mark. There were the usual immigration, police, and customs officers dotted among the crowd looking for heaven knows what or who. But Mark felt that some of them were looking for a specific person, and from their body language, he suspected that he knew who they were looking for.

They were looking Mark Taylor.

It was not like the tricky situation that he had been in, trying to follow one man in a foreign land, in unfamiliar surroundings, with scarce resources. Now he was in Washington, the capital of the land of the free—where there were countless resources. But he thought that the advantage now was his. He was now the one being observed and followed. Tails could be lost. Not that it really mattered.

The passport control let him through without too much drama. His passport had been issued in Peshawar to replace the one that was presumably now sitting in a lost property box either in an Afghan hotel or in the US Embassy in Kabul, or in the hands of the Russians, depending on whoever had bothered to collect their belongings. The officer at the gate spent longer than normal perusing a largely vacant document and used the time to signal to someone waiting inside the gate that their 'target' had arrived. After all he had been through, Mark could only smile at the amateurish way this latest event had unfolded.

Mark viewed the guy through the chaos that was typical of an airport arrival gate. Body language was all that Mark needed. And he got it: the sudden increased awareness after a long day staring at an endless sea of faces. The guy was in an unfamiliar environment, and it showed. He stood out from the customs and immigration staff. They knew what they were about and made no secret of the fact that they were on the lookout for felons or drugs. This guy was possibly CIA, probably FBI.

Mark wandered into the duty-free area and purchased a low-end laptop computer. It would have enough power to get by until he could get his hands on something more in line with what he needed.

After retrieving his bag from the Baggage Claim area, Mark was politely requested to submit to a personal search while the customs officer searched his bag. They did not find anything of interest, much to the amusement of the customs staff, until they came across his sat phone. That revealed nothing. Then they checked his new laptop. That also revealed nothing. The customs officer signalled to one of his buddies, who came across and took both electronic gadgets away 'This won't take long.' Mark smiled politely and waited.

He smiled again when they were returned. The observing officer, who had now been joined by two of his undercover colleagues, were deep in conversation. Then they nodded in unison and then looked across the hall towards where Mark waited. Mark collected his things together, thanked the customs officer, and turned to nod towards the observer. They could do nothing about that. Mark was free to go.

In the circumstances, Mark now had little choice. Someone was on to him, and he was just too tired to play their games. At least for now. He took the next available cab off the rank and gave the driver specific instructions. The cab driver did not complain when Mark threw a fifty-dollar note in his direction and said to 'keep the change.' The nearest hotel was less than a mile away. Far less if the passenger had chosen to walk. Mark smiled as the people following him panicked and split up.

While two of the men went to retrieve their black SUV, the other one piled into the following cab. Mark smiled as he envisaged the scene.

Follow that cab, and don't lose it!'

Instructions delivered with all the arrogance of the FBI's man on a mission. He had a radio clamped to his mouth, and he was talking non-stop and waving at no one. As the cab stopped to slip the driver's card through the reader, Mark observed the guy in the following cab was on the driver-side rear passenger seat and was looking out of the rear window, trying to find his friends in the chaotic traffic which was typical of any airport in the world. Mark quickly tossed the driver another fifty and exited the cab from the passenger side, tumbling onto the ground with his bag. From there, he crawled behind the station and watched as his cab and the following two vehicles sped off into the night.

Mark walked the rest of the way to the hotel.

Once safely installed in his hotel, out of a sense of duty, Mark first called his father. The call went to an answering service, not that he had very much to say in any case. And he did not tell him in his message that he was back in Washington. That is the beauty of satellite telephones.

'Hi, Dad! Just thought I would give you a heads-up on what we are up to. Call me back when you have the time.

In the morning, your time will do fine,' was the message that Mark left with Harold.

Talking to Harold Taylor was not that important, and it was 11:30 pm so Harold was either asleep or otherwise occupied.

Mark next called Brad Morgan on Brad's mobile phone. This time he got through. And this time he revealed where he was. Mark apologized for calling him so late in the evening, but Brad did not seem to mind. Probably because Brad felt partly responsible for whatever had happened to his boss's partner. Partly because Brad was very much awake. He had very definite plans for the rest of the evening. And those plans did not involve anything to do Taylor Software.

'You're in Washington? When did you get back?' were the first two questions that Brad asked.

'Just flown in. Have you heard anything about Debbie?'

The tension was very evident in Mark's voice. The answer was expected, but he had to ask.

No - *How are things at the office?*

The boss had other things on his mind, and Brad was smart enough to recognize the signs.

Brad answered with the simple truth.

'We have not heard anything at all. The FBI says they will handle it and are making reassuring noises about how good they are, but nothing so far. Do you want me to check? I can do that!'

'What's the point?' Mark replied in his cold, clinical style; and Brad knew then that his boss was on the warpath.

'I suspect that I know who is holding her. And why. So, we have some work to do.'

There was a pregnant pause while he let that sink in.

'OK!' Mark continued. 'I have a problem that I need

to get sorted. And I am being followed, probably by the CIA. Maybe the FBI as well. Could you spare a couple of days to join me in Washington? But be aware that you may be followed too. Don't trust anyone!'

That just about summed up the situation. A cold chill crept up Brad's spine. Mark was not the least bit concerned about how things were going at Taylor Software, despite having left Brad in charge. And Brad was rather pleased with his temporary promotion and his performance in the role of boss.

From Mark's attitude, it was obvious that his company, for all the years of dedication, could go to hell. Mark needed resources, and resources he could trust, and he needed them now. Fortunately, Brad had a sixth sense, and although he had never quite returned to his much earlier role of barely speaking, he could quickly sum up a situation. The less he said now, so much the better.

The boss had asked, 'Could you ...,' but Brad knew from the tone of Mark's voice that he really did not have a choice. And he also cared about Debbie, who he assumed would be the focus of Mark's attention.

'Where do I find you?' was all that Brad asked.

'I am at the Holiday Inn by Dulles Airport, just for the night. How soon can you get here?'

Brad managed to keep his voice level.

'You want me to leave *now*?'

Mark's reply was level, and cold.

'You got anything else to do?'

Now that was tricky. And it depended on interpretation.

Brad was young and fit, with all the natural instincts of a single and horny adult male. And he had very definite plans for this evening.

So far in their relationship, Shania had not responded quite as positively and enthusiastically to his overtures as he would have expected. If the truth be known, Brad was shy, and so was Shania, but someone had to make the first move. But what move? And how to make that move without the earth-shattering risk of rejection? But she was at this very moment nestled in his arm, apparently waiting, expectantly, for—well, he did not know what.

He looked down at the shapely legs which were barely covered by the short skirt, threatening to, but not quite, reach over his. Her blouse revealed much more of her breasts from his angle than she probably realized. And when she moved, just for an instant, he could almost see her nipples. She was a very seductive, beautiful, and intoxicating woman! And maybe this was the night when he would finally break through his own reluctance and make that one small move that would turn his desire into action.

It was driving him insane!

Brad sighed.

'OK, I am on my way.'

'And, Brad, bring a couple of satellite phones and a couple of laptops. You know the kind of stuff I need.'

Mark terminated the call, not knowing the frustration that he had caused. And not knowing that he was setting in motion a string of events that would cause that frustration to come to an unexpected end.

Mark had to think long and hard before he made his next move. He did not know who he could trust, or, more correctly, who he could not trust. But it was important that he know where Stephen Rodriguez was now.

Reluctantly, he decided to call Owen on his satellite phone.

'Hi, Owen. How's it going?'

Owen sounded quite pleased to hear Mark's voice.

'Mark! It is all good. More importantly, how are you and Dusty?'

The latter question posed a very real problem. Dusty was still in Peshawar with instructions to only contact Owen as a last resort. It looked as though Dusty had not exercised that option.'

'Fine. Thanks to you!' was Mark's non-committal response. 'Could you just tell me whether Stephen Rodriguez has left?'

There was a pregnant pause before Owen replied. Then Owen almost whispered his reply.

'Leaves Peshawar in two days,' and then his voice returned to normal. 'Found out this morning. Sorry about the cloak-and-dagger stuff.'

Owen did not elaborate.

Mark said thanks and disconnected the call.

The next thing that Mark had to do was to find somebody else who he could trust to do a couple of special jobs. For those jobs, it did not matter whether the people were nice guys, or they were ruffians. He just had to absolutely rely on them to get the job done, quickly and efficiently, without complicating things by asking too many questions. They should be single and have no hang-ups about taking a few days off from their normal routine to get things sorted out. And no hang-ups about taking risks and tweaking the tails of people in power.

Mark knew of such people.

Just because such men had many years of experience in the United States Special Forces did not mean that they were necessarily angels. It is a tough life in military service, in which you can expect to witness some pretty horrible things that men can do to their fellow men, and women, and even children. The problem is that such people often cannot intervene in many situations that they are a witness to for fear of compromising their position, compromising the safety of their colleagues, or of compromising their mission. They often must stay hidden, grit their teeth, and hope that someday they will meet the vermin at some place where they are alone, and then they can vent the anger and the rage that is pent up inside.

But that rarely, if ever, happens. The pain and anger stay inside, never to be released.

Consequently, it should come as no surprise that people who have served in the Special Forces often have difficulty integrating back into the society that they had dedicated their lives trying to protect. Especially one in which people tend to write off the Armed Services as dedicated big boys playing silly little games. It is not at all like that, but they can rarely provide the proof of their commitment to an ill-informed public. In the worst-case scenario, some military personnel completely lose the plot while trying to adjust back into a more normal society and turn to drugs or alcohol as a means of escape. In most cases, they do adjust, but it would still not be a good idea to rile them up. If you do, and they have a reason to dislike you, they could do you some real damage that may seem to be totally out of proportion to your understanding of the situation.

Such men can be extremely dangerous if provoked.

Such men can make lifetime friends of people with whom they share mutual respect and trust.

'Hello,' was all the voice said in response to Mark's call.
'Hi, it's Mark Taylor.'

There was a long pause before the man spoke. 'I might have known it was someone like you!' The man laughed. 'How the hell are you, Major? Where the hell are you?'

Mark also laughed. It had been over five years since he had last spoken face-to-face with Blake Whittaker. They had kept in touch by infrequent e-mails, but that was just not the same thing. Blake spoke as though it was yesterday.

Whittaker was an ex-sergeant, and he still carried himself with the same brutal authority that he had two years before when Uncle Sam had decided that he was just too old for any more missions overseas. Blake had an Afro-American father and a Mexican mother. That made for a strong, laid-back personality tempered with the fire and humour of the Latino. He had been offered a job in the training division, and in that role, his vast experience would have been more than useful to the US Army. But he had declined that offer. He would have expected too much from the trainees—they would have one hell of a time in the hard grind of Fort Bragg without the additional worry of having to put up with a sergeant whose sole aim seemed to be to break them. He was like his father had been before him—the kind that stressed, 'If you aren't moving, you'd better be dead!'

Blake now had another mission. That was to look after his twin daughters, who had escaped the inferno that had engulfed their family SUV in a car crash that killed his beautiful wife and left their two girls without a mother. The drug dealer who had run a red light trying to get away from the police and who had been responsible for the crash was in jail. And that was about the safest place that he could be. If, or when, the drug dealer returned to the community, he would need to deal with Blake Whittaker.

'I am OK. Sorry to call you at such a late hour,' Mark

eased into the conversation. 'I need some help in sorting out a few people here in Washington. You up for it?'

'Sure. How many men do you need, and when?'

Blake was all business. He trusted Mark, so there was no point in his asking for any details, at least at this stage in their conversation. Mark had already said quite enough. *'Sorting out people'* meant they were not your run-of-the-mill petty criminals. *'In Washington'* meant that they were serious players. Mark was not a hoodlum. So, someone had obviously really made him angry. And that was good enough for Blake.

For Mark, the *'When?'* was the easy part of the question. Mark had to think about the *'How many?'* Too few people and the job would become impossible to carry out, as he had recently experienced in Afghanistan. Too many people and the job would become both unmanageable and equally impossible. Whatever the number of men he had at his disposal, security was paramount. Mark had to be able to trust each one to do a specific job, to be able to see the bigger picture and to react accordingly. That is why he had called Blake. There was one man he would trust with his life. But what of the men that Blake would call, and at such short notice?

'My guess would be six,' Mark replied.

No need to spell out the need for absolute trust. Blake would be aware of that. Maybe a need to stress the kind of men that Mark had in mind, but that would also have been insensitive. Mark just had to hope that the people that Blake selected were still as good as they used to be, when they were in a man's world, crawling through the undergrowth, in some godforsaken place, covered in shit, not having washed for days, smelling awful, and loving every minute of it.

'As for the *when* does tomorrow present any problems?' Mark concluded.

'No,' was all the answer he got, and the answer he expected.

'OK. Call me back on this number when you are ready. I will arrange accommodation by then. All I need is numbers and first names. I am being followed—I think they are CIA or FBI—so you will need to be careful! I think I lost the tail at Dulles, but it should not take them too long to figure out what happened, and to be back on my tail. It would help if the men that you have in mind are armed, but you can let me know of anything they may need when they are organised, and I can fix that.'

Blake's curiosity got the better of him.

'Are you planning on starting a war?'

Mark had to laugh.

'I did ask if you were up for it!'

Mark realized that he would need to get some sleep. He was dog-tired from the travel and the worry but drove himself to keep going. There were a few more things that had to be done first.

He had declined the first two rooms that had been offered by the ever-helpful concierge just in case his tails had a *special* room which they used for travellers of his kind. The polite young lady was not the least bit fazed by this awkward and shy customer, which gave Mark some confidence that the CIA had not prearranged anything. Not that it really mattered. They could bug as many rooms as they liked. By morning, he would be gone. He had little doubt that they would eventually track him down. In the meantime, they could try to follow, observe, and listen. It would not do them much good.

Mark logged on to the Internet to find the type of longer-term accommodation that he was looking for. After all, he could hardly mount an operation of the kind that he envisaged from the Holiday Inn. He may have done so, but the various comings and goings that his plan entailed would certainly raise some eyebrows among the law-abiding citizens in the fair city of Washington DC. And that would not be a particularly good idea.

He needed this operation to be kept out of the public eye. He needed a small group of apartments with secure access and egress somewhere close to centre of the city. For the brief time that he needed them, that could be difficult. But not impossible for the right amount of money. And why should Mark worry about that? He had plenty of funds at his disposal.

Nonetheless, he would expect to get reimbursed and thanked by a grateful, if reluctant, government.

Well, at least he would get reimbursed. His, father through the office of the OIG, or the DEA, would be picking up this tab, even though Mark's immediate plan had extraordinarily little to do with the Government.

Mark located a place that was available on the west bank of the Potomac and rang the agent. Calling some people after midnight may seem a little unreasonable. Mark had expected the call to go to the answerphone. Instead, he had to explain his late call to a confused but receptive agent. The conversation calmed a little further when Mark mentioned money. They agreed to meet at 6:30 am later that same morning.

Now he could get some sleep.

But would he?

His mind raged through the plans as he fought to calm down. Where was Debbie? Unlike many people who would have gone raging about like chooks with their heads chopped off, Mark had every confidence that the FBI would eventually find her. Would they be too late? Mark, on his own, could do no better. But he still worried.

Had Stephen Rodriguez or his cronies taken her, or

was she just a victim of a random crime, never to be seen again? Logic said no, this was not a random event. Don't believe in coincidence! But also, never make assumptions! He tried to placate his raging thoughts with confidence that Debbie would be safe, at least until Stephen Rodriguez was back in Washington. And before that happened, Mark planned a little mission of his own. It was nonetheless a worry as the arguments whirled around in circles, spiralling out of control.

He felt that sleep would just not come.

Mark awoke in panic at the ringing of the alarm.

It was five thirty in the morning.

It was time to go and implement the next stage of his plan.

Mark immediately checked out of the Holiday Inn. Being so close to Dulles Airport, it was not unusual to be checking out so early in the morning. He initially thought of paying in cash to avoid the inevitable audit trail that would stem from using his credit card, but what the hell. By the time anyone traced his credit card transactions, and his movements, it would be all over anyway. That was assuming that someone was the least bit interested in where Mark Taylor went and what he spent his money on.

Mark took another cab and was amused to see that his escorts had finally figured out what had happened the night before. They duly resumed following their target. This time they had a couple of black SUVs. At least that was what was visible, but there may have been others. Mark smiled as they weaved through the traffic. He was about to ask the cabbie to give them the shake, but he then thought better of it. All in good time. He would lose his tail anyway.

Mark got to the west bank of the Potomac before the

morning traffic got too snarled up and paid the cab fare. He was pleased to see that the agent that he had arranged to meet had also arrived on time. It was bitterly cold, but Mark declined the invitation to step into the building that he had arranged to see. Instead, the two men sat on a bench in the middle of a park. The wind howled around them, making any chance of anyone overhearing their conversation improbable. After a discussion about the layout of the inside of the property, and a more studied examination of the outside, a deal was struck.

A temporary three-month lease was all that was needed, with a clause for automatic rollover—both conditions to suit the agent. It was a little overboard for less than a week's occupancy, but why the hell should Mark care? His father would need to arrange for reimbursement, if for no other reason than to avoid embarrassment.

The agent left with a clear warning ringing in his ears.

'I will not care in a few days, but meanwhile, if someone asks you what we have just arranged, say nothing.'

'Who are you talking about? Why should anyone ask?'

Mark smiled.

'I am just speculating. If someone asks, that is all. You may not have noticed a couple of black SUVs parked by the roadside. The passengers would be extremely interested in what we were discussing. If asked, you should say that nothing was decided. And be a good fellow —it is important that you do not mention the building we were discussing. You can do that, can't you?'

Their eyes locked. Mark's expression had gone from that of a shy, good-natured human being, to that of a cold, calculating, ruthless killer.

'The keys are with the building manager. I will call him and authorize the pickup.' The frightened agent nodded and left.

Mark waited patiently while the four people stationed around the park decided who should follow the agent. That decided, the remaining three set themselves in typical covert situations and positions. It was classic, straight out of the textbook as had been taught at the Farm or at Quantico. Mark called the agent on his mobile phone and simply described the guy that he would meet shortly and repeated his instruction to say nothing. And added one further instruction: 'Delete this message, now!'

Mark got up and walked down to the banks of the Potomac and stared out across the languid grey waters.

Where was Debbie?

Sure, he was setting up a plan on the assumption that Stephen Rodriguez had somehow got her into his clutches. But what if it was nothing to do with Rodriguez? Tears welled in his eyes. Tears of sheer frustration. He clenched his jaw as he fought back the tears. He had to go on and trust his instincts.

His synchronized followers moved as one to adjust their positions so that they all had a clear uninterrupted view of their target as Mark slowly walked back up towards the road. He then crossed it and strolled along, moving away from the apartments that he had just leased. He waited until the traffic was particularly congested and then flagged down a cab. The instructions he gave to the driver were simple: Get me into that apartment complex in the shortest possible time. That the cab driver did while the following entourage panicked and lost sight of their target.

The apartment turned out to be ideal for the purpose. Mark's next job was to call a rental firm to get some temporary furnishings. That was also not so hard. There are some very shrewd operators in the furniture hiring business, and again, money rules. Within two hours of Mark's arrival, he had what he wanted—living accommodation for up to ten people, both male and female, and a set of rooms that could very easily be used as a prison. He just needed to change the locks so that in one of the rooms, the doors and windows could not be opened from the inside.

Now, all that he needed was people.

The first person to arrive was Brad Morgan. Not that, that was quite as easy as it may have been. The cellular phone rang shortly after Mark had shaken hands with the furniture delivery guy and sent him on his way.

The conversation with Brad was terse for a while. Maybe they were both just tired. Maybe Mark did not expect Shania to have accompanied Brad to Washington. Mark took some convincing before he finally agreed to let Shania in. On the negative side, she was FBI—she had only recently informed Brad of this piece of useful information, although Mark had known and not wanted to spoil a relationship for all the wrong reasons. On the positive side, Mark had met her, had read all the signals, and she was OK. She would not know all the finer details of the plan, so on balance, she could be useful. If she knew all the plans and went along with them, then she may need to start looking for another job and another employer.

Shania was able to confirm that there was no scheduled task at the FBI's Washington office to seek anyone fitting Mark's description, so he had been correct in his original assessment that it was the CIA who had been following him. That made her involvement more palatable. Shania was also streetwise when it came to surveillance and countersurveillance techniques.

However, the deciding and overriding point was that

Shania had been heavily involved in the efforts to find Debbie. Mark also knew that she cared. Not the most convincing of reasons, but even Mark was allowed some deviance from his regimented plans where Debbie was involved. It really came down to his ever-reliable ability to read body language. And that applied to both Shania and Brad.

Mark sent the pair of them out to do some shopping —Brad to get locks and other hardware, including some burner cells, Shania to get some linen and food.

The next person to arrive at the complex was Blake. And he was alone.

Blake was a man who had an infectious grin that belied the dour man and the serious thinker that hid behind it. He was short and stocky, a little under five feet nine and 180 pounds. His head was shaved, and the muscles rippled across his body despite the passage of time since he had been in uniform. He had kept in shape in mind and body.

Blake remained silent while Mark outlined what he had in mind. Apart from the occasional grunt in either agreement or dissent, there was just no way of knowing. He just sat there, his eyes never wavering. Eventually, after Mark had finished, Blake spoke.

'I could only find four men who I can rely on. Others are around, but it is not worth the risk,' he concluded with a shrug.

Mark did not look disappointed.

'That's fine. Better to be one short than risk compromising the operation! I could get Elliott Shannon to make up the numbers—if we can get him.'

Mark had trusted Elliott in the past, and if he knew of a man who would not let Stephen Rodriguez off the hook, it was that likable ex-CIA Irishman.

Blake did not say either Yes or No, but body language said he was OK with that part of the plan. Blake did not know Elliott, but Mark did, and it was Mark's plan. And Mark was the officer!

'So, what do you think? The plan is not perfect, but with limited resources and time, it could work!' Mark eventually speculated.

It was like having a conversation with Dusty. Like Dusty, Blake was an ex-sergeant, and as a breed, they tended to converse in the same symbolic grunts—the difference between agreeing and disagreeing being in only the raising or not raising of an eyebrow. Eventually, Blake spoke again.

'It does not have to be perfect to be the best. It is simple, and that counts. So yes, I think it could work. But I have a few ideas that could help. You want to hear them?'

Mark just nodded. Blake was never one to waste his or anyone else's time on trivia.

'I have been doing some work for a friend in the dirty tricks department at the FBI. And the CIA is involved as well. We are working with a professor of anaesthesiology at Georgetown University Hospital. You want to hear what we came up with?'

Mark again nodded in agreement. It seemed to be Blake's preferred method of communication. And Blake would not have raised the matter if he did not think it was relevant.

'We have been experimenting with a drug called cyclopentolate. You may have heard of the drug—it is commonly used by pediatric surgeons for eye examinations and operations. Delivered in small doses, it just makes the eyes more sensitive to light, and images get blurred for a short time. Apart from those effects, it is relatively harmless.

In slightly larger concentrations, it can render someone virtually paralyzed for a brief time. Again, they would be otherwise unharmed, and that is why the FBI and others are interested. The initial problem that we had to overcome was the time that it takes to have an effect—around thirty minutes. If we could get around this problem and turn it into an aerosol formula, then we have something better than, say, Mace or pepper spray. Mace is a tear gas that irritates the eyes. It is next to useless especially against drug addicts and the like—they are just too spaced out already. So, we now have something under development based on cyclopentolate, which is instantly effective against anybody. Would something like that be useful?'

'What about other side effects?' was the obvious question that Mark had. Yes, he was interested. But that interest would wane rapidly if there were serious side effects. The plan was not to start the World War that Blake had alluded to earlier.

'And there is also the question of traceability,' Mark added as an afterthought.

Blake merely looked at Mark for an instant in frustration. And then he relaxed. He had been through all that with the nutty Professor, and so had the FBI, CIA, and everyone else who had become involved in the project. Here they were— developing something that could revolutionize crime-fighting, and the scientists and crime-fighters involved were more concerned with the side effects! The side effects would be felt by violent criminals, so who really gave a rat's ass about what other effects it had, good or bad! And the Food and Drug Administration would never know of the drug's existence. And neither would the criminals.

From his arguments with the professor, Blake, in fact, had the answer.

'The side effects of a drug like cyclopentolate are rare,' Blake explained. 'Apart from the victim appearing slightly drunk—incoherent speech, blurred eyesight, disorientation, loss of balance—there is nothing of any real concern. We don't expect anything but the same from the aerosol spray. The only significant difference is the reaction time. That is virtually instantaneous.'

'OK,' said Mark. 'What about traces of the drug that are left behind? And if we used it, could someone trace the drug back to you?'

Blake was more confident as he replied.

'We think that the drug would be extremely hard to trace, for the simple reason that the people that it is intended to be used on would already have similar symptoms: incoherent, blurry-eyed, and so on. Would anyone be looking for another drug? I don't think so. As for my involvement, do you really care?'

Blake realized that he had gone too far and held up his hands in supplication before Mark had the time to react.

'OK, I know it matters, but trust me, there is no way it could be traced back to you. In any case, there are so few people who know of this development and its application that it would be an awfully long shot. Anyone looking at a victim would be looking for known drugs and their normal method of delivery. By the time they had figured out what had happened, all trace would be long gone.'

It was Mark's turn to relax. No, Mark did not really care, for the two quite simple reasons that Blake could take care of himself. If this drug helped to get Debbie back, Mark could handle any consequences.

With what Mark had in mind, as a plan began to develop, a drug of this kind could make things a whole lot easier!

Blake knew that he had Mark's interest. He could see the massive advantages of the work he was doing, and what better than to test it in a live situation?

'You want to hear about another drug we have been working on?'

Since Blake would not have asked if he did not think it relevant, Mark again nodded.

'This one is based on a common drug—polyethylene glycol, which is used for clearing out people who are going to have surgery on the stomach or the bowel. It is a powerful form of laxative. It is also used prior to having things like a colonoscopy. We are testing a version that acts a little bit quicker than the normal dosage.' Blake grinned.

'You are saying that you are going to give people something that makes them shit?' Mark laughed in response. He needed something to relieve the pressure he was under.

'Think about it!' said Blake. 'If someone has, and I mean really has, to go to the toilet, they are not going to be a problem for quite a while, are they?'

They both ended up clutching their sides, tears of laughter pouring down their faces. Then they got serious.

They were as prepared as they could be, except that Mark needed one more man. Battling against the weight of the CIA, even if all twenty thousand plus of their employees were not on the same side, and the potential of thirty-four-odd thousands of the FBI, less at least Shania, Mark had to even up the odds somehow. A small band could often outwit a much larger and more cumbersome organization. What they lacked in size and resources, they made up for with their flexibility. And they had at least one advantage: they knew how the larger organization would react.

He called Elliott Shannon on his mobile phone.

'Hi, Elliott, it's Mark Taylor. You may remember me from a couple of months ago?'

The Irishman laughed.

'I wouldn't be forgetting that little episode now, would I? What are you up to now? Still fighting against the system, are we?'

'Dusty and I have just been on a trip to Pakistan and Afghanistan following a friend of yours,' Mark began. 'It turned out to be all that we expected it would be. Now there are some loose ends that need tidying up.'

'Who was my friend?'

Mark told him—just enough to get him fired up.

'OK, I'm on my way. I am in Washington now, down at the marina having my boat serviced. I can be with you in a couple of hours. Just tell me where to go, and I'll see you this afternoon.'

Now they were ready—or at least Mark hoped so.

The plan that Mark had was based on one key element. They were up against the CIA and their colleagues in other divisions of the United States Government. Consequently, the odds were numerically massively stacked against Mark and his small team. But that was Mark's key advantage. When you are a member of a small team on the outside, you are infinitely more maneuverable. And you do not have a procedure manual to trip over. For all their so-called efficiency, the CIA would be slow, making sure that the right people were kept in the loop, and would be forever referring to procedures and rules. And making sure that each one covered their ass should something go wrong.

A small team with the experience that Mark, and the

others brought with them would know exactly what the CIA would, and could, do. And more importantly, they would know what they would not and could not do. The team that Mark was assembling had no rules and could react quickly and proactively to any situation. The CIA could not anticipate what they would do in any given situation, and the CIA would therefore be reactive rather than proactive.

There was also the element of surprise. The bureaucracy expected people to play by some rules or norms, so they were forever profiling their opponents. Such profiling often eliminated certain forms of action as just too preposterous.

There was then only one slight problem.

Stephen Rodriguez, as the growing evidence indicated, was not exactly following the rules either.

Chapter 47

Re-insurance

The black Chevrolet Camaro convertible pulled out of the driveway and turned right. It was bitterly cold in Washington at this time of the year. There was a hint of rain, or even snow, so the hood was in place, and the heater was on. It was late afternoon, and probably the best time of the day to pick up a few things from the supermarket.

As the Camaro pulled out into the traffic, a black Cadillac, also a product of General Motors, with two men inside, eased away from its position one hundred or so yards farther down the road. They took up station at a reasonable distance behind the Chevy. Across the road, a nondescript grey Ford SUV did a rapid U-turn and followed the two vehicles at a more discreet distance.

The driver of the Chevrolet Camaro was a lady called Dayanara. She was a Puerto Rican by birth and had all the Latin and Hispanic fire in her belly that was typical of the people from that country. On her five-feet-nothing frame, she still retained her trim figure and black hair, and although her face was lined with wrinkles that even her expertly applied makeup could not hide, she still took pleasure in the heads that turned her way. The name *Dayanara* had a meaning: it meant 'husband slayer.' That description could have meant something romantic. But it did not. A more correct translation of the name would have been 'husband destroyer.' Now that was a bit of a laugh.

Dayanara had been married for twenty-seven years to one man, and a man that she still loved, despite all the pressures of life in today's world, and the somewhat negative and remote attitude that he had recently displayed towards her and their family. Dayanara and her husband had two beautiful daughters. One of them, the eldest girl named Juanita, was away in Africa tending to the poor and the needy. The other girl, who was two years younger than her sister, named Estefania, was a law student at George Washington University Law School. It was your normal family—part of it trying to save the world, part of it caught up in the rat race.

Her husband was basically a good man. And he did not have an easy job to do, working all hours and in various parts of the world, never knowing when, or *whether*, he would be home. At the constant beck and call of his political and other masters.

Dayanara had got used to it, and she accepted it.

Her second and married name was *Rodriguez*.

Being married to Stephen Rodriguez had its issues, but it was better than the life enjoyed by most of the people from Puerto Rico who were trying to scrape a living in the United States—the land of the free, the land of opportunity. But recently, something had changed—or rather, Stephen had changed. And now Dayanara was worried. Her attempts to discuss the matter with him had become lost in the myriad of issues, only some of them related to work, that men use to avoid such confrontations. And the time would come, sooner rather than later, when Dayanara and Stephen would need to make a choice. With the constant scrutiny that people in their position had to put up with in this city, you could only take so much. Meanwhile, there was a life to live, and you carried on as normally as was possible.

The rules for the protection of senior officers of the CIA and their families were quite straightforward. The lower down the scale you were, the less VIP protection you got. At the highest level, the wives or husbands got some protection usually depending on the attitude of the spouse concerned. Dayanara's attitude was *Do whatever you think is appropriate. I have other things to worry about.* Consequently, there was a discreet form of protection provided to her around the clock.

The United States Secret Service, which was responsible for the protection and surveillance of Presidents and ex-Presidents, had an ambivalent view. There was probably little danger to most people in public office in Washington even in the post-9/11 era. They had received no actual threats, and the threat level, decided by some bureaucrat after perusal of intelligence reports, was at the low end of the scale.

However, there was another side to the question of surveillance, which was generally not made known to the people being *protected*. Someone needed to be sure that these VIPs were not passing information to the other side, so there was good reason to offer them protection, wasn't there? It served two purposes: one of which the VIPs were aware of, the other they would be mortified to learn about.

All this aside, the Secret Service had to show a presence, and they needed some live subjects to enable them to be trained for higher responsibilities. Basically, they needed someone who was live and mobile to 'protect' and hone their skills on, hoping that their more brutal skills would not be needed at this level.

Consequently, the Secret Service allocated three cars and six trainee secret service agents to the wife of the assistant deputy director of intelligence of the CIA to operate three eight-hour shifts, round the clock, seven days a week.

The young and raw agents themselves were enthusiastic when they started their shift. But by the time that their shift was ending, the mind-numbing boredom of the routine had them looking at their watches instead of concentrating on their task. It was just training, but who knows? One day it might be the President of the United States, or the First Lady, they were asked to protect. But right now, it was some Hispanic broad who did not seem to matter much, and who cared even less. She gave the impression that she could have been something of a player in her time, and she still had the looks and a body that would be welcome in the bed of any bored, lonely, and frustrated trainee.

The Chevy pulled off Montgomery Avenue, parked at the supermarket, and Dayanara skipped out and locked the car. She then turned and playfully waved to the guys in the black Cadillac. The driver and the passenger both cheerfully waved back.

Not the recommended move, but it was a training exercise, and no harm could come from it.

The grey Ford SUV cruised to a halt and parked right next to the Cadillac where the two agents inside had wound down the windows and were having a smoke. The two average-looking men got out of their SUV, and the Afro-American sprayed something from a small canister at the driver of the Cadillac. The driver's first move was duck, then to object. Then he saw the Glock 19 that was pointed at him. He turned to his partner for support, but his eyes could not focus. His partner was also looking down the barrel of a similar weapon—a Glock 26—from the other side of the car. The passenger opened his mouth to protest just as the spray hit his face. Suddenly, everything went blurred. They were both fed a small pill through their open mouths.

The two men holding the guns did not say anything. They just opened the car doors and reached over to the control panel to roll up the window and then closed the doors. Within seconds, the spray from the canister had the desired effect.

The Secret Service agents were anaesthetised, courtesy of a new drug that was still not released for widespread use by the security services of this fine country. The second drug would cause them some embarrassment when they recovered from the first.

Then the two average-looking men climbed back into their SUV, and it was just a matter of waiting.

There was no hurry.

Dayanara emerged from the supermarket laden down with packages, which she just threw into the back of her car, giving no more than a casual glance in the direction of her escort. All that she would have seen were the two agents apparently sleeping. They always did that! Dayanara laughed as she noted that the car did not follow her as she sped out of the parking area. She was not well versed in surveillance or countersurveillance techniques, so she did not notice the grey Ford that followed the Chevy back to the Rodriguez residence.

Once there, Dayanara pulled into the drive and drove straight into the garage. A black Cadillac cruised to a halt fifty or so yards down the road. A few moments later, the grey Ford SUV drove straight into the drive, and two men emerged. They were now dressed in FBI jackets.

They tapped on the door, and after a few moments, Dayanara opened it. The shock on her face was obvious. The taller of the two men smiled and held up his hands in a form of supplication. In one hand, he had an official-looking badge that looked suspiciously like an FBI badge.

'I do not want to alarm you, Mrs Rodriguez—this is only a precaution. We have had reports that an attempt to kidnap your husband is planned when he arrives back in the United States early tomorrow morning. We do not know where, and if you want my opinion, the authorities are overreacting. But we have our job to do and to make sure you are safe.' The man shrugged, and he continued to smile.

The second man took up the conversation.

'We want to stake out the house, just in case, and we would not want you to be placed in any danger. We would like you to gather a few things and come with us to a safe house, just as a precaution while we get this sorted.'

At first, Dayanara was suspicious.

'What about the people who are supposed to be watching me?' she said, indicating the Cadillac.

'They know all about this,' he answered.

He turned towards the car and exchanged a brief wave with the man sitting in the passenger seat. All Secret Service personnel and Secret Service wannabes dress and look the same. People usually focused their attention on the bulge from their shoulder holster rather than on their face.

'What about my daughters?' she asked next, the concern obvious in her voice.

The man nodded and again gave her a reassuring smile.

'Arrangements are being made to have Estefania placed in protective custody right now. We are trying to get tabs on Juanita—as you know, that is not so easy,' he said

with a reassuring smile and a laugh. 'She is so far away—
we think that she will be OK. But don't worry, our services
are everywhere, and we will protect her.'

The wife of Stephen Rodriguez was suitably
impressed. The gentlemen knew about her two daughters
and their names. Was there anything that they did not
know? And the man was so handsome!

Dayanara rushed inside and gathered a few things.
As she emerged through the door, she gave the keys of the
house to the surprised agent. He shrugged, locked the
door, and hurried off to join his colleague in the Ford. As
they reversed out of the drive, he again indicated the
Cadillac and simply said that they would stay by the house
until further assistance arrived.

Blake dropped the keys to the house in the
letterbox.

This was going to be a much easier job than they
had anticipated.

Estefania was a typical young student. Fiercely
independent and bullet-proof. Her classes were paused
for a break between semesters, but she still went to the
library for most of the day and studied. She was going to
be the best female criminal lawyer there ever was. That
meant that she had to study, find out where the United
States justice system was going wrong. Find out where the
justice system only occasionally got things right.
Like her sister Juanita, she was determined that the
under-privileged should get a better deal. However, she
did not see the point of working in the obscure back-
blocks in some equally obscure African country to achieve
that. The changes that were necessary had to be made to
the system in the capital of the country that prided itself
in giving all people the same chance as everyone else. Deal

to the cause, and the affects would take care of themselves. Except that the poor people of Puerto Rica seemed to be excluded from this grand principle. Her plan was simple. She would first make some money. And there was certainly plenty of money to be made in the practice of law. Then she would look at the world and fix the problems that it had created for itself!

She packed up her various papers and notes and returned the library books to the box. Estefania could just as easily have returned them to the shelf where she had got them from, but that was not the system. She smiled at the person on the desk and said good night. She had often thought of getting a part-time job working in the library, but the woman on the desk had put her off. She looked like a book—and a little-used one!

Estefania, on the other hand, was a beautiful young lady. She had inherited her stunning looks and wild spirit from her mother. She assumed that she had inherited her cunning and brains from her father. There was no need for her to wear any makeup. All the young men, who were supposed to be studying in the library as well, looked up as she passed and immediately thought of things far removed from the subject of their books. Except, perhaps, those who were studying biology.

Estefania did not live in the Rodriguez household. While she loved her mother, and respected, rather than loved, her father, she still wanted to be free. She rented an apartment which she shared with two other students: a tall and gangly Afro-American girl called Geraldine and a drop-dead gorgeous white male called Kelvin. It was a pity that Kelvin had turned out to be gay, but he was a good flatmate, a good cook, and a faithful friend.

On this evening, Estefania would have the apartment to herself, and so she would spend some time making and then eating lasagne, maybe watch some TV, and just enjoy the peace after a long day of study.

She got to her apartment and got as far as defrosting some meat before there was a knock on the door.

She checked the spyhole to see who her visitor was. The guy must have seen some movement because he held an FBI badge up for her to see through the spyhole. Must have something to do with the disappearance of one of the neighbours, although it would not take a rocket scientist to work out what had happened to him—try the bottom of the Potomac, and good riddance. She opened the door, and there were two of them. They both smiled and held up some form of identification that indicated that they were from the FBI. They looked harmless enough. But Estefania was a law student.

'What can I do for you?' was all she asked.

The question that the shorter of the two men asked in reply did not really answer her question.

'Are you Estefania Rodriguez?'

'Yes. What do you want?'

'Are you alone?' the man replied, still not answering her question.

She did not say anything while her mind battled with the confusion. Her original question of '*What do you want?*' seemed to have been ignored. That did not stop the smile on the face of the FBI agent. He just repeated the question, embellished a little.

'It is important that we talk to you, but first we have to know if you are alone. Otherwise, you can come downtown with us and talk there. It is your choice.' The smile was still there. The tone of his voice had changed. The eyes told a vastly different story.

It was not as she had envisaged for her first confrontation with the legal system, or those responsible for its implementation. The lawyers and other people in the legal profession that she had met so far did not have the highest regard for the people involved in law enforcement. And that was understandable. The law enforcement people were forever trying to prove that people brought to trial were guilty. On the other hand, the lawyers were forever trying to prove that they were innocent, even though they may not have been. In fact, they usually were guilty until a smart lawyer could prove otherwise, or plea bargain to settle for a slap on the wrist with a wet bus ticket. At the end of the day, both groups were just doing their jobs. On balance, it did not really matter who was proven right and who was proven wrong. There are plenty of 'alleged' criminals around, so shit happens! Bring on the next case! The only discernible difference was in their pay-packets. But still, lawyers always liked to win. Law enforcement officers did not like to lose.

Estefania shrugged. They were just doing their job. She stepped aside and invited them in. She was alone, and a little bit of intrigue could brighten her day. And they both seemed very polite and nice enough.

'What do you know of your father's work?' the smaller of the two guys asked.

'I don't know anything. He works for the Government. Is he in trouble?'

Again, the disarming smile. FBI agents were supposed to be arrogant and nasty son-of-bitch–type people, but these two men were anything but. In different circumstances, Estefania could be quite interested in either of the men. Neither of the two men was wearing any rings. If all the FBI guys were this good-looking, and this polite, maybe after graduation she should have a change of plan, and she should look to the FBI for a job!

The agent continued to smile.

'Not trouble! At least not of his own making. But he could be headed for trouble. There is just the threat that someone intends to do him some harm. That is why we already have your mother with us, in protective custody. We do not want to give anybody the opportunity to pressurise your father through his family. That is why we would like to take you in as well. Just as a precaution, you understand?'

That caused Estefania to giggle, which at first took the two apparent FBI agents by surprise. But then it all began to make sense.

'I don't think my father would give a shit! Oops! Sorry … I don't think he would care, especially about me. We are not exactly close.'

Again, the disarming smile.

The agent looked at Estefania for a moment, then took out his mobile phone and selected a number. She did not know who he was talking to, but after a couple of exchanges with whoever had been on the other end of the line, he finally said, 'Oh, hi. She wants to talk to her mother. OK. Just a moment, I'll put her on.' And then he handed the phone to Estefania. The phone was on speaker.

'It's your mother.'

'Hi, Mum. What is going on?'

Mother was quite calm.

'There is something I should have told you long ago, but I did not think that I could. But these guys say it is OK. Your father works for the CIA—in fact, he is fairly high up in the organisation.'

If that news was supposed to shatter the young girl's dreams, it failed.

'I know that! So, what trouble has he got himself into now?'

Kids are kids. While fathers typically spend years trying to cleverly hide things from their children, usually the kids have known all about the 'things' but find them just too plain boring to merit any mention. When Estefania answered the question that the FBI guy had asked about her father's work, she did not lie. She did not know what he did, and she could hardly have cared less. The CIA was just another one of Washington's boring bureaucracies. Estefania certainly did not believe all that claptrap on television that made heroes or villains out of them all.

'I am worried, is all! These guys are nice, but they haven't said much. They have staked out our home and are just waiting to see what happens. Your Dad is due home sometime tomorrow, and there may be some issue with his arrival, is all I know. Meanwhile, I have to stay here, and so should you.'

Dayanara sounded upset, but she was talking like all mothers do.

Estefania sighed. University was not due to start for some weeks, and she had nothing planned that could not wait awhile. 'OK, Mother. Where are you?'

Fortunately, she did not say that she did not know. Because it sounded important, she replied to the question.

'We are at a safe house,' and then added, 'The FBI knows where to bring you. Just pack a few clothes— enough for two or three days should be fine. And don't forget your toothbrush.'

And it was, again, as simple as that.

Ben Chapman got out of the Cadillac, put on a pair of plastic gloves, retrieved the keys from the letterbox. He then went up to the front door, which he opened and went inside the Rodriguez residence, closing the door behind him.

The driver of the Cadillac waited outside in the car. It was now completely dark, but you could never be too careful in suburbia, and they did not anticipate having that much time to achieve what they wanted to do. It was good that Dayanara had left them the keys because that would save time and largely prevent too much interest from nosy neighbours.

The expectation was that the gas that had been inflicted on the hapless Secret Service guys would last for about an hour. Unless the men were fit, in which case it would be less than an hour. And while the trainees may have been a little dumb, they were nonetheless supremely fit young men. They would presumably need to make a visit to the toilet, once or twice, which would slow them down somewhat; but they would nonetheless eventually be back on the job. Somewhat confused, somewhat drained, totally disoriented, but back on the job either in person or by their replacements. So, time was of the essence.

Chapman only needed to place a few listening devices in the various telephones that were scattered around the place. There was no point in putting any other devices in the house because Rodriguez would be on his own and was unlikely to have any meaningful conversations with himself. The man doubted that Rodriguez would scan the place for bugs on his arrival. The house was swept randomly as a part of normal security services procedure, and Stephen would leave that kind of nonsense to lesser mortals. If he did sweep the place and find the bugs, then it was not a big deal. He would be sure as hell mystified at how they had got to be there. He would be more mystified by the brand—they were the same bugs, and the very latest technology currently being used by the FBI. Now wouldn't that be a laugh—bugged by his sister organisation! And the main reason for the bugs being placed where they were was that they would be found sooner rather than later.

His work done, Ben left some lights on in the living room and in the master bedroom. He turned on the TV in the front living room and exited the house through the same door. He snipped the lock, said good night to no one in particular, and went back to the Cadillac.

He did not rush. Everything would appear as normal as was possible to anyone who was watching from behind a curtain, or anyone who was out walking the dog. His timing could not have been better. As Ben settled back in the car, another black Cadillac entered the street. They had no reason to move away—Cadillacs were a common sight in this part of town, and the Secret Service, when they turned up, would have no reason to query who they were or what they were waiting for. Ben and his colleague sat and watched as the other car cruised to a halt on the opposite side of the road.

The guy in the front passenger seat got out and just stood there, looking towards the Rodriguez residence. After a brief conversation with his colleague, he walked across the road and went to the side of the garage and peered in the window. Then he looked confused, turned away with a shrug, and returned to his car. A few moments later, the other agent got out of the car and sprinted towards a house that was five doors down the road, frantically opened the door, and disappeared inside. He had no sooner returned to the car than his partner rushed to the same house and did a similar disappearing act. The polyethylene glycol was obviously working well. The two men would be looking sideways at the people who packed their lunches.

There was only a half hour to pass before the end of their shift, and the Rodriguez Chevy was parked in the garage where it should be, the lady was obviously watching TV, and oblivious to the antics of her protection squad. And the young agents were just too embarrassed to knock on the door and to admit that they had fallen asleep. Must have eaten something! And they were only trainees. And they were only practicing.

All that Blake and Ben had to do now was stay exactly where they were and see what happened next. When something did happen, it was not hard to interpret the body language of the participants.

The change of shift did not go as smoothly as had been anticipated. The new agents checked with the agents they were relieving, and there ensued a heated discussion. Then one of the men walked up to the front door and knocked, more out of courtesy than anything else. When there was no reply, he knocked again and shouted, 'Security.' Still getting no reply, he pulled out his mobile phone, and even in the dim light, you could see the colour drain from his face.

Blake and Ben cruised down the road, leaving the Secret Service with a mess to sort out.

Mark looked at the two Puerto Rican ladies, sitting expectantly side by side on the couch in the Georgetown apartments. They were innocents, brought into a man's world, so that men could fight their evil and wicked battles. There was a deep sadness in his eyes that could not have been conjured up as a part of some act. And the two ladies saw it.

This was the first time they had met Mark Taylor, and they took him to be the boss of this group. The one with all the worries and the weight of the entire world on his shoulders. The one man who would protect them. The one who would ensure the safety of the man who was the husband of one, the father of the other. They assumed that he was also from the FBI. So why did he look so worried?

The members of Mark's team had discussed their next step very carefully before they decided on what they should do, and what they should say. They had only an assumption on which to base their actions, and a few coincidences which may or may not have justified that assumption. In the end, Mark felt that they should tell the ladies the truth as he saw it—what would happen if his assumption was correct.

Mark would not, of course, tell them that he was not from the FBI. Nor would he say who he was.

There was nothing delicate about the way he introduced the subject.

Mark did not sit. He would not be in the room long enough.

The guard stood as well, his arms loosely folded, his hand not far from his pistol. He nodded his head as an acknowledgement to Mark and then turned his attention back to the ladies.

Mark had a cold look on his face and a callous attitude as he spoke, the emotion almost overpowering him.

'We are sorry that you have had to be dragged into this mess, but I will tell you the facts as simply as I can. Stephen Rodriguez is on his way back to the United States and should arrive at Andrews Air Force Base tomorrow morning. When he arrives, I expect to receive a call from him saying that, unless I do certain things, or rather I don't do certain things, a young lady by the name of Debbie Peterson will die. I do not care what happens to Stephen—your husband and father—at the end of all of this. But if he, or any of his cronies, harm as much as one single hair on that lady's head, then we will kill him. I hope that you will have the opportunity to talk some sense into him before it gets to that stage. I wish you luck.'

The reaction from Dayanara was one of shock.

Mark took that to be a natural reaction by someone who had been given so blunt a message concerning her husband. But Mark did not, and could not, know that all was not well in the Rodriguez household.

In fact, Dayanara's shock was brought on by her realisation that the same Stephen Rodriguez could just as easily turn his back on the family that he had once claimed to love. And the further realisation that she and her daughter were now being used as bargaining chips. But would she be worth it? Her thoughts turned cold as the options dawned on her. Had the reasons for her husband becoming so remote anything to do with the story the FBI gentleman had just described? But what could she say?

And what was the FBI up to?

Before she could gather her thoughts, Mark turned his back on them and walked straight out of the room, locking the door behind him.

Before tears overwhelmed him.

Chapter 48

Dusty Miller

Being left behind in Peshawar was not what Dusty would have planned, but then sergeants were supposed to follow orders and not invent them. He had listened to Mark explaining the problems that he had in trusting people. While he thought that Mark had been a little paranoiac, he would respect that view.

Mark had decided that to avoid the catastrophe that they had suffered in Afghanistan, they would each operate independently. They would communicate only by satellite phone, and then only when it was critical.

Owen's job was to track the ADDI for as long as he remained in this part of the world. He did not need to know what the other two members of the team were doing or where they were doing it.

Mark had given Dusty a quite different job to do—of finding enough evidence of the ADDI's involvement in the drug trade. More than that, they needed to know how Rodriguez managed to get the drugs from Peshawar to the United States, apparently with impunity.

So Dusty was now acting alone.

It had been a long time since Archibald Miller, commonly, in fact only, known as Dusty, had the rank of senior sergeant. Then he had been a fighter in Delta Force, the much feared and largely covert branch of the United States Armed Forces. While serving on his third mission in Colombia, he had met up with an officer who went by the rank and name of Major Mark Taylor. The differences between the two of them were quite apparent. Apart from the obvious difference in skin colour, Mark's family had its origins in the peaceful rolling green hills of southern Ireland, and then New England, whereas Dusty had his origins in the brutal and uncompromising world of slavery, oppression, and then prejudice—firstly in Atlanta, Georgia, and then in the Bronx in New York City.

Mark was a professional soldier, who started in the Marines, got himself transferred to Special Forces, and eventually ended up in Delta Force. He carried his rank reluctantly but with quiet authority. Mark was a fighter, and he simply had no time for the petty nuances of officer status. Everyone had a job to do, and so long as they did it to the best of their ability, then the rank was irrelevant. Colour or creed did not enter the equation.

And it was those characteristics that formed the basis of their friendship. Senior sergeants cannot carry their rank with anything other than brutal force. Officers requested their staff to carry out their orders. It was the sergeants who made it all happen. Dusty was such a huge Afro-American that it did not take much to convince anyone to carry out their allotted task. It was only his equally huge smile that prevented the lower ranks from wetting their pants in abject fear when the orders were passed down.

After both Mark and Dusty had left the services, out of sheer frustration at the incredibly naïve attitude of their masters at the Pentagon, they returned to civilian life. Mark formed a computer software company, and Archibald 'Dusty' Miller took up the role that he had studied so hard for—as a lawyer. But Mark and Dusty never really parted company. Dusty acted as Mark's lawyer and oversaw his friend's march into the cutthroat world that is modern business. Mark was ever grateful for his friend's often-candid but well-meaning, advice. It was always the same. The officer having the plans, the sergeant making certain that they would be implemented efficiently and well.

Now Dusty was holed up observing a building located to the southwest of the city of Peshawar in Pakistan, just off the junction of the Ring Road and Kohat Road. It was mostly good luck that had got Dusty this far. But, as in all things, you make your own luck. Dusty had been expecting to find the firm called Aziar Textiles in the place that he had visited a week or so earlier—in an industrial estate just to the northeast of the Hayatabad–Bara Road. But he had been there again, but there was no one there. The factory was deserted. The drug laboratory was gone. Aziar Textiles had quite simply vanished. And there was no sign of the Aziar Toy Factory that had lived next door.

Dusty had two very distinct jobs to do in Peshawar. He had to carry out the instructions that Mark had left him, and first, he had to find out what was going on in the Pakistani city and how it all tied in with this drug business. The second job required a vastly different set of skills: to build a case against Stephen Rodriguez.

At the present time, all the evidence that they had gathered was purely circumstantial. No matter what his personal views about the man were, there was just nothing that Dusty could take into court and avoid being laughed at. Therefore, either he could build a case on circumstantial evidence and hope that something more substantial came out of it, or he could continue following trails and hope. Right now, he had an interesting story, but one that nobody would want to hear.

For once, Dusty got lucky. While he was contemplating what to do next, a truck arrived at the factory address in Hayatabad, and it transpired that the driver was also looking for Aziar Textiles. Ever helpful, Dusty had read through the driver's documents and found a delivery address of an industrial estate alongside Kohat Road, well to the east of where they were now. He advised the driver to go there. To be followed, in due course, by Dusty.

It struck Dusty as rather odd that when he had finally found the new Aziar textile factory—well, really nothing more than a huge shed—there was no sign of the Aziar Toy Factory, as had been the case at the old premises. The connection between the two companies had escaped him at the time, and still did. He had long since given up trying to understand the workings of the business world or the coincidences that may occur. Dusty continued his survey of the surrounding area and eventually found what he had been searching for. There was another shed a few hundred yards away, and sure enough, that was the new premises of the Aziar Toy Factory. Now it was just a matter of being patient and waiting for something else to happen.

And Dusty Miller was exceptionally good at being patient.

Patience that he had learned in his dealings with women. His first love, all those many years ago in Harlem,

New York, had been a lady who was both an enigma and a chameleon. Because he was young and in love, he did not see the downside to the lady he had been smitten with, or to see any harm in their relationship. Sharon was the girl who first invited the virgin and innocent Dusty into her bed, and once she had him there, she had also introduced him to drugs. In a way, he got lucky, although he did not see it that way at the time. She was killed in a senseless drug deal, where both she and the dealer were too stoned to realize that there was really nothing to be upset about. The dealer had quite simply lashed out. Sharon had quite simply died.

It took Dusty several days of quietly and patiently tracking the movements of the dealer, and then in a back alley, in the dead of night, he had ruthlessly beaten the man to death with his bare hands. He had learned a couple of extremely hard lessons. About women—they mess with your mind. About drugs—they mess with your life. Do not ever touch either of them again.

But he had relented on one of these two things. Now he had a relationship that no one, not even his close friend Mark Taylor, knew anything about.

This lady, Claudia, was also a chameleon, but not an enigma. All that Dusty knew of her daytime job was that she worked in the Secretariat Building on Capitol Hill as a legal advisor. Dusty had no idea who she provided legal advice to and on what she advised. All that he knew was that when they were together, it was like a huge euphoric release; and when they made love and then said their reluctant good-byes, he could hardly wait until their next meeting. And he had the impression that the expectation was mutual. But he had to be patient. Claudia had her career. Sometime, eventually, her natural instincts and desire to bear children would overcome her desire to prove her Afro-American talents in a world dominated by white folk and to prove her talents in a world dominated by men.

Patience that he had, had to learn in the brutal backstreets of Mogadishu in Somalia. That was the one time in his life that Dusty had been scared shitless. It was October 1993. They had simply been making a run from the airport where the United States Delta Force group had been based in the Pakistani compound that was supposed to hold a United Nations peacekeeping force. In fact, that was where the CIA had a base, and the CIA was the organisation that dictated a purpose for this trip. The problem was that there was a fight going on at the same time. The United States forces were about to be withdrawn in yet another about-face, either by the politicians or by the military, in the ever-changing world of international politics. But before the US forces were withdrawn, they had to make one more bid to capture members of the Habr Gidr clan, headed by the warlord Mohamed Farrah Aidid.

That meant that more than one heavily armed convoy had to pass along what became known as the Mogadishu Mile. The dense urban nature of that part of Mogadishu meant that they had to travel through a heavily populated area where there could be no distinction between friends and foes—nothing to distinguish the Somali militia from the Somali civilian population, and from every other rat-bag group that made a home in that festering pit. Every building could have housed any number of the many factions that went under the name of the Somali National Alliance.

It was meant to be a fair fight. A couple of hundred highly trained elite troops of the United States forces under the command of Major General William F. Garrison, versus over 4,000 heavily armed, but poorly trained, and equally poorly disciplined, militia under the leadership of Mohamed.

As with all simple plans, it did not quite work out. The original mission was supposed to only take about thirty minutes. A couple of United States Black Hawk helicopters would take the assault force to the target building where the elite troops would rappel down and capture the people they sought. The targets were known to be in the building, so timing was particularly important. Meanwhile, a dozen or so military vehicles would ride up to the building and take away the prisoners and the assault troops. Simple. Job done!

Things almost worked out despite a civilian mob blocking the streets, making it near impossible for the ground troops to get through, which seemed to suggest that something was wrong with the intelligence and the security of the mission. This was made worse when one of the Black Hawk helicopters, call sign Super-6-1 piloted by Cliff 'Elvis' Wolcott, was shot down by a rocket-propelled grenade. Then all hell broke loose.

Dusty could never exactly recall how he got involved because everything seemed to happen in a blur. One minute, they were driving along a street, then there was an explosion, then he found himself under intense fire trying to help the wounded American servicemen into a makeshift shelter. The problem was that the Somali militia was hidden among civilians, firing over their heads, even between the legs of women and children. It was mind-numbing. And some of the children were actively involved in the fight. If there is a ten-year-old boy running towards you carrying an AK-47, do you shoot the kid or smile? The answer is, 'Sayonara, son.' You shoot the kid. You must survive while waiting for the inept response from those responsible for getting you into this mess in the first place. You may be scared, but you need to be unemotional and attempt to stay alive.

And be patient.

And it did not end there. When, finally, the person in charge of the botched operation decided that the US forces needed to be rescued, there was only enough room in the rescue vehicles for all the casualties and some of the troops. And only at this point did they realize they had one additional member in their troop—Dusty Miller. So, four of the men, Dusty included, had to fight their way out through the streets of Mogadishu. Only three of them made it out, and one of those three was so gravely wounded he died later in hospital from loss of blood.

Patience.

The task that Mark had given Dusty was, on the face of it, relatively simple. Gather evidence of what happened to the opiates that Stephen was allegedly responsible for once they had arrived in Peshawar. But this task was, of course, far more complex than that. Dusty was not a criminal lawyer. He had, early in his career, realized that there was far more money to be made in the financial and business world. He had also realised that he simply could not defend people who were so obviously guilty. Nor could he prosecute people who were so obviously innocent but who some dumb-ass cop thought should be convicted, usually based on their race. It was not that Archibald Miller, LLB, thought that the police were biased in any way. He just thought that the justice system was biased. Consequently, he turned his considerable talents to working for people who used the justice system to gain a pecuniary benefit, and he left the criminal elements to someone else.

That said, one of his jobs, sometime soon, would be to build a case against the assistant deputy director of intelligence of the CIA, and that would be difficult. The only advantage that he would have was that it was unlikely that the army of lawyers on the CIA payroll would be involved in defending the ADDI—the reason, same as with everything else the CIA and other organizations who wielded power, deniability. The major, and at the present irreconcilable, disadvantage that he would have been that the present case looked like smoke and mirrors. Dusty was a fine lawyer.

He also knew what it was like pushing shit uphill with a fork.

The security on the property that Dusty was watching now was considerably better than it had been when he had previously visited the Aziar Textile Factory, although nothing quite as scary as it had been in Somalia. With the original Aziar property, it had been almost comical, the ease with which he had been able to get into, and out of, the factory without being seen, or of anyone being aware that he had even been there. Now the door into the new factory had a keypad, and the door was always closed, and apparently locked whether people were in the factory or not. The roller door on the loading dock was also activated from inside with no means of access visible on the outside. The whole loading area was isolated, such that anyone in the area could not gain access to anywhere else in the building without having an access code. Whoever had set this up had either got rapid access to resources to have done it so quickly, or they had chosen a purpose-built facility that just happened to be available. Or the more likely case was that they were able to wield influence in the place that mattered.

So why had the factory been moved? And why had they increased the level of security?

There were two possible scenarios. The first scenario

was that it was just business—the earlier premises had been much larger and more upmarket than where they were now, so it may just have been a matter of economics. The second scenario was that his earlier intrusion into their factory had, in fact, been spotted, so it was really a matter of running, hiding, and securing.

Dusty's pulse raced as a third scenario struck him. The third possibility was that someone had told the Aziar Company what they had to do. If that were so, then that someone was probably connected to Stephen Rodriguez, or to his deceased FBI colleague. Therefore, someone had probably also told the assistant deputy director of intelligence that the security of the factory had been breached. At the time of the earlier infraction, that would not have been a major issue. Now that Stephen Rodriguez was aware of some covert presence in Afghanistan, and probably the city of Peshawar, all bets were off. So, who had spooked them?

Mark's words, when they had landed for the second time in Peshawar, were *I can no longer trust him*. Mark had been talking about Griz.

Griz, their amiable pilot of the Gulfstream from the DEA, had been the only person who could have known. Unless, of course, they had traced the information all the way to its next logical place—the assistant inspector's office back in Washington DC. If the advice had come from there, then their whole mission was in serious trouble.

No, it had to be someone who was close to the action. Griz was the obvious choice, but there could be another. And that gave further justification for the call that Mark had made earlier, to not make any further use of Owen Squires in his actual surveillance. That hurt. Owen had singlehandedly, and without any doubt whatsoever, saved the lives of Dusty and Mark a few days ago. But, putting emotion aside, Owen was part of the DEA team, and the performance of that team was not looking that flash. The decision that Mark had made seemed to have been the correct one, even though he had made it for very different reasons. Dusty would proceed alone, using Owen only as a source of information.

At last, Dusty got at least one more break. A taxi pulled up outside the new premises, and Dusty recognized the passenger who got out. He had first seen him in Marjah in Afghanistan. Jacob Dutton was his name, and he was with the CIA Marjah cell. What the hell was he now doing in Peshawar?

Dusty would have loved to get closer to record the conversation, but he could not risk moving from his position. He watched as Dutton walked from the taxi to the door where he was greeted by a Pakistani gentleman, who certainly knew his visitor. Dusty still had not gotten used to the animated way in which people in this part of the world greeted each other, so he could not tell whether the Pakistani was pleased or not. From the bits of conversation that Dusty could catch, they did not converse in English. They were probably talking in Urdu, which was the national language of Pakistan, so it was even harder to judge what the hell was going on. But Dusty could read body language. His summation of the visit was that Dutton had come to deliver a message. That message was unequivocal. The Pakistani took the message and was not overly pleased. But he appeared to have no choice but to comply. And then Dutton left, looking rather pleased with himself.

Dusty immediately sent a text message to Mark.

Jacob just paid a visit to a factory in East Peshawar. Can u ask Owen to find out where he is going?

The day slowly turned into night, and the people from the factory ended their labours, and headed home. All the lights were extinguished. The only noise coming initially from the building was from the alarm being set. Then, after sixty seconds, even that lapsed into silence.

Still, Dusty waited.

At 9:25 pm, a vehicle arrived at the factory. Of the four men in it, only the driver got out. He was wearing the uniform of the Pakistani Police Force and judging by the insignia, he was of low rank. He proceeded to completely circumnavigate the building, checking every window and potential point of access. He then he scanned the surrounding buildings and terrain before returning to the vehicle. Only then did he open one of the rear doors of the vehicle, and out stepped another man in uniform. Dusty could not be certain from where he was hiding on the opposite side of the road, but he guessed that this was a police officer of at least superintendent level.

This man approached the building, entered a code into the access pad, and opened the door. He then signalled to the vehicle, and the other two occupants got out, and scurried over to the door. The three of them entered the building, closing the door behind them. The driver remained outside, talking on a cellular phone, and it was only after he had waved his arms down the road that anyone would have realized there was even further security spaced out around the vicinity of the factory. That is, except for Dusty.

It was at moments like these that he could be thankful for all the intense training that he had been through all those years ago in Delta Force. That training had honed his skills in hiding his bulky frame almost under the noses of the people he was hiding from. He did not move, his breath hidden by a mask, as were his teeth in case he felt like laughing, his eyes hidden behind non-reflective and tinted plastic. He observed everything that was going on in this remote part of the foreign city.

Still, Dusty waited.

It was 2:30 am the following morning when the entire process of entering the factory was repeated but in reverse. The police superintendent opened the door and issued some instructions to the driver. The driver made a hurried inspection around the building, and made a cursory scan of the surrounding land, before reporting back that all was clear. Only then did the two men scurry out of the building and get into the vehicle. The officer reset the alarm, and they were on their way.

Still, Dusty waited

He was waiting for four security guards to abandon their surveillance. If they were good at their job, they would remain in place for some time, just to make sure that nothing was amiss. And as if on cue, just as they had arrived one hour before the other visitors, two of them departed exactly one hour after the visitors had left, no doubt relieved that another night had passed without any drama. That just left two men whose task it seemed was to make half-hourly circuits of the building and spend the rest of their time smoking in plain view of anyone who might be passing by.

The deadly-boring business of surveillance and countersurveillance was the same the world over. The Pakistani security officers had missed the obvious and had adopted a routine—that was how it should be.

Dusty waited until the guards had taken off on yet another circuit of the building, and then stood for a few seconds and eased his muscles back into working order. He then slowly walked across the street up to the factory door. Now he had to be extremely careful. He was aware that people in the drug business were usually very picky about security, and if nothing else, they could afford the best.

Any breach of security would be rapidly and ruthlessly dealt with. He was taking a risk, but he had to find his way inside. He attached an innocuous-looking fitting to the side of the keypad. Pressing a switch on the side of the device, which was little larger than a flash drive, he had all he needed for the moment—the access code to the door. Just to be certain, he scrolled through the small display and saw that the same access code had been used much earlier in the day, so he had the correct numbers. He knew that he had more than enough time—the guards took well over five minutes to complete their circuit, although he did not know why. He would realize later that the reason was that they had to check two buildings, not one.

He entered the number into the access panel, and the door opened. He crept into the building and closed the door. He held his breath as he waited for an alarm to go off. It didn't, which, thankfully, confirmed that the keypad had deactivated the alarm. He took a special torch out of his pocket, which gave off only a dim red light, and waited until his eyes had adjusted to it. This light would be difficult for anyone to detect from the road outside but was more than adequate for Dusty's purposes. It was also a unique feature. It would detect any point-to-point laser beams that may be activated. There were none, which came as a surprise.

The entranceway had a few doors to his right, none of which appeared to have combination locks. His cursory examination revealed that they were general office and storage space. The corridor ran alongside the loading bay on the left and ended with another door, this one with a keypad for entry. He briefly thought of using the same access code that he had discovered earlier but sighed as he realised there was no hurry. And being careful was critical to the success of his mission. It was better to be sure than to be sorry. What he had to find out would probably take him little more than an hour, so the extra few minutes to find out the access code for this door was no big deal.

He attached a different device that looked like a Blackberry but was, in fact, far simpler, to the side of the keypad. He pressed the Start button and watched as numbers raced across the small screen and then stopped, displaying a four-digit number. Dusty shook his head and wondered at the sheer stupidity of people who profess to be security conscious. This access code was *1234,* which was probably the factory default setting of the company that had manufactured the device. And no one at the Aziar Company had bothered to change it, despite the earlier warning. To Dusty, a more logical number would have been some mathematical addition or subtraction following in sequence from the access code for the main door, but he just smiled and entered *1234.* The door opened, and he was in.

The whole factory consisted of one massive floor with huge piles of packages stacked around the outer walls. There were two forklift trucks parked haphazardly in the middle of the floor, one of them still loaded with several packages—whether arriving or departing, Dusty could not tell. Examination of them revealed nothing. They were the same size and style as all the other packages in the building. He decided to take a chance. He took a knife out of his pocket and slit one of the packages. It contained textiles. He then moved to the side of the building and slit open a few of the packages. They all appeared to contain textiles. There was no sign of drugs. There was also no sign of the laboratory that he had found at the previous premises.

He looked around in search of some clue as to whether any drugs or opiates either arrived or were dispatched, but there was just nothing.

But then, why all the security? And what had the three

gentlemen who had appeared earlier been doing?

Dusty was about to abandon his search when, quite by chance, he came across an area where there was a trapdoor on the floor, and the indications were that the trapdoor had been in regular use. One of the forklift trucks was parked on top of it. Dusty thought of starting the truck to move it, but he thought better of it. He located the handbrake and slowly rolled the truck forwards. He looked around for any indication that the door was linked to an alarm. There was none that he could see, and so he cautiously raised the door and peered down into the hole beneath. The hole went down for at least thirty feet, and then he could dimly see that it linked to a passageway that was at the bottom of the shaft. The whole structure was well made, being lined with wood, and the planks looked to be new.

The direction of the passage meant that it was leading to the rear of the factory, but why? A ladder was attached to the left side and secured by a linking and locking mechanism which took Dusty a few moments to figure out. The ladder, incredibly, was, in fact, a fire escape that was pulled up. That meant that no one could gain access to the factory unless they had some mechanism for lowering the ladder from below. Or, or unless someone from the factory lowered it for them. At the top of the ladder was a crude switch, which Dusty took to be a light switch. He briefly thought about turning it on. Since he did not know what, if anything, was down there, he decided against it. He would have to explore further because this discovery could perhaps explain what went on in the factory.

He still had plenty of time on his side.

His phone vibrated in his pocket, which momentarily

scared the shit out of him. It was a reply from Owen to the message that he had sent to Mark.

J off to US ETD 8am PKT.

Dusty frowned. Now what did that mean?

He replied,

Who with?

He got an almost immediate response.

Alone.

Dusty sent a message to Mark.

Dusty released the catch that held the ladder and was surprised at how quietly it descended to the cavern floor. He climbed onto the ladder and then eased the trapdoor closed above his head. He felt an initial surge of fear as he descended the ladder. Being belowground in a claustrophobic environment was not his idea of fun. He was quite used to cramped conditions but being cramped belowground made the hairs on the back of his neck stand up. The red light did not seem to have the range that it had in the factory. Dusty realized that this was simply his mind playing tricks, and he gritted his teeth.

At the bottom of the shaft, he stood and surveyed the passageway before venturing along it. He had to stoop. The passage was under six feet in height compared to Dusty's six feet plus and was not very wide, which suggested that whatever it was used for, it was for people rather than things. Or else the things that did transit the passage were small and easily carried. It went along for about thirty feet and then ended abruptly. It had a crude lighting arrangement with a wire simply stapled to the right side of the tunnel roof, and two bulbs dangled from sockets. On the left was a flimsy door attached to which was the inevitable keypad.

Dusty was beginning to feel tired and restless, and the perspiration was beginning to run down his face. The dank atmosphere of the tunnel meant that there was little air, and he began to wonder whether he should have turned on the switch. Maybe it was not just for lighting—maybe it was also for air circulation. He tried one of the numbers that he had used earlier to get inside the factory. Fortunately, the number *1234* again worked, and he eased the door open. There was another tunnel. He went through and closed the door behind him. It had a keypad on the opposite side as well.

The tunnel disappeared into the distance, beyond the range of his red light. On the right, and behind the door, was a cupboard that was not locked. Dusty cautiously opened the door to reveal a collection of beams, shovels, picks, and other tools obviously used for the construction or repair of the tunnel. He closed that door. He padded down the passage for maybe 100 feet, where he came across a series of seven steps on his left leading up another door, this one looking far more robust that anything he had encountered so far. It was protected by a keypad, and this time the access code *1234* did not work.

Before tackling the door, he walked farther down the passage until that again came to an abrupt halt, below a shaft that went straight up to another trapdoor. It was similar to the place where he had entered the tunnel, except for one thing: there was no ladder. He had travelled maybe four or five hundred feet from where he had entered the tunnel, so this exit could not be in the same building. The ceiling beams and the walls were new, so it had been purposely built for something. But what?

Dusty retraced his steps back to the door that was in the middle of the tunnel. He attached his gadget to the side of the keypad. Initially, the device could not decipher the code, but with some adjustments and a rerun, he had it. Someone obviously thought that this door should have better protection than had been evident in the building so far.

He was in.
The excitement was immediate.
He had found the laboratory.

The place was certainly more organized than the original factory had been. Here, there was not even an attempt to hide what was going on from anyone other than the casual observer. The whole room was a drug laboratory. Dusty felt sick. He had seen first-hand the effects drugs can have on the lives of people in the back streets of Harlem in New York. It is not so much the recreational users who have an occasional snort, injection, or a smoke. Recreational users were normally among the well-off who could afford the occasional dabble in the odd moments that they were not counting their wealth. The initial surge of euphoria, or rush as it was known, followed by a dry mouth, a warm flushing of the skin, a heaviness in the extremities, and the clouding of mental functions.

The problem was people who found drugs as a means of escape from their demons, and with regular use, tolerance develops that then requires more heroin to achieve the same intensity. That leads to dependence on drugs. Dependence leads to addiction.

The work that went on in this laboratory could hardly be described as highly scientific. Spread out around the room were tables with poppy seeds laid out with almost military precision. The work in the main area consisted of simply making an incision into the pods and leaving them to let the milky white fluid run out and dry. Then the dried fluid was carefully scraped and collected into plastic bags. This is opium, and it contains a mixture of various drugs, the main ones being morphine and codeine. The powder was then transferred to the tables at the left side of the room, where it was quite simply refined into heroin by treating it with lime and a few other compounds. Metal containers were lined up along the wall, and alongside each were microwave ovens to speed up the drying process after the drugs had been boiled. It did not take a degree in chemistry to work out what was going on, nor did it require any skill to perform this task, other than to follow the strict and methodical procedure.

Dusty had witnessed on his previous trip the use of laboratory technicians, so the people who ran this facility were obviously taking no chances despite the menial nature of the work. In a similar way, it was unusual for them to ship the raw poppy buds rather than just the opium all the way from its origins in the south of Afghanistan. Conclusion? The refining process was entirely under the control of these people, and what was being produced here was effectively pure heroin, with little chance that it could be contaminated or cut. That meant that there was some serious money behind the operation.

The heroin that made its way by a variety of means, and from a variety of sources, into the hands of the drug addicts in the United States was probably cut and mixed with all manner of other substances—some harmful, some harmless, but nonetheless substances which rendered the heroin content less and less before it reached the ultimate end-user. This was done to just feed the greed of the dealers, as it passed through the various levels in the distribution network and to ensure that the price remained reasonable. It still meant that people could become addicted. And it would still maintain the evil cycle that meant that people had to turn to crime to fund their habit.

Unless, that is, they already had plenty of money.

But where did it go from here? By far the largest market for heroin was the United States, although that did not necessarily mean that all heroin production was focused solely on the US. It could be destined for the north-east of Pakistan, where there was a more than ample demand. But the only assumption that Dusty could make was that this product was destined to go overseas; otherwise, why the visit from the assistant deputy director of intelligence and his shadow, Jacob Dutton?

In his earlier surveillance at the original premises, Dusty had seen the opiates come into the factory. They were disguised as packages of textiles. But he had yet to see any drugs leave either factory, and without that piece of the puzzle to complete the picture, he had no real proof of what went on, and why.

Frustrated at having got only a part of the answer, Dusty exited the room, reset the keypad, and retraced his steps. He had found another possible method of getting into or out of the factory. There were now two possible exits for the drugs, but where did they lead? From his recollection of the outside of the building, to the left and west of the factory was another shed like structure whose only role in this world seemed to be to house a facility for making kids' toys, so what had that got to do with anything? He exited this part of the tunnel through the door by entering the code 1234 and made his way back to the bottom of the original shaft. But where was the ladder? He peered up the shaft. The ladder was still there. What he had not counted on was it automatically retracting.

Dusty swore.

He was now trapped underground with no physical means of exit. And it was expecting too much of anyone who happened by to offer him a way out. That is, unless Dusty resorted to physical persuasion, which was well within his means, but which was not exactly covert. He had all the skills necessary for unarmed combat, and just to be sure, he had a Glock 19 on his hip. Either way, that would do the trick initially. But what about when he got out of the tunnel? What kind of reception would he get then?

He was mulling over the options when he had another problem. Someone was moving in the room above the trapdoor. He checked his watch. It was only 5:00 am which was far earlier than he had witnessed anybody come to the factory the morning before. And, judging by the noise of the footsteps, there were several people up there. That presented Dusty with a dilemma. He could wait out the people by remaining where he was until they once again departed—that is, unless they decided to come down into the tunnel. However, what if someone came from the other end? Then there could only be one possible outcome: he would need to take them out. And where would that leave him? Still belowground and with people at either end of this miserable underground rabbit warren wondering what had happened to their colleagues.

Dusty strained to hear the conversation coming from above. There was obviously a disagreement going on conducted in Urdu. Then Dusty froze. A loud voice told the people, in English, 'Shut the fuck up!'

It was the voice of Stephen Rodriguez.

That meant that the choice was an easy decision.

He made his way back down the tunnel, opened the door into the secondary tunnel, and then closed it behind him. He then opened the cupboard, squeezed inside between the tools and the beams. He pulled the doors closed.

Dusty had to guess. If anyone came down the tunnel from either direction, they would most probably switch on the lights. They would probably not try to enter the cupboard, as it appeared to only store maintenance materials. They could possibly tell Dusty what he needed to know: What happened to the heroin when it left the laboratory? Other than that, it seemed that Dusty was in for a long wait until the factory was once again vacated.

Patience.

There was no fresh air in the tunnel. It was not airtight, so he would not die from a lack of oxygen. But it would mean that as the day progressed, Dusty would become even more lethargic than he already felt.

The trick in these circumstances was for Dusty to conserve every ounce of energy—no movement, preferably sleeping. And that was OK. His training had taught him all that was needed.

Patience.

While he waited in the cupboard, his only hope was that someone else in his team was having a little more luck than he was.

Chapter 49

Brad Morgan

The task that Mark had given to Brad was massive. It was not helped by the fact that Brad was no longer employed by the CIA. He still had all the skills that he had acquired while working for the Directorate of Science and Technology. He had honed those skills because of knowing Mark Taylor and through his work with Taylor Software. Brad could hack into almost any computer system because that is what he had an aptitude for, and what he had received very specialized training for. The US intelligence services—well, any government service—could not normally pay the remuneration that the top people in the computer profession demanded. But what the services could do is, having caught people doing illegal things, they could bleed them of their knowledge during their rehabilitation back into society.

Or at least get them to reveal their tricks in exchange for a lighter sentence.

But that did not make this task any easier. That was easy when his target was a normal computer system where, despite all the skills that existed in the commercial and private world, they were no match for the vast number crunchers and analytical abilities of the country's security and intelligence networks. This task would have been difficult enough had he still been with the CIA.

But not this task!

And who was to say that the system he had to find, and then penetrate, was computer based? Despite the misgivings in security circles of making assumptions, you had to assume something, and now it was reasonable to *assume* that computers and communications were involved. In fact, if they weren't, there was just nowhere else to look. On the other hand, *computers* meant the immense cyberspace that had been created by the Internet. And in that case, where was he to start?

The conversation between Mark and Brad had been blunt.

'Somehow, people in the CIA, and we assume other organizations within the Government, have access to drugs,' Mark began the debate almost as though he were talking to himself.

'We know that there are drug users in the CIA, the FBI, and elsewhere. They could be simply obtaining their drugs through the usual market sources. However, some people appear to have access to drugs where their suppliers are right there in Langley.'

Let's talk about what we do know. The drug is heroin. We know that the drugs originate in Afghanistan. We have reason to believe that they come into the United States via Peshawar, Pakistan. What we do not know is how they do it, how they ship it, or who the organizers are. There must be a network of some kind. We need to find that network. How does a user working for the CIA order, have shipped, and pay for drugs, and do all that without it being picked up by the existing systems that are already in place to track such activities? Because there are users, the network or whatever drives the system must be hidden in plain sight, and that is why I think someone has a very smart system. I do not care how you do it, but I want you to find out.'

Brad was talking to his boss, so he was not inclined to say what came immediately to his mind, like, 'Time is not exactly on our side!' He knew that Mark was worried, not only about drug users, but about Debbie. But Brad had to concentrate on the former. Brad knew that Mark had other things in motion, and that Mark would tell him if he wished to. Although Brad was curious, that did not seem likely. But that was cool.

Where drugs are involved, there are also two other things involved. Firstly, people who are addicted will do absolutely anything to get their drugs. Secondly, there is just so much money involved. The combination of these two things usually means one thing: if anyone gets in the way, they usually die. Brad also knew that Mark was playing a cat-and-mouse game with the assistant deputy director of intelligence, but that could not last. Like the next twenty-four hours would be critical. It was not that Brad did not want to help, in any way he could.

It was just he did not know where to start.

He asked the next obvious questions.

'What makes you think that the network is controlled by computers? Do you have anything which tells us where to start looking?'

Mark at least grinned, but his reply was nonetheless grim.

'Come on, Brad, it has to be! No, I don't know anything, but no one could organize something on this scale without the use of computers and the use of communications. And that must be via the Internet. Yes, the internet is complex with all sorts of virtual parts and all sorts of places to hide. But that is your area of expertise. As for where we start, there must be a weak link somewhere. Several people in the CIA must know what goes on. Security on such a system must be tight. But to someone with your ability and experience, can it be that tight?'

'You want me to speculate?' Brad asked.

The enormity of the task was made evident by his body language. Brad had been a government servant. The *government* had vast resources and time. The bureaucracy would form a plan, and once it had that in place, it would bulldoze ahead like a tsunami, overturning everything in its path.

Mark remained calm.

'Well, we have to start somewhere!' Mark replied. 'So, think as they would. How would you go about organizing a supply system that could be used for drugs? Think laterally. We do not have the time to go down many blind alleys. Knowing what we do know, could it be done?'

Brad began to think.

'Setting up any supply system is easy enough. Bouncing messages of servers in all parts of the world to hide addresses and avoid recognition is standard procedure for most people who work in the areas that you are talking about—easily done and easily and constantly changed. And the Internet makes it quite simple to arrange shipments and payments, but a drug network over the Internet is bit of a stretch. But ... If I did not want people to know that it was drugs that were being traded or exchanged, then I would obviously call them something else.'

Mark did not display any emotion. That was what he had been thinking, and that was why Dusty had been left in Peshawar following the treacherous trail. Mark's next question was not unexpected.

'What networks do the CIA, and for that matter any government, employees have that they access on a regular basis?' Mark, of course, would already partially know the answer to his own question. He was looking for ideas. Or was he hopelessly lost?

Brad was already on the same page, and Mark could see a flicker of hope. Mark's crazy ideas that he had been mulling over and had prevented him from sleeping could be torn apart by the ever-clinical mind of Brad.

'OK,' said Brad, deep in thought. It was now Brad who was seemingly talking to himself.

'Let's think this thing through. They have a social network that is government-sponsored and maintained. Mostly the academics have got hold of it, so your average bureaucrat does not do any more than exchange opinions on who is going to win the next Super Bowl. But it is, in fact, a vast social network, and only loosely controlled. Because it is only used in-house by bureaucrats, it is not seen as a threat. To return to the question, how would I go about organizing what would be a network within a network? This is where I would go. It would not be impossible to set up something that would be accessible to the selected few. With a username and password logic, you could do almost anything. Hidden in plain sight. It could be done!'

Brad logged in to Google and hit a few keys. Before long, they were on the CIA website home page. To get beyond that, to anything other than general knowledge, you had to enter a username and a password. Presumably, someone had forgotten that Brad no longer worked for the Government, because after trying different combinations, he found a username and a password that still worked— not surprising, given the still relatively innocent nature of this part of the whole website.

As Brad had indicated, most of the web pages and their various links lead down tracks that few outsides of academia, or those bureaucrats who had little better to do with their time, would ever venture. And the website, with all its links, was vast if a little disorganized. Some tracks were blind alleys. Bits that had been only partially developed or features that were there but had been bypassed in some upgrade. Or bits that the *budget* had not allowed to be completed.

There was obviously some part of some organization, somewhere within the bowels of government, which was responsible for maintaining it. Some parts would have been *under development* but had not received funding to continue. In others, the staff may have left mid-project and, as with many computer projects, the new people may not have been able to fathom what the hell was going on, and so the entrails were just left hanging. There was just no incentive to fix things. These networks ended up as a mess. Generally, they also lacked the precision that commercial websites displayed.

It would have been foolish to assume anything.

However, what could be assumed is that if the maintenance of the website was somewhat haphazard, then presumably so was the security. That was why the network could potentially be used by others.

Mark was eager to hear what Brad had to say now.

'Well, you could do it. I do not know if I could trust this network as a cover for what I wanted to do. The idea sounds good. If you set up another secure website, or maybe more than one website, you could access that from here armed with the correct username and password, and if you knew exactly what you were looking for. It could be made totally secure: you would need to be certain that no one got past that security by accident or by design. That is relatively simple to do with smoke and mirrors.

Brad rambled on, lost in the world of bits and bytes. Then he came back to planet Earth.

'What say the methods of access to the network were

passed by word of mouth? And having gained access, the basic operating procedures are communicated in the same way. You could set it up so that you must access things in sequence. Simple, in plain sight. Yes, you could do it. Not necessarily on this website. You could do it on any website, which means that the research into finding the networks is like finding a needle in a haystack. We normally think of access to a website as being self-contained. But in a site set up with a special purpose in mind, why would it be? There is nothing wrong with having a onetime access that you get either from another website or by word of mouth!'

Brad paused and then asked.

'How long have we got?'

Mark went pale when he contemplated how to answer that question. He sighed.

'That is the problem. We either crack this thing in the next twenty-four hours, or we are in serious trouble. Somehow, they have already effectively removed my old man from the scene. I do not know whether it was part of their plan or if the old man just gave up. Either way, we are on our own. We do not have time to search the whole of the Internet. What we need to do, and in a hurry, is find the weak link. We need someone to talk.'

The two men sat staring at the computer screen, almost willing the answer to magically pop out. But of course, that would not happen. The next few hours would be critical, because unless they made some progress, they were in real trouble. They knew what they had to do. But would it be enough? And would it be done in time?

After a long, hard chat, the two of them agreed on the only plan that they could come up with. It was high-risk. Mark would have to stay confined to the apartment until at least another of his plans came to fruition.

But they did have other resources.

Brad called Shania.

Brad and Shania had planned to meet up later in the evening, have a pizza, watch a DVD, have a glass of wine, and maybe, just maybe, Brad could get his leg over this time. That was a false hope. Now his plans for the evening would need to change.

Their relationship was warming up. Neither of them was the type of person to rush into things, and they had not yet made love. They were both shy. They had kissed, passionately, and Brad's hands had explored her body, always stopping just short of touching anything important. Her response had been one of frustration, but her hands had always stopped short as well. Brad was not sure whether that frustration was with him for not going farther, or was it with herself? Only time would tell. She had yet to encourage him. Or was it that Brad could not read the signs? But she was worth waiting for. As with all shy couples, trying to establish the ground rules before they jumped in, when it happened, it would either be one massive disappointment or one glorious event.

It just would not happen tonight.

They met on the banks of the Potomac to discuss what they had to do. Well, it was really Brad that had to do something, but Shania, with all her FBI training, was up for it. They discussed what Mark suggested, and much to Brad's relief, Shania agreed.

As she drove away, Brad could only hope that she would be safe dressed as she was in a stunning business jacket and a skirt, which was a little brief in the jacket and a little brief in the skirt.

Brad was amazed that someone looking so beautiful, and desirable could be packing a Glock 15 in her handbag.

And what is more, she was very capable of using it.

Chapter 50

Lies

Brad Morgan did not like to lie, which probably meant that he had been wrong to choose a career in the CIA. However, it was only a small lie. And no one would come to any harm.

Brad called Mama Christie, who by reputation was the mother of the backroom boys in the division where Brad used to work. She was still at work.

'Hi, Mama. How are you doing?'

Mama never forgot a person or a voice.

'Brad! Where have you been? Why have you not kept in touch? Don't tell me! You boys are off chasing young girls, no time for me. You going to tell me that you are coming back?'

'Good to hear from you too, Mama!' Brad started, wondering how he could try to get some information out of the one person in the CIA who knew what went on.

'Just down in Washington for a couple of days and thought I might catch up with some of the boys. I hear that some people are over from Afghanistan, and it would be good to hear what life is like out there.'

'Some of them will be down the FC tonight. Be glad

to see you again—that is, if they remember that far back. I won't be there, of course!' Mama concluded as though it was the last place she would be seen. Which was true.

Brad headed down the Wilson Boulevard of Arlington towards a favourite CIA waterhole, Ireland's Four Courts. It was probably more in keeping with the psyche of the FBI, but for some reason, the CIA also enjoyed the Irish flavour of the pub to wind down after a hard day at the office. Or was that just an excuse?

There was a mixture of people in the bar. There were several groups who were the obvious regulars, the odd couple quietly chatting and looking forward to spending their evening in more passionate surroundings, and the occasional loner.

It could be a long night. Brad would wait, listen, observe.

One of these *loners* could be what he was looking for, but first, he had to find one that was from the CIA, otherwise, this whole exercise could be a complete waste of time. Eventually, he had narrowed the field down to three possibilities: two of the loners who seemed lost in the bottle and, oddly enough, two men who did not drink much and had spent the whole evening in idle chatter and not much else. All four were men, and all were people who appeared to be known at least to some of the other people who were imbibing in the bar, and to the barman. All four men had the body language of people who had nowhere else to go, and, if the profiling theory was at all accurate, were most likely to be into drugs.

The profile did not work for the first guy that Brad engaged in conversation. This guy was on something, but it was more likely to come out of a bottle than from a small plastic bag or a syringe. But he had much more luck with the odd couple. It turned out that they had been overseas, although neither of them would say whereabouts they had been or what they had been doing. And that was fair enough. They would not say who they worked for, either so that meant that they worked for the Government. And it did not take a rocket scientist to work out the rest.

The first guy introduced himself as Winston.

The second guy was called Jacob.

Brad simply introduced himself as someone who used to work for the Directorate of Science and Technology of the CIA, who had dropped by on a visit to Washington to see some friends who looked like being a no-show. That news was greeted with a shrug that said, *What's new?* And they got on with discussing the political situation with the usual profound knowledge that all bureaucrats, with a fair supply of amber liquid on board, can impart. It soon became apparent that Winston and Jacob were not close friends, and that they were only companions of convenience. They were both accommodated at the Hotel Rosslyn in North Fort Myer Drive in Arlington.

It was a dangerous game. People who work in the inner sanctums of Government have an extraordinary knack for recognising fellow travellers. They are also adept at talking for hours and saying nothing. Brad was no actor. But he had been a part of the inner sanctum, and he knew how these games were played.

Eventually, Brad willingly accepted an invitation to join them for a nightcap at their hotel. He was rapidly running out of ideas of how he was going to progress this investigation, but he had to try, and this seemed to be a fair bet.

And hope that Shania was having much better luck.

At least with the passage of time, back in their own hotel, and with the switch from beer to spirits, Winston and Jacob were getting more vocal. The guy named Jacob finally let it out that he had been posted to Afghanistan, and he did not have many pleasant things to say about the southern part of that country. Whether he had intended to confirm the obvious—that he worked for the CIA—this time of night and with the amount of alcohol that he had consumed was beside the point. There were not much better things to be said about his masters in Langley, and Brad took the opportunity to remind Jacob that he had until recently also worked for that esteemed organization, and therefore he was among friends. Even then, Brad was no closer to learning anything of interest.

Winston finally decided to call it a day and retired. Jacob invited Brad for a nightcap from his minibar in his room, more by way of having somebody to keep him company in this crowded, and at the same time lonely, city. In the process, Jacob revealed that he was on drugs—purely social, he was not an addict, but nonetheless, drugs.

Brad declined the invitation to have a snort, citing some important things that he had to do later that day—after all, it was 1:00 am. Jacob was relaxed. He even joked about how easy drugs were to come by in Afghanistan. He even said, with a knowing wink, how easy it was for people at Langley to acquire drugs. He went further, and he said that he would need to order some more while he was in Washington.

Brad held his breath. He hoped that the realization that the conversation was drifting into his area of interest was not evident from his body language. Jacob had said nothing about how he would acquire drugs, but it was remarkable that Brad had got this far.

But then Jacob made a mistake.

Not that he could be blamed for it. Jacob had no idea

of Brad's skills, or of his background, or what mission he was on, if indeed he was on a mission at all. There are people in this world who often think of computers as just a tool and who do not take much interest in technology. Jacob was such a person.

While Brad had gone to the toilet, Jacob fired up his laptop computer and logged in to a website. Brad returned to the room as Jacob was concluding his transaction. The meaningless mumbo jumbo that flashed across the screen did not mean much to Jacob. It meant something to Brad Morgan. Especially the apparently meaningless rubbish that flashed across the bottom of the screen.

http\\www.......

When Jacob went to the toilet, Brad pulled a flash drive from his pocket and loaded a small program into Jacob's machine. It would not take up much room and be easily hidden away. Not that it mattered. When it had finished its primary task, it would delete itself completely, leaving no trace that it had ever existed. Brad turned away from the laptop, conscious that he would not want to be seen showing any interest when he saw Jacob's mobile phone also just sitting there on the table. It may not reveal anything, but Brad saw an opportunity to get some further information on his new-found friend.

Brad listened for any sign of Jacob coming back, but from the noise emanating from the toilet area, he knew he would have at least a couple of minutes. Brad grabbed the cell and quickly checked for the number. Then he entered a code into his own spare cell followed by Jacob's number and set the two cells side by side. The process of copying data from one to the other commenced, the only problem being that he had no way of knowing how much data there was, or the progress of the transfer.

He heard noises coming from the toilet and then the sound of flushing. A quick glance at his cell indicated that the transfer was still in progress as Jacob came back into the room. Brad leaned back on the table, leafing through a magazine, hoping that Jacob would not notice the two cells. He was not overly worried that Jacob would find a strange number on his unanswered calls list because that would reveal nothing other than a mystery with no solution. However, he was worried that he should see the two cells sitting side by side.

Jacob was, fortunately, in such a mood that alcohol was a higher priority than anything else. He went straight to the refrigerator and was busy examining and choosing from the contents when Brad's cell beeped. Both men reacted to the noise, Brad by grabbing the cell and Jacob looking up with a suspicious look on his face. Brad hoped that he sounded sincere. He pushed a few buttons and then informed Jacob that he had a message from his partner, and *she* wanted him to pick her up. Jacob appeared suspicious, if a little disappointed; but he was, after all, working for one of the most suspicious firms on the planet.

'One for the road?' was all that he asked as he moved from the fridge over to the table where Brad was now standing and thrust a glass into Brad's hand.

He looked at the laptop. The screen had gone to screensaver, but a tap on the keyboard revealed the system to be exactly as he had left it.

Jacob picked up his mobile phone and clicked a button.

That revealed nothing either. He shrugged.

'Bloody technology!' he laughed. 'Never did get involved with computers. I don't know how you guys from DS&T can stay sane!'

'Who said that we are sane?' Brad enquired.

They both had a good laugh.

Brad was in the clear.

More importantly, Jacob Dutton had unwittingly provided some critical information that could ultimately define the outcome of this saga!

Chapter 51

Shania

Shania's task was a little easier than Brad's. It was unfortunate, but that was just the way the world is. She was an extremely attractive, and seemingly promiscuous, young lady.

For no other reason than that she had called her friend Pita to have a drink with while in town, Shania went to the Halo Bar, which was in P Street just outside the Logan Circle. Pita was one of those ladies who did not need to wear any makeup—such was her flawless skin. She had that captivating look that made her special. And she had that attitude that made her need to be the focus of attention. She was tiny, a little over five feet, but had a well-proportioned body, long and wavy auburn hair, and looks that would turn many heads, and break more hearts.

Even more hearts would be broken when they realized that her friend Pita was a lesbian. Hence the choice of bar.

Apart from the fact that the Halo was smoke-free, it was also a part of the LGBT network, the acronym meaning lesbian, gay, bisexual, and transgender. Shania dared not ask Pita whether that was the bar that many people from the

J. Edgar Hoover Building used to wash away the troubles of the day. The question may have been too direct. Shania was confident that she already knew the answer to that question and hoped that some of her other friends that she had made while in training had not succumbed to the same interests as Pita. She hoped that this would be an intimate meeting and that it did not require a crowd.

Shania was interested in drugs, not sexual orientation.

It turned out that the selection of the bar and the company were not a bad choice. It was probably not the best environment in town to practice her not-so-finely-matured instincts, but she had to help Brad in any way she could. She had had it drummed into her during her training: Rely on your instincts. She had chosen this friend deliberately. If they wanted to get a result, and in a hurry, what better way than to find people who were at least vulnerable. And people who were certainly part of the drug scene.

Shania had no hang-up about Pita's sexual orientation. She believed in free choice, and that was that. But Pita was into social drugs. Shania had very definite views on that issue. When she had the time, she would try to change Pita's behaviour.

But not just yet. There were more important priorities.

Maybe, if she was successful in helping Brad solve this case, or at least set him off in the right direction, then he might, just might, stop frigging around, treating her like a delicate and untouchable goddess, and get into her pants!

There is something about the Halo Bar that made it ideal for the purpose that Shania had in mind. The atmosphere was pleasant, relaxed, amicable, and congenial. Despite her good looks, Shania attracted no attention from the males. She got plenty of admiring looks from the females, but because she was with Pita, she was not hassled. The people were in their own little world, where no one cared or cared who they were or what they were. They were among friends—at least until tomorrow, when they would once again have to deal with the everyday problem of simply being different.

And they talked.

They talked about their experiences. Everyone had a different tale to tell of how they had been initially rejected by family and friends. Then they had either slowly gained their understanding, or they had drifted farther apart. They talked about how having access to a bar, like the Halo had brought together people of similar orientation, where they could just be themselves. They talked about their social networking and how that had improved over the years with the Internet, and how the security provided in that environment had helped them and their friends.

And they talked about drugs.

Some even laughed about how easy drugs were to acquire.

Shania was puzzled—at least at first. While the FBI was not the lead United States Government agency chasing down the druggies, they did have at least a moral responsibility to help do something about them. Sure, the FBI was called in by the DEA to deal with prosecutions and the like. But they still had a responsibility to the American people. Even if the *F* for 'fidelity' and the *B* for 'bravery' did not apply in this case, surely the *I* did. *I* for 'integrity.' They had to adhere to moral and ethical principles. Therefore, why were some of these people who worked for the FBI talking about the ease of access to drugs?

The only answer could be that they were not talking about the normal sources of supply. They were talking about a private source of supply which, for reasons best known to the participants, was above the law.

And that could be the answer.

There was such a strong link between drugs and crime, between drug takers and criminals, that often the truth of the matter was obscured. If there were a source of supply that bypassed all the criminal elements, then what was the problem? That had to mean that their source was part of the FBI, or at least part of a government organisation. The logic used by Shania in reaching this conclusion may have been influenced by Mark and Brad. But assuming that Shania was on the correct track, this was leading in the direction of something that was scary. Shania would need to find out more, and Pita could be the source. She did not like to take advantage of her friend, but there were other considerations. Her mind went back to Brad. Maybe she could prove to him that she was more than just a pretty girl.

It was nearing midnight when they started to think of leaving the bar. Pita had had more to drink than was probably wise, while Shania had carefully restricted herself to only a few. Shania offered to give Pita a ride home. The offer was accepted with a little bit more enthusiasm than Shania had anticipated, the reason for which she could not know. At least not yet.

They made their way through the sparse traffic to Pita's apartment, which was just off the Lee Highway on the western side of the Potomac. Once there, Pita invited Shania to come into her apartment for a nightcap, and from the manner of the invitation, she obviously wished it was for something more. Pita would, in fact, be pleasantly surprised.

Shania was aware that there were drugs in the apartment, but neither of the ladies was up for that—at least not yet. Shania did not know any of the protocol involved with the kind of relationship that Pita obviously had in mind, but she had seen her share of pornographic movies in her official capacity and faking an interest in Pita would not be too hard.

They initially sat side by side on the floor with their backs against the couch and chatted while sipping on a glass of wine and watching a quiet DVD of the sultry songs and music by Diana Krall.

Then Pita first took hold of Shania's hand. They looked into each other's eyes, and there was nothing to detract them from the love and respect that they felt for each other. Encouraged by this, Pita playfully brushed Shania's hand over her breasts, and then eased it inside her blouse. The strange shock and sensation of touching the body of another woman and her baby-soft skin, and then the hard nipple, took Shania's breath away.

When Pita sensed no negative signs, she took the hand down towards her waist and nestled the hand at the top of her thigh. Still no negative sign. Slowly, Pita sat forward, moved her head slowly towards Shania, and then very gently kissed her on the cheek. There were positive signs.

Then Pita suddenly hesitated and sat back as she seemed to come out of a trance.

'Shania! I did not think! I am sorry! It is just that it has been so wonderful to see you again, after all this time!'

Shania reached out and hugged her friend.

'I love you, Pita. You are a very dear friend. You don't need to apologise. If we want to show that affection, why shouldn't we?' she added with a laugh, while holding Pita's gaze.

She just hoped that her doubts did not travel to her eyes.

While Shania did not know how far Pita was prepared to go, they continued to fondle and caress each other. Slowly

Pita eased her hand under Shania's blouse, undid the clasp on her bra, and let it fall free. She gasped at her first sight of Shania's nipples, and then leant forward, passionately kissing Shania as though in a trance once again. Before long, they were both semi-naked, and each seemed lost in her own world. Their hands fluttered over each other's body, searching for the spot where they could gain maximum pleasure as their legs wrapped around each other. It came as a complete, but pleasant, surprise when Shania found herself becoming aroused. Pita was becoming more intense, and Shania realised that she was approaching orgasm. Pita closed her eyes and moaned while Shania just continued caressing her. Pita seemed to forget that there was anyone else there, as she finally reached her climax, oblivious to the presence of Shania.

The girls continued massaging and kissing each other as though neither wanted this moment to end. Shania patiently waiting. Pita wrapped in dreams of her own.

No wonder men loved girls so much!

Originally, Shania had no intention of going this far. It had seemed so natural! She felt a brief pang of guilt when she thought of Brad. She should be with him now! She got over it by satisfying herself that she was really doing this to help him, while secretly, she enjoyed the experience. It was with a struggle that she kept some control and eventually managed to free herself. By this time, Pita was just lying back, resting with a contented smile on her face, and she made no attempt to cover her body.

Then Pita sat up and leant into Shania, a dreamy smile on her face. Pita kissed Shania full on the lips and whispered, 'That was wonderful!'

The sat there hugging each other. Shania content to wait to see what would happen next. Pita lost in her own little world. Then she reached up to Shania's face, lovingly held it in her two hands, and then almost whispered, 'Now, how about a snort?'

For just a moment, caught up in the afterglow of her first lesbian experience, Shania did not know what Pita was talking about. Then realised that she was back to talking about drugs. Although it had been hard to concentrate, Shania fought to regain her composure while she continued to snuggle up to her friend.

'I can't have too much. I have got important meetings tomorrow. Let's just have a little,' she added with a giggle, hoping that the insincerity did not creep into her voice. But she needed not have worried. Now that Pita had got something like agreement from her friend, and there was the exciting prospect of even more fun. She rushed to her feet, pulling Shania up after her, and they headed into the bedroom.

The room was surprisingly neat and tidy, except that every available space on shelves and the dressing table seemed to be taken up by soft toys of every description. On the dresser, there was also a laptop computer; but apart from that, it was a typical girl's room. Pita headed to the dresser and playfully teased open the top drawer and rummaged around to find what she was looking for. She did not look overly pleased when she found the small plastic bag of white powder. In fact, she looked quite annoyed as she turned once more to Shania and was very apologetic.

'They have had problems with supply just lately. This is all that I have!' she said, holding up a small plastic bag. 'I will try to order some more. But there should be enough for tonight,' she added with a giggle.

Shania's breath was taken away again. She had to

maintain this moment. Was she close to finding out something important?

She moved closer to Pita and put a loving arm around her.

'I told you, I have meetings tomorrow. And the way things are going at work, I could be up for a random drug test, so it is just not worth the risk. There is enough for you. I do not need drugs to get me started or to keep me going. You take it. I can get some tomorrow after I am through.'

A look of shock appeared on Pita's face, and Shania temporarily froze, unsure whether she had said or done something wrong. However, she needed not have worried, as the words flowed out of Pita.

'Have they fixed the problem? About time!'

Then her mood changed again as she giggled. 'God, if we cannot get drugs, who can?'

Caution did seem the correct way to go, and Shania replied, laughing at her friend's obvious stress,

'Oh, I don't know about the supply issue. All I know is that I can get them again. I will check it out tomorrow and let you know.'

It was the best Shania could come up with by way of an explanation. Again, she needed not have worried. Pita simply gave Shania a huge hug and then devoted her attention to the white powder which she snorted, leaving nothing for Shania. The warm rush enveloped Pita as she lay back on the bed and pulled her friend down with her, her hands fondling Shania's breasts and thrusting her lower body urgently upwards as thought expecting Shania to take her. Shania watched, mesmerised, but had the sense to gently caress Pita's body as she seemed oblivious to the world around her. Pita moaned again, lost in a fantasy world, and she reached orgasm again, this time without seeming to care what her friend did.

Then she suddenly came out of the trance and, as though it had never happened, smiled a dreamy smile, hugged Shania again, and simply said, 'I must get some more!' She seemed oblivious to the risks, content in her own little world, of which Shania was now an integral part.

Pita went to her laptop computer and switched it on. The website that she accessed was not stored among of her favourites, and she seemed to take a very circuitous route to get to the part of the web that she was searching for. Nonetheless, she was quickly into the order process, and Shania just hoped that she could remember the many twists and turns that Pita had followed.

What on earth did Pita want with yet another soft toy?

Chapter 52

Progress

Brad and Shania both returned to the Georgetown Apartments at about the same time. Brad was just firing up his laptop when there was a knock on his door. He suspected that it would be Mark. He was pleasantly surprised to find out that it was Shania. He greeted her with a kiss and went to return to his laptop and began explaining to her what he had discovered after his night at Jacob's hotel room.

But then there was something different about this girl. She clung on to him, and her kiss was more passionate than he would have expected. She was not about to let him go.

'That can wait!' Shania urgently whispered as she pushed him towards the bedroom. She had her jacket on when she came in through the door, but that was soon discarded, and she reached for Brad's belt. He could not know whether that was to stop him from falling, or for some other purpose. Either way, she was not about to let go as he was pushed backward onto the bed. His first thought was that he should protest. The only thing that stopped him was the determined look on Shania's face and the fact that he could feel himself becoming very rapidly aroused. Shania could sense his arousal as she feverishly fought to unbuckle his belt.

Brad did not have time to even think as he lay back and reached up towards her to at least give the impression that he was participating in the event. She sensed his trepidation as she just grabbed his hands in frustration and forced them up to her breasts.

He did not know what she was on or what had suddenly changed in their relationship. She did not appear to be affected by alcohol, or drugs, but he was not about to object. Finally, she got his belt free, pulled down his trousers, and clambered on top of him. She reached orgasm almost immediately. Then she slowed from the hectic pace of her initial assault and continued to move on top of him, and then erupted again as she felt Brad also reaching his climax.

She smothered him with kisses and clung to him as though fearful that this moment would end too soon.

They lay on the bed, Brad still wondering what was happening, Shania seemingly exhausted, yet content. He did not want to spoil the moment, so he just quietly stroked her hair as she snuggled in his arms. After what seemed like hours, but was only a few minutes, Shania let out a sigh, raised herself on one elbow, and looked into his eyes.

'I am sorry, but I love you!'

The words came out, and the eyes told the true story. She kissed him lightly on the lips, a smile on her face. Yes, she really did love him!

'Well! Do you want to tell me what that was all about?' Brad asked in a quiet and gentle voice.

Shania gazed into his innocent brown eyes. How could

she tell him that it had taken a brief and platonic affair with her lady friend to wake up her innermost urges?

She had never had a meaningful relationship with a man. Sure, there had been the odd flirtation—a rush of blood to the head, fuelled by adrenaline or lust. But not love. And afterwards, she had witnessed the cold reality of life in the fast lane.

The brief shrug of the shoulders. The *'I'll call you tomorrow'* line, said in the heat of the moment. And then the long, quiet, lonely nights waiting for the call that never came. Waiting for what?

Shania had embarked on a career that did not exactly make it easy to maintain a relationship with someone who was not part of the same fraternity. But the FBI songbook stressed,

Do not mix business with pleasure!

So what chance was there? Outside of the FBI, guys did not like girls to have real jobs. Within the FBI, a girl did not really have the chance to compete with the boys. It was not as bad as the CIA and some other parts of the security services, where girls were there to be treated as second-class citizens. But it still meant that it was hard work being recognised for competence and performance, rather than just for looks. Despite what was said by politicians, bias based on gender was alive and well in the security services.

And then she had met Brad. A guy who seemed to understand and accept her for what she was. And who treated her as an equal. Then she realised what love really was. And she was then too scared to make a move, least it ended up in disappointment yet again.

She needed to be loved, but she had realised with a shock that she was in danger of finding love where it was available, rather than where her instincts led her. The brief affair with Pita had been her wake-up call. Could she now lie to the man she loved?

'I went out with Pita tonight,' she began, cautiously. 'She is a lesbian, and an incredibly beautiful lady. It came down to a choice—did I want her, or do I want you? Guess what? I want to be with you!'

Brad just looked at her and smiled. He understood.

They kissed again. Brad struggled to find the right words that would say what he felt while trying to get back to the reason for their being in Washington. And get back to the task that he had been given by Mark, with the rapidly approaching deadline.

It was his turn to sigh. 'I love you too—more than you could ever imagine!' And then tried to get some sanity into their relationship. 'I suppose we should do some work, and then, later, we could …'

Shania laughed. 'Typical. Men!' She playfully threw her leg over his, her breasts now fully uncovered; kissed him again; and then, with mock modesty, covered herself up. 'So, are you going to tell me what you have been up to before I tell you what I have discovered?'

That got Brad's attention. 'You have some good news?' he asked while trying, and failing, to stop his hands wandering over her beautiful body.

'I think I have! The way into the network is something to do with stuffed toys.'

That also got Brad's attention.

He had taken notice of the laptop at the hotel. However, he had not taken any notice of the other things that had been lying around Jacob's room. There had been the usual collection of things associated with a traveller— the haphazard bits of clothing, newspapers, scattered as though they had no home in this temporary place of residence. The room was so untidy that there was no ordered state to refer to, and therefore no way of knowing what should have been where. Now there was something else that should have struck him as odd. That man called Jacob had a couple of stuffed toys. They were not placed as though they were to be a present for some half-forgotten child. They were just cast aside as though they were an afterthought and not germane to anything else in the room. And Jacob had said that he was single and had not mentioned any children either past or present.

'Tell me more!' Brad sat up, reluctant to move from his position of extreme comfort and pleasure. Wheels were starting to turn. Fortunately, Shania sensed the mood, and forgot about the fact that she was still half naked.

'It was Pita's room—she had so many soft toys. But when she went onto her laptop, she ordered some more, and I thought she was going to order some more drugs. That is when I thought maybe she was.'

Within seconds, they had moved from a couple, very much in love and making the most of the loss of their inhibitions, to the professionals that they were. They moved to Brad's laptop, went onto Google, and, with a couple more clicks, followed the link that he had seen on Jacob's machine. The trail led them into the intelligence and security services social website. Once on the website, they browsed through all manner of options. They could not find anywhere that offered stuffed toys.

Brad backed out of the website, and he tried searching for toys and came up with a few options—something in excess of 300 million. He narrowed the search by keying in 'stuffed' in front of the word *toys*. That worked. He got under 3 million options. So, what did he do now? Then he tried *Peshawar stuffed toys*. That reduced the options down to a more manageable 9,200.

As a distraction, while he half-heartedly browsed

through the list trying to focus his attention through the kaleidoscope of random thoughts, he fired up the burner cell that he had used earlier that night. That also revealed nothing more than what you would expect. It had a call log that was as meaningless as a supermarket cash-out docket. It also had an address list that meant nothing, except there was one name that Jacob had called frequently within the last few days.

Why then was it encrypted?

Brad again logged on to Google, went to a site that few would know about, and quickly downloaded the appropriate software. Then he connected the cell to his laptop, downloaded the data that he had copied from Jacob's cell, and then ran the de-encryption software over it.

It was time to wake up the boss.

Mark had not been able to sleep. His mind was a kaleidoscope of plans, problems, and a fear of what would happen in the following days. Eventually, he gave up and decided to read a book. Robert Ludlum was his favourite author. Stories that involved the intelligence and security services and the Government of the United States in improbable but realistically described plots that would end the natural order of things but usually ended up OK. Plots that described organizations in which the bad guys *always* seemed to have an endless supply of fully informed, superbly fit, fully equipped, and disposable men. And the good guy who was *usually* on his own cut off from the security of his vast support networks and who could not escape from the clutches of the bad guys until the very end. Mark knew that in real life, this kind of thing just did not happen. Nonetheless, he could to the dilemma.

Mark could not concentrate on the story and ended up staring out over the Potomac River. He was worried about the lady that he loved. He vowed to punish those who had taken her from him. If only he could unravel the kaleidoscope of problems that he faced. And if only his small team was adequate to meet the demands that they faced.

The ringing of the telephone shattered his thoughts. It unnerved him until he realized it was an internal call. At least someone else was still awake. And probably worrying, just like he was.

It was Brad.

The *'Are you awake?'* question caused Mark to laugh. He overcame the desire to make an equally illogical and sarcastic response and simply replied, 'Yeah, what's happening?'

Brad sounded wide awake.

'Could you step down to my room? We have had an interesting evening and have since been searching on the web. I think we are on to something. I may need some help, though. At this stage, I would only describe it as a lead. It is tenuous, but that won't last. We are definitely on the right track.'

Brad tried to sound as positive as was possible. If for no other reason than to give Mark some good news for a change. Besides, Brad was feeling upbeat, and the sooner he got things moving. And the sooner he would find time to attend to other matters of a more pressing and of a more manly nature.

'OK, I am on my way.'

Mark looked at the clothes he was wearing. He had on a dressing gown over a T-shirt and boxers, and on his feet, he had an old pair of slippers. He shrugged. At this time in the morning, who would care?

He set off down the corridor to Brad's room and knocked lightly on the door. He was surprised and embarrassed when Shania answered the door. She laughed and gave Mark a hug, dragging him into the room. Body language always tells its own story. Something had changed, and Mark's reading of the situation was probably spot-on. It was about time that Brad got his rocks off! Mark thought as he smiled to himself.

But Brad was all business.

'Best if I explain what we have been up to,' Brad began. 'I went to an Irish bar—Ireland's Four Courts—where people from the CIA usually hang out. And I got lucky. I latched on to a couple of guys who were from out of town. It turned out that one of them was from Afghanistan. We went back to his hotel for a few more drinks and then up to his room for a nightcap. While I was there, he went on to the Internet, and I am betting he was ordering drugs. I could not see the precise path that he was into, but it had something to do with the CIA network.'

'Was Shania with you?' Mark interjected.

'No,' Shania answered herself. 'I went off to the Halo bar with a friend of mine called Pita, from the FBI. On a similar mission to Brad's, but with the FBI. If you didn't know, the Halo is an LGBT bar.'

Mark interjected again. 'What is LGBT?'

Shania looked embarrassed for a moment. Neither of the two men read anything into her embarrassment, especially when she explained the meaning of the acronym. She hurried on.

'Back at her apartment, Pita also went onto a website. I thought that she was ordering drugs, but she went and ordered some stuffed toys! That was what I explained to Brad. She had stuffed toys all over the place!'

Mark reacted as though he had been shot. He almost whispered to himself. 'Don't tell me that the bloody Brits knew all along!'

Brad did not seem to notice the question and interrupted.

'That got me interested because Jacob also had a couple of stuffed toys—'

'Who is Jacob?' Mark asked, his voice still little more than a whisper.

'Son of a bitch! Is he our man from Afghanistan?'

'Why? Yes, what are you thinking?'

'Jacob is not a particularly uncommon name,' Mark began. 'But less than a week ago, we were tracking a man of that name in the Helmand province in the south of Afghanistan. He was a man that Stephen Rodriguez spent an inordinate amount of time with. We lost track of him when we were in Kabul, but he could have come back to the United States. He is hard to describe. Nondescript summed him up—about five feet ten, 190 pounds, forty-five, maybe fifty years old, a moustache that needs a bit of TLC, thinning brown hair—'

'That's him!' Brad interrupted. 'You know him?'

Mark sat forward. 'I do not exactly know him. I know of him!' Mark almost said to himself as he repeated, 'Jacob was the man with who Stephen Rodriguez spent quite some time traveling around Marjah with. That is a place also in the south of Afghanistan. I know that Jacob subsequently went with Stephen up to Kabul, but there we lost track of him. In fact, we lost track of everything and everyone! He must have slipped back to the US ahead of Rodriguez. As far as I know, Stephen is due back tomorrow—sorry, later today.'

Brad began to smile.

'I also got a peep at his mobile phone and managed to find out who he had been calling recently. Some of his address details and the messages were encrypted, but I got around that. He has been communicating with a guy called Stephen, but not here in Washington. His messages, as well as being encrypted, also use a code. But the structure seems fairly simple. I will work that out shortly.'

Mark looked impressed.

'How can you do that?' And then he sighed. 'Don't tell me you copied his cell phone data!' He turned to Shania. 'You should arrest this guy! He is a menace!' Turning back to Brad, he said, 'Well done! What we need to do now is to confirm who this man Jacob really is.'

'Can't you ask your father to check up?' Brad inquired. 'Jacob is definitely with the CIA.'

Mark sighed. 'I do not think that my old man is of much use to us now. OK, so you called me about being on to something. And I assume that is more than just to brag about how clever you are. What is your theory?'

'Well, it depends on what you discovered in Afghanistan,' Brad began. 'Firstly, we know that the CIA, and probably every other government agency on the planet, are into social networks for the purpose of spying on our friends and foes alike. And every man and his dog are on the Internet for business and other reasons. Secondly, you believe that Stephen Rodriguez is somehow tied up with the supply of drugs from Afghanistan, and we are struggling to find out about his distribution network. Put the two together and assume that something totally unrelated to drugs can be bought and sold on the net. However, drugs are the product that is being sold. That is where stuffed toys come in. What say stuffed toys are the cover?'

Mark smiled. They were on to something. But they had been slow on the uptake. He replied to Brad's comment with an air of bitterness in his voice and with a shake of his head.

'We should have spent more time with MI6. The British secret service has known about the toys long before we found the connection. In Kabul, we had to use the Brits to dig us out of a hole. They gave us a couple of satellite phones and a few other bits of gear. I did not understand it at the time, but I do now. They gave us a teddy bear! Why do they always have to play games? But you have to admire their sense of humour!'

Mark picked up Brad's satellite phone. He did not say a word as he pressed the buttons. After several minutes, the phone was answered in another land and another time zone.

'Hi, Dusty, how are you going?'

'Well, OK. If I can ever get out of this shithole!' Dusty replied while not bothering to explain where *this* shithole was. 'What the fuck are you doing up at this hour?'

Mark ignored the question from Dusty.

'OK, a question for you: What kind of factory was attached to the Aziar Textile Company?'

'Why? It's a toy factory.'

Chapter 53

Circles

The time had seemed to pass slowly for Dusty being buried underground with nothing to refer to or to relate to. He had almost given up. The air was dank. During the time that he had been confined to the cupboard, no one had used the tunnel or the laboratory. The only thought that he had was to be patient and wait until the night came. But he could not sleep. In fact, he must not sleep.

And then his satellite phone started to throb in his pocket. It was 9:00 am, but at least Dusty knew that it would be a friend calling because no one else knew the number. He thanked his lucky stars that he had thought to switch off the ring tone and go to Vibrate. Even so, the throb sounded like a ship's foghorn in the cramped quarters of the cupboard.

It was Mark.

And his question was not exactly riveting. But it meant that he had to get out of this hole and find out some more about the presence or otherwise of a toy factory and what went on at the other end of the tunnel. At least Mark reminded him of one vital piece of information that he had overlooked during all the drama: today was Saturday, and maybe, even in Pakistan, toy factories did not work on the weekends.

Dusty was not so sure about drug laboratories.

Dusty got out of his cupboard, and his relief at no longer being cramped was euphoric. He stretched until he was sure that all his body parts were working, and then moved off down the tunnel to where it ended. He listened carefully but could hear no noise coming from up above. He studied the trapdoor some thirty feet above him and could see no sign of any kind of security. If he could get up to the trapdoor and look inside the building, warehouse, or whatever was up there, that would be fine.

There were three problems: How did he get up? Was the trapdoor bolted from the top? Who would be waiting for him when, or *if*, he made it that far?

Dusty shrugged. He was rapidly concluding that it did not really matter. His part in the scheme of things was at an end. He would be lucky to escape alive.

He made his way back to the cupboard and surveyed the tools and equipment that he had at his disposal. There were enough beams from which he could fashion a ladder. Whether he would have enough strength to lift them was debatable, but at least he had to try. He thought of calling Mark—he had said nothing of his predicament in their earlier conversation and had not informed him of what he was going to attempt to do now.

But no! What was the point in doing that? Mark had enough problems of his own. And Mark was, after all, an officer. So, he would be bereft of any ideas of how Dusty, a mere sergeant, should get out of this mess.

This was a job for the men.

The first thing that Dusty did was to secure a couple of the beams against the door leading to the textile store so that it could not be opened. The good news with that was that no one could distract him while he was working by entering the tunnel from the other end. The bad news was that if anyone came into the tunnel from that factory, they would simply ask the residents at the other end to go check, and that would be the end of that. Still, he could not have everything.

Slowly, he moved the beams and other assorted bits of timber from the cupboard to the end of the tunnel. By the time he had finished, at least two hours had passed, and Dusty was dripping in sweat. If anyone else entered the tunnel now, they were as likely to die from asphyxiation—such was the rancid smell from Dusty's perspiring body. He decided to rest before attempting the final effort. There was still no sound from above, and that encouraged him to continue. But there was no point in reaching the top exhausted because he may have further work to do before this day was over.

Like kill someone, or at least defend himself.

He had nothing to secure the beams, either to the walls or to each other. He decided to lean the longest beams against the opposite side of the shaft and then place one of the shorter beams across. Then, by working his way up the shaft, he could build a ladder-like structure, albeit the steps would be over three feet apart. When he got to the third step, and he was less than halfway up the shaft, he realised that his structure would never support either his weight or the weight of the beams. After a few moments' thought, he overcame this obstacle by placing beams across from the opposite wall of the shaft propping against the ladder-like structure, and that seemed to work. But it all took time. And it all took energy. For a moment, Dusty began to think his whole plan was a waste of time. What if, when he eventually got to the top, he could not open the trapdoor? Then it would all have been a complete waste of time.

One thing was certain: if this attempt failed, then he would not be returning the beams to the cupboard!

Doggedly, Dusty worked on. It was six hours later that he eventually made it so that he could reach the trapdoor. He leant against the wall, conscious of the state he was in, conscious of the possibilities that lay ahead. He knew that if he had to climb back down, then he would never be able to make it back up. Despite his strength, Dusty was exhausted. But sheer willpower kept him moving.

The first tentative push on the trapdoor did nothing. He had expected that and planned for that. He got his feet into a better position and braced himself one more time. This time he had his back against the trapdoor and his knees bent. He had had many hours to think of what might happen. It was almost impossible to thrust a beam upwards and hope to have any chance to break through if the trapdoor had been secured from above. And that would leave him in a very precarious position. The only chance was to use his body strength in one massive thrust that should break any bolts that were holding it closed. This would be his only chance, especially if there happened to be people in the room above. And if there were, he would have a matter of only a split second in which to retrieve his Glock. From what he had already seen with the police presence, and from what he knew of people in the drug trade, they tended to shoot first and ask questions later.

Dusty breathed in one last huge breath. Then with all the strength that his tired body could muster, he pushed upwards in one fast and decisive movement.

The trapdoor was flung open as though hit by a hurricane. It crashed to the floor, making one almighty *thump*, shattering the peace. The door had not been secured, and Dusty almost fell back down the shaft—such was the lack of any resistance. He managed to grab the side of the trapdoor as the top two beams of his ladder broke loose and plummeted down the shaft, crashing and banging as they went. One of them must have connected with a critical beam in Dusty's makeshift ladder, because then, as if in slow motion, the whole structure, slowly at first, and then rapidly, tumbled to the bottom of the shaft.

The din was deafening, and a pillar of dust came up, causing Dusty to choke as he was engulfed. He struggled to maintain his tenuous grip on the edge of the trapdoor but with one last herculean effort, he scrambled his legs to get some purchase on the side of the shaft. There was no time to reach for his Glock or his torch. If anyone came to check on the disturbance, he was a dead man. Despite his size and strength, he was too exhausted to care.

Pure adrenaline drove him on as he scrambled out of the hole and onto the floor of—what?

Dusty lay catching his breath, conscious that at any moment, someone would come to discover what all the noise had been about. But to his complete surprise, no one came. And he was in absolute pitch darkness. He reached for his Glock and took the safety off. He then switched the dim red light on and surveyed his new surroundings.

He was in another cupboard, or at least a small square room! He switched the light off, and to the left of where he had entered, he could just make out the gap between two doors. There was no other way of getting in or out other than via the trapdoor to the tunnel. The only contents of the room were propped against the wall. It was an extension ladder.

Dusty got to his feet, closed the trapdoor, and listened. He could vaguely make out the sounds of someone talking, but it was in a foreign language. It took a few minutes for him to figure out that he was listening to a radio. The door to the cupboard was locked, but that would not be a problem. Dusty had had enough of being in cupboards. And despite his state of exhaustion, he was not going to give it all up just yet. However, he would be much more cautious in getting out of this one.

Using the red light once more, he examined the inside of the doors. The door on the left, was bolted at the top and at the bottom on the inside. The door on the right had a deadbolt on the outside that was locked in place. The easiest way out of the cupboard was to unbolt the left door, which Dusty did, easing the doors slightly ajar.

He was in another factory.

It was mostly inactive. At the far end of the large room, four men were busy going about their business: they were assembling cardboard boxes. To escape the chronic boredom of this task, all of them were wearing headsets, and they were completely oblivious to Dusty's presence or to the catastrophic noise that had been generated on his entrance.

The only exits from this factory were to the front, past the four men, or almost straight ahead of Dusty on the other side of the room. There was, of course, another way—back the way he had come. But that was now out of the question. The door ahead of him was a fire door that looked as though it had never been opened since the day the factory had been built. The area was littered with waste, and although in most Western factories some inspector would have checked it from time to time, it was doubtful this one had been, and therefore doubtful whether it would open without further drama.

Dusty sighed. Provided no one tried to use the tunnel, the safest place for him would be back in the cupboard, and to wait until the four men left. And hope that they were not replaced by others.

It was now approaching 4:00 pm in the afternoon. It

had taken Dusty the best part of seven hours to travel a few hundred feet—less distance if you factored in that some of that distance had been straight up.

No one came near the cupboard, which was just as well for all concerned. Dusty had not washed for approaching three days. He had spent most of that time grovelling on the ground staying hidden while he observed the building. Then he had been underground and hauling beams up a shaft that was thirty feet high. The smell of body odour must have been terrible. Even so, he had resolved that if he had to get out, he had to start shooting. He was dog-tired, and he felt that he did not care anymore.

So tired that he almost missed the departure of the four men.

There was a sudden silence, which really was all that got Dusty's attention. The four men were leaving as the dusk settled in Peshawar. The last man to leave set the alarm and slammed the door behind him as the alarm began its countdown—*beep, beep* … If the alarm was standard, it would cease beeping after one minute. Then, depending on the age of the electronics, it would either recommence the beep once any movement was detected by the infrared sensors, or it would simply wait. And then, on detecting some movement, at the expiry of the prescribed time interval, all hell would break loose as the alarm sounded. Again, if the alarm was standard, that would give Dusty less than one minute to disarm it. Too soon and the departing men could realize that something was wrong, so he patiently waited while the countdown continued. If he were too late switching off the alarm, then they, and everyone else within a five-mile radius of the building, would know that something was wrong.

He had to have faith that normal standards applied. Dusty also had to assume that the alarm was externally monitored and given the type of business that seemed to be going on, he could expect a rapid response.

The countdown of the alarm finally stopped.

The building lapsed into complete silence.

Dusty waited.

He knew that he was tired. But the next minute of activity would be critical, so he had to gather his thoughts, summon what energy he could, and concentrate.

From his position in the cupboard, he scanned the room through the crack in the door. He located two infrared detectors on the opposite wall facing outwards into the factory floor. Again, depending on the type of equipment used, each detector probably had an angle of about 70 degrees left and right, and the two that he could see would be overlapping. What he could not do is to see what was on the wall on his side of the room, but he could assume that there was no need for extra detectors given the coverage already afforded. From the angles, and from the fact that one of the detectors was directly opposite the cupboard door, one thing was clear. As soon as he exited the cupboard, he would be detected, and the alarm countdown would commence.

He then reviewed his options. He could either deactivate the alarm, or he could go back down the tunnel. He preferred the first option, but he had to have a plan B. There was a ladder, so getting back down to the tunnel was not a problem. The problem was that he would then be trapped in the tunnel. If the alarm went off, the first thing that would happen was that there would be a response, particularly from the guards outside, and also from the people who were monitoring the alarm. The security people would surely seal both ends of this elaborate setup. He would be trapped.

He would have one minute before his fate was sealed.

Dusty took a couple of deep breaths, and he was ready.

Dusty crashed out of the door, and before he had even reached the alarm pad, the monotonous *beep, beep* started again. He pulled his scanner out of his pocket to enable him to find the code. Then there was another problem. The scanner was broken. No doubt crushed sometime during his spectacular exit from the shaft. But Dusty told himself that now was not the time to panic. He had now perhaps forty-five seconds to get out, or go back to the cupboard, or find out what the code was. Going out the door seemed like an easy decision. He could not know who or what was out there. He gave himself thirty seconds before he would have to go back to the cupboard, back through the tunnel, and make his escape through the other factory without ever getting to see what he had been looking for. But that was stretching reality.

He first tried the factory setting *1234*. Nothing. He then tried the number that worked at the other factory alarm: *6597*. Nothing. He had ten seconds to decide, maybe twenty-five seconds before all hell broke loose. He had come so far that it would be a shame to waste it. He despaired at the thought of it, but it was back to the cupboard and almost-certain discovery. He could fight his way out, but the odds were very much against that being successful.

He turned away, a beaten man.

Then something caught his eye. A piece of paper with four numbers written on it: *8156*. Surely these people weren't so stupid as to write down so simple a code! *Give it a go!* The ten seconds were gone, so what the hell.

He keyed in the numbers 8156.

The alarm countdown stopped.

But had it stopped because the one-minute set time was up, or because the code that Dusty entered had been correct?

He held his breath, waiting for the alarm to sound.

No alarm sounded.

He was safe.

He felt that he was getting paranoiac. Nonetheless, he waited, hidden behind a table that protected him from the view of anyone entering from the front door, or anyone entering from one of the various offices that were on a mezzanine floor at the back of the building. Only after ten minutes, he began to believe that he was alone.

Dusty stood up and surveyed the factory.

The place where the four men had been working was littered with small cardboard boxes. And there was a strong smell of glue.

He froze as he realized what the men had been doing. They were sealing something between sheets of cardboard. He searched around the area of the bench but could find no evidence of precisely what was being hidden in this way, so he resorted to the obvious. He proceeded to carefully split open one of the boxes. And he had found what he had been looking for. It was well thought out. A thin plastic bag was carefully layered between the sheets of cardboard, and the contents of the plastic bag were what caught his attention.

Heroin.

He pocketed a couple of the plastic bags, not sure at this stage how their presence would be explained to some curious Customs official. They needed hard evidence, and this was as hard as it got. But it was no use to them in Pakistan, and it was also no use to them if Dusty was bailed up in some jail for possession. But Dusty could not worry about that now.

He was puzzled. Why would anyone seek to conceal

a drug in such a way? The boxes were intended to contain whatever was produced by this factory. And from what he had observed in the rest of the factory, that was soft toys. The benches, most of which had sewing machines on them, were littered with a wide variety of materials and dogs, cats, bears, and countless other types of animals in various stages of completion; but they were all the same basic size. The size that would conveniently fit into one of the boxes.

Drug traffickers were very smart and sophisticated and had a long time ago abandoned any plans to conceal drugs for shipment in soft toys. But to conceal the drugs in the packaging was plain dumb.

Unless that is, the plan for shipping them was much subtler, and dumb was good enough.

Getting a soft toy and then destroying it to get at the drugs was not the recommended way of giving a gift or a present to someone. If that someone was into drugs and did not care about the animal or the toy, it would probably be OK; but a more civilized way was to just keep the box. So, it really became a question of what was being ordered, and in the view of Dusty, which did not really matter. All they wanted was the box.

He looked around to see what else these people were up to. Over to the left, there was an area in which the toys were placed in the boxes and prepared for dispatch. The toys were simply put into a box of the appropriate size and packed with soft white paper, and a couple of plastic containers, which were marked as containing silica gel, were also placed in each box, presumably to keep the contents dry. Further back, towards where he had gained entry to the factory, was a workbench where the plastic containers were prepared and filled with the silica— although to Dusty, the entire process did seem a little over the top. It was not normal business practice to go to the trouble of filling their own containers, but who could say what went on in the minds of these people. That is, unless the plastic containers did not, in fact, contain silica gel. Dusty pocketed a couple of the filled plastic containers for later investigation.

The question now was how they got the drug-infested boxes through the postal services or other delivery systems, border controls, and all the other entrapment mechanisms that lay in the path between supplier and recipient of illegal substances. There was only one way to successfully do that: not go through the postal services or freight or courier companies, all of which would involve customs and the other means of entrapment. But that was ridiculous. How else could you get goods from one country to another?

Dusty continued to search the factory until he stumbled on a pallet about a meter square with a layer of boxes of the same standard shape and size. On the bench, adjacent to where the pallet was lying, were several pre-printed address labels. And they were all identical:

Ministry of Foreign Affairs
Islamabad

Dusty went cold. Was the Pakistani Foreign Service involved in drugs? Or was the CIA, or Stephen Rodriguez, using the Pakistanis to ship the goods to the States? It sounded a bit far-fetched. But that was one way of making sure that the goods could avoid customs scrutiny.

Send them via the diplomatic bag!

Dusty had mixed feelings. He felt the thrill that came from a possible understanding, or a realization, of what could be going on. He felt the let-down that came from an understanding that this scenario was highly unlikely unless some enormously powerful and influential people were involved. If this theory was true, then even more people were involved. But some of them were outside the jurisdiction of the US authorities, which would make it difficult to pin anything on the CIA. Dusty searched further but could find no evidence of the boxes being destined for anywhere else other than Pakistan.

He was aware that his luck had to run out eventually as he contemplated what was going on. He returned to the bench and extracted one of the delivery dockets, which also went into his pocket. He then decided to call it quits.

The evidence he had now gathered was finite. He now knew of the location of a drug laboratory and the place where the drugs were packaged, ready for dispatch. He now had more than enough evidence to make an irrefutable case against the owners and the operators of the factory, and a good case against the Pakistani Ministry of Foreign Affairs. However, that was not the case he was trying to build.

As a lawyer, he felt that he now knew the truth. He had nothing but circumstantial evidence that Stephen Rodriguez had anything to do with it. Sure, Stephen had visited the Aziar Company in both their previous and present locations. And he had visited a drug dealer in the Helmand province. The problem was that the drug dealer was dead, probably on the orders of Stephen Rodriguez.

Smoke and mirrors.

Dusty returned to the workplace and reassembled the box, leaving the bench as he had found it. He then made his way towards the rear of the building and relocked the cupboard door as best he could. The people in either factory would eventually realize that something was amiss by the heap of beams that lay at the bottom of the shaft, but Dusty was not about to sort out that mess. He doubted that they would ever figure out what had occurred, so there was no damage done as far as he was concerned. Next, he went to check the fire escape door, but as he had thought earlier, getting out of the building that way was out of the question.

He had to make his exit via the front door.

He scanned the surrounding buildings and could see no sign of life, but now he had another riddle answered. He now knew why the security guards he had witnessed the day before took so long to circuit the building—they were circuiting two buildings. There did not appear to be anyone around, but he was taking no chances.

Dusty waited, and sure enough, two guards eventually appeared outside the door. They were talking in Farsi, so Dusty had no idea what was being said. What he did not know was whether part of their routine was to enter the building, switch off the alarm, and make sure that the building was secure—all windows locked and everything in its correct place. If they did that, then they would immediately realise that the alarm was not set. Their initial response would be that the occupants had not set it, but they would surely call it in, and that could then involve some further action on their part. Dusty was thankful that the alarm was not the type that issued a continuous *beep* once it was set, so he just patiently waited behind the desk to see what would happen.

Nothing happened.

The two guards stood by the door talking and laughing. They had a smoke and did not seem to be in any hurry. Then they left, circulating down the right-hand side of the building, and were gone.

Dusty waited for a couple more minutes.

Patience.

He was surprised that the door was not deadlocked, relying entirely on the keypad. He reset the alarm and gently closed the door behind him. He immediately dropped to the ground and scurried along until he was well clear of the building. Again, he thanked the instructors at Fort Bragg all those years ago. Despite his size, he could move with the stealth of a cat.

Then he had two calls to make.

His first call was to Mark. That call went to answerphone. He left no message.

His second call did get answered. It was to Owen.

'Where the hell have you been?' was the greeting, he got.

'Oh, just been wandering around looking at the sights!' Dusty replied, giving nothing away. 'I may need some help. I must get back to the United States in a hurry. I would prefer to travel by military airplane. I don't want the hassle of travelling by civilian flight. Is there any chance you can arrange that?'

The reply that he got was what he had come to expect from the likeable Welshman. Owen would arrange his return to the United States.

Dusty had originally thought of asking Griz to arrange the trip because he would be better informed of military aircraft going in and out of the Peshawar Air Base but figured he could just as easily find that out from Owen. And perhaps find out in that process whether the two of them were on the same song sheet. Not that it really mattered. Dusty was about the lowest in the pecking order, and he was only trying to return home from a mission.

The fact that he had in his possession a couple of pieces of cardboard, plastic bags, and small containers meant that he wanted to at least avoid the dogs that were everywhere around civilian airports. Other than that, it would be nice to catch up with friends.

At least one friend. But even she would still have to wait until he had debriefed.

Mark had sounded positive when Dusty had told him the product of the adjacent factory.

Mark had not told him the reason why he wanted to know.

But it gave an indication that they were moving in the same direction.

Chapter 54

Wheels

The Gulfstream jet landed at Andrews Air Force Base at around 4:30 pm, and a very tired and grumpy Stephen Rodriguez emerged into a cold, wet, windy, and therefore miserable, Washington DC. He would not have time to sleep for some hours yet, so his mood would not improve. He knew that he was now treading a very thin line. What he was doing was not what he was expected to do by his government. But he had to do it for his own preservation. And to protect the network that he had invested so much of his time into.

He had deceived his boss about his real reason for going to Afghanistan. On balance, which was manageable. The trip could be justified in bureaucratic terms, so that was that.

What he had to do now was different. He would have to be in his office to report back early the next morning, and that meant by 7:30 am at the very latest. That meant he had fifteen hours before he had to report to Jim Schlesinger. Between now and then, he had to sort out this interference in his plans that had apparently been orchestrated by a bunch of amateurs.

He was confident that he could sort them out.

The first thing that he had to do was to get rid of the CIA driver who had been sent to collect him at Andrews. The obvious way to achieve that, without raising any suspicions, was to head home. There his only distractions would then be from his interfering wife and the surveillance team from the Secret Service. Dayanara Rodriguez was manageable, although she may be a little irritated by her husband's apparent preoccupation with matters concerning his work. She would not be able to understand. Women always thought, with their husbands, having been away overseas for a while, that they would be the sole focus of their attention on their return. Rodriguez had been so preoccupied during his trip that he had not even bought Dayanara a gift. Worse still, he had not brought anything for his favourite daughter, Estefania.

Still, he had work to do, and that was of a higher priority than placating the women in his life.

His driver was expecting to take him to Langley but a terse instruction from Rodriguez delivered him to his home in Bethesda, where the driver just shrugged and went off to do his next pickup job. It did not matter to the driver. Although he was a fully trained CIA agent and was equally adept at driving or killing. His current task was to pick up and deliver these arrogant government servants to wherever they wanted to go.

It also did not matter to Rodriguez.

As Stephen got out of the car, he automatically emptied the mailbox and moved to unlock the front door. As he swung the door open, the emptiness of the house registered in his tired mind. The house looked as though it was occupied, but a sixth sense told him that nobody was there. It was unusual to find no one at home. Sure, he had not bothered to call ahead—he rarely did—but that was no excuse for the house being so cold and impersonal! A chilling feeling gripped him. He called out.

'Hello, is anyone home?'

He did not expect, and he did not get, any response.

Becoming irritated, he made to move back towards the door to go check with the surveillance team. But then he thought better of his doing so. In Stephen's younger days, he had experience in surveillance matters. He did not want to become a source of amusement in the Secret Service for being unable to find his dutiful wife. Relations between the CIA and the United States Secret Service were never the best. The CIA felt that it could take care of its own and resented the fact that the Secret Service were even involved. Stephen would not give them an opportunity to have a laugh at his expense.

Then he shrugged. His wife was not that important, and she had probably gone over to town to visit or stay with their daughter Estefania, even though she probably knew of his impending return. And probably to just show him that she could be independent of her globe-trotting husband. Relations between the two of them had not been good of late, but at least for now, that would also have to wait.

Then he had another thought. A shiver ran down his spine as his brain began to overcome the jetlag. Why was the surveillance team still outside the house when there was no one home to watch? That made him both angry and aggressive. He marched out of the house down to the Secret Service car. He did not recognise either of the two men, but they certainly recognised him, and his body language.

'What the fuck are you doing here?' was about as politely as Rodriguez could put the question.

'What do you mean?' the perplexed rookie asked.

The agent did not like the sneer, and he knew that there was trouble just around the corner. Stephen was at his most arrogant self, which was unfortunate for the whole detail.

'If you are supposed to be watching my wife, I suggest that you get your ass into gear and go find her. Or go and find another job.'

Rodriguez immediately turned around and stormed back into the house, feeling rather pleased with himself. And amused that Dayanara had somehow managed to give the much-vaunted Secret Service surveillance team the slip.

He told himself to concentrate. He had much more pressing things to concern himself with.

The first thing he had to do was to check that the drugs were flowing again. He unpacked his laptop, plugged it into the mains, and fired it up. If everything was now working according to plan, his package should be delivered by diplomatic courier in three- or four-days' time. And to his home, and not to his office.

Sure, he could give away the toy that came with it to one of the many middle-aged mothers or grandmothers who seemed to have an insatiable desire for such things. There were, after all, few enough perks to be had in the CIA headquarters, and only on the very rarest of occasions did the boss speak to such mere mortals other than to issue instructions, usually in abrupt terms.

He checked. His order had been acknowledged, and his payment had gone through.

Everything seemed to be returning to normal.

He used a mobile phone to call another phone number from memory. It was not a number that he would store anywhere that it could be found by anyone else. And he would dispose of both phones very soon.

The call was answered by Karl.

'Hello,' was all that Karl said. Then began an exchange that would make any designer of security systems turn green with envy, before they could finally agree that Stephen Rodriguez was who he said he was. Then all that Stephen had to ask was, 'Is everything under control?' And in response to that, he got a simple answer in the affirmative.

He disconnected the call.

Now came the part that was tricky. Stephen looked up the mobile phone number of Mark Taylor, and he called him on a burner phone. One of the advantages of mobile phone technology is that you can ensure that the person you are calling has no idea where you are calling from. However, one of the problems with mobile phone technology is that you can have no way of knowing where the person is that you are calling.

Had Stephen known where Mark was, he would have started the conversation quite differently.

'So, you are back in New York? And how was your trip?' Rodriguez asked, not sure whether his voice would be recognised.

'Who is this?' Mark asked, the annoyance obvious in his voice. Mark was too tired to concentrate, and too hyped up to be able to think clearly.

'There is no need to sound so hostile, Mark! But then, maybe you should,' Stephen began, full of confidence. 'There is no point in us getting involved in idle chatter, or us wasting any more time. Let us talk about your lady friend—Debbie Peterson, I believe her name is. And I will be brief. Back off! Or you will not see her again. Do I make myself quite clear?'

Mark had expected such a call. But not the brutal way the message had been delivered. At that moment, his loathing for the man on the end of the call had no bounds. He belatedly realised that the caller was Stephen Rodriguez.

Mark fought to calm himself and not to react in the way that the caller would have hoped for.

Mark had to believe that he was in a position of strength despite the painfully slow progress that they seemed to be making. He had to have confidence that Debbie would be OK. Mark knew that if he went to anyone in authority with the evidence that he had been able to accumulate, he would be laughed at.

Yes, he was certain that the caller was Stephen Rodriguez. He would not acknowledge that unless the caller stated his name. Mark took a deep breath before he replied.

'Perfectly clear.'

There was a pause and a very awkward silence before Stephen had to ask. 'Well, is that all you have to say?'

So, Rodriguez wanted to play games! Wasn't he in for a surprise!

'Well, we could extend this conversation if you like,' Mark began, hoping that he did not stumble over the words that he had rehearsed in his mind for at least a hundred times.

'How is the wife of Stephen Rodriguez? Dayanara, I believe her name is. And oh, have you heard from Stephen's daughter. I know her name—she is an incredibly attractive young lady, Estefania. Now that is a nice name. Both ladies are our guests. Do you want to see them again? If so, we have to do a deal. It is over to you.'

Now there was fear in the voice of Rodriguez.

'You would not dare harm them!' he screamed into the telephone.

'Hey! I never said that I would harm them.'

Again, Mark paused, not for effect, but because he had to choke back the tears of emotion—or was it anger.

'We do not have the callousness or the arrogance to threaten them in that way. But we can talk to them. And in the process, we can tell them what an asshole they have for a husband and a father.'

'I will get back to you!' Rodriguez shouted.

And with that, he disconnected the call.

Chapter 55

The Gatekeeper

At 6:45 pm Nathan Ryman logged off his computers and headed off down the corridor. He made his way towards the elevator and along a path that would lead him out of the suffocating environment of the CIA headquarters in Langley.

It had been yet another day of absolute boredom. Repetitive stuff, screen after screen of crap that might, or might not, reveal something of interest. For the most part, it did not. It was occasionally fun to hack into a new computer environment, and, unknown to the system's owner, reveal secrets that were previously unknown to others. But such occasions were rare. Sure, it needed someone with his unique skills to get through the mass of data and to find the bit that would lead somewhere. But once there, it was the same old rubbish.

Nathan was about six feet tall, quite well built, and did not look anything like the nerd that he, in fact, was. He was a little overweight, which came from having a sit-down job, but he did not intend to spend much more time doing this drudgery. He carried himself with confidence. He did not have the arrogance that is usually adopted by people in his position. He was respected by his peers, and that was all that he needed. And he knew that he was technically superior to them. He could afford to be relaxed in their company.

He smiled and nodded to his colleagues as he passed by, and he said good night to the other people who occupied this inner sanctum of the Directorate of Science and Technology of the CIA. He went down to the basement carpark and got into his car. It was only a short drive home. Nathan could afford to live in the northern suburbs of Washington alongside the other elite members of society. Others lived in the same area for the status that it gave them among their friends. Such people only wished that they could afford the lifestyle, and they still sought to live the dream. Nathan was one of the few who were living the dream.

His partner, Nancy, and their twin three-year-old girls, Penelope, and Sally were pleased to see him come home so early.

The Rymans were the epitome of the modern family. Except for one thing that differentiated them from the rest of the rabble: they did not have a mortgage to worry about.

Nathan had made a small fortune in private enterprise, before selling out and then accepting a job applying his not-inconsiderable computer skills in the country's leading spy agency. This job he had thought would be at least interesting, and a job that had the possibility of being exciting. What his official job was with the agency was to hack into and to pry into computers, to find out what secrets were hidden behind some complicated, but nonetheless to a man of Nathan's ability crude, data encryption systems.

What he found, in most cases, was porn.

He was not overtly concerned about the job or its nature,

peering unseen and uninvited into peoples' private lives did not concern him. What he was concerned about was the amount of child pornography, and that just made him feel sick. The fact that the people in the CIA, who were found guilty of such criminal activity, were quietly removed from their jobs was not the punishment that they should have received. Nathan was far from pleased about that.

Still, that was not his responsibility. His job was to find evidence of all sorts of misdemeanours, and he was extremely good at doing just that. Someone else had to deal out the punishment. Saving the planet was also someone else's job.

After dinner and the usual game playing and reading that went on with three-year-old children, the girls were finally put to bed and went quickly to sleep. Peace once again descended on the Ryman residence.

Nancy settled down with a glass of wine and a couple of magazines in front of some meaningless soap opera on the television. Nathan helped himself to a cold beer from the refrigerator and went off into his study to check for e-mail traffic on his personal computer.

His computer was not quite the average home personal computer, and any e-mail traffic on this machine would be far from normal. While Nathan was displeased at the people who were involved in what amounted to the criminal activity of storing and exchanging pornographic material, it did not mean that all the work he did by his computer was of necessity, strictly legal, or honest toil either. His machine was, in fact, the central hub of a particularly important network.

And, some may say, a very illegal network.

The network would never be found by Google or any other search engine, either existing or yet to be developed. While Nathan's daytime job was to probe into areas on the web commonly referred to as the *dark web,* his other role in life was to protect a similar part of the web that would never become exposed. And this was a far more vital role than anything else he did.

The very existence of the network was known to very few people. The inner workings of this network were known to only one man.

And that man was Nathan Ryman.

He was the Gatekeeper of that network.

Like many people who had risen at an astonishing speed through the ranks of computer wannabes, Nathan had needed something to keep him going. Programming may be fun, but most of it involved negative thinking, full of 'if-then-else' logic which would drive ordinary people to distraction. And while a mistake made by an office clerk in filing a piece of paper in the wrong cupboard was at most an annoyance, in computer programs mistakes were far more significant. They could turn into life-or-death situations were a programmer to put a 1 instead of a 0 in a program. Add to that the long hours, and the stresses that came with the territory were horrendous, so Nathan could be excused the occasional dalliance, with something exotic. And that something he could easily afford.

Heroin.

Nathan had joined the Central Intelligence Agency after a chance meeting with a couple of very senior people. At least Nathan thought that it was a chance meeting. It was, in fact, a setup. The meeting had been arranged after an incredibly careful and thoroughly researched investigation by the people he was meeting with. That meeting had eventually led to a job offer and a unique opportunity to apply his talents. That opportunity combined four especially important aspects.

Firstly, it would avoid Nathan having to deal with the unsavoury characters who had so far been meeting his need for recreational drugs.

That led to the second aspect: it removed any threat to his family from the aforesaid characters.

Thirdly, and far more importantly, it challenged his skills and ingenuity in handling information technology, and more particularly, the worldwide web, in an incredibly special way.

Fourthly, it would provide all the retirement funds he would ever need.

The first reason was a personal matter. Basically, he would no longer be in any personal danger from the suppliers of the product. Suppliers did not normally mess with their clients so long as the clients paid their bills, and so long as the clients stayed quiet on where their drugs came from. But the same suppliers were unpredictable and could change seamlessly into someone else entirely. Nathan certainly did not like the people he was involved with, and he could not trust them. In relation to his previous suppliers, Nathan had also made the correct assumption that the actual product, heroin, that he was supplied with had been mixed with all manner of different powders. In that, or those processes, it could be rendered far from pure, to the point where it might very well have been contaminated. It seemed that the more people who were involved in the supply chain, the less pure the drug became. All of them trying to clip the ticket, not content with the obscene money that they were already making. But any attempt to circumvent this would be asking for trouble. Now with his new employer, these problems would simply go away.

The second reason was also personal. Nathan had an

unbelievably beautiful partner whom he loved dearly. He thought that Nancy was beautiful. He knew first-hand, that she was sexy. And these two factors made her desirable. Others would think so too. The drug scene was littered with one disaster after another—almost always involving people, usually involving close relationships or friends. The main cause? The abandonment by suppliers and users alike of the normal rules that govern how a society, and people within that society, conduct themselves. And the abandonment of or the total disregard for morals when the choice came down to drugs or no drugs. While he trusted Nancy implicitly, who could say what she would do under the influence of drugs, or when the need for drugs became so urgent that she may falter? And what others would do to feed or to take advantage of that desire. That risk would simply disappear.

The third reason, on the other hand, was much more exciting. His job would be to design a system that his fellow workers would not be aware of. In the very unlikely event that they should become aware of its existence, they would not be able to get into it. That was a given. Nathan reckoned he was far smarter than any of the other nerds who worked alongside him. All that he needed to do was to design the system, and the terms under which it was to be designed in fact ensured that it would be hidden in plain sight. The system had to be simple. The best way to deal with the complex was to eliminate the things that could go wrong. The old KISS principle.

The guts of the system he would design to reside in the dark web, hidden from everyone, including trolls and hackers. The front end of the system would be in plain sight, accessible to anyone and everyone who cared to look. The back end of the system would be so well hidden that no one would know that it even existed. The files that resided in the system would be innocuous to anyone who happened upon them. Transactions would exist only for the time that it took to pass the smallest flag from one file to the next, and then that transaction's purpose, and its very existence, would vanish and simply not be retrievable. The very slightest anomaly would render the transaction void long before it made its way through the first tier of a multilevel encrypted security system. That transaction would also disappear forever, except that it would flag another innocuous file. The file that only the Gatekeeper would have access to.

The information in the file to be used by some of the most powerful people on the planet. If the file located a potential problem, then these people would take steps to eliminate it, or the people responsible for the problem.

The fourth reason was the one that locked everyone into the scheme and ensured secrecy. There was so much money to be made from drugs that it was almost obscene. But this scheme cut out all the middlemen. It cut out all the smuggling and transport issues. It avoided all the losses that were incurred through interceptions—both the loss of drugs themselves and the loss of the means of transport. No more bribes that had to be paid to border control and banking staff. There was no need for all the armies of men paid and employed to ensure that the system worked smoothly and ensured that anyone who stood in the way was brutally and permanently removed. All the myriad of levels that the drugs and the money normally went through each, taking a clip of the ticket—all no longer required. All the time spent, and the people involved in laundering the money, were a thing of the past.

So that was the justification, wasn't it? The scheme removed all the criminal aspects of the drug business, so there was no crime. They were almost doing their proud country a favour, weren't they?

The drug world is complex and ruthless. Of the 10 or more billion dollars spent on illegal drugs in the United States alone in a single year, only a relatively small percentage was spent on Nathan's drug of choice, heroin.

Opium, from which heroin is derived, was one of the world's first known painkillers. And originally, that was all it was. However, in more recent times, people had been able to recognise other effects, and it became the preferred drug of many. While it was relatively easy to become addicted to the drug, and it was also easy to overdose on it, it did have some advantages. Heroin has the effect of giving the user a huge surge of pleasure and a feeling that all is well in the world. The fact that the drug, when injected or sniffed, goes straight to that part of the brain that affects judgement and breathing is offset by the fact that it does not have the more obvious, and troublesome, side effects of other drugs.

For example, your teeth don't usually fall out, so at least you can continue a relatively normal life. Higher grades of heroin are sniffed rather than injected, so that you can get around the problem of needle marks. The problems come from the quality, and that is where the ruthless nature of the drug world becomes a crucial factor. Apart from the problems caused by addiction, which means that people simply need *more* of the drug to get the same high, the drop in the quality, or of mixing it with other drugs can cause side effects and send users down a slippery slope from which there is no return.

Most of the heroin consumed in the United States comes into the country from either Colombia or Mexico. The Mexicans supply mostly a cheap version known as black tar, but despite the Mexicans competitive nature, they are still quite happy to assist the transit and sale of the higher-quality product of Colombia. The reason? Drug dealers and traffickers are only in the game for the money. To generate money, they must have product. To sell the product, they must have a marketing plan, and that plan usually involves giving some of the drugs away for the guaranteed reward of gaining a captive user base.

Given the normal price of heroin, it would sound silly to give the drug away were it not for three factors. Firstly, shots are measured in grams. Secondly, you never get quite the same rush of euphoria from the second shot as you got from the first shot. And that is OK because of the third factor: heroin is extremely addictive.

All these factors caused Nathan to review his life and that of his beautiful drug-addicted partner, Nancy, and their two lovely daughters that they were bringing up in a world that was scary.

Faced with the prospect of being the Gatekeeper in a very clever scheme to acquire heroin, there was the very real prospect of acquiring vast amounts of money. He still had enough control over his thought processes to realise that he could have the best of both worlds—he could have his drugs for purely recreational purposes, and he could also have money. So, both he and Nancy embarked on drug rehabilitation, and consequently, they had become addicted to the drug diacetylmorphine, after first trying a couple of other substitutes: methadone and subutex.

At least they were trying. And with good reason. It was just as easy to become addicted to money.

There was no point in cutting out all the middlemen and all the transportation costs in the scheme and then selling the drugs cheaply, because that would be self-defeating. The drugs were sold at normal market rates, and they could afford to do that because of the superior and consistent quality. That solved a couple of money problems. It meant that they could siphon off some of the money for themselves. But the real clincher was that they could siphon off some of the money into an account that was in the name of the purchaser, thereby establishing a quite legitimate reason for their expense. This in turn solved a couple of other problems: recruitment and security.

In order to do that, the system had to have access to a legitimate savings scheme that would quietly accumulate the wealth and do all the other things, like deduct appropriate administration, management, and other fees that such schemes usually entail, and not to attract much attention from the authorities. And Nathan's contacts within the CIA knew exactly the right organisation who could handle this side of the business.

The Augem Group.

This was an organization that had featured in earlier business with the CIA, and for their sins, Stephen Rodriguez had leaned on the Company to set up a savings scheme to handle the legitimate side of his new plan.

The system then had just one more factor that the scheme would need to consider. While people who were addicted would be the easy mark, it also meant that there were risks. Like the risk of them getting involved in drug wars as people fought for territory. Like the risk of people talking.

They had very meticulously profiled their users. Not that this was particularly difficult. They should be reliable. They should not be addicts. They should be professionals. They should be social drug users, taking a shot maybe once a month, maybe twice at Christmas, Thanksgiving, Valentine's Day, or whatever took their fancy.

It was simple to regulate the supply so that if anyone got a little carried away, they could be quickly identified and disciplined. The threat of losing your job was good enough to discipline most people. If that did not work, then there was a threat to their loved ones. If that did not work, then there was a threat to their life. That always worked.

The key to all this was information.

And there was the massive advantage in the scheme for which Nathan was the Gatekeeper. They had access to all the personal files of their customers in all the meticulous and often-embarrassing detail that the CIA, FBI, DEA, and others in government service seemed to keep on everyone on the planet. In the case of actual employees of the aforesaid, down to how often they burped and farted. It was not the normal profiling exercise the likes of which the FBI was very proficient at, albeit not always correctly. They were not drawing up a profile to identify some unknown suspect. They knew exactly who they were dealing with because they used real live data, and that data was knowingly provided to them.

Ryman checked his e-mail traffic. There would be none of the usual nonsense that people had to pick up. The e-mail address was known to virtually no one, and only known electronically to another address—it was passed-on traffic. Usually, there were no messages.

Today there were only three.

The first one was from Jacob Dutton. OK. What had Dutton been up to now? Surprisingly, nothing. Dutton's e-mail was just a reference for one Brad Morgan. Now, there was also a name that Ryman knew!

The second one had come from one of the secretaries that worked in the office of no less a person than Stephen Rodriguez. That e-mail also contained a reference for Brad Morgan. The attachment that Morgan had attached via Dutton's laptop was obviously working well. Ryman could not have known that.

The third one was from Brad Morgan. It was an application to join the CIA's own savings scheme. Yes, Morgan used to work in the very same room at the CIA as Ryman. Quite a bright lad for an Afro-American. Would never go far, but good enough to handle the vast amounts of boring data that the CIA had to deal with.

Was Morgan the type who used drugs? Maybe an occasional recreational user—they were the best and the most reliable! For once, this would be quite simple. Morgan was a good, reliable guy and nothing like the normal faceless names that Nathan Ryman was used to processing. It should be a mere formality.

He pulled up the copy of the CIA personnel file and looked for a match. Although he personally knew Brad, the system still required that he check every detail. It was not Brad Morgan's latest personnel file—that was difficult to obtain even for someone with the contacts and skills that Ryman had. He made a mental note to talk to the ADDI about that and arrange to get a more up to date one!

This was not Nathan's normal command link. But that was the sheer beauty of their scheme, and he was comfortable with it for these purposes. The situation was typical of bureaucrats—always forgetting that mere mortals at lower levels needed a constant flow of accurate and timely information. And in the business that they were in, the more up to date that information was, so much the better.

Brad Morgan, Directorate of Science and Technology, and on *special assignment,* and he had been for over two years. Well, depending on what the special assignment was, that could drive any guy to drugs. Nathan laughed. He was quite used to finding people who were on 'special assignments,' and it was not too difficult for him to find out some more by digging deeper into the files. But he was not really interested in that.

Nathan Ryman laughed again. Some people were assigned to investigate drug use, but to do that, they were first seconded to the inspectorate. Any unusual movements were checked out, and anything unexplained simply meant that the application would be rejected, and a flag placed on the record.

He entered a username—the e-mail address from which the message had originated—and then searched the net to make sure there was nothing going on in the background. He traced the e-mail address to its point of origin, and then checked through the various Internet services providers (ISP's), who had mindlessly and seamlessly passed the message through to its ultimate destination. Brad Morgan was using his personal computer, and that was good. They did not want people to use the computers at their place of work. That was fine for browsing, just so long as they did not go ordering stuff through the net. And definitely not so good when applying to join the scheme.

Logic said that the security system would have raised a red flag if he had used a workstation at his workplace, and the e-mail would never have arrived. Ryman still checked anyway.

Satisfied with the checks so far, he then entered the username of the original e-mail address once again and allocated a random password of *QA8afo9mnk24* which had no meaning whatsoever. Sure, the password could still be broken by some of the software that was freely available to anyone who knew where to look on the net. The software would struggle with the case of the alpha characters, so good luck with that. It was only a short-term thing and cracking this password would lead nowhere.

The trick in this system was that the password had to be entered twice—the second time in a slightly different sequence and with a couple of random characters thrown in. That was enough to fool most systems most of the time, and all the people all the time. That is, if they even got that far before the unauthorized access was detected, or even suspected, and the path diverted elsewhere. No such rubbish about passwords being invalid. If you cannot spell the name of your dog or cannot enter your own telephone number backward, what is the point!

The people that Ryman had to watch out for were those from the FBI. They could be sneaky little buggers. Some buffoons at the head of this beautifully engineered scheme had decided, not content with members of the CIA and the NSA, that the FBI could be a part of it as well. At least the authorities had drawn the line at agents of the DEA! Or so Ryman believed.

The four organizations—the CIA, the NSA, the FBI, and the DEA—all had divisions whose reason for their very existence was to try to track and trace any organizations that were doing exactly what this scheme did. But the security on this system was so tight that in the blink of an eye, the entire system could simply disappear. And could be reincarnated in another form, in another place.

As was usual, when playing with the system, Nathan was completely engrossed in self-congratulation and self-satisfaction. He was oblivious to what went on in the real world.

Ryman had not heard anyone enter the room.

There was no sound other than the faint humming of the computer fan. He tensed in a state of sheer panic. He felt a momentary cold shiver of fear run down his spine. He felt the hands slip around his throat. But he could not do anything about it as his body became paralyzed. He nearly choked as, in one blinding moment, the enormity of what he was into, and the powerful people that he worked with and for flashed before him.

He worked for the CIA, which employed some of the most ruthless people he could ever wish to meet. And there was one risk that he could not avoid! If he fucked up, retribution would be swift. No warning would be given. He would be dead.

A sudden whimper escaped his lips. The relief! He could relax. He felt the brush of something against his back, just the very faintest of touches, a body that was familiar to him. He smelt a whiff of perfume. Then he felt a kiss on his neck and the hands dropped from his neck and started to explore his lower body.

He slowly turned to find Nancy Ryman, scantily clad in a pair of brief lace pyjamas, both the top part and the bottom part leaving absolutely nothing to the imagination. She playfully skipped away from Nathan, and her hands brushed against her proud nipples before she cupped her breasts and leaned back in a display of erotic pleasure. Slowly, her hands moved down to her lower belly, under the elastic that held the very briefest of pants, and there she started to gently rub herself while her eyes implored Nathan to watch and enjoy. Watch the lady he loved doing to herself what he felt that only he should do.

He looked at Nancy, his eyes mesmerized and drawn by the movement of her hands. He could see that she was already aroused. Had she started without him! But no matter—he was captivated and immediately aroused as he felt the uninvited bulge in his trousers begin to grow.

Nancy was an incredibly beautiful lady. Despite being the mother of his two daughters, she still had kept her trim figure and her good looks. And she knew it.

She moved seductively back towards him. He nestled

his head against her ample breasts, while her hands playfully skipped over her soft mound of hair, and their fingers intertwined. She moved her legs apart on either side of Nathan's as the movement of her hands became more urgent. His hands moved to her waist, then down over the shape of her hips, and then he slowly eased his hands up under her pants and was again drawn to the same place that she was urgently rubbing.

He knew what she wanted, and she would, of course, have it.

They would make love right here on the floor of the study. They would take their time as they always did—there was no hurry. They would each fantasize while they reached their orgasmic climax.

Then they would share a joint.

Then they would go upstairs to their bedroom and make love once again before they fell into a contented and blissful sleep.

Nancy moaned, and Nathan realized that this could not wait any longer. While Nancy started to undo his shirt buttons with one hand, and she ensured that he was still suitably aroused with the other, she was oblivious to what else he was doing.

He moved his left hand into the top of her panties and started to ease them down. With his right hand, he moved his mouse over to the Accept button on his computer screen and clicked.

There were far more important things in life than deciding whether Brad Morgan was to be accepted into their inner sanctum. He was one of the boys! It was unthinkable that someone like Brad would be entering the scheme for anything other than purely legitimate reasons. In any case, if someone like Brad Morgan were trying to infiltrate the system, he would have to be part of an official investigation. Such an investigation would need to be authorized at the highest level. There Nathan had that well covered.

He would have known about any investigation long before it got to this stage. And also in any case, there were plenty more checks and balances to be implemented, long before any drugs, or other benefits, began to flow through to their new member.

Although Brad was regarded by some as a technical whizz, he was not *that* smart!

Not smart enough to be any threat to Nathan and the masterpiece that he had created in the cyberworld.

That is why Nathan Ryman was the Gatekeeper.

Nathan turned his undivided attention to the lady who had interrupted his evening's work.

Chapter 56

The Net

For some people, getting onto the Internet and surfing is their idea of fun, even if they become frustrated with the tedium and idiosyncrasies of search engines. Systems that try to anticipate what you are searching for and come up with some helpful, some not-so-helpful suggestions of what you may want to find or where you may wish to go. Systems that are designed to be *idiot proof* so that they make everyone end up feeling like an idiot. To other people, it is a job, and it can be as boring as watching paint dry because they also must pick their way through the myriads of idiot-proofing to get to where they really want to be. That is, except for the very few who have long since mastered the cyberworld.

In this latter world, although everyone basically uses the same language and procedure, individuals have a style of doing things. Worse than that, the arrogance of some individuals means that they must leave tell-tale signs that *they* have created something. Those signs could be recognised. But it would need a like mind to recognise the style and read the signs. And at this level, everything then becomes child's play.

Brad had received acknowledgement of his application to join the 'insurance scheme' and had been given a username and a password by someone who had blocked their originating IP address. And that was fair enough. Later, that would be another avenue of enquiry, but right now, he had other matters to occupy him. The website that he went on was *www.cia.gov*. The instruction that he had been given was to select the Kids Page, then Related Links, then the Defense Intelligence Agency Kids, and finally, click on the RSS button, which got him into the Really Simple Syndication website, an area where anyone and everyone could place blogs or articles on any subject that they felt needed their attention. Most of such contributions rarely became exposed once they were written and submitted. Apart from Facebook, Twitter, and a few other websites, very few people really bothered with the billions of options that were available on the web. And Brad was now in one such area where no sane person would ever surf.

From the RSS website, it was quite straightforward. Brad clicked on an article submitted by the guy who had the unlikely name of Robert De Niro. This blog would only exist for a restricted time, and for all that he knew, it may have been set up just for him. He then clicked on the link that finally asked him again for a username and a password. He entered the details that he had been provided with and was then routed to another website: www.toys4kyds.com; and at last, he could order what he wanted. Well, almost.

He ordered a stuffed bear. A toy one, of course.

Then he had to complete the delivery details, like the *how* and the *where*. He recalled that he had already supplied this information with his original application, but no matter, it was apparently important that the details be entered exactly as he had done before. He specified that he would like it delivered by special courier to his private address. That resulted in a message that said,

Address Validation

Acknowledgement will be sent to you via e-mail to the nominated e-mail address.

And he was automatically logged out. This was the first time he had used this system, so that also was fair enough.

A frustrating ten minutes later, his system beeped, advising him that he had an e-mail. He opened the e-mail, and it said that his delivery would be confirmed after he had completed registration and payment arrangements. He clicked on the link at the bottom of the e-mail, and the system again asked for the username and passwords. And then it got interesting. The system displayed a message:

You need to confirm your registration for the insurance and confirm the details of your payment arrangements. First, you need to confirm that you have read and accept the terms and conditions of this arrangement. Tick Yes to continue. Tick No to cancel.

Brad clicked the Yes box. He then got a screen that included a link to the Terms and Conditions with the usual boxes which you could tick to say 'Yes – I accept the Terms and Conditions,' or 'No – I do not accept the Terms and Conditions.' The mouse hovered over the Yes option. There was not really the time to read through all the garbage that lawyers seemed to dream up to enable them to escape from any commitments, but reluctantly, Brad opted to read through just in case. And in doing so, he had a shock. He had never taken much notice of such matters in the past. He was a computer expert and excelled at mathematics. But the logic of computers and the symmetry of mathematics made him recognise the style and patterns.

The document was most likely one published by the Augem Group.

He froze. If there was a system in the world that Brad knew about, it was the Augem system. He had worked on it for over two years, first as a CIA spy working undercover for Mark Taylor of Taylor Software, and latterly actually working for Mark as a technician. In that time, he had never enquired about the Augem Group policies or their clients. He was concerned about security and matters of far greater importance than what the internal systems did. Now it was just too much of a coincidence that the Augem Group was once more associated with his investigation. The last time Augem had been involved, all sorts of chaos, and deaths, had resulted. Sure, that had all quieted down—but had it really?

With some trepidation, Brad returned to the page that just asked him to say Yes or No. He clicked on the Yes box. He was then asked by the system to enter either his credit card details, or his bank account details, which he did, opting for his credit card. Again, this was his first time using the system, but he suspected that he would have to re-enter the data each time he made a payment. Some suppliers state that repetition is necessary because they do not store any personal information, and anyone who believes that should take a pill. He knew what was coming. The machine responded with,

Payment Validation

Acknowledgement will be sent to you via e-mail to the nominated address.

He had to wait a little longer for this acknowledgement to come through.

Now all that he had to do was await the arrival of the bear and find out what it looked like.

As well as what it brought along with it, if anything.

Brad's next job was to look at the Augem system a little more closely because that could contain the most clues. What he had gathered from his introduction to the scheme was that he had to join an insurance plan—there was just no other way in. It appeared then that the payments were made as apparently legitimate fees against a policy, so that no payment would appear on his, or any other, bank or credit card statement as anything other than routine transactions. If that payment was, in fact, for drugs, that meant that there was a limit to the amount that he could spend on drugs. Very clever!

The clue, therefore, to the scheme was, who got the benefit the sale of drugs? And more importantly, *how?*

Brad sighed. In the years that he had spent looking at the Augem system, he had been following the leads dictated by what he had been asked to look for—the link between Augem and terrorists, and therefore the link to Augem. And for the most part, that had involved money and could therefore have involved money laundering, depending on how you looked at it. He had found only tenuous links because the bulk of the funds had been paid through the accounts of the chief executive, John Dubois; and that was an account that he did not have access to. The feeling had been that the link had died. Well, John had committed suicide, and that seemed to be the end of that. So much so that Mark Taylor had renewed a contract to support the Augem system now that Dubois was out of the way. And apart from the usual tweaking that Brad had to do to maintain the system or to accommodate various changes, all the fun and games had long since passed.

But now things could be different.

There had to be a way that funds, which were paid apparently via legitimate transactions into the Augem accounts, were either redistributed or redirected. From the model on which the Augem system had been built, each type of policy had its own set of accounts which showed whether that kind of activity was profitable or not. With insurance, the source of income was premiums, and the source of expense, apart from the overheads, was claims. It was not unusual in the insurance business for income to exceed expenditure, but not in all cases. Some liberty was taken with the allocation of the other expense—overheads—that could render a scheme profitable or otherwise depending on what people wanted to achieve, or what they wanted to show.

Slogging through the accounts of an organisation that was primarily into handling vast sums of money was not Brad's favoured past-time. In fact, the entire process was boring. It ceased to be a computer exercise. Getting access to the system was easy. Taylor Software had long since perfected their means of access into the Augem system, and they could do so at any time of day or night without the members of that company being any the wiser. The need for a *back-door* access into the system had dissipated after the change in interest—call it now a total lack of interest—by the FBI and the CIA. But the means of access to the system which Taylor Software had needed was still there, so why not use it?

Somewhere there had to be a link that siphoned money out of the type of policy that Brad had signed up for, and into some other scheme, or into some overhead account that somehow found its way to another beneficiary.

Mark had indicated to Brad that the ultimate beneficiary would go by the name of Stephen Rodriguez, or possibly someone even senior to him, but more probably to some company set up for just that purpose. Even then, probably a pseudonym that would be very difficult to trace.

Mark and Brad believed that they knew how the scheme had been set up because that is the only way that the scheme made any sense.

But where was it?

Probably hidden away in the dark web.

And probably beyond the ability of most people, including the likes of Brad Morgan, to trace.

Chapter 57

The Noose

Mark was terrified as his rented SUV rolled toward the place where they had agreed that they would make the exchange. He had taken as many precautions as he dared. But he was still very uncertain of whether to trust the CIA's assistant deputy director of intelligence. Stephen Rodriguez's recent track record said that Mark should not trust him. But then, did he have any choice?

It was absolute insanity that two grown men, both of whom had seen action in all parts of the world, on behalf of the government of the greatest democracy this world had ever seen, were even embarking on such a plan. The only thing that gave Mark some confidence in his ability to survive the exchange, apart from his training all those years ago, was his trust in human nature.

His reading of the body language of the two ladies that he had in his care meant that he did not believe that either Dayanara or Estefania Rodriguez would condone an act of violence against him. Certainly not against Debbie. And that was probably a fair assumption. Consequently, he would be safe if he was in their presence. But the question was, how long could that position be maintained?

There was an overriding consideration that probably screwed his judgement. All that he was concerned about was that he had to get Debbie Peterson out of the clutches of this madman and into a safe place.

What happened after that was likely to get rough.

He could live with that.

What motive Stephen Rodriguez had for undertaking this exchange beggared belief. Rodriguez was handing over his only means of influencing Mark Taylor, to gain—what? Mark had stated to those whom he had chosen to assist him that his pursuit of Stephen Rodriguez and his alleged drug network was at an end. All that he wanted to do was get his Debbie back, and in order to do that, he had arranged an exchange of Stephen's wife and daughter. Mark had been abandoned by the powers that had set him off on this crazy trail, and he felt that it was just not his fight anymore. So that should have been motive enough for Rodriguez if it was believed.

The arrangements were that Mark and Stephen should come to the rendezvous alone apart from the ladies they were to exchange, and that both men should be unarmed. The area that they had finally agreed on was at the Washington Park Arboretum, in an area of parkland to the south of Highway 50. It was sufficiently close to the civilised world while, at least at night, providing the remoteness and the privacy that was necessary for their purpose.

There were plusses and minuses on both sides in this arrangement. Mark had been in the United States Special Forces and Delta Force, so he knew all about stealth and surveillance. He knew how to escape when cornered. He knew when and how to make his move. He knew when to call off. He knew when to slip away like a thief in the night.

Though, this was not the jungles of Colombia, the

deserts of Iraq, or the brutal desolation of Somalia. This was Washington DC, the capital of the free world. And Mark no longer had the backing of the Pentagon with all its enormous resources in command structure, manpower, equipment, satellites, and surveillance gear. Stephen Rodriguez could not match Mark Taylor in background or in training despite his years in clandestine operations with the CIA. The many years spent on the Farm honing his skills would be no match for someone trained to kill. But he did have behind him the power and strength of the CIA, the FBI, and countless other organizations that made up the United States security and intelligence mechanism. In blunt terms, this all translated into one conclusion.

While the 'exchange' may go according to everyone's plan, the chances of Mark getting away from the park unscathed, or even alive, was a more doubtful proposition. Still, what was the alternative? Mark was not concerned for his own safety—he had the training, and he knew, and took, the risk. Debbie was another matter entirely. She was innocent in all that had happened. He was not going to let her suffer anymore.

The SUV came down a track from the north of the arboretum and cruised to a halt at the appointed place. Mark had seen no sign of anyone else, but up against the might and the stealth of the CIA, who could tell? Mark had kept his part of the bargain, and now it was a matter of trust. The arrangement was that the ladies would decamp from the respective vehicles and walk alone and unhindered across the open ground towards the other vehicle.

Another vehicle slowly approached from the south, then stopped about one hundred yards away. There was a single flash of headlights to acknowledge that the vehicle that was supposed to contain Debbie had arrived.

Then they waited.

The two Rodriguez ladies were visibly nervous. On instructions from Mark, they alighted from the vehicle and took some tentative steps in the direction of the other vehicle. In the darkness ahead, Mark could see what looked like the figure of Debbie. She had also alighted from the vehicle that had brought her to this place. Mark was almost overcome with the urge to rush forward. But training and focus held him back as he waited.

The ladies took tentative steps towards each other. All three of them seemed reluctant to move quickly, glancing back over their shoulders, as if expecting something else to happen. But it appeared that things would go according to the plan.

Until, that is, the ladies came together at roughly the halfway point between the vehicles.
They had all walked slowly, checking what lay ahead of them, checking what was behind them. Unsure and scared.

Then they met.

In fiction, where the exchange of prisoners or hostages occurs, the people involved usually run to join their loved ones, or their protectors, and show little or no interest in the others being exchanged.

However, Dayanara Rodriguez was more than a little curious at what the hell this was all about. She had initially gone along with the original story that she had been told about the threat to her husband that had initiated her incarceration.

Then she had met Mark Taylor. That had told her three things. Firstly, there was no threat to her husband of over twenty years. Secondly, that husband, for whatever reason, had taken something from Mark that he would do anything to recover. Therefore, thirdly, what right did anyone have to involve innocents in their evil play, be it her husband or whoever? Just as she and her daughter Estefania had been dragged into this thing, so had Debbie. Unfortunately, wives, daughters, partners are not privy to the scheming and manipulating that their husbands or friends get up to in whatever line of endeavour they chose. So as Debbie approached the Rodriguez family, Dayanara's curiosity turned to anger when she saw the state that Debbie was in.

The two women embraced, and for some reason, Debbie said that she was sorry, and broke down sobbing in Dayanara's arms.

'What have they done to you?' Dayanara asked, the concern evident in her voice and in her body language. She looked in disbelief at the distraught, dishevelled, and badly bruised woman that she held in her arms. She looked towards the vehicle that she presumed held her husband, as if looking for some explanation of this act of insanity. Dayanara knew that Stephen was an important man. But what could he possibly have to do with this?

He would certainly have some explaining to do when this was all over.

That was Dayanara's last coherent thought.

She heard the faint puff of the bullet leaving the rifle. She felt a sharp stab of excruciating pain in her head. Her mouth opened in exclamation. No sound came out. A white light lit up everything. Then blackness. Then nothing.

The bullet entered Dayanara's left eye socket and then blasted through her head to shatter the rear of her skull as blood, brain matter, and bone scattered around. Both she and Debbie crashed to the ground, locked in a fatal embrace.

From a distance, and in the darkness, it was impossible to tell who had been shot. Only Debbie Peterson knew for certain the direction from which the bullet had come, as she gasped in terror at what had happened.

Dayanara was dead.

That shot had to have come from a sniper rifle. It had been fired by a professional, and someone who was skilled in its use. And from the position of Dayanara's body, that shot had to have come from the direction from which Debbie had just walked.

Estefania stood rooted to the spot. She was trembling in absolute fear for several seconds, petrified and quite unable to move. Suddenly, she felt someone dive at her from behind, and she tumbled to the ground. It was Mark, and from the way he lay over her body while scrambling to also cover Debbie, it was obvious that his first and automatic intuition was to protect them.

But from whom? From her father!

Mark clasped Debbie briefly, and his relief was absolute as he realized she was alive.

He whispered, 'I love you.'

The stone-cold look in his eyes meant that he had other more important things on his mind. The only response that he got from Debbie was a frightened whimper as the three of them huddled together.

Mark's training had instantly kicked in. He was armed with a Smith & Wesson pistol. That would be no match for a sniper rifle. Instead of firing ahead, which would have had the sole effect of revealing his position, Mark rolled over and fired two shots—at his own SUV, instantly extinguishing the lights.

That decision was easy. it would remove the background glare that would make him and the two ladies an easy target for the person who had already shot and killed one of the women. The next decision that Mark had to make would be critical. And that would involve a gamble.

Whoever had fired the shot that had killed Dayanara was presumably just as certain to try to kill Mark, and probably Debbie as well. But would the shooter be prepared to risk killing Estefania? The other acute risk was that, during the initial shock and the chaos that ensued, someone could have crept around to get behind Mark. That was what Mark himself would have done if the positions had been reversed, and that was a risk that he would need to counter.

Mark had his own people not too far away up to the north of where he and the ladies were. Those people would have been alerted by the shot. However, they were trained to evaluate the situation before plunging into the fray. Mark knew extremely well that until that evaluation had been completed, he would get no immediate help no matter the risk to his life or the other ladies. For the moment he was on his own, and he needed to act quickly and decisively.

From a hurried instruction from Mark, the two ladies stayed on the ground. They crawled to the left, away from the headlights of the other vehicle, and towards the treeline. Mark's logic was that by leaving the lights of the Rodriguez vehicle alone, the man with the rifle would focus on what he could see. And, assuming he had night-vision equipment, would be somewhat restricted by the lights. However, vision reacts to movement.

A total of six shots rang out. Five of them sailed harmlessly by. The sixth shot hit Mark in the shoulder as he had positioned himself between the shooter and the two girls. He grimaced as the brutal pain lanced through his body. This was followed by even more excruciating pain as he continued to crawl, and the shoulder had to support his weight. But he would not give up as they made it into the trees.

Then the lights on the Rodriguez vehicle were extinguished.

That was not good news.

Whoever was behind the rifle now had a massive advantage once his eyesight had adjusted. A handgun, no matter how accurate and how proficient its user, was no match for a rifle. And Mark's suspicion that this man had night vision equipment was now confirmed. Mark could not see anything, and it was now only a matter of time before they were overrun. His left arm was beginning to lose all feeling, and the pain from his shoulder told him what he really did not want to know. The bullet had lodged in the joint, and he needed to get to a hospital. And fast.

He tried whispering to the girls that they should be quiet. The sobs coming from both told Mark that they were still alive. But the sobs could also give away their position. The combination of the urgency and the pain meant that his whispered instructions were given in a tone that would leave no doubt as to the intention but would further frighten the two already-terrified people.

What insanity was now transpiring? The shot that had killed Dayanara Rodriguez had been as clinical as an assassination could have been. And it had been fired from the direction of the vehicle that should have been occupied by Stephen Rodriguez.

But was it? While Mark had been the one that had been subsequently hit, was that just a coincidence? Did Rodriguez, or whoever was out there, care what order all four of them were taken out? If Stephen was responsible for the brutal killing of his wife, there simply was no point in maintaining an illusion that love for his daughter would have her stay alive. She would have to live the rest of her life knowing how her mother had been so ruthlessly and callously slain. No amount of fatherly love would ever change what Estefania had seen with her own eyes.

Mark could not stifle a moan as the pain began to get more extreme, but he had to do something. Otherwise, there was no hope. Having reached the treeline, he got unsteadily to his feet. He summoned the ladies to do the same thing. They headed across the park towards the east. Mark knew that he would be cut off by the river if he headed this way. But on balance, he had no other choice. He could only hope that his pursuers would expect him and the girls to head either to the north, south, or west because those were the only ways to freedom.

Think! You need to do the unexpected. And if that doesn't work, do something else unexpected. You need to keep trying. Keep the other side guessing.

If Mark could distract them, then maybe Debbie and Estefania could get back to the SUV. The keys were still in the ignition and the vehicle offered the quickest and most obvious way out. However, that sounded very unlikely to be a viable option.

This was insane! All around them were the lights of the city. Were it not for the security detail, you could walk from where they were now to the White House and have a coffee with the President!

Deep in the woods, Mark called a halt and told them what he planned to do. By this time, he was in so much pain that he had to speak through clenched teeth. He cursed at his own stupidity for failing to have a trusty first aid kit with which he could have relieved some of the pain. However, this was not the jungles of Colombia. Debbie became hysterical as she tried to convince him to stay.

For just a moment, Mark held Debbie close, and for reasons that could never be explained, Estefania joined their embrace. She was careful not to press against Mark's useless left arm.

Amid the racking pain that surged through his shoulder, he tried to think of people that he knew in Washington that he could trust, and he gave directions to Debbie.

'I have some people looking out for us to the north of where we are. But you will want to avoid any contact with people you do not know. You have to get to the Columbia Island Marina at Pentagon Lagoon. Ask for the chief and ask him to get you in touch with Elliott Shannon. He will arrange to get you out of Washington until this thing is all sorted. You know Brad's cellular phone number. He is here in Washington. Call him, but only when you are in a safe place.'

'Who is Elliott? Why would he help? Why do we have to get out of Washington? What are you talking about? What are you going to do?' Debbie whispered, the tears streaming down her face.

Mark had to fight back his own tears—from emotion, from the pain, and from sheer frustration at not being able to do more. Debbie was not going to like his reply to at least one of her questions if he told her the truth. So, he would not.

'Debbie, you are in danger, and we have to get you somewhere safe. I should have realized it sooner, but my accommodation in Washington may be known to these people, so you cannot go there. No one can. The chief at the Columbia marina knows me, and Elliott Shannon is an old friend. They will get you to safety. Just tell them what has happened. As for me, this shoulder is not serious, just a flesh wound. I will be OK. I am going to lead the men who are shooting at us off to the south and will deal with them. You go north. You must trust me. But do not trust anyone else you meet in this park.'

Mark realized that he was making the situation sound worse. But not as bad as it really was. They were in trouble. The only logical conclusion that he could make out of this mess was that Stephen Rodriguez would primarily want Mark permanently out of the way.

Rodriguez would believe that he could then pick off the other two at his leisure.

Mark could do nothing about the first part other than to lead Rodriguez in the opposite direction. He hoped, rather than believed, that Shannon could prevent the second part. He had met Elliott Shannon some months before in an unfortunate incident that had led Mark to the Chesapeake Bay, and later to the marina in Washington where he had met the chief—ex-chief petty officer of the US Navy.

Shannon was also an ex. Ex-CIA. But one who Mark knew that he could absolutely trust. And Elliott Shannon knew Stephen Rodriguez. Now that he had recruited Elliott into his team, Mark hoped he could trust him again to do the right thing. He was only one man against the juggernaut, but he, along with his son Brent, who was with the United States Special Forces, was someone who you would want to be on your side in a fight.

'Will you be, OK?' Debbie asked.

Then Mark knew that she was at least partially back to the Debbie that he knew and loved. Trusting.

'I will be fine!' Mark lied.

He said a quiet goodbye to the two of them. He asked them to stay hidden until they heard the noise of a firefight coming from the south, and then rush out of the parkland and to safely. Mark just hoped and prayed that his plan would work.

Debbie and Estefania reluctantly headed north.

Mark headed south, and then he turned west so that he was in a line parallel with their earlier passage east. Traveling through woods in the dead of night, silent and unseen, was something Mark was particularly good at. His problem was that he did not want to remain silent; otherwise, what was the point of the plan? He had to make a noise to attract the attention of Rodriguez and the other pursuers. Then he had to make an even greater noise to give the signal that the two terrified ladies would be waiting for.

Mark aimed at a tree not more than twenty feet ahead of him and pulled the trigger. In the stillness of the night, the noise was shattering, and Mark could not help but laugh to himself at the commotion the discharge caused among the nightlife of the woods. He could tell the difference between human-made noise and noise made by nature. He paused and put a new magazine into his Smith & Wesson Sigma SWF pistol. That would give him seventeen shots; he hoped this little mission would not need them all.

Mark heard a muffled shout from up ahead, and to his right. That meant that whoever was in the woods was to the north of his present position. He turned south and ran silently, trying to ignore the intense pain in his shoulder and the imbalance caused by the lack of movement in his useless left arm. After traveling about two hundred yards, he stopped behind a tree; took careful aim, this time aiming to miss the trees; and sent a bullet whistling through the woods in the general direction from which he had heard the shout. He was not aiming to hit anyone, but it would sure give a wake-up call to anyone in the vicinity. And it did.

This time there were at least two people because there was a quite distinct and panicked warning issued to someone to *get down!*

Now, Mark had them playing at his game. And playing by his rules. He had all the skills necessary to lead this band of thugs in a merry dance. Skills learned and practiced to deadly effect in the jungles of Colombia, in the hide-and-seek cities of Iraq, and in the badlands of Somalia. He was quite at home in this environment, and before long, his foes would make a mistake. One by one, he would pick them off.

But that was not to be.

He had tolerated the pain and the discomfort from his shoulder in the adrenaline rush that had been the experience of the last few minutes. Now he realised that blood loss was another thing entirely. Mark first noticed the symptoms after crouching down and then dashing across a gap between the trees. He went dizzy, and he had to rest against a tree while his head cleared. He folded the windcheater and his shirt back so that he could examine the wound. The constant movement that he had been making had prevented the blood congealing. Even though his left arm was useless, every movement of his shoulder caused another gusher of blood. How much longer could he keep this up?

He had to keep going!

The body, however, had different ideas. Another dizzy spell. Mark went to lean against the tree.

His mind was the last thing to fail. One minute he was running through the woods. Next thing, his legs would not work. Try as he might, he could no longer lift his feet. He had no control over his limbs. He seemed to drift out of his body and then watch from outside as it slowly crumbled to the ground. And then, as though caught in a whirlwind, he rushed back to his body, and everything went blank.

That was the last thing that Mark remembered.

Debbie and Estefania followed the instructions that they had been given by Mark and headed towards the lights that indicated north. Except that they were so petrified that they crept from cover to cover rather than ran. Their progress was pitifully slow. Debbie was the older of the two by about ten years, such that she felt an obligation to provide leadership. Turning that thought into reality just did not happen.

Estefania, being younger, and a student, and carrying the arrogance that made her bulletproof, felt an obligation to be brave and somehow avenge her mother's callous killing. However, she was so emotionally drained that her normal bulletproof attitude deserted her. They were both scared shitless.

They crept towards the north-western exit to the parkland, cringing each time they heard a noise, terrified when it was silent. Debbie could only think of Mark—out there trying to distract these horrible men who obviously planned to end his life. And probably both hers and Estefania's as well.

She had only really known Mark for so short a time. In that time, she had rejoiced that at last she had met someone who really cared for her. She loved him unconditionally and she knew that he genuinely loved her. Now it looked as though it would all end at the hands of these frightening men.

Estefania Rodriguez could only think of her mother, Dayanara, her body lying in the dirt. So callously abandoned, while her father was also out there involved in some insane game in which, she realised now, that no one could win. Her life, which up until now had been a bit of a laugh showing the usual petulance of a young and confident lady making her way in the world, was wrecked. It was all shattered now—her parents estranged in so brutal a fashion.

The one remaining parent she would fear, and loathe, for the rest of her life.

It all became too much for the two of them as they sought yet another place of concealment.

They sat down with their arms around each other, sobbing and wishing that they were in some other place, unable to go any farther.

Then they heard a gunshot. Debbie let out a startled cry, and Estefania started to sob again. The stood up and looked around, not sure of which direction they should go. Then they heard another gunshot, and now, petrified, they started to run in the opposite direction from the noise.

A body emerged from the bushes. Estefania saw it first and nodded her head in that direction. At first, the two of them dived behind a bush, continuing to cling to each other, hoping that the body would just go away. Hoping that it had not seen them.

It was creeping forward, not making even the slightest sound, just like they had tried to do. But it continued inexorably towards them. Despite the darkness, it was as though it could see them. They were so terrified that they just buried their heads. Mark had told them to trust no one, and, more than anything else, to keep silent. They remained frigid and alone, absolutely petrified with fear. They were resigned. If this was how it was to end, then so be it!

A hand reached out and touched Debbie on the shoulder. It was a natural reaction to scream, but the fear was so stifling that all that came out was a gasp. Then the hand had immediately travelled to her mouth to stifle the scream that would surely come as she stared over her shoulder into the face of the man.

The man had been following the ladies on a parallel course through the woods. He had been between the girls and where he knew that other less-friendly folks were intent on finding them.

It was not that he really cared about the girls. He was on a mission and as an ex-CIA field operative, he viewed them as a nuisance and merely thought of them as potential collateral damage. His primary interest was quite simply,

Where was Mark Taylor?

He put his finger to his lips and, with his eyes, pleaded with the girls to be quiet. Only when he thought that they had got the message did he speak in the lilting Irish brogue that had never left him. And the smile that attracted the ladies, that put fear into the hearts of men.

'You have nothing to fear from me. Where is Mark?'

At first, Debbie would not say anything. She had before, and more recently, met too many men who would cause her harm. This one looked genuine, kind, and considerate. There was nothing to be lost by telling the absolute truth. But all men are the same. This one would get nothing that would help him.

'I don't know. He told us to head this way—that is all I know,' she replied, desperately hoping that her answer would satisfy the man.

'Well now, what would Mark Taylor be doing leaving two lovely young ladies to fend for themselves in these lonely woods, and at this time of the night?' the man answered, though his body language became much more aggressive.

Mark had stressed to the girls that they should trust no one. Debbie was torn between not trusting this man and finding help. And she realized with a shock that it was not for herself. It was for Mark. He was out there on his own, injured, and exchanging gunfire with men who had already killed Estefania's mother! At times like these, it was hard. The tears welled up in her eyes as she found herself angling to protect Estefania.

'Who are you?' she asked their visitor in an aggressive and accusatory tone, almost as though she had predetermined the answer as one that she would not want to hear.

The man was clearly puzzled by the show of aggression.

'My name is Elliott Shannon,' he said with a smile and a slight bow.

'Not that the name would be meaning much to you.'

Chapter 58

In from the Cold

The lights blazed down out of a pure white background. So bright that it hurt his eyes.

Where was he?

The pain in his left shoulder, which he recalled as a series of sharp spasms, had been reduced to a dull throbbing ache. But there was something else wrong! He was neither warm nor cold. He felt that he had clothes on, but he did not have any clothes on. Someone was holding his right hand—gentle, soothing, caring. Someone was holding his left hand—in a vice-like grip from which there would be no escape. Something was attached to his face, and a cold flow of air was being forced up his nostrils. He wanted to shout out, but no words would come from his parched throat. What was going on? He moved his head to his right-hand side, and he could dimly make out a fuzzy form. He moved his head to the left, and there were three more forms moving into and out of focus.

Shadows without any discernible shape.

Where was he? Where were they? What were they?

No! They had to be people.

Who were these people? And what were they doing?

Why could he not speak to them?

Mark fought to concentrate and to focus, but the effort was too much for his tired body.

His eyes closed again, and his body slipped back into its unconscious state.

His mind was still working, but in a manner in which he had no control.

That was what really terrified him. Mark was used to being in situations where he was very much in control. Now things were totally out of control. There were voices in the background that occasionally made sense, but for the most part, they did not. The voices sounded far away, so why could he hear them? Talking about someone who may or may not live. He was certain it was him that they were talking about! But he could not communicate with them and remind them that he was alive!

Or was he?

It was the constant nightmares that scared him the most. Was this what it was like to die? Alone and heading for a place that was nothing like the heaven or hell that he had been taught about as a young boy? It certainly was not any heaven that he was in, and the hell was far worse than he could ever have imagined in his wildest nightmares.

Mark shook his head to try to get some clarity into his thinking. This had to be a hospital. It was not on a ship. He had had an operation, which explained the odd clothes he was covered with and the various attachments. Prior to his operation, he had a very vague recollection of being warned about the effects that the drugs would have, as is standard procedure in hospitals the world over. He had also been told of the risks that were involved in the operation that the surgeons were about to perform. Had he signed something? At some stage, he must have signed a form of agreement that said something like *If he died, it was no one's fault but his own, and therefore he could not sue.*

No one could check whether or not he was capable of understanding what was written in the documents. In a practical sense, he probably felt that he just wanted his body restored to something resembling its former state.

Suing people was not high on his list of priorities.

The warnings, the risks, the pain all made sense to the people delivering the message. They were irrelevant in the mind of the patient. They would only be recalled long after the events that relentlessly besieged his tired and confused mind. In moments of semiconsciousness, all he could sense was the crushing pain on his upper chest, his left shoulder, and down his left arm. It was not that the intensity of the pain that was a problem. It was consistency that caused the waves of nausea to sweep through his body. And his mind would be dragged back to the nightmares that were a new and terrifying experience.

The nightmares seemed to follow a rigid pattern which, try as he might, Mark could not vary. And he could not escape them.

It started as he seemed to drift over a dry, desolate, dusty, and barren surface. There was no sign of life, no sound, no light, and he was desperately alone. It was as though in his mind he was searching for a drink which he would not find in this place. That alone caused him to panic.

The surface also had a pattern which slowly came into focus to reveal what could only be endless featureless coffins stretching to eternity in all directions. The only other constant being the absolute dryness. He was both in the middle of an endless sea of sameness, and at the same time trapped in an environment where there was no sky and no horizon. And no light.

Or was it his eyesight? His mind seemed to be trying,

and failing, to prevent him focusing on one spot. But the sameness of everything that surrounded him meant that his eyes were rapidly flickering, trying to find *the* spot. He started to panic again. Was he experiencing death? Did you go to a place where you just drifted, frantically searching for something or someone, but never finding anything or anyone in the vast sea of nothing? And it went on and on, into eternity, with absolutely no end and no escape.

Try as he might to see beyond the terracotta-coloured landscape, his body was drawn closer to one of the coffins as the lid slowly opened and beckoned him to enter. He desperately fought against it, unsure of *what* or *why*. Try as he might to will his body away from the inevitable, he was drawn down into the depths of a coffin. And then suddenly, he was somewhere else even more frightening than before.

It was as though he had entered another world. The dry, dusty, barren terracotta landscape was gone. It was replaced with a black sea of slowly swirling glutinous black oil or treacle. At first, his mind momentarily relaxed, having escaped from the terrors of his previous world. Maybe there was some hope.

Even this dream was shattered. His unfamiliar environment became worse than anything he could have imagined. The sea of slimy black goo began to close in all around him. He tried to turn away from it, but it was the same view everywhere he turned. His eyes were riveted on what was slowly coming into focus. At first, shapes began to appear, and his mind struggled to discern what they were. The more his mind struggled, the more focused he became. At last, some clarity!

And then the horrible truth slowly dawned on him.

They were human bodies, seemingly caught in the terrifying and agonising throes of death. This had to be caused by something so painful, catastrophic, and unexpected that they were screaming in fear, anger, frustration, and agony. But they could not die. Their bodies would be forever locked in that tormented and tortured state. It was so horrible that Mark screamed out. He did not know whether it was from the sights that he had witnessed or from fear that he would suffer the same terrible fate. But his throat felt that it was so parched that nothing would come out.

Then he had the feeling that he had been viciously dumped on a solid surface. Every bone in his body felt the impact, and he felt himself thrashing around to try desperately to escape from this torment and the nightmares.

In fact, all that happened was that he had opened his eyes. The fear and the panic evident as his eyes scanned wildly around him. The bodies were gone, but the paralyzing fear remained. And there were the bright lights.

He gulped in air as he took a deep breath and immediately regretted it as the pain racked his chest. He tried to clear his throat, but his tongue wasn't working. He tried to cry out for some water, which attempt just resulted in a meaningless croak. No one seemed to take any notice of him.

But at last, someone did.

'Ah, so the warrior awakes!'

It was a kindly male voice, the voice of someone that sounded pleased with himself. Mark's focus partially improved as he scanned the three green-robed people who were staring intently at his left shoulder, one of them holding a piece of equipment that seemed more at home in an automotive workshop than in a hospital. Such was the cocktail of drugs coursing through his system that Mark could not know what he did not know. What seemed like an expected normal movement to him was, in fact, the movement of someone who was chronically disabled.

Mark looked to his left again and focused on a nurse whose sole job in life seemed to be to smile and to try to make the patient feel comfortable. On his right side, he could also vaguely make out numerous wires that were hooked up to a complex electronic machine. There were two plastic bottles whose clear liquid inexorably dripped, as though choreographed, into two tubes. He painfully followed the tubes down to the bottom, where they turned out to be intravenous drips that were feeding something into his right arm.

His immediate reaction was to tear them out. While still not fully conscious, he was fearful that they were part of a plot to end his life. He couldn't. His arms were pinned, and panic again assaulted his mind. He was used to being in control, but his inner voice told him that he would never be the same again. The male voice continued in a cold, detached monotone, oblivious to the panic that was going on in his patient's mind.

'You are one lucky guy. The shoulder will be as good as new in a couple of weeks. I hope you have a good explanation ready for the police! I do not like to waste my time fixing up criminals. Your friends tell me you are not a criminal. But they would say that, now, wouldn't they?'

The smiling doctor continued to compare the readout from a monitor with what he had on a clipboard. The smile never travelling to his eyes. Then, apparently satisfied, he abruptly turned and muttered.

'We will see what else has to be done,' and left, without any further comment or acknowledgement of the patient. The cold and clinical attitude of the professional dealing with just one more problem to add to an already lengthy list. The cold professional who had long since decided on the priority of this patient.

Mark tried to focus his attention on the nurse. Although his words were slurred, and without realising it, he repeated the message he did manage to communicate. 'Where the hell am I?'

'You have lost a lot of blood!' the nurse answered, still smiling. 'They brought you in here last night. The *here* is a hospital, and if my reading of you is correct, you are no stranger to this environment. You certainly seem to have made a habit of getting on the wrong end of a gun. It is fortunate that you appear to be very fit, and that is what saved you! Now I suggest you get some rest. You have had major surgery to fix your shoulder. When the drugs wear off, there will be some pain. We need to monitor that to make sure everything is OK. And then you will need many weeks of physiotherapy and rehab.'

Mark stared at the nurse as she slipped a couple of tablets into his mouth. He would have spit them out had she not quickly followed with a paper cup containing water. Just enough to wet his parched lips. Just enough to swallow the tablets. It wasn't enough to quench his terrible thirst. But it was all that there was.

She smiled again. Body language! Did Mark detect some sympathy? Or was he in fear of the inevitable? Was he going to die? Hospitals do that, he told himself. Keep patients alive just long enough so that the medics could complete some insane thesis, and then, 'Good-bye. Sorry we could not do more. Now off you go. We need the bed for the next one!'

'What is your name?' he croaked.

Again, the smile. She cared!

'My name is Michelle. Now get some rest.'

And she drifted away.

Michelle! There was something about the lady that Mark recognised. What was it?

He tried to rationalise. Yeah, his body did have the odd bullet wound, and he was as aware as anyone of the need for rest while the body repaired itself. His previous medical treatment had been on board a United States Navy ship, where the medical treatment had been first-class. And the pain relief and post-operative patient care virtually non-existent. On board the Navy ship, he had endured the pain without the problems and side effects caused by drugs.

He knew that he was tired. But he was frightened of closing his eyes again. Out of fear he would once more descend into the depths of that dry, barren place. That would inexorably lead to the sea of black, and to the screaming of people in agony. Despite thinking about that and fighting desperately to stay awake, his body was just too exhausted. He drifted back into his nightmares.

The one relieving thing was that although the nightmares went through the same sequence—the only difference being the initial patterns and colours of the parched landscape changed—they went quicker. There was less time to be scared by the actual scenes. It was the fear of what might happen next that scared him the most. He desperately tried to seek some logic to it all to belie the fear, and he tried to make some sense of what had become an integral part of his immediate life. None could be found.

He went through the same terrifying nightmare and then woke with a start. It was almost as though his mind had been separated from his body and allowed to float through another world and then joined again. He felt that he had been thrashing around wildly, trying to escape, and then reunited with, the inert corpse.

The next time that he was awake, he was all alone —just man and the machines. While he had absolutely no idea what time it was, or even what day it was, he had the impression that it was night-time. The nurse—was it Michelle? —came to see him as if on cue, gave him a mixture of pills and a glass of water to wash them down while she checked the IV's and made some notes. Nothing else other than a reassuring smile, and then she was gone.

He wondered why he did not ask her some questions. Apart from saving 'Thank you,' no words would come. It was only after her third visit, when she was about to leave him, that his fuddled brain said to ask— something, anything, just to get his life back together.

'How is Del?'

It was as though Michelle had been shot with a Taser. No amount of training could have concealed her reaction. She hurried back to his bedside in a state of near panic. She looked at the notes to read his name, and she turned white.

'Major Taylor! How did you end up here?'

Mark could only smile.

'I did not come here by choice, if that is what you mean. More to the point, what are you doing here?'

Michelle furtively looked around, before coming closer to Mark, and she whispered, 'Mr Darrington is also in this hospital. He is in an induced coma and will be for some time. I am here in case he wakes up. I have other duties as a nurse. You know how these things work!' she added as an afterthought.

And then she was gone.

Scared of going to sleep again, Mark's mind battled vainly against the drugs—probably morphine based, which were meant to both kill the pain and give him some rest. The doctors failed to mention that these drugs also played havoc with the mind. But they could only fix one thing at a time, couldn't they?

Mark tried to focus on the events that had led up to his being in hospital. The problem was that his mind could not, or would not, fill in all the gaps. He just did not know what had happened. He could vaguely recall running through some woods, and then everything went blank. He had been doing what? Had he been dreaming, or was he having the nightmares that people with his background tend to get from time to time? Were these feelings and thoughts what PTSD was like?

Very slowly, the memory of the events of what must have been the previous day started to come back to him.

He had been to a meeting with Stephen Rodriguez, which had turned out horribly wrong, and they had to escape—that much he knew. There had been gunfire. Someone was dead!

But who?

No! It was not Debbie.

He had left Debbie in the woods. Why had he left her? He had told her to contact someone—but who? Where had she gone, and who was the other girl that was with her? They were both crying.

But why?

It was immensely frustrating as his mind fought to reach some logic, fought the drugs that were trying to drag him back into the depths. Eventually, he drifted back into his drug-induced coma that the hospital staff called rest and sleep. And back to his nightmares.

During yet another nightmare, he was shaken by some movement. Before he could recall anything further, he saw two faces peering through a window. They looked out of context. They were familiar! He felt an enormous sense of relief as he recognized the pair.

It was Brad Morgan and Blake Whittaker.

If these two were in any way feeling sorry for Mark, it was not evident from the grins on their faces. The nurse, who was once again fussing over the IV drips, finally left. But not before admonishing the two visitors: they would need to be gone in five minutes—the patient had had a long and traumatic day and needed to rest!

They both shook hands with Mark, careful not to disturb the drips and monitoring lines that were festooned around him. They were both unsure whether Mark would be in any condition to discuss what had to be discussed. Neither visitor was inclined to speak first. Until Brad gently tried.

'How are you feeling? And what the hell happened to you?'

From the confused look on Mark's face, it was apparent that he had little recollection, as he desperately fought to bring his mind into focus. It was not that he did not want to answer Brad's question. It was simply that he couldn't. His mind was still confused with the drugs. They were meant to lessen the pain. However, they were laced with antibiotics and whatever other cocktails the medical people deemed appropriate. This resulted in a very confused patient.

He asked a question of his own.

'How did I get here?'

That got a reply from Brad Morgan.

'You can thank Blake for that. He found you in the woods and was lucky to get you out, what with all the other people floundering around. He got you straight into Walter Reed—he thought it better to get you to an Army Hospital,' Brad added with a shrug. 'But he saw nothing of the ladies—either the Rodriguez girl or Debbie. So, I say again, what the hell happened?'

Mark tried to hard concentrate. Had he left Debbie

with someone else? But there were only two of them, whereas there should have been three. Where would he have told Debbie to go? And then he struggled to concentrate as his thoughts drifted in and out of his consciousness.

One of the ladies, Dayanara Rodriguez, was dead!

The other two ladies, together with Mark, were getting away from the killers. Mark had tried to create a diversion. But why could he not remember the finer details? He looked at the other two men and saw the same blank expression on their faces.

Knowing what the answer would be, he asked,

'Where would I have told Debbie to go?'

Blake answered that with a couple of questions of his own.

'I assume that, for some reason, you did not tell her to go to the Georgetown Apartments. That turned out to be a good call. Who else do you know in Washington that you would trust? I would speculate that it would have to be either someone connected with the Special Forces or with your father. Come on, think!'

There was no one in Washington that Mark would trust—that is, apart from his father and his mother. But he surely would not have sent Debbie to them, for two reasons. Firstly, Rodriguez would assume that Mark would try to contact his family residence and at least check that line. So, that line was closed. Secondly, his mother would be at the residence, and from his recent experience, it would not be a clever idea to send anyone connected with Mark or his father anywhere near an angry and frustrated woman.

Where his father was, he had absolutely no idea. Mark would not have told Debbie to try to go see them— for both her physical and mental safety. Mark again tried to concentrate.

Where would *he* go if *he* was in trouble when he could not know how much the other side in this crazy mix knew? He would go to friends who would get him away from Washington, and quickly. By water. The Potomac. Go down the river and lose yourself in the vast spaces of the Chesapeake Bay. He had done something along these lines before, not so long ago. He had a contact. Had he told Debbie to go and seek out Elliott Shannon? In which case she would first need to contact the chief, an ex–US Navy chief petty officer who ran a marina at the Pentagon Lagoon. But at the time of night that this had all unfolded, what were the chances of the chief being there? Nil. Although it seemed a bit far-fetched, that was the only safe thing that he could think of.

'I would have told her to go to the Columbia Island Marina,' Mark blurted out.

He looked at his two friends for confirmation. He did not exactly get that confirmation.

'Who do you know at the marina?' Brad asked.

It is funny how things seem so clear when stated with enough authority. Find the chief! In and around the Pentagon Lagoon, there would be any number of ex-US Navy people variously employed, and contrary to widely held belief, not many of them would be likely to snub their noses at authority. And not many would be around, or sober, at this time of the night. Mark had to laugh. It was a bitter sound.

'I cannot remember the chief's name. I don't know that I ever actually knew it. He was just the chief. That is what everyone called him. We must get there and find Debbie! I'll come with you!'

Mark moved to uncouple himself from the tangle of wires and tubes. The movement caused the nurse to come rushing into the room. Her concern was evident. The barked command was incisive.

'Get out!' she screamed at Brad and Blake. She clamped hold of Mark's hand to prevent him from removing the IV and then yelled for assistance from the two orderlies who had followed her into the room.

Mark gave a weak smile.

'I don't suppose that was very smart!' he said to the nurse.

'Go. Find Debbie!' was his instruction to the backs of his two friends.

Brad and Blake left while the hospital staff checked the IVs and the wires. Fortunately for Mark, they found that none of them had been disconnected.

Mark had an innocence about him that could have helped him charm his way out of this situation. The doctor who came next into the room would not fall for that. He stood with his hands on his hips and addressed Mark as he would any intern or patient of lower rank than he was.

'If you want to kill yourself, you have my permission to get up and leave. Now! If you want to live, I suggest you should do as you are instructed.'

The doctor sighed. Why did military men always assume they are indestructible? He continued in a kinder tone, but the message was still clear.

'You have lost a lot of blood. Too much blood if the truth be known. You don't know how lucky you have been to still be alive. And we are not out of the woods yet if you will excuse the pun. I have done my best, and now the rest is up to you. If you tried to leave, you would make it perhaps as far as that door. Now make the choice. Leave and die, or stay and do as you are told, and live. Do I make myself perfectly clear?'

'Yes, Doc,' was Mark's meek reply.

The doctor was right. That wasn't going to help find

Debbie, and Mark's contribution to any search would be futile. He had to leave it to Brad and Blake.

That did not make it any easier for him. A plan, which had been in cruise mode, was now shot to pieces. Stephen Rodriguez was out there with his band of thugs, Mark was no nearer to solving the riddle of the CIA drug network, and he was now banged up in hospital. One lady was dead, two more were missing, the gatekeepers of the plan were, unbeknown to Mark and his friends, off bonking each other. For all his adventures in Afghanistan, he had come back to—what? Chaos and not much else.

The doctor finally decided that Mark had got the message and left storming out of the room. Soon to be followed by the two orderlies who had seemed more amused than concerned. That just left the nurse.

Michelle could not bring herself to stay mad. Mark had been to hell and back. Compared with other patients, he was generally well-mannered and uncomplaining. She knew that he was lucky to have come this far. He had appeared so close to death during the frantic rush of last night to get him to the operating table. And into the hands of the team of surgeons, anaesthetists, and nursing staff who, between them, could save his life.

Mark could not yet know that he owed his life to the people who had worked all night to put his shoulder back to where there was the chance of a full recovery. But the shoulder was a minor issue. The bullet had passed so close to vital organs that it was nothing short of a miracle that there wasn't more fatal damage.

Michelle leaned over the bed, holding Mark's hand.

'Is there something that is worrying you? Is there anything I can do? You need to get some rest! Do you want a stronger sedative to calm you down?'

Tears came into Mark's eyes. It was uncharacteristic, but he could not help it. The drugs he was on may have deadened his pain, but they did nothing to strengthen his state of mind. In his drug-induced calm, he knew that he had never felt weaker. He felt so helpless, and it was not for the first time. It was happening once more in his short life.

The person he loved was in danger. Yet he had arrogantly decided on a course of action that now he could see would only increase that danger. And now he was paying the price. He could not move, nor could he do anything to remedy the situation. He would have to leave it to others, which was not a condition that Mark was used to. And now his nurse was proposing an even stronger drug to maintain his escape into cuckoo-land. He bit his tongue.

'There is nothing you can do,' Mark said in a whisper that the nurse had to lean over him to hear. She was an attractive young lady and used her looks to advantageous effect in getting the patients to overcome what demons they had in their minds. But not this time. Mark's eyes told the story. He continued to whisper.

'I will get some rest. Thank you!'

Then he closed his eyes, and he felt, rather than saw, the nurse squeeze his right hand. He was sure he felt her lips brush against his forehead. Then the lights dimmed, and Michelle left the room.

Now Mark could grapple with the other problem that had now been raised. How much did the senior doctor know of the background to Mark's injury? Saying that Mark was *not* out of the woods was a common throwaway line in most circumstances.

But why had the doctor regarded it as a pun?

At some time in the evening, Mark had a visit from the Washington police. Even in his befuddled state, it appeared to be quite pointless. The two officers came into the room and introduced themselves as Sergeants O'Malley and Rawson. They consulted some notes and then asked a couple of questions.

'You are Mark Taylor from New York City?'

Mark nodded his head in the affirmative.

'When did you arrive in Washington?'

That resulted in a blank stare, before Mark muttered, 'A few days ago.'

The two officers exchanged a look. Mark could read their body language. They were going through the motions and not expecting to gain much from this interview.

'You got shot in the arboretum woods. What were you doing there?'

A similar blank stare as Mark tried to recall what had happened. How did he explain the crazy notion that he was trying to get his lady back? And how did he explain the dead body?

'I can't remember.'

'Have you any idea who shot you?'

This question would have been greeted with a shrug. Except that any movement of his shoulders was restricted by the sling that held his arm firmly in place and by the pain that racked his body at even the slightest hint of movement.

The two officers merely shrugged at the lack of response. In fact, they looked totally disinterested.

'We will come back tomorrow when you will perhaps be a little more coherent. Then we will require some answers.'

Mark drifted off to sleep despite fighting to stay awake to avoid the nightmares that would surely come. With all the stress that he had been under during the visit of his two friends, the nightmares seemed to get worse and more disjointed. This time he descended into an even darker place. It was still dry and dusty, but this time it was very cold. The human shapes in their agonizing and fruitless struggle with death took on a whole new meaning. They seemed to appear out of nowhere and then disappear in abject terror into the black oily mess as the lids of coffins banged shut. Only to slowly open again, beckoning Mark to get inside. No matter how hard he fought, he was drawn to take another look, and he ended up drenched in sweat as his body simulated the intense struggle to stay alive and avoid sharing the fate of those silent screamers.

Then he had the overwhelming urge to have a pee, and he rushed around looking for a place to go. He awoke in a state of panic. He desperately reached for a bedpan, and he relieved himself. It was the most beautiful feeling he had ever encountered, and he laughed inwardly as he realized that so simple a thing could only mean that he was alive and that he would get better.

And that was what saved him.

He sensed someone entering the room. All those years with the Special Forces, where you trained to be acutely aware of your environment and everything in it, came back to him through the drug-induced fog. There was someone in his room, and a sixth sense told him that they were not friendly.

Whoever it was had crept towards his bed and examined the IV drips. Mark lay quiet and still, ready, waiting. The person did not appear to be armed. Then he or she reached up to the bag that contained the fluids that Mark was slowly absorbing into his bloodstream, one relentless drip after the other. It could have been a perfectly legitimate action. Except the person had been hiding a syringe in their left hand. They pricked it into the top of the bag and then emptied its contents into the IV plastic bag.

Content with their action, the person crept out of the room without a second glance at their intended victim.

Fear gripped Mark as he lay there helpless. He did not know much about hospital routines. But he did know a few things. Almost all staff usually came into the ward, whether in intensive care as Mark was or in much lesser facilities, with lights on and making enough noise to wake the dead. Also, they usually explained what they were doing even though most patients had no idea what they meant.

Mark had experiences that could lead him to only one terrible conclusion. The drip had been contaminated with another un-prescribed drug or drugs. It could be something like morphine that was readily available in most hospitals. That drug was essential in the present circumstances. When delivered in a high dose, it would seek to end Mark's life on planet Earth.

And no one would be any the wiser.

He grappled with the logic of it. It was insane! Because he was in one of the most respected hospitals in the world there would be an investigation. So, he knew that the drug would need to be one that was in his system anyway. But would it be morphine? Why not use potassium chloride? Mark's limited knowledge of drugs suggested that this would be a better bet. A body produces its own potassium, and an excess supply could cause the heart to stop quite simply. The post-mortem would reveal nothing. No cause. No murder. Just a dead body. Cause of death - Heart failure.

Mark experienced real fear. He knew that he could be hallucinating and that this whole affair could just be a figment of his drug-induced, confused state of mind. But warning bells had gone off as he had watched the entire episode. His mind struggled with the logic of injecting the bag. Intravenous drips were very carefully prepared. There should be no need to inject anything into the bag except in very exceptional and critical conditions. Maybe it was the correct procedure. Maybe he was just being paranoid. The problem was that the only way to prove it was to just die. Then he would find out for sure whether his nightmares had been realistic!

Battling against the pain, Mark reached up and turned off the feed from both bags. Then he disconnected the IV tubes from the bags and from then the lures into his arm. He threw the tubes onto the floor. He was taking no chances about whether he got the correct lead.

He was taking a chance because he was sure that the fluids were critical to his recovery. And there was the other obvious risk - they would probably be carrying the bulk of his pain relief. He had endured pain before, so at least that part of the risk was acceptable. The additional risk was that, without the fluids, he could dehydrate. And that was acceptable as well. It took a while to die from dehydration.

The question then was - what did he do now?

For all that he knew, the assailant could have been the nurse. Or it could have been one of the orderlies. Or, for that matter, it could have even been one of the doctors.

He was in the Walter Reed Hospital, which was an Army establishment. And, for all its other faults, that came with a military discipline and a security system that should be second to none. The intravenous drips that Mark had been connected to were intended to build up his fluids as well as carry various drugs which were released in a predetermined way, at a predetermined rate. What they had added would be evident in the drip-feed but would probably not be so evident when it made its way into his body. He did not intend that the latter would be the case.

Reaching over as best he could, he pulled the IV feeder towards him and then removed the bags, placed them carefully in his locker, so that the pinprick made by the syringe was at the top, then locked the door. He would, at the proper time, have some explaining to do to the doctor or the nurse. And he would then rely on his reading of body language to reveal what they did, or did not, already know.

There would be no sleep for Mark, and he could only speculate on the effect that the lack of legitimate fluids would have on his body and on his recovery. Previously, he had strived to stay awake to avoid nightmares. Now he had to stay awake just to stay alive and to avoid turning the nightmares into reality. It was an intense struggle fighting off the effects of the drugs which were still coursing through his body. He felt the pain start to increase, but in his confused state, he could not know whether that was real or imagined.

It was an hour later that the night nurse came to check on Mark. He went through the usual routine of checking the data that was held on a clipboard at the end of the bed, before checking the IV and the monitor. It was a quiet night in this ward as the nurse went methodically about his business, seemingly unconcerned and expecting nothing out of the ordinary. But then he turned apoplectic. Because there were two IV lures on the patient with nothing connected to them, he first returned to the notes. Then he seemed undecided. And then he panicked.

He rushed out of the room, and he returned within a few seconds, accompanied by a young doctor. They went through the notes again before deciding on a course of action.

They woke Mark up.

The young doctor was obviously new, and he did not want to make a mistake. In hospitals the world over, the young and inexperienced always get the graveyard shift, and the Walter Reed Hospital was no exception. Except, that is, it was still subject to military discipline, which meant that this doctor would be subjected to the arrogant wrath of his superiors should he make even the slightest error. If he got it right, there would be nothing said—such was the way of the world.

'Who disconnected the drips?' the doctor asked of the nurse in as stern a voice as he could muster. When the nurse could offer no explanation, he addressed the same question to Mark.

Mark had prepared himself for this, and he answered as placidly as he could. 'Someone took them out because they weren't feeding correctly and said they would return with another couple. I thought that was what you guys were doing.'

The doctor simply wrote up his notes. Someone had made a mistake, and it was of primary importance that the notes made it clear that it was not him. He then dispatched the nurse, who returned in a matter of minutes with another two bags and tubes, which they rapidly connected.

Mark froze for a moment.

He had the dreadful thought that these two could have connected him up to another lethal dose of whatever it was that had contaminated the earlier bag. On balance, he thought he was safe, judging by the body language of the two men. But, how could he be sure?

The fact of the matter was, he couldn't.

Peace descended once again on the room as the two men exited, the young doctor giving clear and concise instructions to the nurse regarding the future monitoring of Mark. The instructions were met with the normal reaction of a senior and vastly experienced nurse receiving words of wisdom from a junior and inexperienced doctor. That gave Mark some comfort in believing that these two would not be part of a plot to harm him in any way.

When all was quiet, Mark sent a straightforward text message to Brad.

We have a problem. Get here as fast as you can.

The hospital woke up later in the morning with the usual noises that accompanied a handover from the night staff to the day staff. The tired briefing fell on receptive, eager ears.

The fact that this occurred far earlier in the day than most mere mortals who would regard the invasion of their sleep as unreasonable, escaped everyone. The patients because they had nothing else to do. The hospital staff because their roster said that it should be so.

Brad had still not returned Mark's text message, and Mark began to get increasingly worried as the morning people slowly made their way down the ward. Someone would probably be quite surprised to find that Mark was still in the land of the living. And they would not be overly pleased about it. That is if Mark's action had not been provoked by a simple case of extreme paranoia.

If it wasn't paranoia, then who was involved?

The only defence that Mark could muster was his ability to read body language.

And he had his answer as soon as the doctor from the previous evening joined the crowd of medics. The medical doctor, who in the army was Colonel Ian McPherson, read the notes that had been added to the mass of paperwork hanging on the clipboard. It is always the eyes that give people away. The doctor was the usually outwardly calm person that had been here last evening—or was it also earlier on this day? But the shock revealed itself in the flickering of the eyes as he tried to comprehend what had taken place. Today he was still the cold and clinical doctor that he had been before.

McPherson's body language said far more than that. There was still a chance that he was merely annoyed that someone had failed to carry out his instructions up. Mark did not think so. Logically, Mark would need to get out of this place and do so quickly.

But could he get out before there was yet another attempt on his life?

It was later in the morning that Brad came back into the hospital to see Mark, frustrated by the hospital rules and regulations that prevented him from coming earlier. Brad had still not been able to locate either Debbie Peterson or Estefania Rodriguez. Mark's heart ached as he hoped that Debbie had made the connection with his friends and that the reason for Brad's lack of progress was that the security blanket around the girls would be tight. Rodriguez would still be out there.

Mark was worried, so he had no difficulty convincing Brad of his concern. Brad, in turn, had his own concerns about the CIA. He told Mark of his progress and his hopes, but it sounded to Mark as though things were spiralling out of control.

And they were going to get further out of control.

Brad listened in silence, and with a sense of mounting anger, as Mark recounted the events of the night. He took the two IV plastic bags that Mark had managed to keep hidden in his locker, with instructions to get them to Blake, who in turn should get them to the Professor of Anaesthesiology at the Georgetown University Hospital. The significance of which escaped Brad, but orders were orders.

He was, however, even more alarmed when Mark explained what else he wanted him to do.

'You have got to keep on the track of the Rodriguez network. I may not survive, but you must bring Stephen to account. That is your primarily priority. I am sure Debbie is safely holed up out of harm's way,' said Mark, with enough urgency in his voice to ensure that Brad got the message.

Still, Brad protested that it was safer to get Mark away from the hospital. But Mark would not hear of it. It took some even firmer words before Brad reluctantly agreed to do as Mark wished.

The nightshift came on, and the nurses did their usual and routine handover checks. Then the hospital settled down, the lights were dimmed, and those who could sleep did so despite the cacophony of noise that pervades hospitals the world over. The banging of doors and bedpans, trolleys wheeled here and there, conversations between professionals concerning all manner of subjects—all noises that in the daytime would be accepted. Occasionally, there would be conversations between doctor and patient, which were not in the least bit restricted by the curtains that nurses insisted on drawing to partition off the bed where the confidential conversation was taking place.

Mark was in a state of stress, having slept little the night before and still in need of a good rest. Despite the need to stay awake and alert, he found himself drifting in and out of sleep, and eventually, he succumbed. Thankfully, the nightmares decreased in intensity so that it was now more the uncomfortable strapping on his left shoulder, and the fact that he had to lie on his back, which caused his sleep to be restless and fitful. The years of training would always apply. The slightest movement on his ward was enough to wake him.

A person came into Mark's room at 11:00 pm and examined the IV drips. They were both over half full. He glanced around to make certain that there was no danger of him being seen. Mark appeared to be asleep, although with the various tubes and wires attached to his body, he did stir from time to time, endeavouring to get into a more comfortable position. The syringe would have entered the IV bag and silently discharged its fatal contents into the feed—a feed that was to end the life that so desperately needed fluids, but one that would leave little trace in the resultant dead body.

Mark's life would be at an end, leaving to others the now-insurmountable task of bringing a powerful man, in one of the world's most powerful and secretive organizations, to account.

The CIA just had too much power in this city.

Mark's right arm shot out from under the sheets, grabbing the left wrist of the intruder, twisting it backward with all the strength that he could muster. Although Mark was weak from the drugs and all that had gone before, his skill was more than enough to bring a shriek from the intruder, and an agonized moan as the intruder's wrist was broken. Mark was relentless as he seethed.

'What are you doing?'

The man tried to get released from the grip. When he could not, he turned to Mark to try to reason with him. And in the dimly lit ward, he revealed who he was. He seemed quite oblivious to the pain in his wrist, and oblivious to the fact that Mark would instantly recognize him.

'What is the meaning of this, Mr. Taylor? You come to my hospital, where there is no doubt that we saved your life, and now you attack me! Why would you do that?'

Mark did not answer the doctor's question. He asked one of his own.

'So, tell me Colonel McPherson—what were you about to do?'

'I am trying to give you some medication, you idiot. Now the syringe is broken, so I will need to go and replace it. Would you be so kind as to release my arm?'

Mark gave his wrist another twist, which brought a gasp from the doctor. 'Come now, Doctor. Don't you think it is somewhat preposterous for a doctor of your standing to be doing something as menial as delivering medication, at this time of night, and in the darkness? Let me tell you what I think you were doing. You were trying to inject a lethal dose of something into the IV bag. Why I do not know, but it is hardly true to your Hippocratic oath. Now let me tell you what you are going to do now.'

The CIA had, almost since the day it was formed, recruited some of the very best doctors in the country and elsewhere to assist it in many ways. Most of these doctors were occasionally paid, but often than not provide their services as a contribution to the society that they all served. From time to time, their task merely consisted of looking at photographs or videos of 'people of interest' and assessing their state of health. That may sound like a strange way to run so powerful an organization like the CIA. But there were times, more often than you would expect when there was just no other way. If they sought information concerning someone's well-being from the normal and more obvious sources, such as people within the medical fraternity, then they took the risk that the people being asked the questions would talk. Or it was simply too expensive to travel to somewhere like Moscow,

Tehran, Beijing, and other such places just to find out if someone was likely to die anytime soon.

Consequently, they took the straightforward way of asking a qualified doctor to assess the subject based on pictures. And, unlikely as it may seem, doctors were often correct in such assessments. The fact that some such subjects would die, or otherwise disappear shortly after the assessment, would play havoc with their Hippocratic principles was a small price to pay for this rather unconventional yet convenient method.

And Doctor McPherson was one such participant in this informal arrangement. Unfortunately, this arrangement did not turn out to be exactly as intended. Some six months prior to the present day, a senior CIA official by the name of Stephen Rodriguez had approached the doctor with a fistful of pictures for an opinion on the health of the subject. No names or places were mentioned. But it was obvious to McPherson from the first couple of pictures that the man was obviously in vigorously good health. At least he was satisfying the lady in the picture more than adequately. From the later pictures, he was clearly a man of power and influence, and it was hard not to recognize the head of state in an overseas country. The name of this man was known to McPherson, and he made the mistake of mentioning it. This meant that Rodriguez would have to take some other action.

Shortly after this meeting, the two men met again. This time socially. And this time Rodriguez introduced McPherson to another side of his work at the Agency. How the CIA, or more specifically Stephen Rodriguez, knew that the good doctor was a user of heroin, was one of the many mysteries of life. Shortly afterward, McPherson was recruited into another simple scheme. One that ensured he would get top-quality heroin without his having to deal with the usual scum in the drug world. That seemed to be a harmless and convenient arrangement that merely meant that the doctor was drawn closer to the bosom of probably the most powerful organization on planet Earth.

And now the wheels were coming off the whole sorry arrangements. This time, the doctor was approached by a young lady who was a nasty piece of work. She claimed to work for the CIA and wanted to talk about one of his recent patients. A man who had been brought into his hospital suffering from a severe loss of blood with a shoulder injury caused by bullets. It was requested that this patient be carried out in a body bag.

McPherson, quite naturally, protested. However, several things were made clear. The primary one was that it would not look good if McPherson was revealed to his colleagues as a druggie.

Unfortunately, that meant that, despite the brutal way in which Mark Taylor had instructed McPherson as to his next course of action, that was simply not going to happen.

One man against the might of the CIA was not going to work.

Chapter 59

Mind Games

Dusty Miller was not best known as someone who was easily frightened. But he was now as he approached the address that he had been given.

He had agreed to meet with Harold Taylor on his return to the United States for two reasons. Firstly, the game had started to turn ugly; people were getting killed. Secondly, Dusty was a lawyer.

Dusty had originally been tasked to accompany Mark Taylor on a trip to Afghanistan to provide a service for which he was more than adequately qualified. His ability to exercise brute force when needed and as efficiently and effectively as circumstances required.

And at the time of accepting the mission, for which his background made him entirely suitable, that had seemed like fun.

But Dusty had another role. He was also tasked with building a case against the CIA, and against Stephen Rodriguez, and he was more than adequately qualified for that role too.

He had done both of his jobs.

Now it depended on other people.

It was not that he was frightened of having a meeting with an assistant inspector of the OIG of the CIA. Maybe when he was a sergeant in the Special Forces, he would have been somewhat over-awed, even fearful. But he had long since got over the aura of meeting high-level government officials. And this one was the father of his close buddy, so he knew of Harold, and was known by him.

The problem was that this whole business had turned pear-shaped. And rightly or wrongly, a fair amount of the blame for that rested on the shoulders of Harold Taylor. In Dusty's view, had Harold done his job, things could well have turned out differently.

After a long trip back from Afghanistan, Dusty had managed to track down Brad Morgan, and Brad had told him the shocking details of what had happened to Mark. Brad had also informed Dusty of the involvement of Blake, so at least there was some good news. That had led to Dusty having a rather terse conversation with Harold Taylor, which in turn led to their arranging this bizarre meeting.

Meetings in Washington DC would normally be conducted over lunch or dinner. After all, this was a city dominated by bureaucrats, and the one thing that bureaucrats were very good at was using a government-funded expense account. When Dusty was given a residential address in Bethesda, he was suspicious. Given the time of the meeting as 10:00 pm, he was even more suspicious.

He arranged for Blake and his colleagues to check it out. More specifically to check out the people who were already in and around the address. They had staked it out, registered who came and went, and they knew exactly who would be waiting when Dusty arrived for his meeting.

Although well-intentioned, that surveillance turned out to be overkill.

The address was the residence of Karen Marshall, director intelligence of the Drug Enforcement Administration.

Was it the intention of this meeting to inform Dusty that the matter was at an end? That no action would be taken? Dusty was frightened that he would not be able to control his rage if this was the case.

Harold Taylor made no apology for the lateness of the appointment. He made no mention of the fate of his son. Nor did he as much as thank Dusty for his efforts over the previous couple of weeks.

He was pleasant enough, but he offered coffee rather than beer. He sat on the couch next to Karen Marshall. He was somewhat closer than would be appropriate for a meeting of any kind, which for some reason made Dusty even more annoyed than he already was. Dusty's annoyance had been caused by Harold Taylor having caused considerable stress by not doing his job. He should have been supporting his son while he had been on a mission overseas.

To Dusty, that was unforgivable.

But for now, the lawyer in him took over.

'We do not have sufficient evidence to bring a case against Stephen Rodriguez, nor do we have sufficient proof of any wrongdoing on his part. We have a ton of circumstantial evidence, but you know where that will get us don't you?' was Dusty's opening statement.

Harold looked about as concerned as someone receiving the news that the sun would rise in the morning.

'Tell me what you know—then we can judge for ourselves,' replied Harold. There was no arrogance involved. It just came out that way: the elder white American who held a prestigious position in the Government seeking information from his younger black Afro-American who had been on an overseas mission, the objective of which was to obtain it.

Dusty's initial reaction—that of a Special Forces operator who was once again to be let down by officialdom —was to just get up and walk away.

However, he recognized that he was talking to some profoundly serious officials, and they just might be able to make something out of this. He was also a lawyer, not a judge or a jury. He also had an overriding responsibility to his friend Mark Taylor. And he knew that this was his only chance of telling his story with the end objective of getting revenge for what had happened. Dusty was convinced that the assumption Mark had made about Rodriguez's involvement in their near-death experience in Afghanistan was correct. But how do you convince an American court that one of their top Government officials would have been involved in such nonsense? Especially since the best witnesses were either Russians who were part of a shady ex-KGB organization or Afghani soldiers whose respect for law and order was not exactly well known.

He ignored his immediate reaction and spent the next half hour telling them of their experiences in Afghanistan and Pakistan.

Dusty dealt with the facts and left out any emotion. He explained that their first hint that drugs were involved was at the laboratory when they first arrived in Peshawar. After that, there had been nothing until they had followed the assistant director in the Marjah district of Afghanistan. Then things started to get interesting. They had followed Rodriguez and his friend Jacob Dutton from the CIA cell in Marjah to a meeting with Wakil Hekmatyar, the local Afghani who controlled much of what went on in the drug trade in that part of the world. Whatever reason Rodriguez had for meeting with Hekmatyar it was highly unlikely to have been on legitimate business.

He explained that he did not at the time see the significance of Rodriguez's next meeting with the dealer. Although Hekmatyar certainly did. Mark subsequently found out that this was probably Wakil's last meeting with anyone in this world. Although it would be difficult to pin his death on the ADDI or anyone in the CIA.

Dusty skipped over most of the drama that had been the Battle of Ghazni. Except to mention the brief meeting between Rodriguez and Mark Taylor. And the suspicion that Mark had been recognized. He briefly mentioned the death of Stephen's FBI boyfriend earlier on that day, and their suspicion that Rodriguez may have had a hand in this too.

He skipped over their experience in Kabul, except to mention their theory that it was Stephen Rodriguez who had set them up, and to let them know that Owen Squires had saved them from certain death. He told them what he had discovered back in Peshawar but skipped any mention of the day he had spent buried alive.

On his return to Washington, Dusty had been informed of the death of Dayanara Rodriguez following the apparent kidnapping of Debbie Peterson. Mark was accused of the former. Rodriguez, or one of his cronies, was apparently responsible for the latter.

He told them what they already knew—the attempt on Mark's life carried out at the Walter Reed military hospital. He told them of Brad's theory of how the drug network was set up and how it worked.

They already knew about the funeral of Dayanara, which was scheduled for the next day. Harold would attend because that would be expected of him. Karen would attend as a show of solidarity. Dusty made no comment.

When Dusty had finished, all three of them just sat there, lost in thought. It was an incredible story. But the truth of the matter was, although Dusty had some proof of the involvement of drugs, he had nothing except suspicions and assumptions about the exact involvement of Stephen Rodriguez.

It was Karen who asked the obvious questions.

'Do you now believe that Rodriguez is behind all this? That he was responsible for the death of the drug dealer in Afghanistan? That he may have been responsible for the death of an FBI agent? That he tried to have all three of you killed in Kabul? That he killed his own wife? That he arranged to have Mark killed in a United States military hospital? All to protect a drug network that he himself set up. Are you serious?'

The enormity of what she said was only just sinking in with Harold, but Dusty was on the same page.

And Dusty was at his best when people drew their own conclusions. Especially when the lady had accurately summed up his story, and she was focused on the very reason that Mark and Dusty had been involved.

'Yes, I am,' Dusty replied.

'And how are we going to prove it?' Harold inquired.

Dusty had to think for a moment. He could have been annoyed at the way Taylor had bypassed the obvious. It was surely the job of the Office of the Inspectorate to assemble the proof. Instead, Harold, an assistant inspector of that very office, was putting the onus on Dusty to prove everything.

Or was Harold just being Harold?

If Dusty's understanding of the origins of this mess was correct, it was these two people who had originated the plot that they had humorously called the Porto Plan, with the clear intention of finding proof. But Dusty was not swayed by the evasion. He was aware, from his various discussions with Mark, that having a meaningful conversation with Harold was difficult at best. You never knew what was going on in the old man's fertile imagination.

The question now was, could Dusty get these two officials to go along with what Mark had in mind?

There was an element of risk. It would require a very carefully choreographed plan. And everyone would need to be singing from the same song sheet.

Except for Stephen Rodriguez.

'I think we can get to the truth if we put Rodriguez under pressure,' Dusty opined. 'To do that, we may need some help.'

Dusty talked for a few minutes, explaining the plan. Neither Harold Taylor nor Karen Marshall reacted at all, at least initially. When he had finished his explanation, he just sat and waited for a reaction.

It was Harold who asked the next question.

'I know that the FBI would just love a situation where they could get stuck into the CIA. There is little love lost between the two organizations. But they would need to be convinced that there was a more than fair chance of success. Are we confident that they could be convinced to take that chance?'

Dusty knew extremely well the fickle nature of bureaucrats, and of the politics that would be involved in getting three organizations to work together. The FBI and the DEA would be relatively painless. However, involving the OIG of the CIA would probably result in fireworks. And he was also aware of the immense pressure that these two high-powered people would find themselves under, especially if the plan failed.

Nonetheless, the plan would be entirely dependent

on the assistance of the FBI—the one organization that so far had no idea of the importance or of the many issues that would be raised.

'What choice have we got?' Dusty offered.

That got no response.

'Or have you got a better idea?'

That got no response either.

Dusty was about to get up and leave when his phone vibrated in his pocket. He glanced at the screen, and he leaped to his feet.

'That call is from Mark. He is in trouble. I have to go! Mark is leaving the Walter Reed hospital—does anyone know where else he can go?'

'Can you get him to the Johns Hopkins Hospital in Baltimore? We will meet you there. Come on, Harold—it is your son!' said Karen as she headed for the door.

Chapter 60

Johns Hopkins

The gurney made its way along the corridor towards the ramp where the ambulance was waiting. On the right side of the gurney strode the doctor, with his left hand apparently steadying the passage of the precious cargo. In his right hand, he held the two IV bags that were still attached to the lures feeding into the patient's right arm.

Behind the doctor walked Blake, who was never far from the doctor. He held under his jacket a Glock 19. Ahead of them walked Ben Chapman, checking to see that they had a clear passage. To the rear of the gurney was a nurse—the same male nurse who had discovered the mess that Mark had caused the day before. Behind him strode a very unhappy Dusty, who was also armed. On the left of the gurney were two nurses, one of whom was frantically whispering into the patient's ear. Eventually, Michelle got a nod in the affirmative, and she raced off to carry out her task.

The arrangements that were now being implemented had not been easy. Mark had first called Blake, while still holding the doctor's shattered left wrist in his vice-like grip. The instructions that he gave to Blake were brief.

Next, he texted Dusty asking for help.

Then he had instructed the doctor to arrange for an ambulance to be available to transport him to a place yet to be defined. Mark then waited, hoping that his grip on the doctor's left wrist would not weaken, as he fought his own demons trying to stay awake. And hoping that the doctor would not do anything silly.

Fortunately, Blake was the first to arrive, having talked his way through the various security checks, and immediately took control of the situation. His first reaction was to dispose of the doctor, but Mark said no. They may still need the doctor's authority to escape the rabbit warren of hospital corridors. Once they had reached the ambulance, then Blake was free to deal with the doctor as he saw fit.

Dusty arrived next, and he had the same sentiments as Blake. In the case of Dusty, Mark had to be more affirmative in restraining his old friend.

Now the team had arrived at the ambulance loading area, where things moved at a rather hectic pace. The inquiry from the paramedic and the driver as to their destination was answered by Blake.

'You do not need to know that.'

He took them to one side and expanded on his comment in a whisper.

'The gentleman on the gurney has a rare disease, and we have to get him to another facility as soon as possible for treatment. It is important that you say nothing of this transfer until tomorrow, or never, depending on how you feel. I will tell you where we are going when we are on the road.'

Blake smiled at the two men, and he nodded his head towards where the doctor was standing by the gurney and then added, 'For security reasons, it is important that the good doctor does not know our destination. Is that clear?'

Both ambulance men looked totally un-surprised by anything that Blake had said. The driver replied with a shrug.

'I just drive the bus.'

While they were manoeuvring Mark into the rear of the ambulance, another gurney arrived at the loading bay, with a now-breathless Michelle and a male fussing around. Dusty took control of that situation. He faced the doctor, and in as polite a voice as he could muster, he asked for his assistance.

'Would you be so kind as to authorize another ambulance? There are a couple in the bay, so that should not be too difficult for you.'

The doctor started to protest, and Dusty nearly lost it. He showed the doctor the Glock 19 that he held and simply said, 'Do it now, or accept the consequences.' In a voice that barely resembled that of a colonel, he replied and complied. De Lawrence was loaded into a second ambulance. Blake gave the same instruction to the personnel of the second ambulance as he had given to the first one.

He got the same response.

Blake then turned his attention to the doctor.

'I hope you can explain to your masters what you have done here. Good luck with that. You will be hearing from us later. If your career is not already over, it will be shortly, if you get my drift.'

Again, the doctor started to protest, but that was cut short as he collapsed to the floor, after Blake sprayed him in the face from his aerosol can. And then Blake had another idea. He slipped a couple of pills between the doctor's teeth.

Dusty, who had moved to drag the inert body towards a closet, could not help but laugh. 'I have heard about your little pill! You really do not like this guy.'

They bundled the body into the closet and closed the door before Blake replied. 'I hope he rots in hell!'

Dusty shrugged. 'Me too!'

While Blake went to give instructions to the two drivers, Dusty rounded up the nurses who had accompanied the two gurneys to the loading bay, and he said, 'Come on, into the ambulances. You are coming with us.'

Everyone was too scared to argue.

While Dusty and Ben each rode in one of the ambulances, Blake climbed into his SUV, and the small convoy started its journey north. The ambulances only had their lights flashing. There was no need for the sirens—there was hardly any traffic on the roads at this time of night, and nobody was in any imminent danger of dying—at least not yet.

The journey was conducted in silence. Mark was asleep, lulled by the gentle movement of the vehicle. Del was still in an induced coma. The medical staff carried out their assigned routines. Dusty just glared at them, almost begging them to try one false move so that he could spring into action—anything to help his friend.

Their arrival at the Johns Hopkins hospital was the exact opposite to their departure from Walter Reed. The gurneys from the two ambulances were quickly, and efficiently, off-loaded and rushed off to a part of the facility that had been apparently set aside for the DEA.

A doctor was assigned to each patient, and they were ushered around by Karen Marshall, who made certain that their every need was met. Harold Taylor looked a little out of place, but he busied himself in conversations with Dusty and Blake. Mark and Del each had a room that was fully outfitted with every conceivable medical aid, and both opened onto a large area where any visitors would be well looked after.

The medical staff was informed that they would be staying with their patients, and they were each assigned to a room where they could take rest breaks if they so wished. The four people who had manned the ambulances were informed that they would be stood down for twenty-four hours and that they would also be treated as guests of Johns Hopkins.

The number of heavily armed police who were around the vicinity made compliance a non-too-difficult task. Nor was it too difficult to implement one cardinal rule: all mobile phones to be collected, and any communications with the outside world banned until further notice. Everyone seemed to reluctantly accept this, although no reason was given. Only the message that no one, outside of this group, was to know where the people who had earlier left Walter Reed had gone.

It was just the way the message was delivered. Everyone on the receiving end of the message was scared shitless.

When everyone had settled down, a small group gathered in the room that had been allocated to Mark. The group consisted of Harold, Dusty, Blake, and Brad, who had mysteriously appeared out of nowhere.

The following day would be a watershed moment, so it was critical that they each get their act together. They each explained what they knew of the case against Stephen Rodriguez. They all agreed that it was all circumstantial, but they generally agreed that they could make it work.

When, finally, the whole thing was over and they took their leave,

Brad had one further message to deliver to his boss.

'Mark, I know you are tired and probably want to sleep, but there is one other thing that has been sorted. There is someone who wants to see you.'

Brad turned and held the door.

Debbie Petersen came rushing in.

Brad quietly closed the door behind her.

Chapter 61

Endgame

The funeral got underway at 11:00 am the following morning. It was cold in Washington, but on this day, the sun shone.

There was a hint of warmth filtering through as the grim crowd sat huddled together in the small chapel, their attention focused on the ornate casket that was wreathed in flowers and mementos. As with all funerals, there was a mixture of people in attendance. The people who had no choice. Some people were there out of a sense of duty. Other people who were there out of a commitment to the family. Others who were there just to watch—drawn to a funeral as flies are drawn to rubbish.

And then there were the people who could not be there. People who could not trust the sanctity of the environment. Or those who felt nothing but loathing for the man who would be the centre of attention.

Stephen Rodriguez sat at the left front of the funeral hall, alone in his own private little world. Where were his daughters? Where was his family?

The official story was that the risk was too high and that attempts could be made on their lives. Until such time as all the suspects were rounded up, they would stay out of public view.

Rodriguez himself had to attend surrounded by an ample force of undercover security agents. That was the risk that you took! Part of the cost of being a high-ranking state servant. And part of the cost of being the loving husband of the body that lay in the casket.

He stared straight ahead, unable to comprehend what had gone wrong. Was it worth it?

On balance, he thought yes, it was. His relationship with his wife of some twenty-five years had become strained, and it had become more or less a marriage of convenience. Stephen Rodriguez had recently taken a liking to his young and dear friend from the FBI. They had shared a beautiful but tragically short relationship before Edward Hennessey had been senselessly killed in that hellhole that was Afghanistan. Well, that could not be helped, could it? If only Hennessey had kept his nose out of matters that did not concern him!

Despite Stephen's grief at the loss of his friend, he could have maintained the charade of the model family. If only the bitch Dayanara had not recently chosen to ask too many questions about his business. And then, more recently, she had allowed herself to be influenced by Mark Taylor and his associates. Now there was no choice. She had to be eliminated, and what better way to do that than in the presence of his other tormentor.

Rodriguez was not the only one who knew who had pulled that fatal trigger. But he was also not the only one that would say that Mark Taylor had fired the shot. The weight of the office of the CIA, and the 20,000-plus employees, against a lone maverick, was simply no contest.

Stephen Rodriguez was safe, at least for now.

Mark Taylor had got his woman back. But at what

cost? Mark had now paid the ultimate price. Instead of simply crawling back into his hole, he had tried to prevent Rodriguez from eliminating all witnesses.

And now Mark was no more. How stupid could a man possibly be? He gets injured in a gunfight. So, he checks into a US military hospital, where there is any number of people available to do the CIA's bidding. And who could doubt the ability of some of those people to be able to terminate Mark as easily as they will have eaten breakfast? Dead from any one of any number of causes, and the only one who could have a hope of challenging the cause of death were friends of Stephen Rodriguez's.

Sure, there were rumours that someone was hassling to have the case reopened. And they could only originate from one source. That was one more loose end to clear up in this saga.

Stephen should have read the situation much better —there were more people involved—but now it was clear.

Once the funeral was over, he would find and eliminate Archibald Dusty Miller.

Stephen had no recollection of having met the Afro-American friend of Mark Taylor's. He knew little about the man, except that he had a similar disposition as Mark. He had the annoying habit of turning up. So, he would be eliminated. Then Stephen's life and business could return to normal, explanations given and accepted

The service droned on, the priest saying the usual things about feelings and emotions that only some of those present felt. Saying things about a loving wife, and someone's daughter, and someone's mother, who had been so tragically taken from this world. About a husband and a father who had to now live in this world without his beloved companion, and with all the pain and suffering that would be involved. A husband and a father who was just too traumatized by the events of recent days to be able to address this assembly of his friends and his peers. A father who was so frightened that the attendance of his two daughters at the funeral would attract the killers of their mother, that he had been forced to keep them away.

Tears were shed as people listened to the priest, as they thought of happier times when the marriage of Stephen and Dayanara had seemed like a dream. Others cringed at the false sincerity of it all. Others looked on dispassionately, lost in the world of their own demons.

As is the way with such matters, Stephen's boss and a few other associates from the CIA stayed in the background, acknowledged by no one. The director, Jim Schlesinger, did not really want to be there at all, but he thought that he owed Stephen at least something. By the end of this day, things may well have changed in a most unexpected way.

Schlesinger had received a telephone call from the FBI not half an hour before he left his office to attend the funeral. A sort of heads-up, except that his contact had failed to tell him the details of what it was all about. Typical of the FBI! He would quietly drift away, his duty done, and await eventualities.

Also in the background was Harold Taylor, who knew what was going to happen. In another part of the chapel sat Karen Marshall. She also knew what was going down. She also knew it would be inappropriate to be alongside the AI of the OIG of the CIA. It was, after all, a funeral. There were just too many Government people around.

Later perhaps.

The service finally ended. The pallbearers took up

their places, and the rest of the crowd filed out of the chapel behind the coffin. To add to the drama and to the emotion, the casket was carried rather than driven to the burial place where everyone gathered around to witness the final commitment of the body into the ground.

Tears flowed one more time from many eyes as the priest read the final words. He waved his hand as everyone focused for the last time on the casket that held the body of Dayanara Rodriguez, beloved wife of Stephen, beloved mother of Estefania and Juanita.

Stephen Rodriguez was absolutely stunned.

On the end of the coffin, closest to where he was standing, and sitting among the flowers and wreaths was a stuffed bear. Clutched in its arms was a small plastic bag. While apparently looking at the coffin, Stephen's eyes frantically searched the crowd. Where had the toy come from? Who had placed it there? Was he being paranoid? He watched in fear as the coffin was slowly lowered into its final resting place. It was as though the toy bear was accusing him, the bright but lifeless eyes knowing what had really happened.

He shook his head as people filed past, some grabbing a handful of soil and dropping it into the grave on top of the casket. Stephen did the same. His first thought was to hurl the soil at that fucking bear. Sanity prevailed, and he just let the coarse particles dribble through his fingers. His grim face would be read as the appropriate response to an overwhelmingly tragic end to the life of his much-loved companion of many years. Only Rodriguez would know that there was both fear and commitment on his face.

Fear of what had happened and why.

Commitment to kill those responsible for this latest

insult.

A slight shift in the balance of the coffin caused the bear to roll off and silently plummet down into the abyss of the grave where it would be crushed and forever buried.

Unseen and insignificant to all except Stephen Rodriguez.

Refreshments were served in the small building just to the left of the entrance to the cemetery. This was an essential part of the funeral ritual. It enabled people to pay their last respects before they returned to the cutthroat world where they would no longer be as amicable as they would be on this day and in this place.

Rodriguez loathed it. He had to speak to those he barely knew, accept their sympathy, express his deep sorrow at the loss of his dear wife, repeat the same platitudes.

But there was something wrong with this gathering.

Several people had taken their leave without having spoken to the bereaved husband. And there were at least four *guests* who looked out of place to the seasoned observer. They did not say a word. They did not approach the host. They did not avail themselves of the refreshments on offer. They politely acknowledged the other people who had attended the requiem. Nobody thought to ask them who they were, or why they were there. Surely, nobody came to a funeral uninvited! Many came and sat silently in the background, watching, and waiting.

These four men, strategically positioned around the room, were watching one man.

When most of the important people had finally taken their leave, Rodriguez found out who they were.

All four of the men approached him at the same time,

just as he had made his escape from another bunch of teary-eyed women whom he did not really know. From the way the men carried themselves, and positioned themselves, they did not look like normal attendees at a funeral. They positioned themselves carefully, blocking any exit or avenue of escape.

They looked as though they were FBI agents, but without the bold lettering on their jackets that normally announced the presence.

'Mr. Rodriguez, we would like you to accompany us downtown now that the formalities appear to be over. The FBI has some questions that we would like answers to.'

The eldest of the four men was pleasant as he addressed Stephen and showed his identification badge. But there was an ominous tone to the way his message was delivered.

Stephen was rigid with fear, but still maintained the outwardly calm and arrogant attitude of a senior bureaucrat.

'What is this all about? Can't it wait? It has not exactly been the easiest of days!'

The guy remained pleasant, although his words were delivered with the cold indifference of a man who had seen and heard it all before.

'No, I'm afraid not,' he said. Then he added, 'We would like you to come and talk with your daughter Estefania about the events of the last few days.'

Stephen looked around the room in a panic. Looking for some means of support. Looking for some means of escape. Looking for the comfort of the men who had supported him during his career. He could not find anybody!

In his mind, he grappled with the conflicting thoughts that were bombarding his brain. There was no family to turn to. He had not been able to talk to either of his daughters since the tragic death of their mother, so he had been unable to explain to them what had happened. Well, his official version of a story that would be correct in fact, if not in substance.

Estefania had refused to answer his calls, and so he had decided that the situation was just too dangerous for her. And she had apparently got the message. The press had had a field day, and at least Estefania would be both aware of the speculation about her mother's death. And she would be aware of the many and varied theories about *what* and *who* had caused it.

Telling the reporters from the news media the official line and having them dutifully report it, albeit with all the twists and turns that would spin it into a newsworthy who-done-it was one thing. Having a daughter, who was present when it happened, was quite another. And she was either scared and frightened enough to stay away, or she had been got at by others with a vastly different story and was now scared. Maybe she now hated her father enough to stay away from her mother's funeral. The other daughter was away in Central Africa trying to save the world and could not be contacted easily. Messages had been sent, but whether they had been received, he had no way of knowing.

Stephen Rodriguez sighed.

There were two other tormentors to be dealt with.

In the end, he went quietly, excusing himself from the remaining people and explaining that he had to go to see his daughter. It was to be expected that one so important as the assistant deputy director of intelligence would be accompanied by men in suits. They looked outwards from their little group as though expecting trouble. And they looked as though they would kill without a second thought. Which everyone fully understood for all the wrong reasons.

Except, Stephen Rodriguez.

Chapter 62

FBI Headquarters

The FBI drove their black SUV through Washington in silence and into the carpark basement of the J. Edgar Hoover Building. Ironically, this was Stephen Rodriguez's first visit to the premises occupied by the CIA's sister and domestic organisation. Consequently, he had no prior knowledge of whereabouts in the building they were headed.

The entrance to the Hoover Building was not as dramatic as that at Langley. But it still gave the impression that you were in the presence of immense power.

They went through the usual security checks, which gave the distinct impression that this party had been expected. The leading agent exchanged a few words with a couple of the guards, and there was a noticeable increase in the tension around the foyer as they moved towards the escalator. They rode the car up three floors, and then they meandered along a corridor until they entered a conference room that was already crowded with people. The room was large and cold. The table was immense. The only other piece of furnishings, other than the table and giving no information on the reason for the gathering.

Silence descended on the room as the men entered, but for all the reaction, the meeting may have been to organize an office thanksgiving party, except for the status of some of those present.

The person seated at the head was completely unknown to Rodriguez, but he recognized at least two of the others. And he had a fair idea who some of the others were. All those years of training, and many more in the field, allowed him to scan the room and the people in attendance without appearing to look at any individual.

Brad Morgan had made the effort. He was dressed in a charcoal-grey suit, looking very smart but also looking nervous. Harold Taylor, on the other hand, looked totally relaxed. He was in his usual attire of dark-blue pinstriped suit, white shirt, red tie—the epitome of the stoic professional bureaucrat, his eyes icy cold and missing nothing. The lady sitting next to Harold—now she was interesting! She sat a little closer than the normal regimented seating arrangement the FBI allowed, and she must be Karen Marshall from the DEA. The huge Afro-American guy sitting between Brad and Harold was perhaps the most imposing figure who Stephen vaguely recognized from somewhere. Afghanistan, was it?

Was this the infamous Archibald 'Dusty' Miller?

None of those in attendance looked particularly friendly. In fact, the two Afro-Americans seemed particularly hostile. The people on the other side of the table had a sameness and an indifferent air about them that said that they were *bureaucrats*. People who could well have just come from the funeral—it was their duty to be there. They would probably take no active role in whatever it was that was about to unfold. Just taking notes. Watching as others played their silly little games. Like vultures just waiting to pounce.

Rodriguez was motioned into a chair at the end of the

table. They all sat exchanging glances for a disquieting few moments, and that caused Stephen to make the first call. Appear confident. Put them on the defensive.

'So, what is this all about?' Stephen inquired. 'And where is my daughter?'

The gentleman at the opposite end of the table smiled.

'All in good time, Stephen! I am sure that you would like to see her, but I am not sure, yet, whether she wants to see you.'

He let the message sink in while he surveyed those present and then continued. 'It is hard for me to know where to start. My name is Peyton Reed, and I am an assistant director of the Federal Bureau of Investigation. My job is to try to make some sense out of this puzzling, and quite intriguing, story. I suppose my first responsibility is to advise you, Stephen Rodriguez, of your rights.'

'I know my rights! What is this all about?' Stephen almost shouted.

Body language can be terribly revealing, and there was nothing that Stephen could do about that. He felt that he was trapped, but a plan immediately formed in his mind as to what he would do now.

The mind plays funny games in trying to rationalize a situation. He did not know! Who would have the necessary authority to call these people to this place? But he could hazard a guess. He no doubt would be told what the meeting was about, but he had to try to keep one step ahead. Assume that they thought that they knew everything, so listen to what they had to say. Be patient. Listen to what they had to ask, without his lawyer present. Deny everything. Then he could claim all sorts of indiscriminate and misleading methods that had been used at what was obviously set up as an interrogation. Like everyone else in this country, he had his rights. And as he saw it now, those rights had been denied him. He would let them prattle on, and then they would have to let him go.

Were they here to find out what had happened to his wife? Well, they were out of luck there. What they could not get out of him was any kind of confession, for the simple reason that he had not been the one that pulled the trigger. Then he would have the final say, and he would throw it all back in their faces. Harold Taylor would find that his son Mark Taylor was the one who was accused of being the killer. This meeting could well be about the death of his wife, but no one could prove that Stephen was even there, could they? Mark Taylor, the man who had set up that gathering in the park, could only *assume* that Stephen was also there. And Stephen knew what this gathering at the FBI thought of assumptions. And now Mark Taylor was no longer in the land of the living. The doctors at Walter Reed had taken care of that, hadn't they?

This meeting could be about his involvement with drugs. But he had absolute faith in the security of his network, and in the people responsible for its security. It could be about the death of a couple of people in Afghanistan. One of them was a well-known criminal and drug dealer with more enemies than friends, and those who were his friends were all criminals. He had been killed by the Afghanis. The life expectancy of people in this country was about half the life expectancy of a person living in the United States! The death of one more was a matter that would be swept under the table, and soon forgotten about. In any case, that had absolutely nothing to do with the FBI. And good luck with trying to prove that Stephen Rodriguez had anything at all to do with that.

Sure, the FBI had lost a man. That man had been taken to Afghanistan by Rodriguez to do a job for the CIA. So what? Edward Hennessey had gone of his own volition, and presumably with the knowledge of his superiors. Good old institutional cooperation. And then he had been killed. In a convoy that had been under attack by enemy insurgents. He had died as a result of a bullet from an AK-47 rifle. Good luck ever locating that weapon! Maybe he was killed by friendly fire. Well, shit happens! If you cannot take the heat, get out of the kitchen!

The thoughts rapidly tumbled through Stephen Rodriguez's mind as he formulated his plan. So, what was it about? It could not be just about his wife; otherwise, what were all these people doing here? Therefore, it had to be about drugs, which helped explain why Karen Marshall was here. And something to do with his recent trip to Afghanistan; otherwise, what was Archibald Miller doing here? Therefore, there was only one reasonable conclusion that could be drawn.

It could be that the FBI was simply hosting this meeting at someone else's behest.

That was very unlike them.

The FBI was on a fishing trip.

Peyton Reed rested his head on his intertwined fingers, looking at Stephen with a not-unkindly expression.

'What is this about? That is what we are all here to find out! I have so far heard several theories, and while the investigations are ongoing, none of them seem to make much sense to me. The Washington Police are investigating the death of Dayanara Rodriguez, and they have referred the matter to me as they are puzzled by a couple of factors. Call it a conspiracy theory. That involves personnel from the CIA, and involves a couple of kidnappings which, of course, we are concerned about. Hence the involvement of the FBI. Then there are a few matters that concern your recent visit to Afghanistan. The reasons why you went there are a matter for the CIA. But your activities on your return are of interest to the FBI.'

He then turned to Harold Taylor.

'Perhaps we could start with you. For the benefit of all present, if you could just state your position, and then your role, we should be able to get some clarity into this extraordinary tale.'

The people around the table immediately got out their pens.

Chapter 63

The Evidence

Harold was the best person to begin, if for no other reason than that this whole affair had started with him. That he probably knew the least about how it had all ended did not matter.

'For the record, I am Harold Taylor, assistant inspector of the OIG attached to the Central Intelligence Agency. Together with our friends in the DEA, we set out to investigate the involvement of certain people of the CIA in drug trafficking. This was not an investigation that had anything to do with the CIA policy on drugs. This was an investigation into whether certain people within the CIA were buying and selling drugs for their own use, and for their own gain.'

Stephen riveted his attention on Peyton Reed.

'What has this got to do with my wife, and her death?' Stephen laughed. But since no one immediately replied he continued,

'You are not trying to imply that she was killed in a drug deal gone wrong, are you?

Typical, thought Harold. This was just the beginning of a complex story. He had faith in the theories that had been presented to him. And faith in the people who had presented them. But it was really a house of cards. One small slip, and the house would collapse, and Stephen was then off the hook. One small slip, and Peyton Reed would close this enquiry. Harold had managed to get the FBI to hold what was really an informal hearing solely, he believed, based on two unexplained kidnappings, one of which had resulted in death. Both of those kidnappings had occurred because of activities half a world away in Afghanistan. The aim was to find out if Stephen Rodriguez had a case to answer for his role in Afghanistan. And the last thing on Harold's mind at the present was Stephen's domestic problems.

Harold had the floor. The years that Harold had spent in the service of his country, working closely with diplomats, hiding his feelings, waiting for the opportunity were his strengths. Repeating the same thing but in a different way. Ignoring interruptions.

Harold fixed Stephen with his cold grey eyes. He hoped that the look conveyed his loathing for the man who he had once worked for. And, he had to admit, once respected.

'The FBI asked me to speak first because we see a connection between your trip to Afghanistan and various other events which have occurred both during and since. You may claim to be unaware, but I am sure that you were aware that you were followed on your travels abroad. We have a theory that these occurrences and the people involved are all connected. I am sure that you would want to know if they are!'

The ADDI of the CIA could read body language like many people in the intelligence business. Harold Taylor was on very shaky ground. What Stephen did not know was that his own arrogance could be his downfall.

Rodriguez just shrugged and let Harold continue.

'Because of the sensitive nature of the subject, and my own reluctance to involve any CIA personnel in my investigation, I instead came to an arrangement with the DEA. We formed a small team made up of two ex-Special Forces officers and a DEA agent to carry out an investigation and to follow the trail from its source to the end-user. We have evidence that the CIA has been involved in drugs and that there was some concern that the supply, for whatever reason, was being interrupted. One of the reasons for your trip to Afghanistan was to find out why. The task of the team that we sent to Afghanistan was to investigate the operations of the DEA teams that were already in the country. But they did have another purpose. Their specific job was to find out how the drugs were being purchased by someone in the CIA, how they were brought into this country, and how they were distributed. We did not alert the FBI for the simple reason that we had cause to believe that the use of drugs and their distribution network also involved people from within the FBI. After the shambles that you will recall were described as the second 9/11, you will understand why this investigation needed to be kept covert. Even at this late stage, this mission is still an unsanctioned operation, and this is the first time we have made this information known to people outside the immediate group of those directly involved.'

'Does the President, or anyone in the White House, know?'

The unexpected question came from a man who was sitting just to the right of Peyton Reed. Like many of the others in the room, the unnamed man was dressed in an immaculate dark suit. His body language said that he was someone quite senior. And the fact that he did not volunteer his name and Reed never asked him to state it told the others all they needed to know about his place at the feeding trough. He was from the National Security Agency, and probably outranked, by some margin, everyone in the room including Harold Taylor and Stephen Rodriguez, and probably Peyton Reed.

Not that it really mattered. The FBI is part of the Department of Justice, whereas most of the other principal sixteen players in the US security and intelligence services are part of the Defense structure. The CIA is an independent agency, but the real question was, who had the most say at the top table? And the answer to that question was probably the NSA.

Harold Taylor did not even blink at this further interruption.

'With respect, I should sincerely hope not!' Harold began. 'I understand that the President was not overly impressed by the recent performance of his intelligence and security services. Because we had no hard evidence in this case, and we felt that it was a relatively minor investigation, nothing would have been achieved if the President had been informed. Other than to further weaken his faith in the services. I should not need to add that the White House staff is not immune from our investigation. Or from the FBI's investigation. I am not sure that we want to open up that particular can of worms in this particular company, do we?'

Initially, that seemed to take the wind out of the NSA. There was yet another theory, but no, the NSA did not want to go down that track, and certainly not in front of this group of people! But the NSA persisted.

'Well, when do you intend to tell him? Now that your *investigation* is, shall I say, coming to its logical conclusion.'

Again, Harold did not appear to be under any pressure, which Brad and Dusty had to admire in Mark's old man.

They had heard all about the mind games that people in Washington loved to play. Their assessment was that, by interrupting so early in the piece, the overweight gentleman with slick black hair, greasy skin, and thick black glasses was simply making the point that he was senior and that he could get to the President. Well, at least more so than the peasants in this room. But Harold had made a none-too-subtle suggestion, which clearly unnerved the man. And proved beyond doubt that the man from the NSA had no idea where this investigation was going to lead.

Harold knew of the man—in fact, he had a dossier on all the senior staff, albeit edited somewhat at his level. He knew his name - one Joseph Klein - but resisted the temptation to use it. White House insiders regarded him as slimy and arrogant. And as evidenced by his performance thus far - they were probably right.

There was not a hint of a victory, or of any arrogance, as Harold continued.

'The decision of when, or whether, the President should be informed is not my decision. That is yours. You will know who I have to report to and also know that I do not eat out of the same trough as you do. I assume that is why you are here—to listen and to judge the story on its merits. Then we will all know what should be done.'

So, shove that up your ass! Harold thought.

This was not going to be an easy day at the office! thought Reed. There would be diversions at every step. The questions were - how good was the case? And how good were the people trying to prove it?

The briefing that he had received had sounded far-fetched, as well as far-ranging. He was mainly interested in the death of one of his own men in Afghanistan and the apparent fact that there had been two kidnappings here in Washington. How these were related to each other was anyone's guess. But the story was intriguing. This was the only reason that he had agreed to host this gathering.

The reports that he had received from his own people was that Edward Hennessey had died from an AK-47 fired at point-blank range. So why had the other members of the party not suffered the same fate? No one else in the whole convoy had been shot at so close a range. Those who had been killed by bullets had been shot from a distance. And there was zero evidence that any Taliban or other insurgents had been shot or killed in the battle. So how did someone walk up to a vehicle, in the middle of a convoy, shoot the only FBI agent within hundreds of miles. And then quietly disappear?

Now they were hearing a story that told of a CIA official being followed by an investigating team that appeared to be totally unrelated to the matters that concerned the FBI. Or was there more intrigue to follow?

Karen Marshall took over the discussion, as everyone waited in anticipation now that the knives were out.

'I am Karen Marshall, director of intelligence of the DEA. My agent, together with the two unassigned officers, followed the trail of the ADDI, first to Peshawar, Pakistan, then into Afghanistan, and then back to Peshawar. The team discovered that the drug opiates were sent from the south of Afghanistan, over the border into Pakistan, where they were refined into heroin at a laboratory in Peshawar. We have evidence that this was arranged with the cooperation of certain CIA operatives in both Afghanistan and Pakistan. We have reason to believe that the agency was shipping the drugs for sale to its own people. Our problem was finding out how they were imported into the United States, and then how they were ordered and distributed. We found some evidence that they were distributed strictly within the Government. We know that there has been a drug problem in the United States military as well as in other organisations, including the CIA and the FBI, and it looks as though someone has established a very clever network to distribute drugs from the inside. The exact extent of the network we do not know yet. It probably extends to include even the DEA.'

Her last comment raised a few eyebrows, but it was made with the candour of someone who was used to telling the truth. Still, there had to be questions, as all the bureaucrats in the room looked sideways at each other. Reed, as chair of the meeting, felt obliged to comment.

'That is a serious allegation. We will need positive proof! How certain are you that the scheme even exists? More to the point, how certain are you of the people involved—and I mean both the people organising the scheme and the people who claim to have uncovered it.'

Marshall focused her attention on Stephen Rodriguez. There was no accusation in her voice, just the facts.

'My people followed the Central Intelligence Agency ADDI to Afghanistan and Pakistan. Apart from the fact the agents were lucky to survive the trip, we have ample evidence of Rodriguez's direct involvement in drug trafficking. Evidence that is good enough for the DEA to take to a court. As for the integrity of the people employed on this mission, you will find that they were very well qualified and have impeccable references.'

'Well, we had better hear from them,' Reed said as he followed Marshall's gaze towards where Dusty was sitting.

'No!' Harold responded. 'I think you first need to hear

our conclusions as to how the scheme works. I would like to introduce Brad Morgan. He has led the investigation since our agents returned from Afghanistan. He is known to Stephen Rodriguez, so he will need no introduction there.'

Attention shifted to Brad, who had been sitting quietly at the back of the room. He now stood and, in silence, purposefully made his way to the whiteboard.

'I am Brad Morgan, employed in a company called Taylor Software as a specialist in computer security systems. Immediately prior to joining Taylor Software, I was with the DS&T at the CIA. With the CIA, I was employed as a professional computer hacker.'

That comment brought a nervous titter from the assembled crowd. They all thought that computer system hacking was the province of geeks and crooks, and people who hid from sight. Now they had met one, and he did not look like a geek, even if he was Afro-American and was wearing glasses.

Morgan drew a series of four horizontal parallel lines across the board, each interspersed with several boxes. On the top line, he labelled each box as he described the flow of opiates through Afghanistan, and then finishing up in Peshawar. On the bottom line, he made similar notations while talking about the usual needs of the drug user and how they would normally obtain their supplies. Then he came to the middle two lines and, for the first time, turned to face his audience.

'This is how I think the scheme works. The potential users contact an existing user from within their own organization, and they are sponsored to apply for their subscription and connection to the network. Their details are screened by a gatekeeper. For those of you who are unfamiliar with the computer lingo, the term *gatekeeper* in this case means someone who controls access to a network. Usually, such people are employed in what we refer to as the dark web, but they are not limited to that. Suffice to say that no one gets into their website or scheme unless they are suitably vetted by the gatekeeper. If they are successfully vetted, then they are given a username and a password. In this case, they are also given instructions on how to access the ordering system via the Internet. Each order, each delivery, each payment is screened by the gatekeeper, or, more correctly, by a computer system controlled by the gatekeeper. If anything looks even remotely suspicious, the link is immediately discontinued. The access to this link is hidden in plain sight on a government social network. If you know where to go and where to look, you will find a website where you can order the goods of your choice, namely, stuffed animals. Innocent enough! But if you use your password, you can turn the order into one for drugs. The order goes to the same place. It gets filled in the same way, and you still get your teddy bear. Except, in this case, it gets shipped via diplomatic bag, so that it does not get checked by customs. If it were, your teddy bear will be found to be packed in a box that holds small plastic packages. These contain the drugs. Heroin, to be exact.'

Brad paused while he filled in notations on lines two and three on the board.

'So now I have written up how this all relates to what we are here for. I have shown the links between this kind of scheme and the flow of drugs. We think that the drugs are shipped to order in small packages out of Peshawar, Pakistan. That is why we could not find any evidence of actual shipment into the United States. There isn't any shipment. The factory in Peshawar, where the opiates are delivered from Afghanistan, and where they are refined into heroin simply hand them over for storage and eventual sale in a sister organization, which is, you guessed it, a toy factory. As for the Internet connection, that is secure. There are, in fact, two networks: one a private system that the gatekeeper uses and controls, and one which we can call a public connection that any and everyone has access to. The first monitors the second, and at the slightest hint of something not right, the gatekeeper and the link from the public network both disappear and get rebuilt. The strongest features of the network are its security and its communications. No one is trusted. There is a three-tier system to the access the ordering system—all controlled by the gatekeeper.'

'Do you know who the gatekeeper is?'

The question came from Peyton Reed, but it may as well have been asked by anyone in the room—they all had the same thought.

The reply he got was just a shrug of the shoulders and a brief comment from Brad.

'If you knew who he was, and you had access to his server, then you could close down the network. But in the Internet world, he would be extremely hard to find. He must be one very clever guy!'

If anyone could read body language, they would know that what Brad had told them was the truth. But he had avoided answering the question. His answer could have been 'Yes.' But his instructions were not to reveal that, especially since Stephen Rodriguez was in the room.

At this point, Brad resumed his seat. There was no point in telling this auspicious gathering everything that he knew. Brad was not on the Government payroll, so he did not have to. He also did not need to reveal that there was a certain amount of assumption involved. Nor did he need to reveal that he had an incredibly good idea where the gatekeeper plied his trade. But he had to smile to himself.

Taylor Software had a few tricks of its own and had recruited Brad from the ranks of the CIA. Using a thief to catch a thief.

Dusty took over the discussion. In his real life, Archibald Miller was quite accustomed to addressing himself to gatherings of people. In fact, addressing himself to gatherings that had some of the smartest brains in the city, if not beyond. This group of people was all bureaucrats, so when, or if, they needed to think, they tended to do so slowly. There was little point in trying anything clever. Dusty stuck to the basic facts.

But first, he had to let these people know just how difficult the task had been, and who was responsible. And he hoped to get an early reaction, which would make the rest of his presentation so much more manageable.

'I am Dusty Miller, a lawyer by trade, but ex-Special Forces sergeant and I was hired to accompany the team that was sent to Afghanistan.'

That brought another reaction from the NSA man, Joseph Klein.

'How does that qualify you to undertake an investigation into drug trafficking? I would have thought that the DEA had more suitably qualified people!'

Dusty eyed the insipid man with a cold stare that would have made most men crumble. But Dusty had a smile on his face as he replied.

'I guess I am not qualified to answer that. You should direct your question to the people who did the hiring. However, let me speculate. Firstly, I am the right colour to blend in with the locals, especially in Pakistan. Secondly, I have been involved in several drug-related investigations and am familiar with the trade. Thirdly, I am experienced in covert operations. And, should the need arise, in killing people. But the facts before us now are that I was one of the three who went to Afghanistan – as a team. I have been asked to comment on my experience – which I have done. So, are you happy that I should continue? Or do you want to continue bickering about whose territory we are stepping into?'

The first comment caused a few gasps around the table. It was the final comment that had the best reaction. No one had ever spoken to Klein in that way, and he was not about to take that now. If it were not for Peyton Reed, there could have been a bloodbath.

'Mr. Miller! Would you please continue? I am sure any questions that others may have will be dealt with at the proper time,' Peyton calmed the situation.

Dusty continued as though he had been discussing the weather.

'Afghanistan is a third-world country,' he began. 'You neither expect nor are given many of the comforts we are used to in our United States. When my colleagues and I got a first-hand experience of the fragility of life, we were aghast at the ease with which one of our own adapted to the local custom of complete disregard for the life of his fellow human beings. I refer, of course, to Mr. Rodriguez.'

Dusty paused and took a drink of water, staring over the rim of the glass at Stephen Rodriguez.

'Has anyone in this room ever suffered from hypothermia? Has anyone in this room been left to die in the wilderness? In a freezing-cold blizzard, with next to no clothes on, tied hand and foot and with no hope of being rescued?'

In the absence of any response, he continued.

'I thought not! Well, I have during my recent visit to Afghanistan. And I can tell you, as one who is not easily scared, it is frightening. Gives you a whole new outlook on life.'

'What is your point?'

The question came from the NSA. It was predictable. It gave Dusty the moral ground on which to continue.

'My point is this: I am a lawyer. I went to Afghanistan with my friends to investigate a scheme that was involved in shipping drugs into the United States. Before we left Washington, some research had already been done, so the plan was to find out what Stephen Rodriguez was up to, and, if circumstances warrant, build a case against him. Our job was the simple task of finding out how someone had arranged for drugs to be smuggled from Afghanistan into the United States. Why me, you may ask? In the past, and before I left the military service, I have been involved in many drug investigations. This time, apart from riding shotgun, my role as a lawyer was to make sure that we had a watertight case. And we had little tangible evidence until someone tried to kill us. The fact that he failed then meant that he had to react. That reaction is what led us to the truth.'

'I am sorry. But I do not follow you.' Again, the interruption came from the NSA.

Again, Dusty just smiled. There had been no reaction from Stephen Rodriguez.

But a reaction was coming.

'As I said, if you were listening, I am a lawyer,' Dusty replied, addressing himself to the originator of the statement. Being a lawyer meant that Dusty could not care who held what rank in this muddled world of bureaucrats. Being a lawyer meant that he had facts, but he did not have to reveal what they were. Everyone was waiting. Dusty was waiting. Patience.

Something had to give. And Rodriguez was the first to draw a line in the sand.

'You are not seriously suggesting that I had anything

to do with that, are you?'

'To do with what?' Dusty asked in a quiet voice.

'Your whole role in Afghanistan was what!' Rodriguez retorted, with an air of triumph.

'And what was our role?' Dusty addressed the question to Stephen. He got an answer from Joseph Klein.

I would expect you to tell us!'

So, Dusty did.

'Since this is just an informal meeting, as I understand it, the objective of which is to present the plain facts for those of us who do not have the complete story, I will be brief. We went from Washington to Peshawar, Pakistan, via England and Tel Aviv. While in Peshawar, both the assistant deputy director and his FBI friend visited a drug laboratory on the outskirts of that city. I also went there, at slightly different times of the day, you will understand.'

The ADDI went to interrupt, but Dusty just held up his hand.

'Your friend in this meeting said that he expected me to tell the people who are assembled here, and that is what I am trying to do. I am sure you will have the opportunity of rebuttal. Meanwhile, do you have something you would like to add or deny? You are not going to tell us that you did not know that it was a drug laboratory, are you? Or should I continue?'

The room was totally silent. The ADDI looked defiant, but ill at ease. So, the assumption that Mark had made back in Afghanistan had been wrong—maybe the pilot of the DEA Gulfstream had been on their side after all! Otherwise, what was the point in Rodriguez denying anything?

Dusty continued.

'From there, we went into Afghanistan, first to the capital, Kabul, and then we went down into the southern part, the Helmand province, and to the district of Marjah. There we found where the drugs originated. And there the ADDI had meetings with a well-known criminal, and drug dealer who went by the name of Wakil Hekmatyar. Sorry, I forgot to mention—the late Wakil Hekmatyar. You see, Hekmatyar was killed in suspicious circumstances, while the ADDI was in Marjah.'

Another drink of water. Another few moments staring over the rim of the glass at Stephen Rodriguez. It always worked.

Dusty continued.

'Then things got exciting. On the road from Kandahar to Kabul, we were attacked, by insurgents, probably the Taliban, in a battle that later became known as the Battle of Ghazni. We were there because we were following the drugs. The ADDI and his boyfriend were there—'

The reaction of Stephen Rodriguez was comical and entirely expected—at least by Dusty. But the question came from Joseph Klein.

'What are you talking about?' the NSA enquired. 'Are you suggesting that the assistant director was somehow responsible for the actions of a group of insurgents?'

The questions from the NSA distracted the meeting from what Dusty had alluded to. But they did not distract either Stephen or Dusty.

'I am not suggesting anything!' Dusty addressed his reply to the NSA man. 'I am simply trying to tell you what happened out there in Afghanistan. Unless you have some information that can shed some light on the events of that day, I would like to continue. This is supposed to be an informal meeting, so we are not at this stage having to prove anything. Unless you would like me to?'

The body language said it all. The tension in the room

was noticeably increasing, while the mind of Stephen Rodriguez was doing cartwheels. The NSA just nodded.

Dusty just waited, and then continued with his story.

'When the convoy was first attacked, my colleague and I checked that the ADDI was OK, and we found that the FBI agent accompanying the ADDI was dead. How that occurred, we did not know at that time, except that he was shot with an AK-47 at close range. And the only person close enough who had a rifle of this type was the ADDI. At the time, we simply ensured that the ADDI himself was safe without his boyfriend—'

'What are you saying now? What is this "boyfriend" nonsense? And what has the FBI got to do with it?' The almost-shouted question once again came from the NSA representative.

Dusty was not interested in the question. He was more interested in the reaction of Rodriguez. A confidence, almost a smugness, which belied what Dusty knew of the relationship. But Reed came to his rescue.

'Please carry on, Mr. Miller. We were aware of the relationship before we agreed to let Edward Hennessey travel to Afghanistan. We quite obviously have questions about Hennessey's passing, but that can wait until later.'

Now Dusty was interested in the reaction from Peyton Reed. So, the FBI *knew* about the relationship! The ADDI was going apoplectic at this new piece of information. But Dusty continued as though this bombshell had not dropped.

'Then we went towards the front of the convoy where the major damage had occurred. We went to offer whatever assistance we could with the defence of our convoy, and then our extraction back to Ghazni. You will understand that the troops had suffered heavy losses, and we were extremely willing to help. We can thank the Brits for getting us out of that pickle. In fact, you can thank Harold Taylor's son, Mark Taylor, for our survival. We did not receive a lot of help from others who would have been expected to help.'

Dusty took another drink from his glass.

'Back in Ghazni, the ADDI came to thank the team, and that is where he recognised Mark Taylor, despite the beard and the unkempt appearance of someone who had just placed his own life on the line to protect this scum! For those of you who do not know the background, Mark Taylor and Stephen Rodriguez were associated in the events that occurred a few months ago in the second 9/11. You can also thank Mark Taylor for sorting out that mess. But no thanks from the CIA. From the time that the ADDI realised he was being followed in Afghanistan, our lives turned to shit. We were apparently accused of an attempt to kill the President—'

'What! Why did I know nothing of this?' The blurted-out response again came from the NSA's Joseph Klein.

Dusty smiled. He held up his hands in mock surrender.

'Don't worry! That was exactly our reaction at the time. But no, not our President. The President of Afghanistan. How the Russians got on to us—'

'What are you talking about? What have the Russians got to do with it?'

Dusty was not smiling now as he addressed the NSA, but he was conscious of the reaction he was getting from Rodriguez.

'Sir, have you actually been to Afghanistan? Or, for that matter, anywhere where there is actually a war going on?'

A pause, then Dusty continued.

'No, I thought not. Well, let me tell you—things are a

little different out there. The Afghan intelligence service is a joke, with apologies to our CIA's attempts to make it otherwise. And the Russians take advantage of that. So, anyone who falls into the Afghani clutches, especially Western men, become guests of the Russians until such time as they are of no further use. Then the "guests" go back to the Afghanis for disposal. I am sure you will understand, the Russians would not want the world in general to know of their involvement. The guests are just made to disappear. And that is exactly what happened to us. However, we were fortunate. Someone just happened to find us before it was too late, and before we froze to death. Again, we were fortunate to receive some help from the British MI6. And we now have more than enough evidence, backed up by the Brits, of who was to blame for this fiasco.'

Dusty just stared straight ahead into the eyes of Rodriguez. He saw fear. The mention of MI6 was what caused that fear. And he saw a worried look appear on the face of Joseph Klein. While the cooperation between the UK and the USA at government level was well known, the cooperation between their respective intelligence organizations was a different matter. It was most unlikely that MI6 would share with the CIA even a smidgen of information on what they knew of this affair.

If nothing else, the Brits were masters at using information to the embarrassment of their enemies. And the embarrassment of their friends when the circumstances warranted such action.

Harold Taylor took over the commentary.

'Now, before we get into accusing anyone of orchestrating this scheme, we need to think about the cost.'

The bureaucrats in the room again sniggered as one of their fellows got down to the important business of talking about money. Harold ignored them. He was not talking about money.

'I believe that while in Afghanistan, contact was made with a Russian who goes by the name of Yuri Alekseyev. Most of you will not know that name, but Alexseyev and I go way back to the days when the KGB and the CIA were fighting the Cold War. He tells me that instructions were given for three of our agents to be disposed of. That instruction came from the CIA. Our agents managed to extricate themselves from that situation, and I am sure you will want to question Mr Miller on how that was achieved.' He nodded his head towards Dusty, who continued to stare at Stephen Rodriguez, remembering how close he had come to being literally frozen to death.

Harold continued.

'Suffice to say at this stage that our agents were able to continue with their mission, until one of them got back to Washington, only to have further threats on his life. During this stage, the wife of Mr. Rodriguez was unfortunately killed, as you are all aware. Also, there were two attempts on the life of our agent who was wounded and in hospital, the second attempt being more successful than the first.'

'What has all this got to do with Mr. Rodriguez? Don't you think the man has had enough to deal with—he has only just buried his wife! Surely you are not saying that these things are in some way connected!'

The question, again, came from the NSA man.

Harold held the man's eyes in a bitter stare. The NSA would be of no use in resolving this issue. It seemed to Harold that the drug network had possibly spread to that organisation as well. Well, so be it. It was now time to play his other card. He turned to the man standing by the door and asked him to open the door.

'Would you please ask the gentleman to come in now?'

Mark Taylor entered the room.

Chapter 64

Resurrection

The fact that Mark had survived the last few days was as a result of his determination to deal to the man who now faced him across the table. And it was against considerable odds.

The staff at the Walter Reed National Military Medical Center were as dedicated as any in their field of work. But the mix of dedication to things such as the Hippocratic oath and military discipline sometimes did complicate things. Involving the CIA just made it more complicated.

When Mark had issued instructions to Colonel McPherson, he had no real idea whether or not he would carry them out. It was clear to Mark that the colonel was under some form of instruction, and that instruction must have come from the CIA, or at least from someone who had connections to Stephen Rodriguez. The problem was that it did not matter that much. Having involved an officer with rank in a military hospital, the fallback position would be to protect the reputation of the hospital, and the senior staff, having made certain that there was no possible connection to the security service.

It was therefore important that Mark make a judgment call on what was going on. That meant he had to make some assumptions. Mark was aware of CIA involvement with medical people. He had to assume that McPherson was a medical officer known to and trusted by the CIA.

What, then, could have happened that would cause the good doctor to stray from his principles? From what Mark knew of Rodriguez, that link had to be drugs. There was just no other logical explanation. Therefore, the assumption was that the CIA, or Rodriguez, had proof that the doctor was using drugs and could make his life exceedingly difficult should they choose to reveal that. By a word to the media, or a chat with some other medical people or a word to his boss, McPherson's distinguished career would be brought to a shattering halt. And whatever else was going on in the mind of the doctor, the prospect of such an end to a military career was an easy decision. He would kill for it.

The question Mark now had to answer was, how to counter the might of the CIA? And how to threaten McPherson with a fate worse than that which he already faced?

That answer was to add a new factor to the McPherson dilemma. He had to make it clear that McPherson would be killed if he did not comply.

Mark felt sorry for McPherson. That would have been evident in the way he addressed him, were it not for the fact that the man had tried to end his life. Mark's attitude had been stone cold as he spoke.

'You are aware of the reason I am in this hospital? You must have seen the people who brought me here. And you would be aware that they are not the kind of people you would want to get on the wrong side of. You will have seen many injuries in your time but have probably never been involved in many activities that would have endangered you. Well, let me now tell you who *we* are. We are the people who do the nasty and dirty work under instruction from our friends in the security services. So now you are on notice. If you make any further attempt on my life, my people will ensure that you will be dead within twenty hours of my demise. Do you understand the full implications of what I have just said?'

The doctor's face drained of colour, and he struggled to get the words out. And then Mark was surprised at what happened next. McPherson crashed into a chair and burst into tears.

'I should not have done this, I know, but what could I do?' he sputtered between sobs. 'The man gave me orders and left me in no doubt of what would happen if I failed to carry them out!'

Mark very nearly lost it.

'You could have reported the matter to higher authority where you would have found someone with the guts and principle to do something about it. We are supposed to live in the capital of the free world. And yet you were prepared to accept such orders to protect, what? Your military career? What is that career worth if it means taking an innocent life to protect it? You make me sick!'

The doctor probably had not heard a word of the outburst from Mark. He was now a blubbering mess. But he would need to get himself under control, and quickly. There was much to be done.

'Doctor! Get yourself under control! There is something that you now must do,' Mark barked out this command.

McPherson initially looked as though he hadn't heard.

'Doctor, you are going to sign my death certificate

and arrange for me to be carried from here in a hearse. Except that I will not be dead, and I will be on my way to another hospital. One that actually cares for its patients!'

'I can't do that!' McPherson protested.

'Oh yes, you can. And you will.'

The hearse that had been commandeered had no sooner made it onto Interstate 95 than Mark emerged from the black plastic bag that he was encased in.

'Where are we going?' he asked the driver.

The driver, who had shown absolutely zero surprise at being spoken to by a corpse, turned around and grinned.

Blake had kept quiet up to this point, thinking that Mark had about enough for one day.

'We are going to Johns Hopkins in Baltimore. I spoke to the professor at Georgetown, and that is what he recommends. And I have every reason to believe him since Marshall of the DEA also recommends Hopkins. And we have a little surprise waiting for you at Hopkins.'

'What is that? I've had more than my share of surprises to last me a lifetime.'

'Ah, then it would not be a surprise, would it?'

Mark was about to argue, but his heart wasn't in it. Blake was right. It was probably Dusty back from Pakistan; and while he would be pleased to see his old friend, it did mean there was more work to be done. In any case, he was unlikely to get any sympathy from Dusty, having left him halfway around the world. While he was thinking about that, Mark fell asleep, and the next thing he was aware of, he was being wheeled into Hopkins on a gurney.

Mark was wheeled into a private room in a secluded part of the hospital, where a rather pleasant young female doctor waited to take his vitals. But that was not all. Sitting on a chair in a darkened corner of the room was another person, who said and did nothing. When Mark had been settled in the bed and the doctor had finished her essential work, Blake said a few quiet words to the doctor and then turned to Mark.

'We will leave you to get some rest, but do not worry. We will be close enough if you need anything. And then, grinning like a Cheshire cat, he and the doctor walked quickly out of the room. Only then did the other person stand up and rush over to the bed.

'Mark, thank God you are OK!' And then burst into tears as she cradled his head. Mark could never really understand women, especially Debbie.

The following morning, after the medical staff had completed their rounds and announced that Mark was in excellent condition under the circumstances, Blake Whittaker and Brad Morgan appeared alongside their boss, anxious to hear what he now had to say. Although first, Blake explained what had so far been arranged.

'We have arranged for this suite to be available to you for the next couple of weeks. Debbie is in the next cubicle. The place is guarded by the local police, although they have no idea what they are guarding. When you are ready, we can talk about what you want to do next. The important thing is that you recover from what you have been through. We don't want you rushing off again on some madcap escapade trying to fix everything yourself!'

Mark had to smile at the summation of the last few days. But first, he had to get his head around what was happening now.

'Blake, thank you for all you have done. But you cannot have done this all on your own. So, what goes on?'

It was Brad that handled the reply.

'You have some friends in high places.' He grinned. 'This has all been arranged by the DEA and the CIA's OIG, so that is all above our pay grade. You are safer than the President, and everything is being done to keep it that way.'

Then Blake took over the conversation.

'Sooner, rather than later, you need to talk the Harold. This whole business has taken some serious twists lately where people have died, and there could have been more deaths if it weren't for some good luck. I know that you hold your father responsible for a failure to react when you were in trouble in Afghanistan. And we can debate the rights and wrongs of that all day long. But the facts are that you need him, if you are to get justice out of this mess and to not waste all the excellent work that you have done.'

Mark sighed. 'Yeah, you are right, of course,' he said as he reached for a phone.

It was no use trying to get some sympathy out of his father, so he went straight for the jugular. 'How do we get Stephen Rodriguez to face justice? And how do we avoid him slipping off the hook again?'

Harold had come to Hopkins within the hour of receiving the call from Mark. He was aware of the circumstances that had led to the situation, although he did for once enquire as to Mark's health.

'We need to get the FBI on our side,' Harold began. 'I can pull some strings there that should help. But getting Rodriguez in a position where he can be called to account —well, that could take years!'

Again, Mark sighed. 'When is his wife's funeral?' he asked.

Harold was surprised by the question but answered

it before thinking.

'The day after tomorrow.'

Mark thought about that for a second or two.

'That would be the time to pick him up for a chat. Stephen would be at his most vulnerable when Dayanara is buried. He would be relieved that the funeral was over, and at the same time, he would be apprehensive. Can we get the FBI to arrange that?'

Harold shrugged. 'On what possible grounds could they do that? Your friend Dusty is still not convinced that he has the evidence that is strong enough to bring a conviction.'

Mark was not put off by the bureaucratic answer. 'If we have proof that Rodriguez was personally responsible for the death of their agent in Afghanistan, do you think that could spark them into action?'

'Yes, that would work,' was the reply.

Chapter 65

Turning the Screw

It had been a difficult few days since he was declared
dead at Walter Reed Hospital. And Mark did not look
particularly well even now. He had lost quite a few pounds
in weight, and he was unusually pale in complexion. His
left arm was immobilized by a sling, and his entire upper
body was stiff and sore, every movement seems an effort.
The staff at Johns Hopkins had insisted that Mark come to
the meeting in a wheelchair, but that had been discarded
at the door. He now had a determined and not particularly
friendly look on his face as he leaned across the table to
place a teddy bear in front of Stephen Rodriguez. Clutched
in its tiny arms was a small plastic bag. Stephen looked at
the bag, and the colour drained from his face.

It was identical to the bear that he had watched
disappear into Dayanara's grave but a few hours ago.

'You were dead!' Stephen whispered.

Mark held the man's gaze, and he could not avoid
the smile. This was Mark's first experience of coming back
from the dead. Not his first experience of being
frighteningly close to death. But his first experience of
being personally involved in the intrigue and deception that

had engineered his removal from Walter Reed on that fateful night.

Harold continued talking as Mark took a seat next to Dusty Miller.

'Let me introduce Mark Taylor. Chief executive officer of Taylor Software, ex-Special Forces and Delta Force—the person who was in charge of our mission into Afghanistan. He was also the person who, some of you may or may not know, was responsible for unravelling the second 9/11 in New York City. Mark, together with his colleague Mr. Miller, has been on several overseas missions on behalf of the Government of the United States, tracking down our enemies in the drug trafficking business. Perhaps I should ask Mark to state the obvious. There have been several attempts on his life, mostly courtesy of our friend Stephen Rodriguez, but as you can see, he is very much alive!' Harold smiled.

Mark fixed Stephen Rodriguez a cold stare. He had got over the hate. But there was nothing that could hide his feeling towards the man. His voice was quiet as his words descended on a deathly quiet room.

'It seems that people who attempt to get in your way end up dead,' he began. 'First, there was a gentleman by the name of Wakil Hekmatyar, who you had disposed of by your Afghan friends. Sure, who cares? Just another crook who made money at other people's expense!'

A deathly hush hung over the room. They were aware of the intensity with which Mark spoke, and aware of the fascinated look on Rodriguez's face. All were shocked by what Mark said next.

'For the second person that died, you made a critical mistake. Do you remember the little gift that you picked up at Hekmatyar's warehouse? It was an AK-47. The investigators could not understand what that weapon was doing discarded on the side of a road, which happened to be adjacent to where your truck had stopped during the battle. Where Edward Hennessey was shot at point-blank range. What confused the investigators, even more, was the gun carry case and the silencer. Not one single insurgent in Afghanistan has a case, and there has never been a situation in living memory where a silencer has been used in a battle of this kind. But you had one, didn't you? And that was discarded as well. The FBI now has a match between that rifle and the bullet that killed your *friend*.

Rodriguez laughed.

'This is preposterous! I—'

Peyton Reed abruptly stepped in and turned to Mark.

'How do you know about the rifle? And why did you not tell the investigators?'

Mark had expected that. His information on what forensics had concluded was pure speculation. Nonetheless, it was a good guess. He doubted whether they would find any evidence, especially fingerprints, on the rifle. Rodriguez was too clever for that. But the fact that he did have an AK-47 was probably news to everyone except Stephen Rodriguez; Jacob Dutton; the deceased Edward Hennessey; the deceased Wakil Hekmatyar, an Afghan soldier who was unlikely to come under the FBI's radar anytime soon; and, of course, Mark, Dusty, and Owen, who had witnessed the transfer.

Mark addressed the two questions in reverse order.

'I said nothing to the investigators because I wasn't asked. In fact, I was not spoken to by any of your team. But it was unlikely I would have said anything anyway. At the time, I had no reason to suspect that our mission had been blown, so in the true tradition of covert operations, I would have said nothing. That is, I would have been unlikely to tell anyone that my team had witnessed the transfer of an

AK-47 from an Afghan soldier to Stephen Rodriguez. However, I am now happy to fill in any gaps in your information.'

'So, your evidence is just speculation!' This comment came from the NSA.

Mark sighed, and thankfully, so did Peyton Reed, who again intervened.

'This is not a court, Joe!' Reed smiled at the NSA man. 'We are just trying to understand what happened, and we are getting the views of the people involved.'

Reed nodded to Mark while writing furiously on his pad. 'Please continue, Mr. Taylor. I believe you were talking to Mr. Rodriguez.'

Mark had to smile, but his eyes again focused on his adversary.

'Back in Afghanistan, when I, unfortunately, saved your ass in what became known as the Battle of Ghazni, you recognized me and tried to set me up through Yuri Alekseyev as a suspect in a plot to kill the President of that country, one Hamid Karzai. When it turned out that you had misled our Russian friends, they had no option but to hand me over to the Afghanis to dispose of. Thanks to the services of an insignificant one-legged Welshman, who is, incidentally, standing in the queue of people who want to see you get your just desserts, I got out of that one. Alongside the Welshman is the Russian head of the SVR people in Kabul—Yuri Alekseyev. He is pretty annoyed at you for using him, and for your misinformation. But you need to remember that Alexseyev is really a mercenary. He needs to have the United States, rather than just the assistant deputy director of intelligence of the CIA, on his side. Somewhere in all of this, you arranged to kidnap my partner, Debbie Peterson. That was another big mistake that you made. And that is how your wife got involved.'

'I do not follow. How does one thing lead to another?'

The question came from Peyton Reed but was on the minds of most of the people present.

Mark remained outwardly cold and calm, although his emotions were running slightly out of control.

'Quite simple!' Mark replied. 'I had some of my people ask his wife, Dayanara, and his daughter Estefania Rodriguez, to assist us. And they agreed.'

'You mean you kidnapped Dayanara and my daughter,' snarled Rodriguez.

Peyton Reed had to say something.

'You need to be careful—both of you! Kidnapping is a serious offense!'

'Well, you can call it what you like!' Mark replied, then turned his attention back to Rodriguez.

'Are you going to deny that you arranged to kidnap Debbie Peterson? Our conversation about the exchange of people that you agreed to makes it clear that you did *kidnap* Debbie. That conversation is recorded on tape. Do you want us to play it back for you?'

Reed again stepped in.

'Kidnapping is an offense that we take very seriously. No matter what the circumstance, you could both be in real trouble with the law!'

Mark acknowledged the interruption with a shrug while staying focused on Stephen Rodriguez.

'OK. Prove it!' said Mark. 'Dayanara Rodriguez is dead. The only living person who can vouch for what I have said is your daughter Estefania. Ok, Mr. Smart Guy, I will take a chance here if you will. Let us see which story the daughter of Stephen Rodriguez supports.'

Mark got stiffly out of his chair and opened the door. Ignoring the guard and ignoring the bulge under the guard's left shoulder that no doubt held the current sidearm issued to members of the FBI. Estefania and Debbie walked in.

Mark had to hold Estefania back as she burst into tears and took a wild swing at her father.

For the first time on this terrible day, Rodriguez looked defeated.

The mention of the death of her mother would set Estefania off into another wild rage. He first tried a small diversion before he had to mention it again. Now was as good a time as any to mention the Rodriguez attempts on Mark's life.

'We have had an analysis of the drug that you arranged with a friendly doctor to be fed into my IV at Walter Reed. Not only once, but twice. It was a drug that causes myocardial infarction. For the uninitiated, the drug causes the heart to at first race and then to virtually explode under the pressure. Had that got into my body, then I would have had no chance of recovery. And the drug is virtually untraceable in the human body. That was two failed attempts on my life. Not to mention the attempt that resulted in my being in the hospital in the first place. And of course, we will not mention your role in trying to have my team terminated in Afghanistan. Not a very impressive hit rate for a man who works for one of the most powerful, brutal, and callous organizations on the planet. You could say that is all conjecture. And your friends may say that it is further speculation on my part. But that is not important.

'Much more important is your dear wife, Dayanara. You did manage to have her murdered. You probably did not fire the shot. That would have required a skilled sniper and marksman—a skill that you quite simply do not have. You can try to say that the shot was intended for me or for Ms Peterson who was standing at her side. But the shot was too precise to have been an accident.'

'Why would I want to kill my own wife?' Rodriguez shouted, turning as he asked the question to his friend from the NSA.

Klein at least acknowledged the question with a nod of his head.

While Rodriguez protested, his gaze shifted to his daughter. There he got no sympathy whatsoever. Just a cold loathing that only a father caught in a trap could comprehend.

'Because she found out about your little drug game!' Mark almost whispered.

The damage was done.

Rodriguez suddenly sprang to his feet, pulling a Beretta from his pocket. The group in the room tensed, half from the realization that Stephen should have been searched. And half from fear of what might happen now.

He pointed the gun directly at Mark.

The glazed look in Stephen's eyes was that of a madman.

'I have apparently tried to have you killed, so why don't I finish the job now?' Stephen yelled.

Those were almost his last words.

The guard by the door had his gun out, pointed directly at Stephen. In a voice that was devoid of any emotion spoke to the madman.

'Don't make me do this, sir. Please put the gun down. Now!'

Mark looked outwardly calm. He had faced more than his share of gunmen in his short life. Now he relied on his judgment and his reading of the body language of this madman. He hoped that he was right. He focused, not on the gun but on Stephen's eyes. Looking for intent. Debbie started to cry and move forward, but she was held back by Dusty, so she buried her head in his shoulder, unable to watch as the drama unfolded. The other people in the room seemed frozen, unable to do anything. Unwilling to say anything that may upset the delicate balance which would determine who would die.

An insane smile erupted on the face of Rodriguez.

That was the moment Mark had been waiting for. His left arm shot out across the table, clutching Stephen's right wrist in a vice-like grip and twisting the gun up, pointing it at the ceiling. There was a sharp crack as the gun discharged harmlessly into the air. That caused the people in the room to erupt into chaos. Dusty launched his body across the table and slammed Stephen to the floor, his huge hands gripping his neck and sending the pistol flying.

'So why don't I finish my job now, you weasel?'

Everyone felt relieved that no one was hurt.

Dusty dragged Stephen Rodriguez to his feet, as though he was playing with a rag doll. He glanced at Mark as he sat down nursing his shoulder, and in obvious pain from the effort. But he smiled.

Stephen's shoulders slumped, and he crumpled back into a chair. Now two FBI officers stood next to his chair, their hands at the ready to deal with any further commotion. But Stephen's body language said that he had given up. The stress of all that had happened over the last few weeks was just too much for a man who had become used to barking orders at people so that they jumped. Now he was a vastly different man. He buried his head in his hands as the room lapsed into a tense and total silence. Around the table, several people shifted uneasily in their seats. Many of them were used to reviewing cases that were brought against some of the most brutal and vicious criminals in the United States. They could see that, despite the emotion of the moment and all that had been said, the case against Stephen was still circumstantial, and would take a massive amount of investigation before a case could be laid. A half-decent lawyer would drill so many holes in the case as it had been presented so far that they would be lucky if Stephen even served time for any of the crimes he had been accused of.

The alleged architect of the CIA drug network, the alleged murderer of FBI agent Edward Hennessey, mastermind of the attempted murder of Mark Taylor and friends, and alleged murderer of his wife, the assistant deputy director of intelligence, Stephen Rodriguez, appeared to at least have a case to answer. And he was a broken man.

But this was Washington.

And anything could, and usually did happen.

Peyton Reed cleared his throat.

'Well, I believe there is a case to answer. But since this is not a court of law, we have to let matters take their course.'

For the first time in the meeting, Reed stood and addressed the ADDI. 'Stephen Rodriguez, you are under arrest on a charge of homicide. Other charges may be laid against you at the proper time. I assume that you are aware of your rights, but I must inform you of them. You have the right to remain silent. Anything you say can, and will, be used against you in a court of law. You have the right to an attorney. If you cannot afford an attorney, one will be appointed for you. Do you understand those rights?'

Rodriguez remained silent, staring sullenly at the table. Dusty stood to one side as the two agents lifted Stephen to his feet and locked his hands behind his back using handcuffs.

Reed simply said, 'I will take your silence as an answer in the affirmative.'

There was still no response from Rodriguez, so he continued,

'These two gentlemen will escort you to the Third District Police Station, where you will be placed in their custody and held for further questioning. There you will be able to contact your attorney. Is there anything that you do not understand?'

Rodriguez raised his head and just stared at Mark, a look of hate in his eyes. Then he muttered almost incoherently, 'I want to make a call now. I am entitled to my attorney. This is all nonsense.'

Mark held Stephen's gaze while Reed replied.

'All in suitable time, Mr. Rodriguez! I am sure you would rather make your call in private rather than in a room full of people. Especially some of the people in this particular room.'

Mark knew then that the Washington machine had already started working. There was no reason why Stephen could not have called his attorney from this room. There must have been enough telephones. Had Reed made a mistake or was he already gearing himself for a long and pointless legal battle that would eventually see the Federal Government backed into a corner. And a man that had destroyed the lives of so many people escape the punishment that he so richly deserved.

Unable to face the man any longer, Mark turned away, put his good arm around Debbie, and they walked out of the room. Dusty and Brad followed.

Outside the room, Mark turned to Dusty.

'Why transfer Rodriguez to the Washington Police Department? I can understand that the WPD would be responsible for a murder on their patch. But surely, there is much more involved that would make it a federal matter. And given his position in the CIA, that makes it hardly a local police matter.'

The two friends looked at each other as though reading the other's mind.

Dusty nodded.

'You think that someone is going to take him out? Or worse still, try to snatch him? What easier way is there than take him while he is being transferred?'

This time, Mark nodded.

'It is a puzzling combination of things that have happened over the last few weeks. Stephen Rodriguez, for all his faults, always seemed to be one step ahead. That means he has contacts in places that we would not expect. That is, until now,' Mark thought out loud.

'We have been concentrating on finding evidence of his involvement in drugs. What we should have been doing is finding out more about the extent of the network. How far does it go, into what organizations, but especially, how high up? And it was something that the Russians said back in Kabul about the nature of us Americans. The NSA, with the aid of the FBI, is going to attempt to sweep this business quietly away under the carpet. Now that would not suit the Russians. Then you have the druggies to think of. They are probably divided into three distinct groups: users who are loyal, users who are not, and suppliers. None of them would want to have their identities revealed. The users because ... well, we don't know who they are, but you can bet your bottom dollar there are some very powerful people involved. Some would want to get Stephen before he can reveal who he is working with. Others would just want him dead. On the other hand, the suppliers are running a business worth many billions of dollars, and that is worth protecting. All three groups would be fearful of what might be said to incriminate them if Stephen wants to do a deal with the authorities. He faces the gas chamber, so he has nothing to lose.'

'Shit!' was the response from Dusty. 'Why did you not

suggest that they hold Rodriguez here?'

'Well, you know the answer to that,' Mark replied. 'How do we know which side these people are on? Peyton Reed looks OK. But he was being pushed by that arrogant prick from the NSA. And there is little doubt that the NSA was controlling things, despite appearances—that is why they were here!'

'What are we going to do?' Dusty asked, although he probably knew the answer.

'We are going to try to ensure that Stephen has his day in court. If I am right, there should be at least three groups out there trying to get him—two groups who want to kill him, and the other group that wants to assist him escape. With a bit of luck, they may end up trying to shoot each other.'

He was almost correct.

Chapter 66

Justice

The mood in Evgeny Ovsyannikov's office at the Russian Cultural Centre had changed, from one of anticipation to one of anger. Word had come through of what had happened at the FBI headquarters, and of the likely fate of Stephen Rodriguez. His contact was so good that Ovsyannikov might as well have bugged the room in which the Americans were meeting. But this was much better. Bugs could be found and traced. The Americans were particularly good at that. The Americans were not so good at catching moles.

The Russian shook his head as he tried, and once again failed, to understand the people of his host country. And he doubted whether his masters in Moscow would do anything about it.

He had kept his masters informed about the ongoing saga, and the potential embarrassment it would cause when it was revealed to the American media. But no. It would be another case swept under the rug, and the people involved would quietly disappear to who knows where. Not like the old Soviet Union, where they would disappear, either executed or banished for life to a labour camp in outer Siberia. The worst-case scenario was that these Americans would disappear into a cosy jail, three meals a day, TV, and all the comforts of home, at the expense of the long-suffering American taxpayer.

Ovsyannikov had had a lengthy conversation with Yuri Alexseyev, his contact in Afghanistan. Alexseyev was also not overly impressed with the Americans. And he was pretty angry at the CIA and that clown Rodriguez.

Although Evgeny was philosophical about the tricks Stephen Rodriguez had played on his friend, there was still the matter of honour. Now it was looking most likely that this Rodriguez fellow would be out of the reach of the Russians forever. He would no longer be a threat. He would also be someone with whom they could never get even.

But there was a far more sinister matter that the Russians had to think about, and that was the working of the American justice system. In Russia, things would have been much simpler. After being tortured, during which every snippet of information would be squeezed out of him, Rodriguez would be made to disappear, never to be heard from again. People would speculate that he may be alive, living out his remaining years with hard labour breaking rocks in the outback's of Siberia. The people that knew the truth would know that he was dead.

The American system could result in similar secrecy. But for quite distinct reasons. And with a vastly different outcome.

They would quite happily negotiate a deal. And the strange thing about the Americans is that they would stick to it. Rodriguez would know this. He would no doubt come up with a deal that they could hardly refuse. Like, if he were to reveal the name of a mole in the higher echelons of the security and intelligence services in exchange for a new identity and a life of relaxation in some faraway place where no one would ever know who he had been. And where no one would ever find him.

Such an outcome presented a *clear and present danger* to the Russians.

Well, he would see about that!

Ovsyannikov stepped out onto the street and started walking rapidly towards the Potomac River. Then he pulled a cellular telephone out from his hip pocket and tapped in a number. The person on the receiving end did not need to say who he was. Neither did Evgeny.

'Stephen Rodriguez is on his way to the Third District Station. Make sure that he does not get inside.'

He closed the telephone, picked up a handful of gravel from the pathway, and started tossing stones into the water. When he was sure that no one was taking any notice, he tossed the cellular phone into the river as well.

Nathan Ryman was scared shitless, but he had to do something. While he regarded Stephen Rodriguez as someone he would not choose as a friend, all things being equal, Ryman still owed the man a debt of gratitude. And more to the point, while Rodriguez appeared to have been charged with murder, there was still the network to consider.

The scheme was so clever that Ryman was confident that it could be protected, and that it was safe. But he needed someone with the skills and the knowledge of the government bureaucracy to make it operate. If that person was no longer employed by the CIA, then another person would need to take his place. Ideally, the existing incumbent would have to engineer an escape and do it quickly before they got him out of sight.

The one advantage Ryman had was that only he knew by name, if not by sight, all the people who were a part of the network. He had heard what had happened in the Hoover Building. Sometimes the reception had been a little distorted—that was the chance you took with cellular telephones switched through the Internet and hidden from plain sight—but he knew the important stuff. His man had somehow managed to have Rodriguez transferred to the Washington Police Department, and that gave his men the opportunity they needed. Sure, some people may have to die during the escape attempt.

That was just collateral damage.

Ryman had heard about such damage. He had no clue what it meant. Nor did he realize that he could be part of it.

Nathan had been given several emergency procedures to be followed in the event of trouble. And he judged that this was such an occasion. One had been set up by the ADDI, and that involved making a phone call to a rescue party. He grabbed the mobile phone and hit the speed dial. The message asked for Nathan's code, which he dialled in and hit the # key. All that the message said was 'Call acknowledged,' and the phone went dead.

For a few moments, he just stared at the phone. Why had they not practiced the emergency procedure before? What would happen now? Stephen Rodriguez was the man in trouble, but what about the network? Surely that was more important!

Now in a state of panic, he grabbed his own mobile phone and punched in the number of the only other contact that he had. He got a little irritated when the call wasn't answered immediately. They had to move, and move now, otherwise, the opportunity would be lost.

Finally, William Prendergast of the NSA answered in his usual arrogant tone, even though so few people had this number that he must know where the call had originated.

He just said, 'Yes?'

'Ryman here!' were the words that came out, his voice sounding unnaturally high.

'I have just received information that Stephen Rodriguez is being transferred from the FBI Building down to the Third Precinct right now. I think we should mount an operation to grab him. I have followed my instructions, and I assume that a team is on the way, but we may need you to arrange a little interference.'

Prendergast never hesitated. After all, he had his own representatives in the meeting at the Hoover Building, and they were instrumental in having Rodriguez transferred to the care of the Washington Police Department. This Ryman character was a nerd who might understand his computers. He had no idea what happened in the real world. He may well have had someone in the room who was feeding him information, and that was good. The system was obviously working. But by 'I have a team' translated into the truth, he had keyed in an alert to the system, and now matters were way beyond anything Ryman could do. Now it was time for men to get involved and to sort out this mess that Stephen Rodriguez had got himself into.

'How many men are in your team?' was what he asked, knowing that Nathan could not know. Hence the sputtered reply.

'I am not sure.'

'OK, leave it to me. It will be taken care of.'

Prendergast disconnected the call without any further acknowledgment.

Chapter 67

Pawns

The three of them waited in a side street on the route that they had to assume the police would take to the Third Precinct. They had to depend on their spotters to keep them informed of any change of plan.

Dusty was of the view that it did not really matter, and it was just not their problem whatever happened to Stephen Rodriguez. Mark was of a different view. He felt, despite the politics of the situation, that Rodriguez should be pushed through the legal system and should not be allowed to escape even into a world where he no longer enjoyed the privileges that he had become accustomed to.

The drug world can be very unforgiving of those who happened to get themselves caught, irrespective of the reasons, or of the logic. Someone would want to see Stephen Rodriguez dead. Killing him would be a just reward for all his crimes. But even that would not satisfy Mark. Rodriguez should face the law, if for no other reason than to account for the years he had drawn from the public purse while screwing the entire system to meet his own selfish ends.

Mark and Dusty had their problems, not the least of

which was the fact that the Washington Police did not see the transport of their prisoner as any big deal, so there was no concern about security. But following a police car that was to depart from the FBI headquarters did present a few problems. There was just nowhere to hide.

Once the transfer was underway, they could only follow at a discreet distance. And hope that, in the event of any attempt to grab the prisoner, they could either intervene or at least witness his demise.

The Russians had positioned a total of five snipers at various places around the Third Precinct, confident that at least one of them would get the drop on the man as he was driven by. The Washington Police were not very smart. They would use the same approach that they always did. They would drive up Sixteenth Avenue, turn left into V Street, and then turn left through the entrance to the police station.

The traffic at this time of the day was a nightmare. That meant that the target would be barely moving at various times as the vehicle made its way toward the destination. It also meant that the response to gunfire in the crowded streets would be one of total chaos, thereby enabling the Russians to quickly disappear into their surroundings.

The decision had been made.

Stefan Rodriguez would not live to see another day.

Prendergast was already at the Third Precinct Police Station. His stated reason for being there was that he had to make sure that Stephen Rodriguez arrived safely and that he was treated with due care and attention. Besides the fact that he was an important person, the NSA representative needed to be certain that no one could, or would, interfere with due process. And Rodriguez was entitled to an attorney at his arraignment, which Prendergast would provide.

However, William Prendergast's actual plan was to handle the situation slightly differently than he had stated. A call would be received at the time of the arrival of Rodriguez that would authorize the NSA to assume custody of the prisoner. The reason given would be national security issues.

The Washington Police would be extremely pleased to get rid of their VIP visitor and they would comply.

The squad car slowly made its way up Sixteenth Avenue and then ground to a halt in the traffic. The SUV that Dusty was driving was about four vehicles behind and in the outside lane. The expectation was that the vehicle carrying Stephen Rodriguez would need to turn left into V Street. The din from the traffic was only compounded by the honking of horns, which did little more than allow the drivers to vent their frustration at the delays.

Then it happened.

Mark grabbed the door handle and leaped out of the SUV.

'Someone just took a pot-shot at the squad car!'

With Dusty and Blake following, Mark ran up the street towards the vehicle, oblivious to any personal danger. All three men had spent time under fire, but not exactly in these circumstances. The sniper could be anywhere out there, but the odds were that the sniper was in a building. The sniper had to be to their north and on their right. The three men sprinted the short distance up the left side of the line of traffic, taking cover as best they could.

Mark was first to arrive and assessed the situation.

The driver of the squad car and his partner were dead. The windscreen was shattered and there was glass everywhere.

Mark glanced in the back passenger window and saw that Rodriguez was lying prone behind the front seats. Dusty yanked at the left-side door, but to no avail. The back doors were deadlocked from the front. Blake was the first to react to this. He smashed the window with his pistol and popped his head up to call the occupant to get out.

That got a reaction. Both from the sniper and from Stephen Rodriguez. A bullet pinged off the car inches from Blake's head, and that caused Rodriguez to crouch even lower behind the seats.

They had never expected to get into this kind of situation so close to the White House in downtown Washington. Dusty had experience in Mogadishu, and Mark and Blake had had moments of fun in Bagdad. There they had all worn protective gear, and they been supported by others with the firepower necessary to handle the trouble. But this was different. More so because they had no way of knowing exactly who they were up against or why.

The three men had a quick consultation. The odds were that someone had reported what they had just witnessed, and that police would be flooding in to surround the area in short order. The sniper would probably have to reload and re-sight his rifle after each shot, so they would have about five seconds to act. The question, then, was, how long was the sniper prepared to stay and take the risk of his escape path being blocked?

And then another question was, Was the sniper alone?

Probably not.

As by far the smallest of the team, Blake volunteered. It brought back memories of what had occurred in the Battle of Ghazni. They had to get Rodriguez out of the vehicle otherwise it was only a matter of time before he was killed.

Dusty attempted to draw the attention of the shooter, while Mark focused his attention on a five-story building at about forty-five degrees to their forward right. It had the desired effect. A further shot rang out, and Dusty gave a sharp intake of breath as blood started to ooze down his neck from where the bullet nicked his right ear. Mark pinpointed the exact location of the shooter and fired his Smith & Wesson in that direction. Not that he had any real chance of making contact at that distance. More to signal to the sniper that now they had the position spotted. While that went on, Blake threw himself through the window space and tumbled into the car, unceremoniously landing on top of Rodriguez. He called out to his colleagues in the street.

'He is alive!'

They then had to make another decision, but it was not really a choice. While they were anxious to ensure that Rodriguez would get to his destination, he was not the most important person. To get him out of the car meant that he would be exposed to the sniper for a couple of seconds, and that was the chance that they just had to take. They were lucky that the sniper had probably taken his first shot a little too early because had the angle been narrowed, he could have quite easily shot anyone in the rear seats. Dusty once more raised his bleeding body off the ground, and another shot was aimed, this time ricocheting off the roof of the car and flying harmlessly over the traffic. By the time the whine had died, Stephen was pushed out of the window and landed with a crash on the ground, followed almost immediately by Blake, who again landed on top of him.

Sirens started to sound, with police cars seemingly coming from all directions. However, they were unable to get through the vehicles on the road, many of which had simply been abandoned, as their terrified drivers and passengers sought to escape. Mark pointed to his right, and after a pause to catch their breath, Dusty and Blake gathered up Rodriguez, and all four men rushed to take cover in a shop. Mark expected further shots, but fortunately, none came.

For now, they had escaped.

And probably so had the sniper.

Ovsyannikov was not at all worried that the sniper attack had failed to kill their target. The object of this stage of the exercise was to get Rodriguez out of the car. Hitting a man in the rear passenger seat of the vehicle was always going to be difficult. Taking out the driver and front-seat passenger was a breeze. Now the man was on foot, and that made him a much easier target. Evgeny had no idea who the people were that had interfered, but he doubted that they would be either able or willing to put their lives on the line for a prisoner.

The first sniper had to abandon his position because they now knew where he was. He just left the rifle and the tripod and disappeared into the crowd. There were four other people strategically located farther up Sixteenth Avenue, and it was only a matter of time before one of them could get a line on their man. The sniper thumbed his mobile phone, sending a text message to the others to be ready.

Mark Taylor called the only people he knew who

could handle this situation. He called Fort Bragg, who then patched him through to the detachment of Special Forces located at Andrews Air Base. It was almost like ordering a taxi or a pizza, except that Mark hoped it would be an armoured vehicle that turned up.

The avenue was now crawling with police, who, understandably, were initially more concerned that two of their own had been shot than they were about their missing prisoner. But eventually, sanity prevailed, and they located the four men hiding in the shop. Blake, with his usual cheerful disposition and the FBI badge, got them to hunker down while the chaos on the avenue was slowly brought under control.

The Humvee that arrived about an hour later drove right up to the door so that even the most expert marksman would gain only a fleeting glimpse of the men as they emerged from their hiding place and scrambled on board. With the number of police in the vicinity, it would be a foolish man who was still out there with a sniper rifle, but they still took no chances. Mark volunteered to recover their SUV from where it had been left on the avenue and followed the Hummer around the corner towards the Third Precinct.

The journey had taken far longer than planned, but at least they would arrive. Except that was not the plan.

Now it was the turn of Evgeny Ovsyannikov to be frustrated. Someone who was helping Stephen Rodriguez had some immensely powerful friends and was obviously aware of the problems and solutions involved in extracting people from a tight situation in the middle of a city.

He sighed and told his men to stand down.

He then went to plan B.

Ovsyannikov called his friend at the *Washington Post*.

The NSA contingent at the police station had nothing to do but wait for the arrival of the prisoner from the FBI headquarters. They had heard about the sniper attack in Sixteenth Avenue but were powerless to do anything about that. The arrival of the Humvee caused a stir of excitement. On cue, the call came through from the NSA advising that responsibility for the prisoner would now move away from both the police and the FBI and to their representative. The fracas that had occurred on Sixteenth Avenue would only improve their chances of pulling it off. And the Washington Police would be extremely pleased to be rid of the troublesome and high-ranking federal official.

What they got instead of a new guest was a visit from Mark Taylor.

Mark came through the door of the Third Precinct and approached the desk. 'You were expecting a prisoner from the FBI?'

'Yes! You one of the guys who got caught up in the shootout?'

'That's right.'

Mark turned and looked at the group of men who had been sitting in the waiting area but who now rose to their feet and rushed over to where Mark was standing.

'I suppose these guys are expecting the prisoner as well?' Mark deliberately addressed his remarks to someone who was obviously not the one in charge.

Prendergast bristled at Mark's tone, as well as reacted to the size and shape of the man who stood before him.

'There has been a change of plan,' Prendergast shouted.

'The prisoner is to be handed over to us on his arrival. Where is he?'

Mark smiled, but that did not alter his tone.

'And you are ...?'

'This is a matter of national security, and way above your pay grade, son!' Prendergast fired back.

The sergeant at the desk smirked as the comments flowed, and then cringed at Mark's reply.

'You can deliver a message to your associate Joseph Klein. Tell him that by the time he gets the message, the White House will have been informed—about this and other matters. I am sure that he will understand. Meanwhile, he will not be able to see the prisoner. And certainly not until such time as it is authorized by someone on a much higher pay grade than either you or him.'

And then, being content to have seen the flabbergasted look on Prendergast's face, turned and headed toward the door.

Mark left the building.

He had other matters to attend to.

Chapter 68

Pragmatism

The knock on the door was soft and polite, almost apologetic. Nancy Ryman placed her half-finished glass of white wine on the table and skipped to the door. She had settled their two young girls into their beds. Nathan Ryman had read them a night-time story and had then gone off to do whatever he had to do on his pesky computers, and now was the time to relax. She was now in the mood for some fun, and whoever was knocking on the door would not delay her for long. She had put on a housecoat, which was just as well because underneath the coat, there was little to hide her beautiful body that she hoped would soon be ravaged by her man.

The door was fitted with a spyhole, and through it, she surveyed the two gentlemen who were standing on the porch. They looked very official! And the badge that they held up to the spyhole said that they were FBI officials. Her reaction at first was tense. A visit from the FBI usually meant trouble. But then, Nathan often had visits from people from one or the other of the many Government and quasi-Government organizations, who seemed to have little regard for times of the day or for people's private lives.

Nathan Ryman worked for the CIA, and although Nancy had little idea of what he did, she knew it was important. She also knew that he was well respected in the intelligence and security community. She opened the door and asked them to come in. They asked if they could see Mr. Ryman. She simply escorted the two visitors to Nathan's study, closed the door behind them, and returned to her wine to continue her preparation for the exciting evening's entertainment.

She would be oblivious to the discussion that ensued.

Nathan Ryman was equally undisturbed by the late-night visitors. There were certain things that quite simply could not be discussed at his official place of work, even though that was in the inner sanctum of the CIA headquarters at Langley. The room that was his study was the hub of a network that was far too important to risk even the faintest chance of discovery by the prying eyes of bureaucrats, although some of their colleagues were the main beneficiaries. This was not the first time that he had mysterious visitors at odd times of day or night. Nor would it be the last—or so he thought.

But the opening remarks from the FBI agent made him cringe.

'It is over!' was all that was said.

Ryman's right hand moved imperceptibly on his keyboard as he rapidly typed in a simple command that would cause the network to disappear, removing access to everything. Especially the database that contained the list of the people who were privileged to have access to it.

The FBI agent just smiled.

'It is OK! We know what you have just done. That does not matter, provided you will agree to what we will propose to you now. Otherwise, we may have to leave you to the mercy of the judicial system. With the charges that you could face and the time you could spend locked up, you will never see your beautiful wife again. Except through a steel grill.'

'I do not know what you are talking about,' replied Nathan with a shrug. The smugness of a genius talking to ignorant cretins.

He was far too clever for these guys, and his system was just too secure. No one could possibly defeat or replicate what he had set up.

Again, the agent smiled.

'Well, just for the record. We have been talking to your friend Stephen Rodriguez, and to other people who are members of the CIA Directorate of Science and Technology. They confirm that you are the Gatekeeper of a certain network. We now know all about what it does, who uses it, and who controls it. So, your efforts to destroy the evidence were a bit of a waste of time. The game is up, Nathan. We have enough evidence, courtesy of your leader, to make your life miserable. Now I say again—we will not pursue that issue, provided you agree to what we propose.'

Now Ryman was tense and apprehensive. How had they managed to get information out of the ADDI? Sure, Rodriguez was under some pressure with the sudden death of his wife. But that had all been dealt with and covered up. From what he could gather, Dayanara Rodriguez was no great loss. She did not feature as a high priority in the grand scheme of things. Either they were bluffing, or Rodriguez had indeed given up Nathan's identity. Or someone had!

The question formed in his mind. When it came out, his tone and his body language said that for once in his privileged life, he was scared.

'What are you proposing?' he almost whispered.

'Oh, nothing much,' the FBI agent replied. 'I have to inform you that your employment with the CIA has been terminated, effective immediately. Your choice now is to take the risks involved in a long legal battle where we will aim to put you behind bars for the rest of your natural life. Or to seek other employment of our choosing.'

He paused, while the significance of what he had to say sank in.

'What we now propose is that you come and work for the FBI under the executive assistant director – in our Science and Technology Branch. You will be doing the reverse of what you have been doing. You will be trying to locate and track down Internet sites that allow illicit or illegal activity. We will be interested in terrorism, financial dealings, or drug activity, which I am sure you already know something about. We are primarily interested in finding rather than designing networks and in finding people within our own and our sister organizations that are involved in extra-curricular activities if you get my drift. You could find this new work quite interesting! There would be some loss of privileges, without a doubt, but that is a small price to pay, don't you think? At the very least, your life could carry on as normal. You would, of course, need to behave yourself—otherwise, what we are offering you would be cancelled, and you would then have to take your chance with the justice system.'

The atmosphere in the study was cold. Or was it just Nathan?

Why was the FBI not saying exactly what he had done wrong? Maybe they did not know, and they were just bluffing! He fought within himself. It had been fun. Surely Stephen Rodriguez would not have given up all that they had worked for all these years! They had built the perfect network. They had established as perfect a security system as they ever could have envisaged. Where had it gone wrong? And what were they now saying?

The FBI had offered him the straightforward way out. What if this was a bluff? So, he asked the obvious question.

'What will become of Stephen Rodriguez?'

The two agents exchanged glances as Nathan looked from one to the other. Then one of them replied.

'In case you have not heard the news, Stephen Rodriguez was taken into custody this afternoon. He is facing various charges, including murder, kidnapping, drug trafficking, and conspiracy, as well as employment-related matters. There probably will not be a trail as such. These things very rarely see the inside of a courtroom. But he can expect to spend the rest of his life locked away in Leavenworth.'

Tears came to Nathan's eyes. It was not so much that he liked Rodriguez. In fact, he did not like him at all. In many ways, he hated that arrogant son of a bitch. But the grand scheme had been orchestrated by Stephen Rodriguez, and he had to admire him for that. Now that which was Nathan's creation was apparently to be destroyed. The real sad thing was that he would not know how on earth that had happened. Drugs he could get from anywhere. Being able to get them through the very organizations that were supposed to prevent them was sheer poetry. Beautiful in its simplicity. Brutal in its implementation.

'I take it your answer is Yes?' the FBI agent prodded.

Ryman could only nod his head.

Someone out there had either outsmarted him or betrayed him. At least this time. But give him access to a computer, and who knew what magic lay in store. He had created one network under the very noses of the people that he worked with and for.

He could do it all again!

The FBI agent seemed to be blissfully unaware of the possibilities and almost looked sorry for Nathan.

'You will need to come with us now. There are several questions that we need to ask, and it may take some time. We will of course need answers, which may take a little longer. And the authorities will need to be sure that you can hold up your side of the bargain—you do understand that?'

Nathan again nodded. Then another truth dawned on him. And the fear that had gripped earlier returned.

'You will not tell Nancy, err ... Mrs. Ryman?'

'That is your call, Mr. Ryman'

'Could I just have a private word with her?'

'Sure, we'll be just outside. And don't do anything silly!'

Nathan had seen the FBI agents to the door of the lounge and had returned to his study without a word to, or a glance at, his wife. He was dependent on them to keep their word and to leave him to tell his own story.

What was he to say? The truth? Or would he continue lying to the person he loved? He returned to the seat at his computer and buried his head in his hands.

He neither saw nor heard Nancy come into the study and did not react at all as she placed her hands on his shoulders. He was crying! She bent forward, running her hands down his body, but there was no bulge that would have given her the hint that he was ready to make love to her. What had the discussion been about that had caused him to be so visibly upset?

'What is the matter?' she asked, unsure of how to handle this unusual state for her man who had always been so supremely confident in everything that he did or said.

A huge sigh rippled through his body, and he sobbed again. And then he seemed to partially recover himself. He slowly turned his chair around and roughly pulled open Nancy's housecoat, burying his head between her breasts, and running his hands over her smooth buttocks. He knew that her body beckoned for his attention.

But his heart was not in it.

'I have a new job—we will talk about it later. For now, I have to go downtown with these two gentlemen to sort out the details.'

'At this time of night?' was Nancy's startled response. 'Surely that can wait until tomorrow!'

Nancy reached down to undo the buckle on his trousers, talking to him, encouraging him to take her body. Nathan tried to obliterate the other thoughts that were bombarding his mind. Nancy was easily aroused, especially fortified with a couple of glasses of wine. She could see and feel that Nathan was not exactly switched on. That would change. It always did.

The immediate problem for Nathan was the same one faced at some time in their lives by most men.

It was almost impossible at times such as these to get a hard-on.

He felt that he had to try.

But in the end, it was no use. He had to admit defeat as he murmured that he had to go, leaving a barely clad Nancy standing there in tears. Tears of frustration.

There would be no lovemaking tonight.

The FBI agents moved back into the office to collect Nathan Ryman. And to collect the recorder that they had left behind. They had overheard the conversation between Nathan and Nancy.

They could hardly stifle a grin.

Chapter 69

Revenge

The man waited in the shadows until there was no pedestrian traffic around. Then he made his way across the street and approached the door of the apartment building.

The weather was wet and bitterly cold. The wind cut through his jacket as though trying to wrench it from his body. There were particularly good reasons why few people would venture out on such a night. But for him, there was important work to do. The weather would play no part.

It was much easier than Blake had anticipated with the conditions coming to their aid. He studied the surrounding buildings and ascertained that there were no CCTV cameras operating in the area, other than one that covered the door that he was focused on. That he disabled with spray paint and then turned his attention to the door.

He examined the lock, took a small tool from his pocket, and easily defeated the mechanism. Then, satisfied that all was clear, he made a signal to Mark Taylor and Elliott Shannon, who were waiting some 100 yards away. The three of them entered the building together. They were all well wrapped and hooded against the wind and rain, so it was unlikely that anyone but the most observant would ever be able to identify them. And even if they did, that would be of little use. What they were about to do was to merely pay a visit to one of the residents.

Mark Taylor would have preferred to do this job himself and alone. There was nothing strictly illegal about what he had in mind. Well, the result could be stretching the ethics governing legality a little bit, but then why should he, or anybody else, have any sympathy for their target this evening?

Mark had been the one who had been in danger. The man they were after was the one who had tried to take his life. And he was also a man who had demonstrated that he would stop at nothing to protect the evil trade that was being run from the nation's capital.

The FBI would be unable, or unwilling, to do anything about it. That was why Mark had not bothered to file reports on the attempts on his life that had been made while he was in Walter Reed. He knew how the system worked. It had been made clear that there had been two attempts on his life. But when it came to seeking revenge on those responsible, he would be laughed at for making such ridiculous accusations against a man with so distinguished a military career and a man who was working for such a prestigious organization.

Consequently, he had a simple plan.

Mark was, however, in no physical condition to handle a situation where things could easily get out of hand. There was just no point in his trying to be a hero. The target just wasn't worth that much.

He had initially toyed with the idea of using Dusty for the mission, and he was certain Dusty would have leaped at the chance. But Dusty was an officer of the court. While Dusty may very well have approved of the planned course of action, he would nonetheless have prejudiced his position with the legal fraternity, as well as being contrary to the commitment that he made on admission to the bar, and that would be unfair. Dusty would be annoyed at being left out but would see the logic of the decision. Maybe.

Mark would tell him later what had happened. And he did not look forward to his friend's blast, as Dusty would go apoplectic about being excluded.

Mark had got Blake and Elliott to front, giving the operation a semblance of respectability. Expertise and experience in covert and clandestine operations. One was ex-Special Forces. The other was ex-CIA. They knew how these games should, and would, be played out.

They had located the exact apartment unit that they were aiming for—a very plush penthouse suite on the top floor of this twenty-story building. They knew that the man was in residence. They knew that he lived alone after a turbulent marriage that had been wrecked, like so many others, by the stresses that went with life in the military service of one's country. They had carried out surveillance on the property and its residents as best they could, and they were reasonably certain that he was alone.

And that Doctor Colonel Ian McPherson was not entertaining friends this evening.

They were lucky. A brief tap on the door to his unit caused the door to open in one hell of a hurry to reveal the good doctor casually dressed and obviously expecting someone else, judging by the startled reaction. Blake immediately pushed him through the doorway and propelled him back into a chair.

Mark quickly scanned the room to make sure there was no one else there, while Elliott checked that no one had seen them enter the apartment. Then he also entered the apartment, locking the door behind him.

'Who were you expecting?' Blake asked in as pleasant

a tone as he could muster.

'No one!' came the reply from the colonel, a little too quickly and obviously a lie.

Blake gripped the doctor by his shoulder with both hands, demonstrating a clear understanding of the human body and the points that would give the most pain. 'I will ask you one more time, Doctor McPherson. Who were you expecting when you answered the door? I can promise you that they will come to no harm—at least not from our hands—so long as you behave!'

'Just a friend!' the doctor blurted out, for once in his life not in control of the situation. And unable to exercise his usual arrogant contempt for his fellow human beings.

Elliott picked up the cellular phone that was on the side table.

'Give me the name. I suppose he or she must be in your list of names?'

'You have no right ...'

'Ah! Now you are being petty,' Blake cut him off. 'You must know how this is supposed to work. You are a military man, as well as a doctor. We did not introduce ourselves, but that is hardly necessary. We are with the security services, and right now we can do anything because we are unsanctioned, and therefore we make the rules. Tell me his or her name, or we will simply wait for them to turn up and kill them. Get my drift?'

The colonel was a realist. He grabbed the phone off Elliott, hit a couple of keys on speed dial, and began speaking.

It was pathetic. Blake sat opposite him, levelling his gun at the doctor's head, and smiling. The doctor told the person on the phone that he had an unexpected visitor. He was obviously talking to a lady. And it was obvious who was in charge.

It was not the doctor.

When that conversation ended, the doctor desperately tried to seize the initiative.

'Now, what is this all about?' he demanded.

It was then that Mark turned and, for the first time this evening, came face-to-face with the doctor. And it was then that the doctor appeared to shrink, the reality of the situation clear. He had come face-to-face with a man who he had attempted and failed, to kill.

'You know what this is about!' Mark said in a voice devoid of any emotion, except utter contempt.

'I can explain!' the doctor almost screamed.

'OK. Try me,' Mark answered.

'I come into your hospital to be fixed up with a gunshot wound. And end up fighting for my life against not one, but two attempts to murder me. Now explain that if you can.'

'I had no choice!' The tears welled up in the doctor's eyes. 'They would have killed me! They gave orders!'

'I would have thought that a man in your position would not take orders from anyone, particularly where those orders run somewhat contrary to your Hippocratic oath! Does not that oath say, at least in original Greek form, something about *"neither will I administer a poison to anybody when asked to do so"?*'

'You don't understand! They are everywhere. They can do anything!' the doctor whimpered.

'Who can do anything?' Mark asked.

That question caused the doctor to pause. His body language said that he was not being evasive. Mark could feel the chill creeping through his spine. It was inconceivable that McPherson did not know the answer to what should have been a simple question.

Blake stepped in.

'They are not the only ones who can do anything.' He put on a pair of surgical gloves. He then poured a large glass of Jack Daniels from the bottle that was on the table, handed it to the doctor, and just said, 'Drink.'

'I usually have ice with Jack Daniels' said the doctor as he started to rise.

Blake shoved him back down and repeated his message.

'Drink! You won't be needing any ice!'

The doctor took a sip.

And that was where things started to turn ugly.

Blake again pulled out a Glock and levelled it at the doctor's head. 'All of it!'

When the glass was empty, Blake filled the glass again, this time to the top, and pushed it in front of the doctor. The look of panic from the shock of seeing Blake wearing gloves, and the amount of Jack Daniels whisky that he had already consumed was somewhat mellowed by the doctor's state of inebriation. He nonetheless tried to protest.

'I have a procedure to perform in the morning. I don't think I should have another one.'

Blake smiled.

'All your procedures have been cancelled, so it is quite OK.'

'But ... how?'

'Well, they will be cancelled, or someone else will do the procedures for you. You will not be going anywhere near the hospital tomorrow.'

The doctor still did not get it. Since Blake still had the gun, and the glass was full, McPherson took another drink.

It was then that Mark entered the conversation again.

'What was it that you injected into my IV in the hospital?' he asked in a tone that said that he already knew the answer.

That brought a shrug and a simple answer. 'Morphine.'

'And the dose?' Mark asked.

Despite his condition, the doctor did look embarrassed. His capacity for alcohol must have been tremendous, and Mark began to worry about whether their plans for the doctor would work. They still required him to assist them, and that meant that he should be totally drunk. At least the doctor laughed.

'Enough to kill a horse! You must be one strong son of a bitch!'

'Oh, I am. But not quite in the way you might envisage,' Mark replied. 'So why don't you have another drink?'

The doctor obliged, draining the glass.

'OK,' Blake pulled something from his pocket and placed four small packets on the table. Body language said that the doctor knew what they were. He had seen them before: Firstly, because he was a doctor and would know these things, and secondly, because he was a member of the scheme organised by Stephen Rodriguez and his Gatekeeper, Nathan. The only thing missing here was the teddy bear.

And that was when the doctor finally did get it.

Blake poured another glass of Jack Daniels and pushed the four plastic packets in front of him.

In a state of near hysteria, the doctor protested. 'That amount of heroin would kill. And with the amount of alcohol ...'

'That's correct. Enough to kill a horse!' said Mark. 'You will be familiar with its origins and its chemical structure. It is morphine based. You will get a high as soon as you take your first shot. Later, you will probably lapse into unconsciousness. When you awake, we will be gone, so it is not all unwelcome news!'

'But I may never wake up!' the doctor cried, tears streaming down his face. 'You cannot do this! This is murder. You will never get away with it!'

'Oh, but we will. When you recover—or should I say *if* you recover, you are going to retire from both the Walter Reed hospital and the Army. If you don't, the recording of what you have said will be given to the media and you can take your chance in the court of public opinion.

'So off you go,' Blake intervened. 'Take it! This is not murder. It is assisted suicide, euthanasia, or whatever you wish to call it. We are not going to waste a bullet on vermin like you.'

The tone of Blake's voice left little doubt that he could not have cared less. Elliott, who had been along simply as backup, sat impassive watching the doctor with loathing. Mark, who had seen his share of broken lives because of drug addiction, saw no difference between the death of a low life and the death of a social druggie who just so happened to have a very responsible job in a hospital. In fact, the doctor was the worst case. The doctor did not steal to feed his drug habit, because on his salary, he could afford the asking price. But what he had done was try to administer a fatal dose of a perfectly legitimate drug to protect his source, and to protect the whole illicit organisation. Which was the worse?

The three men sat there and watched Colonel Ian McPherson as he rambled on about his involvement with the military and the hospital, and then finally, he told them of his involvement with drugs of a different kind.

Eventually, he sank into a drug-induced coma, his mind and body unable to handle any more.

That was when Blake picked up the doctor's mobile phone and rang for an ambulance. He thought seriously about injecting a couple more vials into McPherson's system, thereby ensuring that he would never awaken from his coma, but he decided against it. There was little point in leaving even the faintest hint that this was anything but self-inflicted. He was just not worth the trouble.

he doctor had virtually committed suicide, certainly as far as his career as a doctor was concerned. Since he crossed paths with Mark and failed in his duty of *Primum non nocere*—First do no harm—his military career was over as well.

They left the apartment locking the door behind them without a second thought, or even a hint of remorse.

Chapter 70

Leavenworth

When Stephen Rodriguez had been handed over to Special Forces troops, they had to get him away from Washington and all the nonsense that was going on there. The solution was to have him placed in a military correction facility where access to him could at least be controlled until someone in authority got their act together.

He was whisked away to the US Disciplinary Barracks in Kansas, a place better known as Leavenworth. This was a maximum-security place where those incarcerated could either be held in solitary confinement or allowed to coexist with others who had got on the wrong side of the military. Because of Stephen's background, and because of the nature of his arrival, nobody knew what to do with him. Therefore, it was decided that he should be confined in solitary and not allowed to have any access to anyone, and vice versa.

However, such a situation could not last. From the noises coming out of Washington DC, there were obviously a few different people who urgently wanted to speak to Rodriguez. The military people took the defensive view that until someone could decide who had jurisdiction in this case, nobody would be allowed access. And the intriguing thing was that Rodriguez did not seem all that keen on talking to anybody.

Eventually, after several days where absolutely nothing happened, a request came through from the FBI to transfer Rodriguez to a federal civilian penitentiary. That meant a trip of about five miles, which was the distance between the Leavenworth military and Leavenworth civilian establishments. The latter was, of course, controlled by the same Department of Justice that also ran the FBI.

The military people were glad to see the back of their unwanted guest. But for reasons that would have been obvious to anyone involved with his case, Rodriguez was far from happy.

Rodriguez immediately asked to speak with his lawyer, and of course, the prison authorities were eager to grant his request. The fact that his lawyer would need to travel from Washington gave the people in Leavenworth ample time to prepare. And gave Rodriguez ample time to contemplate his future.

Little had been said when he was checked in other than to repeat what had been said when he was originally arraigned back in Washington.

With nothing else to do, the prisoner had several options to consider—to plead Guilty or Not Guilty being the most obvious one. But what was he guilty or not guilty of?

In chronological order, Stephen's first apparent misdemeanour was his involvement in the death of, or at least the disappearance of, Wakil Hekmatyar in Marjah.

Contrary to what was often portrayed in the movies,

the CIA very rarely got involved in killing people. And in the case of Wakil Hekmatyar, Rodriguez had certainly not pulled the trigger. Even if he had, and even if he pleaded guilty to any involvement, he would have had the full support of many of the people on both sides of the Afghan conflict. But there was an apparent witness that could place Rodriguez at the last time and in the last place, that Hekmatyar had been seen alive. Coincidence? It was not as though anyone in Washington DC would be terribly interested in the goings-on in Afghanistan or the fate of one of the local criminals. The problem was that there was an *apparent witness* who had seen an AK-47 rifle being handed over to the ADDI at the same time and in the same place that Wakil Hekmatyar had been dragged away from.

What was that all about?

Now the second event had occurred at what had become known as the Battle of Ghazni. The theory was that Rodriguez really had little choice but to dispose of Edward Hennessey. Edward, the man who had professed to be his lover, was a plant by the FBI, and therefore deserved to die. And his death could not have been achieved at a more convenient time. In the middle of a battle in a far-off place, people tended to get killed, and Hennessey was just another of the unfortunate casualties of that terrible day. Collateral damage it was called. The fact that some investigating people had found a discarded AK-47 rifle on the side of the road did not prove anything. And the finding of a so-called suppressor and a bag nearby like the bag handed to Rodriguez also did *not* prove anything. Sure, it was unlikely to have been left by any of the terrorists who were around that day. Terrorists were not well known for using sophisticated devices or for carrying their weapons in *bags*. But that did not mean that you had to *assume* that only Western people would use suppressors and gun bags. You could take all these so-called facts and make whatever story you wanted to make.

The third event was a little more difficult to explain. However, it was unlikely that the FBI would call on the Russian Yuri Alekseyev as a witness in any trial. It was only the meddling Harold Taylor, and his Teflon son Mark Taylor, who had somehow reached the conclusion that Rodriguez had contacted Alexseyev and *arranged* for Mark's team to be incarcerated. It was unfortunate that the Tajiks had messed up their assassination attempt on President Karzai. And it was just a matter of poor timing, that had resulted in Alexseyev's panicked effort to get rid of the Americans. Unfortunately, the Afghanis had once again failed to perform the simple task of disposing of the bodies, which could have saved everyone a whole heap of trouble. But whether Rodriguez was involved in any of this was pure speculation and assumption.

As was the alleged involvement of Rodriguez in the kidnapping of Debbie Peterson. No amount of digging would reveal any connection to anyone in the CIA. Her kidnapping could just have been an attempt by some criminals to get Mark Taylor to part with some of his cash. The criminals were just unfortunate that Mark had been overseas at the time, was probably up to his ass in other matters, and would have been difficult, if not impossible, to contact. Rodriguez was also overseas at the time the alleged kidnapping would have been carried out, and so he could not have been involved. The problem was that Mark had automatically *assumed* that Rodriguez had been involved.

Acting on this assumption, Mark had kidnapped Dayanara and her daughter Estefania. At the FBI conference, it had been very eloquently described to anyone who cared to listen that these two ladies had *volunteered* to help Mark locate his girlfriend. Well, who wouldn't if they were held in captivity? So much for the FBI's profiling effort on the relationship between the kidnapped and the kidnapper. And the ladies appeared to have been brainwashed, such that Stephen Rodriguez's own daughter would not even attend her mother's funeral.

Yes, there were questions about how her mother had died. And for reasons yet to be revealed, the FBI had believed the Taylor theory that Rodriguez was somehow responsible for that. A more logical explanation of the death was, both intuitively and from the FBI's own *profiling*, that Mark Taylor had been responsible.

How about a scenario that said Mark Taylor had his woman back, shot Dayanara out of sheer frustration, and got himself shot in the process by someone who was simply reacting to his brutal and callous act? But the death of Dayanara had been the reason given by the FBI for the incarceration of Rodriguez. Well, they could try to prove it.

Good luck with that.

Then came the other fantasy. Mark Taylor had been *rushed* to the Walter Reed Army Medical Center by some unknown good Samaritan to get his arm repaired after a gunshot wound. The fact that Mark had turned up at a military hospital suggested that the Samaritan had a military background and was probably strongly associated with what went on that night. And was more likely to have the necessary firearm skills to be responsible for the shot that killed the dear wife of Rodriguez. And who knows? No one had so far owned up to having fired the shot that injured Mark, but it was known that it was fired from a military-style rifle, which, of course, meant that it could not have come from any CIA employee. And then, despite being in the absolute best care of people who had probably saved his life, and at a hospital with a worldwide reputation for the excellence of its services, Mark Taylor had come up with a theory that someone had talked a senior officer into trying to kill his patient. Not only once, but twice. The good doctor so accused was an Army colonel who had seen action in all parts of the world. So as an aside to the suggested lunacy of it all, if the vastly experienced colonel/doctor had really wanted to kill someone who was drugged up to the eyeballs in a post-operation stupor, would not the patient be long dead?

Rodriguez was supposed to be the architect of all this nonsense.

Really?

However, despite the flimsy nature of all this so-called evidence against Stephen Rodriguez, there were a couple of things that Stephen had to worry about. While he was being held at Leavenworth, he could not attend to matters of much greater importance. And meanwhile, there were people who would take advantage of his incarceration.

It was alluded to at the FBI conference that there were suspicions that the CIA had been involved in some drug deal in Afghanistan, and that Stephen Rodriguez was at the centre of that. The CIA had been involved with drugs, and drug dealers, from the get-go. It was, some would say, unfortunately, part of the scene which all countries had to deal with.

Although a theory had been presented of a grant scheme for the sale and distribution of drugs, no one could pin down who was responsible for what. And the redeeming feature for Rodriguez in all of this was that nobody could say for certain how high up in Government the so-called *scheme* went.

So, Rodriguez had a bail-out position. While his high ranking in the CIA gave him access to all sorts of information, it also enabled him to establish his own network of information and informants, not all of which he had to share with the authorities. And this would enable him to negotiate his way out of this mess.

What surprised the staff at the federal prison was that Rodriguez asked that they have a man attend his first meeting, which they duly did when Benjamin Dale and a trail of supporting staff arrived from Washington.

Dale came from a highly prodigious firm of criminal lawyers, and he had the reputation of a no-nonsense guy who had won more cases than he had lost. And those cases that he failed to win, he at least managed to get his clients heavily reduced sentences.

The lawyer's first comment at his first meeting with Stephen Rodriguez was to ask why he had asked for a federal officer to be present. He was quickly assured by Rodriguez that there was a reason, and that was the end of that. Benjamin Dale could see from the get-go that this was going to be a difficult case. But this meeting would be short.

The first question came from Rodriguez, and it was directed at the federal officer.

'Why was I transferred from the military to the civilian prison?'

Dale was astonished. He had a lot of questions to ask, and it did not matter a toss which prison they were in.

'What has that got to do with anything? You are in serious trouble here. Shouldn't we concentrate on your defence?'

'Well, that depends!' Stephen began.

'I am not sure what I have been charged with at this stage. Are you?'

'Well, your charge sheet says that you have been arraigned on a charge of homicide. But we suspect there are more charges to follow. This is serious!'

'OK, so I suggest that you find out what those other

charges are. In the meantime, I was quite content to be in a military penitentiary. And I do not appreciate being moved to this excuse for prison without knowing why.'

Dale looked puzzled.

'What difference does that make?'

Rodriguez stood and signalled to the guards that the meeting was over. As they led him from the room, he turned.

'Until you can answer that question, I have nothing to say.'

And that was the end of that.

The meeting of the NSA officials who had an interest in the case of the state versus Stephen Rodriguez did not occur in any Government office building but instead took place at the residence of Joseph Klein. There was only one other person there—William Prendergast. By their body language, you would have thought that neither had a care in the world.

Klein cut straight to the point.

'Rodriguez has been successfully transferred to the federal prison, so he will be much easier to have access to than if he had remained with the military. So now what do we do? He will most likely start a plea bargain to get him off the hook, which means he will start pointing the finger at other people who are involved in the scheme.'

Prendergast took a sip from his brandy before replying.

'Yeah, what a mess he has got himself into. I guess we need to consider termination.'

'I agree, William, but we have to be careful how we do that. The Feds are all over his case. Why did he need to go and tap an FBI agent?'

'Come on, Joe. Give the guy a break! You are assuming that he did kill the agent. It may have had nothing to do with

Rodriguez. And the FBI will need a miracle to assemble enough evidence to solve that one.'

'Yeah, maybe,' Joe countered. 'But we can't afford to wait, can we? Should Stephen get wind of the fact that normal service has been resumed, he will first shit himself. Then he will sing his head off.'

'Put yourself in his position,' Prendergast speculated. 'He has to go for a deal—he has lost everything and faces the rest of his life in the pen. With the information he has in his head, the CIA certainly cannot afford to let him out. But and here is the fact, he can and will negotiate to have an extremely comfortable life behind bars. The only bargaining chip he has is not his knowledge of the CIA, but the knowledge he has of those like us who have been benefiting from undercover activity that we would rather not have made public.'

'Yeah, you are right, of course. So, I suspect you have a plan?'

'Yes, I do. Little has been said about the whereabouts of Stephen's offsider from Afghanistan. Now he has everything to gain by cooperating. According to all the reports I have seen, he has had nothing to do with people being kidnapped or killed. He is languishing in a penitentiary here in Washington as an accessory after the fact and awaiting the outcome of investigations into Stephen's misdemeanours. And that could take years. Now he would not be involved in any killing or any of that nonsense. But if he had access, he could get Stephen talking. If that reveals that Stephen is contemplating doing a deal with the FBI, then all we have to do is put the word out to the druggies already at Leavenworth in such a way that they will do the job.'

'OK, that sounds like a plan. Can you get the FBI to transfer your man from Washington to Leavenworth?'

'Does the bear shit in the forest?'

The meeting of those at the FBI who had responsibility for various aspects of the case against Stephen Rodriguez was gathered in a room on the seventh floor of the J. Edgar Hoover Building. It was not ideal in terms of timing or location. Over the years, since the FBI had moved in, this building had become both run-down due to a lack of adequate maintenance and not fit for purpose, as the FBI staff were now scattered all over the city. There had been various attempts to have it replaced or rebuilt, but they had all floundered somewhere between planning and decision making. Still, a job had to be done, and the state of his office accommodation was far from the mind of Peyton Reed as he surveyed his team.

There was enough evidence to have Rodriguez put away for a long time on any one of several charges, but life was not quite that simple. Apart from the various high-powered government agencies involved—including the CIA, NSA, DEA, and FBI, all of whom would have a critical, and not necessarily objective, interest in *how* the process was conducted, the case itself was enormously complex. It would take months, if not years, to untangle this mess, and that would disrupt the normally efficient workings of the system.

With the passage of time, everything would get diluted. With the complexity of the case, and the consequent need to employ different people to investigate every aspect, each with their different agendas and time frames, bringing a case before a judge would be a nightmare.

The FBI did, at least, have a place to start. They had originally got an indication that Stephen Rodriguez was a person of interest in what seemed like a simple case of involvement in the drug business. And that was why Edward

Hennessey had been on a covert mission to track what was going on. That had escalated somewhat when the FBI had discovered that the CIA and the DEA had launched their own covert mission on the same person, and presumably on the same subject. They had found that out, more by good luck than anything else.

The FBI had a source within the DEA who was intended to give them a heads-up on possible criminal activity resulting from money laundering as a by-product of drug activity. This source was, of course, sanctioned by the DEA. But it was a closely held secret within the DEA. Consequently, when the FBI was notified by their source, Brian 'Griz' McKinley, that he was about to fly a team overseas following a CIA plane that would have Stephen Rodriguez on board, they had to move quickly. That meant that they had to somehow delay the departure of two Gulfstream Jets while they cranked up their agent to a slightly higher level of preparedness. The fact that the agent, Edward Hennessey, had died on this mission made the FBI people brutally dedicated, but no less objective, in their pursuit of justice.

It is unusual for the FBI to take the action that it did in this case. The suggested course of action came from the NSA, which did present some problems. The NSA often saw the end game as more important and simplistic than the means of getting there. But did the FBI have a choice in the matter?

Reed sighed as he addressed his team.

'I think we need to get inside the head of Rodriguez, and the only way to do that is to have someone on the inside at Leavenworth. As far as we know, he has not volunteered any information that can shed any light on what went on in Afghanistan. He is obviously holding out for a deal, but I cannot see that happening on my watch. Any comments so far?'

'You mean we have an informant in Leavenworth?'

The question came from Daniel Crosby—the agent who had been assigned to investigate the death of Edward Hennessey. Crosby was due to leave the following day for Afghanistan, a trip that he was far from looking forward to. And finding out what was in the head of Rodriguez was not high on his list of priorities. He was probably the most senior agent on the team, and he did not want his investigation screwed up by someone else being too clever. But if he could find a justification for not having to travel to a warzone, he would take that.

Reed could lie like the best of them, although he hated to do it to members of his own team. And the FBI had strict rules for the use and handling of informants, and with particularly good reasons. That is, apart from the strictly moral perspective and the Constitutional rights of the target. But this one would not be an FBI informant.

'Currently, no,' Reed began. 'However, one is about to be transferred to Leavenworth, and he will be good to go.'

'How good is he?' another agent asked.

Reed smiled at that.

'Good question! As with all informants, we must wait and see what happens. But he should be able to get Rodriguez to talk.'

'You seem confident!' Daniel noted. 'Are we allowed to know who he is?'

'Sure! But although the name probably does not mean much to you - this must stay within this team. His name is Jacob Dutton.'

The boring routine of life in a penitentiary was starting to get to Stephen Rodriguez. Although in his normal day job he had been used to early rises, whether as part of normal life or as required by the exigencies of the

CIA, this was different. Firstly, he had no reason to get up in the morning. Secondly, the noise started at a ridiculous time, meaning a peaceful 'lie-in' was out of the question.

He shuffled along to the showers like a zombie with his hands and feet tied together, for no reason that Stephen could think of. But then, he was on the other side of the law this time! There was a piece of soap, but no flannel. The water was only lukewarm. But it was a moment of peace and the only time when he was not confined to his cell when he could wash away the stench that came from being confined in this miserable place.

The shower was over too soon, and then they shuffled off for breakfast. Some of the inmates had made *friends* with their fellow prisoners and collected in small groups where they chattered in hushed tones, their eyes ever glancing around the hall, from time to time sniggering at some perceived action or mannerism of some other group or individual. Others, Stephen included, isolated themselves, apparently content to eat their food and take no part in the prison's social life.

After breakfast, some were escorted back to their cells, where they would spend the rest of the day contemplating the four grey walls of their ten-by-fifteen—feet box, which had become their home. Some—and on this day it was Stephen's turn—were escorted to a small courtyard about the size of a basketball court, where they could catch a glimpse of the sky and catch a moment's fresh air.

But this day was different for Stephen.

Leaning against the far wall was someone that he recognized.

Jacob Dutton.

'Jacob! - What are you doing here?' Stephen asked,

out of earshot of the other prisoners and guards.

'You tell me!' Jacob replied with a grimace. 'They just told me yesterday that I was being moved. I thought that I was being released, but got bundled into a van, then a plane, and here I am at Leavenworth. I have not been charged with anything other than an accessory after the fact, whatever that means. All that they will say is that I can talk to my lawyer *later*. And so, what about you?

'Oh, I have been charged with homicide, would you believe' Stephen asked. 'And I have spoken to my lawyer— fat lot of use that was! He reckons they have a lot more to charge me with, that it will take years to build the case and that will give me plenty of time to build my defence. That is if I don't die first! But if anyone thinks I am going to sit on my ass in the god-forsaken place for even a couple of months, they should think again. I know enough to incriminate some people in extremely high places. And I am not going to take the rap while they all get off scot-free.'

'You may wish to think again before you embark on that course of action,' Dutton replied. 'Those same people can be pretty ruthless when it comes to protecting their investments.'

'Yeah, well, they will see, won't they?' Stephen replied with a smugness that came from years of getting his way.

The call from Jacob was brief.

'He is going to do it!'

'OK. Now let me tell you what you are going to do. In a few days' time, you will be given a new passport, a new identity, and airline tickets to take you to your new home. A bank account will be opened under your new name with enough money to see you through a comfortable life. You will leave the USA for New Zealand,

and I suggest you do not return to these shores anytime soon. Good luck.'

Joseph Klein just hung up the telephone.

Stephen Rodriguez did not see Jacob Dutton again, which struck him as rather strange. But he shrugged his shoulders. He had far more important things to worry about. Later this day, he had a scheduled meeting with a lawyer, Benjamin Dale, and he would get the ball rolling. There had been enough stuffing around. Now it was time to start playing by his rules.

Meanwhile, he went through the mindless morning prison routine and plodded down the ramp towards the shower block. His mind was full of all bits of the strategy that he had worked on over the previous few days. It was coming together nicely.

The two guys in the left shower cubicle started arguing about something irrelevant, which Stephen chose to ignore. But then they started to fight and spilled over into the cubicle where Rodriguez was. At first, he stepped aside, before his natural reactions took over.

'Oi, fuck off!'

One of the men involved in the fight turned to Rodriguez with an evil grin on his face.

'You talking to me?'

The other man stopped fighting and pushed Stephen against the wall, his arm covered in tattoos held against the throat.

Rodriguez never saw what had been pushed into the left side of his stomach and then twisted up, causing fatal damage as the instrument pierced his heart. He looked down in disbelief as blood gushed down his body, quickly washed away by the flow of water, and spiralled down the drain. And then he saw his life pass before him as he crumbled to the floor.

Chapter 71

Unsatisfactory Conclusions

The problem was just that Mark did not understand women. Even the ones that were closest to him and the ones that he loved. Sure, he could read their body language better than most people. But that did not mean that he could fully understand what drove them to make what he regarded as irrational decisions.

But if he put his mind to it, he could probably understand why Debbie had been upset by recent events. She was not used to being kidnapped. Not used to having a lady that she barely knew shot dead millimetres from where she was standing. And not used to the chief architect of this piece of misery being a highly respected member of the government of her country.

Well, the architect had first threatened Mark with the same fate, and, while Mark was aware that Stephen Rodriguez would have been blown into the next world by the FBI marksman the instant his finger tightened on that trigger, Debbie was not used to the complexities of situations that men seemed to get themselves into. She was petrified at the time, and still envisaged quite vividly what so easily could have happened.

And she had not got over it.

Nor could she understand the orchestration of the fate that would become of Stephen Rodriguez. While she had not interfered in any way with Mark and his methods, she honestly thought that this episode in their lives should be over.

But it wasn't.

She thought that Mark would leave it to others to deal with the aftermath.

But he wouldn't.

After the shambles that had occurred in Afghanistan and the chaos that had ensued after his return to the United States, Mark would not trust anyone in authority. So, he had dictated his story of the whole sorry affair and placed the disk in escrow with a quite simple message: If Rodriguez was freed or got a mere slap on the wrist with a wet bus ticket, then the disk would be released to the media. Mark did not want the matter to be opened to public scrutiny, but he expected the authorities to take a responsible attitude and punish those responsible. He had absolutely zero faith in that happening without some form of coercion.

She cried long and hard as she explained to Mark that she had to go. They had made love, passionate and intense, as though both knew it would be for the last time in a while, if not for the very last time. She clung to him as though her life depended on it, at the same time telling him that she could not live with him.

The adage 'I would rather live with you in your world, than live without you in mine' simply did not apply.

Mark truly did not understand, but his love for Debbie was enough to let her go. She was off to Sudan Africa, along with Estefania, to sort out another set of problems that men had imposed on their fellow human beings.

Now Mark sat in his office, once more without a personal assistant. He contemplated the week ahead with not a lot of enthusiasm and not a lot of confidence. Wishing that it was Friday rather than Monday.

Brad Morgan had done an excellent job of running Taylor Software during Mark's absence, and the Styris project was about to get underway, which provided a guarantee of cash flow for at least the next two years. That should have been more than enough to lift his spirit. But Mark could not dispel the feelings of loneliness and isolation.

Life was very unfair. Brad had a girlfriend who was, in many respects, the complete opposite of Debbie. Shania greeted every day like it was a new beginning: Bring it on! But Mark longed for what had been. He would not swap Debbie for the world or change the slightest thing about their relationship. He still loved her, and maybe, one day, they would be together again.

His telephone rang and disrupted his musing. Since it was still before 7:30 am and he was the only one in the office, he had to take the call.

He answered it with a very formal 'Good morning. Taylor Software.'

It was quite a surprise to hear from his father, and even more of a surprise so early in the day.

'Morning, Father. You're up and about early!'

His father laughed.

'It is not that unusual! But I knew I would find you in the office. Did Debbie get away OK?'

It was like a knife through the guts. Why did other people fail to realize the pain that the separation from Debbie had caused him?

And especially his own father!

Mark answered amicably enough.

'Yes, she was fine. We probably will not see her for a few years. I took her and Estefania to the airport. They both seemed quite excited.'

Mark rambled on, trying, and failing, to get the image of Debbie. First, turning her back to him, and then turning for a final wave, the tears streaming down her face. At the same time, a resolute set to her jaw which said there would be no turning back.

Harold was oblivious to the pain that he had caused. After all, he had lived in the world that Mark knew. A world of intense calm, interspersed with moments of intense activity and brutality. A world of truth and a world of deceit. There was no room for personal feelings.

'How about joining us for lunch? We have a couple of things that we need to discuss, and your business seems to run OK with Brad at the helm', Harold asked in the tone of voice that did not expect a refusal.

Yeah, sure! His father had always assumed that running a computer software company was child's play. He had always assumed that the modern technology coming into the market at an ever-increasing, faster rate just seamlessly dropped into place. Harold had assumed that there was always someone smarter than his own son. So how come on no less than two occasions in recent times, Harold had called on his son to do his, or his master's, dirty work in various parts of the world?

Mark did not understand women. But he sure as hell did not understand his father.

It was mutual.

'Who is *we?* And what do we need to discuss?' Mark asked in a somewhat sarcastic tone, the inference of which was not lost on Harold.

'You do realise that this business is not over?' Harold began. 'It also raises some wider issues which we cannot avoid. But for now, the DEA director would like to talk to you. I cannot say too much, but she is thinking about offering you a contract to sort out the computer systems in the DEA.'

So 'wider issues' took second place to matters that Karen wanted to discuss!

The mention of a possible government contract caused Mark to be temporarily interested, but, at the same time, cautious. Getting money from the Government was always an exciting prospect. It was usually the other way around: the Government did the taking.

It was extremely rare for a small software company to land a government contract. It was even rarer to have one offered without having to bid for it.

Mark had often dreamed of accepting Government contracts. In that scenario, you had to compete with the egos of innumerable state servants who were forever trying to score brownie points off each other rather than getting on with the job at hand. More specifically, their information technology people preferred off-the-shelf packaged solutions rather than take a risk, going out on a limb, and getting something that worked. An outside 'consultant' was like a pariah to them, and while that could be fun, it was a case of forever looking over your shoulder to see where the knives were coming from next. But the income you could make typically far exceeded the expense.

'What do they want to be done?' was Mark's obvious next question.

'I had better let Karen tell you that.'

Mark wondered what he was letting himself in for. He was too intrigued to say no. But then it all came down to trust.

Would all the bureaucrats and politicians involved display the same trust? They were incredibly good at making decisions that fell within their jurisdiction. And, when the shit hit the fan, morality and other principles went out of the window.

That phenomenon may have explained why Harold Taylor, had not informed his son of the fate that had befallen Stephen Rodriguez. On the other hand, the reason could be much simpler.

Harold did not know.

The first thing that happened after the fight in the showers at Leavenworth was that the warden panicked. He called the FBI and asked a simple question.

'What the hell do I do now?'

The answer that he got was also simple.

'Say nothing to anyone. A van will take Stephen Rodriguez to a nominated FBI-controlled hospital for the post-mortem.'

The FBI was concerned that the *attempt* on the life of Rodriguez could have been made by any one of several groups who would want him dead. And until such time as they found out which one, nothing would be said.

The rationale was that the group could be revealed by the FBI announcing that Rodriguez was still alive, and simply observing the reactions to that piece of news. The fact that this subterfuge did not work was really beside the point. The whole business was in danger of getting out of hand, and the FBI was not able to let the demise of a senior official of their sister organization be made public before they had a lot more information on what had happened.

In fact, any information would have been good.

The CIA was in a similar state. The revelations that

had been made at the earlier meeting at the FBI headquarters, where all the Rodriguez dirty laundry had been aired, had rocked the bureaucracy to the core. The fact that one of their own had been accused of the murder of his wife, and the murder of a serving FBI agent, and was embroiled in drug trafficking was just too much.

The FBI had little choice but to inform the director of the CIA that one of his staff had been attacked. The director was a political appointment. Therefore, it was debatable whether the story could remain quiet for long.

The immediate response was to take a more pragmatic approach. Whatever else would come out of the chaos, there was ample evidence that most of the issues had origins in the remote town of Marjah Afghanistan. The CIA dispatched a senior and very experienced, agent to the CIA cell. Ostensibly, this agent was to replace Jacob Dutton. Because of seniority issues, he would effectively become the head of station in Marjah.

His name was Peter Ross.

Chapter 72

Afghanistan

It was a bitterly freezing day with the relentless wind blowing down from the angry snow-packed mountains away to the northeast. The clouds rolled down towards Marjah, and another storm threatened. The direction of the wind and the gathering clouds indicated that it would be snowing before long. It was unusual for snow to fall this far south and at this time of year. But the residents took it in their stride.

There were only a few boys who were brave enough to come to play football this day, and they just passed the ball around, running in a vain attempt to try to get warm. There would be very few goals scored today.

Naeem Sediqyar sat on his customary rocky perch, watching the boys at play. He was wrapped up against the wind, only the wooden stump of what had been his right leg exposed to the elements. It did not matter to him. It did not matter to him how many boys played or how many goals they scored.

Naeem had a job to do, no matter what the weather. He had a message to deliver, the significance of which he had absolutely no idea.

On this day, he was watching and waiting for someone to come out from behind the wall of the allied forces compound. He had heard from Nurul Hadi that there had been some changes in personnel behind the wall and that Jacob Dutton had been 'reassigned.'

Naeem had not had enough education to be able to know the full meaning or the implications of that word. He had even less idea of the subtle nuances that went on in Jacob's world.

But he would never see Jacob Dutton again.

People came and people went.

Nothing ever changed.

All that it meant to Naeem was that Jacob was no longer his contact.

Another person by the name of Ross would now receive the messages.

For one Afghani per day.

Suddenly there was pandemonium.

A man who had been quietly watching the game leaped to his feet as an M1117 Armoured Security Vehicle approached the compound gates. There was just no time for anyone to react. The soldiers in the ASV were relaxed as they ended their patrol and did not see the man literally throw himself at their vehicle, at the same time activating the detonator on his vest.

The explosion was massive. It sent the ASV tumbling and crashing into the compound wall. It was the driver who came off the worst as the windscreen burst inwards, instantly blinding him, and sending him into the life hereafter. The other three passengers were badly hurt, as they were tossed around and would forever carry their injuries from this random event.

And then there was silence.

The only thing moving was the dust.

This was followed by a burst of action. A dozen marines rushed out of the compound and immediately formed a defensive perimeter around the crash scene. The explosion had obliterated the man who had worn the vest. The occupants of the ASV had been partially protected by the armour. It had been insufficient to prevent considerable damage to men and machines.

A group of medics followed the marines out of the compound, hastily recovered the four soldiers, and rushed their gruesome baggage back into the compound. A heavily armed truck next came out and dragged the remains of the ASV back into the compound. Then the marines walked backwards towards the wall. The perimeter was withdrawn, and the gates were slammed shut.

The whole episode barely took more than a few minutes.

And then the silence was restored.

Then the only thing moving was the dust.

And then life returned to normal.

Naeem was the first one to resume what he had been doing before. Sitting on the same rock, waiting.

The boys came out and resumed their game, albeit more watchful and more aware of their surroundings.

Finally, a man came out of the gates of the compound and furtively looked around as though he had landed on another planet. Was he scared? Was he unsure?

He huddled into his thick coat, a hat pulled down to cover his ears, gloves on although he had his hands thrust deep into his pockets. He looked just like an actor in an old movie: dressed up to look like a spook. His breath came in short bursts, made evident from the gasps of condensation that hung in the air. And then these were whisked away by the wind. It was as though they had never happened. It was as though nothing that happened in this place mattered.

The American eventually made his way over to the rock where Naeem was seated. He sat down next to the Afghani boy. The boy could not have been much over fourteen years old, but he looked twice that age. The man stirred the dirt with his boots, seemingly unsure how to begin his conversation with the boy who he had been told to contact.

'Is everything set?' was all that he eventually asked.

'Yes' was the simple reply from Naeem.

So, the next shipment of opiates was about to head north. Through the rugged and unforgiving terrain that existed in this inhospitable land, all the way to Peshawar in Pakistan. The ultimate destination was the United States, there to satisfy the unrelenting demand for heroin.

No matter how much it cost in money.

No matter how much it cost in human lives.

Peter Ross rose to his feet and gazed over the killing field.

What a hell of a place! he thought.

Then he hurried back inside the compound to send an innocuous e-mail to his masters in the warm air-conditioned peace and quiet of the Central Intelligence Agency headquarters at Langley, Virginia.

Nothing else mattered.

Nothing ever changed.

Epilogue

The lunch was not quite what Mark had been used to. Apart from the occasional luncheon with Dusty and some of his clients, he usually settled for a sandwich while reading through programs or reports. Or while trying to decipher a client's needs from scrappy and incomplete notes.

The restaurant was plush and elegant. It had that hushed atmosphere that only money, or power, or both could engender.

When Mark arrived, Karen and Harold were already there, and deep in a conversation that it seemed like an intrusion to break. Harold had his back to the wall in typical spook fashion.

'Hello, Mark. Thanks for coming!' Karen gushed.

Mark smiled. 'I was not exactly given a choice, but it is good to see you again and under somewhat better circumstances.'

Karen turned to Harold.

'You have told him!'

The excitement in her voice said one thing, her body language suggesting that whatever it was, was not the reason that Mark had been summoned to a meeting.

Harold looked a little bit embarrassed.

'Well, no, we did not get around to talking about that. I will tell him now, and then we can get on with that other business.'

Mark was about to ask the question *What the hell are you talking about now?* but didn't, as he tried to understand the different body language of these two people. The female one was excited. The male one looked as though he had wanted to be somewhere else.

'Mark, I am going to file for a divorce from your mother.'

Oh, yippy-do. Karen was clearly disappointed with Mark's reaction. There was none. Just a noncommittal *You have to do what you think is right.*

Harold also looked nonplussed.

'You are not surprised?'

Mark studied his father's face, seeking a reaction, but finding nothing. He was certain that the invitation to lunch was not to discuss his father's matrimonial affairs. Mark just shrugged, and almost as an afterthought, he said, 'No.'

Harold persisted. 'You don't mind?'

Then Mark showed his exasperation.

'Who cares whether I mind or not? If you had thought that I would mind, then maybe you would have thought about that while I was running around in Afghanistan, being shot at and nearly frozen to death, doing your dirty work. And, I might add, while you were not exactly helping!'

There! He had said it now. The one time in his life that he could recall his father not being dedicated to his job was the one time that Mark needed him to be. And Mark and his small team had almost perished as a result.

Karen Marshall came to Harold's rescue.

'That was my fault,' she almost whispered. 'We had to keep details of your mission to a select few. And when the shit hit the fan with Harold under intense pressure from above, we had no choice but to duck. The fact is, however, that when the crunch came, we were too slow to react. I am so deeply sorry—it should not have happened, and it will not happen again.'

'Do I care whether it happens again?' Mark asked, and then felt the anger rising within. 'You do realize for all we went through in Afghanistan; all we did was to shuffle the deck. The game goes on!'

But he could not help but smile. The farther away from the DEA and the CIA he spent the rest of his life, so much the better, so there would not be the next time, would there?

'Well, maybe,' Karen replied. She had that infectious way of saying things. No wonder his father had been infatuated!

'I was about to offer you a consulting contract. You interested?'

Mark looked from Karen to Harold, looking for a clue, but receiving nothing and not sure how to answer.

Surprisingly, it was Harold who continued.

'The DEA has recognized the vulnerability of their computer systems to interference from both inside and outside the organization. While we have been worrying about computer hacking, security, and all that kind of stuff, we have forgotten about what we need the systems for. Following on from your work on the CIA business, Karen and some others have recognized a problem. The IT people we have in both of our organizations, and who we depend so much on, we have now recognized as our weakness. We used to think that their insistence on standardization and staying with the latest in technology was correct. But the other side of that begs the question— heaven forbid that someone should use some initiative and develop something that does what we want it to do. I have checked. All Government departments have the same approach—not only just in the United States, and the result is that the big players in the computer business control what we can and cannot do. But if you go to the White House and see what those people do, especially the Secret Service, they get what they *need*, and nobody dictates to them!'

'Like accountants have taken over the CIA so that everything is reduced to dollars, now the IT people have taken over systems so that everything is reduced to parameters. The United States Secret Service uses a little-known database system that every other IT department would reject on the grounds of a simple question: 'Who are these people?' But they use it because it is more secure than anything else. The fact that it is also more powerful and flexible, and probably so, seems to escape the IT experts who are primarily concerned with covering their own butts. It is a system that we should use, but we are prevented from doing so by our own bureaucracy.'

'So,' Karen interjected, 'we want you to come in as a consultant and review the rubbish that we have had to put up with for so long—and, hopefully, turn the system around so that we can get systems that actually do what we want, rather than what someone who doesn't understand our needs says that we want. And at the same time, we want you to check on what other weird and wonderful things people get up to while apparently doing what they are supposed to be doing. At the DEA we tolerate people 'surfing the web,' as you call it. But how much of what goes on is real work, we wouldn't have a clue. What is more, we suspect that our IT department's so-called experts are just looking for new systems to impose on us mere mortals to justify the ridiculous salaries we pay them, and to keep them in a job.'

Mark had to laugh. In most organizations, the story

was the same. At too high a level, the people were impressed by the credentials of their consultants and did not understand the needs of the people that did the work. At too low a level, the people knew what was wanted but were too far removed from the decision-making process to be able to have any influence. The IT people were too clever or too aloof to deal with peasants and so the massive expenditure on IT continued unabated, and with little real benefit.

'What makes you think that I can make a difference?' asked Mark, the suspicion very evident in his voice.

Harold laughed.

'You don't know what effect your recent work on our networks had on our IT departments. You put the fear of God into them because they quite simply did not know what was going on, or what could go on. Or, rather, you put the fear of God into the controllers who expected our 'experts' to know much more than they evidently do. Now they do not know whether to trust them or not, so they want an audit done by someone from outside. Your appointment will be approved by the administrator of the DEA, so you will have all the official backing that you need. But that is just the DEA. The CIA wants to buy into it too.'

Mark could not resist the temptation to ask,

'Does the White House know?'

His father saw the joke.

Mark was unsure whether Karen did, but it was Karen who answered.

'The President has been told that we are conducting an inquiry. That includes the CIA, the DEA, FBI, and several other organizations in the intelligence and security business. But no, the personnel involved will not be known in the White House or to anyone other than a few who sign the formal agreement.'

'How do you see this playing out? Mark began. 'If we are not known, how do we stay unknown? Surely, someone will know, and you know what keeping secrets is like in government—Chinese whispers, but nonetheless, it will not remain a secret for awfully long.'

Harold was out of his depth in understanding what Mark was alluding to However, Karen seemed to know how it would work.

'You will set up as a shell company. You will be given access rights to all the computer systems at the highest level, but neither you nor your staff will ever set foot in any office of the DEA. The investigation will be electronic, and Harold tells me you are particularly good at that kind of thing.'

Mark was startled.

'That is placing a lot of power in my hands. How do you justify that?'

Karen just smiled.

'Trust.'

'It will be expensive!' was the next thought that entered Mark's head. He thought of the deal he had made with the Augem Group not that long ago. A sum of 10 million dollars seemed a lot of money at the time, but in retrospect, the amount paled into insignificance. That exercise had cost a lot in terms of human lives, and he could put no price on the lives of two of his close friends who had been killed in that insane encounter with those involved. And as usual, if you were to look for a single reason, the answer was drugs.

This most recent exercise, chasing drugs, had not been quite so costly, at least from Mark's point of view; but it had still disrupted his life in ways that could never be repaired. It had to stop. And money was no compensation. Now he was offered access to what would be the most privileged information on the planet. That came at a cost. Sure, they needed to do something, but could it be done without giving away the family jewels? Through access to the various systems, Mark could, if he wanted to, find out a whole heap of things that had bothered him in the past. Maybe not *Who killed JFK?* but much simpler things like who fouled up his exploits in Delta Force down in Colombia all those years ago.

They would know that, given this amount of power, he could do that. In the small print of the agreement that Mark would have to sign, there would be some clause that reads something like a death sentence if he, or one of his employees, put a foot even slightly out of line. And the problem was that line would be determined by an official who was high enough up the totem pole to make their own rules and to choose their own timing.

Or would they?

Karen must have been able to read the body language. She had a caring and sympathetic look on her face as her eyes scanned first, Mark, and then Harold.

'Well, we will just have to make sure that you are suitably recompensed. I have written down a few figures.' She turned the piece of paper for Mark to look at.

Someone had clearly misunderstood the size of the task, even with the added annoyance of dealing with bureaucrats and their petty rules.

That amount of money would not be easy to refuse.

That amount of money should make a difference.

Mark was somewhat unique. The principle came before financial reward. And he would never betray the trust that these people were prepared to put in him. The same principles existed for his company and his people. Whether they knew it or not, Brad Morgan would be a critical player in Taylor Software being in this game. Mark trusted Brad, even though Brad was ex-CIA, and even though

Brad's girlfriend was currently with the FBI.

Well, Mark had to laugh. Mark's father was an assistant inspector of OIG, and here he was, talking to the director of intelligence of the DEA, who, the way things looked, could end up being his stepmother. The whole of his working life had been dedicated to his country. And it was all based on one thing.

Trust.

Review by Ron Davies CA

This was a fascinating and enjoyable book with all kinds of interesting angles.

There was an uncensored portrayal of Afghanistan the country seemingly in everlasting conflicts.

And the actions of the big superpowers were intriguing and not widely available to the public. They had various interests that they want to secure and defend at all costs by fair or foul means.

The author has done a great job in introducing characters that were relevant with paths that crossed and kept us surprised.

The main character Mark was an interesting person with many honed skills, and these were well outlined in the book which kept me guessing on the outcome to the end.

The authors research and background of the people, countries and the US and the Russian Military showed an extensive knowledge of these normally confidential subjects.

I could not put it down and as it was a good size book it was an enjoyable read over the Covid-19 lockdown period.

I have recommended this book to my friends as it is a very good book which they should enjoy.

View video on https://youtu.be/1kimcis-omk

Visit Website on www.donaldpetersbooks.nz